CAPTAIN HAWK;

OR,

THE SHADOW OF DEATH

A ROMANCE.

LONDON:

PUBLISHED BY E. LLOYD, SALISBURY-SQUARE, FLEET-STREET.

MDCCCLI.

PREFACE.

In presenting to the public the romance of "Captain Hawk; or, The Shadow of Death," the writer has a twofold object.

In the first instance, it was thought that a vivid and truthful picture of those times, which, although really so near at hand, have passed away never to return, when the highwayman made the suburbs of London his own, would be amusing to a large portion of the public.

In the second place, it was the desire of the author to show what complete and direful misery was sure to result from the unbridled licence which such a man as Gerald Clifton gave to temper and to passion.

In both of these objects the author has reason, from the large share of public patronage the work has received, to believe he has succeeded.

London, October, 1851.

OR,

MAY BOYES AND THE SHADOW OF DEATH.

No. 1.

CAPTAIN HAWK;

OR,

THE SHADOW OF DEATH.

CHAPTER I.

THE DOG AND THE GLOVE.

In what huge flakes the snow falls, obscuring the very air with a white mist, and lodging in the strangest and most inaccessible places the fancy could suggest. It has continued, too, for hours; no flitting shower coming in whirling gusts, but an even down descent of the icy particles, until, for miles around, nothing was presented to the eye but one uninterrupted sheet of white.

The wind, too, was just sufficient, after it had fallen, to sweep it gently from the heights into the hollows, so that as the snow shower, for it could not be called a storm, continued, undulating surfaces became level; hedge-fences and enclosures seemed gradually to sink into the earth; cottages, that might under ordinary circumstances be called small, assumed the aspect of dolls' houses, so pigmy did they look, peeping up like specks upon the snow-clothed landscape; trees of goodly growth seemed to shrink in their proportions; and still on, on came the descending shower, noiseless and steady, until field, road, path, and meadow were alike confounded and impossible to be distinguished each from each. The night, too, is coming—coming with a strange and sullen gloom; the cold becomes more intense, and now and then a wailing wind sweeps moaningly across the wide expanse of Hounslow Heath, carrying with it in its progress clouds of frozen particles, small and cutting, colder than rain, and glittering even in that faint light, like powdered glass.

It was not a fearful night; but it was a quiet, deliberate, and most uncomfortable one. There was no war of the elements, but the snow-drift was more dangerous to the chance passenger, who, with benumbed skin, dazzled eyes, and floundering steps, might seek in vain to find his home by old familiar paths, known to him even from his very childhood.

The sky, too, which bounded the heath's horizon, assumed, as it touched the snowy surface, so great a similarity of colour to the earth, that the prospect looked confusing and boundless.

But the reader will remember that more than a hundred years have rolled down the stream of time since that night of January, 1720, when this continued fall of snow wrapped all objects in its icy embrace.

London had not then stretched its mighty arms far beyond what were once its suburbs; the wants and the wishes of men were more centred in the spots they inhabited; and but few and far between, on such a night as that, were the passengers who, with abated breath and terrified gestures, struggled across the heath. But almost in the midst of this stirring scene—even in that very seeming desert of loneliness—man had set up his dwelling place, and nearly a hundred joyous, jocund hearts were then defying the sternness of the winter, and despite that falling sheet of snow, were revelling to the heart's delight of young and old.

To the southern side of the heath—a spot now covered by suburban villas—there stood a long, low, rambling, ancient inn—it was called the Talbot, and what man can say how many snow storms had wasted their bootless fury on its friendly thatch? It stood alone, for within a half mile circuit no human habitation could be found, and in the gloomy winter time that house upon the heath looked cold and desolate, that is to say, until nightfall, and then what a cheering, ruddy glow flowed from its windows and its ancient doorway.

It seemed to stand in the very centre of that desolate region on purpose to mock at hoary-headed winter; and as the wreaths of smoke curled from its fantastic chimneys, and roars of hearts' laughter came from within its ancient walls, he who listened might well have doubted if ever the season's difference, that lightest of human cares, affected any of the denizens of the old Talbot.

There was a roaring fire on the hearth—a fire of massive knotted logs, which hissed and fumed, and sent up curling wreaths of flame, warming slightly the vast apartments—for they were vast—of the time-hallowed place. And what cared they who sat in the ruddy glow from the consuming embers — what cared they that the old swing sing without creaked and shrieked in winter's howling blasts? they only laughed the more. What cared they that the rain battered at the window panes, like some hungry guest longing to find food, and warmth, and shelter? And as for the snow, the deep snow-drift, was it not a new delight to see some whitened passenger come in, looking blue and frozen, to tell of the state of things without, and then gradually to thaw and become most lamentably wet under the influence of the bright log fire?

And then there was the song and the jest, the dance—no courtly minuet, with its fantastic airs and graces, as if the gentlemen were afflicted with corns and the ladies trod on eggs, but real dancing, fun, and frolic, in which a hundred couple joined in boisterous merriment, and the old house never even shook to the busy patter of so many feet. There were musicians, too, in plenty, and what a fluttering of damsels' hair and flushing of goodly cheeks did down the middle of one of those old country dances produce; truly it was no joke, and yet full of the most glorious hilarity. A misanthrope would have cut his throat to see the guests any one night at the old Talbot.

And those were the days when the substantial yeoman, with his stalwart sons, his portly wife, and buxom daughters, scrupled not to foot it featly on the sanded floor of the inn.

And once a year, it was in January, a glorious anniversary was kept, for some old chronicle had said that the first beam of the old house was laid in that month, and so those who loved it then thronged to it.

Young and old, rich and poor, gentle and simple, never disdained to spend a happy hour beneath its roof.

Time was then when it was thought well even for the the high and noble to condescend now and then to be happy and a little natural. It was no unusual thing for titled personages to cross the threshold of the Talbot—at least, those in the vicinity, who respected the house and its inhabitants, seldom even liked to pass its doors without a smile or a nod of recognition from Peter Butts, the landlord.

And it so happened that on this very night, when the snow lay so deep and thick upon the heath, the anniversary time of jollity, had in the fullness of time come round. Brighter beams of light than usual glowed forth from the windows of the Talbot; louder sounds of mirth came from the long, low apartment on the ground floor, in which the dance was held.

But the mirth was not of so boisterous a character, for in addition to the farmers' dames of the neighbourhood, and a few families, who, early in the day, had made an arduous journey even from the city to keep up the old cherished custom of their youth, there were several families in the neighbourhood who thought it not beneath them to grace with their presence what might be called the ball at the Talbot.

It was the presence of some of these latter persons, which—it by no means decreased the real amount of mirth—subdued some of the more boisterous of the guests to quietude, so that the gambols were not of quite so rough a character, although in every respect quite as amusing.

Among these guests was a Sir John Boyes, his lady, and his two daughters, Philippa the elder, and May, her junior by some three years, both young and amiable girls, but May, so sweetly beautiful, with her calm, Madonna-looking face, that no wonder she had crowds of worshippers, and seemed destined to move through the world blessing and blessed wherever she appeared.

And yet was she no miracle of virtue, clad in stateliness. She had ever a laugh for the gay, and she did not think that inconsistent with the tear of tenderness and sympathy she was ever ready to shed for real distress. But not so much in delineation of character do we wish to occupy our pages as in stirring action. The Lady May, as she was called, will speak for herself, and during the progress of those events, of which she little dreamt to be the heroine, we shall see enough by which to judge her well and truly.

Sir John Boyes was rather stately; he thought he had a fascinating smile, and he always hoped his presence cast an overbearing weight upon—he did not say commoner people, but with a gracious wave of a jewelled hand, and a fascinating smile, he left it to be inferred.

It is ten o'clock, and the revelry is at its height. The Lady May had already turned the heads of dozens of the neighbouring youths, and we sadly fear had sowed the seeds of much dissension among them. Philippa was engaged in the dance, from which May had excused herself, on the plea of fatigue, as the measure which had preceded the one now in progress, had been decidedly of a boisterous character.

She approached her father, and with a familiar fondness hung upon his arm, as looking up in his face—oh! such a blank in comparison with hers—she said—

"Father, did you not expect ere this Ratchley to be here? It is getting very late!"

"Ratchley, my dear," said Sir John, and he waved his arm, shivering his fingers, in order that anybody who might be looking should see the dazzle of diamond rings. "Ratchley, my dear, received my orders to be here from Oxford. 'Tis a long ride, though, and rough weather. Having, however, my dear, as I before observed, and without repetition, received my orders, he will be here ——"

"And—and, father ——"

She paused, and Sir John, with a look of offended dignity, said—

"My dear, I have frequently occasion to inform you that the non-completion of a sentence was extremely reprehensible. It looks as if the intellect were in the state of a—in the state of a ——"

"Yes, father," said May, "it does indeed."

"Certainly — certainly — precisely; and I may likewise remark that interruptions betray bad breeding."

"I was only going to say, father, do you think Ratchley will bring young Gerald Clifton with him? Oh! how he dances! What a grace in every step! and always something new. He seems by inspiration to have caught the dance of nations, who excel in that sweet pastime."

"My dear," said Sir John, "upon this point you and I most incontestibly differ. You are perfectly aware that anything French is peculiarly dreadful to me; and as for *Gummany* ——"

"They call it Germany now, father," said May.

"An innovation," said Sir John, "an innovation. May, you don't know what you're talking about, and by allowing your hand to remain so long upon my wrist, you have taken the starch completely out of one of those magnificent ruffles—that is a—to say—one of the most magnificent ruffles."

"But you have not answered my question, father. Do you think Gerald Clifton will come with Ratchley?"

"I invited him," said Sir John, "and after that, thought were superfluous. It is not usually necessary for a person in my station in life to repeat anything, but I have no hesitation in again saying that I invited him."

"Ay, then you think he will come?" said May, her eyes sparkling with pleasure. "Oh! that charming dance he half taught Philippa and I when he was last at the Hall!"

"What charming dance?"

"He called it the *tours de grace*."

"The what?" said Sir John, and his countenance fell. "I have not the slightest hesitation, my dear, in saying, that it is some abominable French importation, and I must take leave to remark ——"

"Oh! they want somebody else to make up a set," cried May, and she flew from her father's side, and was in another moment engaged in the evolutions of a new measure, which had just been struck up.

Sir John arranged the long ties of his cambric cravat, settled his sword more comfortably by his side, and then sought consolation by making to himself a series of very small bows in a little mirror that hung over the massive chimney-piece.

"It's worse than ever," said a farmer, as he came into the ball-room, bringing with him a cold atmosphere, which everybody shrunk from. "It's worse than ever."

"Do you mean the snow?" said rather a starched old maiden-lady, with a formidable head-dress.

"Yes, I do, ma'am; it's up to your kness."

"Gracious goodness!" said the lady, with a faint scream, "some people are always thinking of what they shouldn't; as if," she added, in a whisper to a lady acquaintance, "as if any respectable female ever had knees."

Some of the guests now flattened their faces against the latticed panes of the windows, and agreed with the last new comer, that it was worse than ever.

That particular dance then being over, there ensued one of those strange and sudden pauses in the general hum of conversation, which even in the largest assemblies will be noticed occasionally to take place, when every one present, as if by common consent, pauses in what they may be doing or saying.

Such a circumstance must be familiar to all who have mingled in society. It is not for us to speculate on the fact—suffice it, that precisely at half past ten o'clock that evening at the Talbot, for the space of about half a minute, every sound was hushed.

It was no human voice that broke that solemn stillness, no casual remark from some bold and free speaker, as is usually the case, dispelled the charm which held all hearts in bondage; but just at the moment when one might have supposed that the silence would be broken, there came from without the inn a loud melancholy wail of a dog, such a sound as that animal utters in its sagacity, when much distressed by some event which it wishes to communicate to human understanding.

The howl struck upon every ear most powerfully, and not one present was there, but who seemed at once to have a presentiment that something fearful had occurred. Even Sir John Boyes assumed a natural attitude and listened, forgetting everything in the expectation of some catastrophe which had occurred without.

Again, in a more wailing tone than before, came that lengthened howl.

"It's only a dog," whispered some one, and then there was an universal movement. After which, May cried in a voice of alarm—

"Father—father, I know the voice. It's our old dog Rupert. Something has happened; you know his sagacity."

"Hush—hush," said Sir John. "In my opinion it may or it may not be Rupert; but, still——"

The Lady May did not wait for the conclusion of his speech, but she moved swiftly towards the door. Before, however, she had reached half way, several persons had opened it, and there at once entered among the crowded assemblage a large mastiff dog. He was covered with snow, and, as he stepped, he appeared either to be lame or foot wearied. In his mouth he carried some dark object, from which a liquid stream came drop by drop upon the old oaken floor. He paused not until he reached the feet of the Lady May, and there, with a low whining sound of supplication, he laid the object which he carried.

A dozen hands were stretched to take it from the floor. It was a horseman's glove, so sopped in blood, that as it was held up to the light, the ensanguined fluid dropped from its fingers' ends with a sullen plash.

For a few brief moments every one seemed petrified with astonishment and dismay. It was the Lady Philippa Boyes who then, with a shriek exclaimed—

"That glove is Ratchley's! that glove is Ratchley's! He is murdered!"

Lady Boyes, at the mention of her son's name, in connection with such a catastrophe, fainted in the arms of those around her, and the scene of hurry and confusion that immediately ensued, baffles all description. No one knew what to do, though every one seemed to have much to say; and as for poor Sir John Boyes, the equilibrium of his intellect seemed to be completely overturned.

"What is it—what is it?" he said. "Good God, what is is! My son Ratchley, heir to a baronetcy, murdered—six feet two on his stocking soles—killed, who says he's killed? He's the image of me. Lady Boyes, don't be a fool. Good gracious, do something, somebody. Is this the world, or have we all become common people?"

The Lady Philippa seemed unable to move or to speak, after uttering that dreadful suggestion; but the beautiful May, who many would have supposed the least capable of any active exertion, seemed instantly to arouse herself to meet the emergency.

"If there be men here who know not fear, let them follow me. He may be hurt, but not killed. If this be my brother's glove, is he to bleed to death on the snow for want of aid? Is there no humanity in your breasts? Do you come here to enjoy the revel and the dance, and leave your better feelings at your homes? To the heath—to the heath! let us search the heath!"

There needed scarcely half such an appeal as this to induce such a rush towards the door of the old hall, that it would seem, by the eagerness with which the younger men pressed to leave it, as if each, heedless of personal safety, was but intent upon showing to the Lady May how readily he was to do her bidding.

But ere they could leave, for the door opened inwards, and a small space was forced to be cleared, there appeared upon the threshold of the hall a young man richly habited. A winning smile was upon his face. He wore a horseman's cloak, which, partially thrown aside, disclosed the costly nature of his apparel. He had one of those pale oval faces, in which resides so much calm intelligence. The slightest indication of a moustache embraced his upper lip — there was witchery itself in the smile that played around his almost feminine mouth. He was booted and spurred, as though he had come off a journey. A jewel glittered in the cap he wore, and as he looked from face to face of the astonished throng, he said, with the softest and most winning grace and manner—

"I should much grieve if my untoward presence should disturb the hilarity of this happy meeting. I fear——"

Ere he could proceed further, the Lady May had rushed towards him, and seized him by the arm.

"Gerald Clifton—Gerald Clifton!" she cried, "where is Ratchley—where is Ratchley? Tell us, oh, tell us he is safe! Ratchley, my brother—your friend Ratchley. You could not come here and smile, if aught had happened to him. He lives—he lives, and is unhurt! Oh, speak—speak, Gerald, speak!"

"Gracious heavens!" said Gerald, "amazement sits at my heart. We parted half a day's journey from hence, and—but you jest—he is here—a Christmas jest—I see it now—and I to be so faint at heart! and yet 'twas cruel."

"And yet," gasped the Lady May, "it is too true."

But for the protecting arm of Gerald Clifton, she would have sunk insensible on the ball-room floor.

CHAPTER III.

THE KNIGHT OF THE ROAD.

While these stirring events were occurring in the long room of the old Talbot, it must not be supposed that even the desolate heath without was destitute of its scenes of bustle and excitement. Somewhere about an hour before the Lady May had began to ask her father if it was not full time for the appearance of Ratchley and his friend, a horseman had emerged from among a thick clump of leafless trees, bordering one of the hedges of the common land.

This figure appeared in bold relief against the snow, and as such was the case, it may be well that we present our readers with a brief sketch of his personal appearance.

Man and horse seemed both to be as well appointed as it was at all possible to be. The latter was coal black, and of that rather elegant symmetry, which showed that it was much better calculated for speed than for strength. Its coat shone like silk, and its small feet and short arched neck, sufficiently indicated the pureness of its breed. Its trappings were only just sufficient to enable its rider to maintain his seat, and exercise the most perfect control over its movements.

So much for the steed, and now for the rider. He was slim, and appeared of the middle size. There was about him that appearance of roundness and flexibility of muscle which gave promise of great personal activity, and as with easy grace he bent with the movements of his horse, his perfect self-possession and skill as a rider might easily be adduced.

He wore a scarlet coat, trimmed with

silver lace, horseman's boots up to his knees, and the ruffles that hung from his wrists, if he allowed his hands to drop, reached to his finger nails; a rich lace cravat, the long ends of which were thrust into the carelessly buttoned-up breast of his coat, was around his neck; some costly rings glistened on his fingers, and his hat was looped back with a jewel; his saddle was provided with holsters, and the heavily silver-mounted hilts of a pair of pistols presented themselves to his hands.

And yet with all this, although his apparel was of the finest, and his general appointments of the most costly character, no one could have mistaken this man, as he then appeared, for a gentleman. There was a swaggering ruffianly air about him, which looked as if he were trying to be something, which it was evidently quite out of his power to become; and yet among a certain class, such a man as this was looked up to as something almost more than human. His very vices assumed in their eyes the garb of virtues; and his ruffianly disregard to all his social relations of life, seemed to place him upon a pinnacle of perfection.

Our readers, although they may not know who, will have no difficulty in guessing what he was. In the mounted stranger we recognise the highwayman of the old school—a knight of the road; one of those bold, daring, insolent spirits which have became extinct within the last half century, and now belong entirely to history. He paused and listened acutely, while the horse pawed the snow up with his feet.

"Yo! ho! Angelo," he said, patting the neck of his steed; "be still," he said, "we have work to do to-night. I will give you a reputation that shall stick to you in tale and legend, for, by all that's good, I'll stop the Oxford mail to-night; I have been dared to do the deed; but the snow lies deep, the air is biting cold, and drowsy benumbed passengers, in such a night as this, are little able to make resistance to one with the warm blood dancing through his veins as mine is. Nay, Angelo, Angelo, how impatient you are—yo! ho! my steed; and that's not the only job we have to do. I have a plot which must be carried out —a bold one, and a necessary one; for my exchequer presents a melancholy aspect, and I will not meet fair eyes and smiling lips a penniless adventurer. I know not how this will end. I do not wish to hurt him; but with me it must be as it ever has been—your money or your life. It is my trade, and I will not dishonour the calling. Ah! Angelo, you prick your ears. Rare steed! you have never failed me; and before I, with the minutest attention, can hear the slightest sound, you have often warned me of friend or foe."

He wheeled the horse round, and again entered the clump of trees from whence he had emerged. The sound of the horse's feet upon the snow was completely hushed as if it trod upon many folds of velvet; and then all was still for the space of nearly five minutes in duration.

Even then but faintly could be heard the beat of a horse's feet at a hand gallop, but when the sound had once broken upon the stillness, it momentarily increased in power, until at last it was clear and evident that some mounted man was about to pass close to the ambuscade.

And now with a *sang froid* that was one of the most remarkable characteristics of the highwayman, he just trotted out from his place of concealment, and, whistling a popular air of the day, he placed himself in such a position in the way of the advancing stranger as made it evident he meant to interrupt him.

He who was coming on at so good a pace seemed to be at once aware that he would not be allowed to pass so readily that little clump of wood as he had at first supposed. He reined in his steed, so as to come up only at a short trot; and then when he got so near to the highwayman that it required no exertion of voice to make anything heard upon either side, the latter said, with a careless intonation, and a kind of cadence in his voice,—

"Hilloa! sir traveller, whither so fast? We collect a toll here, and we leave it to the generosity of a gentleman to make it worth our while to keep the gate."

"What do you mean by that?" said the stranger; "are you mad or drunk?"

"Neither, my good sir; but if you must have it in plainer language, I have a difficulty in telling the right time of day, and, therefore, will trouble you for your watch. I admire jewellery, and if you have any, will wear it for your sake. Dame Fortune has jilted me at cards—I will revenge myself for her frowns by levying a contribution from you; and if that won't do, why, have it shorter or plainer still—your money or your life!"

"A highwayman!" said the stranger. "Tell me one thing before I punish this insolence as it deserves. Are you Captain Hawk, who is sometimes called the double knight, in consequence of the rapidity of your movements from place to place?"

"Most devotedly at your service," said the highwayman, and he slightly lifted the hat from his head. "I admire your delicacy; you would not be robbed by a lesser hand than mine."

"I'm afraid," said the stranger, "I shall scarcely merit your thanks; I asked you who you were, in order that I might be quite sure that I was ridding society of one of its greatest pests; and as I am about to make a sojourn in the neighbourhood, it's as well that I should commence by ridding it of you."

The young man—for young he was—spoke these words with rapidity, and while the last were upon his lips, he drew from his saddle a pistol, and fired it directly at the head of the highwayman.

The report in the dense cool air was loud and clear, and it appeared absolutely impossible that the knight of the road could have escaped the shock.

"That was well meant," said Captain Hawk, as his horse reared, and he had some difficulty to bring him round again.

"And have I missed him?" said the young man. "Confusion!"

"It's my turn now," said the highwayman; and he at once fired upon his adversary; and it appeared with a better aim, for the young man reeled in his seat, although he did not actually fall off his horse, and one of his arms fell powerless to his side. Captain Hawk was close to him in a moment, with his hand upon his bridle.

"Fool!" he said; "if you are now taking your last look of this world, it's not my fault. I would have spared you if I could."

With professional dexterity, then, he helped himself to the valuables the young man had about him. They consisted of a watch, a considerable sum of money, and some papers, which, although of no intrinsic value in themselves, were so mingled with the cash, that the highwayman took all together, without taking the trouble to separate them.

"Scoundrel!" muttered the young stranger, between his clenched teeth; "I'm badly hurt, but we shall meet again."

"I will hope for that pleasure," said the highwayman; "and when we do meet again, be a little more carful of your mode of reception. I have a charmed life; but for all that, I will not be attempted by every one who is foolhardy enough to think that he can cope with the Hawk. Adieu."

Humming an air, he, with all the nonchalance in the world, turned his horse's head, and trotted gently from the spot.

"To be robbed," said the wounded man; "robbed on the highway by one man! How faint I am—I cannot raise my arm; and I can feel the blood pouring from the finger-ends of my glove; and there he goes in triumph. Yet, no. Why should he? I have another weapon here; there may be virtue in a second bullet; 'tis not a long shot; and I have hit my mark at a far greater distance. If—if, now, I could but bring him down!"

With his left hand—for it was his right arm that had been broken by the shot of the highwayman—he drew his second pistol from his saddle-case, and taking as steady an aim as he could, he fired after the retreating horseman.

In an instant the highwayman wheeled round, and came back to him.

"Ratchley Boyes," he said, "I know you. For this second shot, I owe you one. I will not pay you now, because the score will keep; but remember that the Hawk owes you one, and pay-day always comes. There's your bullet."

He thrust into the hands of the bewildered young man a leaden bullet, and then clapping spurs to his horse, he galloped at a hard pace from the spot.

Bewildered by the singularity of the adventure, and exhausted with the loss of blood, young Ratchley Boyes—for it was indeed he—felt a film gather over his eyes. He reeled to and fro in the saddle for a few moments, and then, with a heavy plunge, he fell from his horse.

The sagacious animal seemed to know that something fearful was amiss. It threw up its head, snorted, and pawed the ground for a minute or two, then, with a sudden plunge, he darted furiously and wildly across the heath, while the blood of its rider was changing the hue of the snow about him, as it flowed from the serious wound he had received in his arm.

CHAPTER IV.

THE OXFORD MAIL.

"Main cold, ain't it? Them as is at home is best off. Be yer got any toes, neighbour?"

These words were uttered by a rough countryman, at the top of the Oxford mail, to a shivering passenger who sat beside him, and who only vouchsafed to say in reply, in a sulky tone—

"Don't bother."

"Well," added the countryman, "I do say it be main cold; it's enough to take the nose off the face of a Christian. What do you say, marm? How do you feel?"

"I haven't had any feeling," said the female who was addressed, "for never so many miles, always except a kind of tingling from the sole of my head to the crown of my foot, ever since we was told that that dreadful Captain Hawk was in the neighbourhood; the monster, they say, is partial to females."

"Oh, it be too cold to be robbed such a night as this," said the farmer; "besides, what do you think I have done? I say, mister, what do you think I have done?"

"D—e!" muttered the man who sat next him. "Don't keep on pinching me in the ribs in that way. I tell you I'm too cold to speak; so don't bother."

"Merciful Providence!" cried the woman, "how the coach is a swagging."

"Hilloa!" cried the guard to the coachman, "where are you going to? We're off the road for a guinea."

"Who can see the road?" said the coachman. "It's road and no road here. I shan't know Hounslow Heath when I see it."

"There's a state of things," said the woman; "and I a lone female on the coach; and Hounslow Heath not to be known. It's a coming down, too, prodigious! and I've got another lapful already."

The coachman was extremely careful now, for the coach had evidently strayed from the high road, and now and then it shook so ominously from side to side as the wheels got into deep ruts, that the alarm of the passengers momentarily increased, and an impression that it would end in an upset became extremely prevalent.

"Hold hard," said the guard; "there's somebody a coming as can tell us, perhaps, where we're going."

"I see's him," said the coachman; "I think we're all right, for he's coming exactly in our line, and he's a whistling away as if there was no such thing as being frizzed to death."

Such a dense mist rose from the horses, that each of them appeared to be in a vapour-bath, and the lamps of the mail loomed strangely through that mimic fog.

"Hilloa!" cried the guard, as the horseman trotted carelessly up to the vehicle. "Can you tell us where we are?"

"Yes, on Hounslow Heath. You'll want a good story to tell when you get to the inn to-night. You can say you were stopped and robbed by Captain Hawk."

The female passenger on the outside gave a loud shriek, and that roused an old lady within, who answered by a succession of screams. The passengers who had still circulation of blood to do so, swore, while the guard kept on saying—

"Hush—hush—hush!" to every one about him, while he prepared his huge bell-mouthed blunderbuss for action.

"Hush—hush—hurrah! I'll have him. Don't speak—don't breath—here's a go. I'll have him. Now for it, here's a nob-scuttler."

Click went the lock. No other effect ensued.

"Why, you d—d fool," said the man who didn't like to be disturbed. "It's been snowing into the barrel of that thing for the last two hours and a-half."

"La!" said the guard. "My eye!

who'd athought of that?" and he looked carefully into the hugh brass-mounted blunderbuss. "Well, all I can say, if it had gone off, it would have split him to pieces nicely. There's twopen'orth of iron tacks in it, besides a dozen of buttons."

Whether the highwayman calculated upon the disabled state of the guard's blunderbuss or not, it is difficult to say, but certain it is he took no notice of that individual, or his presumed powers of mischief, but calling to the coachman, he said—

"You, Tom Bown, driver of the coach, I'll lodge a couple of ounces of lead amongst your fat, if you drive on, so now don't be a fool." He was at the coach-door in a moment, and with a rapid glance he saw that no effectual opposition would be offered to him from those within. "Gentlemen," he said, "you will be so kind as to hand me your valuables, and be as quick about it as you please. Ladies, your contributions will be thankfully received; but if there be any little article you may wish to preserve, such as a ring, a locket, a brooch, a *gage d'amour*, I always return it for a kiss."

"He's a very nice man, ma," said a young girl, who was in the extreme corner of the coach.

"Hold your tongue, you hussy—how dare you speak! A highwayman a nice man! He'd think no more of—a-hem! than nothing in the world."

"Have mercy upon us, sir," said a young gentleman who had been amusing the passengers, for the last twenty miles, with anecdotes of his feats of courage. "Have mercy upon us, dear sir, if you please. I have a tender parent, sir. I'm only nineteen, sir. Take everything, but don't hurt us."

Rings, watches, and purses, were handed tolerably freely. The highwayman's policy was always to take as much as he could, and as quickly as possible, but the appeal of the young gentleman appeared to excite his indignation.

"Why, you ape in boy's clothes," he said, "what do you mean?—open your mouth!"

"Oh, no; oh! no—no—no! Oh, mercy! Oh, don't. I believe in the Holy Ghost—the forgiveness of sins. Don't, Mr. Highwayman, don't—think of my mother."

The whole of this scene did not take more than a few minutes enacting, and then the highwayman cried out with a clear voice—

"You can go on all, and good night. Tom Brown, don't boast at the Swan again that you've never been robbed."

He was about to move off, when most unexpectedly two stout fellows, who had descended from the roof of the coach, seized his horse's bridle.

"Hurrah—hurrah!" cried the guard. "Nabbed him at last."

A blow on the head from the heavy butt-end of one of the pistols released the highwayman from one of his assailants, who instantly dropped; but the other clung to him with a desperate tenacity, so that he was compelled, from the bounds of the horse, and the manner in which he was held, to release his feet from the stirrups, and slip from the saddle. The struggle on foot was short and decisive. The highwayman gave his opponent a terrific fall, and then, as fast as he could through the snow, he strove to recall his horse, which had bounded off to some distance.

"He's afoot now—he's afoot now, Tom," cried the guard. "Hurrah! after him."

"Here goes," said the fat coachman, "and blow everything."

He turned the horses' heads in the direction the highwayman had taken, and for about half a minute there was the phenomenon of a coach and four horses pursuing a man—then there was a heavy lurch of the cumbrous vehicle—loud shrieks from its occupants, and over it went into the drift.

Captain Hawk had caught his horse, and sprung to his saddle with one bound from the earth. A glance showed him the state of affairs as regarded the Oxford mail, and with a loud righing laugh he pushed his horse at full speed towards it. A tremendous leap cleared the whole obstruction, and before any one dared to look up for fear of the horse's heels, he was out of sight.

CHAPTER V.

THE HIGHWAYMAN'S HOME.

THE occurrences which we have related, are not of a nature to be without their serious consequences. The very sound of the name of so redoubted a highwayman as Captain Hawk, was at any time sufficient to produce a large amount of consternation in any district.

His reputation was certainly not quite European, but it extended over every county in England, although the most daring of his depredations were usually committed in the immediate neighbourhood of the metropolis. There can be no doubt that rumour and popular exaggeration had done much more for the fame of this redoubtable highwayman, than he had ever done himself. But yet, notwithstanding all this, and that a great many feats of skill and valour were attributed to him wrongfully, he was, as our readers will perceive, a man of no mean accomplishments.

That he had escaped the fangs of justice so long, was, a hundred years ago, by no means so wonderful a circumstance as it would be now. We have at the present day a better organised police. The counties of England are more highly cultivated and better known; consequently, the hiding places of such depredators are much fewer, and the opportunities of perpetrating crime in lonely spots are now, indeed, few and far between.

And is it because the race of highwaymen, such as Captain Hawk, is now extinct, that these doings are now invested with the halo of romance. In the memory of our grandfathers, some of these heroes of the road still hold a place; but to us they have become matters of history, and never again, in such a country as this, can there ensue circumstances which can bring such persons into existence.

Hence, in our opinion, is it the very ecstasy of foolish apprehension to suppose that the history of such a man as Captain Hawk, with all his skill and boldness, his affected chivalric bearing, and his peculiar notions of generous feeling, can incite even the most unreasoning individual to pursue a similar course.

The opportunity for making even the attempt to follow in the footsteps of such a man is gone. Hence we join not in the outcry against such historical episodes, and we shall paint with some degree of pleasure the hair-breadth escapes, by flood and field, of this thorough-paced knight of the road.

After the two perilous adventures in which he had been engaged—for, indeed, both were most perilous—he sped on with a rapidity that showed he still had something upon his mind to do, which presented itself to him under a more important aspect than anything which he had already that night accomplished.

In his attack upon Ratchley Boyes, he had been deliberate and calm almost to an excess. His assault upon the mail, too, had been conducted as he had ample time at his disposal, and cared not how much of it the adventure occupied.

This, probably, was a portion of his system of tactics—one of the means, perhaps, by which he overcame inferior spirits, and taught them to respect his powers; but if we might judge from his after conduct, Captain Hawk was really on that night in a most desperate hurry about something.

It was a tangled and most troublesome bit of country into which he plunged after that adventure with the Oxford mail; overgrown with thick brushwood, and interspersed with tall trees, with here and there a marshy bit, on which a chance traveller might, to his great mortification, come most unexpectedly.

This, however, scarcely seemed to be an obstacle to the bold highwayman. With a knowledge of the locality which must have been most intimate, he threaded his way onwards, making a speed even in that apparent labyrinth, which few, in so inclement an evening, would have thought of accomplishing even on the open heath.

After he had proceed in this manner about half a mile, the wood in which he was, increased in density; the thick branches of the trees hung closer to the ground, and the place assumed all the appearance of a preserve, allowed naturally to become replete with vegetation, expressly so thickly planted in order that it might become a cover for game.

Without a moment's consideration, but as if he had arrived at some particular spot at which it had been his fixed intention to do what he was about to do, he flung himself from his horse, and with great celerity drawing the bridle over the animal's head, he tied it to the stump of a tree; after which, speaking a word of friendly admonition to the creature, he proceeded forward on foot, through a tangled mass of vegetation which a horseman could not have hoped to thread.

The boughs under which he walked produced a darkness beneath them almost as intense as if they had been clothed in all the beauty of their summer foliage; for so interlaced had they become, that the snow flakes falling thickly upon them had, in many instances, filled up the small interstices, producing all the appearances of a thatch of spotless whiteness above, but underneath, as dark as Erebus.

Suddenly he merged on to a small clear space, and then a few steps brought him to the door of a small hovel, which, standing as it did in that waste of nature, shut out apparently from all companionship with civilization, must surely, if inhabited at all, be the home of some person of most singular tastes and habits.

It was evident, though, that Captain Hawk presumed upon finding some one to welcome him, even in that wretched, lonely hut; and it would appear, too, that he judged but a slight summons would be sufficient to announce his presence, for the tap he gave at the door was but with his hand, as he exclaimed, in a voice more distinct than loud—

"Time—time!"

There was a flash of light from a wretched-looking casement. The low growl of a dog, and then the door was flung open, and a man with a small lantern in his hand appeared, holding back, by a firm grip of the collar, a strange mongrel-looking cur, which seemed ready at once to dart upon the intruder.

"Ah," captain," said the man, "Beauty only heard the knock, and not your voice, or she wouldn't show her teeth in this way. You're welcome—walk in, captain. Any luck to-night?"

"What's that to you?" said Hawk, as he strode across the threshold. "And as for being welcome, it would be hard indeed if a man were not welcome to his own."

"So it would—so it would," said the other; "so you're welcome as flowers in May. What about the Oxford mail, captain?"

"Robbed," said Hawk, "and left in a snow-drift."

The fellow put down the light he carried, and burst into such a roaring laugh, that Hawk turned fiercely upon him, saying—

"D—n you! I've no time for your folly—how is she?—better or worse—alive or dead?"

"Raving away, and singing the old songs over again."

"Curse the old songs!" muttered Captain Hawk. "Take care of these things till I return; and mind you keep an eye upon her—if she escape you, look to it; I've not brought her here for nothing. You will remain here till you see me again. Be very cautious; show no light at night. I—I—shall be in the neighbourhood, and have a keen sight. Here, give me the light."

While he was speaking, Captain Hawk had taken off the scarlet coat he wore, and cast it on the floor of the hut. He then divested himself of his hat, and twitched from his head a light brown wig which had covered far more luxurious locks of raven blackness. His huge horseman's boots he likewise got rid of, and then, snatching his lantern from the man, who now again lifted it from the floor, he opened a small door at the end of the hut, through while he passed, and closed it behind him.

"Hilloa, captain!" cried the man, who did not seem at all to relish being left in the dark. "Captain, I say, don't put out the light; it's the only one I have here, and there's no fire—or at least what's not much better than none, for the wet wood only smoulders on the hearth. Captain! captain! I say."

The door was flung open, and Hawk appeared, saying, in an angry voice—

"What is it—what are you bellowing at?"

"Oh, I only asked you not to blow out the light."

"Hush!—What's that?"

The fellow pointed with his thumb up to the ceiling of the hut, as he replied, in a low tone—

"It's her—her above. I thought you'd hear something of her before you went. There, that's the way she goes on day and night. A nice, d—d sort of life this for a fellow to lead—keeper to a mad woman that doesn't know how to say, pretty well, thank ye, if you ask her how she does. There she goes again; and all her talk is about——"

"What?" said Hawk.

"Newgate."

At this moment a strange, half-smothered, wailing noise from above, came upon their ears—it was that of a female; and if, from its tones, an indication of the state of the speaker's mind could be obtained, some frightful amount of anguish must have found there a home.

"Innocent!—innocent!—innocent!" she cried; "I am innocent; again and again I tell you, I'm innocent! Such a deed were too dreadful to think of—and this is Newgate—Newgate—Newgate!—the home of despair—the grave of hope. I feel the influence of its suffocating atmosphere; the air is heavy with the hot sighs of despairing wretches. Newgate—Newgate! why am I in Newgate? I did not do it—I did not do it—God knows I did not do it! I never saw it eyes—it never look upon me! Help—help!—help!"

"My eye," said the man, "there's a screech! Captain, did you hear that? That's just the sort of thing I has to go through. Now and then when I feels a little drowsy and sleepy like, she pitches it strong in the wocal line, and up I jumps, thinking the place is a fire, or something or other. I say, captain, can you give an idea of how long it's to last? It's out of my line, and that's the truth. 'Twas but this morning I went up to her, and I says 'What do you bring it in now, marm?'—'Murder!' says she. Here's a mark on my nose! D—d if I think she'd leave me such an article on my face. Blow me if some people knows what manners is."

Captain Hawk said not a word; but very slowly, as if he feared to make the least disturbing noise, that might give the shrieking maniac above an intimation of his presence, he closed the door again, which separated the two lower apartments of the hut.

"Well," said the man, whom he had now again left in the dark, "I can't say as I knows the rights of it, but the captain does, I suppose. He said he was afraid she'd lay violent hands on herself. No such luck, say I; 'twas but yesterday I chucked her an old piece of rope and a gimblet, just to give her a chance of hanging herself, but it was no go. Women are the very deuce when they does get disagreeable. Die, indeed! they'll see you d—d first! I think I see 'em at that caper. I say captain, if I was you, captain—what an odd fish he is. Now he won't speak. I don't hear him either. I'll be hanged if he ain't gone—he's popped out by the other way—and now I hear the sound of his horse's feet. There can be no mistake about it. If he's put out the light now, I'd just as soon be hung at once."

The supposition that Captain Hawk had left the hut was perfectly correct. Probably he had only come there to effect one of those remarkable changes of costume at which he had such surprising tact, and which had so frequently enabled him to elude the consequences of his numerous criminalities; but certain it is he was off, whatever had been his object, and in a few moments the sound of his horse's feet had died away upon the night air, and all was still again as the very grave, save an occasional low moaning wail from that heart-stricken being in the loft above the lower rooms of the hovel, and the muttered curses of the man, who seemed half inclined to defy, and yet to dread doing so, the orders of Captain Hawk to remain where he was as a sentinel over that luckless and ill-starred creature.

In the meantime, how or by what means the dog belonging to the Boyes family had found the glove saturated with the gore of the young Ratchely, no one knew.

Possibly, having accompanied the remainder of the family to the farmhouse, and not being considered a fit guest for the well-filled ball-room of the Talbot, he had taken, of his own accord, a stroll upon the common, and the scent of blood might have taken him to the spot where the young man had met with his misadventure.

We cannot say this fortunate finding of the glove was the means of saving the life of Ratchley Boyes, for although he had now fainted from exhaustion, where he lay, the intense cold of the night, and the still falling snow, prevened the further effusion of blood from the wound; but still he migth have been subject to other accidents by flood and field, but for the timely aid which came to him in consequence of the discovery made by the dog.

We left our guests at the Talbot in a state of the greatest apprehension and alarm. May Boyes was quickly taken from the arms of Gerald Clifton, and consigned to the guardianship of the portly Mrs. Butts, who, folding her in an embrace that perfectly extinguished her, called out for water, as the poor thing had fainted.

"And the poor thing," said Peter Butts, "will be suffocated too, if you don't let her go. For heaven's sake, wife, set her down. It's like being embraced by a state bed, with full chintz hangings."

Poor May was rescued from the overwhelming kindness of Mrs. Butts, and seated near to a window, where she soon began to show signs of returning consciousness, while poor Sir John, without speaking to any one, went about wringing his hands, and looking curiously in everybody's face he came to, as if he expected there to see written the exact particulars of what had occurred to his son Ratchley.

"My dear Sir John," said Gerald Clifton, "let my feelings of friendship for your family, and admiration for yourself, plead my excuse for being so rude as to request to know really what is the matter."

"Ratchley—Ratchley!" exclaimed May, who had now sufficiently recovered to hear and understand what was going on around her. "Where is Ratchley? Gerald Clifton, where is he? came he not with you?"

"A great part of the way he certainly did; we separated some few miles off; I had a call to make, and we took separate routes."

"Oh, seek him—seek him! he is murdered!"

"Lights—lights, my masters," cried Peter Butts; "the dog hasn't come far, I'll be bound, and if young Master Ratchley has met with any accident, you may depend it's on the common. We'll soon find him. Cheer up, Miss May; a little blood makes a great show; and after all, if this be Master Ratchley's glove, which I don't see how you can be quite sure of, he may not be much hurt. Come on—come on; we'll have a hunt for him in the snow. Lay hold of all the candles you can, my men, and follow me."

"And how many candles," said Gerald Clifton, "do you expect will live out of doors on such a night as this? A stable lantern will answer all the purpose; and yonder dog, no doubt, will guide you accurately to the spot where any mischief lies."

"Will you come with us, sir?"

"Most certainly. Bear with me a moment, and I'm with you."

He stooped till his lips touched the ear of May Boyes.

"Be not alarmed," he said; "always sufficient for the hour is its evil. A thousand circumstances short of anything serious may have occurred to Ratchley. I love him for his own sake, as well as for the sake of one whom I love better. I will not return to you without news of him. Adieu, dear May! Let me live in your remembrance."

Before May Boyes could return to him even a word of thanks, he was gone, but his words had filled her with a strange and new delight. A delight that even successfully struggled into existence, notwithstanding the cloud of depression that was on her spirits, and the dreadful feeling of uncertainty that hung around the fate of her brother.

Did she love Gerald Clifton? she had not yet asked the question of her own heart. Had she asked it, she would have feared to reply to it; and yet truthfulness was an inherent principle in the mind of May Boyes. What was it, then, in the few and simple words Gerald Clifton had uttered, which brought so exquisite a sensation of pleasure to her heart? How was it that he, by merely speaking of hope, by merely starting a favourable supposition on the subject of her anxieties, could make so great a change in her feelings?

Could it be possible that that single word "dear," which he had appended to her name, had solved some weighty riddle at her heart? Did she from that feel that he loved her? or was the word one of those chance-spoken ones which slipped from the unguarded tongue in a moment of generous emotion, breathing really nothing of passion, and meaning nothing but a kindly sentiment of humanity?

We shall see; but much we fear that the heart of the beautiful May Boyes is already ensnared; much we fear that we shall have to sigh over the ruin of her fondest and best affections, and that she is already far from being fancy free.

But does not Gerald Clifton love her? and if loving her, why would we not bestow her on him? These are questions that time will answer, and in the solution of which our readers will share with us.

That we have paused for a brief moment to pity May Boyes, has arisen from an irresistible emotion. It is a sequence to that with which we are acquainted, to that sad tale of terror, anguish, and despair, which we have charged ourselves to tell, and which shall bring woe to thee, thou most beautiful and just.

But to our tale. Fifty ready hands were ready to do any good servive for May Boyes. Peter Butts had no want of assistance in the search he proposed upon the snow-clad common, and that large, thronged room in the old Talbot Inn, which had so lately appeared crammed almost to uneasiness with guests, wore a desert aspect, while the ruddy glare from the fires within the house shone forth now from the open doors and casements; for those who went not forth for the search followed with straining eyes those who did, as they saw them, like black specks upon the snow, following the track of the dog, who now bounded towards the spot where Ratchley Boyes lay in the seeming sleep of death.

The direct route which the dog took caused many a tumble in the deep snow drift, and there were some laggards on the way ere the party got half the distance between the Talbot Inn and that spot of ground which had witnessed the encounter between Ratchley and the highwayman.

Quite enough, however, sped forward to render every asssistance that might be requisite, and when the dog suddenly paused and set up a lengthened howl, old Peter Butts, who was the foremost of the cavalcade, stepped forward but another pace, and then held his lantern to the ground, as he exclaimed—

"Good God! my masters, he is indeed murdered! Here's a sight! God help us all!"

There lay Ratchley, in the midst of such a mass of snow and blood, that it was terrible to look upon him; and although the throng of persons, impelled by intense curiosity, first crowded round what they supposed to be the body, a a kind of terror soon came over them, and with one accord they shrank back, making a wider circle round that fearful spectacle.

Gerald Clifton without a word took the lantern from the hand of the landlord, and regardless of the half-frozen pool of blood around, he flung himself upon one knee by the body, and tearing open the vest, he astonished every one by placing his ear flat upon the region of the heart, as if he were intent upon nestling on the bosom of the dead.

It was but for an instant he thus remained, and then springing to his feet, he cried—

"He lives! and, if I may judge from his appearance, he is not much hurt. Carry him at once to the inn; he is insensible, but when there we shall soon hear from his own lips some account of what has reduced him to this said condition."

This round assertion, spoken so confidently, with regard to the existence of Ratchley Boyes, exercised an effect quite magical upon all present. The strange solemnity and the awe-struck appearaace that had sat upon every countenance while they thought they were in the presence of death, immediately fled, and many who probably could not have been induced by any bribe to touch the dead body, now that they believed life only for a time suspended, were the most eager in rendering efficient assistance in the conveyance of the wounded man to a place of safety.

Poor Ratchley had become completely frozen to the ground, and it required quite an effort to disengage his apparel from among the snow. Four persons, however, lifted him in their arms, and Gerald Clifton, leading the way with the lantern, and taking rapid strides along the same path they had so lately traversed, they all proceeded with their ghastly burden, with far greater speed than they had left the inn, back again to its friendly shelter.

When they arrived within sight of its time-hallowed porch, Gerald Clifton handed the lantern to the landlord, and then dashed forward alone with great speed, so that he reached the long, low dancing-room some minutes before those who carried the wounded man. He dashed in without the slightest ceremony or preparation.

"He lives, he lives!" he cried; "Ratchley lives. He is but slightly hurt. May Boyes, where is she?"

"He lives!" cried Sir John, and thought he was sinking into a chair, but in reality fell on the floor. "Lives! Then the baronetcy will not be extinct, and the glory of the Boyeses will continue unfaded."

"Where is May?" said Gerald.

"Young sir," said Sir John, "there ought to have been a chair behind me—some miscreant has removed it; and as for my daughter, the Lady May, she is in a chamber precisely above this room, as I am informed, carefully tended by——"

"Thank you—thank you," said Gerald, and turning upon his heel, he dashed from the ball-room, and up the first staircase that presented itself, in a moment.

The old inn was exceedingly intricate, and it required a person to be most amazingly well acquainted with all its various staircases and corners to find even any particular chamber that was described to him. It was, therefore, not much to be wondered at that, having but the vague direction of a chamber above the ball-room to go to, Gerald Clifton should be somewhat out in his topography when he reached the landing.

He paused now, as a natural consequence, to think; not that he did himself any good by so doing, because he really had no basis for reflection; never before had he been above the ground-floor of the old inn, and he presented the phenomenon of a man making an apparently laborious effort to remember what he had never known.

"Confound these old rambling places," he said; "one cannot guess which way to turn. Sir John mentioned the room immediately above the hall. Let me consider. The staircase runs up in a spiral—Surely I must be right. What a strange light the snow casts from its reflected surface into this old corridor. Ah! I hear the sound of voices; that must be the room; the news I bring sanctions my intrusion. Pretty May Boyes, if I do not this night advance myself somewhat in your favour, it will be an astonishing fact, and no fault of mine."

It was the murmur of female voices which broke upon the ear of Gerald Clifton, and he doubted not for a moment that they proceeded from the room into which the beautiful May Boyes had been conveyed. His purpose was no vacilating one, however much his progress from the ball-room partook of that character; and, now that he no longer doubted that he was on the right path, he sprang forward in the direction of the sounds he had heard, and pushing rudely open a door which yielded to his touch, he found himself in the principal bedchamber of the old inn—a large room, the roof of which was crossed and interspersed with huge beams of wood.

An exclamation of surprise arose from some one at his entrance, and then a scream from some one else produced universal confusion among the inmates of that chamber.

But Gerald Clifton was intent upon his purpose, and little he heeded what might be thought or what might be said by others. On the bed, partially covered by its ample coverlet, lay May Boyes, her hair dishevelled, her face pale, and apparently far, very far, from recovered from the mental shock she had so recently received. For the bold intruder to spring to her side was the work of a moment; casting aside all scruples and punctilios of time and place, he seized her hand, exclaiming—

"He lives—he lives! May, look up, he lives!"

"My brother?" half screamed the beautiful girl.

"Yes, Ratchley; and is but little hurt."

It was with an hysteric scream of delight that she raised herself partially from the bed, and in the impulse of the moment, as if she could not thank him enough who brought her such gladsome tidings, she flung herself upon the breast of Gerald Clifton, and while his arms encircled her for a brief moment, a gush of tears relieved her overladen heart.

In another moment she fell backward again upon the bed, and then the young man, turning to the astonished females

THE MIDNIGHT RIDE.

who were in the room, lifted his hat, which he still wore, gracefully from his head, as he said, in such bland and musical accents that they imparted a grace to every word he uttered—

"Ladies, place your gentlest construction upon this intrusion; as I am a gentleman, and one who I hope will ever feel sensations of honour, I meant no wrong in coming hither. I know that my presence here is unsanctioned by custom: let my excuse be, that I brought news of joy to her who is afflicted, and that I profoundly appreciate the extreme courtesy I have received from such a collection of wit, beauty, and intelligence as I now see before me. Ladies, adieu!"

And so he vanished.

"Quite the gentleman!" said the landlady. "Did you ever, my dear, see such a nice young man? Intruding, indeed—not him. There's a air and a grace. We's wit, beauty, and intelligence; there's judgment. He'll die young, I know he will; such as him always goes first. There's my husband, now, as different a sort of man as may be, no more delicacy than a pig, and stronger than a rum puncheon. When will he go, I wonder?—ladies, never!"

"Ah, you've had a great deal to put up with in your time, Mrs. Butts," said one; "and I must say, if I was asked on my bible oath to say who I thought was the most elegant young man I had ever seen, it would be Mr. Clifton."

"He lives—he lives!" murmured May, "and in those words I live again. Let me rise; I am much better now. Where is he? where is Ratchley?"

At this moment the sound of many voices, and the trampling of feet in the lower part of the inn, announced the arrival of the cavalcade bearing the still insensible Ratchley Boyes.

May sprang from the bed, and despite a feeble effort to retain her, rushed from the room, meeting the supporters of that corpse-like form, stiffened in blood, before they had well crossed the threshold of the inn with their ghastly looking burden.

She was about to utter some exclamation of terror and surprise at seeing Ratchley so immovable, when a voice whispered gently in her ear—

"Hush—hush! dear May. Believe me, there is no danger; he lives—on my sacred word, he lives!"

It was Gerald Clifton.

"I will be calm," she said; "I will be calm," and she hung heavily upon his arm. "With your assurance that he lives, I can be calm."

"Carry him up stairs," cried Sir John; "no, I mean down stairs; that is to say, leave him here—or take him into that room, or this, or something. Great minds are always prompt in danger. Do something, somebody, for Heaven's sake; and then I'll direct you. This way—no, the other way. That it should come to this!—one of our family covered with snow and bleeding; the precious blood of the Boyeses mixing itself up with sand on the floor of an inn. Run for all the doctors, somebody. What would you do without me? Bless my heart and soul, how we rise with the occasion; that's always the way with great minds, too."

In a clear, audible voice, Gerald Clifton directed that the frozen, bleeding form of Ratchley Boyes be conveyed into the ball-room, at the further end of which, and sufficiently from the fire to prevent any ill effects from too sudden a change of temperature, he had him comfortably bestowed upon some chairs, and then, with a skill and readiness which no one thought him capable of possessing, he proceeded not only to examine the wound, but to use such means as it was possible for him to procure for the recovery to consciousness of his friend Ratchley.

"Bless my heart," said Sir John—"and the nearest doctor lives a dozen miles off. What's to be done now? The heir-at-law of the great Boyes' family waiting for a surgeon. These physical people ought always to be following about persons of distinction, in case of being wanted; but it's always the way with the lower orders, they prefer their own ease and idleness to their most sacred duties."

"Let me have some water," said Gerald Clifton, "and a sponge. I think, Sir John, you may safely trust me, in the absence of the regular practitioner, to do what is requisite here. I have made human maladies much by study; and, moreover, I do not conceive this to be a case which will call largely upon any one's skill. I want some water and a sponge."

"Yes, yes; ah, to be sure," said Sir John; "water and a sponge; run everybody for water, and the rest of you for a sponge."

"I'll go," said May; "those requisites that you require, Gerald, are in the room above."

She was holding the head of Ratchley, and Gerald Clifton saw she was unwilling to forego her trust.

"I will go more expeditiously than any one," he whispered.

"A thousand thanks," said May; and away he started to go again to that apartment which he had at first so great a difficulty in finding. He rushed up the staircase with rapid strides, and now he paused not for one moment in that corridor where he had before held council with himself, but, guided by the moonlight which at intervals struggled in through the latticed windows, he made his way towards the door of the apartment. He was within a few paces of reaching it, when a sudden and a fearful yell burst upon his ears. It seemed more like a shout of some wild animal in mockery of a human cry, than aught human, reduced even to the most dire extremity.

Well might Gerald Clifton stagger back in terror and amazement; and he staggered back but just in time to save himself from a more furious attack than was really made upon him. With a rush, as if propelled by some unseen power, there came sweeping on a human form along that corridor; to grapple him by the throat was the work of a moment—a brief but furious struggle brought them to the stair-head, and as if he had been an infant in the arms of a giant was Gerald Clifton hurled down the whole flight.

All this was the work of a moment. Those who were attending upon Ratchley heard the singular cry from above, and many had made their way to the foot of the staircase; among the foremost of them was Sir John, who, indeed, had ascended a few steps, not knowing what he was doing or where he was going.

The consequence, however, of this was, that he was immediately encountered by the falling form of Gerald Clifton, and such was the rapidity with which they for a few moments rolled over together, that those around could only look on in speechless wonder as to what was going to happen next.

It was Clifton who, notwithstanding the severe fall he had had, sprang to his feet first, leaving poor Sir John stretched out upon his back, apparently without sense or motion. Fury was in every look and gesture of Clifton, and every eye followed his as he bent an earnest gaze up the staircase. Something dark appeared a considerable distance up, which moved slightly. Clifton had seen it, and before any one could make a remark upon the circumstance, he drew a small pistol from his pocket, and fired it up the stairs.

A short crack came fluttering down; but when the sound of the pistol's discharge had ceased, nothing was heard, and so intense was the dismay and astonishment which had taken possession of all present, that each remained in a fixed attitude except Sir John, who now sat up and was woefully touching his nose, from which drops of blood came drop by drop upon the floor between his feet.

"Gracious Heavens!" exclaimed May, as she clung to Clifton, for she had rushed from the ball-room upon hearing the pistol-shot; "what has happened? are this night's terrors never to be done?"

"Yes," said Clifton, "they're over; some one attacked me in the corridor above, and I fell down the staircase. I think I have had my revenge, but am not sure; let those search who will, I care not."

He turned from the staircase, and May Boyes saw it was with a shudder that he did so, and she suspected that dread had more to do than carelessness with his determination not to proceed up the staircase again.

"I don't see," said Sir John Boyes, "why I should be knocked down and trampled upon under any possible circumstances. I had certainly no idea that society was in such a state, I beg leave to remark. Murder!"

He was assisted to his feet, and then Clifton said to him—

"Forgive me, Sir John; it was unintentional. May Boyes, I have forgotten something, but will see you to-morrow morning at breakfast in your father's hall. Adieu!" and then he added, in a whisper, "remember me."

Without a word of greeting or adieu to another person, he turned and left the inn, encountering, nearly upon the threshold, a melancholy cavalcade, made up of all the passengers of the Oxford mail, headed by the guard, with his amiable and peaceable blunderbuss in one hand and his horn at his lips, upon which he blew a long and horrible blast, as if they were knights of old arrived at some castle gate, whose frowning portal looked angrily down upon them.

CHAPTER VI.

THE LOVERS' VOWS.

A WEEK has elapsed, the snow has melted off the heath, one of those sudden and delicious changes has taken place in the aspect of the season which speak to all hearts gently and sweetly of the coming summer. It was a day suggestive of thoughts of deep sunshine, many-tinted and fragrant flowers, songs of birds, and all those sights and sounds which make the vernal season such a dream of delight. The breath of the south wind had melted the icy manacles in which the earth had been bound, the congealed streams again bubbled forth their pleasant music; there was a pleasant freshness in the air, and the light fleecy clouds lent the charm of spring-time to the deep blue sky.

It was on such an eve as this, one little hour before the coming shadows of the night would envelope all objects, that two figures stood upon a raised terrace which ran along the southern side of Boyes Hall. Some former owner of the large estate must have travelled in Italy, and there contracted a taste for the style of gardening prevalent in that sunny clime. The gardens of Boyes Hall were laid out in that style, half formal, half picturesque, which is ascribed to the Italian school.

There were vases, grottoes, and fountains; long straight walks, with here and there the statue of some sylvan deity or ancient god; while the terrace upon which these two persons stood seemed to have been constructed as a stately walk from which to view the far-stretching beauties that lay beneath.

The light of day was gradually decreasing, and the soft, damp, warm wind which had brought about the wondrous change upon the face of nature, was beginning, now that the brief sunshine was sinking, to show more power, as if it felt more independence. It came occasionally with a briefer and a lustier gust, moaning among the old trees, and bending down their leafless branches with its unseen agency.

One of those forms was that of a man, not tall, but of that middle height and symmetrical proportion which betokens more agility than brutal strength. His companion is young and beautiful, her hands are locked around one of his, while his disengaged arm encircles that slender waist so seemingly fragile; and they are not looking on the gardens or the glowing sunset; his eyes are fixed with searching earnestness upon her face, while hers, in downcast, maiden meditation, seem but to see the marble flags upon which they stand.

It is Gerald Clifton—bold, handsome, and full of talent—who has stolen out at this sweet evening hour to whisper such a tale to May Boyes as may well make her ears tingle with delight, and her young heart to beat as though it would burst its dwelling-place.

She loves him! she loves him with a love such as a being of such sensibility and intelligence alone can feel. She loves him, not with the ordinary affection which may rather be called a preference than a passion, but with her whole mind, her whole genius, her heart, and her soul; as she loves Heaven she loves that man. Such persons as May Boyes never love but once, and then the gushing, headlong passion sweeps away all obstacles, and it is the well spring of a thousand happinesses or the tomb of slaughtered hope; she has no being but in him; he is her idol, her breath, her life itself.

Let those who would blame her for the impetuosity of her passions, blame rather the prodigality of nature that made her a being of such rare gifts. She could do nothing weakly or tamely. Alas! for the happiness of such beings; they build the houses of their joy on the quicksands of delusion, and at one moment of betrayal all is wrecked.

Woe be to those who, like May Boyes, are not of the common heard; woe be to those who are gifted with the disastrous privilege—godlike though the gift appear—of nobler, higher aspirations than their compeers. Fatal gift, that light of genius, which illumines the heart but to destroy it!

Yes, she loved him. There need no words of ours to paint the pure devotion of her spirit; nor could she now, so deep-seated was that idol of her heart in its innermost shrine, by any ordinary circumstances of conduct or of action, pluck his image from that dear abiding place. Yes, she loved him! and in those brief words are concentrated, as regards May Boyes, a whole world of devotion.

And did he return with like affection that young girl's happier, better feelings? Was he the man to feel for her that torrent of blessed emotion which she deserved, as but a fit recompense for the soul-absorbing tenderness in which she held him? Fearful question! one that must be answered by acts, not words.

Let us listen to the lovers.

It was Gerald Cliftou who spoke, after the silence which had been maintained for nearly the fourth part of an hour; he spoke, too, with enthusiasm, and that rich, glossy tone which we will not say always masks hypocrisy, but which clever hypocrisy is never without.

"I have long loved you," he said; "since first I saw you here on this terrace, when your brother and I returned from Oxford at the period of our last happy sojourn in this, to me, sacred and sainted house, I loved you. You'll say the passion was of sudden growth, but not the less majestic was it, not the less glorious the fruitage that it bore. That love which wants such careful tending, that from a tender sapling it must be fostered till it grow gigantic, is not of my complexion. I loved you, May, from the first not better than I love you now, and now I love you not the less because I feel that heart responds to heart. Is it not so, my sweet May?"

"Gerald Clifton," was all she could say, and then she seemed to be rather communing with herself, and repeating to her own heart that name which bore about it the halo of a magic spell.

There was a silence now again for a few moments' duration, and again Gerald spoke.

"Can you be mine," he said, "knowing so little of me; feeling, even, that the shroud of mystery is around me? Can you yet be mine?"

"For ever!"

"Bold words, May Boyes; and yet such as I should not quarrel with. I never loved before I saw you."

"It is destiny," said May. "Let us walk upon the terrace."

"Yes, yes, it may be destiny. We will walk; the air grows chill."

"I felt it not. I knew not that it touched my cheek."

"And, so, May, despite of all your father's anger, perchance, and malediction, a mother's tears, and a brother's fury, you will yet be mine?"

"In my own thoughts of thee, Gerald Clifton, I have no father, no mother, no brother. 'Tis you who can make or who can destroy me! I am yours, yours only! To live, or to die, to joy, or to suffer, I say again, it is my destiny!"

"A strange feeling, May, and yet so closely bordering on my own, for I am not one to make a superstitious clamour of it,—I do despair, dearest, of your friends' sanction to our union."

"Then," said May, "our union must want our friends' sanction. What are friends to me?"

"You are young, and you are enthusiastic; as yet you have not known the pressure of a single want. What if I am poor?"

"I care not. We'll live as live the forest birds."

"Nay, May Boyes, you know not that great world of which you speak. But if we fly from here, surely we might take with us something?"

"Yes," said May, "a mutual love, scorning all things but itself."

"Nay, I hear your family have jewels."

"We have one of priceless lustre."

"Indeed!"

"Yes, in our hearts—fit casket for such a treasure."

"Yes, yes; oh, yes. But can we live, dear May, on air or herbs, on flowers, or on romance?"

"We can beg."

"A most unsentimental employment. But wherefore talk we thus? There is much treasure in this house, so I've heard; we do not value it, for to us the brightest gold is but a speck of dross compared to our pure affections; still, however, would we be glad to have the power of holding out the hand of fellowship to deep distress."

"Ah! now I know your motive; but it may not be—but we will touch nothing. Friendless and penniless, if it must be so, we will go forth. I would not lay a hand upon that Indian cabinet, the glittering contents of which my father sets such store by, to save my life; it would seem such profanation to my love to mingle it with such grosser feelings. That Heaven, Gerald, which has brought us together, and which has fashioned us of sympathetic souls, will not desert its creatures. We will trust in that, and we will grieve not that the luxuries of life are taken from us, for we shall look upon even its privations through such a medium, as ten times more glorious than its ordinary choicest blessings."

"Yes, yes," said Gerald Clifton, "who can do other with such sentiment expressed so eloquently? My beautiful May, it is a pride as well as a delight to hear you. I sometimes wonder to myself what I could have said or done to win you."

"And I," said May Boyes, with a touch of mournfulness in her tone, "and I believed myself for ever fancy free, and that the trammels of what the world calls love would never fall upon me; and I was told by those who had felt the soft influence, of such a delicious dream, that when I did love, it would be a passion past all bounds of reason; such a love as sets experience, counsel of friends, and all the world's usual habits, at defiance."

"And have you found that to be true?"

"Most true—most true."

"And yet——"

"Why do you pause, Gerald Clifton? Have you a doubt? If you have you love not. To doubt affection is at once to discard it for ever form the mind."

"No—no, my beautiful May, I have no doubt of thee. How well and prettily you turned aside my notions of worldly wisdom when you spoke about the Indian cabinet, which, after all, I dare say contains nothing but such curiosities as old folks doat upon, things of no intrinsic value, although they may occasion a gape of astonishment from the unlettered multitude."

"You're wrong, dear Gerald. But this is a theme scarcely worth our talking of."

"Most true, except as a matter of mere curiosity. There is wealth, you say, in the Indian cabinet?"

"A large amount. One of our ancestors was curious in precious stones. Living in a style far below the commonest and meanest income, he expended nearly the whole of his revenue in the purchase of gems; he was half a madman, they say, and had some fancy of huge profits eventually from the disposal of them. He died, though, without his dream of ambition being fulfilled; and, as he left an estate completely unencumbered, the next heir let the precious stones remain, and so the next, and the next, which was my father."

What a strange fancy. Dear May, oh! if I could find but words to tell you how I love you."

"None are required; I ask for no asseverations. When I meet you, look upon me as you now look, and I shall be content. Speak gently, yet not timidly; and when we part, do it with a tenderness of regret, mingling yet with happiness at the thought of how soon we'll meet again. Our interview has already been prolonged beyond the bounds of prudence; I am about to visit Ratchley, and will pass into the house by the picture-gallery. Gerald Clifton, come weal or woe, I will love you! Heaven itself may interpose; and even then, if it be impiety to love you, I am impious."

She suddenly paused and trembled. Gerald flew to her side.

"You're unwell," he said anxiously; "your colour flits like the sunshine of an April day."

"A sudden pang," she said, "from what cause I know not—'tis over, and all is well. Farewell, until a few short hours, and then joy again. It is night till then."

She walked slowly down the terrace, until she came to one of the deep bay windows that opened upon it, through which she passed into the mamon.

Gerald Clifton gazed after her musingly; his brows contracted, and he compressed his lips as if he feared to give utterance, even to the idling evening air, to his thoughts. He muttered something, but so inaudibly that the words were not half formed, and then he turned off in another direction and entered the house.

CHAPTER VII.

THE BROTHER AND SISTER.

Oh! what a change had come over the spirit of the beautiful May Boyes; she was now far, very far, from being the gladsome, happy spirit which she was some short time since. The wild extravagance of her devotion to Gerald Clifton seemed to have robbed her pure spirit of all its gaiety, and so sudden had been the transformation from the happy, laughing girl to the deep-think woman, that those who had known and admired her a few short months since, would scarce have recognised her, so altered was her mien and general bearing.

She no longer walked with the same light, dancing step, but with a swan-like gliding movement she passed from place to place. In her very smile there seemed a melancholy, and that boundless passion which had taken possession of her very soul had evidently drowned in its overwhelming torrent all previous pleasures.

We will not say that those whom she loved before no longer shared her affections; her love for Gerald Clifton was of a different character. Her tenderness for these who were allied to her, and with whom she had passed many of her happiest days, knew no diminution since the accession of this wondrous passion.

It had yet to be seen if they would place themselves in hostile array against it when it should become known to them—which would be the victim; those old household loves and feelings which had grown with her growth, and strengthened with her strength, or this new love for a stranger, which appeared so boundless as to carry her to the verge of credulity?

We will follow her to her brother's room.

Although the wound which Ratchley Boyes had received was by no means a serious one in itself, yet the consequences which had ensued upon it had been of a character to excite serious alarm.

He was a young man in the prime of health and vigour; he had ridden hard to be present as early as possible in the ball-room at the old Talbot Inn, and his blood was heated and fevered when he received the wound from the highwayman's pistol bullet.

Notwithstanding, therefore, the considerable loss of blood which, of course, had tended greatly to delay the danger of inflamatory symptoms, poor Ratchley had lain for several days in a most precarious condition.

The strictest orders had been given by the medical men attending upon him, that he should not be pestered with questions concerning the manner in which he had received his wound, and now that he had sufficiently recovered that this interdict was removed, the young man himself was taciture and distant upon the subject, turning off the conversation always into another channel, as if it were one he would fain not converse on.

Sir John Boyes had been the most curious of the whole family to know the particulars of how anybody could forget so far what was due to his patrician blood as to spill any of it upon any pretence whatever.

But Ratchley had answered his father distantly, merely saying that the man who had attacked him was a highwayman, and that further he could say nothing.

Sir John Boyes had, therefore, only the melancholy satisfaction of writing a letter to the secretary of state for the time being, to whom he detailed the atrocious circumstance, and requested the government, through him, the secretary of state, to take some uncommon steps in the proceeding, and to offer instantly a large reward for the discovery of the offender.

To this proposition, he had a reply full of politeness and terms of consideration, the gist of which was, however, that the goverment was very sorry through him, the secretary of state, but that, on the whole, it rather advised him to offer the reward himself.

It was May Boyes alone, who seemed to read in the eyes of Ratchley that there was surely some secret connected with the mode and manner of the attack. She did not long to know, but yet she had a feeling as if it would have have much gratified her to be made acquainted with its minutest particular.

Noiselessly she enters the sick chamber; Ratchley was sleeping, and she places a chair by the bedside, on which she sinks to watch his repose, and after indulge herself in the dreary thoughts incidental to her passionate love.

The sleep of Ratchley was anything but profound, moans and impatient murmurs came from his lips, and at times he tossed his arms to and fro, saying, as he did so—

"Off—off—off. Murderer, off!"

May watched him intently, and believing that a sleep like that could be in no way refreshing, she gently awakened him, and holding his hand in both of hers, she whispered to him in soothing accents—

"Ratchley, Ratchley, awake; 'tis I, your sister, May. What visions are those that disturb your slumbers?"

He gazed upon her for a moment in silence, and then, in a low voice, he said—

"Have I spoken, May? What have I uttered?"

"Nothing, Ratchley, of reason. Nothing, that the judgment could come to any conclusion from."

"It is well—it is well," he said. "Oh, that I were off this bed of pain and suffering. Where is Gerald Clifton?"

"In the house, brother, an honoured guest, for your sake as well as for his own."

"Sister," said Ratchley, "are we quite alone?"

"Yes, yes; what would you say?"

"It is a secret which I thought to hide deep in the recesses of my own bosom until I could myself, hand to hand, meet him of whom I am now about to speak."

"What means this preparation? Speak freely, Ratchley, and at once, to me."

"Before I go further, sister May, answer me some questions. I fancied that at our last vacation here you had a kindness for this Gerald Clifton, my college friend; but whether that has proved fleeting, or has deepened, I know it will not prevent you answering me truly that which I shall ask of you."

"It will not," said May, in so low a voice, that it scarcely reached her brother's ears.

"Then, does Gerald Clifton pass his evenings with the family?"

"No, brother; he has a sick friend some miles off, and let the weather be what it may, hail, rain, sleet, or snow—let the loudest wind that ever howled from Heaven be blowing, he mounts his horse, and goes upon his pious errand. It is not great and noble of him?"

"Very," said Ratchley.

"That *very*," said May, "sounds not like a genuine affirmation of the sentiment. Beware, brother, for one moment breating aught evil of Gerald Clifton."

"Why beware, May?"

"Because it is impossible you should be right."

"Alas! my sister, this is blind faith—intolerant bigotry. I am not strong enough to carry on a long discourse; but beneath yon table lies a small vallise; some two hours since it was brought to me by our faithful servant, Andrew. For the first time he found it unlocked in Gerald Clifton's chamber."

"Brother!" exclaimed May, "do I hear aright, or is this some dream? Is not Gerald Clifton our guest, and has any one, knowing him to be such, dared so far to violate the holiest rights of hospitality, as to pry into that which alone belongs to him?"

"Hush! sister, hush; you take too inflated and romantic a view of this business. It remains yet to be seen who has violated the rights of hospitality; honest Andrew, who has acted under my directions, or Gerald Clifton."

"What mean you? What hideous mummery is this? Brother, brother, you know not what you say."

"Open the vallise, and look at its contents."

"Never!"

"This is infatuation. In that vallise is a suit of clothing that I have seen before; or, at all events, one of a similar pattern. A scarlet coat, richly trimmed, horseman's boots, lightly made, and folded up into a small compass, a cap looped with a jewel, the arms and the accoutrements of him who——"

"What, what, brother—what? Is this a time to pause?"

"It is not—I will finish—who shot me on the heath."

A wild kind of laugh came from May Boyes' lips, as she cried—

"This is madness—this is madness! rank insanity—the delirium of fever. Oh! Ratchley, Ratchley, speak of this to none but me!"

"Ah, ah! I do perceive but too truly," said Ratchley, "that you have warmed this serpent in your bosom but to sting you!"

"Serpent!"

"Yes, May; I tell you now I have a feeling as strong as that I have in Heaven's mercy, that it was Gerald Clifton's

MAY, DISGUISED AS HAWK, STOPS THE WAGGON.

self who stopped me on the heath; at the very time, and when the cold moonbeams fell upon the face, each moment, well disguised as it was, it grew more familiar to me, and I knew him. Hush, sister, not a word—not a word till I am up and stirring; but keep you an eye upon him for my sake, for your own sake, and for the sake of all you love that are in this house. I tell you, sister, that man is not what he seems."

May Boyes sat for some moments

motionless as a statue. She then rose from the chair by her brother's bedside, and moving to the door with a strange gliding movement, she muttered—

"Oh, yes, I will watch him—who will watch him as I shall? Gerald Clifton, Gerald Clifton, this of thee!"

She reached her own chamber, she clasped her brow for a moment, and then she wrung her hands.

"No—no—no!" she cried, and then, as if alarmed at the sound of her own voice, she placed her finger on her lips and added—"Hush, hush! if it be so, it is my destiny. I love him still."

She dashed a quantity of cold water upon her face. She was death-like pale as she mechanically arranged the long tresses of her silk-like hair, and then she walked down to the principal hall, where well she knew that Gerald Clifton was wont to linger ere he went on what she had described as his deed of greatness and piety, with the hope of a glance from her, or some fond pressure of the hand, ere he mounted his steed and was away.

Sir John and his lady were in the hall, and Philippa, as well as Gerald Clifton, who was smiling in his own fascinating way.

"Ah, May," he said, "I'm off again; my poor friend is no better. He calls my visits like angels, few and far between, and yet I see him every day; is not that wilful of him? Adieu, adieu, we shall meet in the morning; or, perchance, I may be in early."

May gave him her hand, but the smile with which she accompanied it was forced and painful. In the hurry of the adieu he noticed it not, and in another moment he had mounted his horse, and was trotting slowly down the avenue of ancient trees that led to the lodge gates.

"My dear May," said Sir John, "it strikes me, that in consequence of an improvement in the symptoms attendant upon Ratchley's wounds, we may pronounce him a little better, and I do not myself entertain the slightest doubt in the world, that if he goes on continually improving, and don't get any worse, he will eventually get well—that's my private opinion. I don't tell it to everybody, but in the bosom of one's family one may be confidential."

"Certainly, father," said May, as she suddenly left the room.

"Dear me," said Sir John, "that's a very abrupt mode of replying to me. Ah! it's a fatiguing thing to have to think for a whole family, and when, after immense mental labour you have, as it were, arrived at a singularly happy conclusion, all you get is 'certainly,' as if people knew it before."

"But you know, Sir John," said Lady Boyes, "that May has been rather strange of late."

"Then, it's very wrong, my lady," said Sir John; "it's very wrong, and things that are wrong, you know, are directly erroneous—that's my opinion again. I have arrived at some conclusions to-day, and I wish to give my family the benefit of them. Philippa, how dare you laugh; one would think that you did not belong to the family of the Boyes, for we very seldom laugh—laughing betrays a vacant mind, and so we don't laugh."

"But not for fear of betraying ourselves, I hope, father," said Philippa.

"What do you mean?" said Sir John, wrinkling up his brows,—"What can you mean? I never desire any of you to think about anything; I am quite willing to do it all, and when I do it all, I don't expect anybody to laugh."

Sir John was highly affronted, and he went with a majestic air out of the room, carrying his majestic mind with him, to the great delight of his wife and daughter.

But it is of May that we must now speak. Whither went she when she left the room so hurriedly? She was not won't to behave rudely, even to her tiresome father.

She has a stern purpose, a sudden one, and yet inflexibly strong. The words of her brother had fallen like melten lead upon her brain. She must prove him wrong before she sleeps that night; at least, so she tells herself. The idea of of verifying them never for a moment crossed her imagination.

With a quick light step she seeks the stables of the mansion—her own favourite palfrey is reposing in its stall—the sound of her well-known voice is sufficient, and the animal is roused. She seeks no idle, lounging groom, but, with her own hands, as quick as thought, she caparisons her steed; but a few minutes have elapsed since she left the hall, and she is mounted —a hazardous leap takes her into a meadow—a hard gallop across its surface brings her to a point beyond the lodge gates—there is a thick hedge of evergreen, and there she pauses; both horse and rider are still, as if sculptured—to watch Gerald Clifton.

Yes, she had now determined upon watching him. He cannot escape her; he always walks his horse idly down the avenue; she has seen him do so often from the windows of the hall, and then the porter has to be roused, and the lodge gates opened. Oh, she has plenty of time; but how furiously her heart beats! Hark! he comes. She presses her hands upon her throbbing bosom to still its tumultuous beating. He comes —he somes—him in whom her very existence is centred; he comes. She hears the sound of his horse's feet: there is to her heart a magic in the very tread of the animal who bears him. In the dim and dusky eve she sees him; he passes: all is still, save the solemn tread of that horse's feet upon the hardened ground. She scarcely breathes till he has passed some distance; then she speaks, which is to the horse.

"On—on!" she cries; and like the wind she skirts the road across the meadows, and makes a rapid detour; she feels that at at the pace she has been going, she must be far a-head of him again, and then she pauses—horse and rider motionless as before.

Oh! what a dreadful chase was that for such a heart as was then wildly beating in the bosom of poor May Boyes. Heaven help her, then! Alas! she has much need of its assistance—ample need, and surely it will not desert her.

Breathless again—and still again, as a painted horse and a painted rider, do they stand.

Again he comes. He has increased his pace to a trot: and as he nears her, the trot becomes a canter. Faster—faster still he comes: and now he sweeps by most rapidly.

"A chase—a chase!" she cries. "Let it lead me where it will, I'll join it."

She has cleared the hedge—her steed is put to a gallop—they are on the heath —the pursued and the pursuer. Surely some evidence of what was following so hard upon his track had reached Gerald Clifton's mind, for his fleet horse was put to its utmost pace, and, for a time, he was gaining rapidly.

A kind of madness seized on May. By voice and gesture she urged that favourite palfrey to a perfect fury; the hot breath steamed from dilated nostrils—foam gathered at its mouth, and drop by drop the heavy perspiration reeked from its sides; but never did wild steed carry a wild rider with more velocity, over hillock and glen, or brake, bush, and brier, than did that small, favoured steed carry its fearless burden.

And now she paused again, breathless and motionless as a statue, until Gerald should again reach the spot, which she knew he must pass. She felt convinced that she had distanced him, and that, in the gloom of the evening, she had far outstripped even the headlong progress of that wild, daring steed of his, that seemed to know no curb, but heedlessly to spring forward, as if inspired with the very soul of its heedless rider. She could feel the palpitation of her own heart; and, to her perception, that sounded louder than the tramp of Gerald Clifton's horse's feet, as now she felt assured that she was in advance of his progress.

The small, fragile figure of that girl, mounted upon that slender-limbed and now panting palfrey, was in clear keeping against the pale night sky; and, as so motionless they both stood, the appearance of the horse and its rider was strangely spectral. It was but the dim outline of both that could be seen, for, ever and anon, a darker and gloomier cloud would sweep across the horizon, and then May and her steed seemed both to vanish into thin air, but to rise again, like spectres, from the earth, when the temporary obstruction had passed away.

Did she really wish now that Gerald Clifton should see her? It would almost seem as if she did, for still and statue-like she stood in his very path.

But he was sweeping onward, and his chief attention was directed to what sounds might come upon his track behind. The thought that he was pursued had once found a place in his heart;

and now the most trivial sounds that came upon the night air were, to his imagination, full of danger, and the heralds of capture, and, perchance, of death.

And so was it that he came upon the form of that young girl so suddenly and unawares, that it appeared to him as if from the very night air around her she had sprung into existence, and stood there like some warning spectre to turn him from his path. The sudden movement he gave to the rein of his steed imparted terror to the animal—for no living creature is so soon aware of its master's fears or hesitation as the horse. Then, too, he gave a short, sharp, sudden cry of surprise, and the animal reared upon its hinder feet, with a snort of alarm, almost throwing from his seat even the skilful, daring rider that bestrode him.

May Boyes remained as motionless as though she had determined, to the very life, to enact the part which Gerald Clifton's fears assigned to her; and yet how little did she dream of personating aught unearthly! How far — very far distant from her imagination was such a thought. Perhaps there was a lingering, clinging hope that he might pause —that he might know her even amid that universal gloom of nature—that his heart might tell him who she was, and fitly translate her errand. She thought that the most distant sound of Gerald Clifton's footsteps would to her be a charm to awaken a consciousness that he who was the fond dream of all her hopes was near, and if so blessed and mysterious an influence attached her soul to his, wherefore should not the fond delusion linger, too, at his heart?

It was a dream—one of those romantic dreams that such a being as May Boyes might well be supposed to indulge in. The only sensation that Gerald Clifton felt was one of terror. He fancied that some spectre of the past had risen to dispute his pathway across the heath; he fancied that, at the next moment, he should hear some denunciation upon his head. Alas! had he stayed, he might have had a blessing; but the Heaven above, that knew him unworthy of it, urged him on, and not for one brief moment did he pause, except to battle with his steed and to dash away the sudden gush of perspiration that broke out upon his brow, as he made a complete circuit to avoid what he considered the spectral appearance which seemed to stay his path.

Then May Boyes smote her hands.

"He does not love me," she cried. "He does not love me. Just Heaven! there must be a victim! God grant that I may be born to suffer, not avenge. On—on—on!"

Clifton was now far distant; terror had added speed to the flight of his horse. He had plunged the spurs rowel-deep in the before sufficiently goaded animal's flanks. Some half-remembered prayer of childhood had at the moment risen to his lips, but soon it was changed to curses, and he seemed to wish to defy rather than wish to propitiate the supernatural power which had, to his imagination, appeared to warn him of his destruction.

And then again he heard his wild pursuer speeding on; there was the sullen beat of the horse's hoofs upon the heath.

"Curses!" he cried. "There are but two beings this night on Hounslow Heath—myself, and some demon, who would chase me to the gallows! Oh, for the shelter of the hut! Oh, for bars and bolts to keep the grim intruder out. I shake in every limb. What fiend is this that chases me across the heath?"

With lips pale and compressed—eyes preternaturally fixed and open, and the damp hair hanging about his brows, did Gerald Clifton at length arrive at that thick plantation, nearly in the centre of which was the hut where the highwayman so short a time before had halted for change of raiment and refreshment.

Need we attempt to keep a secret our readers have already guessed?—that the knight of the road and the accomplished Gerald Clifton, the lover of the beautiful May Boyes, the almost murderer of her brother, the winner of all hearts, the graceful, the gay, the witty, and the intelligent, are—one!

We wish not to deal in mystery. We trust not the interest of our eventful narrative upon such a foundation. Rather would we that our readers went with us in their interest in what we tell them, than in dreamy conjecture of what we keep from them. How it was that talent was misapplied—how it was that the dearest results of education were cast away, and how it was that an intellect of a really powerful order should, in the case of Gerald Clifton, have resulted in nothing more than the production of an accomplished highwayman, we must leave to those who have more leisure than ourselves to search into the hidden sympathies of the human mind, and to find causes for effects.

We aspire but to be the faithful chroniclers of times gone past; we rather say what people did than why they did it. We can provide the material for reflection, but we cannot pause to reflect; events hurry us on, and we will not for another moment forget that beautiful and enthusiastic being, who was now, as it were, trembling between life and death, as hopes or fears predominated in her mind.

Conviction surely must have reached her now. Could she longer doubt? was there a suspicion of her brother now unverified? not one, if she could have suffered her heart to obey its soberer dictates.

But yet she would see with her own eyes further evidence that Gerald Clifton's was the arm which had been raised against her brother's life. She saw his form disappear on the precincts of that little wood; and, ere she was aware, she reached a point where stood his panting steed tied to the overhanging limb of an aged beech, while its master, on foot, was threading the intricacies of the plantation.

"Here will I pause," she said, and she said it in the strange false tone of one whose heart is bursting with suppressed emotion. "Here will I pause, and wait for him."

Into the gloom she rode her horse, and there, completely hidden, she paused for the coming forth again of that being who might have been the blessing, but who was the bane of her existence.

No heed had she of time or place, she saw nothing but the horse without its rider, she thought of nothing but that very rider, and the only words she spoke were, once, when the sighing wind even among the leafless trees created a not ungentle murmur, that almost with an echoing answer as to sound, she said—

"I love him still—I love him still!"

How long she waited she knew not; the biting cold affected her not—she felt not the keen breeze that now blew across the heath, for, as the night advanced, stern winter once again seemed to have assumed his sceptre, and to have swept from off the earth's fair surface all those gladsome indications of the coming spring, that had made daylight so beautiful.

And what had now promised to become a gentle rain, descended in slow flakes, mingled with sharper icy particles; but still she waited. Ay, and until the break of dawn would she have waited there, if human nature could have supported her, rather than not see Gerald Clifton as he should come back again.

And now her straining ears catch the sound of some hasty footsteps, and she knew that he was coming. This, indeed, was a crisis in her fate. How would he come, and what appearance would he bear? Will the idol of her heart be changed, or will he wear the self-same aspect that he wore?—Momentous question! If back he came the Gerald Clifton that he went, unchanged in outward seeming, she might be happy yet.

But, hark! nearer—nearer he comes, and now she hears his voice. His courage is returned—the brief attack of horror he has shaken off—the courage and the daring of the wine-cup is now in him. She hears his voice, she knows it is his voice; but, oh! it is not the voice that has spoken to her in the low, soft accents of affection—'tis not the voice in which seemed to her imagination divinity in every tone. No, no! No more is he the Gerald Clifton of her dreams—no more is he that pure spirit—God's masterpiece—without fear, without reproach.

"God of Heaven!" she exclaimad, "I loved an angel—he has become a man."

A ribald song was coming from his lips, with such a half-tipsy laugh as might have graced the purlieus of St. Giles's. She heard him emphasis the coarser jests with which it teemed; and now forth he came into the dim light, by which she could observe him. Oh, what a change was there!

We have already described to our readers the dashing highwayman, the foppery of his half military costume, the elaborate decoration, and the brilliant colouring of his clothing, the assumption of a desire to shine in his iniquity, and to affect its being a fancy pursuit, to require an elaboration of toilet to set it off. Our readers know all this, but it was new to poor May Boyes.

She saw him tighten his saddle-girths, she heard him talk to the horse, and then she saw him mount. She could not speak, but she stretched forth her arms. She felt at that moment that she must for ever loathe him, or for ever love him. The scales hung even, and then surely some evil spirit whispered him to make disgust kick the beam. He paused a moment ere he galloped to the heath, and with one of those old and well-remembered sighs, that ever seemed to come from the very bottom of a heart replete with the best and noblest of the human sympathies, he said—

"Poor May Boyes, I am sorry that she loves me; she deserves a better fate."

In an instant he was gone.

"Gerald—Gerald!" cried May. "Gerald Clifton, yet a moment! turn, Gerald, turn. He is gone. Oh, Heaven! where are your friendly lightnings now? here, at least, is a head that will not shrink from the fell stroke. Gerald Clifton—Gerald Clifton, I love you! yes, I love you still."

She drooped her head upon the neck of her steed, tears fell fast from those sweet eyes, that were proverbial through the country for their laughing joy. Her heart was breaking—the night of her destiny had come. Never—never again would the sun of joy illumine the best and dearest heart that ever beat in human bosom.

CHAPTER VIII.

SIR JOHN SURMISES.—AN ACTIVE-MINDED MAGISTRATE.

Sir John Boyes sat in great state that night in his own hall. The eccentric combination of notions which he called his mind, was uncommonly severe, and from about mid-day had been extremely dictatorial. The fact is, he had been dreadfully alarmed at Ratchley's situation, but now that he had been assured by so cunning a leech, that he looked upon him as a kind of Solomon in the physical way, to use an expression of his own, of the certain convalescence of the young man, Sir John had dismissed all his fears, and continually spoke in aphorisms upon the most trifling subject.

He had put on his most elaborate laced cravat, and his fingers were loaded with those family rings that made so graceful a scintillation, and spread out such coruscations of light, whenever he imparted to his illustrious hand that tremulous motion for which he was so celebrated.

"Lady Boyes," he said, "upon casting my eyes around this apartment, and observing that our daughter May is not present, I am irresistibly led to the conclusion that she is a—a—in a manner of speaking, somewhere else. Let her be summoned."

And the Lady May was summoned, but she came not, and so half an hour more passed away, and Sir John began to get a little fidgetty. The family rings somehow did not look quite so bright, and the faultless tie of the cravat no longer fixed his gaze in the mirror opposite to him, for Sir John always looked at a mirror, and took care to sit in such a position in the room, that he always had that opportunity.

Moreover, he began to perceive that Lady Boyes went in and out of the room repeatedly with an anxious expression of countenance, so that the idea of there being something amiss, began gradually to develop itself through the intellectual fog which generally obscured his perception.

He heard, too, a great deal of running up and down the stairs, and finally, when he turned round to address an observation to Philippa, to his astonishment he found that he was left completely alone.

"What's the meaning of this?" he said; "the heir of all the Boyeses left by himself! I never did hear of such a thing in all my life—it's monstrous. Perhaps they expect me to fall back upon my own thoughts, but I can't do it; and my unequivocal opinion is, that when a man's left alone, he has not a soul to talk to. God bless my soul, who are you?"

This exclamation arose from the fact that the door was slowly opened, and a strange, rough-looking fellow made his appearance, who, immediately that he saw Sir John observed him, placed his finger on his lips, and said most mysteriously—

"Hush! don't say anything, old cock. Have you any idea where I shall find any of them?"

We certainly feel quite unqualified to present to the reader anything like a literal picture of Sir John's face at this moment. It was so expressive of mingled feelings, that if we were to describe it in any one of its phases, we should be doing an injustice to it in some other particular; but from what our readers already know of that illustrious baronet, they can have but little difficulty in supposing the effect so singular and so sudden an intrusion was likely to have upon him.

The idea of any one walking into his ancestral home, and unannounced getting to him, face to face, and then and there addressing him as an old cock, amounted to a series of extravagant propositions which completely bewildered poor Sir John, and at the same it induced a belief that the whole framework of society was shattered to pieces. It completely choked his utterance, so that he could do nothing for some moments but glare at the visitor with something of the singular expression of some great fish newly dragged from his native element into the open air.

"Mum's the word," said the man. "Snug as poss. Eh! is there anybody at home? Why, what's the matter with you?"

"Eh, eh!" said Sir John; "who am I?"

"Well, I don't know, you look like a thundering fool. I want to see Sir John Boyes. What sort of a fellow is he? active, bold—eh?"

"Where am I?" said Sir John.

"D—n it all," said the man; "is this a lunatic asylum? If it is so, it's very badly guarded, for the deuce a soul I met as I walked in here. But my business won't bear delay—I want to see some of the family."

"I am the family," gasped Sir John. "What do you want here? and how came you into the presence of the thirteenth baronet of this house in such a manner?"

"You?" said the man; "you don't mean to say that you are Sir John Boyes?"

"Well, I think I am," said Sir John.

"Really, sir, I beg your pardon; but as I found you sitting here all by yourself, and that anybody might walk in, I couldn't believe it was you. I have come all the way from London to see you. The Secretary of State—you understand ——"

"The Secretary of State!" exclaimed Sir John, and he immediately raised his cravat. "Sir, are you a government messenger?"

"Why, yes, in a manner of speaking, Sir John, I may be called a government messenger. I'm a runner."

"A what—a rummer, did you say?" asked Sir John.

"No; a runner — a Bow-street runner."

"A thief-taker?"

"Precisely, whenever I can catch them. My name's Long, and I'm rather, you see, long by nature. The Secretary of State has received information that Captain Hawk, the famous highwayman, had been in this district. The fact is, the Oxford mail has been robbed. But there wouldn't have been much fuss about that, only that there happened to be in the mail-bag some correspondence of his lordship, which has fallen into the hands of somebody — Heaven knows who; at all events, as it was all through Captain Hawk that the confusion arose, his lordship, after swearing some tremendous oaths, has made up his mind to have him nabbed."

"Oh!" said Sir John, who was rather bewildered at the rapidity with which the Bow-street runner spoke.

"You will, therefore, perceive," he continued, "why I'm down here. Hawk never leaves a district without perpetrating some outrageous robbery by way of leaving a little relic behind him. Now, the probability is, that he will take an opportunity of breaking into your house; for, as his lordship says, the greater the goose, the greater the danger."

"The greater the what?" said Sir John.

"Oh, never mind that; I want to

know if Captain Hawk has been seen in the vicinity?"

"I can't tell you, Mr. Strong," said Sir John.

"I beg your pardon, my name's Long."

"D—n your name, you're an impertinent fellow!"

"Very good, go on," said Long, and he gave his hands such a clap together that Sir John jumped again; "go on, go on, don't mind me."

"Confound you!" said Sir John, "if ever I met with your equal. There's my son, sir, the representative that will be of the Boyeses, six feet two and a quarter in pumps, and amazingly like the family, has been shot at by this very Captain Hawk; and I've no objection to offer a hundred—that is to say I mean fifty—or ten pounds or so, to anybody who will catch him; but I don't want to have anything to say to you, Mr. Gong."

"D—n it, Sir John, my name's Long!"

"I don't care what your name is—get out off my house! You may be Long and Strong, and Strong and Long, and Gong too, for what I care."

"Oh, stuff, stuff, stuff," said the officer, as he threw himself into a chair; "don't expose yourself."

"Don't do what?"

"Now, my dear sir—now, my dear sir——"

"Was ever a great Boyes so insulted? But I'll pretty soon put an end to this! D—n it, sir, I'll have you tossed in a horsepond and dipped in a blanket!"

Sir John rose as he spoke, and rang the bell violently.

"There he goes again," said the officer, as if he were addressing some third person; "just the very character I heard of him—an ass to the backbone."

Sir John's summons to the bell was so powerful a one, that not only did he succeed in alarming the whole house, but he brought the rope down in his hand, and there he stood, looking like a maniac, as two or three of the servants rushed into the hall.

"Turn this Mr. Prong out!" said Sir John. "Kick him out! Am I to be insulted in my own house? By the bones of my ancestors—kick him out, kick him out!"

"Well," said the officer, rising, "of all the infernal fools that ever I met with at pronouncing a fellow's name, you're about the worst. You know my name's Long, well enough—L-o-n-g, stupid!"

Sir John danced in agony, exclaiming—

"Am I to put up with this? Is the whole family to put up with this? Are the Boyeses to be nonentities? Is this to become a family tale, to be told to the family ears?"

"Oh," said Long, "you acknowledge to have some asinine appendages, do you? Come, now, Sir John, we'll make it all square over a bottle. I'll forgive you—perhaps it's natural."

"D—n all the world!" roared Sir John; "is this fellow to be turned out or not?"

There were two or three stout serving men who had come into the apartment; and now that they had really got over their first surprise at the astonishing impertinence of the stranger, they flung themselves upon him, and lifting him up bodily, they carried him from the room.

"Thank you, thank you," said the imperturbable Mr. Long. "Now this is kind—easy there, mind that corner. By-by, Sir John; turn it over in your mind, and I'll look in again in an hour. As for all of you, my good fellows, you'll find a jug of ale apiece at the Talbott Heaven forbid that I should be ungrateful; and mind, never forget, whatever your master may say, that my name it Long—L-o-n-g, and that I came about Captain Hawk, the celebrated highwayman—remember that, will you?"

He was flung down the hall steps without much ceremony, whilst Sir John sat puffing like a grampus, and in a state of mind which, as the novelists say, transcends description. Never before had his dignity been so cruelly insulted; never before had anybody hinted to him a suspicion that he was not to the full as great a man as he believed himself; but now to be told plumply to his face that he was an ass—to have the chances of his house being broken into first speculated upon because he was the greatest goose in the county! It was too bad, and Sir John felt certain, although he wanted breath just then to say it, that some great social revolution was at hand, which was probably a precursor of the end of the world.

He forgot for the moment the anxious search for May; all his senses and all his feelings were absorbed in a contemplation of the dreadful insults he had received; and at length, when Lady Boyes and Philippa entered the apartment, he was so bewildered, that they found him quite incapable of answering, even as rationally as usual, to what might be said to him.

RATCHLEY COMMUNICATES HIS SUSPICIONS TO MAY BOYES.

"Oh! Sir John," said Lady Boyes, "we cannot find May anywhere."

"D—n Strong!" said Sir John.

"We've searched for her," said Philippa, "through the whole house. Ratchley says she was with him about an hour ago, but no one has seen her since."

"That scoundrel, Gong!"

"Mother, what is he talking of?" said Philippa.

"I don't know," said Lady Boyes;

"but I'm afraid his poor wits are gone."

"Poor wits!" said Sir John; "d—n it! I wonder what next? Is my own family joining that villain Strong against me? Am I to be continually abused by everybody? I'll have him smashed, pounded, and destroyed, root and branch! Confound him, say I!"

"It is in vain," said Lady Boyes, "to appeal to your father, Philippa; it is evident he knows not what he says."

"Yes, I do," said Sir John. "There's been a rascal here of the name of Gong, or something of that kind, and he's been insulting me past all bounds of moderation. I can't stand it, and I won't!"

There was a tremendous knocking at the hall door of the mansion, and in a few moments a servant came into the room and said—

"If you please, Sir John, Mr. Long's come back again. He says he's only one observation to make, which he wishes you particularly to hear."

"The devil!" roared Sir John. "Knock him down! Good God Almighty! am I to be tormented all my life with this Long? Don't let him into the house on an account; throw buckets of water over him—kill him, if you like!"

The servant left the room, and then Sir John wiped the perspiration from his brow with the end of his cravat.

"This is rather too dreadful," he said. "I'll write to the secretary of state to-morrow, and claim his protection against Long. What were you saying, Lady Boyes, when you came in?"

"That our child May has disappeared, Sir John."

"May—May! You don't mean May Boyes—a scion of our illustrious house disappeared?—We never disappear!"

"Alas!" said Lady Boyes, "it is too true."

She sat down and burst into tears, and the moment she did so, the door of the apartment opened, and May glidden in. She was very pale, but with a voice of perfect composure she said—

"What is too true, mother?"

A scream of joy escaped from Lady Boyes, and she flung herself round the neck of May, while Philippa clasped her sisters hands and looked all the joy she felt at her return.

Poor Sir John sat and fidgetted about in the most ludicrous manner.

"I don't understand what you're all about," he said. "Here's been Long, and Strong, and Gong, and Prong, here; and then you set to crying, and then May's gone and May comes. I don't understand it; and I believe I may remark, that when I don't understand anything, I don't comprehend it."

"What is it all about?" said May. "I very much fear that a heedless ramble I took upon the heath has caused you all disquietude."

"Oh! my child," said Lady Boyes, "how could you go out at such a time and so alarm us?"

"I am very sorry, mother," said May.

"And you look pale, and worn, and ill!" said Philippa. "Tell me, dear May, has anything happened to harass you?"

"Nothing," said May; "all is well—very well—very well. I was careless of me, at such a time, to ramble to the heath; but now you see I'm returned, think nothing of it. I have some letters to write, and shall be in my room an hour or more."

She smiled as she spoke, and left the room—but it was not that smile that of yore made her look so beautiful. It was very sad, pitifully sad; and none present, not even the apathetic Sir John, could fail to notice it.

"Let her be," said Lady Boyes. "Of late I have observed that these melancholy moods have seized upon her; 'tis best to leave her to herself, for I have found that she recovers more quickly and more completely."

"Very good," said Sir John; "but I don't see why anybody should be melancholy but me. Nobody has been insulted but me, and of course that makes all the difference. Is the library lighted?"

"Yes," said Lady Boyes, "it has been for some time."

"Then I shall go there," added Sir John, "and endeavour to quiet my nerves by consulting the works of one of those great men of antiquity who remind me so much of myself. I always feel like Julius Cæsar—don't let me be disturbed unless I ring."

So saying, and having recovered a

good deal of his solemn gravity, Sir John rose, and took a small lamp from a side table; but before he could reach the door of the apartment, it was opened again, and one of the domestics stood in a very hesitating manner upon the threshold.

"I beg your pardon, Sir John," he said, and then he paused.

"What is it?" said Sir John. "Speak freely, my man—what is it?"

"Why, Sir John, I hope you won't be offended with me—but—but——"

"Will you have the goodness to explain your errand? Is the representative of one of the oldest baronetcies in this country to be kept waiting your leisure?"

"Certainly not, Sir John. I only beg your pardon; but since your worship gives me leave to speak, I've come to say that Mr. Long has come again, and he says——"

"Fire and fury!" said Sir John; "when is this Long persecution to end? Am I to be bull-baited here by a Long? Am I a badger—that's what I ask you all—am I a badger, Lady Boyes—do you take me for a badger?"

"Beg pardon, Sir John," said the servant; "I thought you'd be angry, sir, but really, sir, Mr. Long is so civil, and such a gentlemanly man, that we hardly knew him again. Of course, Sir John, we kept him outside till your pleasure was known."

"A thousand devils!" said Sir John. "Hang his civility! souse him with buckets of water, and then thrash him off the premises!—I'll hold you harmless of the consequences."

"Yes, sir, John, if it's your pleasure; but he says he comes from the secretary of state."

"I know it, the hardened ruffian! D—n the secretary of state and him too! —do as I bid you, or I'll turn every man Jack of you out of the house!"

The servant went his way, and from the general confusion which in the course of five minutes ensued, it may well be presumed that Sir John's instructions were being amply carried out, and that the unfortunate Long at length met with a due reward for his impertinence. Somehow or another he seemed rather surprised when he was soused with buckets of water, and well cudgelled to boot. He protested that his name was Long, but the servants said they knew it, and then when he said that he came from the secretary of state about Captain Hawk, they told him that they knew that too, but that it was Sir John's orders, so that Long was effectually silenced, as well as effectually beaten, and the last any of the establishment saw of him was, his crawling like a half-drowned rat from the estate.

Sir John was told all this, and he felt profoundly satisfied; Long was punished, and so his wounded spirit was appeased. He went into the library almost with a smile.

Such folks as Sir John Boyes have always a sufficient fund of personal vanity to draw upon under any emergency, and, therefore, it was, that he so easily got over the effects of the highly injurious expressions used by that impertinent Long when talking of his, Sir John's, mental endowments.

He sat down quite in a comparatively amiable frame of mind, and it so happened that he sat directly opposite to one of the long windows, stretching from the roof to the floor, and which opened door-like into that indentical terrace where the beautiful May Boyes had, at an earlier hour of the evening, held that enthusiastic discourse, which we have recorded, with Gerald Clifton.

He reached a volume from one of the shelves around him, and commenced reading, fancying that he fully understood the authour's meaning, looking exceedingly pompous the while, and occasionally tapping the front of his forehead, as if to give a hint to any part of his intellectual organisation which might be slumbering, that he fully expected it to up, and at work.

"Ah!" he exclaimed, "that is precisely my opinion. It is an astonishing fact how, from age to age, and from period to period, when great minds commence a course of—of rational thought, how they continually go on, in a manner of speaking—that is to say, from age to age, and from period to period."

Sir John looked up at the ceiling, as if he he had uttered something profound; but he was soon recalled from this formidable metaphysical flight by a noise at the window opposite to which he sat. Sir John's mouth opened to an alarming width, and so did his eyes, as one half of the window swung gently into the room upon its hinges, and a figure appeared, such as he had never seen before, but of which common report had frequently given him rather an accurate opinion. There was the scarlet coat, trimmed with rich lace, the costly cravat, the riding-boots, the hat and feathers, looped with a diamond, all the insignia complete of no less a personage than the celebrated Captain Hawk, the highwayman.

"I beg your pardon, Sir John Boyes," said this apparition, "but I've left my watch at home; can you lend me yours?"

Sir John could not speak. The impudence of Long was nothing to this; and then, before he uttered a word, the highwayman stepped lightly into the room, and taking up Sir John's watch, which lay by the book beside him, he held it close to its owner's face, saying—

"You will remember on your oath that it is half-past ten."

A half-mask was upon this mysterious visitor's face, and the voice was evidently an assumed one; then, before Sir John could at all recover sufficiently to do more than, with one vacant look at the watch, see that it was half-past ten, the highwayman had glided away, and closed the window again, leaving all as profoundly still as before, so that Sir John Boyes, if he had chosen it, might have gone on being as philosophical as he pleased, the only alteration in circumstances being the abstraction of his watch,

So utterly astonished was he, that after the highwayman was gone, he began pushing his chair backwards from the window until he caught the hind legs of it in a ruck in the carpet, when over he went, and there we shall leave him lying for some time, while we again take up our station on the desolate heath, and listen to the sobs of the beautiful May Boyes, as tear-drops fell like rain from those sweet eyes which surely were marred by destiny, or they would ever have beamed with serenity and joy.

CHAPTER IX.

THE SACRIFICE.

VAIN would be the task to attempt to describe fully the state of feeling in which May Boyes was left, when assurance became doubly sure that he to whom she had given her heart's best affections, was not that which he assumed to be, and which her more than partial fondness had pictured him.

Our readers must for themselves depict to their own imaginations the desolation of spirit which swept over that young and beautiful being; and if, as we hope, those who have sought to beguile an hour by the perusal of these pages, have gone with us in an appreciation of the excellence of such a character as May Boyes, there will be no difficulty in conceiving how fearful a void must have been left in such a bosom by the occurrence of the last few hours.

We do not hold her up to human nature as a model of discretion and worldly wisdom; all we seek to paint her is as a being to be loved, and one whose very foibles look so like excellencies, and lean so much to virtue, that we love her not the less that she is human enough to have some faults.

For some moments she remained in the attitude which we have depicted, and the all-searching eye of Heaven alone could at such a moment see the world of emotions which found a place in her imagination. At length she spoke, and as if the mind had exerted so much power over the physical frame as to alter the very voice, the tones in which she spoke were not those which any one who knew her in her happiness would have recognised as hers; but, in a strange and altered manner, she thus gave utterance to the aspirations of her deep afflictions—

"'Tis past—there is no struggle now—all is over—the romance of life has fled for ever, and a cold reality, sterner far than ever man pictured, has usurped its place! and what, now, is life to me? Can I longer joy in the sweet sunshine, or think the green earth beautiful! No! I cannot live for love, but I can die for devotion! Gerald Clifton, it is not by reproach that I will wring your soul, but by a contray course from that which pride might dictate. I shall hope that even you may feel your triumph too complete. There shall be a sacrifice, and there shall be an opportunity of redemption!"

She raised her head from the inclined posture which it assumed, and gazed around her; then slowly she bent in an attitude of listening, and she heard the sound of his horse's hoofs in a particular direction.

"My soul tells me," she exclaimed, "that to-night will be some crisis in Gerald Clifton's fate! He is bent upon some deed, which, perchance, to his imagination, paints itself in glowing colours. Oh! if but for one moment I could make him listen! and if Heaven would gift me with the persuasive eloquence to turn him from this path of life, methinks that I could die content!"

She urged her steed some distance from the margin of the wood, and scarcely had she emerged fully upon the open heath, when some one hailed her; and, with a familiarity which showed that, seeing her at such an hour, and unattended, he guessed not her real social position, he cried—

"Hillo! my lass, can you tell me which is Sir John Boyes' mansion?"

"It is the first house you come to," said May, "by pursuing the bridle path you are on."

"Thanks. I wonder that you venture abroad alone at such a time!"

"Wherefore?"

"Are you not aware that the celebrated highwayman, Captain Hawk, is in the district, and it is well known that he has sworn to stop and rob Judge Holme on his way from the assizes?"

"And will he keep his word?" said May.

"I think not; but I know he'll try it. Get home, my lass, as quick as you can. There's likely to be rough work on Hounslow-heath to-night."

"I thank you," said May.

The man passed on, and at the moment she heard the neighbouring clock strike the hour of ten.

She counted carefully the strokes, and then muttered to herself, in a low, strange tone—

"Ten o'clock. Let me consider; he has gone to the commission of that crime which surely Heaven in its own way has given me notice of. Ten o'clock? Can I save him? Can I have now revenge for his duplicity which, if he be human, shall touch him to the quick? I can—I can! Home—home—home!"

She urged her palfrey again to its speed, and in a short time reached the Hall. Alighting from the steed, she tied it to the garden gate, as it was called, a small private entrance, of which the actual members of the family alone availed themselves. Then she entered the house, with that strange appearance of firmness and self-possession which sometimes shows itself when the feelings are wrought up to the very highest pitch. With many minds under such circumstances, there must be a furious storm or an absolute calm; it was the latter with May Boyes, but she was as pale as a statue, her lips were colourless, and her features wore a fixed and rigid aspect.

Some twenty minutes might have elapsed when, from that same garden gate, again there emerged a figure, which, had Gerald Clifton seen it, would have made Gerald Clifton think he saw himself, so perfect was it in imitation of him when in his real character of the bold, daring knight of the road. There was that scarlet coat, with its meretricious profusion of lace, that rich cravat, the diamond looped hat, the ostentatious display of finery to catch the vulgar eye—surely it must be he.

And yet a different route he took across that heath; and now, upon a second glance, we shall perceive a slimness and a symmetry about the figure that belongs not to the stronger sex. Thought crowds on thought—that valise which had been removed from Clifton's chamber surely has provided the devoted May the means of assuming outwardly an aspect so foreign to the mind within.

His figure was not the tallest or the most robust for that of a man; hers was about the middle height of woman. She looked in outward seeming all that he could look, for a half mask hid that face of sweet intelligence and beauty, which else had made the glaring costume so incongruous.

She does not mount her steed, but passes onward through the grounds of the old hall by old familiar paths. The terrace steps are reached, and once again she stands upon the spot where she had plighted such sweet vows with that idol of her heart, now rudely torn from its shrine, but still so dear to her. He had fallen, fallen from his high estate in her pure thoughts, but with him she was content to fall likewise.

A light beamed from the windows of the library; she reaches one of them, and looking into that spacious room, it is her father whom she sees, and, for a moment, her face was as a tablet of unutterable thoughts. We know what followed. It was May Boyes, the beautiful and gifted, who so much astonished Sir John, and who robbed him, under his own roof, of his ancestral watch, and left him speechless with amazement.

Then with a light step she again proceeds the way she came, and, ere five minutes more have elapsed, she is mounted and on the heath. For a moment she pauses, as if considering her route, and then turning her horse's head directly away from the path she was certain Gerald Clifton had taken, she swept onwards at a speed which, considering the nature of the ground and the darkness of the night, was most terrific.

Mansion after mansion was passed, and she paused not. The inclemency of the weather kept all but those whom sheer necessity forced abroad, within their homes, and after four or five miles of hard riding, she first met a heavy waggon slowly making its sleepy progress along the country road.

As if with all the speed of a preconcerted design, she rode forward, and arrested the progress of the lumbering vehicle, that is to say she stopped the half asleep leading horse, and then all the rest tumbled one against the other, and stopped in regular succession, till the whole concern was at a standstill, when, the jingling of the bells having ceased, they all fell asleep at once, to the dismay of the waggoner, who saw not the obstruction in front.

It must have been by the force of habit that he cried "whoa!" for there was no occasion for it, or perhaps he could not himself think of stopping in his lazy, lounging march without the use of that conventional order to stand still. Certain it is that he did then come to a halt, and give a loud crack with his whip; but the acquired momentum of the team and the waggon was gone, and such a machine was not to be set in motion again so easily.

He took a lantern which hung suspended from the shaft, and walked along the whole eight horses to see what was the matter, a proceeding which finally brought him to May Boyes, who had yet not spoken.

The waggoner held the lantern so as to throw a full light upon her figure, and then, with an assumed carelessness of tone, she said—

"Have you anybody worth robbing in the waggon?"

This was a cool piece of effrontery which so astonished the man that he only stared the more, but made no reply.

"Can you not speak?" added May.

Then he gathered courage, and, in a broad provincial dialect, which we should despair of putting upon paper, he said—

"This be the fast fly to Uxbridge and Kingston; there's two old women and one young one. Who are you?"

"Captain Hawk, the highwayman. What's the time, my friend?"

"It wanted a minute of eleven, at last 'pike. Take our throats, but don't cut our money, good sir. The Lord have mercy upon us! I've heard of you."

He flopped down upon his knees in the road, and began bellowing like some great lubberly schoolboy. May Boyes gave the rein to the palfrey, and like an arrow from a bow she shot past him, and was gone.

"On—on—on," was all she said, as she dashed from her beautiful face some of the stray ringlets from her beautiful hair that escaped from beneath the confinement of her hat. "On—on, my steed, to London; I will save him yet, and he shall feel that it is to her whom he has deceived that he owes redemption. I will die yet, to prove to him the sincerity of my affection, which should have been a blessing, but has become a theme for despair."

By voice and gesture she still urged that steed beyond its ordinary powers, and soon the huge metropolis—even then huge, comparatively, with the villages that studded its suburbs, but many of which now form integral portions of it—loomed upon her sight.

The redundancy of vegetation vanished, intervals without houses became less and less frequent, and the roads began to be dimly and duskily lighted by the old, inefficient lamps, which cast about as much radiance round them as the faint halo of a glow-worm in a mist.

She passed the royal abode at Kensington; and Tyburn-gate, then in all its glory and all its celebrity, was close at hand. But still she slackened not her speed; for a moment it occurred to her that she was penniless, and that should she be stopped at that gate she must retrace her steps. Two horsemen seemed to be taking change of the toll-keeper, who, shading his eyes with his hands from the glare of the light which came from a lantern with a strong reflector that was placed over the door of the toll-house, remarked—

"There's somebody coming in a hurry, at all events. Bob, look out; close the gate, it's a bilk. No, no, by all that's good; d—n it, it's Captain Hawk. Hurrah! hurrah! there he goes; there's the fellow for my money. Ah! lacks-a-daisey, if I was only him; dear, dear. Gentlemen, that's Captain Hawk, the highwayman. Bless yer, I knows him. I never takes no toll of him. Oh, he's an out-and-outer; he'll be a matter of history, he will; there he goes. I tells you what, gentlemen, if you, and me, and the blessed gate, and ever so many more obstructibles had been all in the way, d—d if he'd have stopped—not he; he's a rum 'un."

The long straggling line of Oxford-street was half traversed, and then May Boyes drew up at what was then a little, low change house, with a roof half of thatch and half of broken tile; the door was ingeniously contrived that every one had to stoop at entrance, and there was a step so ingeniously placed that if a stranger failed to fall over it, and measure his length on the sanded floor, he might well cry out, "A miracle!" The sign was that of the Goat in Boots. It was a well-know house, and stretched far away backward, containing numberless low-roofed and odd-fashioned rooms, such as would take a full month of residence in the place to become acquainted with.

There were some loungers at the door, from whence issued but a faint stream of light, that rendered objects but puzzlingly distinct.

There was a visible sensation among all present when May Boyes drew up close to the kerb.

"The captain, by jingo!" cried a man.

"Wine," said May; "wine!"

There was a rush into the house to see which should obey the order first; and in less time than it would seem possible to do so, a very fat man, with a bald, shiny head, rushed out with a brimming cup of some ruddy-looking liquid in his hand.

"Here you are, captain—here you are. Lord love us, the sight of you's good for sore eyes. Why, let me see, it's a matter of one—two—three——"

May Boyes was fearfully exhausted, and she drank a drop out of the wine-cup—the residue she threw, accompanied by the cup itself, at the landlord's head, and then, without another word, she spurred onwards.

"Ah! that's like him," said the fat landlord, "for all the world. I knew he'd do that. Never mind—who cares?—he's the best customer that ever crossed the threshold of the Goat in Boots. He knows the way to do business; he flings a full purse, now and then, into the door, and he says, says he, 'Landlord, keep score, and be d—d to you, till that's gone."

"Enough—enough!" said May, in low, plantive accents, when she was out of sight of that thieves' house, which, in the inefficiently lighted state of the streets at that period, she might very soon be—"enough; and now for home again."

She turned her horse's head up a narrow thoroughfare to the left, and then, making a large detour, she came out somewhere beyond the village of Bayswater; and still, with her face wearing that marble-like expression, she forced the horse to gallop onward along the track she had so recently passed, until once more the home of her race—the ancient halls, within which she had first drawn the breath of life—rose before her; and more like an automaton than a living, sentient being, she paused again at that garden-gate, whence, so short a time before, she had emerged to take her nearly twenty miles' ride in so incredibly short a space of time.

She dismounted, and tottered to the

gate; she spoke kindly to the horse, but the animal heeded not the well-known call. It had done its work; a shudder pervaded its frame, and it fell dead at her feet.

May clasped her hands, and seemed on the point of uttering some frantic exclamation of grief; but she suddenly checked herself; and, in a deep sepulchral voice, she whispered—

"Be it so. One by one, and my turn next. I have saved you, Gerald Clifton —I have saved you!"

Then, like one walking in a dream, she sought her chamber. Along the dim and dusky passages, she crept up the mansion staircase, and along the echoing corridors.

She met no one; but, like some perturbed spirit, glided to that sweetly-adorned apartment, where she had passed so many happy hours of girlish joy. She's safe!—the door is closed—the key turned in the lock. She staggers to the bed, with a half shriek pronounces the name of Gerald Clifton, and then she falls, alike insensible of joy and sorrow.

CHAPTER X.

THE MURDER ON THE HEATH.

The mists of night, like a routed army, had disappeared before the marshalled hosts which attended upon the sweet sunshine. Once again stern winter seemed, shivering, to have crept into some icy cave, leaving the day to the influence of kindlier spirits—sweet precursors of the dear delights of summer, who wooed the soft west wind once more to play gratefully upon the brows of all who looked with hope upon that smiling morn.

The streams again ran free, murmuring their sweet music to the upper air; moist exhalations hung on every bough, and those free denizens of nature, the forest birds, lifted up to heaven many a song of mirth to think that the dear sunhine had come once again.

It was a soft and lustrous morn; the damp freshness of the invigorating air lent life and energy to all thing animate, awaking once again a hope that the stern season had, for a time, bidden adieu to the young spring time, and no longer, like some lusty warrior, thought it great to do unequal battle with the lithesome young antagonist.

There was a breakfast in the Hall—such a breakfast as puts to shame the puny delicacies of the modern repast of that name. Flagons of old ale, hissing from the cask, and bearing on their surface a mantling cream, were side by side with substantialities such as are now undreamt of.

The rich paraphernalia of the tea equipage was unknown at Boyes' Hall, where it had been the pride and delight of Sir John, during his ownership of the family estates, to ape the good living of his ancestors, if he could not come up to them in his intellectual endowments.

And the whole family breakfasted together at what was considered a very respectable late hour, namely, eight o'clock. Such a man as Sir John Boyes, in the present day, would, with his views and perceptions engrafted upon modern fashion, have shrunk to show himself at so plebeian at hour.

About a hundred years ago we were not so refined a race; an those who had escaped the primeval curse of earning their bread by the sweat of their brows, did not at all consider it necessary to turn night into day, for the purpose of thoroughly establishing such a fact.

Sir John was always very great at breakfast-time, and uncommonly fresh and vigorous. "The mind," as he himself frequently expressed it—"the mind, when it is resting, tastes of repose, and heirs of illustrious houses rise in the morning, when they get up with a kind of a—a—precisely."

And as this was an opinion of Sir John's, and one, too, uttered at his own table, it would be extremely unpolite to quarrel with it, or to hint at the possibility of it being a wit more intelligible.

Still, however, upon this particular morning, notwithstanding the mental freshness, vigour, and serenity which might be supposed to result from his illustrious slumbers, the circumstances of the over night would most uncomfortably intrude themselve between him and his ale, his haunch of venison, his pasties, and, more than all, his personal appreciation of himself.

Sir John was not confidential upon the point; and, therefore, we cannot say how long he laid upon his back in the library, after being so coolly robbed of the ancestral timekeeper. Certain it is, however, that when he did resume a perpendicular position, he remained some time in an attitude which fully indicated that some unusually elaborate effort of cunning was developing itself in the chambers of his brain.

The attitude was that expressive one

during which the forefinger is placed upon the side of the nose, whilst the eye which answers to that side of the face occasionally executes a wink at nothing. We are told that a shake of the head from Lord Burleigh meant a great deal: and so, when a man like Sir John Boyes winks and looks so amazingly cunning, we may, perhaps, be excused for almost expecting in a short time to see the Thames in a blaze.

Assuming that privilege, which we certainly have, of listening to everybody, we shall take the liberty of overhearing the profoundly sagacious remarks of Sir John concerning the untoward event which made him dependant upon an ancestral clock in the hall, instead of an ancestral watch in his pocket, to know what the time of day was.

The idea of being robbed at all, and of his watch, too, was most certainly gall itself, and for that robbery to be committed under his own roof, nay, under his own nose, implied certainly an unlimited quantity of wormwood added to the gall; therefore was it that Sir John set the rather eccentric piece of machinery which he called his mind in motion, for the purpose of getting out of the dilemma in some more dignified way than by a candid confession of the fact that a thief had walked in at his window, asked him what a clock it was, and pocketed his watch, without so much as a word of remonstrance from him, the great representative of all the Boyes.

Alas! poor Sir John. Heaven help you in the concoction of a plot, for, without some extraneous aid, we have terrible suspicions that you may go on thinking for an unlimited period of time, without taking anything by the motion.

But Sir John himself, notwithstanding the prevailing opinion of every one else, could not be very well expected to become impressed with an opinion of his own want of capacity to get up something stunning in the way of an excuse for the absence of his watch; so that after a considerable time spent in doubts and hesitations, he had thoroughly made up his mind to say, that for the first time in human remembrance, something had gone wrong in the internal economy of his time-keeper, and that he had sent it to London to be repaired, but never expected to see it again, inasmuch as, with a too generous confidence in human nature, he had intrusted it to one of the most decided rogues in existence.

Who that rogue was, moreover, he intended to decline stating, for fear he should be thought censorious, so that he fully considered that, take the thing all in all, he was getting out of the affair as nicely and pleasantly as any one could expect.

Indeed, so admirable did he consider this device, that it almost reconciled him to its loss, and he considered that the skilful and elaborate manner in which he was getting out of the scrape, might fairly be pitted against the want of nerve he had exhibited when the daring highwayman so very unexpectedly made his appearance before him.

It was at this very breakfast time, on the following morning, that Sir John had determined to carry out this little piece of domestic duplicity; but somehow or another, in the most extraordinary manner, nobody would give him the least opportunity of do so, and he rather dreaded plunging into the matter in such a way as to make it amount to nothing.

In vain he angled for a question as to the time; nobody seemed to care at all what o'clock it was, or if they did, they quietly satisfied themselves in some other way, so that at last, when the morning meal was nearly completed, and in a few moments Sir John knew the family would be dispersed throughout the house, a feeling of desperation came over him, and, by way of quelling all suspicion, he gave one of the most eccentric and singular laughs that could be imagined, and then, having thus attracted all eyes, he with great cleverness, said—

"It may appear to you all extremely improbable, when you come to consider the intellectual and fundamental nature of my mental organization, what I am going simply to state, but it carries a truth upon the face of it, so let nobody doubt it, or think for a moment that it is not just the fact. Ha—ha! something's gone wrong with my watch."

"Indeed!" said Lady Boyes. "I'm not surprised; it never went well."

"And now it's gone altogether," said Sir John, with a grim look.

"Gone, Sir John!" said Lady Boyes.

"Yes, my lady; I have intrusted it to a skilful artizan, who has promised to amend its irregularities. He has gone to London, and it's extremely droll, but I don't expect it to come back again, and I believe I may say, as a general thing, that what I don't expect I don't anticipate, and, consequently, if it comes to pass I aint surprised, and if it don't, it don't astonish me. So you understand, all of you, it's no use your asking me what the time is."

"But goodness gracious, Sir John," said Lady Boyes, "you've surely not given that handsome watch into the care of a stranger—an article, too, of such taste and value, and such skilful workmanship, though it was a little out of order. I declare it was quite a curiosity; to think that the works could be got into such a space; I don't think it measured above six inches across it, and was not a bit thicker than a toilet pincushion."

"My lady, my lady," said Sir John, "drop it."

"Drop the watch, Sir John?"

This was a happy suggestion; Sir John gave himself a gracious smile, and then added—

"The fact is, I dropped it, my lady—that put it out of order. It's gone to London, and that's all I know about it, and all I shall; the individual who has it, I am afraid, will be dilatory in returning it; but you all perceive that the affair is extremely simple, and that it is, in fact, just as I tell you, and that there's nothing at all to conceal. It is by no means — quite the other way — don't think so, for a moment; but allow me to remark, that what I have stated is a fact."

"No one, Sir John, dreams of doubting it," said Lady Boyes.

"They'd better not," said Sir John. "When was I ever doubted?—I believe never; and when such a thing does occur, the institutions of this country will be in rather a ticklish position. As is my highly intellectual custom, I'm now going to converse with ancient authors for an hour; do not let me be interrupted. When I'm thinking, you may always assume that I am engaged in thought. You know, my dear Lady Boyes, that when I was anticipating being called to the councils of the king, I was compelled to adopt the somewhat novel expedient of sticking a green wafer on the extremity of my nose when my thoughts were of too abstruse a character to be intruded upon by any of the common details of every-day life; I discontinued that wafer when advisers of superior ability prevented his majesty from requesting me to form a ministry; but if I am interrupted during my converse with the ancient authors, I shall be compelled to again append a green wafer to my nose, at even the personal inconvenience of squinting, which you may recollet it gave rise to on the last occasion."

Sir John rose as he spoke, and walked gracefully from the room, occupying an amazing space, and sending the full skirts of his coat with a sway, first to the one side and then to the other, as he proceeded in a style of progression peculiar to himself, when he was on the happiest terms with what he called his intellectual organisation.

"I believe," he said, rubbing his hands together, "I have managed that matter with my usual exquisite tact, and that I have accounted for the loss of my ancestral watch in a manner which will procure me sympathy and reputation, instead of a smile of astonishment that I should had been robbed by any single individual."

He walked into the library with a solemn movement, adjusting his cravat as he went. He smiled benignly in the glass, and made a bew to his own reflected figure in it, then sinking into a luxuriously easy chair, he remarked—

"I am rather inclined to be of opinion, that the present representative of the great Boyes is a remarkable individual."

He then looked at the calves of his legs complacently, and smiled.

"I managed that affair of the watch amazingly well," he added, after a pause. "Tact, tact, tact—what a remarkable thing is tact—ha! who could have done it better?"

He rose, and paced the long apartment, with his hands clasped behind his back, and with such an ineffable look of self-satisfaction upon his face, that it was quite delightful to see him.

Turning, then, at the end of his long march, when he had got to the farther end of the room, he came up again towards the ancient fire-place with a light and airy footstep, and then he stopped abruptly, and his jaw fell, for exactly opposite to his nose, above the chimney-piece, was the ancestral watch hanging on an ancestral hook, where it was wont to dangle time out of mind, while Sir John held communion with the ancient authors.

Poor Sir John! his face was the finest exhibition of bewilderment and dismay that any one could imagine. He retreated back a few steps, and then advanced, and then he retreated again, and then he rubbed his eyes and looked the very picture of the most intense astonishment.

"My— my— ancestral watch!" he gasped; and, in the silence of the apartment, he heard the sonorous tick, tick, of the unwieldy machine. "What shall I do now?—here's a circumstantial circumstance! How came it here—how came it to go, and how went it to come? Gracious Providence! I don't know what to think. There's some more tact wanted now—God bless me, what shall I do?"

He staggered into the great chair, and there he commenced patting his forehead in the vain hope by so doing of awaking some brilliant suggestion which would get him out of the dreadful fix in which he found himself.

"Oh, why was I so precipitate?" he said. "If I had but found it before I lost it; or, after finding that I had lost it, if I'd only thought now, with my usual tact, of losing it, then the finding of it would have been all right; but now, here I am, the victim of an ancestral watch, and its very ticking will proclaim the untruth I have uttered, which is a mechanical means of giving me the lie. Oh! if I had thought for a moment that there were wheels within wheels! What shall I do? that's the question."

Sir John resorted to all the attitudes suggestive of profound thought, that he had ever seen, read, or heard of; but it was of no use—there was the watch, a damning evidence of the fact that it had not gone to London, and that he had invented the tale of its being intrusted to the cunning artizan, with the defective perception of *meum* and *tuum*.

"You wretch," he apostrophised the watch; "you ancestral mortification. You—no, no. What an idea—glorious! I wonder I didn't think of that before now; but great men never come to hasty conclusions. We take a long while to think, but when we do decide, it is a decision rather. I'll hide it. Ha! ha! a good idea, a capital mental suggestion of the mind. One of those refulgences of thought which, in a manner of speaking, are of a kind—of—of —Yes. I'll hide it, and nobody shall know what the time of day is from my ancestral watch again, till some of these days—ha! ha!—I'll produce it, and say, that dread of me, and my distinguished position in society, has compelled the ordinarily dishonest watchmaker to bring it back. Oh! a capital idea—there's tact."

At this moment the door of the library was flung open with such irreverent haste as it had never been opened before, and one of the servants made such a rush in, that he came within an inch of Sir John's very nose, before he could stop himself.

"Oh-o-o-o-o-o!"

"Murder! what do you want here? Hilloa," cried Sir John. "D—n it—come, come, keep off. My watch aint hanging over the mantel-shelf—there's tact."

He had placed his back against the watch, and putting up one of his arms behind him, he took it off the hook, but somehow or another it unfortunately slipped through his fingers, and fell with a terrible crash on to the marble hearth.

"Oh-o-o-o-o-o!" said the servant, "such a smash. Oh! Sir John."

"Villain! it's all through you," said his master.

"Me, Sir John? I didn't kill him."

"Kill him!"

"Yes, Sir John, that's what I come to tell you. Oh, such a spectacle."

"What do you mean? What's a spectacle?"

"My hair stood a hend, and the blood crept jingle-jingle, from the crown of my foot to the sole of my head. Oh! Sir John, excuse haste—somebody's done it!"

"Done what, you character? How dare you come here and break my ancestral chronometer, and then say, somebody's done it?"

"I can't explain. Jervis found him, and all the world and his wife's coming to you, Sir John."

"What next?" said Sir John. "Here's a world. There'll be more tact wanted now."

Through the open library door now came two or three persons, among whom were Lady Boyes and Sir John's private secretary, a youth more learned than his master, and who immediately said—

"Sir John, there's been a dreadful murder on the heath—a murder which will live in the recollections of men fo many a day. Judge Holme is murdered—his dead body was found beneath the wheels of his own carriage, from which the horses had escaped, and further on, in a ditch by the road-side, lay his coachman, badly wounded."

"Judge Holme murdered! one of the judges of assize?"

"Yes, Sir John, and this house being the nearest, his body now lies below."

"Good God! why didn't they take it to the Talbot? Here's a perplexity. I shall have to go to the Secretary of State. Who has done this?"

"The notorious Captain Hawk, Sir John, the highwayman, if any one. Who will sleep safe in their beds after this?"

"It will require a wonderful deal of tact," said Sir John. "Have they caught him?"

"We know nothing but of the finding of the dead body."

"Hark—hark! What means that shout?"

"He's caught—he's caught," cried a man, rushing into the room. "They've caught the murderer. The officers have him, and are taking him to London. He may be seen from the window. There—there, passing the end of the avenue. Look, Sir John, 'tis he in the scarlet coat, with the rich trimming—that's Captain Hawk, Sir John, the great highwayman. If you step out upon the terrace, you'll see him at the turn of the road plainly again."

This advice was at once adopted, and the whole family, with a most unexpected addition in the person of Ratchley, who, suddenly, half-dressed, appeared among them, looking pale and haggard, from the effects of his recent wound.

And the beautiful May, too, was there; she stood with hands clasped, lips rigidly closed, and as immovable as if even carved in stone, gazing in the direction indicated by the last speaker, and apparently oblivious of every other thought but the one of seeing that bold, bad man, for whose sake she had made such incredible exertions, conducted past her own home in custody.

Not a word was spoken, for intense curiosity fixed every one, and in a few moments, as the road wound round a clump of trees, half-a-dozen mounted men appeared, in the midst of whom could be caught a tolerable glance of the knight of the road, attired in his gay and glittering costume, presenting, as he did, a marked contrast to the dark and sombre habiliments of the officers.

His hands were fastened behind him, and the face, for even that was caught sight of for a moment, was nearly as white as the driven snow. In places, too, his apparel was torn and soiled. Some blood had trickled from a gash above his brow; perhaps it was the presence of that ruddy stream which tended to give the remainder of his countenance that absolute colourless appearance, as if, indeed, 'twere painted white.

It was but for a moment that the cavalcade could be seen, but it appeared to all upon the terrace as if the captured man turned his eyes towards the assembled forms thus looking at him. If he did so, it was but a glance—stern, cold, and passionless, and then he was gone.

"I know him," gasped Ratchley.

A shudder pervaded the frame of May Boyes, as she added—

"And I."

Sir John heard these low uttered expressions, and with a groan, he appended to them—

"D—n it, and so do I. Now it'll all come out, I suppose. More tact—more tact. Here's a situation for one of the oldest baronets in the kingdom—here's a pretty predicament for the justice of the peace, and a custos rotulorum. I'll—I'll—yes—I'll do something—I don't know what it's to be exactly, but it shall be something with a wonderful deal of tact about it."

"A murderer," murmured May. "A murderer. God of Heaven! not in vain was the warning given. Taken, taken—the heath—the murder—the gaol—the trial, and the scaffold."

"May—May, you're ill," said Ratchley.

"All is lost—lost to me; but he shall live. And, oh! that the mysterious circumstances which shall now become developed, may turn his soul to Heaven, blood-spotted though it be. Oh! that he may live to pray—then—then shall I have not toiled in vain."

"May—May, what means this strange insanity? Sister, why do you fix your eyes upon vacancy? Do you dream?"

"No, Ratchley, no; and why are you here?"

"To look at him—to feel—to know that in the highwayman, the thief, the murderer, the blood-stained ruffian, I beheld——"

"Hush!" said May; "hush! brother. I know what you would say."

"Gerald Clifton, sister, that is the name that I would utter. The apostate—the false friend—the betrayer—the glozing fiend in human shape—but he will die a felon's death, to expiate my wrongs."

"Indeed!" said May, and she looked calmly in her brother's face. "Indeed, Ratchley, you think so?"

"I am certain. Caught, taken in the very act."

"And yet saved," said May. "Saved by the very act."

"Saved?"

"Yes, saved yet for repentance—yet for good—yet for mercy. There will be a sacrifice—there must be. The blood of the murdered will not cry out alone to Heaven in vain, for vengeance. I say, brother, there will be a sacrifice. And, oh! God, let that sacrifice be one of expiation. There is one who yet will die for Gerald Clifton. Not for love of him as he is on earth—not for love of the intoxicating dream of being his for ever—not to bask in those sweet seductive smiles, which might win an angel out of paradise—not to listen to those tones of eloquence which are, in themselves, a whole world of beauty, but for the sake of that better part of him—his immortal soul—shall there be a sacrifice: he shall not die."

"Sister, sister, you are mad. You know not what you say."

"Too well, too well," said May, and in another moment she was gone.

CHAPTER XI.

THE CRIMINAL.

A more desperate deed than that which had been committed upon Hounslow-heath, as was supposed by the redoubted Captain Hawk, had never inflamed the imagination of the lovers of the terrific.

Judge Holme, who had been murdered on his return from the assizes, was a man, although rather moulded of the sterner elements of humanity, universally respected and esteemed. He held a high place in his profession, and most deservedly so, for, indeed, there seemed to be in almost his every action a sort of Roman rigidity of virtue, such as is rarely found.

Not the slightest breath of calumny or censure had ever assailed his name, and, indeed, he was considered as a man who had borne himself well amid much domestic suffering. It was generally known that in a moment of indiscretion he had contracted a marriage early in life with one he could never raise to his own high state, one having no sympathies in common with himself, and towards whom, if he accorded that deference due to her position as his wife, it must evidently proceed from a strong sense of duty, rather than from that affectionate longing to do honour, where both honour and affection are due.

And so the world had praised Judge Holme for his forbearance, and many had wondered that such a man should for a moment have dreamt of uniting himself to such a one, who could so ill supply the place to him of an affectionate, domestic companion.

That, in his marriage, this man of haughty resolution and stern modes of thought had made a fatal mistake, there cannot be a shadow of a doubt; but if the mistake were to him fatal, how much more fearfully so must it have been to her, who held the state and dignity of his wife, but yet felt that in every word, and in every action, she was an alien to his heart.

Alas! such a state of things is but too common. Men of judgment and of intellect—of elevated aspirations and nobility of thought—men with a keen sense of the beautiful, a high appreciation of the great, and that delicacy of mental structure which doats upon all the intellectual refinements of existence—these are the men who most commonly unite themselves to the pretty plaything of the moment, whom, as if by the magic of their own breath, they have invested with a thousand mental charms, each one of which has no more a substantial status than the fabric of a fertile brain making its own beauty from the slenderest foundation.

And then, alas! too soon the stern realities of life strip the goddess of her beauty. The mental fever fit is passed, and, as she is, they find the being to whom they have tied themselves irrevocably, not as she was.

Blaming, then, not as they fairly ought to do, their own romance, which, like an *ignis fatuus*, has led them far astray, they call that being changed whom they themselves had made so beautiful, but after a time to strip her of her gorgeous decoration, and mourn over the delusion and the sacrifice.

And then ensues the fearful struggle between duty, honour, religion, and all those attributes of moral feeling men hold dear, and the dread chill of a disappointment which searches to the heart's very inmost core. There may be men who can triumph over this—men whose strong sense of right may enable them themselves to be the sacrifice, and unselfishly perchance to pass a long life, wandering among the fading flowers of their once radiant hopes, scarcely catching, as they tread upon those withered leaves, a reminiscence of their once fancied perfume. There may be men who can do this, but they are few and far between. To the world, Judge Holme was one of them; but if the curtain of domestic privacy were drawn aside, some who gazed with admiration upon what passed before its ample folds, would shrink to see its secrets revealed, and dethrone from their high estimation their godlike idol.

There were years of suffering, and then Lady Holme was found dead in her bed; the stern judge wept; some feeling, transient yet beautiful, of early love had touched the chords of feeling, even in his breast; they answered gently, and the stern man wept—once, and once only—then, again, all was cold and passionless, and that portion of a dread domestic drama was over.

The grave had closed over her whom, it may be truly said, he had wooed to her destruction. Oh! it was cruel to take her from her lowly state, and then mock her that she had not the attributes of his! But the deed was done, and now she had passed away in all her beauty—for beautiful she was—and such beauty as might well have adorned a humble home and graced a lowlier station.

But there was one to whom that stern judge owed words of explanation; there was one before whom even he shrank, and whose keen glance he dared not abide; one before whom he shook and trembled, ay, even more than the veriest wretch who ever, at the bar of justice, heard from his stern lips the fiat of his destiny.

And that one was his son. A son combining much of the intellectual power of his father with the weaker, but gentler, attributes of his mother. A son who had no affection to struggle against, for cold and stern had been that father to him, and if in his heart there really was a well-spring of affection for his child, he had ever kept its fountains sealed, wherefore, no one knew; perchance he saw too much of the mother in the boy.

Let not our readers fancy we are wandering from our tale in talking thus of the dead. It is not so; much that is hidden will yet be known, and the issues of that which have occurred have yet to be declared; and now we will paint a picture which, pages after this, will show itself before the mind's eye of the attentive reader, bringing with it its own explanation.

We will step back ten years, to present to those who have followed us so far this living sketch.

There is an antique chamber in a gorgeous house, and in it are two person; one on whom time has placed some of its most significant marks, the other in the very spring-tide of his youth and beauty, a youth physically matured beyond his age, and looking with a stern and seemingly passionless gaze upon his senior.

They are the haughty judge and his son, and it is the evening of that day on which the wife and the mother has been consigned to her last, cold resting-place, and yet, to her, less cold than those arms which once had circled her so fondly, and, in the whispering accents of the tenderest affection, vowed a love which was as fleeting and unsubstantial as Heaven's prismatic bow in a summer sky.

There was a silence of many minutes' duration; thought was fearfully busy in both their hearts, and yet each seemed to fear to speak, and the elder man, for old he looked, trembled as he gazed upon that slim and youthful form which stood so silently before him.

It was evident a conference must ensue, of what nature we shall now record. Finding, probably, that his father would not speak, it was the son who first gave utterance to the thoughts which were swelling in his bosom.

"Father," he said, "my mother was unhappy; she has told me so a hundred times. She is dead! tell me now, before I again sleep beneath this roof, is there nothing at your heart that tells you 'conscience doth make cowards of us all?'"

"Nothing!" said the judge.

"I would probe you to the quick. Did she die broken-hearted? Was her whole life bitterness and disappointment? Did you make for her a sunshine or a gloom? Speak to me, and speak truly. Did she die of your unkindness, or has nature in its due course snatched her from the world some scruple not to say you made so hateful to her?"

"She is dead!" said the judge. "I know no more."

"I adjure you," cried the young man, "by every hope of peace you have here, or happiness hereafter—I adjure you, most solemnly, by the great God above, whose ordinances you even make a great parade in keeping—I adjure you to tell me if but one word of kindness to my mother has passed your lips within twelve months?"

"Not one," said the judge.

"I'm answered," said the youth. "Henceforward we are strangers—more strange than strangers even, for the remembrance of what we might have been shall place a gulf between us, which I will not, and which you dare not, pass."

He strode from the apartment with a gasping sob; the stern man called to him. He wrung his hands for a moment.

"Stay, stay," he cried; "my son—my boy!" and then all was still, cold, and passionless as heretofore.

With scrupulous care he arrayed himself to receive some sympathising guests; and never was the calmness of dignified grief so well acted as by Judge Holme that night.

And now our little episode is over. We again rush onwards in the chariot of Time: and without another glance behind, we proceed to detail those stirring events consequent upon what has already been related to the reader.

It was dreadfully to the chagin of Sir John Boyes that Judge Holmes's body should be brought to the Hall; but having once been brought there, he shrank from ordering its removal; so that now he walked about with a distressed look, making a curious chuck-chucking noise with his mouth, indicative of affairs not being at all in their proper trim.

Poor Sir John, as his lady frequently remarked, was not the best hand at seeing what was passing under his nose; and so the occurrences upon the terrace of his own house, although most significant of some pregone conclusion to any acute observer, passed away quite unheeded by Sir John.

In fact, his mind was so fixed upon the mysterious circumstance connected with the abstraction, and then the return of the ancestral watch, that the most transparent plot in the world might have been carried on around him without his being a bit the wiser.

After his wonder at Ratchley being so well as to be able to get up—for that was the only view he took of it—he had nothing further to remark about, except, indeed, a passing wonder as to what had become of Gerald Clifton, who had only gone out to visit a friend, and had made so protracted a stay.

This he tormented everybody with for about half a day, but as the only two parties in the household, namely, May and Ratchley, who could give him any informatiom upon that subject, were silent, he gathered no information.

And it was strange, too, how these two seemed, as if by mutual consent, to avoid speaking of Gerald Clifton. It was not likely to be a theme upon which May Boyes would wish to converse; and as, so far as Ratchley knew, she was only suffering that kind of gentle affliction which was consequent upon finding that she had misplaced an affectionate preference, he thought it best to let her grief, if it amounted to so much, take its course, and to say nothing whatever to her upon the subject.

This was a strange, anomalous state of

things when their hearts were so full of the matter.

Poor May Boyes could not remove herself out of the belief that the captured highwayman and Gerald were the same. If he were not the murderer, then she had gone through a frightful scene, in her disguise, in vain. Alas! what a

THE CONSTERNATION OF SIR JOHN BOYES ON FINDING THE FAMILY WATCH.

frightful contest was waging in her brain! But it now becomes our duty to avert to the murder upon the heath more particularly, and the consequences of that most unhappy act.

That Captain Hawk was actively employing himself in the neighbourhood none could doubt. The conviction of such a truth would naturally follow—a fact which the robbery of the Oxford mail sufficiently attested.

There was no direct evidence, however, of any one who had seen the deed committed. The judge's servant, although not quite dead when picked up, had ceased to breathe very shortly afterwards, being quite unable, in so brief an interval, to detail anything with sufficient accuracy to be relied upon.

However, his capture in the immediate vicinity of the spot at which the murder was committed, his manner when charged with the deed, and his general appearance, were more than sufficient to stamp him with its authorship, and, accordingly, the jury returned a verdict of wilful murder against —— Hawk, commonly called Captain Hawk, for no one knew him by any other name.

To be sure, Sir John made some remarkable observations upon the jury, but as our readers may form for themselves a pretty good estimate of what that illustrious person was likely to remark, we need not transfer those observations to our pages.

At that time there was no squabbling between coroners and magistrates. Hawk had been taken to London at once, inasmuch as a warrant for his apprehension on the charge of robbing the Oxford mail had been placed in the hands of some of the most experienced officers, so that, irrespective of the new and much more serious charge in which he was involved, they had taken him to London by virtue of the warrant they held, and it was not until late the next evening, that Sir John received notice that the prisoner would be brought back again to undergo his examination before the local magistracy regarding the murder.

This was done as much for the convenience of witnesses as to keep the forms of justice intact, because, if he had been apprehended for the murder, as he was not, the officers would not have taken him past a local magistrate residing on the spot where the deed was committed.

Our readers will imagine the consternation of Sir John when he received a note from the chief magistrate of London, announcing that the prisoner would be sent down to him, and, doubtless, he would see the expediency of committing him for trial on the charge of murder, when he could be at once safely lodged in Newgate.

"God bless me!" exclaimed Sir John, when he read the note, "it's not over yet, and consequently it's not done. It'll all come out now about the watch, and I shan't know very well what to say. To be sure it's quite right to bring him here to me. The authorities in London, no doubt, have heard of me, and they know that if I commit him, there can be no mistake. But what if he says anything to me about the ancestral watch, what shall I reply? I should like to know how he got it back again, and hung it upon the hook; but I tremble to ask him, and I shall sit upon nothing but hooks all the while he is here. The rascal, to place one of the oldest baronets in the kingdom in such a situation. I'll commit him as quick as I can, and get him out of the place. The deuce take it, why did they send him here? I did think, at all events, I'd got rid of him."

There was a terrible combat between Sir John's gratified dignity and his dread lest this affair of the watch should come to light, so that by the time the prisoner was expected at the Hall, he worked himself into a perfect fever, and so strangely did he feel the necessity of doing something clever upon the occasion, that after many qualms of conscience, he made up his mind to consult his young secretary as to the most advisable course to pursue, not being entirely, perhaps, without a faint hope that that individual might be kind enough to take upon himself some of the onus of the transaction, and so relieve his great principal from his difficulty.

"Good Master Lucas," began Sir John, "I am extremely satisfied with you; you are a remarkable youth."

"Thank you, Sir John."

"Ha! ha! it's very funny, aint it? I've got something here," and he tapped his forehead mysteriously. "You wouldn't think it, Lucas, but I've got something here."

"No, Sir John," said the lad drily, "I shouldn't think it, indeed."

"Well, you must know, Lucas, that when I intend to do anything for the benefit of society at large, and human nature generally, in the—the—great—the great—what do you call it?—of thought, I search about for the best method of proceeding."

"Certainly, Sir John, I've no doubt you do."

"And sometimes the vast mental resources which I am forced to bring into play become dreadfully complicated. I'm thinking of something now, and as I wish to push you on in life, you shall be the sharer of the enterprise. Not to confuse you, you know, I mean not to tell you how it will end; but you shall say that you were sitting in my library, you know, after I told you, you know, to give my watch to a very doubtful character to clean, and that Captain Hawk came in and took it from me, and he then brought it back again, you don't know how—you understand me, Lucas?"

"But you didn't, Sir John, and I didn't, and Captain Hawk didn't."

"That's the beauty of the plot, and if nothing's said about it, you needn't say anything; but if anything is said, you can say that, and I'll forgive you. The human mind, you know, Lucas, resembles a—a—which is precisely like it, you know."

"But, Sir John, I really can't understand you."

"Then you are not the intelligent character I took you for. I cannot supply you with comprehension, you know, Lucas. If you cannot understand what I have said to you, I am sorry, very sorry, may I say extremely sorry, which is equivalent, generally speaking, to regretting the circumstance."

Lucas, upon this, saw that it was highly necessary that he should comprehend, and, perhaps, with some degree of reluctance, he was going to say that he would endeavour to obey Sir John's orders, when, fortunately for him, the conversation was interrupted by an announcement that nearly drove Sir John frantic, and made him dance round the library table like a madman. This was no other than a statement by a servant of the arrival of the indefatigable Long, who, as usual, had something of importance to say.

"D—n him! I thought he was dead!" said Sir John. "Turn him out, turn him out! Kick him, and pummel him!"

"Sir John Boyes," said a quiet and gentlemanly man, entering the room, "I have perhaps rudely followed your servant into your presence, because I feel it to be necessary, before I commence proceedings against you, that I should ask you if you've any rational excuse for the extraordinary course of conduct you have pursued towards me?"

"Towards you?" said Sir John. "Why I never saw you in my life."

"I know that well enough. Sir John."

"D—n it! then what do you mean?"

"Why, d—n it, sir, I mean you took good care not to see me, by having me tossed in a blanket, and buckets of water thrown over me for the mere attempt."

"You?"

"Now, Sir John, it's very well to try and shuffle out of it, but I feel myself much aggrieved, and shall seek redress."

"And who the devil may you be?"

"Long, sir, Long. My name's Long, sir."

Sir John staggered.

"Pooh! pooh!" he said, "I know better; you ain't Long, nor Strong either."

"I shall be strong enough, Sir John, to let you know that when I am sent here by the secretary of state to do you a service, I'm not to be half killed with impunity. I mean to trounce you, Sir John, for your conduct. I shall bring my action against you, and I tell you that's the only way to make men such as yourself feel; and now, sir, having settle my private business with you, I assume my public and official capacity."

"But you aint Long," said Sir John. "Where's Long?"

"I am Long, sir. This is the coolest piece of effrontery that ever I met with, to treat a man as I have been treated, and then try to bamboozle him out of his name."

"Did you apply the term bamboozle to me?" said Sir John.

"I did."

"And do you know who I am?"

"Yes; the d——t fool that ever I came across!"

Sir John took up an inkstand and flung it at Long's head, which, however, it missed, but it hit the devoted watch which had been restored to its hook, and further added to the derangement of that ancestral heir-loom, by knocking off a corner of its physiognomy.

"I'm glad of that," said Long; "and there's evidence in the room, too."

"Sir John, Sir John," cried Lucas, "I'm quite certain that this is not the Mr. Long who called first upon you."

"Yes, he is," said Sir John; "he knows that. I'm a d—d fool! and that is what he called me before. Did you or did you not, Sir, come and advise me not to be an ass?"

"This is the first moment I set foot in your presence," said Long; "but I must confess that you are in need of some such friendly admonition. I came here, Sir John, from the secretary of state, who received private information that in your house, under an assumed name, was the celebrated Captain Hawk, the highwayman."

"In my house?"

"Hold!" cried May Boyes, as she suddenly appeared at the door, accompanied by Ratchley.

"Under what name?" roared Sir John. "I will know."

"Let it be spoken," said Ratchley; "let it be spoken, May, at once."

"Under the name of Gerald Clifton," said Long.

CHAPTER XII.

THE MYSTERY.

Sir John was bewildered, and well he might be; a wiser man than Sir John Boyes would have been bewildered at being suddenly told that a cherished guest, whom he had considered the pink of gentility, was a highwayman. Indeed, the whole party, with the exception of Ratchley and May, looked the astonishment which such an announcement was calculated to produce. Lady Boyes and Philippa, both of whom had glided into the apartment upon hearing high words between Sir John and some one, uttered exclamations of the greatest surprise, while Ratchley whispered to May—

"Fear nothing, sister—say nothing. This is a truth which sooner or later must have been known. Let it be a relief to you that it is known so soon."

"I am content," said May.

"But, Mr. What's-your-name," said Sir John, "you don't mean to tell me that there's no such a person as Mr. Gerald Clifton?"

"Sir John," said Long, "you may obliterate from your memory either of the personages you please, but that Captain Hawk, the celebrated highwayman, has been staying at your house under the name of Gerald Clifton, is a truth of which you may be assured."

"Well, then," said Sir John, "'tis one of the most extraordinary things in the world. Here are two men suddenly proved to be only one; while to make up for the deficiency, Mr. Long, there are two of you, for most certainly you are not the Long that was here before."

"I have it," said Long; "I now begin to see what has occurred. You've been imposed upon, Sir John. The tricks and finesse of Captain Hawk are familiar to the police; I have no doubt at all that one of his own associates, ascertaining by some means what was in the wind, got here before me and personated me."

Sir John tapped his head, and, with a melancholy look, assented to the proposition, on which he and Long became much better friends, and a hint at some little pecuniary compensation soon put matters to rights, so that Sir John felt more at his ease, and began to talk of the approaching examination of the prisoner with some sort of satisfaction.

"Of course," he said, "we shall confine ourselves solely to a consideration of the murder; we have nothing to do with anything else he has done; for instance, if he had stolen anybody's watch, that's of no consequence in comparison to the more serious charge?"

"Certainly not," said Long, "except it be in some manner collaterally connected with it; then, it would become a matter of some importance, especially if it had anything to do with the question of time in regard to the manner in which the prisoner was engaged on the night of the murder."

Sir John gave half a groan, for he recollected well how particularly his attention had been called to the hour when his watch had been taken from him. He felt half inclined to divulge to Long the difficulty he was in; and, indeed, it seemed highly probable that the politic

Sir John would, by degrees, tell everybody, under a plea of strict secrecy, and get such a multitude of advice, that, if such a state of things were possible, he would be more confused than ever.

However, upon second thoughts, he said nothing more to Long ; and now as the intervening time before the examination of the prisoner took place was more full of anxiety than interest, we will pass it over, and proceed at once to more stirring incidents of action.

Sir John was what the whole county considered a very painstaking magistrate ; that is to say, he took twice the time that any one else would have taken to deliver a result, and whenever anybody else considered a case as finished, he had a sad knack of beginning it over again.

This mode of procedure as regarded the petty larcenies, trespasses, and offences against the game laws, which chiefly occupied the attention of the suburban magistracy, was of little importance, but should he take it into his head to come out terrifically strong upon the murder case, there was no knowing where it would end.

Our readers will fancy the great hall, in which justice was administered in that ancient mansion, crowded with wondering spectators. There had been time enough for the bruit of the transaction to reach all the surrounding gentry, and that kind of curiosity which casts such a halo of romance around extraordinary criminals, had induced a large concourse of spectators to assemble at Boyes Hall, for the purpose of seeing the celebrated highwayman, whose numerous escapes from the hands of justice had been themes of wondering gossip throughout nearly the whole of England.

This kind of attention was rather flattering to Sir John, for, as he meant to be enormously didactic upon the occasion, of course the larger the audience, the greater would be the amount of self-glorification he was likely to feel.

At each new arrival he seemed to stand at least an inch taller, and he assumed such an air of profundity that he could not at all look where he was going, but stumbled over every table and chair that was in his way.

The prisoner had not arrived, but he was momentarily expected, and as Sir John considered it *infra dig.* for him to take his place in the hall of justice before the proceedings actually commenced, the spectators had some time to gossip among themselves concerning what they considered the unprecedented circumstances of the whole affair ; and yet how little did they know of the real nature of these circumstances, or of the extraordinary mystery in which some of them were still enshrouded.

It was about a quarter before twelve when Sir John, who was pacing the library to and fro, received information that the prisoner had arrived, and that everything was ready to commence the examination.

Assuming, then, a withering look, he walked with a stately air across a corridor, which led him to a large hall, from whence he could already hear the hum of many voices. On his own account, he intended to demolish the prisoner by a glance ; for, although he had intended not to allude to the fact of his having been an inmate of his house, yet he felt that there was something due to himself for so grievous a take in.

He was preceded by two servants, for Sir John had a tolerable eye to effect, and fully intended that his entry should be of as imposing a character as possible.

But, alas! for human intentions! had Sir John been a little less proud, he unquestionably would have walked in prouder, but when a man's eyes are fixed upon a ceiling, he cannot be expected to see obstructions in his path, and, consequently, Sir John's first appearance in the great hall was head foremost, and in a horizonal position over a strip of matting he had himself placed to increase the effect of the preparations.

His most sanguine notions of the effect he should produce upon his entrance were a long way off that which he really effected, and the universal glare of astonishment to see only the upper part of Sir John's illustrious person, while his long, rambling-looking legs were out in the corridor, and the two domestics, with horror in their looks, appeared as if they had just knocked him down, altogether presented a picture of magisterial dignity such as poor Sir John had never anticipated.

Sir John had never heard the quotation, or he would have wished himself five hundred fathoms under the Rialto at that moment; and when he did rise to his feet, how sadly the dignity of the judge was marred by a ruddy stream from the apex of his promontory, which had come in extremely forcible contact with the oaken floor.

Everybody was full of commiseration, but that was so disgustingly different from admiration, that Sir John sank into his seat with a deep groan, and, far from casting a withering look upon the audacious prisoner, he felt completely withered himself.

He could hardly muster courage enough to order the proceedings to commence, and when they had fairly done so, it was a great relief to him to see a roly-poly little man suddenly advance and put himself into an oratorical attitude. It was most likely somebody to quarrel with, and Sir John began to feel that if he could successfully put anybody down he should be more himself again.

"Who are you?" said Sir John.

"A very apposite question," said the little roly-poly man; "I am Mr. Pump of the Temple."

"And pray what's that to me," said Sir John, "whether you're Mr. Pump of the Temple, or Mr. Temple of the Pump?"

"I dare say not much," said the little man; "but I come here as the advocate of the prisoner before you. By my advice he offers no objection to your committing him for trial, although so entirely innocent of the crime that is laid to his charge; therefore, Sir John, if you please, you can commit him upon the smallest amount of circumstantial evidence which you may think may justify you in so doing."

This was spoken in an off-handed sort of a manner, as if he would have added—

"We really would rather be committed than have the trouble of explaining to you that we didn't do it," and consequently, it became a sore place now in poor Sir John's mind.

Although he could not look witheringly upon the prisoner, he did upon Mr. Pump, as he said—

"Sir, I'll commit you, if you don't behave yourself with greater decorum before the representative of majesty."

Mr. Pump smiled and bowed, as he replied in bland accents—

"Your worship is very much mistaken if you consider, for one moment, I wish to treat you with disrespect; attached to the law and the legal authorities as I am, the office you hold would, in my eyes, sanctify a donkey."

There was a titter, which human nature could not suppress, among the audience, and young Lucas whispered to Sir John—

"Pray, sir, treat him with silent contempt. It's Mr. Pump, the well-known thieves' advocate: he don't care what he says, sir; and he always tries to pick a quarrel with the magistracy. Treat him with silent contempt, sir—that's the only way."

"I will—I will," said Sir John; "for 'tis difficult to know what to say. It's beneath one's dignity to be witty or sharp with such a man. Call the witnesses; I will hear the case."

The evidence, as we before remarked, as it at present stood, was much more of a negative than of a positive character. Without finding, in any one respect, Captain Hawk to be guilty of the murder, it rather, by implication, made him so, by clearing everybody else, and leaving the onus of the deed upon him, as the most likely person to have committed it.

And then the proceedings were necessarily narrowed, because the prisoner's counsel said nothing, contradicted nothing, but smiled so blandly at the witnesses, that every one left off in a state of great aggravation, and with an indistinct notion that, in some mysterious manner, he had put his foot in it, and that, among the notes Mr. Pump made in a memorandum book, something or another would come out hereafter, of a most uncomfortable character.

This was all dreadfully unsatisfactory to Sir John, who had no idea of acting so purely a mechanical part in the business, as that which seemed to be thrown upon him; and when the evidence was finished, he looked as stern as possible at the prisoner, as he said—

"Young man—young man—young man—what have you got to say to all this?"

"Nothing," said Mr. Pump; "but a reiteration of our entire innocence."

"But that won't do," said Sir John. "You must not be entirely innocent. Pray understand me: I do not wish to prejudge your case; but when anything comes before me, in a manner of speaking, I see it."

"Sir," said Mr. Pump, "my client has not the smallest doubt in the world but that your worship is one of those gentlemen who can see quite as far through a mill-stone as through a large Cheshire cheese; and with that conviction, we do not want to waste our valuable time."

Sir John looked sage. He was not quite sure whether this was a compliment from Mr. Pump or something quite the reverse; but for once in his life he was wise enough to choose the pleasanter alternative, and with rather a stately inclination of his magisterial head, he said—

"It appears to me—a-hem!—that sitting here as I sit, and being, as I may say, the representative of majesty, that—a-hem!—there has been a murder committed; and when a man commits a murder it is equally clear that he has slain somebody; and although the law does not take upon itself to say who a man shall slay in order to commit a murder, it does take upon itself to say—a-hem!—that, indeed, and in fact, criminality is injurious to public peace."

"It is impossible, Sir John," said Mr. Pump, "that anything can be clearer than your mode of laying down the law in the case, and I shall take a note of your luminous speech, and astonish the profession with it when I get to London, if you will permit me."

"Sir, you may astonish the profession, if you please, with my judgment. I rather believe my judgment is the astonishment of this large and, I may say, influential neighbourhood."

"No doubt, Sir John, they watch you with care."

"Watch! Oh, did you say anything about a watch, sir, or did you not?—for I can inform you, sir, that, magisterially, I know nothing about a watch—not even an ancestral watch. What have you to say to that, sir."

"Nothing at all, your worship; but my private opinion is that there can be no need of any watch or clock either, in the neighbourhood of your worship, who is so wide awake that it is quite impossible you can be otherwise than always cognizant of the time of day."

"Ah—hem! I may say that, presiding here, in a manner of speaking, here I sit. It is a grievous thing to think that a judge who was upon his road from where he had been vindicating the law, should be nobbed on the head within sight almost of Boyes Hall, and that I should be called upon to adjudicate, in a manner of speaking—

Mr. Pump was getting very fidgetty.

"Pray," said Sir John, "will the prisoner apologise?"

"What?"

"I say, will the prisoner apologise for his treatment of me? After breathing the air of this place, it requires an apology from him after then going upon the highway and committing a murder. Come—come, prisoner, look at me!"

Captain Hawk turned his solemn and sad gaze upon the face of Sir John, but he did not speak. They, indeed, looked at each other for a few moments in silence, and a more striking contrast than these two men exhibited surely could not have been found in all the world.

Then was in good truth mind and matter brought into juxtaposition with each other. The pompous stupidity of Sir John Boyes and the looks of solemn nothingness that was upon his face, contrasted most vividly with the speaking features of Gerald Clifton.

Sir John slowly shook his head.

A scornful look passed over the pale features of the prisoner, and then it died away, giving place to the calm glance of inward suffering which at times since his capture he had worn, and which seemed to be the prevailing expression of his feelings when he forgot that any one was looking at him for a moment.

"Well?" said Sir John.

Gerald Clifton only bowed.

Perhaps the respectful character of the bow had some effect in soothing the feelings of the great Sir John Boyes, for it was in a softer tone, and with evidently more of feeling towards the prisoner, that he spoke, when after a solemn pause he condescended to do so.

"It will be my duty," said Sir John, "to commit you to Newgate."

"Very good," said Mr. Pump; "we're willing to go; and, when our innocence becomes apparent, as it will, we shall not blame you for doing your duty."

"Have you anything to say to me?" said Sir John, as he thumped his fist upon the table.

"Do you address me?" said Captain Hawk, for the first time breaking the silence he had maintained.

"Yes, you vagabond; you came into my house in the disguise of a gentleman."

"I don't know you," said the prisoner.

"You don't know me! Come—come, Mr. Clifton; you know very well you've eaten and drunk at my table, sir. You shot my son; and you made yourself agreeable, sir, d—n you! to my daughter. But I shall have the pleasure of seeing you hung. It's a pleasant ride, sir, from here to Tyburn, on a fine morning, and d—e, I'll come, if it rains, even."

"Very good," said Mr. Pump, "very good, indeed. Pray go on, your worship. This is delightful, because it comes fresh from the heart. Pray go on, sir, you're a pleasant speaker to follow. I've got it all down in my memorandum-book."

"I won't go on," said Sir John.

"Then stop, sir."

"No, I won't stop. Mr. Clifton—can you look me in the face? I'll have the spoons counted when you're gone."

"Not forgetting yourself in," said Mr. Pump, "as the largest family specimen of that article in the house."

"Did you hear that, Lucas?" said Sir John. "Lucas — did you hear that?"

"Yes, nearly," said Lucas, very reluctantly.

"Can I commit everybody?" said Sir John.

"I rather think not, if you please, sir."

"Can I put Pump in the stocks, eh?"

"Why, I wouldn't do it, sir. Treat him with silent contempt, sir."

"Silent contempt be d—d, Lucas! I suppose, if somebody were to kick me round my own hall, you'd advise me to take no notice of what passes behind my back."

"Kick you, Sir John! oh! dear that's impossible. I should humbly advise that you calmly commit the prisoner, and break up the proceedings."

"I will," said Sir John; "but, sooner or later, this shall be a dreadful day for Pump."

The committal was accordingly drawn out; and Hawk was delivered into the custody of the officers who had brought him from London. It was evident that throughout the whole affair he had been acting a part; and the cold, silent aspect he wore, was the result of some preconceived plan of action. He walked from the hall with the same calm demeanour he had entered it, and probably he thought to leave that house unnerved; but such was not to be. As he passed through the outer hall which led to the flight of stone steps, he was intercepted for a moment by a female form; and then, for the first time, he shrank, for he knew that it was May. She laid both hands upon his fettered arm, and while a crimson flush now mounted to his face she spoke—

"You will be saved—saved for repentance."

"No," he said, "no. Farewell for ever—my destiny is fulfilled—no human power now——

"Hush!" said May; "you will be saved. Make peace with God. Man will yet hold ye harmless."

Mr. Pump, who was close at hand, heard these words, and addressing May he said—

"If you have any evidence that will be of service, communicate with me."

May answered him not, but, turning slowly, she glided from the hall. Gerald Clifton perceptibly trembled as he looked after her; he seemed about to speak, but one of the officers plucked him by the arm, and he gave up the intention. The mantling colour again left his cheeks, and, probably from the contrast, they looked paler than before. He said nothing, but allowed himself to be conducted into the open air and mounted on a horse; an officer rode on each side of him, one led the way, and another brought up the rear. They showed him, before starting, that they were well armed, and warned him that death, or some grievous wound, would be the result of any attempt to escape.

He looked vacantly at them, and then shuddered.

The officers gazed at their prisoner, and then winked at each other as much as to say—"Ah, he is beginning to feel it now!"—"His courage is breaking down!"—But how little they, in reality, knew of the kind of soul-stricken terror that was stealing over the heart and

SIR JOHN BOYES SURPRISED BY THE ENTRANCE OF LONG.

bosom of Captain Hawk. He saw nothing but May Boyes. In his mind's-eye he saw her, and he heard her last words telling him to make his peace with God, and he felt that henceforward between him and her there rolled an ocean, which she dared not, and which he could not cross.

"Yes," he said, mournfully, "it is over now!—God! it is all over now Poor May!"

CHAPTER XIII.

CAPTAIN HAWK MAKES A DESPERATE ATTEMPT TO ESCAPE.

To the apprehensions of the officers, no prisoner could be more thoroughly depressed than was Captain Hawk. They had been accustomed, in their dealings with the criminal portion of human nature, to encounter all shades of temperament, and all classes of feelings. At times they would find that the bravado that had been the temptation to crime, would vanish completely when its consequences began to be apparent. At other times they would find, that the cool collected courage of the prisoner was only the more apparent as his difficulties and his dangers increased around him.

But as regarded Captain Hawk, those superficial readers of human nature, the officers, fancied, when they looked upon the pale face—pale almost to whiteness—and saw the quivering lip, that it was fear produced such symptoms.

How wonderfully they were mistaken!

Fear was a sentiment with which Hawk was totally unacquainted, and it was not likely that now so great a moral change should take place in his disposition, as to bring him within the slavish influence of such a feeling.

No, it was not fear that blanched the cheeks of Captain Hawk. It was not a dread of what might too soon be his fate, that made his lips quiver, and started thus the blood into the fine vessels of his eyes, but it was feeling—feeling awakened, if you please, merely, and at a time when it could do little good for May Boyes.

He had not thought that she loved him so much, as now he felt convinced that she did.

It was not until he looked upon her fair face, and saw it in the controlled agony of the moment when he was leaving the hall, that he felt convinced what a wreck he had left her; and all for what? The idle gratification of a passing moment—the mere elaboration of a sentiment of admiration for one of nature's masterpieces of beauty.

Yes, Hawk did feel that there he was criminal.

The murder upon the heath—the attack upon Ratchley—all his crimes seemed to sink into insignificance compared with that one deliberate social offence that he committed against poor May Boyes: at least, such was his state of feeling.

There was a point in the road from which a distant and yet a clear view of Boyes Hall could be got. He knew that point well, and when the officers were close upon it, he spoke to them.

"Stop!" he said; "only for a moment stop!"

The tone in which he spoke was so strange and so sepulchral, that they paused involuntarily, and looked at him with pity, and some feeling that was near akin to terror.

Slowly, as well as his manacles would allow him to do, he turned upon the horse, and looked through the vista in the trees at the old house. His gaze continued for the space of about half a minute, and then he turned his eyes away.

"On—on!" he said. "It is the last, perhaps."

"Why, what's the matter with you, Captain Hawk?" said one of the officers. "You seem regularly done up, old fellow. There's many a knight of the road been in the same fix that you are now; ay, and got out of it again. You ain't hung yet."

"No, not a bit of it," said one of the others. They really pitied him, and wanted to rouse his spirits a little. Officers do not feel towards such persons as the general public do.

"Besides," said a third, "when you went on the road, you knew that you run this chance, and you ought to have made up your mind to it; and when you are taken, you ought not to begin snivelling in this odd kind of way."

Captain Hawk looked at them all, and his eyes flashed as he said,—

"What do you mean? I have but half attended to what you were saying. Are you speaking to me?"

"Yes, we were. We were only saying that you need not be so cast down; for, after all, you might get off, and if you don't, it is but the rational kind of end you were sure to come to."

"Cast down?"

"Yes; you look as grave as possible."

"My good fellows, I was no more thinking of you nor of my captivity, nor of its consequences, than I was thinking of the means of escaping all such little troubles. I had other thoughts. But if you fancy that the fear of death is upon me, you are much mistaken, indeed!"

The tone in which he pronounced these words opened the eyes of the officers to the fact that they had made a grand mistake with regard to the state of mind of their prisoner, and the principal one said to him,—

"Captain Hawk, you have used one word that always sounds rather suspicious in the ears of officers."

"And what is that?"

"The word, escape!"

"Oh, certainly; and pray, my good sir, if it so chanced that you were being carried off to be hanged, would not that be a word that would in all human probability come across your mind?"

"It might; but that is not the question; and let me tell you, Captain Hawk, that we are all well armed, and quite ready to use our arms. If you try to give us the slip, we must, however much we should regret such a thing, be under the disagreeable necessity of shooting you!"

"Oh, don't mention it," said Hawk. "I beg you will make no excuses about it. You do your duty, and I will try to do mine."

"Humph!" muttered the officers, "what the deuce does he mean by that I wonder? His duty? What can that be?"

Captain Hawk did not feel disposed to be more explicit, so the officers felt themselves compelled to make the most of what he had said; but they exchanged with each other significant looks, as though they would intimate that they thought their prisoner rather inclined to be just a little dangerous, and that it was needful to keep a keen watch upon his movements.

In order to enable him to manage the horse that he rode, they had been compelled to take the handcuffs off his wrist; but as a slight measure of protection, they connected his elbows together by a rope, which, while it left his arms at sufficient freedom as regarded the control of the horse, would still have been a very serious impediment to anything like personal exertion in any other way, if he should feel disposed to attempt it.

As regards his safety as their prisoner, they might be said to rely wholly upon the watch that they kept upon him, and the fact that it must be well known to him that any attempt upon his part to escape must prove instant death, as long before he could even disengage himself from the horse, the pistols of the officers would be ready for use.

"Come, Hawk," said he who was in command of the little party, "you may as well be good friends with us as bad. I don't mean to say that we can do you much good as regards what you will be put upon your trial for, as that is an affair in which we none of us had anything to do; but as regards your own comfort, it is quite another affair."

"What do you require of me?" said Hawk.

"Give us your word of honour that you won't try to escape from us, and we will take off the cord that fastens your elbows together; and you will find your progress along the road much more pleasant, as you needn't then be stared at by everybody so much, as no one need know you are our prisoner."

"No."

"What do you mean by no?"

"Simply, that I decline the offer, although I feel it's politeness fully. For all I know, you may all be taken ill suddenly, and then, what a fool I should look like if I had made a promise not to ride away, but had to take charge of you all to London!"

"Oh, stuff! that's not likely."

"And yet, what very unlikely things come to pass at times, do they not?"

"Oh, well, if you won't, you won't. Come, friends, there is the place where we will make a bait not far before us. All we have to do is to look sharp after our prisoner."

The object of the officers had been to get into London by the Oxford Road, and they had, therefore, made their way into it, or rather, the Uxbridge Road, previous to arriving at it at a point a little on the London side of Ealing; and the house at which they intended to bait was no other than the Old Hats Inn.

This inn, which is still existing as an inn, was then a very old place. We need hardly say that the original old structure is long since gone, and that the present inn, with its good accommodation, bears no relationship to it. It was at the time of our story a long, low-roofed building of no particular shape of architecture, as it seemed to have been added to by succeeding generations that had had anything to do with it.

The greatest portion of the building was of wood, and the gardens that were then attached to it were more extensive than they are now.

We find in an old work upon the History of London, the following passage regarding this inn:—

"This day we went to the Old Hats Inn, on the Uxbridge Road, and dined in the garden, under the large cedar-tree. Home early, though, for fear of the highwaymen who infest the road, and are so daring that only last week they stopped the Secretary of State, who had been to Berry-Mead Priory, and took his watch from him, although he had two outriders and a gentleman with him in his carriage. It was thought to be one Captain Hawk who did this."

The place called Berry-Mead Priory, mentioned in this little extract, is still in existence just at the entrance to Acton, and was up till very lately the residence of some nuns.

To return to our story. The old sign of the inn was soon seen among the trees, swinging across the road, and creaking in the rather smart breeze that was blowing at the time.

"There it is," said one of the officers. "We can get something good both in the eating and the drinking way, there, I rather think. I suppose, Captain Hawk, you have no objection to stand treat?"

"None in the least," said Hawk, "and I hope you will consider yourselves as my guests upon this occasion, and partake of the best that the inn will afford to you, at my cost."

"He isn't a bad fellow, after all," said one of the officers, whose heart was very much softened towards the prisoner, at the prospect of a treat at his expense, "and I'm rather sorry he is nabbed."

"Oh, gammon," said the other.

As regarded Hawk himself, he had evidently by this time managed to shake off very much of the depression that had come over him; and whether it was merely stifled, as it were, or utterly extinguished for the time, he certainly did not show it as he had done. The colour had come back to his face again, and his eyes looked much as usual, if we may except a certain restlessness, and ever shifting glance about them that was not habitual to him, and which probably now was the result of over-anxiety to become clearly cognisant of every little circumstance that might aid him in his attempt to escape from the officers.

That he had made up his made to escape, was a proposition that there could be no dispute about. How it was to be completed, was the only remaining question.

As they now neared the Old Hats, the officers slightly quickened their pace, and the horses seemed not at all loath to do so, since they no doubt knew from experience that there would be a bait there, for which they were by no means disinclined at any time. And now it could be seen how exquisite a rider Captain Hawk was, for he rode his horse at a rate which the officers had not thought it was in the power of the creature to do, go at as good a pace as they, although they cantered; and when the party stopped at the door of the old inn, Hawk brought his steed to a stand, with a graceful bound, at once, that was as different as possible to the struggling manner in which the officers pulled up.

"Ah, you can ride, captain," said one.

"A little," said Hawk.

"Just a little, I should say. I only wish I could manage it half so well. But come in here. Here we are, and although we may disagree about the road that each of us would like to travel, there is no need why we should not be good friends for all that. Come in. House! house! hilloa!"

The landlord of the Old Hats was soon at the door, and one glance at the group of horsemen showed him the state of affairs. That he saw before him a party of officers with a prisoner of importance, he could not doubt.

"Hilloa! Mr. King," he said, addressing one of the officers by name, "who have you got now?"

"Only Captain Hawk!"

"You don't say so?"

"Look at him, and then you will be convinced."

"Look at him? Why, what's the use of my looking at him, Mr. King? Thank my stars, I never saw him before, and don't know him a bit. This is a respectable house, and I don't think any of your highway gentry would be likely to stop here in a hurry. Besides, don't you know that I am a constable, and that I should feel myself bound to apprehend him at once if he did? Of course I should."

"I don't know what you would feel yourself bound to do, landlord," said the officer with a laugh, as he dismounted, "but I know what you would do."

"And what is that?"

"Why, if all the highwaymen in the country were to come here and ask for a bottle of wine, you would serve them, and be as civil as possible."

"Ah, Mr. King, I grant you that. If all the highwaymen in the country were to come here, pray what could one constable do in the matter, I should like to know, but just lose his life if he was not civil to them, eh, Mr. King?"

The officer laughed.

"You have me there, I admit, landlord. But no matter. Let us have a table spread with the best your house affords, and Captain Hawk will pay."

"Willingly," said Hawk.

"Oh, then, if that is the case," said the landlord, "I can only say that I don't mind how often you come here, Captain Hawk."

"These gentlemen," said Hawk, with a smile, "will tell you that this is my last visit."

"Well, well," cried King, "we won't speak about that."

It would have amused any spectator to see the business-like way in which the officers kept close to Captain Hawk—one in front of him, one behind him, and one on each side of him, after he had dismounted; so that turn which way he would, he found a foe ready to dispute his passage. In this manner they conducted him into the inn.

The officers seemed to know the premises well, and, to tell the truth, so did Captain Hawk, although the landlord found it so very convenient to disown even a knowledge of him by sight; and they all proceeded to a square room at the back part of the house, which opened on to the garden by a window with three stone steps under it. The garden was of considerable extent, and the officers knew that the room itself had but one door to it.

The first thing they all did was to close the window and carefully fasten it. Then one of them took possession of the key of the room-door, and signified his intention to keep it locked while they remained there.

"I can easily let the landlord or the waiter in and out," he said. "It won't be much bother that, and it will be all the more snug for our friend Captain Hawk."

"You have quite forgotten the chimney," said Hawk.

"Oh, we ain't afraid of that."

"Well, you can please yourselves, gentlemen; but if I were you, I would certainly see among you which was to get into the chimney so as properly to wedge it up against any attempt of mine to escape by that way."

"Ha! ha!" laughed King, "you can try it, captain."

Hawk shook his head.

"No," he said, "I see well enough that the disposition to escape, and the means to carry it out, do not always go together. I only wish they did. I must even be content to go to Newgate with you."

"That's sensibly spoken," said one of the officers; "and here comes the landlord with something good."

CHAPTER XIII.

CAPTAIN HAWK PLAYS THE OFFICERS A TRICK THAT THEY DID NOT EXPECT.

The landlord considered that he had received an order that was quite comprehensive enough to include the choicest repast that he could lay before his guests, and, consequently, he presented for their approval so well spread a table that they looked quite delighted at it.

"Let us have a few bottles of your best wine," said Hawk. "If I am to live a short life, let it be a merry one."

"Capital!" cried King. "Capital! Upon my word, you are a trump, after all, Captain Hawk; and if it was not that such things must happen, you know, I should be sorry to see you at Tyburn Tree!"

"Thank you!"

"Oh, indeed I should. It's quite true, I assure you; and I hope you have no malice towards us for only doing our duty."

"None in the least. It is not in my nature."

"That's right; and here's the wine!"

The wine was really good, and after a couple of bottles of it had disappeared down the throats of the officers, they got quite social, and quite communicative. But still it was wonderful to see what an eye they kept upon their prisoner, and how carefully the door of the room was locked and unlocked each time that it was necessary so to do.

"Come, King," said one of his companions, "you sing a good song. Let us hear one now."

"Oh, no—no! I would rather not."

"Nay, no excuses. Let us have it!"

"If you will oblige," said Captain Hawk, "I am sure that I shall be delighted."

"Well," said King, trying to look as modest as possible; "I am an officer, you know, but it's a very funny thing that the only songs I know are highwayman songs."

"Which will just suit me," said Captain Hawk, "seeing that you all of you will have it that I do a little professional business in that line. Let us have it."

"Hem! Well then, comrades, if you must you must; but you must all give me a chorus, you know."

"Oh, yes—yes! We will do that."

Mr. King now, after a few preparatory Hems! fixed his eyes upon a fly-cage that was hanging to the ceiling, and in by no means a bad voice, sung the following:—

The night was dark—the night was dim,
  No star was in the sky;
And Hounslow Heath lay like a pall
  Before my weary eye.
The wind, it came in little gusts,
  The rain was pattering down;
And o'er all the bright green world,
  The heavens then did frown.
    Patter, patter, patter. Hilloa, boys, ah!

"Chorus! Come, gentlemen.

  Patter, patter, patter. Hilloa, boys, ah!

I picked my way through rain and slough,
  And as on the heath went I,
A voice came on the night wind low,
  Just like a human sigh.
"I'm the ghost," it said, "of one who was scragged
  On ancient Tyburn-tree.
And now I go whistling o'er the heath
  As the storm wind fall and free."
    Patter, patter, patter. Hilloa, boys ah!

Another then came, and walked on my right,
  And he hissed these words in my ear—
"I'm the ghost," said he, "of Sixteen-string Jack:
  Oh, let your soul creep with fear."
Then just in front, as I thought to go on,
  Stood a grizly ghost, so thin;
"Stand!" it said, "for your gold I'll have;
  I'm the ghost of Dick Turpin."
    Patter, patter, patter. Hilloa, boys, ah!

Then back I stepped, but I trod on the toes
  Of a spirit that stood behind.
With a hissing laugh it stepped aside,
  Like a crash of winter's wind.
"List to me," said the last come ghost,
  "And let not your spirits fall,
For I'm the shadow that you saw scragged,
  And they called me Claude Duval."
    Patter, patter, patter. Hilloa boys, ah!

My clothes they stuck to my back with fear,
  Mid those spectres gaunt and tall;
I didn't know whether to stand upright,
  To move, or to downward fall.
I raised a shout in that hour of dread,
  It was more like a dying *scrich*,
And then, *wide awake* I found myself,
  Lying snug in a weedy ditch.
    Patter, patter, patter. Hilloa boys, ah!

And ever since then, when I'd had a glass,
  And perhaps just a dozen beside,
I never would cross that ancient heath,
  But kept by the chimney side,
It may be a dream, or it may be true,
  But I thought I heard them talk;
And sorry am, I to think that soon
  They will welcome Captain Hawk.
    Patter, patter, patter. Hilloa, boys, ah!

This song met with the most vociferous applause from the brother officers of Mr. King, as well as from Captain Hawk.

"Capital!" he said. "You have a good voice, King; but I don't call that a highwayman's song, for if I had been going across the heath, and had met with such goodly company, I should have been more pleased than frightened, I rather think."

"Ah, captain, I don't know that!"

"Well, perhaps not. These things all

iepend upon the frame of mind you are n But do you belive in ghosts, Mr. King?"

"Well, no, I can't say I do exactly. But let us talk of something more cheerful. And now, captain, we are waiting for your song!"

"My song?"

"Yes, to be sure: I call upon you for a song. You have got a singing face, and I'm quite sure you can give us a stave. Attention to Captain Hawk, gentlemen, if you please!"

"I really am very sorry," said Hawk, "that I can't sing, but I will tell you an anecdote, if you please to listen to it, which may amuse you quite as well. The only fear I have about it is, that you may not like the subject, and that you may still less like the conclusion."

"What's it about, then, captain?"

"A ghost!"

"Oh, never mind that. It will do. But what's the conclusion?"

"Oh I must not tell you that beforehand, for if I do, it will not only spoil my story, but all the interest you will take in it. But if you are inclined to listen to it, say so, and I will begin."

"Yes—yes—yes!"

"Very good! Fill your glasses, then, and now for it."

During all the wine drinking, Captain Hawk had as yet taken but one glass, and he had hardly tasted any of the repast that was placed before the officers, save a crust of hard, stale bread. He knew that he had his work before him.

The officers, if they had had their wits about them as they ought to have had upon such an occasion, must have seen the abstemious manner in which he conducted himself, and that fact alone should have had the impression to them that he had some scheme in contemplation.

They were, however, too intent upon indulging themselves to take notice of whether he filled his glass or not after the first time the bottle went round the table. The fact is, they were over-confident in their strength to resist any attempt he might make to escape; and as they had not released him from the cord that held his elbows to his sides, they thought him quite secure.

We shall soon see whether this belief of the officers was a reality or a delusion.

There cannot have been a doubt but that the landlord thought something was going on which would end in a riot, for the nervous manner in which he went out and came into the room was quite sufficient to show that he had a heart ill at ease in the affair; and although probably his sympathies and his feelings went more with Hawk than with the officers, for the highwaymen were capital customers of the road-side public-houses, yet he dreaded nothing so much as a disturbance at the Old Hats. Captain Hawk or any one else might have hung twenty times over for all he cared, as long as his house did not attract the attention of the justices.

There was a something, too, about the looks of Hawk which, if the officers had not imbibed the quantity of wine that they so imprudently had done, must have given to such men a hint that their prisoner had something upon his mind more than he would like just then to declare to them.

CHAPTER XIV.

THE ESCAPE.

"Come, captain," said one of the officers, in a half-tipsy tone, "if you won't sing us a song, what will you do, eh? You know we are all good fellows, and you must do something. The man who can sing and won't sing, ought to be made to sing. That is my sentiment, and my idea."

"Hear—hear!" cried all the others. "That is right—that is quite right."

"Well, gentlemen," said Hawk, "I will to some extent admit that you are right in your very excellently expressed sentiments, but some goldfinches, you know, won't sing while caged."

"Oh, stuff—stuff, captain; and, besides, you can't say you are caged yet, though you may be on the way to it."

"Certainly not; but as I have given up all idea of getting away from such clever fellows as you are, I consider myself caged."

The officers were all drunk enough to take this as a compliment, and they tried to look as grave and as cunning as possible, upon the strength of it.

"Why, the fact is," said one, as he gave his hair a fierce rub up about the crown. "The fact is, we know what we are about; and if anybody got the better of us, I should say there was only one other that they couldn't cheat, and that is——"

"Old Nick, I suppose?" said another.

"Yes, that is just what I was going to say, but as you said it first, you are a humbug."

"What?"

"A hum—bug."

"How dare you call me suca a name, I should like to know?"

"Gentlemen—gentlemen!" said Captain Hawk, "if you quarrel, I shall certainly take the opportunity of escaping, for I know perfectly well that if you fight there won't be one of you left alive in five minutes, for you will all-but eat each other up."

These words of Captain Hawk's put a stop to the affray which was all but beginning, and the officers saw that it would be the height of imprudence for them to get up a quarrel among themselves.

"Let it be so," said one. "There' lots of time for disputing when we get to London, where I think we had better be off to at once now."

"Stop!" cried another, "we have not heard the captain sing."

"Nor are you likely to hear it," said Hawk, "for I don't sing; but the truth is, I feel that I ought to do something or another to promote the general harmony; so, as I cannot sing, I will tell you a pleasant little anecdote."

"Hear! hear!"

"It may, or it may not amuse you, gentlemen. That will all depend upon the light in which you choose to view it when you have heard it; but I can tell you that I think it a good one."

"Let's hear it—let's hear it."

"Very good."

Hawk affected to be recollecting for a few moments the heads of the story, and then he said, in a low and confidential tone of voice—

"You must know, then, that about eighty years ago, there was a highwayman upon this road, that went by the nickname of the 'Twister;' and how he acquired that name was by a barbarous and shocking practice he had of twisting the necks of those who opposed him."

"Twisting their necks?" cried the chief officer.

"Yes, so they say. He would seize them by their heads, and twist their necks—just as you, no doubt, would not scruple to twist the neck of a fowl—till their back-bone went crackle crackle, and then the eyes of the poor devils' used to fall out of their heads."

"Lor!"

"How horrid!"

"Pah! It makes one ill to think of it. Go on—go on."

"It was by such a practice, then, gentlemen, queer as you think it, that this highwayman got the name of the 'Twister.' What was his real name, nobody ever knew, but he used to be upon this road, and report says, that he used to put up his horse at this very house, at times, and sleep here, of course quite unknown to the landlord."

"Oh, ah," said the principal officer; "we quite underatand the ignorance of the landlords in these cases. But go on, Captain Hawk."

"Well, then, you must know, that at last a reward of three hundred pounds was offered for him, and that was a great sum in those days, so that it was a serious temptation to all the officers then to have a try at his capture, and six of them, one rather stormy night in February, went out upon this road, quite determined to take the Twister, dead or alive.

"The wind blew in such gusts that they could hardly keep their seats on their horses, and the rain came down in such a way, that all idea of being other than soaked through was out of the question; but still they proceeded, for they were quite determined, if possible, to catch the man they were after."

"It wasn't likely, captain, he would be out on such a night."

"Yes, they thought there was a chance for one reason. The Twister well knew that he was dreaded upon the road, and that people would rather choose a night such as that to pass it, when they might naturally think he would not be out at all, than when the weather was fine; so out he was, to catch any one who might make the attempt to get clear of him with anything worth the taking, under cover of the storm."

"And the officers nabbed him?"

"You shall hear. There were no less than six of these officers, as I tell you, and the way they managed was very clever. They chose a narrow part of the road not far from this house, and one of them got on one side of the road, and one on the other; another two took up such a post that they could get into the middle of the road at any moment, and the last two did the same, a little

MAY TRACKING THE MOVEMENTS OF CAPTAIN HAWK.

further on; so that, in fact, the disposition of the force constituted quite a troop, which if the Twister rode into would place him with a couple of foes each way, well armed."

"Good! and that did it?"

"Wait a bit. The officers had not been many minutes in the position they had occupied, when they heard the sound of a horse's feet coming along the sloppy road, for it was half a pool with the quantity of rain that had fallen.

They all considered that it could be no other than the Twister, and exhorting each other to stand firmly, they were ready to meet him. On he come, no doubt little suspecting the little ambuscade that was laid for him, and the moment he passed the two foremost officers, they rode out into the middle of the road, and then the whole six called out, in loud voices,—"Stand! you are our our prisoner, dead or alive!" Upon hearing all those voices upon all sides of him, the highwayman was so completely taken about that the officers were able to make a rush upon him and bind him hand and foot in a moment or two, and thus he was nabbed at last."

"Is that all?"

"Certainly not. The best of it is still to come. It was rather a strange thing, but his capture did not seem to put the Twister at all out of the way, and he spoke as coolly as possible.

"'Gentlemen,' he said, 'I have an appointment at daybreak, thirty miles from here, and I regret that as you particularly wish for my company, that I really can't keep it.' 'Keep it, if you can,' said the officers. 'We have no objection if you can get away from us. 'Very good!' said the Twister, 'we shall see.'"

"You don't mean to say, Captain Hawk, that he got away from no less than six of them, do you?"

"Wait a bit. I never met with fellows like you who are so fond of trying to spoil a story, by anticipating its conclusion. That will come quite soon enough, and I wish it to surprise you."

"Oh, very well; go on—go on."

"The officers then felt tolerably confident in their numbers, and they thought that it was impossible the highwayman could escape them, and that all his talk about doing so was only that kind of bravado which some people indulge in under any circumstances that they may be placed in; so they brought him to this inn."

"What? To the Old Hats?"

"Exactly so. They brought him, while they sent to London to say that they had him, and to get a still stronger force to take him up to town; and now, just out of curiosity, I'll show you as well as I can what he did."

Captain Hawk rose.

The officers all looked at him with intense curiosity in their faces; but they did not make the least objection about letting him get up.

"Oh, I can't show you," he said, suddenly.

"Oh, yes—yes. Show us—show us."

"But I tell you I can't. I would in a minute, if it wasn't for this rope tying my elbows together. I don't ask you to take it off, but there's an end of the story, for I can't show you with it on."

"Shall we take it off?" said one.

"To be sure," said another. "He's all right enough."

"Off with it—off with it!" said the chief officer. "I'm as anxious as possible to know what the Twister did. Off with the rope!"

Captain Hawk betrayed no sort of exultation when the rope was taken off his elbows; on the contrary, he looked as calm, and cool, and serious as it was possible for any human being to look.

"You can put it on again," he said, "if you should think it necessary, when I have finished the story!"

"That will do, Captain Hawk. That will do. You go on with your story. That's what we want to hear."

"Very well, you shall. The fact is, then, that the officers were imprudent enough to take just a little too much wine, so that they had not their ordinary judgment about them, and they were completely taken in by the highwayman, who, with the alertness and skill of a harlequin, pulled his hat over his eyes this way, and took a flying leap through the window."

To the amazement of the bewildered officers, Captain Hawk suddenly pulled his hat down over his face, and suiting the action to the word, he went right through the window into the garden, with a crash that was tremendous, and at once disappeared in the night air from before their astonished eyes.

For the space of about two minutes, the officers all sat staring at each other in as thorough a state of amazement as it was possible for men to get into. The suddenness of the affair, combined with their total want of expectation that anything of the sort would be attempted, seemed to completely paralyse them.

It was the chief of the party who at

length sprang to his feet, and cried out in a loud voice—

"By Jove, we are done!"

Hastily, then, drawing a pistol from his pocket, he fired it after the fugitive through the window, and the other officers did the same.

"Come on, comrades," then cried the chief officer. "It will be a disgrace to us as long as we live, if we don't nab him again. Come on; he can't be very far off."

They snatched the lights from the table, and while some of them went by the door to get into the open air, others rushed towards the garden through the broken window, and in a moment or two more the room was completely empty.

From the little space, then, close under the balcony that was outside the window, up rose Captain Hawk, and coolly entered the room again. There was an old fashioned screen in one corner, which hid a cupboard, and a kind of sideboard, full of knives and folks, and plates, and dishes. He carried a chair behind the screen, and he calmly sat down, and waited the course of events.

The landlord and the landlady entered into the room.

"Oh, lor! oh, lor!" cried the landlord. "There's a lot of glass gone! The blessed window all broke to smash! But I'll make the county pay for it, as I'm a sinner. I only wish some of those plaguy officers may get their brains blown out before the morning."

"And the idea, too," said the landlady, "of apprehending the captain, who is one of the nicest, one of the handsomest, one of the——"

"Hold your tongue, wife, will you!"

"No, I will not hold my tongue. Hoity-toity. Marry come up, indeed! Ain't a body to have eyes in their head because they have got a sot of a husband, who is good for nothing that I know off?"

"Oh, be quiet!"

"I won't be quiet. It's all very well to say, 'Oh, be quiet.' Quiet, indeed! I should like to see the respectable female who will be quiet, that I should. A nice thing, indeed, to have one's house pulled all to small bits by officers and highwaymen!"

"Well—well, my dear, it can't be helped. Dear me, and here's no less than three of the best cut wine's broken, too, and a decanter, too, as I'm a sinner."

"Never you mind that," said the landlady. "Captain Hawk is too much of a gentleman to let us be the sufferers. He will pay for it all, I'll warrant you."

"With pleasure, madam," said Hawk, emerging from behind the screen.

The landlady gave a scream, and the landlord, who had collected a number of the glasses upon a tray, dropped it, and smashed the whole lot.

"Heaven preserve us!" he said; "who are you?"

"Don't you know me?"

"Yes—yes, you look like the captain."

"And I am the captain, too.'

"But—but I thought you went through there—that hole in the window, and all the officers pelted after you?"

"Yes, and that is the very reason, landlord, why I thought it would be the most prudent thing I could do to come back again. If the officers had remained here, I should have remained there outside, but the same place don't exactly agree with both of us; and now as they may come back, hide me at once."

"Oh, dear, where can I hide you, captain?"

"Anywhere that is secure. My dear madam, I will throw myself upon your kindness and your abilities to hide me from my foes."

"Of course I will, captain," said the landlady. "Be so good as to come with me up stairs, at once, to our bedroom. John, you can stay here, if you please, and gather up all the broken glass, and don't hurry. The captain is only going up stairs with me to the bedroom, that is all, John."

"Is it!" said the landlord. "I think, wife, that you may as well pick up the broken glass, while I show the captain up stairs. If it's all the same to you, wife, I rather prefer that arrangment."

"But it isn't all the same to me, you horrid wretch."

"No, I'll be hanged if I thought it was."

"Oh, ye powers!" cried the landlady, sinking into a chair; "John is getting jealous! Jealous of me, his faithful wife and partner—jealous of me, that might have married one-half of the fine men in the country, if I hadn't have taken up with him instead, and imprisoned myself for life."

"Oh, bother the fine men!" said the landlord.

"It seems to me," said Captain Hawk, "with due deference to you both, that while you are disputing here, I'm as likely as possible to be nabbed again; so I will end the matter by finding my way up stairs by myself."

"Yes, captain, and I'll soon come," said the landlady, "and see if you are all right."

"No you won't, ma'am," said the landlord, "for that will be, to my thinking, all wrong; so I will trouble you to do no such thing."

"Indeed, you brute!"

"Yes, indeed, ma'am."

The dispute was growing fast and furious, so Captain Hawk, seeing no likelihood of a termination of it, left the room, and dashed up the staircase of the inn, just as some of the officers were returning through the garden, after their fruitless search for him. There was no light at all in the upper part of the inn to guide the captain, but he knew that it was only a one-storied house, so when he got to the landing he began to grope about to find the door of some room in which he could hide himself. He did not suppose for one moment that the officers would suspect that he had come back to the Old Hats, so all he wanted was just to get somewhere where he would be out of their sight in case they should take it into their heads to remain for a little time at the inn to talk over their disappointment.

After some little trouble, and stumbling over several articles upon the landing, Captain Hawk at length touched the handle of a door, which at once yielded, and he stepped into a room which, by the dim night light that came through the window, he saw was a bedroom.

Nearly in the centre of this room was a huge bedstead, the hangings of which were of some dingy kind of material that at night looked quite black. Captain Hawk, with some difficulty, found the key of the door, and locked the room on the inside, for, to tell the truth, he was almost as alarmed at the idea of a visit from the landlady as he was at one from the officers.

Sitting, then, upon the side of the bed, he folded his arms across his breast and began to think of the various events of the last twelve hours of his existence. Gradually, however, his thoughts turned to May Boyes, to the exclusion of all other topics.

Perhaps, for the first time in his life, the heart of Captain Hawk had been really touched by his acquaintanceship with the beautiful May Boyes; and if ever a feeling of real remorse came over him, it did at the reflection that he had made all but a wreck of the happiness of that innocent and lovely being—and all for what? For the mere gratification of a few leisure hours spent in her society! That was all. Oh, what will not we do in pursuit of self-gratifications! What ruin—what destruction will they not spread far and wide!

"Oh, that I had never seen her," said Hawk, "or that, having seen her, I had not loved her, or that I loving her, she had scorned me. But so it was: love begets love; and when I little thought that it was my image that filled up her heart and brain, I found at length that I was doomed to be the shadow of her young life. Well, it is done now, and cannot be undone. She thinks that I am taken to London to die. Of that delusion she must be cured soon, for I must and will see her once again, if it be but to implore her to forget me."

Captain Hawk started, for he distinctly heard some one gently trying the lock of the bed-room door.

Advancing to the door, he placed his ear against the panel and listened.

"Captain, captain," said a voice. "Are you here, captain?"

"Confound it," muttered Hawk, "it's the landlady. Now, I shall have the husband betrying me to the officers, from pure jealousy and revenge. Truly, one of the most fearful things in life, is to inspire an old woman with an affection for you."

"Captain, captain!" said the voice again.

There was no resource for it. Captain Hawk was compelled to open the door, or rather to turn the key so that she could open it; but he made no noise, and he still had a hope that he might hide from her. Slipping away from the door, he got behind the hangings of the bed.

"Dear me," said the landlady, as the door now suddenly yielded to her touch, "it is open, after all. I wonder where the captain can be?"

She entered the room with a lighted candle in her hand, and glancing all around, she said in a whisper—

"Captain, captain! It's only me!"

Hawk was profoundly silent.

"Well, how very provoking, to be sure; and John is safe in the cellar, too. Where can he be? Ah, me! He is such a very nice man is the captain, while John—bah! John isn't fit to hold a candle to the captain, that he isn't, that's flat! Oh, captain, you love of a captain, where are you, and John is in the cellar?"

The landlady, to Captain Hawk's aggravation, sat down on one side of the bed and began to cry.

"Plague take her," thought Captain Hawk, "I wish she was at the bottom of the sea."

"The idea, now," sobbed the landlady, "of not being able to find the captain, and John in the cellar, too. Oh, dear, oh, dear!"

After a few moments more indulgence in grief, the landlady went out of the room, to the great relief of Captain Hawk, who was quite in terror lest she should institute a search, and so discover him, which she would immediately have done, if she had once begun to look about her.

Hawk, now that he was alone again, began to consider the best means of leaving the inn, for he longed to get into the country again, and to procure, if possible, an interview with May Boyes.

CHAPTER XV.

RETURNS TO BOYES HALL, AND THE PROCEEDINGS THEREIN.

It is now night at Boyes Hall, and the fair May sits in her own chamber, with the window open to the garden. Her head is resting upon her hands, and the tears are trickling down her cheeks. She is thinking of the past!

Deeper and deeper grows the darkness without, and then a light footstep suddenly comes upon her ears, and looking round, she sees that it is her sister Philippa.

May did not speak.

"Sister, oh, sister May!" said Philippa, "what is the meaning of this blight that has come across your spirits? Am I not worthy to know?"

"Oh, yes, yes," sobbed May.

"Then you will tell me all, and if it be within the power of a sister's love to cheer your drooping soul, you have but to speak, and you know, dear May, how gladly I will do anything to make you smile again."

"You cannot—you cannot! I shall never smile again!"

"Oh, May! let me hope that you know not what you say, or that you do not mean all that you express. You are suffering from some fresh grief, and time has not yet sufficiently elapsed to enable you to feel that it may be softened."

"A new grief!" said May. "Oh, God! it is a grief!"

"And you will tell me all?"

Philippa sat down by the side of May, and took her hand in hers, and the young girl sobbed as though her life would pass away in the tears that came from her heart; but she made no revelation to her sister.

"You do not speak," said Philippa.

"I dare not—I must not!"

"Oh, say not so!"

"It is true, sister! Ask me no more! That which I could tell I must not tell! It shall never pass my lips! It is in vain to urge me! I have a grief; but I can suffer, and I will suffer alone!"

"Oh, no—no!"

"Sister, do not urge me! When I say it must be so, you should believe me that it must. It is in vain to urge me! I will say no more—no more!"

At that juncture, the door of the apartment was opened, and Sir John himself stalked in.

"Philippa," he said, "in a manner of speaking, has our daughter, May, told you why she is melancholy, and, consequently, not mirthful?"

"No, father."

"Then we command that our daughter May should tell us the reason that she weeps, which we take to be a very different thing from laughter; and as there is a marked difference between the two feelings, we may take upon ourselves to say that that establishes a distinction."

Of late, Sir John, when he wished to be rather grand and impressive, had adopted the regal style, and called himself "we."

No doubt there was a look of very elaborate wisdom upon the face of Sir John at this moment; but, owing to the darkness in the apartment, it certainly escaped observation.

"Father," said May, "is it to me you speak?"

"We do."

"Then, father, as you have always been kind to me, I ask you, in the name of that kindness, to ask me no more questions."

"Oh!—ah! Why, that's equivalent to getting no information, I think—that is to say, I am sure it is so."

"It is, father."

"Under those circumstances, then, we disclaim the proposition, for a very cogent and substantial reason, which is, that we want to know what is the matter."

"Nothing—nothing!—oh, nothing!"

"She will throw no light upon the subject," said Philippa.

"Light!" exclaimed Sir John. "That puts me in mind that we are in the dark with our daughters, Philippa and May. Our daughter Philippa will be so good as to order lights."

"No," said May.

"Eh?" cried Sir John. "Does our daughter May dispute our orders?"

"Father," said May, "this is not one of the public and common apartments of the house. This is the room which, in your goodness, you permit me to call my own; and as such, let me beg of you that you will allow me to have exclusive possession of it, and, at the same time, to keep it in darkness, if it be my wish to do so."

"Humph!" said Sir John. "The meaning of that is, that in a manner of speaking, we may go."

For once, Sir John had hit the right nail upon the head.

"Under those circumstances," he added, "we take our leave. Come, daughter Philippa, let us now leave our daughter, May, which is much the same thing as walking off, and we beg to command, May, that you come to our library at eleven of the clock to-morrow morning, and tell us all that disturbs you. Farewell!"

"Farewell, father! Farewell, Philippa."

Philippa embraced her sister in silence, and then followed Sir John from the room. She knew May too well to suppose that anything of the subject that occupied her mind so much would now be got from her after she had declared her intention not to be communicative upon the subject.

Perhaps Philippa had a pretty shrewd guess upon the affair; but yet she would have liked to hear from May's own lips how far her entanglement or engagement with Gerald Clifton, alias Captain Hawk, the highwayman, had really gone.

When May was again alone, she tottered, rather than walked, to the window, and sat down by it. The sight of the dark trees and the gentle sighing of the wind among them soothed her spirit a little, and after a time, she asked herself—

"Can I ever hope to forget?"

This was a question not easily to be answered, and with a shudder, she repeated it, and then in mournful accents she added—

"Oh, no—no—no! It is not possible. I have loved, and the memory of the feeling will abide with me. Oh, God, how strange it is that one who has mind and culture to be something noble, should be something base. It is a contradiction that I thought could hardly be in nature, and yet I see it is. Gerald Clifton, what have you in common with Captain Hawk, the highwayman?"

This was a question that might have well puzzled more astute philosophers than poor May Boyes; but we well know that human nature, in its endless varieties, furnishes such seeming contrarities to the mind's-eye every day.

To May Boyes, in all the innocence and all the purity of her soul, it might, indeed, appear strange to meet with an accomplished villain, because Gerald Clifton was the first one that she had met with; but that there are many in the world, experience amply and quickly proves.

The state of mind that May was in might be taken to constitute quite a crisis in her fate. If she could upon that evening but have managed to call reason to her aid sufficiently to enable her to get rid of the imaginative feeling that made her think Gerald Clifton a paragon of perfection, and Captain Hawk a kind of deviation only from his real character, she would have done well; but, alas! she could not do so. Her youthful imagination was so completely and entirely enthralled, that she found it quite impossible to throw off the spell that was wound around her.

Woe be to him who had cast such a spell of unholy persecution around such a fair spirit!

"Oh, God!" said May, as her tears fell afresh, "if he had been anything but what he is—if he had been poor to destitution—if he had followed any occupation, however humble, so that it was respectable and honest, I could have still loved him; but now I feel that I ought not, and that I dared not, and yet that I do. Alas! alas! was ever any one so unhappy as I? And they will now take his life. They will murder him in their revenge, because he has murdered another! Oh, no—no, he shall not, he must not die. I will save him—I can save him!"

May now began to reflect upon the means she had taken to enable Hawk to prove an alibi upon his trial; and, although she was enabled to keep that means a secret from himself, yet she never for a moment faltered in her intention of supplying to whoever would have the task of defending him all the necessary information upon that point of the subject.

"I will see him," she said. "Yes, I will see him!"

Perhaps there was yet in the imagination of May Boyes some dreamy idea that he might change his mode of life, and, repenting of his crimes, be the Gerald Clifton that she had thought he alone was, without being the Captain Hawk that she had found him to be.

Alas! poor May! It is, indeed, a hard thing that thus, in the very dawn of life as it were, you are to experience some of its most bitter griefs—griefs which better befit the dim autumn of existence, when enlarged appreciation of life and its valueless possession softens the pangs of feeling.

And still the darkness crept more and more fully over the scene, and still poor May felt more and more dark in spirit, and the clouds of fate appeared as completely to envelop her young soul, as did those natural clouds that she could see from the open window of her apartment envelop the dim night in a mantle of gloom.

"Oh, Gerald! Gerald!" she said, "what would I not even now give for the assurance that you are not what you seem!"

These words, uttered with an intensity of feeling that only such an enthusiastic being as May Boyes could at all be sensible of, were uttered aloud.

Hardly had they escaped her lips when she heard a rustling sound in the garden below, and then a voice said,—

"Hist!—hist!"

A cold shudder came over the soul of May.

"Hist!" said the voice again. "Hush!—oh, hush!"

She thought at the moment that she should surely lapse into insensibility, the blood seemed to pause so at her heart, for something seemed to whisper to her that, dead or alive, it was Gerald Clifton who was in the garden below, and who spoke to her.

All was still now for a few moments, and as busy fancy set to work in the brain of May Boyes to forge probabilities out of remote possibilities, she thought that surely in some desperate attempt to elude the vigilance of his captors, Hawk was dead!

"Oh, Heaven!" she whispered, "it may be that he is now no more, and that even now his spirit is at hand, listening to me, and watching the emotions of my soul!"

She strained her sense of sight in order to catch, if she could, any indication of his presence in the garden; and she thought she saw a dim figure standing amid the trees.

The bed-chamber in which May was opened upon the terrace that has been before spoken of as commanding an extensive view of the garden of the mansion; and the window opened like folding-doors on to that terrace, so that May Boyes had no sort of difficulty in stepping out at once on to it, and in the night air gazing still upon that spot where she thought she had seen the outline of a figure.

It was there still.

With a desperate resolution, now, which few in her position could have summoned, and which, perhaps, she would hardly have been capable of if she had not been in the state of excitement that she was, May now went towards a flight of steps that led from the terrace right down to the garden, and began rapidly to descend them.

"Gerald, Gerald!" she said, "I am here. If you are really no more, and your spirit haunts this place, it can only be for my spirit's sake, and so I am here. You loved me in life, and you will not, if you have the power so to do, injure me in death!"

With these words upon her lips, May reached the level of the garden, below the terrace.

CHAPTER XVI.

MAY BOYES HAS AN INTERVIEW WITH CAPTAIN HAWK.

The darkness in the garden was so intense, that if May Boyes had shrunk from it with terror, it would have been only the sort of feeling one might well have expected from a young and sensitive female; but she was well accustomed, under all circumstances and in all states of the atmosphere, to stroll amid the intricacies of that exquisitely kept piece of ground.

Often when some storm had swept over the lanscape, even at the dreary and solemn hour of midnight, May had sallied forth from her chamber, when all others in the mansion slept, to indulge in a poetic vein by the light of the lurid lightning in that garden; and in day or in night, every tree, every bush, nay, one might almost say, every flower in it was well known to her.

Under such circumstances, now, she had no hesitation in at once going across one of the pastures in pursuit of the figure that she had seen, and which appeared to fade away in the darkness, as she would fain have approached it.

This circumstance more than ever impressed upon the fancy of May that it was the spirit of Gerald Clifton that was in the garden; and, with a feeling almost bordering upon distraction, she still pursued what she thought was a phantom.

"Oh, pause—pause!" she said. "Why do you fly me!—Why should you seek to elude my presence? If it be your spirit, Gerald, you should not fly from me, for in death even, I will yet speak to you, if I may not love you!"

As she uttered these words, the phantom seemed to make its way right among a group of trees that hid it entirely from her sight.

Maddened now by the excitement she had gone through, and the thought that the apparition shunned her, she darted forward, and entered the shadow of the trees.

"Stay! oh, stay!" she said. "It is May Boyes who calls after you, Gerald Clifton, to stay! I am here—I am here!"

The thought at this moment struck her that the only object the dim spectral looking figure could have had in shunning her so for was, to get so far from the mansion that any conference they might have together should be totally unobserved. She recollected how the ghost of Hamlet's father is supposed to beckon him away to a distant part of the platform, where the guard held their nightly watch, in order that its fearful revelations might meet with no other ears than those for which they were intended; and so May Boyes thought such might be the object of the spirit that she supposed she had been pursuing.

As this wild kind of idea gathered strength in her mind, she was shaken by a variety of emotions. Fear, anxiety, and deep interest chained her to the spot, and she clung to a low branch of one of the trees for support.

Gazing around her, then, with the expectation each moment of casting her eyes upon some sepulchral being, it was quite a wonder that May preserved her reason in that all-exciting state in which she was.

"Speak!" she said, in a whisper; "oh, speak, Gerald Clifton!—I am here! —Dead or alive, I implore you to speak to me!"

"May," said a voice.

"Yes—yes!" gasped May, "I hear you! "Speak again!"

"May," said the voice, again. "Dear May!"

"Yes—yes! Oh, yes, I am here!"

"You are alarmed—you are shocked!"

"No, Gerald Clifton, I am not! Not even at the fact that I am speaking to your spirit, which has been permitted to visit this world to hold this converse with me!"

"Oh, May, I pray you to disburden your mind of that idea! I live!—I live!"

SIR JOHN SURPRISED BY MAY, DISGUISED AS CAPTAIN HAWK.

"Oh, God! No!"

"Yes, May, indeed, I do live. Are you full of sorrow that such is the fact? Can you not bear to think that I am in life?"

"Oh, yes, yes!"

"Oh, May, I did love you—I do love you still. Unworthy as I am, I love you still!"

May could not answer for the gush of feeling that came over her mind at these words, in the well-known tones of Gerald Clifton—the tones that she had heard so often, under circumstances when they were a joy to her to hear them; but now, what different and conflicting emotions did they not produce—emotions of joy and of sorrow!

"If you live, Gerald," she said. Her voice shook then, and she could not utter another word.

"Go on, May; oh, go on!"

It was nearly a minute before she could add—

"If you do live, let me look upon your face, Gerald Clifton; or I shall still think that I talk only to the dead."

She now, upon this invocation to the real, living Gerald Clifton to make his appearance, heard a rustling amid the branches of one of the trees, and in another moment he dropped to the ground, close to her feet; and, falling upon his knees, he seized her hand in both of his, and in imploring accents, he said—

"May Boyes, can you—is it possible for you to forgive me? Tell me, if in the angelic mercy of your nature, you can look again, except with loathing, upon the man who has made a wreck of your affections?"

"He lives!—he lives!"

"Yes, May, I do indeed live. I have escaped from the officers who held me in custody, and who thought to find it an easy thing to convey me to a prison; and my object in that escape was that I might thus kneel at your feet, and ask you to forgive me."

"Oh, Gerald—Gerald!"

May sobbed bitterly.

"Nay, I am unworthy to cause you so much suffering. Learn to hate me. I wish your young and noble spirit to look with loathing and abhorrence upon me; and I will bear it without a moan. I have but one hope now, and that is that you will awaken from your dream of misplaced affection, and with another, in the time to come, be happy."

"Another?"

"Yes—yes. I never can think of that, for well I know what joy it would be to call you mine; but as I dare not hope—Oh, this is madness! What am I saying—what am I saying?"

"Gerald?"

"Yes, May, yes, go on. I know what you would say."

"What would I say, Gerald?"

"You would ask me what you had done to me that I should seek your destruction as I have done by enthralling your young spirit in the bonds of an affection which cannot lead to good."

"No—no!"

"What else?—what else is it possible that you can say to me? May, speak, if you have words of greater wrong to utter to me."

"I have words of greater wrong."

"Do not utter them."

"You but now asked me to speak them if I had such words to utter."

"I did—I did; but it was when I thought you heard them not. I feel that now they would blast me as I kneel to you. Worse than reproaches would they be to me. Oh, May, think such daggers, but do not speak them to me."

"I must, Gerald—I must. It is my nature to forgive you, and so I must forgive you."

"Wretch—wretch that I am!"

"No, Gerald, we are both to blame; but yet with all that, I see that we must part now, and for ever. Go your path, and leave me to go mine. Oh, Gerald, would that those paths had been as wide apart as the poles."

"I will go—I will go," said Captain Hawk, with real or assumed mournfulness.

"Not yet, villain!" cried a voice. "Not till you have answered to me for your crimes!" and Ratchley Boyes at once strode between May and Captain Hawk.

CHAPTER XVII.

THE DUEL ON THE COMMON.

Nothing could very well be more unexpected either to Captain Hawk or to May Boyes than this sudden appearance of Ratchley upon the spot.

The fact was that Philippa, after the unsuccessful attempt she had made to get from May the secret of her love, had repaired to Ratchley to acquaint him with the fact that she had made such an attempt, and that it had so signally failed.

Ratchley, since the apprehension of Captain Hawk, had made no sort of secret of the fact that it was to him that he owed his wound upon the heath, and that in him he recognised his quondam friend, Gerald Clifton, so that Philippa had nothing to learn from her brother; only he had certainly hoped that she would have been able to get from May the fact of how far her heart had got entangled in the meshes of a wild love for the highwayman.

Upon finding that Philippa could tell him nothing, Ratchley was much disturbed, and unable to control his feelings upon the subject, he resolved upon seeking an explanation with May himself.

Acting upon the idea, he had sought her in her apartment, but finding it empty, and the window open, he had, in search of her, taken the same route that she had taken, and guided by the sound of voices he heard, reached the spot of the meeting between May and Captain Hawk just in time to hear the few last words of the conference.

May, upon the sudden appearance of her brother, uttered a cry of fear, and her first and most natural impulse was to fly from the spot; but that she controlled, for the idea flashed across her that if she did so, a deadly conflict would no doubt ensue between the two beings who in all the world were the dearest to her.

She remained.

Captain Hawk, the moment he found that there was an addition to the party, and that that addition was in the shape of Ratchley Boyes, sprang to his feet from his suppliant posture, and probably from habit or from a disposition to show that he had pacific intentions, he crossed his arms on his chest and waited for Ratchley to speak again.

"Thief!" cried Ratchley.

Captain Hawk shook a little.

"Say on, Ratchley Boyes," he said. "I am upon your premises, and am, I know, an interloper. I am quite unarmed, too, so that it is a brave thing to say what you please to me. Go on, sir!"

"Oh, brother—brother!" said May.

"Silence, May!" cried Ratchley; "this is no time nor place in which you ought to speak. To your chamber. It is sufficiently grievous to me, that I find you at such a time holding clandestine interviews with a felon. To your chamber, sister. You and I will talk of this to-morrow."

"And when you do, sir," said Captain Hawk, "I advise you to talk very gently or you will hear from me."

"Hear from you?"

"Yes, from me, Ratchley Boyes. If one harsh word is uttered in yonder house to May, I know that it will be upon my account, and, therefore, I feel that it will be my duty to resent it."

Ratchley was staggered for a moment, as well indeed he might be, at the cool effrontery of this speech. For some few moments, he could only try to look in the face of the man who could utter it, but the darkness of the night effectually prevented him from noticing the expression that was upon that face, or he might have had a gentler opinion of the highwayman.

Turning again to May, Ratchley said—

"Sister, I again ask you to leave us."

"And so do I," said Captain Hawk.

"No—no! There will be bloodshed!"

"I am unarmed," said Ratchley.

"And so am I," said Hawk.

"Will you both promise—will you give me your words—that you will neither of you attempt violence, and I will go? Gerald Clifton, I expect such a promise from you."

"I freely give it," said Hawk.

"And from you, brother, I likewise expect such a promise."

"I will make no promise, sister. I have my own honour and yours to look to, and I can make no promises that may in this matter have the effect of compromising either."

"Then I remain."

"Not so, May," said Captain Hawk. "Two persons are required of one mind in order to come to a collision. Your brother will not provoke me to any conflict. He is too much of a gentleman to continue abusing me, and it is quite out of the question that he should suddenly become an amateur police-officer, and seek to take me into custody."

Ratchley bit his lips with vexation.

"Go, therefore, May, and go in confidence that all will be well."

These words were spoken in so quiet and cool a manner that May was completely deceived by them, and thought that they promised anything but a continued disagreement between Captain Hawk and Ratchley. She began to think that perhaps if they were alone, Hawk might make such explanations to her brother as might have the effect of soothing down somewhat the apparently implacable resentment that he had to him.

"I will go," she said, "in the confidence that you will not break your word to me, Gerald."

"I will not. Farewell, May, for we may never meet again."

"It is better that you should not," said Ratchley.

"It is better," said Captain Hawk, in a tone of deep pathos. "It is very much better that we should not."

"Oh, Gerald!—Gerald!"

"Hush! hush! May. Let me implore you to console your feelings!"

"I will! I do!"

She pressed her hands tightly upon her head, and with a slow and tottering step she left the spot. Did she really think that they would never meet again? Ah, no! If such a thought had but taken a firm root in her mind, not twenty brothers could have forced her from the side of Gerald Clifton, notwithstanding all that had passed. But she knew that they would meet again. She knew that Gerald Clifton loved her, and that loving her, he would again seek to look upon her face, and hear the tenor of her mind.

It was with that feeling that she proceeded towards the house, and left the two former friends, but now determined enemies, alone in that sequestered and dark spot of the old garden

They both listened to her retreating footsteps upon the gravel path that she took to reach the house, and when that light sound had fairly and entirely died away, Ratchley spoke:—

"Now, villain, we are alone."

"Yes, Ratchley Boyes, we are alone; and still you can't keep your tongue from evil speaking. Now, listen to me. Ratchley, you and I are men, and as men we should quarrel, if we must quarrel at all, and not brawl like women. What have you to say to me? Be it what it may, say it in a manner that becomes you, and not in a manner that is more disgraceful for you to utter then it is for me to listen to."

"I have nothing to say but that I thank heaven the hour has come when I can be avenged!"

"Indeed!"

"Yes, Gerald Clifton, or Captain Hawk, or whatever you may choose to call yourself, I say I will be avenged for the wrong you have done to my sister. For the attack upon me, and the wound you gave me, I freely forgive you. I would rather avenge the wrong of another than one of my own."

"And, pray, what is the wrong?"

"Dare you ask such a question?"

"Yes! Because I much fear you misunderstand its nature and extent. And now I tell you to your face, Ratchley Boyes, that there is not an angel in Heaven more pure and sinless than is your sister, May, at this present moment, and that were she otherwise, I should think of her without the pang that I do not mind confessing rends my heart now when the remembrance of her comes across my soul."

"Dare you say so much?"

"Rather, Ratchley Boyes, let me ask if you dare assert the contrary. Is it to me that you will leave the conservation of your sister's honour? Can such a thing be possible! Oh, Ratchley, where is your manhood? Where is the chivalrous spirit that used to be yours?"

"Gerald Clifton, if instead of speaking as you have done of May, you had only for one half moment breathed a word derogatory to her honour, I would have laid you dead at my feet."

"Easier said than done, Ratchley," said Hawk. "But we will not quarrel about that. Let it suffice that I am willing, whenever my lips could form themselves to the utterance of one word derogatory to May Boyes, that you or any one should take my life. If I live, though, until that happens, I shall be, indeed, a fine specimen of longevity."

"You speak lightly, Clifton; but you stand upon a mine."

"Let it explode."

"It will explode in good time. I do not know whether it has been by force or by fraud that you have escaped from the officers of justice; but you are too notorious a criminal now, to be suffered to be for long at large. You must soon be taken again."

"By fraud it was," said Captain Hawk. "They were too many for me to use force with; and as to my being soon taken again, I presume that is a fact not very interesting, after all, to Ratchley Boyes."

"It is not!"

"So I thought; and, therefore, if you have nothing further to add to the few brief remarks you have favoured me with, Ratchley, I will do myself the honour of bidding you good night, sir."

"Hold!"

"I wait your pleasure."

"I do not, and cannot forget that once you were companionable to me, and that I looked upon you as my equal; and although circumstances now have convinced me of the contrary, I am still willing to give you the advantage of your former position, and will meet you in this garden, of course as if you were a gentleman."

"Go on."

"You will thus feel that I condescend when I say, that I demand of you the satisfaction which, if I had never known you to be what you really are, I should have requested, and, I hope, obtained."

"Oh, you want to fight a duel, do you?"

"I am not aware of any other mode, save blowing your brains out upon the first occasion that presents itself that I have the means with me of doing such an act, by which I can in any way satisfy my feelings with regard to you now."

"Do not mention it, Ratchley. I revert to our ancient friendship, now passed away, to give you every indulgence in my power; and now, upon the spot, if you can provide the weapons, let the affair terminate."

"No. Not within the precincts of my father's house."

"Where you please, then."

"It wants, now, about six hours to sunrise. I will meet you, as soon as we can see each other, at the dawn of the new day, upon Ealing Common. Will that suit you?"

"Excellently well. Good night."

Captain Hawk turned upon his heel, and disappeared in the surrounding gloom so instantaneously, that it looked as though he had absolutely vanished into the air like a spirit.

Poor Ratchley stood upon the spot where Hawk had left him for some few minutes in silence, and then in a low voice, he said—

"Oh, villain—villain! That ever I should have been fooled by such an accomplished scoundrel as this Gerald Clifton, and so introduced him to the bosom of my family, to the destruction of the peace of a member of it! Alas, poor—poor May!"

May Boyes had always been the favourite sister of Ratchley. She had ever most sympathised with him, and with all his failings, and an affection had grown up between them of the most endearing description, so that everything that affected her peace of mind or happiness, touched Ratchley far more nearly than anything would have done that had only interfered with himself.

With his feelings in a sad state of depression, and yet without a thought of doing otherwise than meeting Gerald Clifton on Ealing Common at the time that had been agreed upon between them, Ratchley now sought the house again.

The fact was, that he was still weak from the wound he had suffered from, and he was in anything but a fit state to engage in the conflict that he had insisted upon having with Captain Hawk, and he felt how slender was the chance of his ever visiting that house again alive, after he should quit it to meet the highwayman.

Full of this feeling, Ratchley sought his chamber, there to pen such an epistle to May as should best, according to his judgment, have the effect of soothing her feelings, in case the duel should end fatally to him.

Nothing could show more clearly the sort of appreciation in which Ratchley Boyes held his father, than the fact that he did not write to him. It was not that Ratchley was destitute of affection for Sir John, but he could not conceal from himself that the deficiencies in Sir John's headpiece were of so serious a character, that if he wrote to him at all, it would be much more likely that he would mistake the letter than understand it.

"It is better to leave him alone," thought Ratchley. "May must tell all or nothing, or a part of the affair, just as, in the course of time, she may feel induced to do."

With this determination, then, Ratchley spent an hour in carefully preparing his pistols for the combat, and it was not until he had got everything in readiness that the singularity of fighting a duel without seconds struck him forcibly.

"What can I do?" he said. "Dare I tell any one that it is with Hawk, the highwayman, that I am going to fight? No—no! If I were, it is quite out of the question that any gentleman should accompany me upon such an errand; so the thing must rest as it is, and let the issue of the conflict be what it may, the world will have to put its own construction upon the results of the meeting."

After, then, he had got his pistols in order, Ratchley found that he had still four hours to spare before he need start from the house to meet Captain Hawk upon the heath.

"I will try to sleep," he said. "A few hours' repose may steady my nerves a little, and give me a better chance for my life."

With this object, then, Ratchley threw himself upon a couch. He was afraid to go regularly to bed, for fear that he should oversleep himself, and so most unwittingly break the appointment he had made with Captain Hawk.

It seemed to Ratchley as though he had not slept half an hour, when he suddenly started to his feet with a mind full of apprehension, for he heard, as he thought, a noise in the room. All was profound darkness, and after remaining for a moment or two in silence, he cried out—

"Who is here—who is here?"

There was no reply.

"I am certain," he added, "that some one was in the room. Speak, I charge you, be you friend or foe."

Still, not a sound disturbed the stillness of the place, and Ratchley then began to think that his imagination must have deceived him, and converted some accidental and distant noise into one seemingly in his chamber.

"I am glad I am awake, though," he said, "for I will now note the progress of the time."

With some difficulty, Ratchley got a light, and then upon consulting his watch, he found that there was but half an hour to spare before he ought to set out for Ealing Common to meet Captain Hawk.

More than once, now, did Ratchley felicitate himself upon the noise, be it what it might, that had awakened him from slumbers that might else have continued for hours longer, and he hastily made his preparations for leaving the house.

Ratchley wrapped around him a large blue cloth travelling cloak, and placed a cap upon his head of the same material. Hiding, then, his pistols in the breast of his apparel, he opened the window to sally forth by the terrace.

The moment Ratchley put his foot outside the door he trod upon something that crackled under it. Upon stooping to see what it was, he found, and he could only just by the dim dawn see as much, that it was a large watch that lay there. A little examination of it, broken as it was, convinced him that it was the ancestral watch that his father thought so much of.

How it came there, was to Ratchley a very profound mystery, indeed; but he could not for a moment doubt the identity of the ancient time-keeper.

"This is strange," he said; "but I have now no time to inquire into it, or even to indulge in speculations concerning it; so it may as well remain where it is."

With this remark, Ratchley laid the watch on the stone floor of the terrace again, and then hastened along the garden towards one of the small doors in the wall that opened to the surrounding country, and which, by a short cut, would enable him in a very few minutes to be on the road to Ealing Common.

How raw and cold that early hour of the morning was! It seemed as if the keen, whistling air got admittance to the very heart of Ratchley, and stopped its beating. He shuddered as he proceeded, and wrapt his cloak closer and closer about him.

CHAPTER XVIII.

SHOWS HOW SIR JOHN GOT RID OF THE ANCESTRAL WATCH.

We shall not have to detain the reader many minutes from the proceedings of Ratchley Boyes upon Ealing Common with Captain Hawk, while we inform the reader how the ancestral watch of Sir John Boyes found its way to the stone floor of the terrace.

The fact is, that that watch still continued to be the bugbear of Sir John's imagination. What to do with it he did not know; and he certainly had a notion that in some mysterious way it would come back to him, even if he tried ever so much to get rid of it.

There was quite enough criminality in the career of Captain Hawk to crush him without anything being said about the ancestral watch; and to avoid the necessity of saying anything about it on the trial, which he, Sir John, fully expected would take place shortly, was with him a great object.

Of course, he, Sir John Boyes, had not the remotest idea that Hawk had escaped from the officers; and, indeed, the notion that such a thing was at all possible, had not entered into his mind.

"If," resumed Sir John, "I say nothing about the ancestral watch, they cannot hear anything from my lips upon the subject; but if I say anything, then they will be cognisant of what I do say."

Starting from this point in the affair, which everybody will be very much inclined to concede to the reasoning powers of Sir John, he began to think of what he had already said.

Poor Sir John! He found, upon reflection, that he had floundered about in so extraordinary a manner about the watch, and told such a multiplicity of untruths about it, that, for the representative of a great family, and the sovereign, to boot, he would, if they were all known, cut rather a ridiculous figure.

"What shall I do?" he said. "Oh, what shall I do? I must invent something very cunning to cover up all that I have hitherto said upon the subject to any one; but what shall that be? That is the question."

In truth, that was the question, and if it were to be anything very cunning in reality, the reader will despair of Sir John Boyes being able to make a satisfactory answer to it.

"What I want," said Sir John, and he glared at vacancy as he spoke. "What I want is some natural way of having the watch in my possession again, so that nobody should wonder about it. What, suppose I were to pretend to find it somewhere?"

This was quite a bright idea to the perceptions of Sir John, and from it he very naturally got to another, which was, that it would be just as well if some one else were to find the watch.

Whenever Sir John got this length, he became almost lost in the mazes of his own cleverness; but by dint of keeping his finger on the side of his nose, and shaking his head to and fro for about a quarter of an hour, he thoroughly digested an idea.

That idea was, that from his bedroom window he would drop the ancestral watch to the terrace below, and then the servants whose duty it was to attend to it in the morning would, no doubt, there find it, and bring it into the breakfast-room; and after that, as he was not at all bound to explain how it came to be upon the terrace, it could again be recognised as an article in the house legitimately theirs.

It was with this notion, then, that Sir John, with great mystery, got the watch up to his bed-room, and just as poor Ratchley was sleeping—and would, no doubt, have over-slept himself—Sir John opened the window and cast over the ancestral watch to the terrace below.

"That's done it, I rather think," said Sir John. "They will be clever fellows that make anything out of that. To be sure, I should not at all wonder, now, if the ancestral watch were to go a little wrong; but then, if a watch does not go right, you may generally conclude that it will go wrong, unless it stops altogether."

With this piece of practical wisdom upon his lips, Sir John Boyes closed the window again, just before Ratchley made his appearance on the terrace; so he missed what might have been possibly enough, considering the errand that Ratchley was going upon, the last sight of his son in life.

Poor Sir John went very comfortably to bed again, quite convinced in his own mind that, as far as he was concerned, he had got rid of the watch; so, leaving him in that happy state, we will follow Ratchley to Ealing Common to meet Captain Hawk.

Ratchley had young blood in his veins; but the wound, that he could not be said to be as yet recovered from, had had the effect of very much damping his youthful energies, and he certainly had not about him above a half of his usual strength.

He made the attempt to restore a new circulation to his blood by walking rapidly, but he soon found that even such a modified violent exercise was too much for his strength, and he was compelled to adopt a slow step.

It was well for him, Ratchley, that, after all, the distance from Boyes Hall to the heath was not very great, or he could hardly have completed it in the time that he had before him.

The eastern sky, by the period that he had traversed about half the distance, was brilliantly lighted up, and although as yet it was anything but daylight, yet every object was getting each moment more and more distinctly visible to him.

Hurrying, then, forward, with the dread upon his mind of being thought to shrink in any way from the conflict he had himself insisted, Ratchley at length stood upon the verge of Ealing Common.

To his great chagrin, now, he found that the common was completely enveloped in a white mist, which made it impossible for him to see any object upon it beyond the distance of a few feet from him. Under such circumstances, Ratchley had no recourse but to walk right on to the common, wading through the dew that lay thickly upon it, and there to wait until some accidental means should arise of enabling him to see his foe.

"Hilloa!" said a voice, before Ratchley had proceeded many steps in a forward direction through the mist.

Ratchley paused.

"Who comes?" said a voice, again; and then Ratchley recognised it as the voice of Gerald Clifton.

"I come to my time," said Ratchley.

"Oh, it is you, old friend, is it?"

"I shall be obliged if you will drop the title of friend," said Ratchley, "to one who scorns even the acquaintance!"

"As you please. I am here to my time; and when the mist clears off, which it will do now, I daresay, in a very few minutes, we shall see to murder each other according to the most approved fashion in such matters."

To this, Ratchley made no reply. There was a jeering derision about the speech which he did not choose to answer to.

And now the prophecy of Captain Hawk, that the white mist that obscured the common would soon pass away, seemed upon the point of being manifested, for suddenly the whole mass of it seemed to be agitated by some mysterious convulsive impulse, and to be rolling about in huge masses, like the sea in a storm. Then, from one corner before a light wind that had sprung up, it began to clear away, wrapping itself up in itself, as it were, and creeping along the ground, leaving the short grass with the light sparkling dew upon it in all its rich green tint, that was so great a contrast to the dull white mass with which the atmosphere had been so loaded.

Another moment, and the mist was gone.

Captain Hawk, to the surprise of Ratchley, was some eight or ten paces of him.

"Well," said the captain, "I am here, and you are here. What is to happen next?"

"This is neither a time nor place for jesting, Gerald Clifton. One or both of us may not leave this place alive."

"Very likely."

"We do not come here to talk, but to act."

"Just so; but as I came here upon your invitation, I will get you to be so kind as to take the arrangements upon yourself, and to say what you wish me to do, now you have got me here."

"Fight."

"That is very definite, Mr. Ratchley. Are you armed?"

"I am. I have my pistols here, of which you may make choice, if it so please you. I am well aware that this duel, if it may be properly called such, is contrary to all rule and form, inasmuch as we are alone—We have no seconds."

"No. Nor do we want them, either. Publicity is not my aim at this present time, I assure you, Ratchley."

"Take one of these pistols, then, and stand where you are. I will go to a stated distance with the other, and you may give the signal yourself to fire. Will that satisfy you?"

"Anything you like, my dear sir, will satisfy me. It is to satisfy you that I

SIR JOHN OVERHEARS A LITTLE LOVE-MAKING BETWEEN HAWK AND MAY.

came here, for, to tell the truth, I had business elsewhere, and should have been much better satisfied not to come; but I never break an appointment if I can possibly help it."

"Very well. Take the pistol, then."

"I have weapons of my own."

"Use them, then. Doubtless you are better accustomed to them, and have more faith in them than in mine."

"Much more so."

Ratchley made no reply to this remark, but turning with his back towards Captain Hawk, he stepped carelessly about fifteen paces, and then facing him again, he said—

"Will this distance do?"

"Perfectly well, Ratchley."

"Give the word to fire, then."

"Pray do so yourself. I positively decline it. I am the challenged party, and I presume that all I am bound to to do is to come and stand up and be shot at. I don't see that there is any obligation upon my part to give the word that shall herald me to another world."

"Do not speak with such levity," cried Ratchley, "of an affair that you, in your heart, if you have one, must feel was forced upon me. I came here in defence of my sister's honour."

"As you please. This is not a time for me to reason with you upon the objects of our duel. Go on. Give the word, and let this matter end."

"Then, if you will not give the word to fire yourself, I must; but recollect, Gerald Clifton, that, let the issue of this circumstance be what it may, I offered you all the advantages in my power."

"Oh, yes—yes. Nobody, Ratchley Boyes, ever yet doubted your honour or your generosity; so now, with that admission sounding in your ears, fire away."

"One," said Ratchley—"two—three—Fire!"

He raised his pistol and fired; but, to his surprise, Captain Hawk did not return the fire.

"Fire!" shouted Ratchley. "Fire, I say!"

"Pardon me," said Hawk. "I presume I have the right to fire or not to fire, as I think proper."

Ratchley dropped the discharged pistol to the ground.

"Do you mean to tell me," he said, "that you will not fire?"

"I do."

"Rash man, why, then, should you risk your life against my shot?"

"You would have it so; but I tell you now, Ratchley Boyes, that when I do fire I never miss, and I feel that I have inflicted pangs enough upon the innocent heart of May, without adding to them the murder of her brother."

Ratchley stepped up to him.

"And yet you deserve death at my hands."

Captain Hawk looked at him with flashing eyes.

"Ratchley Boyes, if you wish to kill me, say so: I will stand here and be your target until you hit me, and then your thirst for my blood may be assuaged; but I will not, so help me Heaven, lift my arm against you! You hear my answer, and you now know my determination. Take your own course."

A fearful emotion came over the features of Ratchley; and after a few moments he spoke, saying—

"Gerald Clifton, if you were only poor, ignoble of birth—if you had only committed some one crime that had been the result of a moment of thoughtlessness or of passion—I might still have called you friend; but your are—you are——"

"A highwayman," said Captain Hawk.

He spoke the words rapidly, for he seemed to have been afraid that the name Ratchley was about to call him, would be one sounding harsher still in his ears. He recollected what in his anger Ratchley had called him in the garden of Boyes Hall, and the name had stung him to the quick. It was the name of thief.

"Yes," said Ratchley, "you are what you say, and, therefore, there is a gulf between us which I will not, and which you dare not, attempt to cross. Farewell!"

"As you please. Farewell!"

Without another word, Ratchley turned to leave the spot.

"Hold!" cried Hawk.

"What would you say?" said Ratchley, turning to him.

"If ever," added Hawk, with bitterness, "you feel inclined again to have a try at my life, you have but to make the wish commonly known, and it will reach my ears, when I will adopt some means of letting you know where to find me."

"There speaks the highwayman," said Ratchley. "It was Gerald Clifton who spoke before."

Ratchley walked across the common at a quick pace. Once he heard a voice calling after him, but he would not stop. No doubt it was Gerald Clifton·

but yet, what was the use of him, Ratchley, staying to prolong a conversation with one he never could know again as he once had known, and towards whom he could have no feeling of a more kindly nature than would amount to pity?

No doubt Captain Hawk had called after Ratchley, but he did not think proper to pursue him—the haughty spirit could not stoop to that; and so these two young men, who were very similar in disposition in some respects, separated to pursue their different paths in life: the one of honour—the other of disgrace.

CHAPTER XIX.

CAPTAIN HAWK GOES TO HIS MYSTERIOUS HOME.

Captain Hawk, upon the occasion of his duel, if it could be called such, since only one of the combatants fired, with Ratchley Boyes, was attired in a very different style to that which he mostly adopted when upon his marauding expeditions.

He no longer wore the scarlet coat, with its lace trimmings, that looked so showy and military in its cut, nor was there the cap with its drooping feather. On the contrary, he was so plainly attired, that few who had been in the habit of seeing him in his full dress, would have recognised him now as the same man.

The coat he wore was of plain grey cloth, and the cut of it was of the most commonplace description. Upon his head, he had a three-cornered hat, quite destitue of any ornaments, and the only part of his regular attire that he wore, were the high polished horseman's boots, highly polished, with which he was seldom seen without.

No one would have taken him, though, for anything, now, but a gentleman farmer out for a morning stroll.

As Captain Hawk walked from the spot of the encounter, he accidentally trod upon the pistol that Ratchley had fired, and which he had left upon the ground after letting it fall from his hands in his surprise at not having that fire returned by Captain Hawk.

The highwayman picked it up and looked at it.

"A pretty enough weapon of its kind," he said. "The bullet whistled past my face in tolerably close proximity. I will keep this, at all events, Ratchley Boyes, until we meet again."

With these words, he placed the pistol in his pocket, and then at a very rapid pace he made his way towards a clump of trees that was close at hand, and plunging in among them, he proceeded to untie a horse from the lowest branch of one of them, to which he had secured the creature by the bridle.

Captain Hawk had taken that horse from a groom, who was riding to town with it, only half an hour before he had met with Ratchley upon the common.

"I don't know," he said, as he glanced at the horse's feet, "whether you are good for much or not; but as the officers have thought proper to make free with my steed, why, I suppose I must make you do till I can pick up a better. Perhaps I shall hear of some one who has got a first-rate hunter for sale, and then if it suits me I will try to take it in some way or another. We shall see—we shall see."

With this rather cool determination regarding somebody's horse, Captain Hawk mounted the animal he had stolen that morning, and went out on to the heath at a canter.

The horse was a better one than it looked.

"Ah!" said Hawk, "this pace is not at all a bad one; and if you can leap a little, you will do very well for a make-shift."

There was a hedge close at hand, leading into a meadow; and as across that meadow was the nearest route that Captain Hawk could take where he was going, he thought it a good opportunity to try the capabilities of his steed.

In a moment he put him to the hedge, when the creature went over it with an ease and a grace that astonished Hawk.

"Well," he said, "men say that a poor-looking horse is a bad one till you try him. I shall not like to part with you, my new friend, even if I see anything that looks as though it would suit me better."

The object of Hawk now was to reach the hut where he had what he considered a kind of home, inasmuch as he kept a man there always ready to attend upon him; and as it was there, too, that he kept the unfortunate creature of whom the reader has already heard something.

That great exertions would be made by the authorities to re-capture him, Captain Hawk was well aware; and the propriety of lying by for a day or two, at all events, was not to be mistaken. He only hoped that he might get to the hut unmolested in any way.

In this hope, it will be seen, that Captain Hawk was doomed to be rather disappointed.

The meadow into which his new horse had jumped so cleverly, was a very large one, occupying, in fact, some fifteen acres in extent, and it wound round a farm-yard that was near to Hanger Hill. Captain Hawk wished to get past the farm-yard, if he could, without observation, but he hardly hoped to be able to do so at such an hour in the morning, when the farm-labourers would naturally be upon the stir.

Of course it was possible enough for Captain Hawk to have made a rather wide detour, and so have escaped going close to the farm-yard; but he feared that if he did so the object of such a course would be so transparent, that it would bring upon him more suspicion and danger than if he went on the even course.

The moment he got near to the farm-yard he saw a man looking over a gate at him.

"I will ask this fellow some trivial question," thought Captain Hawk, "and that will have the effect of calming down any suspicions he may have of me, if he has any at all."

With this object, Hawk rode up to the gate and said—

"My friend, can you tell me how far I am off the village of Hanwell, which is somewhere hereabouts, I think?"

"Oh, lor! Murder—murder! Help!" cried the man.

"Why, what's the matter with you?"

"Help—help! Here he is, Mr. Giles; bring out the gun. Here's the very fellow as took master's hunter from me, and here he is on it now. Murder—fire! Bring out the gun!"

There could not have been a more decidedly malapropos meeting than that.

The fact is, that Captain Hawk had stopped the man with the horse before it was at all daylight, and had taken it from him in the course of a few moments; and as regards knowing the man again, it was not to be expected that he could do so, nor would the man have known him, Captain Hawk, had he not been mounted upon the horse with which he was perfectly well acquainted; and, of course, then he at once jumped to the conclusion that this was the person who had, with such audacity, taken the creature from him.

Captain Hawk faced the horse about in a moment, and uttering an execration at his ill-luck between his clenched teeth, he set off at a gallop across the meadow again.

Bang! went a gun from the farm-yard, but as Captain Hawk was some fifty feet beyond the range of it, his danger was not very great from the discharge.

Still, in the open country in broad daylight, the situation of the highwayman was now sufficiently perilous to cause him to feel rather uncomfortable, and he kept the horse at speed until they reached the hedge again which led to the common.

The leap, as before, was done capitally.

"Now for a gallop on a good road," said Hawk, "and I shall be in a position to see what this horse can really do. Off, and away!"

The horse, when put to the gallop upon the road, went like the wind, although Captain Hawk was not what might be called exactly a light weight. The little village of Hanwell—then a much smaller and more retired place than it is now—was rapidly passed through, but it was no part of Captain Hawk's intention to show himself upon the rising ground beyond it.

He kept in the hollow, where the Brent River is in wet weather a tolerable stream, but where in summer, when there has been but little rain, it shrinks to rather insignificant dimensions. It was in about its medium upon this occasion, and Captain Hawk found no difficulty in leaping it.

In the course of a few minutes, then, he dashed into a narrow lane that would only allow one vehicle to go at a time in it, and which, consequently, was just about size sufficient for a horse to proceed in at a gallop.

"Safe enough, now, I think," said Hawk, as he drew up, after going a short distance down the lane.

His great object now was to discover if he were pursued, and by whom the pursuit was kept up. With this view he dismounted, and scrambled to the top of a bank, that gave him, when he was upon its summit, a pretty extensive view, although the vegetation around sheltered him from any observation, except it might be of an uncommonly keen and ardent character.

Coming right across the fields, in the direction of the lane, he saw about half a dozen horsemen.

To jump from the bank and mount his steed again was the work of a moment, now.

"Let them come," he said. "It will be a bad day's work for those who have the ill luck to overtake me. I need not wish them to have a worse."

Holding the bridle of the horse in his teeth now, Captain Hawk went through a rapid examination of his pistols, and arranged the priming in them, so that he ran the least risk of failing in a shot by a miss-fire. The unerring percussion cap was not then invented, so that the use of the pistol was always accompanied by a certain amount of doubt.

The point at which the lane went out into the main road again was about half a mile further on than where Captain Hawk was, but he had no intention whatever of going out of the lane while his enemies were so close at hand. It was too good a cover for him to desert so easily; and, besides, if compelled to endure an attack, it was much better in such a place than in more open ground.

CHAPTER XX.

CAPTAIN HAWK ENCOUNTERS GREAT PERIL.

It was still rather questionable whether the horsemen who were coming across the meadows were in pursuit of Captain Hawk or not. It was just possible enough that they might have business in that part of the country of a very different character to hunting a highwayman.

Then, again, if they were in pursuit of him, he had no positive evidence that they saw him, except, we may say, that he was warranted in thinking so, from the fact that they were so evidently making for the lane in which he was.

Yet, with all these grounds for conjecture and hope that he might not be in so much danger as, at the first glance, would seem to surround him, Captain Hawk felt that his position was sufficiently ticklish to call upon him to use the utmost caution in his movements.

In the course of a very few minutes, the horsemen had reached the little river, and some of them jumped it at once, while some others, who did not seem to have so much faith in the leaping capabilities of their steeds, went along the bank, with the hope of finding some narrower spot, or, perchance, some place at which the little stream might be fordable.

About five men, well mounted, entered the lane.

During this time, however, Captain Hawk had not been idle. He felt that to engage in a conflict with so many foes could only end in a way fatal to himself, if they had but the courage to persevere in the fight; so his obvious course was to hide from them, if he possibly could.

The lane was flanked on each side by a very tall bank, upon the top of which grew a straggling kind of hedge-row, composed of all the common hedge shrubs of England. In the fields, on each side over the hedge, there were many trees, which shot up and spread their tall foliage right into the lane.

The idea of Captain Hawk was to get into the meadows, if such a thing were possible; but, although there were no difficulties to prevent him from doing so, it did not appear to be a very easy thing to get the horse with him.

With Captain Hawk, however, to determine upon anything was half to do it, and, accordingly, he dismounted, and led his horse along the lane, looking for some likely spot at which he could get the animal over the high bank and through the hedge-row.

It was all in vain. If anything, the bank appeared to rise in height as he proceeded, and the vegetation at the top of it to be still more luxuriant and impervious.

Captain Hawk paused and looked about him.

"No," he said, "there is not space enough for a leap. It would be folly to attempt it; and yet it is possible enough that if I had hold of the bridle and tempted him on, the horse might scramble up the bank. I will try it."

Full of this idea, Hawk got the bridle of the horse over the creature's head, and then holding it over his arm, he proceeded to get up the bank himself, and soon reached the top of it. His next care was to clear away some of the twining hedge, so that it should offer no baulk to the horse in climbing the bank.

Captain Hawk set about this work in a systematic manner, which soon enabled him to make rapid progress in it. By the aid of a long-bladed sharp knife that he had, he cut asunder the strongest stems of the hedge, now, close to the top of the bank, and by that means he got rid of large masses of it in a very short space of time.

"That will do," he said, as he carefully replaced the knife in a leathern sheath that he had for it. "That will do; and now if, by persuasion or by force, I can only get the horse over, all will be well enough yet, and I shall be out of the way of those fellows in the lane."

As he spoke, Captain Hawk could hear as plainly as might be the sound of horses' feet in the lane, and he felt that if he did not succeed very shortly in getting his horse over the hedge, that the foe would be upon him.

When men do such extraordinary things with such alacrity, too, it is when they have the smallest possible amount of time to do them in. There is no leisure then to think of imaginary difficulties, and the thing gets done, which, otherwise, upon mature reflection, would hardly be at all attempted.

It was with something like a feeling of desperation that Captain Hawk now set about trying to get his horse over the bank.

The animal was evidently rather disinclined to make the attempt; but yet, with that rare sagacity which the horse is honoured for, it soon found out what was required of it; and, after a little while, it placed its fore-feet upon the bank.

That first movement was a failure, for the bank was not hard enough to stand the pressure, and gave way beneath the feet of the horse, crumbling down into the lane.

"It won't do," said Captain Hawk, "I am afraid it won't do. I must think, or try to think, of some other mode of operation."

The horse was evidently thinking, as well as Captain Hawk; and it would appear, now, that the creature thought with rather more effect than the man, who, by right of conquest, considered himself to be its master.

Suddenly, with a toss of its head, the horse got the rein out of the hand of Captain Hawk, and was free.

"Ah," cried Captain Hawk. "I have lost you, have I?"

He was about, upon this, to jump into the lane to get possession of the horse again, when he was stopped by the movements of the animal; and he soon saw that what he wanted done would be done much better by the sagacity of his steed than by any means that he could adopt in the matter.

As soon as Captain Hawk became convinced of such a fact, he was resolved to give the horse every latitude and opportunity. Accordingly, he stepped aside from the gap in the hedge, so as not to baulk him in his attempt.

The creature now retired to as great a distance as he possibly could get from the hedge, of the capabilities of which he had had experience; and Captain Hawk really thought at one moment that he was going to try to jump it. He soon corrected that opinion upon watching the horse still more attentively.

After a moment or two spent in calculating his distance from the hedge, the horse made a sudden dash forward, and by the impetus which he gave himself, he went right up the bank without displacing any of it, and got safely with a bound on the other side of it.

"Bravo! bravo!" said Captain Hawk. "That is capital!"

The horse shook his tail, and tossed his head, and looked as pleased as possible that he had succeeded in doing what his master wished him to do; and from that moment Captain Hawk took an affection for the creature, which induced him to resolve not to part with it, except by force, or under such disastrous circumstances, should they occur, as would make his death the probability of remaining with it.

The level of the meadow was some few feet higher than that of the lane, for the latter had been cut through the fields, to get as near as possible a level; but yet the bank even upon the field-side was in many places high enough effectually to shield the horse from observation, if he stood close to it.

Captain Hawk now led the horse close under the bank; in fact, he made him stand right in the little water drain that was there, so that he was completely hidden; and then hastily replacing the bushes that he had removed, he restored the hedge to pretty much its former condition to the eye.

Scarcely had he completed these highly necessary arrangements, when the mounted men who had compelled him to take so much trouble reached the spot.

To the surprise of Captain Hawk, they halted within a very little of the place where he and his horse had got over the hedge.

"This will do!" cried one. "This will do."

"But is there any chance?" said another.

"Every chance," said the first speaker. "Two of you must keep good watch here, for it's the shadiest place in all the lane, and it is as likely as not that he will come down it. Now, who will stay?"

To this question there was no answer for a few moments, and then at last one of the men said in a rough voice—

"Oh, well, I will, then."

"If you will, Brown," said another, "so will I."

"Very well," said the man who had first spoken. "That is so far settled, then, that you, Brown and Arrowsmith, will remain here upon this spot, and not stir till I come to you, or till the old man himself comes."

"Yes—yes, it's all right."

"But is it quite understood what we are to do?" said the other.

"Of course it is. Sir Michael O'Leary has made up his mind to that, and I thought you all knew it well enough."

"I heard something, but I did not feel quite positive that he meant us to kill the young fellow."

"Of course he did."

"Oh, well, then, it don't matter a bit to me. I will do it. If I am paid, it's all right enough, I take it."

"Certainly; you are a sensible man, Arrowsmith, and all you have got to do is to earn your money, and look to Brown to tell you what to be at. Brown knows all about it, and has done from the first."

"Oh, yes," growled Brown. "I know all about it."

"Then I am perfectly satisfied," said Arrowsmith, "and will do whatever Brown thinks I ought to do."

"Go to the deuce," said Brown. "If you did what I think you ought to do, you would hang yourself upon one of those trees yonder, and I should do the same thing myself if I did what I ought to do; so don't talk in that way."

"What do you mean, Brown?"

"What do I mean? Why, I mean that we will do what we are paid to do, and what is to our interest to do; but that's a very different thing, I take it, to what we ought to do, ain't it? Don't try to gammon me with your nonsense."

"Well," said the man who appeared to be the chief of the party, "I must say, Brown, that you are about as amiable as a bear with a sore head; but if Sir Michael O'Leary trusts you, that's all I need care about."

"Go along with you."

"Good-day. I am going, and you will be all the more richer the sooner you come to the lodge with the news that you have shot the Ensign, I can tell you. We will take the horses back."

"No," growled Brown.

"What do you mean by no?"

"I mean the cattle here. Do you think I am going to walk two miles, perhaps in the middle of the day, too, back to the lodge? No, I rather think not. Leave the horses. They won't come to any hurt if they don't get anything else now for these six hours; they have had a good feed already."

"Well, I will leave them. Here, Joe, tie the horses to the branch of an alder tree. Tie them loose, and it will only just keep them from straying."

Brown and his companion stood in the lane and looked after the other party as they went off at a trot; and Captain Hawk was in a state of perfect bewilderment as to what it could possibly all mean.

CHAPTER XXI.

HAWK MIGHT DO A GOOD ACTION, BUT PREFERS DOING A BAD ONE.

The curiosity of Captain Hawk was very much excited by what he saw in the lane, as, indeed, it might well be; for, from the moment he found, which he soon did, that the party of mounted men were not in pursuit of him, curiosity got the better of every other feeling, and he listened intently to what they were saying.

He had had a hope each moment that something of an explanatory character would be uttered by some of the men; but that hope was quickly disappointed, for the main body rode off, leaving the two men, named Brown and Arrowsmith, to hold a mysterious watch for somebody.

"I would give something," thought Captain Hawk to himself, "to know what these two rascals are here for; and if I were not so much engaged with my own private affairs, I would take the trouble to force them to be communicative upon the subject."

Captain Hawk had an idea now of leaving the spot, for he was very anxious indeed to reach the hut which he called his home, and where he fully meant to lie by for a little time until the hot pursuit, which he knew would, in a very few hours, be instituted all over that part of the country for him, should have subsided; but Arrowsmith suddenly said to Brown—

"Brown, old friend, do you really know all about this affair?"

"I do!"

"Then I wish you would tell me."

Brown was silent for a moment or two, and then he said—

"I don't know why I shouldn't tell you. I'm sure I don't see why I ought to be so mighty particular with that old rascal, O'Leary's, secrets."

"Nor I."

"Oh, Arrowsmith, there isn't such a rogue unhung as our master, Sir Michae O'Leary. You don't half know him as I do, that you don't. He'll be a sweet nut for the devil to crack."

"Will he, Brown?"

"Will he? To be sure he will, the rascal; and so old, too, as he is getting! Well—well, he can't last very long."

"That's just what I have been thinking, do you know, lately, Brown. He seems a good deal shaken, and I should say he is on the go."

"And a good job too."

"But, Brown?"

"Well?"

"I am afraid of offending you by what I was going to say, or else I was just going to make a remark."

"Make it."

"Will you promise, Brown, not to take it amiss? for I do not mean it for any offence against you, indeed I do not. Will you promise that you won't fly in a rage about it, now, Brown?"

"I do promise."

"Well, then, I was going to say, that I wonder, with your feelings towards O'Leary, and your knowledge of what a rogue he is, that you are the very man that Mr. Brian, the steward, always puts upon awkward jobs that old Sir Michael want's done. How is that Brown?"

Brown was silent.

"Ah, now I see," said Arrowsmith, "that, without intending it, I have offended you, and I wouldn't do that for the world, for though people say you are a rough sort of fellow, and haven't a civil word for any one, yet you have been the kindest and the best friend to me that ever I met with in all the world, and I respect and revere you for it, Brown!"

"Peace—peace, I say!"

"Oh, yes—yes. If you wish it, I will not say another word upon the subject. Not one, Brown. No, not half a word."

"Are you never going to be quiet?"

"Yes, I am. Oh, yes, Brown, if you wish it. There are very few things that I would not do, if you wished it, Brown!"

Poor Arrowsmith was evidently very much indeed afraid of his dear friend Brown, who had done, according to his own account of the matter, so much for him.

There was now a silence of some few

moments' duration between this oddly assorted pair, and then Brown said suddenly—

"And so you don't know why old O'Leary wants to take the life of the young Ensign?"

"How should I know? Sir Michael don't tell me his secrets."

CAPTAIN HAWK AND MAY SURPRISED BY RATCHLEY IN THE GARDEN.

"No; nor me, either. But I found them out for myself."

"Ah! Brown, you have a tact, a cleverness, a means about you, that I cannot pretend to."

"Go along with you, will you?"

"Now you think I flatter you, but I don't."

"Well, I will believe that you don't. But I will say this much of you, that I have always found you the same man under all circumstances; so, sit down here by this bank, and I will tell you all I know about this remarkable affair."

"Thank you, Brown. Thank you."

Arrowsmith did not know how to be thankful enough for the great condescension of his friend in saying that he would tell him all; and they sat down upon the bank together. As these two men now sat, they were so close to Captain Hawk, that he could with ease have, merely by stretching out his hand, touched their heads, so that there was no likelihood of his losing any portion of their conversation.

Brown spoke hurriedly, as though he wished to get the story over as quickly as possible; and it was evident that the other paid the most profound attention to what he said.

"You know that Sir Michael O'Leary, our master," he said, "is one of those men who live hard and fast, as it is called. Did you ever know him go to bed sober, or be five minutes out of bed without his glass?"

"Never."

"Well, it may be that there's enough upon his conscience to make him take to drink to try to forget it. They say that he has had three wives, but nobody seems to like to say what has become of any of them."

"Perhaps nobody knows."

"Oh, yes, they do. But that is not the question, just now, my friend, so we will let that drop. You know that Miss Isabel is Sir Michael's niece. She was the orphan daughter of his only brother, who was as different a man from Sir Michael as day is different from night."

"Did you know him, Brown?"

"I did—I did."

"And he was a nice man, was he?"

"Hush! He was. Don't speak of him to me. He is dead—dead!—murdered!"

"Murdered?"

"To be sure. What are you starting at, now, eh? Is he the first person in all the world that has been murdered that you should start at it as though it were quite a wonder?"

"Oh, no—no. But ——"

"But what? Go on. I will hear all that you have to say."

"Nothing, Brown. Nothing. The idea only came upon me unawares, that was all.—Nothing else, I assure you."

"Oh, that's well. I was afraid you might think that I had any hand in it, my old friend."

"You, Brown? Oh, no, no. I could not think such a thing of you, I am quite certain. But go on—do go on. I long to hear all that you will be so good as to tell me, Brown. It is quite a treat to me."

"Is it? Well, where was I?"

"At the murder of the brother!"

"Ah—ah, to be sure I was. I was at the murder of the brother of Sir Michael O'Leary; and, as I say, Isabel is his only daughter, and, you see, the brother left all he was worth in the world to Isabel, and when he was dead, Sir, Michael persuaded her, she being then little more than a child, to come to his house, and since then he has spent her money for her, as he had pretty nearly got through all his own, and was some thousands of pounds in debt besides."

"Then I suppose that's why Sir Michael is so savage at the idea of her marrying?"

"To be sure it is! Hush! Did you hear anything? It sounded like the snort of a horse, and our beasts are quite still."

CHAPTER XXII.

CAPTAIN HAWK LEARNS MORE OF THE AFFAIRS OF SIR MICHAEL.

It was the horse of Captain Hawk which at that most inopportune moment had thought proper to make a noise, and had attracted the attention of Mr. Brown and his friend.

There was nothing for it but to take the consequences of the affair, and let the two men be scared or not at the sound, as they might think proper; so Captain Hawk did not move an inch.

"Didn't you hear the sound, Arrowsmith?" said Brown.

"I heard something."

"And where did you think it came from?"

"From one of our own horses, of course; but the fact is, you were at the moment very much engaged in what you were saying, so that it came upon you with rather a surprise, that was all."

"It must be so."

"To be sure it is. Sit down and go on with what you were being so good as to tell me, for I assure you I am very much interested with it."

"No wonder—no wonder. I will not make a half confidence with you, but I will tell you all. The fortune of Miss Isabel is about two thousand pounds a-year, and old Sir Michael has been spending it for her, and will continue to do so."

"If she don't marry."

"Ah, that's it. Now, you know that Ensign Chester was thrown from his horse quite close to the lodge gates, and that the servants took him into the house, and there being no one at home but Isabel, she had him properly attended to."

"Where was Sir Michael?"

"In town, as usual, drinking hard, and gaming with young Isabel's money, to be sure; or, you may be quite sure, the Ensign would never have got a footing in his house."

"Certainly not."

"Well, the Ensign he falls head-over-ears in love with Isabel, and she does the same with him, and then they, all of a sudden, had to meet Sir Michael, who came home while they were snugly taking tea in the old summer-house in the garden."

"Wasn't he in a rage?"

"A rage? I never saw a man in such a state, in all my life. I did think that it would be the death of him outright. He talked of kicking Mr. Chester out of the house, but that was easier to be talked of than done; and at last he swore dreadful oaths—that all Isabel had in the world was one hundred a-year; and then the Ensign, he said he was glad of that, as all he had was another; and as, with such a sum, she must be quite a charge to Sir Michael, he would take her away at once, and marry her."

"And did he?"

"No, certainly not. Sir Michael had a kind of a fight with him, which ended in Sir Michael being thrown over the balustrade of one of the staircases, and the Ensign walking out of the house as if nothing in the world were amiss."

"And that was all?"

"Not quite. Sir Michael had to lay up for a fortnight from the hurts he received in his fall; and the Ensign, during that time, used to visit Miss Isabel in the garden; but only yesterday, some one sent Sir Michael a letter, telling him that some time to-day the Ensign was going to carry off Miss Isabel, and then he sent for me and spoke about it."

"What did he say?"

"'Brown,' he said, 'Ensign Chester and Isabel will pass down the old lane by the Brent some time this morning. Take some of the fellows with you, and mind you bring Isabel back with you, after you have shot the Ensign.'"

"Was that all?"

"About it. He knew that I would not—he knew I could not say 'No' to the plan; and so here I am."

"And here I am; and here I should not be, but for the fact that Sir Michael screens me from the law, knowing I am, or rather that I was, a footpad. I suppose, Brown, that he has some sort of a hold upon you in the same kind of way?"

"Ha! ha!"

"Why do you laugh, Brown?"

"At your simplicity. You think that I am a footpad, or perhaps a cracksman, do you?"

"Well, I —— You will excuse me Brown?"

"Oh, don't be at all delicate about it I am neither the one nor the other; and yet Sir Michael has as good a hold of me as he has of you, Arrowsmith."

"Then you must have done something."

"How true!"

"I hope it hasn't been a—a—"

"What?"

"A murder?"

"Yes, it has. What do you think of me now? It has been a murder; and that is the sort of hold that Sir Michael O'Leary, villain as he is, has of me; and that is why he says to me, commit such and such a crime, and I am obliged to do it. Well, you are a little staggered at that, are you not?"

"I rather am. I did not think—I did not guess that it was even quite so bad as that, I assure you, Brown."

"No, of course, you couldn't—How the deuce could you? A man don't carry a placard upon his neck, with the word, 'Murderer,' written upon it, does he?"

"Don't be angry, Brown—don't."

"Angry? But I will be angry—and why not? Why should I—even I, although there is blood upon my hands, be the slave of such a wretch as that Irish Baronet, that we are forced to call master, because he is the only man in all the world who will permit me to do so for want of character!"

"Ah! there it is,' said Arrowsmith. "I had no character; and when you met me and told me Sir Michael would take me on that very account, and rather preferred it than otherwise, I thought I had dropped into a good thing; but now I find ——"

"What?"

"That he only likes bad characters about him, because he wants bad things done."

This seemed to touch Brown a little, for he was silent; and the pause that ensued lasted several minutes. At length, Brown spoke again:—

"You are right," he said; "you are right."

"Well, it's something to hear you say that. I was afraid ——"

"Of what?"

"That you would only fly into a rage about it at once, and, perhaps, strike at me as you have done before to-day. But, oh! Brown, believe me, I never felt any ill-will at you for doing so, as I took it to be the infirmity of a better nature."

"Arrowsmith, I shall never strike at you again."

"Won't you, though?"

"I will not; and if I should say a harsh thing to you ever again, don't you believe that I mean it, for I do not. And now let me tell you a bit of my mind, Arrowsmith."

"I am all attention."

"Then, to be frank and candid with you, and you may be off and tell Sir Michael, if you like, I would as soon think of putting my own head in the fire as of behaving in such a way to the young Lady Isabel as he wishes me to do."

"You won't do it?"

"As Heaven is my judge, I won't."

"You—you mean to say you won't shoot the Ensign? Not shoot Ensign Chester? That you won't bring the Lady Isabel back to the lodge? You really mean it, Brown?"

"I do—I do."

"Bless you, Brown! Oh, what a happy fellow I am, in comparison to what I was a little while ago! I could cry now for joy, that I could. He won't do it—he won't do it! I thought in my own heart that he would not do it, and now I am sure of it."

Arrowsmith held both his hands over his face, and wept plentifully.

"Well," said Brown, with a sigh, "all this is very odd, it is very odd, indeed. You say you feel happier, Arrowsmith?"

"I do—I do. It is true as gospel, Brown."

"And so do I. It's a very strange thing, but from the moment that I made up my mind not to shoot the Ensign, nor do the wicked commands of Sir Michael O'Leary, something seemed to go crack in my heart, and a kind of weight that had been on it appeared to be lifted off, and I feel quite a new man. I say, Arrowsmith."

"Well, go on, Brown."

"We have been both of us very bad fellows in our time."

"Very bad, indeed."

"Well, then—what, suppose we were to make a try from this time to be good and honest, and to do what's right? What do you think of it? Is it too late, or are we too old?"

"No—no. Something seems to tell me, no."

"And so it does me, too. I feel that it is never too late, and that man is never too old till the grave closes over him; and so from this moment, here, in the face of God's bright daylight, I swear that I will never willingly do a bad act again, and that far from acting as Sir Michael would have me to the Lady Isabel and her young lover, the Ensign, I will help them off if I see them, and wish them joy."

"So will I—so will I, Brown; and shan't we sleep all the sounder to-night for it, and awaken all the happier, too? But, of course, after this we have no home at Sir Michael's. Have you thought of what is to become of us, Brown?"

"Not I, and I won't, either. If we make up our minds to do well, who can help us? Suppose that for a time we don't know which way to turn, it will be, perhaps, all for the best in the long run. Virtue is a great property, and a scarce one."

"Indeed!" said Captain Hawk to himself, as he leant in a reflecting attitude upon the bank. "So these men, unwittingly, are giving me a lesson, are they? Well, it may not be too late for them, but it is too late for me. I have no further business here."

He was now upon the point of creeping away from the spot, when he heard the gallop of a horse's feet, and in a moment the man who had stationed Brown and Arrowsmith in the lane, reached the spot.

"Hide yourselves," he said. "They come—they come."

"Who come?" said Brown.

"Why, Ensign Chester, and the young lady, to be sure. Remember that you are to make sure of him by a pistol-shot, but you are not to injure her in the slightest degree, for if she dies, her money goes away from Sir Michael."

"Oh, that's it, is it?" said Brown calmly. "Who is that now in the lane on horseback? Ha, they come!"

"Oh. it's only some of our friends, that's all. We will all hide here in the bushes, and then come out upon the chaise the moment it gets opposite to this spot."

At this minute three more of the mounted men reached the place, so that Brown and his friend Arrowsmith were in a decided minority upon the occasion; but yet, with a coolness and a courage that did him infinate honour, Brown spoke out his former sentiments.

"How long will it be before the Ensign is here?" he said.

"About five minutes," was the reply.

"Very good; then there is ample time for me to tell you on my own behalf, and in behalf of Arrowsmith too, that I don't like this job at all, and that we don't mean to carry it out."

"You don't like it, and you don't mean to carry it out?"

"Certainly not."

"Are you mad?"

"I hope not. I think I have been, but it seems to me, that only within these last few minutes, or say the last half hour, I have recovered my senses, and the first use I make of them is, to say that I will not commit the murder."

The leader in the business looked staggered.

"It is a foul murder," added Brown, with increasing vehemence, "and foul will be the soul that is stained with such guilt."

"Well," said the leader, "this is pretty, certainly. And, pray, what do you expect that Sir Michael O'Leary will say of all this?"

"He may say what he pleases, but Sir Michael O'Leary had better beware. A poor tool may be used until it gets so sharp, that it may wound its owner."

"Ah, you think so, do you? Well, I am too far gone in his affairs to become so wonderfully upright and penitent all of a sudden; and as I don't choose to run any risks, I will put it out of your power to do me or my companions any harm." Turning to his partners in guilt, he said, "If this fellow, Brown, whom I have long suspected, leaves this spot alive, it will be the worst day's work for us that could possibly occur. Shoot him down at once. We have the majority, and must conquer. Down with him!"

"Hold!" said Captain, Hawk rising up, and just showing himself above the hedge, with a pistol in each hand. "Allow me to have something to do in this little affair. Who will have the first shot?"

The consternation of the villains, who, no doubt, would have murdered Brown and Arrowsmith, was so great at the sudden appearance of Captain Hawk, that they at once turned to fly from the spot; but at that minute the sound of carriage-wheels reached the ears of the whole party, and as though by general consent, there was a pause.

Another moment, and coming down the lane was seen a chariot, making all the speed it could along the uneaven ground.

"They are here!" said Brown.

"Confusion!" muttered the man of business of Sir Michael. "Yes, they are here, and I am powerless."

The carriage came on rapidly, and then suddenly raising his arm, that man who was true to the villany of his master, fired a pistol right through the front window of the vehicle. Captain Hawk shot him through the head in a minute, and then at a bound dashed into the lane.

The carriage stopped, for the postilion, in his fright, fell from his saddle. The other men who still remained true to the interests of Sir Michael O'Leary, at once made off, and no one thought it worth while to interrupt them in their progress. In another minute the carriage door was dashed open, and a young man, with a drawn sword in his hands, and his face flushed with excitement, leaped out of the vehicle.

"What is all this!" he cried. "Where are my foes?"

"Gone, sir," said Captain Hawk. "Is the young lady hurt?"

"Thank God, no!"

"Then all is well. I see the shot has missed you. You were to be murdered upon the spot, if a certain Sir Michael O'Leary had had his way!"

"Sir Michael?"

"Yes, the same; but I and these two honest fellows, I rather think, have saved you, and the worst of the villains lies there."

The Ensign, for it was, indeed, he, walked up to the dead body, and after gazing at it for a moment or two, he said—

"It is Sir Michael's secretary and steward. What an awful piece of business is this. Isabel—Isabel, they would have murdered us."

"Oh, no—no!" cried a female voice from the carriage, and then there stepped out of it a young lady of such ravishing beauty that Captain Hawk stood gazing at her like a man enchanted. He quite forgot May Boyes while he gazed upon the charms of Lady Isabel.

"My darling," said Ensign Chester, "all is well. There was, indeed, as it appears, a plot against my life; but it has, thank Heaven, signally failed, and we can now, I hope, pursue our journey in peace."

"Yes," said Captain Hawk, "God, she is beautiful!"

Upon this, the young lady hastened into the chaise again, and Captain Hawk, starting from the reverie into which he had fallen, added—

"Pardon me for saying so much, but the words were but the echo to my heart's thoughts. Sir, allow me to tell you that it is to those two men you owe your life."

"And to you," said the Ensign.

"Never mind me. I am in no need of any manifestation of your gratitude, but they are very much in need of it."

"Who are you both?" said the Ensign. "Why—why, is this possible. I have seen you both at Sir Michael's. How comes it that you are servants of his, and yet such friends to me?"

"We have repented of our evil life," said Arrowsmith, "and being sent here to murder you, we made up our minds rather to assist you, and we shall go no more to the lodge."

"Then come to me in London, whither I am at once going with the Lady Isabel. You will easily find me by an inquiry at where my regiment is stationed, which is now in St. James's Park. I will see that you are well provided for, and most amply repaid for all that you could possibly have lost in the service of Sir Michael O'Leary."

"Ah!" cried Brown, pointing along the lane, "there is one of the men come back again, who would have done the deed of blood, and felt no sort of compunction at the doing of it. There he is, peeping behind yonder old chestnut tree. He is mounted, too."

"I must have him!" cried the Ensign. "Lend me one of those horses. All's right. I won't let the animal go. Guard the lady with your lives!"

Before, then, any one could say one word to dissuade him from the step, or in any manner interfere to stop him, the impetuous young soldier flung himself upon the back of one of the horses, and galloped off down the lane after the fellow who had been evidently watching from behind the chestnut tree.

"Oh, save him—save him!" cried the young lady. "What will become of him now? Will no one help him?"

"Do not be alarmed," said Hawk, as he once again fixed his eyes upon her beautiful form, and felt a delirium of passion stealing over him. "Do not be alarmed. Oh, how happy is Ensign Chester!"

"Happy, sir?"

"Yes—yes. You love him: is not that sufficient?"

Rapidly, then, turning to the two men, Brown and Arrowsmith, he cried—

"Go at once after the Ensign. You may be in time to render him the most effectual assistance, and, perhaps, to save his life. I will guard the lady."

Brown and Arrowsmith set off at once as hard as they could now in the direction that the Ensign had taken. A feeling almost approaching to madness took possession of Captain Hawk now, as once more he turned his attention to the beautiful Isabel. She was weeping, and wringing her hands frantically.

"Do not weep," he said. "Oh, do not weep. Tears should never come from those eyes that were only made to win all hearts. How beautiful! How more than beautiful you are!"

The young girl was by far too beautiful to pay the degree of attention that she ought to the expressions of admiration that came thick and fast from the lips of Captain Hawk, for now that he was alone with her, he did not scruple to say what he really thought.

When we say that he was alone with her, we must not forget the postilion, who was lying upon his back, looking up to the sky with his mouth wide open, and afraid to move from the spot, for fear of being murdered at once, if he did so.

"I will fly to him. They will kill him," cried Isabel.

"Oh, no—no; but if you would with your own eyes see him—if you really wish to be able to look upon him——"

"If I wish? Oh, show me how to do so!"

"There is a bank of earth close to here, upon which you can get with my assistance, and from it you will see well."

"Yes, I will go—I will go. Where is it?"

Poor Isabel would have gone anywhere at that moment that would have promised her a view of her lover, and, besides, had she not every reason in the world to put faith in Captain Hawk—for was he not, as it were, presented to her as the preserver of her lover? Besides, she had the most guileless virtue the world ever saw, and so she was even more apt to trust any one, than to be suspectful of them. If she had not been of such a disposition, her bad uncle, Sir Michael O'Leary, could never for so long have robbed her in the rascally manner he had done, as described by Brown and Arrowsmith in their confabulation together in the lane, to which Captain Hawk had listened.

"Take me where I can see that he is safe!" cried Isabel, as Captain Hawk now assisted her from the carriage. "That is all I ask of you."

"I will do so. Trust to me."

"I do. Heaven knows I do. You have saved him, and that is enough for me."

Captain Hawk flung one arm round her waist and almost lifted her upon the bank. By a powerful effort he caught with his right hand the branch of a tree that grew in the hedge-row, and as his left was round Isabel, he so hove her on the bank in a moment.

"Can you see him?" he said.

"No—no. The trees prevent me."

"Come this way then."

Before she could either assent or dissent to his proceedings, he took her in his arms and jumped with her into the meadow on the other side of the hedge. If anything like reason or a feeling of honour was left in the heart of Captain Hawk before the fact of holding Isabel in his arms, from that moment he banished it, and he gave up any idea but the mad one of adoring her to distraction.

"You cannot see him yet?" he said.

"No—no!"

"But from the back of my horse you can. Let me lift you to the saddle; you will be then high enough to see over the hedge-top, and you will observe how gallantly your lover acts—you will see if he is in the least hurt. Ah, that was a pistol-shot."

With one bound from the ground, Captain Hawk now placed Isabel upon the saddle of his horse. She strained her eyes in the direction that the Ensign had gone.

"I do not see him," she said; "I cannot see him."

"Then we will go after him," said Captain Hawk. "Sit still, and all will be well."

Placing his right hand upon the horse's back, he at once vaulted on to it behind Isabel. Flinging, then, his right arm round her waist, he with his left caught the bridle. Dashing the spurs he wore, then, against the horse's flanks, he cried,—

"Away—away! By the earth, air, sea, and Heaven, I love you, Isabel, with all my heart and soul!"

She raised a shriek, and then the horse, smarting under the goad of the spurs, made a mad bound in the air that would have unseated any less skilful rider than Captain Hawk; but he not only kept his own seat adroitly, but prevented Isabel from slipping off the saddle, by the powerful grasp that he kept round her waist.

The horse then went off at a wild gallop, as if it, too, like its master, had gone mad under the influence of some powerful passion.

Whether it was absolute fright at the wild speed of the horse, or that she had really fainted, that kept Isabel now quiet, it is hard to say; but certain it is, that she did not utter but the one shriek, that let Captain Hawk know that she was no longer a stranger to his designs upon her liberty—perhaps her life. Then she was profoundly still.

The object of Hawk was now to get to the hut that he called his own; and in the midst of the whirlwind of passion that had come across his heart by the sight of the angelic beauty of Isabel, he had just perception enough left to know that he was guiding his terrified steed in the right direction for that miserable and dreary place.

The notion that he was exposing himself to the greatest possible danger of being apprehended, did not seem at all to come over Captain Hawk's mind. He certainly showed that he thought of nothing and cared for nothing but to get clear off with Isabel from that spot; and so, regardless of whether he was seen or not, he made the best of his way across fields — over roads — breaking through hedges, and forcing the horse to several wild leaps, that in his right senses he would never have thought of testing the animal's powers to do, until he got very near to his place of destination, indeed.

Then, and not till then, did Captain Hawk restrain his rate of riding a little, and glance around him. Not a soul was to be seen; and on he went still at a gallop. Now he had to cross a narrow lane, and the moment he got into it he saw a man staring at him with his mouth and eyes wide open, as if he were an apparition.

"Take that for your curiosity," cried Hawk, as he drew a pistol from his pocket, and fired it at the man, who immediately fell headlong to the ground, roaring out murder, althought the bullet had really missed him. In another moment Captain Hawk was out of sight on the other side of the hedge.

CHAPTER XXIII.

RETURNS TO BOYES HALL, AND TO MAY.

It would be quite impossible for any person to do justice to a description of the state of mind of May Boyes, now that she knew Captain Hawk was about again, and free as before upon the face of the world.

She had so completely made up her mind that his capture was his positive destruction, that the fact of his escape came upon her like a thunder clap; and yet she knew not why she should have thought it so impossible, or at all events so improbable, that he should by one bold manœuvre release himself from the custody of the officers.

Concerning the duel that took place between him and her brother Ratchley, she knew nothing; but in about an hour after that duel took place, Ratchley suddenly appeared in his sister's presence.

May had been sitting alone by that same window through which she had passed the night before, when she met Captain Hawk in the garden, and she started at the sound of her brother's voice, for her heart was not with any one who was in the house. It was upon the road with the daring highwayman, who had first taught it to love, and who, whatever might be his actions, could never wholly eradicate the feeling from that noble and affectionate bosom.

"Sister May," said Ratchley.

May rose with a cry of surprise; and then pressing both her hands upon her bosom, she said softly—

"Oh, it is you, Ratchley?"

"Yes, dear May. It is I."

There was a softened tone about his voice, and a subdued moan, that was very different to that in which he had lately spoken to her. She looked up into his face, and she then saw no feeling expressed but one of profound sorrow.

"You are suffering?" she said.

"I am—I am."

"Your wound vexes you yet."

"Ah! would that I had no other cause of suffering but that, May! The physical injuries of our frame will pass away; but when the spirit is wounded,

THE DUEL BETWEEN CAPTAIN HAWK AND RATCHLEY BOYES.

no act will heal it again, and make all sound as before."

May sunk into her seat again, and sighed deeply.

"Sister," added Ratchley, "I have come upon a perilous errand to you."

"Perilous?"

"Yes. I come to ask you for your confidence, if you will give it to me—your whole and unreserved confidence. Do you think you can?"

"I do not know, Ratchley," said

May, as she rested her head upon her hands and wept. "I do not know."

Ratchley drew a chair close to her, and gently moving her hands from before her face, he said—

"I have one thing to tell you, sister, which, perhaps, you will be glad to hear."

"I shall never know what gladness is again," she said.

"Oh, you—you are young yet, and the light of a young heart is not so easily quenched—you will smile again in the time to come, and, I hope, yet be the joy of us all, as you ever have been until this sad, very sad cloud came over your spirits."

"It is a cloud, indeed."

"But, like all other clouds, it will pass away, and then the sun will shine out again as before, and all will be well."

"Ah, brother, you speak more as you wish than as you think. But you had something to tell me. What is it?"

"Yes, sister, I have something to tell you, and I will not keep you in suspense regarding what it is. I—you shall hear it."

It was evident that Ratchley yet hesitated about saying to May what he had in reality come to her to say.

"Oh, tell me," she said "if it be good news. If evil, I can spare it, Ratchley, for I have had enough of that, heaven knows."

"It is not news at all, sister. It is but a personal matter of my own, and relates to a resolve that I have come to."

May shuddered. She thought to be sure it must be some violent resolution regarding Captain Hawk, or Gerald Clifton as she liked much better to call him to herself. That name of Captain Hawk always made her feel faint and sick when she heard it.

"Provided," added Ratchley, "Gerald Clifton——"

"Ah! it is of him?"

"It is, sister; but I pray you listen to me. Provided Gerald Clifton adds no other to his offences against me and my family, I will never, while I live, lift up my hand against him."

"You will not?—Do I hear aright? You who were so full of anger? Oh, Ratchley, are you speaking the truth to me, or is this but a snare to catch my unwary heart and make it show itself more fully to you than it does? If so, Ratchley, it is most unworthy of you."

"May," said Ratchley in a cold tone as he rose, "the unworthiness is with you, who can suspect me of such wicked duplicity. I no longer, after what you have now said, ask your confidence. Farewell, sister."

"No—no!"

She sprang after and caught him before he reached the door.

"Forgive me, brother. Oh, if you knew how much I have suffered, you would not find it so very hard to forgive me for a few idle words."

"It is not hard at all, dear May," said Ratchley, who was deeply affected at her pathetic manner of speaking. "It is not difficult at all. I do forgive you, dear May, with all my heart. But you will not doubt me again?"

"I will not, indeed. I did not then. I cannot tell what it was that made me say what I did; but, of late, I say and think strange things."

"Your mind, dear sister, is thrown off its balance. Time will restore you to yourself. And now fully understand me—that from this time forth, unless some new attempt, or some new villany makes a new offence, I have done with Gerald Clifton."

"And this is for my sake?"

"No—no. Do not tempt me to assume a virtue that I have not any pretensions to, and do not ask me why it is I came to such a determination. Let it suffice that I have come to it, and then let the matter so far rest. And now, dear sister, will you not tell me that you will at once and for ever shake off the thraldom of a feeling which, while it was awakened by Gerald Clifton the gentleman, was nothing amiss, but which, if it belong to Captain Hawk the highwayman, is most reprehensible?"

May was silent.

"Ah, sister, you do not answer me."

"What would you have me say, brother?"

"I would have you unequivocally renounce all further idea of that bold, bad man, who but too plainly enthralled your young heart in the wiles of his elaborate cunning. I would have you be yourself, and with the proper pride of your youth, sex, and your condition, I would have you spurn the idea of wasting another moment's thought upon such an object."

May spoke in a low tone of voice.

"Brother, I will be true to you, and I will be candid with you: I did love Gerald Clifton."

"Alas! alas!"

"Nay, do not lament that I loved one who was so lovable, but hear me say all that I would say. To my affections, Gerald Clifton is dead, and although we may say that from his ashes this Captain Hawk has arisen, it does not follow that I should love him. I will still at times, for I cannot help myself from doing so, think of Gerald Clifton; and I now aver that from this hour I have nothing in common with Captain Hawk. Do you understand me, brother, fully?"

"I do. And I am satisfied."

"Murder!" cried Sir John Boyes, at this moment hastening into the room with an open letter in his hand. "Murder That is to say, when I say murder, I mean something else altother, and not the same thing."

Poor Sir John was in an evident state of great excitement, and he stood in such an odd attitude with his mouth wide open, and his legs far asunder like a pair of compasses, that both Ratchley and May were afraid that something very serious was the matter with him.

"What is the matter, sir?" said Ratchley. "I hope you are quite well?"

"Oh, father, you terrify me," cried May.

Sir John dropped into a chair, but it gave such a crack, that suspecting at was intent upon treacherously giving way with him, he suddenly started up again, and said—"Oh!" Then observing that both Ratchley and May were looking at him with amazement, he put himself into what he considered a fine attitude, and swinging the letter he had in his hand round and round in a circle, he said—

"The Secretary of State for the Home Department has taken advantage of an obvious opportunity of writing to me, or in other words he has sent me this letter—hem! He has sent it to me. The next thing to possessing an extraordinary intellect yourself, is to—to—dear me, what was I going to say? It was some sentiment Ratchley, which you would have done well to put down in your memorandum book; but I quite forget it, so let it pass, or, in a manner of speaking, think no more of it."

"But what is the letter about, sir?" said Ratchley.

"Permit me to say that that is the question," said Sir John. "When any one receives a letter, and in the profound abyss of his ignorance does not know who it comes from, he is ignorant of the sender, and, no doubt, is lost in a sea of conjectures regarding the contents, until he reads them, and then he knows them."

"Certainly, sir."

"Dear me, it is quite singular, what a flow of felicitous language I have today. It is really wonderful—admirable I may say, and wonderful, and odd—very."

To this rather egotistical remark, neither May nor Ratchley thought proper to make any reply. They both, though, guessed pretty well what was likely to be the subject matter of the letter which Sir John had received from the Secretary of State. That it concerned the escape of Captain Hawk was but too probable.

"Of course," added Sir John, "when the Secretary of State of this great country sits down to write a letter, he naturally asks himself to whom it is to be directed, and the answer is, Sir John Boyes, the representative of all the Boyes; and here it is

"Perhaps, sir," said Ratchley, "you will read it to us?"

"In a manner of speaking, I will. Hem! Listen, both of you. It is a very dreadful communication, indeed, not that it in any way concerns you, May; but still, out of courtesy, you may as well hear it! Hem! the letter proceeds thus, or, I should rather say, begins thus—Dear me, what an astonishing flow of language I have to-day, to be sure! It is quite remarkable."

"That is a very odd beginning to a letter, sir," said Ratchley.

Sir John looked at his son with what he intended should be great dignity, as he replied—

"Ratchley Boyes, Esq.—who, in the course of time, when the world loses me, in a manner of speaking, will be Sir Ratchley Boyes—allow me to state that that was not the beginning of the letter, and, consequently, that it was not the commencement of it."

"Oh," said Ratchley, "that was my mistake."

"I rather believe it was. This is the letter :—

"'Downing Street.

"'Dear Sir John Boyes—I have to inform you that the criminal, named Hawk, who was apprehended near to your estate, upon the charge of murdering Judge Holme on the highway, has contrived to elude the vigilance of the officers, and is now at large. Allow me to request that you will, in your magisterial capacity, do all you possibly can to capture the criminal again, as it is thought that he is very likely to infest your immediate neighbourhood. An active officer, of the name of Long, will put himself into communication with you, and I request that you will be good enough for the public service to give him every possible assistance and countenance.

"'I have the honour to be,
"'Dear Sir John Boyes,
"'Your obedient servant,
"'NORTH.'

"There," said Sir John, when he had finished the epistle, "Lord North thinks proper to write to me upon the subject, and here is the letter, so that there is nothing to do now but to arrest the criminal."

"Then Captain Hawk," said Ratchley, "is upon the road again ?"

"In a manner of speaking, he is. But—I don't know whether I ought to name it before I have consulted some of the old authors upon the subject—but there is an expression in the Secretary of State's letter that puzzles me rather, and so, I may say, confuses me, and as I don't understand it, it has to me the character of incomprehensibility."

"What is it, sir?"

"The Secretary requests me to give Long every countenance I can ; now, how can I give Long any other countenance than he has already, I should like to know ? Nature has given Long a countenance, and with that he must be satisfied."

Ratchley could hardly forbear smiling as he said—

"Perhaps, sir, the ancient authors may throw some light upon the subject."

"Perhaps they may—perhaps they may," said Sir John, as he left the room with a stately step to go to his library."

CHAPTER XXIV.

SHOWS HOW CAPTAIN HAWK REPENTED OF HIS VILLANY.

WE left Captain Hawk not very far from the hut, or cottage, in which he found a rough home, and a rougher welcome usually, from the man who kept it for him. In that cottage, too, we may suppose, that there was still one who, from reasons which will appear as we proceed, was bereft of that greatest gift of Heaven to man—reason ; but whether or not Hawk was accountable for the fact of the derangement of that poor creature, we must not now say.

His right arm was still clasped around the waist of Isabel, that most beautiful young creature, towards whom he felt a wild love that had overstepped all reason most completely.

With his left hand he guided the horse in safety.

It was quite evident that either from actually fainting or from fright the young girl was not able to speak a word or to make the least effort to free herself from the thraldom in which she now was, and, consequently, Captain Hawk had no difficulty in proceeding with the poor victim of his mad passion towards the cottage, which was now close at hand, and the little single chimney of which could he readily seen among the trees that shaded the rest of the building upon that side from observation.

"At last," said Captain Hawk—"at last I reach a haven of safety, for I have the means of hiding in that hut, which I have nowhere else, and oh ! what a mad delight it is to feel that I have this treasure of beauty all to myself ! That I can hold her in my arms, and defy all the world to tear her from me."

It was, indeed, a mad delight.

Two or three bounds of the still affrighted horse was sufficient to bring it and its two riders to the door of the hut, against which Captain Hawk gave a kick with his heavy riding-boots that was enough to send it in off its hinges at once.

There was a scuffling noise inside the hut, but no one opened the door, and Captain Hawk, who was never very renowned for patience, gave it another kick that split the upper panel.

"Hilloa!" he cried. "Open! open! It is I."

He knew that his voice would be known, and there was no occasion to proclaim any more to the man within. In another moment the door was flung open, and the rough-looking fellow who has been before presented to our readers appeared.

"Oh, captain, is that you? Oh, lor, ain't I glad to see you! They said—"

"Silence!"

"Oh, yes, but they say as——"

Hawk gave him a kick, and shouted "Silence!" in a voice, that if it did not quite stop the man's loquacity, had the effect of making him speak only in a whisper.

"They said as how you was nabbed."

"Bah! you ought to know better."

"Wasn't you, then?"

"What is that to you? Let it suffice that I am here now; and if you were to hear that I was hanged, you might still expect to see me."

"Oh, lor, I hope not. But, gracious goodness, who is this?"

"Hush! Hold the horse's head."

"I'll help her down, captain."

"Hold the horse's head, will you? unless you want a bullet through your own. Your long tongue will be the death of you, I know, some day. Dare to lay a finger upon the girl, and I will kill you at once."

The man held the horse while Captain Hawk managed to alight, still holding Isabel from falling. He then took her tenderly and carefully in his arms, and at once carried her into the hut.

"Take the horse away to safety," he cried.

"Yes—yes. I will take him. Oh, lor!" muttered the man, as he walked the horse away, "this is a nice caper, rather. The idea of his bringing a little bit of a girl here! She is pretty, though, if it wasn't for her pale face. Lor bless me, he hasn't no taste! Why I know a woman who stands six feet one in her shoes, and whose face is so big and red, you could see it a mile off, looking like the setting sun in a fog. Ah! that is a fine woman! Dear me, how people can take a fancy to little bits of delicate girls amazes me, that it does."

Captain Hawk had taken but three strides to reached the principal room in the cottage. With his foot he kicked an old couch from the wall to a more convenient situation, near the fire that was smouldering in the grate, and then he gently laid Isabel upon the couch.

"Speak—oh, speak to me!" he cried. "Tell me that you do not hate me—that you do not loathe me, for I love you with a despeate passion that knows no bounds. It is the very insanity of love."

A slight shudder passed through the form of the fair young creature. It seemed as if she heard that something was being said to her, but had scarcely the power to understand it, or to thoroughly awaken to reply to it.

Captain Hawk started from the side of the couch, and repairing to the back of the cottage, he procured a jug full of cold water, with which he speedily returned, and dashed gently a few particles of the chilly fluid upon Isabel's face.

She opened her eyes.

"Oh, God! Oh, God!" she said.

"Hush!" said Hawk. "Hush!"

He did not like to hear that name then pronounced, for it put him in mind of the villany of the act that he had committed in taking that young and innocent creature away from him whom she loved, and with whom she would have been happy, to make her listen to the ravings of his wild passion.

With a startled glance, Isabel looked around her upon the rough and rude appointments of the cottage, and then she looked at Hawk. Her mind was evidently still in a state of great confusion, and she found it impossible to assure herself of the reality of what she saw.

"A dream!" she said, in a low, faint voice. "Oh, it is only a dream!"

Hawk was silent: he dreaded to assure her that it was reality, and to open her eyes to the fact of what a villain he really was.

For the space of about half a minute, now, Isabel covered her fair face with both her hands, as though, by shutting out the objects that had alarmed her, she could entirely dissipate them. When she looked again around her she began to shudder.

"Were am I?" she said. "Oh, it is real! Where am I?"

She half rose from the couch.

Captain Hawk dropped upon one knee by the side of the humble resting-place of the fair girl, and spoke in a low, silvery tone to her.

"Rest in peace," he said. "Oh, rest in peace! What are such beings as you are brought into this great world for but to be loved—to be madly worshipped, as I love, as I worship you? I have looked upon many a fair face, but, oh! I never saw real beauty—real exquisite loveliness, until I looked upon you. Do not tremble. What can you have to fear from one who loves you as I love you? You look alarmed!—Oh, banish such a feeling, and in the adoration of my heart find rather cause for great safety, than any sentiment for fear."

"Help! Oh, help me!" she cried. "Help!"

"Hush!"

"No—no. I am in the hands of a villain! Help! Mercy! Help! Oh, who has dragged me from him whom I truly love? Take me back to him! Where am I—what dreadful place is this?"

She sprang up from the couch, but Captain Hawk flung his arms around her and held her fast.

"Peace—peace!" he said, in a high, cracked voice. "You will drive me mad!—Do not think so despairingly Live only for love and joy."

"Help! Murder! Unhand me ruffian! Oh, can God look down upon me now and hold out no succour to me? Off—off—wretch—Help!"

Hawk had kissed her cheeks and lips—he held her to his heart, and in that mad moment, if all the world had tried to tear her from him, it would have been in vain. Had he been quite certain that death would come to him in the next hour, if he continued that wild embrace, he must still have held her to his heart.

"Are you human?" she said. "Had you a mother?"

"Peace! Do not speak to me."

"D—n it, captain, fair play!" cried a voice.

Hawk started round and saw his rough friend, the keeper of the hut, at the door.

"Be off with you, will you, or I'll shoot you!" he cried.

"No you won't," said the man, "or, if you will, why you will, and all I have got to say is, do it. This won't do—it is unworthy of you, and I tell you it won't do. If this young thing—why, she is but a child—had come here with her own free will and made a fool of herself, I would have said nothing about it; but, I say, it's the act of a coward to bring a fainting girl here, and then attack her like a savage. For shame, captain—for shame! If any one had told me as much of you I wouldn't have believed them; and now that I have said my say, shoot me if you like."

Captain Hawk had drawn a pistol from his pocket, and levelled it at the head of the man, who stood firm and collected waiting for the shot.

"I don't forget," he said, "that you saved my life once, captain; so you think it your property, and you may take it, I suppose. Well, do so; murder me, and then have your will of a weak, young child. Oh, that will be brave!"

Hawk's hand shook, and he dropped the pistol from his grasp. He staggered back from the couch, and leant against the wall in silence.

"Oh, captain," said the man, "I knew you would think better of it. It is not in your nature to do the act of a villain."

"Go—go—go!"

"No—don't tell me to go. Look at that young creature all of a shake, and half frightened out of her wits; and she is pretty too—a pretty toy—and just like a wax doll, poor girl. Don't you be frightened, miss. The captain will take a better thought of it, and you will be all right."

Hawk staggered to a chair.

"If you wish to kill me," said Isabel, "do so. I can meet death calmly, but not dishonour. Take my life, if you must do so, and I will pray God to forgive you."

"Oh, stuff!" said Captain Hawk's rough friend, "I tell you he don't mean it. Lor bless you, at times he's as mild as a babby; only, you see, if he is put out of his way a little, he is rather hasty. Come, now, captain, just tell the little creature that you don't mean no harm, and that she may go."

Hawk advanced to Isabel. He seemed about to speak; but after two or three efforts, his voice failed him, and he darted out of the hut and disappeared among the trees that were close to it, and which formed the commencement of quite a little wood, extending about half a mile to the eastward.

"I am a villain!" he cried, as he rushed along at headlong speed—"I am a villain, and I deserve death and excommunication!"

The low bough of a sycamore struck him on the head. He reeled back for a moment or two, and then fell heavily to the ground in a state of insensibility, while the blood flowed copiously from the wound that the rough bark of the tree had given to him.

This sudden departure of Captain Hawk from the hut had astounded the man and had astonished Isabel. She did not, as yet, feel able to decide upon whether he repented of the evil he had done her, and of the further evil he had meant to do her, or not; but she had heard enough from the man who kept the hut to know that he had a friendly feeling towards her; and now, clasping her hands and looking at him imploringly, she said—

"You will let me go from here? You will, for you have said kind things to me already. Oh, save me—save me!"

"All's right. There's nothing to fear. The captain will take a better thought of it. He isn't quite so bad as to be a thorough out-and-out scoundrel, if he only takes a thought of it."

"But, may I not go?"

"Where to? Just tell me where you came from, my dear, and then I shall know better what to say to you."

Thus questioned, Isabel related to him all that had taken place, so far as she knew it, and told him who she was, concluding by imploring him to let her go forth at once in search of the Ensign.

"Oh, lor, what would be the use of that?" said the man. "You are most likely some miles away from him, and, besides, you don't know where he has gone by this time, my dear. Oh, won't he be in a way, to be sure!"

"Yes—yes. What will become of him? Oh, how cruel it was of this man you call the captain to bring me here! But he must be in the interest of my cruel, bad uncle, who would have killed Ensign Chester."

"No," said the man of the hut, as he shook his head "you may take your oath of it that Captain Hawk is in nobody's interest but his own. If he does a queer thing, it is on his own account, I can tell you, and no one else's. It must have been your pretty face that at the moment drove him out of his wits, that is all; and now, I daresay, he is as sorry for it as he can very well be, poor fellow, It's a mercy I was at home, that's all; and that he just had sense enough left him not to shoot me, as he meant to do at one time."

"But what can I do? What shall I do to get to the Ensign again? I cannot—I dare not stay here!"

"You must, my dear, till the captain comes back; you will find him in quite a different mood, I am sure, when he does; and then, you may depend, he will find a way of making it all right again."

"Oh, no—no—I will not wait!"

"Oh, yes, do; that's a nice little girl. Now, do. Don't you be rash, now, and go doing things that you oughtn't. Do stay."

"Heaven help me!"

"In course, that's all right. Now, I give you my word that I'll stay by you, and no harm shall come to you.

That ought to satisfy you; and as for the captain, I know now that he will take a better thought of the affair, and he will take you back to that young man of yours as soon as he comes."

Isabel wept. She dreaded that if she did not, with some appearance of willingness, follow the advice of the man of the hut, that she should jeopardise her hold upon his friendship and sympathy; so she gave a kind of enforced consent to stay where she was until the return of Captain Hawk.

That return, however, appeared to be far distant, for half an hour passed without it taking place, and she was now getting evidently alarmed.

"I will go into the little wood," he said, "and look for him. You stay here, and make yourself comfortable, if you can, but don't stir: and, mind, if any one knocks at the door, don't answer."

"I will not."

"That will do. If anybody knocks, and there's no answer, they will, of course, conclude that I am out, and away they will go again; but I shan't be long gone. The fire is burning up, you see, so you will be quite comfortable—Good-by."

"Good-by," said Isabel, mournfully.

She heard the man carefully secure the door of the hut on the outside, and then, with a timid look, she glanced around her, saying mournfully—

"And here I am alone and a prisoner in this strange place! Even yet I can scarcely believe myself that it is real—it seems so very strange and so dreamlike. Will that man repent of his wickedness, and come back to me as a friend instead of an enemy; or is this, after all, but some subtle device of my enemies, and is he whom I love no more?"

The idea that it was possible her lover might be murdered by that time, was too much for the strength of mind of Isabel, and she wept bitterly. She felt that if he really were dead, her situation was indeed most desolate, and that the only haven of peace she could look to was the grave, which she wished in such a case might soon close over her.

In the midst of her weeping she heard a kicking at the door of the hut, and although she made no answer, and indeed, scarcely dared to breath, it continued as though, whoever it was, he was resolved not to fail in getting admittance for want of perseverance.

CHAPTER XXV.

CAPTAIN HAWK MAKES A PERILOUS JOURNEY WITH ISABEL.

THE man of the hut was really in a state of considerable alarm regarding what had become of Captain Hawk, and he went into the wood to seek for him with a dread that he should discover some catastrophe. By mere good fortune he happened in a few moments to come to the spot upon which Hawk was lying.

The first impression of the man, and a reasonable enough one it was too, was that Captain Hawk had shot himself, for the blood had covered his face, and there was every appearance of a bullet having entered his brain.

"Well," he said, after indulging in a long meditation, "there is an end of him at last, is there? Poor fellow! Dead is he? Well we must all die some day; but I should like to have gone before you, captain, for it ain't my weakness to care much for anybody, and yet I would have gone through fire and water for you, though at times I have had a harsh word from you, and at times a blow that was rather too much to bear. I'd lay down my life now, if I could only see you with your eyes open, and hear you swear a little. Oh dear—oh dear, I shall leave England now, and go and die in some outlandish place or another, I suppose; and the sooner the better, too—the sooner the better. But I'll take that little gir home to her young man first, if I can only find him."

A groan from the seemingly dead body of Captain Hawk came rather startlingly upon the ears of the man.

"What the deuce is that?" he said.

Another long-drawn groan.

"Why, he ain't dead, or if he is, I'll be hanged if that ain't his ghostesses. Hilloa, captain, is that you, or isn't it?"

"Joe?" said Captain Hawk.

"Lor! he says, 'Joe,' and if that don't mean me, I'm a Dutchman, that's all! Perhaps it's all right, after all. How do you find yourself, captain? Is it all up with you, or isn't it?"

"I don't know. Are you Joe?"

"Yes, to be sure I is. I ain't changed in this little time."

"What is amiss, then?"

"That you ought to know, captain, for I'm quite sure I don't. I found

THE PAINFUL INTERVIEW BETWEEN RATCHLEY AND HIS SISTER, MAY.

you here all over blood, and thought you had kicked the bucket to a certainty, and precious sorry I was, too. I didn't expect to hear you say 'Joe' again, I can tell you. What has happened—eh? Has anybody given you a bullet or a blow?"

"Neither, Joe," said Captain Hawk. "My recollection is now coming back to me and I understand what has happened. I was running headlong through the wood here, and was foolish enough to hit my head against a bough of a tree, and it stunned me for the time."

"Oh, that won't last long, captain; you will soon get the better of that, I'm sure. Do you think you can get up?"

"Yes—yes."

With Joe's assistance, Captain Hawk got to his feet, but for a few moments he was forced to cling to his friend's arm, for all the wood seemed to be spinning round him at a tremendous rate. The blow had given a little shake to the brain, and it was sure to take a little time to recover itself again.

"Better now?" said Joe.

"Oh, yes, a great deal. I shall be myself again in a few moments. The trees are not going round and round me in such a mad sort of way. I am very rapidly recovering, Joe, and shall be as usual in a few moments."

"That's all right."

"Yes—yes. It is all right, now. It was a foolish trick to run against the branch of the tree, and I cannot tell how I came to do it."

"Why, the fact is, captain, you were not pleased with yourself."

"How do you mean?"

"Why, you were trying to run away from yourself, and that was the fact, captain, so you didn't look where you were going; and all I have to say to you is, now, that I beg you will take that little creature of a girl at the hut back to the young fellow as she has set her heart upon, or she will just go out of her mind."

"Oh, heaven!" said Hawk, placing his hand upon his brow, "I recollect now."

"Recollect?"

"Yes, Joe, yes, I had quite forgotten all about her. It shows what a confusion there was made in my brain by the blow I had. But now it all comes back freshly to my mind, and I know all about it quite well. Oh, yes—yes, I know now—Oh, how mad I have been!"

"A little," said Joe.

"Quite mad—quite mad! The idea that I should dream for a moment of dragging that young creature away from joy and repute, to try and make her the wretch she might have been! What can I do to replace her with him who loves her?"

"Well, it's hard to say, captain; but where there is a will there is a way, and you must just turn it over in your mind, you know, and see how it can be done. But come back to the little dear, and wash your face, for you don't look very engaging just now, I can tell you."

"There is blood upon my face, I suppose?"

"Yes, and upon your hands, too."

Captain Hawk turned round fiercely the man.

"How dare you, of all men in this great world, taunt me with that fact? I know that there is blood upon my hands, and innocent blood, too; but you should not take notice of it. There is blood upon my soul, and I shall never get it off again! Never—never!"

Joe looked staggered for a moment or two at the vehemence of Captain Hawk, and then stretching out his hand, he said—

"Captain, you mistake me. If I meant to say such a thing as you speak of, I only wish this hand may drop off me. I didn't dream of such a thing for half a moment. Look at your hand. There is blood upon it, and that was the blood I saw and spoke of. It is your own."

"Yes—yes, it is my own. Let it pass, Joe. I know you did not mean to taunt me. Let it pass."

"All's right, captain, so long as you know what I did mean, and what I didn't. Come back to the kennel, and speak to the young creature that's there. I daresay she is in fright enough now to be left all alone."

"Yes—oh, yes! No doubt she is. I will go to her at once, and assure her of her absolute safety. Come on, Joe—come on."

At the moment they arrived within sight of the hut, they saw four men approach the door of it, and knock. That was the knock that Isabel heard, and to which she made no reply. Captain Hawk and Joe hid among the trees, but still kept themselves in such a position that they could keep an eye upon the door of the hut. They saw the four men knock again, and then, upon finding that they got no reply to that, they held a short consultation together, and then hurried from the spot.

"What does all that mean?" said Joe.

"They are officers, I daresay," said Captain Hawk; "and it is just as well that we have seen them. We can make our way in by the back of the cottage easily. I find that I must have been traced to this place by some means, Joe."

"Ah!" said Joe, "that was when you brought the little bit of a girl with you, no doubt. Somebody has seen you, and given the information to the grabs; but they haven't quite got you yet, captain."

"Nor will they. Come on, and don't jeopardise our common safety by talking too loudly."

"Not I. I considers myself as down as a hammer, and as fly as any lark as never was."

With this luminous remark, Mr. Joe followed Captain Hawk by a roundabout way to the back of the cottage; and then, by dint of scrambling over a neglected little patch of garden ground, they at length got into the little dwelling by a window that Joe opened readily enough from without.

"I will be off at once," said Captain Hawk.

"Oh, no—no! Recollect who is in the neighbourhood."

"Never mind that. I must and will seek the only person who has a right to assume the office of protector to the young girl who is at hand. Better thoughts have come across me, and she shall suffer as little suspense as possible."

"Do you mean to take her away, then, captain?"

"I do. Get my horse ready while I speak to her, and endeavour to make her believe that I can be her friend instead of her enemy."

Joe had no resource but to do as he was directed, although he highly disapproved of what he considered the indiscretion of leaving the hut at such a juncture, when he (Hawk) knew so well that the officers were about, and only waiting to pounce upon him.

There was a special reason, too, why Joe preferred that Captain Hawk should have remained in the hut; and that consisted in the fact that there was a cleverly constructed hiding-place under the flooring of the little room, where he (Captain Hawk) and Joe, too, and half-a-dozen other persons, might have remained in perfect security.

The value of that hiding-place had never yet been tested; but it was so well contrived that there could not be two opinions about its excellence.

Joe knew, however, that if Captain Hawk once made a determination, that it was quite useless to attempt to turn him from his purpose; so he wisely forbore to aggravate him by making the attempt.

Joe was, in his way, quite a philosopher.

If ever Hawk felt a degree of nervous embarrassment that was nearly equal to that which oppressed him when he was brought before Sir John Boyes as a determined criminal, he did now that he was about to come into the presence of the young girl whom he had done so much wrong to, and to whom, but for the intervention of Joe, who had given him time to think, he would have done so much more wrong to.

"Thus feel the guilty," muttered Hawk, "when they are going into the presence of those who alone have the right to judge them."

In another moment he was in the room. Isabel raised a cry of alarm at beholding him, and well she might, for his appearance was ghastly in the extreme. The clotted blood from his wound was smeared over his face, and he looked as though he had risen from the dead upon some field of carnage.

He spoke to her in a low tone.

"Have no fear of me now," he said. "If my deep and sincere repentance for the rash and most unconsidered act that brought you here will avail me in getting your pity and forgiveness, let it. If not, I yet feel that I have what reparation to make I can, and that will consist in freeing you as shortly as possible from all constraint in this place, and in taking you to the arms of him from whom I tore you."

"Oh! can I believe such happy tidings?"

"You can, and may. The wild delirium of passion that made me gallop off with you from your protector has passed away. I can still look upon your beauty with admiration, and yet be just."

"If such be the case," said Isabel, "let the past be as freely forgotten as it will be forgiven."

"Can you really forgive [illegible] h[illegible]

"Ah, indeed, I can. [illegible]o muc[illegible] need we all of us have for forgiveness from one, who, if he could not forgive, might leave us desolate, indeed! Say no more upon that subject. All I ask of you is to redeem your promise, and to take me to him from whom you draged me so short a time ago."

"I will—I will."

"But you are wounded—there is blood upon your face!"

"A mere trifle. I struck my head against a bough of a tree. It is nothing. But I will cleanse myself from such a ghastly witness of injury, as the blood that now covers my features would have to all whom we might meet. Have but a little patience, and I will soon again be with you, and will leave this place at once for any other that you yourself may select."

"Take me to London, then. Any of the officers of the regiment to which he who is to be my husband belongs, will protect me."

"It shall be so. Ah, they come again!"

A violent kicking at the door of the hut now ensued, and soon had the effect of summoning Joe into the room.

"There's a lot of 'em now, captain," said Joe. "I rather think we are in for it this time."

"No—no. Hush!"

Bang! bang! went two heavy blows upon the door, which, if it had been an ordinary one, such as might be expected to belong to such a cottage-like place, would soon have given way; but from time to time Joe had so strengthened it, that it was by no means a bad barricade.

"Oh, captain, your life hangs upon a thread now. Get into the hiding-place, and I daresay the young lady will say nothing at all about it, will you, miss?"

"Oh, no—no!" said Isabel. "If I could do anything to save you I would. But what is it that you fear? Who are these men without, of whom you have a dread?"

"They are the officers of police," said Captain Hawk, coolly; "and as I am a highwayman, they naturally wish to take me into custody, that is all.'

"A highwayman! Why, surely you are not—not———"

"Go on. I am not ashamed of my name."

"You are not Captain Hawk?"

"I am."

"Oh, Heaven! into what dreadful hands have I fallen! Save me—oh, save me! What faith can I put in the word of a man who is stained by such crimes as you have committed?"

"You will see," said Hawk. "I regret that you should think as you speak, and I am sure that you speak as you think; but I cannot help it. Time alone will show what and who I am."

CHAPTER XXVI.

HAWK ESCAPES FROM THE HUT.

Captain Hawk was evidently very much affected at the idea that the young girl felt that she could not trust to his word in consequence of his being the well-known highwayman. It had always been a grand effort upon his part to keep as much as possible his private character free from the reproaches that might be justly heaped upon what he, no doubt, would have called his public career in life.

There was not now, however, much time for reflection, for those who were on the outside of the hut were getting very clamorous for admission, and the door was being battered at a great rate.

Suddenly, then, there was a complete cessation of the violent attack upon the door, and a voice cried—

"Villain! we know that you are here. You were seen to come to this cottage, and I will have you out, if I pull it piecemeal about your ears.

Coward as well as villain—come forth, I say!"

"Oh, 'tis he! 'Tis he!" said Isabel.

"Hush!" said Captain Hawk.—"Tell me calmly who that is who spoke just outside the hut-door?"

"Yes, I will tell you. It is Ensign Chester."

"Ah!"

"Yes; he has followed me here. Let me go to him, and all that you have done will be forgiven; your repentance of the act shall be sufficient. I implore you to let me go to him, and all will be well again."

"I will do so as well," said Captain Hawk, "for I will bring him to you. Unbar the door, Joe."

"Unbar it, captain?"

"Yes, unbar the door, I tell you, while I speak to this young gentleman who is without." Captain Hawk then raised his voice. "Say—is it a gentleman named Chester to whom I address myself?"

"Yes," replied the voice. "My name is Chester. Who is it speaks? If you can give me any news of Isabel, oh, say what else you will, and I will bless you if you tell me she is safe!"

"Come close to the door, and listen."

"I am close to it."

"He will shoot you, sir, through the panel of the door," cried out another voice from without. "You had better come away, sir."

"I care nothing," replied the Ensign, "so that I hear news of Isabel."

Joe had fully obeyed the orders of Captain Hawk, with regard to the unfastening of the door, so that it was now only secured by a little latch, and the slightest touch would suffice to open it. Captain Hawk gave it that touch, and suddenly stretching out his hand, he caught the Ensign by the collar and dragged him into the hut.

"Bar the door again!" he cried. "Bar the door again, Joe!"

"As good as done, captain!" shouted Joe, as he sprang to tho door, and had it fast again in a moment.

The Ensign was so bewildered at this sudden attack that had been made upon his personal liberty, and the extraordinary manner in which he had been dragged into the hut, that for some few moments he could make no resistance, although, probably, the idea that he was about to be murdered was the most prominent one in his mind then.

Captain Hawk took the advantage of his confusion to speak; but he had scarcely opened his lips to do so, before Isabel, with a cry of joy, rushed forward, and flew into her lover's arms.

In their mutual happiness, now, at their meeting, they both forgot that there was any danger, or any probability of danger about them; but with all the fervour of youthful affection, they twined their arms around each other, and Isabel wept convulsively upon the Ensign's breast.

A loud shout from the people without now awakened the Ensign to the facts by which he was surrounded.

"My sword!" he cried. "Where is my sword?"

"Hold!" said Captain Hawk, advancing. "If you had twenty lives, and I chose to take them, they would all be lost to you; but I am not your enemy now—I never was; but you may be mine, doubtless. Here is my heart. Send a bullet into it if you have the means and wish to do so."

"Villain!" cried the Ensign, "what is the meaning of this mummery?"

"It is no mummery. You have a right to revenge upon this occasion, and I will not resist it."

"Oh, cease this altercation," said Isabel. "It is true that a wrong was done, but not an irreparable one, and this man repents that he took me from you. It was done in a moment of thoughtlessness, and when thought came back again, he bitterly repented of it."

"That is true," said Captain Hawk. "Ensign Chester, I here resign to you the fair object of your affections. She is as pure as when you last saw her. In a moment of mad passion, influenced by her beauty, I brought her here; but reflection came to my aid ere it was too late, and I resign her to you again, thanking Heaven that I did so reflect, and that I have been spared the commission of another crime to those which already sit heavily upon my soul."

"Is this so, Isabel?" said the Ensign.

"It is. It is, indeed."

The Ensign was silent, and could only look at Captain Hawk with mingled feelings of dread and dislike, and, perhaps, just a little dash of admiration at the chivalrous manner in which he had sought to atone, as far as he could, for the atrocious abduction of Isabel.

But now the danger of all within the hut became rather imminent, for those without had obtained a reinforcement, and seemed now determined to force the door open at any hazard.

One of the principals spoke in a loud, clear voice.

"Captain Hawk," he said, "we have certain information that you are in this place, and it is our determination to take you dead or alive. You cannot possibly better yourself by any resistance to us. You may cause the effusion of blood, but you must be taken."

"And then I assuredly die!" said Hawk, in a low voice.

"Oh, no—no!" said Isabel, "it is too horrible to think of!"

She glanced at her lover as she spoke, and he seemed for a few moments to be lost in thought; then suddenly looking up, he said—

"Captain Hawk, you have done me a wrong, but it was evidently rather one of impulse than of intention, and so I can and will forgive it. I do not like to see you, criminal as you are, taken prisoner, if I can help it, without seeming to be actually your friend. Is there no means by which you can leave the place now, at once?"

"Yes, if yonder yelping curs were only kept off my track for a few minutes, I could easily find a place of safety."

Such a tremendous knocking at the door of the hut now ensued, that it shook again, and it was quite clear it could not for many minutes resist the efforts that were being made to break it down.

"Let me get at it," cried a voice; "this will do it."

"Ah! that's it!—that's it!" shouted every one else.

Captain Hawk and the Ensign were both a little curious to know what it was that was to do it so easily and rea ily.

Suddenly there came a blow upon the upper panel of the door that sent splinters flying in all directions, and then it became evident that a sledge-hammer was the weapon from which so much was expected, and which, without a doubt, would very soon remove the obstacle of the door.

"Go," said the Ensign to Hawk. "I will speak to these men, and keep them in parley for a few minutes while you escape."

"Will you, indeed, do so generous an act?"

"I will, and freely, too. Go while there is time. A few more such blows as that, and the door will be down."

"It will—it will. Come, Joe."

Bang went the sledge-hammer again, and again the door creaked with the weight of the blow. Captain Hawk saw that there was no time to lose; and after one glance more at the face of Isabel, which he felt would be a face to haunt him with its wondrous beauty while he lived, he rushed from the first room of the cottage, followed closely by Joe.

"Hilloa!" said the Ensign. "Stop that hammering. It's all right."

"What's right?" said half-a-dozen voices at once.

"Don't you know my voice?" added the Ensign.

"It's Mr. Chester," cried one.

"Yes, you are right, and I have found the Lady Isabel. There is no need to knock down the door. Be quiet, and I will open it for you in less time. Have a little patience. It is well secured."

The Ensign was resolved to give Captain Hawk all the time he could to get away; so he affected to find a difficulty in opening the door, which in reality did not exist.

"You had better let us break it down, sir," said one of the men from without. "Here's a blacksmith, who will soon knock it through."

"No—no. I am undoing the bolts. All is right. The door is cased partly with metal on the inside, too; so you would not find it quite so easy. Do not be impatient. It is coming, now."

Poor Isabel sat with her hands clasped, and speechless with terror, looking so pale and wan, that it was evident that the terror and excitement of the last hour had been too much for her, and it would be a wonder if some illness did not succeed that fearful day's proceedings.

The Ensign found that he could procrastinate really no longer, but that he must either open the door himself or allow those who were outside to do so. He preferred the former alternative; and shooting back the last bolt, he raised the latch, and the half-broken door swung back upon its hinges at once.

"Come in," he cried. "There is no danger."

Upon this intimation, which was an exceedingly grateful one to the ears of all who were without, there was quite a rush into the cottage, and then a look of blank disappointment, as nobody but the Ensign and the Lady Isabel were to be seen within.

The general impression evidently had been that the Ensign had Captain Hawk as a prisoner; and to find him not there was quite a grievous disappointment, indeed.

"Why, where's the highwayman?" said one.

"That I cannot tell you," said the Ensign, as with Isabel upon his arm he made his way through the throng of persons to the outside of the hut.

"But wasn't he here, sir?"

"Perhaps he was; you all saw me pulled into the hut?"

"Yes—yes!"

"Well, the first thing I saw when I got in was yonder couch."

"Yes—yes."

"And sitting upon it was the Lady Isabel. After that, I had no eyes for anything else; my first and foremost duty was to protect her, and I have done so. What became of those who were likewise in the place, I really cannot tell you; but it seems that you have frightened them, for they are nowhere to be seen at all."

The officers and their assistants looked at each other as blankly as possible. Of course, they could not say anything to the Ensign in the matter, for he had done all that he came about, namely, rescued Isabel; and it would have been too ridiculous to find fault with him, because he did not neglect doing that, but, on the contrary, took up his time in trying to apprehend a highwayman.

"Then, we are done at last," said the principal officer.

Ensign Chester made no reply to this, but left the cottage, with Isabel upon his arm.

The carriage that long before that would have taken them to London was in the immediate vicinity of the spot, and towards it the young lover conducted the beautiful girl.

"Calm yourself, dear one," he said, "all will be well. 'The course of true love never yet ran smooth,' and we will learn to regard the evils of the day as some of the inevitable accidents attending our true and constant passion."

"Yes—yes!"

She trembled as she spoke.

The carriage was now reached, and then was the postilion aroused somewhat from the state of fright that he had been in when the affray in the lane took place. But as he had been a witness to the manner in which the Lady Isabel had been taken away by Captain Hawk, he had been able to give a relation of that circumstance to the Ensign, and to point out the route that Captain Hawk in his wild gallop had taken.

The Ensign assisted the still trembling girl into the carriage, and then, springing in himself, he cried to the postilion—

"Get on to London, now, as quickly as you possibly can. Time is everything to us, for I have already extended my leave of absence from my regiment."

Off set the postilion at good speed, for he was not at all sorry to get out of a neighbourhood which was so full of dangers to him and to every one with whom he was concerned.

In the meantime, the officers had made a hasty search of the little cottage, and found nothing to warrant them in supposing it to be other than the house of some labourer who, in all probability, they thought was at some distance at work. The conclusion they came to was that Captain Hawk, feeling himself hard pressed, had got into the little dwelling as a temporary place of security, and that he really had nothing further to do with it.

After an inspection of the garden, they saw that a portion of the paling had been torn down, and about that spot the deep indentations of horse's hoofs sufficiently showed that it was there that Captain Hawk had mounted his horse and gone off. After that fact they did not entertain the smallest hope of finding him in the neighbourhood.

Captain Hawk had gone alone. The fact was that Joe was hiding in the immediate vicinity of the cottage until the officers should have left it, and that they were not very long in doing; and when he felt quite satisfied that such was the case, he emerged from the thicket in which he was hidden, and began to whistle a tune.

After indulging himself in this way for some time, Joe shook his head very sagely from side to side, and spoke—

"Well," he said, "I never knew the captain come such a mean trick as this of to-day in all my life. He certainly is an odd chap. Why, a little while ago he was quite a different fellow, but now he seems rather flighty about his upper-works, and don't appear to know what he is going to do next. Ah, well, I suppose I ought to look forward to his coming to some queer end some of these days; but I like the fellow, after all, so I shall be sorry enough when he does."

With this sentiment, which was a genuine one, however strangely it might have been expressed, Joe went cautiously into the cottage again. The fact is, he did not greatly fear the officers, for if they had come back and found him there, he would just have said that the cottage was his, and that he had just come home, and pleaded the most complete ignorance of anything that had recently happened within it.

But the officers were too well satisfied that there was no hope now of laying hands upon Captain Hawk, and in rather a moody frame of mind they turned their horses heads towards London again, wondering when they would have the pleasure of seeing Hawk on the gallows-tree.

CHAPTER XXVII.

CAPTAIN HAWK ROBS TWO TRAVELLERS.

THE keen perceptions of the rather considerable experience of Captain Hawk were quite sufficient to enable him to decide, with some degree of accuracy, regarding his position and its chances. He soon made up his mind that the officers, partly from fear and partly from a firm convictoin that it would be anything but an easy thing to lay hands upon him, had given up the chase, and gone towards London.

Hawk, from that moment, felt that he had a little time to be inactive in, that is to say, to think over his own affairs, which were pretty sure to produce such a feeling.

There was much in the past situation of Hawk to afford such a reckless spirit as his ample food for the most painful reflection; and now that he had time for such an indulgence, he gave it full scope, and the wild and wayward fancies that beset his brain were about enough to topple reason from her seat.

Amid all his thoughts, the image of May Boyes ever was uppermost, and he could almost have persuaded himself hat something like an apparition of her was now ever at his elbow. More than once he started round with her name upon his lips, and a half uttered demand of why she haunted him in such a fashion; and then, with a shudder, he would recollect that he was quite alone.

These were thoughts and surmises that could only be got rid of in the wild activities of such a life that he was in the habit of leading; and so, heedless of all resolves of a contrary tendency—heedless of the state of confusion in which he might leave affairs at the little cottage, and in so desperate a frame of mind that he was ripe and ready for anything, and at a tearing, headlong gallop, he went up the first road that presented itself to him.

"Oh, that some one would only meet me," he said, "and put an end to all these horrors, and kill me at once! That would be the greatest joy of all, and I could, and I would, forgive any ony one my death."

The horse appeared to partake in its actions of the maddened character of its rider, and the tremendous pace at which it went was certainly one that could not be kept up very many minutes. Strange to say, that headlong pace had the effect of soothing down Hawk a little, and producing a more agreeable frame of mind. He now made an effort to pull up and find out where he was. for trees and cottages had flitted past him in his headlong gallop like the confused spectrums of a dream, and he knew not to what part of the country he was speeding.

Suddedly he heard the dash and gurgle of water, and as his horse sped down the declivity he saw a little stream rushing along at good speed in the hollow.

Upon the opposite bank were two

JOE FINDS CAPTAIN HAWK APPARENTLY DEAD, UNDER A TREE.

gentlemen on horseback. They seemed to be regarding the stream with some hesitation, as if they wished to pass it, but rather afraid that the jump was too wide a one for their cattle.

Of course, these two persons could not but both hear and see the approach of Captain Hawk, thundering on, and to their surprise, he and his horse were over the stream in an instant, with a good two feet to spare upon the opposite bank.

The leap was a tremendous one, and it had the effect of sobering the horse a little, so that after a bound or two, that took him some twenty feet from the bank of the stream, he stopped and shook himself a little.

The two gentlemen said something to each other, and then they both came up to Captain Hawk, at a walk, and one of them, in a drawling, affected accent, said :—

"A good horse, sir. Will you sell him?"

"To be sure," cried Hawk.

"Oh, very well—ah! He will sell him, Jobson. Well, what's the figure, eh?"

"What do you think he's worth?"

"Well, ah—really Jobson, what do you think he is worth?"

"A cool hundred, my lord, I should say," replied Jobson, in a very deferential tone.

"Ah, very well," said the decidedly weak-minded individual who was named 'my lord' by his deferential companion, Jobson; "very well, if you say a hundred, let it be so. Will you take that for him?"

"Have you got the money with you?" said Hawk, with a sudden fierceness that quite alarmed his lordship.

"Oh, yes—yes, I have it in my pocket-book."

"Very good, you will want a receipt, and here is one in full of all demands; and by the Heavens above us, I will blow out the small quantity of brains you have out of that stpuid looking skull of yours, if you do not give up your money this instant."

This threat was seconded by a pistol, the long bright barrel of which was so correctly pointed at his lordship's head, that it might well give him a very ugly sensation of alarm.

"Now, my lord, be quick!"

The entreaties of both Jobson and the nobleman, whose humble friend he was, was quite ludicrous. His lordship's face turned almost blue with terror, and Jobson took his hat and held it partially before his face, as though that would be sufficint to save him from the effects of any chance bullet that might come in that direction.

"Oh, oh!" was all his lordship could say.

"Murder!" said Jobson, but he pronounced the word in such a tender and delicate voice, that such a word of such significance was never uttered so before.

"Your money, or your money and your life!" cried Hawk, "which you please. I am in the humour to blow out your brains as soon as look at you, if you have any sort of inclination for the process."

"Oh, gracious, no!"

"Very well; then give up your cash."

"Oh, dear, yes, good Mr. Highwayman, take it all. What is money compared with one's present safety? I'd rather raise twenty thousand pounds from the Jews, at a hundred per cent., than be hurt ever so little."

"Yes, my lord," faltered Jobson.

"That will do," said Hawk, as he took a pocket-book from the trembling hands of his lordship, and at a glance found that it contained bank notes. That is sufficient. I have a very good watch of my own, your lordship, but it is now out of repair. How does yours go?"

"Oh, excellent—that is, I mean—oh, dear!"

"Murder!" whispered Jobson again.

"Your watch, then, if you please, my lord. Thank you. It does look a good one. Are these brilliants round the case real?"

"Yes, they are."

"So much the better. When one takes things of this sort, one likes them to be of the best quality; I should be quite ashamed to take a shabby watch from any one. And now I have the honour of bidding your lordship good-day, and a pleasant ride."

"Murder!" said Jobson.

"What did you say, sir?"

"Oh, nothing, Mr. Highwayman—nothing, I assure you, but thank you—that's all I said, I—I—that is, thank you, sir."

"Very well—go on, now, at once."

"And without my purse and my

watch?" said his lordship. "Oh, it is a joke surely!"

"Your best plan, my lord," said Hawk, "will be for the future, if you can, to consider it as such; but at persent I am afraid, if you and Mr. Jobson do not be off at once, you will find it is no joke."

"Come along, my lord," said Jobson, whose teeth were chattering in his head from fear. "Come along, my lord, if you please. It ain't worth while saying any more to the—the—"

"What?" cried Hawk.

"Gentleman," added Jobson. "I was going to say gentleman, upon my word of honour. How could I say anything else? I have lived too long in polite society to mistake a gentleman when I see him. Good-day, sir, and thank you — good-day, sir, if you please."

It was quite clear that Jobson was in such a state of fright he did not know a bit what he was saying; so he and his lordship rode off.

CHAPTER XXVIII.

CAPTAIN HAWK MEETS WITH A LITTLE ACCIDENT.

HAWK felt a little soothed after perpetrating this daring robbery upon the highway. A glance at the contents of the pocket-book belonging to his lordship showed him that it contained notes to the amount of four hundred pounds, and the largeness of the amount set him thinking a little.

"Now," he said, "I have, if I like to make it, the opportunity of doing what I have often thought of doing, namely, of leaving England at once, and for ever. These notes could be very well changed on the continent, but it may be dangerous to try to convert them into gold here. I could go to Paris at once; but can I leave you, May Boyes?—Ah, no! My heart still clings to you, although I feel that there is such a barrier between us as you dare not, and I cannot leap. No—no! I cannot leave the country which is your home, unless I take you with me. Is that impossible?"

This was a new idea to Captain Hawk, and it set him thinking of its very remote possibility. He told himself that, if he could get together about a thousand pounds, there would be no difficulty in living in the south of France with perfect ease for the remainder of their lives, provided he could induce May to go with him.

"What has she to lose by so doing?" he said. "Her father she cannot even respect, much less love.' Captain Hawk did not seem to know that it was very possible to love without much respect. "There, then, is the rest of the family—Ratchley, with his violent temper, and the cold sisters. No, May has nothing to lose by bidding adieu to them; and what, then, has she to gain by attaching herself to me? Everything, for does she not love me?"

Hawk smiled as he uttered these last words. They were specially pleasing to his vanity. That he should be loved by such a creature as May Boyes, despite her knowledge now of what he was, constituted the most flattering incense that could be offered to his heart.

"Yes," he added, "she does love me. She loves me as she will never love another; therefore, with no one can she ever be so happy as with me; and if I could only work upon her feelings sufficiently to induce her to take the step of leaving her home with me, all would be well."

Well enough for him, Captain Hawk, it might be, but would it be well for the young girl who, by such a step, would, for the wayward and fickle affection of such a man, barter friends, fame, and all that she ought to hold most dear as the sacred possessions which never can be torn from any one, but by their own indiscretions? Alas! no.

Captain Hawk was so pleased with this picture of the future that he drew, that it quite got him over the state of mind he had been in, and he thought of going back to the cottage where his comrade and servant, for he deemed him both, would be, no doubt, glad to see him.

"Yes," he said. "I will go there, and hide the money that chance has thrown into my possession. I will now make a point of adding to it as much as possible; and as soon as there is a sufficient sum, I will seek May Boyes and tell her, that with me in another land she may be very happy. I will tell her that not only will she have the delight of being with the person who was her first love, but that she will have the additional satisfaction of effectually withdrawing me from a line of life she cannot but look upon with horror and alarm. That argument will speak trumpet-tongued to her. Oh, she will consent."

Hitherto Captain Hawk had certainly not been a saving character. In fact, he had, with the greatest recklessness, squandered right and left all that he acquired during the practice of his nefarious profession, and he had always gone upon the principle of merely supplying his wants by his robberies on the highway. If he had his pockets well filled, the most lonely traveller upon the most lonely bit of road was perfectly safe from him; but if his purse happened to empty, then he was ready to commit the most daring acts for the purpose of filling it again. Now, however, he made up his mind that the case should be different, and that he would not stop in his career until he had possessed himself of the amount of money that he thought would suffice to carry him and May Boyes to a secure retreat on the continent.

Full of this idea, he set spurs to his horse again, and at a gallop—although not such a pace as he had gone at before—he went on with the hope of meeting some one who would tell him what road he was upon—for it was an unknown one to him.

That the little river he had crossed was the Brent he felt assured, because there was no other stream of such appearance in the neighbourhood; so that he knew he was somewhere between Hounslow Heath and Southall; but as he had got into a bye-road, it rather puzzled him.

"Hilloa!" he said to a country lad whom he met, "where does this road lead to, my lad?"

"Right on," said the boy.

"Yes, I know that; but where does right on go to?"

"Why, to the river, to be sure. Every fool knows that."

Captain Hawk made a slash at him with his riding-whip; but the boy set off at a good pace, and reaching the bank of the same stream which Duval had jumped over before, although not near that place, he dexterously crossed it by some stepping-stones, and when he got to the opposite side, he grinned defiance at Captain Hawk.

"Ah!" he said, "you'll find it ain't quite so easy to get over this, old feller. If you try to come over without the horse, I'll pelt him, and he'll run away; and if you try to come over with him, souse you will go into the water. How do you feel now, stupid—eh?"

To say that Captain Hawk was positively angry at the lad for his impertinence would be, perhaps, saying too much. Perhaps he was rather amused than otherwise; and yet he felt that he ought to correct him for it. He thought that the horse which had jumped over the Brent once that day, would do it again; and so, without a word to the boy, Captain Hawk turned from the stream for the purpose of giving the animal the advantage of a gallop before his jump.

Crack! came a stone against Captain Hawk's hat.

"You rascal," he muttered between his teeth, for he knew the boy had cast it at him—"I'll soon give you a lash of my whip."

About a hundred feet from the side of the little brawling stream, Captain Hawk turned his horse's head towards it again, and put him at it for the leap. The boy looked frightened, and the horse rushed forward gallantly; but he was fatigued with the hard work he had had so short a time before, and although he took the leap as well as he could, he failed at it.

The fore-feet of the creature only touched the opposite bank, and in another moment he fell backwards right into the stream, carrying Captain Hawk with him.

"Hoora!" said the boy. "Blest if I didn't think that was just what he'd go for to do."

By great good luck—or certainly there would have been an end of his career there and then—Captain Hawk got his feet out of the stirrups, and slipping off the horse's back got clear of it, and began to swim for his life. The horse, too, took to the same process, and went down the stream, quietly, the way of the current, snorting and looking right and left for a secure landing-place. Captain Hawk swam right across, and laid hold of some weeds on the bank; but they came away in his hand, and over head and ears he went backwards into the water again.

"There he goes again," said the boy. "Hilloa! Never say die, old feller. Try it again. Lor bless you, our old cow can swim a deal better nor you."

The mud at the bottom of the stream was thick, and it held Captain Hawk there by its tenacity for the space of time during which you might count twelve slowly. That was nearly sufficient to kill him, and when he rose to the surface again, he was really in a dreadful state of exhaustion.

"Help!" he cried.

Then he fancied he saw a mob of people on the banks of the stream; and he thought he heard voices and cries; and then he thought something caught him by the hair of his head; but after that he knew nothing. It seemed to him as if the world had suddenly slid away from him, leaving him swinging to and fro in space.

CHAPTER XXIX.

CAPTAIN HAWK FINDS HIMSELF IN GOOD QUARTERS.

How long a time elapsed before Captain Hawk opened his eyes to the world, was to him a complete mystery. Suffice it to say, that he did open them at last, and then quickly enough shut them again. It was a natural instinct that made him open them, and it was a glare of light that made him shut them.

How very ill he felt! What a throbbing there was in his brain! and what a deadly feeling of sickness at his stomach! The light that had glared so upon his weakened sight was an artificial one, and he much wondered how it came to be in his way, for as yet he had not sufficiently recovered his senses to be fully alive to what was happening, or to what had happened.

This state of mental oblivion, though, was sure not to last very long; and as he lay upon his back, there gradually came to him a recollection of the past, together with some perception of the present.

The intense stillness around him was very favourable to reflection and to the complete recovery of his faculties; so that in a very little time he was able to reason with tolerable clearness and memory regarding things in general, and his own fate in particular.

"What is the meaning of all this?" he said. "Let me consider: I tried to leap a little river, aggravated as I very foolishly allowed myself to be by the vulgar insolence and stupid wit of a boy, and the horse leaped short and in I went—Yes, I recollect that well enough."

It was rather a mortification to recollect that so well; but there the memory halted and refused to aid him any further, except with s confused kind of remembrance of fighting with the water, and trying to scramble up a bank, which only gave way as he attempted to grasp it.

"No," he thought after in vain trying to connect the fall into the water with his present condition in some way. "No, I remember clearly nothing further; so I must just put up with that hiatus in my life, and begin to think of where I am."

With this view, it was tolerably evident that the use of his eyes were of very great importance, so he opened them again.

The glare of artificial light came upon them as he did so, but by this time Captain Hawk was a little stronger, and by dint of perseverance, he first succeeded in keeping one eye open and then both, so that he was able to look about him tolerably well.

The apartment in which he found himself deserves some sort of description.

Imagine a room about twenty feet square, with a handsome bedstead nearly in the centre of it—with rich hangings at the windows—with a costly carpet on the floor—with the walls hung with looking-glasses and pictures, of very great worth, and you will have an idea of the chamber in which Captain

Hawk, to his intense surprise, found himself.

"Is this a dream?" he said.

As he spoke, he raised himself upon his elbow, and looked about him.

"It's all real. Here I am, in a very luxurious sort of bed, and upon that chair lies my clothes, and there is my hat and feather, too—ah, and upon that table, I see, are my pistols, my two watches, and everything else that I had in my pockets. This must be surely enchantment."

Captain Hawk felt so puzzled that he thought the best way would be to lay down again and try to think a little, for he felt quite assured in his own mind that there must be some portion of his recent history that would sufficiently explain all that was at that present time so mysterious, but which for the minute had escaped his observation and recollection.

"What can it be?" he said; "that is the question. Where am I? Ah, that is what I should like to be able to answer; but this place is as strange and as wonderful to me as Aladdin's Palace would be to me, or was to him, or to the worthy old file his father-in-law, when he woke up in the morning and for the first time saw its golden fruits. Hilloa!"

The exclamation with which Captain Hawk concluded his reflections about Aladdin, was from the fact of hearing a door suddenly open and shut, and a footstep in the room.

"How is he now?" said a voice.

Captain Hawk thought the best way of getting some information to start with would be by listening, and the best way of listening would be to feign a continuance of the state of insensibility, from the which he had in truth fully and completely emerged.

"He don't seem any better, sir," said another voice.

"That is odd," said the first speaker. "Perhaps it would be as well to let the marquis knew."

"I think it would, sir, for Doctor Pogsworth can be sent for again, then, although he did say that he would be all right again, and that there was nothing serious the matter."

"Yes, but Doctor Pogsworth likewise said that he would recover before now."

"So he did, sir."

"And such is not the case, so that it is, in fact, incumbent upon us to go to the marquis with the intelligence. How very still he is."

"Very, sir."

"He—he ain't——"

"Ain't what, sir?—lor, sir, how you frighten me!"

"He ain't dead, Samuel, think you?"

"Dead, sir? goodness gracious, I did not think of that. I wouldn't have him dead on any account."

"You are very feeling, Samuel, for the gentleman is a perfect stranger to you, and yet you are so solicitous about his life."

"Oh, dear, yes, sir; but it's myself I am thinking of, not of him at all."

"How do you mean, Samuel?"

"Why, sir, I can't abide the idea of having a dead body in the house. I'm rather given to what some folks call *surreptitious*."

"What?"

"Surreptitious, sir."

"Good gracious, Samuel, how you do mispronounce words! You mean superstitious, I suppose?"

"Very likely I do, sir; but I can't be expected, being only a footman, to be so learned in long names as you, sir, who is the marquis's secretary."

"So," thought Captain Hawk, "I now know something, at all events. This is the house of a marquis, who keeps a private secretary."

"Well, Samuel," said the secretary, "I quite agree with you there, that it is absurd upon my part to expect you to know things concerning which your station in life prevents you from learning information; but as regards this gentleman, I shall now go and inform my lord that I think it a very serious case, and one that ought to have some medical advice directly."

"Do so, sir. I'm sure it don't look well, as a body may say, in a way of speaking, to see any Christian be so long without once moving hand or foot, do it sir?"

"Certainly not. You will remain here, Samuel, while I go and inform the marquis of the fact."

"Me, sir?"

"Yes, and why not? Are you afraid,

Samuel? Let it never be said that you are afraid."

"Oh, no, sir, I ain't afraid—I'm only a little bit scared out of my courage, that be all, sir. No, not afraid; that wouldn't do, would it?"

"Certainly not, Samuel; and allow me to remark, to you that the very b st way of recovering your courage again, will be to stay where you are, and give your imagination full play. Picture to yourself as many horrors as you can, Samuel, and then you will accustom your mind to such a species of excitement, and in time you will think nothing of it."

"Eh?"

"Oh, I see—I see——"

"You see what, sir? Oh, lor! I do hope you don't see anything as a Christian man ought to be afraid of? Where do you see it, sir?"

"My good fellow, I merely wanted to observe, that I perceived the language in which I addressed you was much too elegant and refined for your simple comprehension, that was all; so you need not be in the least alarmed."

"Oh, thank you, sir."

"Not in the least. Stay where you are, and I will go to the marquis, who is in the blue drawing-room with the marchioness and the young ladies."

Captain Hawk thought that now he had obtained all the information that he was likely to get without positively asking questions, so he considered that now his best plan would be to give some indications of returning consciousness, so as, at all events, to stop the doctor from being sent for again. He made a low groan, and moved one of his feet.

"Oh, lor! he's a-coming-to!" cried Samuel.

"Is he? Are you sure, Samuel?"

"Yes, sir; he's gived a groan, and a kick, and that's the sort o' symptomatics, sir, of his coming to, I take it."

"So they are—so they are!—Hem! Speak to him, Samuel, and let us find out, if we can, if the gentleman is exactly in his right mind, for if he is not, I shall rather decline staying in the room with him."

"Oh, don't you go, sir—don't you go."

"Speak to him, I say."

"Yes, sir; but don't you go and leave a poor fellow like me alone with him, if he isn't in his right mind. Please, sir, how be's you now?"

"Better," said Captain Hawk, in the mildest and most honied tones he could assume. "Better, thank you. But I am much surprised to find myself here. Pray, where am I?"

"Oh, it's all right," said Samuel. "He's as mild as fresh butter, sir. He speaks quite soft, like curds and whey, sir."

"So I hear, Samuel," said the secretary, advancing; "but, of course, it would have been all the same to me; and whatever state this unfortunate gentlman had been in, I should still have felt it to be my duty to do all in my power for his welfare, and his comfort. Pray, sir, how do you do?"

"I am getting better each moment, thank you," said Captain Hawk. "Pray, sir, can you, and will you tell me where I am?"

"Certainly, sir; you are in Pembroke Lodge, a country seat of the most noble the Marquis of Pembroke."

"And where is this country seat situated?"

"Within one mile of old Brentford."

"Oh!"

"And permit me to add, sir, that you will receive every attention here, by order of the marquis himself, who very much commiserates your situation, indeed, and will omit no means of ameliorating it."

"I have some confused recollection of falling into the Brent."

"You may consider that confused recollection, sir, to be quite positive," said the secretary, with great pomposity of manner and tone; "for the fact is, sir, you did fall into the Brent in trying to jump your horse across it; and as the Marquis of Pembroke, with his lady, the marchioness, and the Honourable Georgiana Augusta Olive Fokes, was in the carriage, and saw the accident, they had you pulled out by the hair of your head, and brought here; and that is the whole story."

"And who is the lady named Fokes?"

"Oh, sir, that is the marquis's daughter, aged sixteen exactly. Fokes is the family name, you see, sir."

"Oh, yes—yes, certainly. I am

much better. Will you give my compliments to the marquis. and say that Colonel Luck is much obliged to him?"

CHAPTER XXX.

CAPTAIN HAWK MEETS WITH A DISAGREEABLE SUSPRISE.

Captain Hawk had felt the necessity of immediately adopting some name, for that he would be asked who he was, either by master or by man, was a matter of certainty. The name of Captain Hawk was, of course, quite out of the question; and since the proceedings with the Boyes family, the other name of Gerald Clifton had become unfortunately notorious; so that upon the spur of the moment he called himself by the rather singular name of Luck, and added the military rank of colonel to it.

At that time, Europe was so overrun with military adventurers of all sorts, that any one might call himself captain, or colonel, or even general, without being much questioned upon the subject; and if he were questioned, all he had to assert was, that it was in the Austrian or the Prussian service, and the questioner was effectually silenced.

"I shall, sir, have positive pleasure," said the secretary, "in carrying to the marquis you kind message; and I feel sure that it will be quite delightful to that nobleman to receive the assurance of your bodily welfare. I, therefore, now, sir, very respectfully take my leave of you."

With these rather profound words, the secretary left the room, and Captain Hawk was alone with Samuel, who, finding what a soft-spoken, highly rational person the stranger was, had no disinclination to remain with him, the more particularly as he thought there would be a good chance of getting some very handsome present for his services.

"I am afraid I have given a deal of trouble to this amiable family," said Gaptain Hawk to Samuel.

"Yes, sir, a deal of trouble."

"Indeed?"

"Oh, yes, sir; and much of it has fell upon me, sir; but I said to myself, says I, 'It's as clear as mud, that the gentleman is a gentleman; and such being the case, as soon as he gets all right again, he will remember you, Samuel.'"

"You are quite right, Samuel. Those are my clothes, I believe, there?"

"Yes, sir, they is. We have dried 'em all nicely, by putting them in the oven in a large dish; and there are all the things that were in your pockets, sir, if you please. The secretary, sir, took an *involuntary* of 'em, sir."

"An inventory, I suppose you mean, Samuel?"

"Yes, sir, that's it. Lor! bless you, sir, it's words with no end of *syllabies* as bothers me, you see, sir."

"Not a doubt of it. I see that my purse is upon the table there; so you will oblige me by handing it to me."

"With all the pleasure in life, sir. There it is, sir, and I hope it will be always full, sir, for a gentleman as is a gentleman, and knows what to do with his money, ought to have plenty to do it with."

"That's a capital toast, Samuel; so here are five guineas for you, and I have great pleasure in handing them to so deserving a person."

"Oh, sir—oh, colonel!"

"Nay, I want no thanks. It is I who still feel myself the debtor of every one in the house; so now, as I really am pretty well again, after my ducking in the Brent, I will get up and thank the marquis in person for his great kindness to me. Hand me my clothes, Samuel. Thank you—that will do."

With the charateristic speed that was quite a portion of Captain Hawk's conduct, he soon dressed himself; and as he was putting his hair in order, he told Samuel to go to the marquis, and say that he was up and dressed, and, if he had no objection, would wait upon him at once, to thank him for the kindly service he had done him.

Captain Hawk did not feel much the worse for his submersion in the little river; but he was rather anxious to get away from the house, for while he was there he not only felt that he was losing time, but, likewise, that he ran some risks of an awkward rencontre with some one who might know him.

Captain Hawk did not think that such a rencontre was so soon to happen as it did.

"I will go, sir, at once, and tell John to tell William to tell the secretary to tell the marquis just what you say, sir."

"Do so."

Samuel left the room, and Captain Hawk hastily completed his toilet.

CAPTAIN HAWK STOPS LORD RHOLEY AND MR. JOBSON

"I must leave this house," he said, "with all convenient expedition. Confound the malapropos adventure that has brought me into it! I will but thank my noble host for his kindness, and then be off. Ah, my horse! I forgot him completely. How very unwise of me not to ask that fellow, Samuel, who was here just now, about the creature. I hope it got safely to land. If it be lost, it is, in good truth, a most cruel loss to me."

Captain Hawk had just secured all his valuables, including the pocket-book and the watch th he had so recently taken from Lord somebody on the highway, in his pocket, when the door of the apartment was tapped at by some one.

"Come in," said Captain Hawk, who did not doubt but that it was either the secretary or Samuel come back again. The door was opened, and a voice said—

"I hear that you are better, sir; and as my friend, the marquis, is rather busy just now with his letters, I have just stepped up to congratulate you."

"The devil!" said Captain Hawk.

"Murder!" said the visitor.

Hawk, with one bound, reached the door of the room, and seizing the visitor by the collar with one hand, he dragged him in, and with the other he closed the door and locked it.

"Not a word—not the least cry of alarm, upon your life," he said.

The visitor was no other than the very person whom he had so recently robbed of the purse containing the notes upon the highway.

"Oh, gracious! How came you here?—that is to say, how came I here —no, I mean—how—oh, dear—oh, dear!"

"Silence, my lord—another word, and——"

"Oh—oh—oh!"

"You will speak, then? You are weary of your life, and will throw it away life a fool, for the mere love of hearing your own stupid voice?"

"Oh—oh, no—no!"

"Silence, my lord, and listen to me!"

"Yes—yes—yes!"

"You are in great danger."

"So I should say!"

"Hush! don't interrupt me while I tell you how you may easily escape it. I am here by accident, and I am quite willing and ready to go away again, as soon as I can. There is a gang of exactly twenty-four of us, bound together by the most frightful oaths, to avenge each other's wrongs, so that if through your instrumentality I am apprehended, you will have no less than twenty-three men all intent upon some mode of murdering you, at theearliest possible opportunity."

"Mercy!"

"Hush! But if, on the contrary, you keep locked up as a perfect secret in your own breast what has taken place upon the road betwen you and me, all will be well, and I shall never in any way again revert to the circumstance, and you will be as safe as any one possibly can be. Do you understand me?"

"Yes, I do."

"Then, what is your answer?"

"Answer? Do you think I am an ass?"

"Oh, dear no. Quite the reverse."

"Of course, I shall say nothing about it; and I only hope you will be as good as your word, and be off as speedily as possible."

"That I will do. You know sufficient of the affair that brought me here to be perfectly aware that it was quite an involuntary intrusion upon my part, so that you must not for one moment imagine that by your silence concerning who and what I am you are in any way aiding and abetting me in any scheme. I assure you that I have but one wish regarding this house and its noble owner, and that is, to get out of it as quickly as possible. I hope, therefore, my lord, that we fully understand each other?"

"Yes—yes; of course we do."

"What is your title, my lord? I only thought that you were a lord, but I did not hear your friend Jobson give you any other name. It will be better that I should know it."

"Oh, yes. I am Lord Rholey."

"Lord Rholey? Very well. Now, can your lordship tell me what became of my horse?"

"No, I know nothing about it at all. I only came here after the whole affair, or else I should have seen you, I dare say. I knew you at once as the—the gentleman who stopped me on the highway."

"Call me the highwayman at once, my lord. I am not very particular upon such matters, and if you keep faith with me, I will keep faith with you."

"There is one little thing—"

"What is it, my lord? If in any

way I can oblige you, it will give me great pleasure."

"It is my watch. I should very much like that back again."

"You shall have it before I leave; nay, you shall have your pocket-book back likewise, for I have no right to rob you and then count upon your patience towards me. We will part as clear of each other, my lord, as we met."

"Oh, hang the money! I don't care a straw about that. You may keep that, and welcome; but the watch was a present from my sister."

"And who is you sister?"

"The Marchioness of Pembroke."

"Oh, indeed. Well, my lord, you are generous; and all that I can say is, that I am grateful to you for being so. It may be even in my power some day to do you a good turn: and if it should, I will not scruple to do it, though it be nigh to cost me my life."

"Oh, don't mention that. The fact is, I have a very good income, and so I ain't such a fool as to run into any danger if I can help it, I can assure you. It's all very well for a man who has nothing to be thrusting his stupid head into scrapes; but when a fellow has four thousand a-year, the least thing he can do is to take care of himself."

"You are quite a philosopher, my lord."

At this moment there came a tap at the chamber-door, and Captain Hawk opened it at once, and allowed Samuel to enter.

"Please, sir," he said, "master will be glad to see you in the blue drawing-room."

"I shall attend him with pleasure."

Captain Hawk and Lord Rholey bowed to each other at the door of the room.

"After you, Lord Rholey."

"Nay, colonel, after you, if you please," said Lord Rholey. "After you, Colonel Luck. I always think that military men ought to be given a certain degree of precedence."

"You are too good, my lord."

"Well," said Samuel, "by gosh, it's a fine thing to see gentlefolks bowing away at such a rate to each other. I haven't been long in the family, but it's good wages, and lots to eat and drink; and as for that colonel, who has given me five guineas, I means for to go for to say as he is the king of trumps, and no mistake in life."

Captain Hawk and Lord Rholey went together to the blue drawing-room of the Marquis of Pembroke in the most amicable manner in the world; and one would have thought that they were quite old acquaintances, and had the most remarkable respect for each other, instead of standing in the comical kind of relation they did to one another.

A couple of footmen were upon the landing at the door of the drawing-room, and they flung open the door for Captain Hawk and his lordship; and in another moment Hawk found himself in the blaze of light of a gorgeous drawing-room, in which were several ladies and gentlemen.

CHAPTER XXXI.

HAWK RATHER ASTONISHES MR. JOBSON.

There was quite a sensation in the drawing-room when Captain Hawk appeared with Lord Rholey. The reader is already aware, that for personal appearance, Hawk stood unrivalled; and the handsomest man of his day, walking into a well-lighted apartment, even although he may not be dressed exactly in the costume he would have chosen for such an occasion, was sure to produce some effect among the ladies.

"Allow me," said Lord Rholey, but he made rather an odd face over it. "Allow me to be the medium of introducing Colonel Luck—hem!"

Hawk bowed.

"This is the gentleman who fell into the Brent, if I mistake not," said the Marquis of Pembroke, advancing.

"The same," said Lord Rholey.

There was a slight titter among the young ladies at this, which brought a crimson flush to the brow of Captain Hawk, for there was nothing in all the world he was so keenly alive to as ridicule, and especially when it came from young ladies. Looking up, he cast a glace around him, as he said—

"Yes, I am the man whose horse

threw him into the Brent; but I rejoice very much now at the circumstance, as it affords some amusement to those whose most trifling pleasures I would die to procure."

The young ladies were all serious in a moment, and the Marquis of Pembroke, with a smile, said—

"Come—come, Colonel Luck, never mind what they say, or how much they laugh. You have the best of the joke, you know; for although you did fall into the Brent, you got out again, and here you are, without any injury, I hope."

"Thanks to the kindness of all in this house, I am not the least the worse from the affair, my lord."

There was a young lady in the room who wascompelled to hide her cherry lips with a bouquet of flowers to conceal her laughter; but, oh! how her eyes laughed.

Captain Hawk made his way to the part of the room where she was sitting, and took a seat by her, which did not seem to displease her in the least.

"You heard of my visit to the bottom of the Brent?" he said.

"Oh, I saw it. It was truly——"

"Ridiculous?"

"Well, it was a little."

"I thought you were there," added Hawk, "for something dazzled my eyes, or I do think I should not have fallen. It must have been your eyes on the opposite bank that, like two stars, startled the horse."

"Oh, no!"

"Oh, yes. I never saw their equals. You are very—very beautiful."

Of course, Captain Hawk took good care that no one else heard a word of this confabulation that he was having with the young lady all to himself. The fact was, that the parties in the drawing-room had broken up into little groups, so that no attention was paid to what Hawk was about; and although in the line of life in which the young lady with the bright eyes moved, it was something new for a stranger after five minutes' acquaintance, if it might be called so much, to tell her boldly that she was very, very beautiful—still it was one of those offences which a young lady is exceedingly apt to forgive, indeed, and the more especially so, if she thought nobody heard it but herself.

"Really, sir," she said, "I do not understand you."

"Can that be possible?"

"What did you presume to say?"

"That you were very, very beautiful indeed; and if your glass does not tell you as much every time you glance into it, it is a false mirror, I shall never see a face that I can call so truly lovely—so enchantingly youthful in the very bloom of its exquisite fascination, as yours."

This was getting on at a good rate!

"Oh, you don't believe what you say," said the young lady, who was all of a flutter at the extravagant compliments Captain Hawk paid to her, "I am sure you don't believe one word you say; and this little badinage is just out of revenge for my laughing at your falling into the Brent."

"Oh, no, no!"

"Confess, now, like a good man—confess that such is the case, and that you think me very plain."

"Impossible! The only thing that is quite plain is, that you are quite lovely. That is so plain, that it is like saying it is daylight when the sun is shining upon us."

"Ah, you are one of those general lovers, or rather, I should say, general flatterers of whom there are so many in the world, and who never really love."

Hawk smiled slightly, for he had said nothing at all about love: that was the young lady's idea solely.

"You do me a great injustice," he said.

"Nay, look about you; there are other young ladies in this apartment, and I make no doubt but that you would just say the same to them that you have said to me, if by chance you were sitting next to them."

"Oh, no, no!"

"But I say, oh yes. I can tell in a moment what you are; you are, in fact, one of those butterflies of men, who fancy that the last flower they see is ever the fairest and the most worth the winning. Look at the other ladies, sir."

"Yes, I am willing enough to look

at the stars when the light and beautiful moon is not shining."

"Oh, but you compared my eyes to stars just now."

"Oh, but you objected to that, so I began upon the moon."

The young lady shook her head, and her pretty lips were just opening again to say something, no doubt, very serious indeed to Captain Hawk, when a gentleman came up to them, and in a mighty civil voice said—

"Sir, I congratulate you upon your narrow escape from what might have been a very dangerous fall indeed. I was not there, but I heard that your horse left you in the Brent. Now, sir, the Brent is a river."

"That, no doubt, continually flows into the sea," said Captain Hawk. "I am very much obliged to you, sir, indeed."

"Why—why! Hilloa! Bless me!"

Upon heaing these exclamations, Hawk looked more earnestly at the gentleman, and then he saw that it was the satellite of Lord Rholey, the humble friend who flattered and attended upon his lordship. Hawk made up his mind in a moment to face it out, and looking Mr. Jobson full in the face, he said—

"Well, sir?"

"Why—I—that is—oh, it must be!"

"What, sir?"

"What do you mean, Mr. Jobson?" said the young lady: "really, sir, this conduct is, to say the least of it, rather rude. What do you mean, sir, by it?"

"Ah, what do you mean?" added Captain Hawk. "As this young lady says, and says with perfect truth, your conduct is contemptible and absurd!"

"I am staggered!" said Jobson.

"Very well, sir; fall down, then, for all I care."

"Oh, go away altogether, and leave the house," said the young lady. "You are very rude, Mr. Jobson. This gentleman, Colonel Luck, is just telling me a little anecdote about—about—"

"The deserts of Central Africa," said Hawk.

"Yes, exactly; and here you come interfering and intruding, Mr. Jobson. in the most extraordinary and remarkr able way. I am surprised at you, sir, fo you, at least, used to have the worthy nature of being quiet and only speaking when you were spoken to."

Poor Jobson staggered under the weight of all these reproaches; but so certain was he of the identity of Hawk with the man who had robbed Lord Rholey on the highway, when in his company, that he did the boldest thing he ever adventured in his life—a thing which, had it been successful at the moment, would have set him up as a man of the greatest nerve and resolution in all time to come. Suddenly facing about, he called out in a loud tone—

"Thieves! thieves! A highwayman! a highwayman, my Lord Pembroke!—a highwayman, ladies and gentlemen! I can identify him, and so can Lord Rholey! This man is a highwayman, and one of the most daring that ever I heard of in all my life; and as true as I now stand here, I——Murder!"

In the irritation of the moment, Hawk could not control himself, but lifting up his foot, he gave Mr. Jobson such a kick behind, that he sent him sprawling to the floor, when the first thing he caught hold of was the ankle of rather a corpulent old lady, who immediately fell on top of him, shrieking.

All this, although it took place in the short period of half a minute at the utmost, created a confusion in the room of the greatest character. The ladies screamed, and the gentlemen swore, and when Jobson was lifted up, he pointed at Captain Hawk, and cried—

"That's the fellow!—That's the highwayman!—That's the thief!—Hold him tight!—He will rob and murder everybody in the house!—He is no more a colonel than I am!—He is a highwayman, and robbed Lord Rholey early this morning, that he did!—Where is Lord Rholey to identify him?"

"I am here!" said Lord Rholey.

"Well, my lord, look at that villain."

"What villain?"

"There, my lord. That vagabond who calls himself Colonel Luck. Look at him well. Don't you recognise him, my lord?"

"Yes."

"I told you so—I told you so! Oh, we have him at last!"

"I recognise him as the gentleman who fell into the Brent, owing to the fault of his horse in not taking the leap so clearly as it might. I believe it is the same gentleman?"

"The same, my lord," said Hawk.

"Well, but, my lord," cried Jobson, "don't you recognise him as the highwayman who robbed your lordship this morning on the road?"

"Oh, dear no!"

Upon this there was quite a sensation. Jobson, with his mouth open, and his eyes goggling much wider than usual, stared at Lord Rholey and then at Captain Hawk, and Lord Pembroke and his guests looked on with amazement.

"Shame!" said some. "This is too bad."

"But, my lord," added Jobson, "my dear Lord Rholey, look at him again: I say he is the man. Don't you know him, my lord? Oh, do look at him and recognise him at once."

"Oh, dear no!"

"What, my lord! do you mean to say that this is not the highwayman who robbed us this morning upon the road?"

"My answer to that," said Lord Rholey, "is, that it is quite news to me that I have been robbed at all."

Upon this there was a great cry of execration at poor Jobson, who looked then as if he were going out of his wits. He rubbed his eyes several times, and looked all round the room, and then he said—

"Will anybody pinch me to convince me that I am awake?"

"With pleasure," said Hawk, and he seized Jobson by the nose, and gave it such an awful nip, that the unfortunate man roared again, to the intense delight and amusement of everybody in the room except himself.

"Now are you wide awake?" said Captain Hawk.

"Oh—oh—my—my——Oh, dear—oh, dear! I must be going out of my mind, for I assure you, ladies and gentlemen, that my impression is, that Lord Rholey and myself were stopped this morning by a highwayman upon the high road, and his lordship was robbed, and this is the very man."

"Quite mad," said Hawk.

"Oh, quite — quite," said Lord Rholey. "I fancy, poor fellow, he is going to be very ill. Brain fever, perhaps."

"Something like it," said Captain Hawk. "You may depend upon it, ladies and gentlemen, you are taking about your last look at poor Jobson. He is changing colour even now."

"Oh, no—no!" cried Jobson. "I know I am right. I won't be argued out of my senses. You are the highwayman, and Lord Rholey was robbed! I know it—I was there—I saw it—I heard it—I—I—will swear it!"

"Is it at all likely," said Captain Hawk, "that Lord Rholey, accompanied by Mr. Jobson, would both allow themselves to be robbed by a single highwayman? I put it to all the company if that be probable."

"Oh, no, no, no!"

"Poor Jobson! I think he had better be sent off to bed at once," said the marquis, "and we will send to Brentford for a medical man to attend upon him, poor fellow! He does look very bad."

Jobson shook again, and for once in his life, in spite of his patience, he got into a passion.

"Say what you like all of you," he said. "I have my opinion, and I will keep it. I am neither mad nor ill; but as the general opinion is against me, why, I will say no more about it, of course. I yield to you, Lord Rholey, and to your superior judgment in this affair."

"It don't require any judgment," said Lord Rholey. "It is a matter of fact. But as Mr. Jobson gives it up, I hope Colonel Luck will think no more about it, but let it pass over as a harmless hallucination."

"Oh, certainly," said Hawk.

"Then we will let it drop, gentlemen," said the marquis, "and we can only hope that Mr. Jobson will not commit himself again in such a manner."

Everybody looked daggers at poor Jobson, who yet felt in his own breast that he was right, and that it was only the fears of Lord Rholey that kept him quiet. Had his lordship not denied the fact of the robbery taking place altogether, he, Jobson, might have thought himself liable to a mistake in the identity of the robber; but that at ance convinced him the affair was just so he in his own mind thought it.

CHAPTER XXXII.

CAPTAIN HAWK FINDS A REFUGE FROM DANGER.

HAWK was very much amused, indeed, at the scene that had taken place with poor Jobson, pregnant as it was with peril to him. It was so truly ludicrous to see that person almost persuaded out of his own senses; but as it was, Hawk thought the danger was over. In that idea, though, he was mistaken, as the events of the next few hours sufficiently proved.

Of course, Captain Hawk had no desire to remain one moment longer at the Marquis of Pembroke's than necessary, and he was just debating in his own mind how in the most handsome manner he could take his leave, when a gentleman came up to him, and offering his snuff-box, said—

"Do you do anything in this way, Colonel Luck?"

"At times I do, but not often," said Hawk. "Allow me to offer you a pinch from my box, sir."

It was a very fool-hardy and hazardous thing to do, but as he spoke these words, Captain Hawk actually took from his pocket the elegant snuff-box that belonged to Lord Rholey, and handed it to the gentleman, who took a pinch from it, and was in the act of returning it to Hawk, when, with a cry of exultation, Jobson darted forward and laid hold of it, shouting,

"Here's proof—here's proof! His lordship's snuff-box!—Ha! ha! It's all right now. Who will doubt it now? Here is Lord Rholey's snuff-box in the fellow's possession! The very snuff-box that he robbed his lordship of this day. Capital—oh, capital!"

"What is the meaning of all this?" said Hawk.

"Is the man mad again?" said the gentleman who had taken the pinch of snuff.

"Oh, dear, no!" cried Jobson, "the man is not mad, nor was he ever, nor is he likely to be, only the man is right after all—ha! ha! ha! Oh, this is excellent! Lord Rholey! My lord—my lord!"

"Bless me, Jobson, what is the matter now?" said Lord Rholey, as, along with all the other guests, he came towards where Jobson stood with the snuff-box in his hand.

"Ah! what now?" said the Marquis of Pembroke. "Has my poor friend Jobson found another horse's nest, I wonder?"

Everybody laughed at this, but Jobson was no whit disconcerted at it, but holding the snuff-box as high as he could above his head, he cried—

"The proof—the proof! Here it is! Ha—ha! Here it is! Now am I wrong, or am I right? Now am I mad? The proof is in the snuff-box! Oh, this is unexpected, but capital! The proof is in the snuff-box!"

"Pray open it, then," said the marquis, "and let me see it."

"But I mean the snuff-box itself is the proof—here it is. Hurrah! Hip! hip! hip! hurrah!"

"Oh, the man is quite mad," said Hawk. "I cannot feel angry at a madman, but I hope he will be made to return me my snuff-box."

"Upon my word this is too bad," said the Marquis of Pembroke. "Lord Rholey, this Mr. Jobson is a friend of yours; you brought him here, and, therefore, it is your duty to look to the poor fellow, for his wits are deranged."

"Oh, decidedly—decidedly!" cried everybody.

"No, they ain't," cried Jobson, "no they ain't. Come here, my Lord Rholey. Do me the favour, my lord, of coming forward, if you please, my lord."

Lord Rholey stepped forward.

"Now, if your lordship will be so kind as to look at this snuff-box—a slight glance will suffice, my lord; but yet, for the satisfaction of other people, I advise you to look at it well. Now, my lord, now?"

"Well?" said Lord Rholey.

"Well!" cried Jobson.

"I say, well? and I say it in the interrogative sense. What are your wishes, Mr. Jobson?"

"Look at that snuff-box, my lord."

"I am looking at it."

"What do you say to it?"

"Nothing."

Jobson staggered back, and trod upon the Marquis of Pembroke's toes, and then he glared at Lord Rholey as though he considered that the end of the world must surely be close at hand.

"Do you mean to say, my lord, that —that——"

"That what?"

"That you never saw that snuff-box before?"

Lord Rholey shook his head.

"Oh, dear, no! Before nor behind nor any way. Poor Jobson!"

"Ah! poor fellow!" cried everybody.

"If you have now done with my snuff-box, Mr. Jobson," said Captain Hawk, "I shall be very much obliged to you for it again. You can take a pinch, if you like. Perhaps it will clear your head a little."

"Stop!" roared Jobson. "Stop! My Lord Rholey, is not this your snuff-box?"

"Mine? Oh, dear, no."

"No?"

"Certainly not. It is that gentleman's, I presume. Here, Colonel Luck, take your snuff-box, and pray look over these eccentricities of our poor friend, Jobson."

"I am mad, then!" gasped Jobson.

"You certainly are," said everybody. "You certainly are, Mr. Jobson, as mad as you possibly can be. You had better go to bed, my good sir."

Jobson sat upon the floor, looking rather wildly about him; and Captain Hawk advancing with the snuff-box in his hand, and very adroitly blowing about half of its contents into Jobson's face, said—

"I think that a good sneeze would do the poor fellow good. You may depend he will see all the clearer after it. How are you now, Jobson?"

Poor Jobson sneezed so dreadfully, that he could not tell how he was, and he rushed about among the guests in such an outrageous way, under the influence of the snuff, that the Marquis of Pembroke, by the advice of the ladies, backed by Lord Rholey and Captain Hawk, rang for a couple of stout footmen, who carried Jobson off to bed, in spite of all the opposition he could offer to such a summary mode of disposing of him.

"We will see how he is," said the marquis, "in a few hours; and if he should be no better, we will get medical assistance for him."

Jobson was not a person of any consideration, so he was soon enough forgotten by all but by Captain Hawk and Lord Rholey. The former was anxious to get away; and the latter, aggravated as he had been at the conduct of his humble friend, could not but feel that he had been treated very ill. Captain Hawk would have left at once, but he was afraid by so doing to give a colour to the accuastions of Jobson. There were two gentlemen in the dining-room, likewise, who had not joined in the vociferations against Jobson, but who had looked at him, Hawk, with countenances of serious inquiry, so that he had a slight idea, that they had suspected there was more in the matter than met the eye exactly.

One of these gentlemen took the Marquis of Pembroke into the recess of one of the windows, and engaged him in earnest conversation. This was, to the apprehension of Captain Hawk, a very suspicious circumstance. The other gentleman walked up to him, and in a very off-hand sort of style, said—

"Are you attached, colonel?"

"No, sir."

"Oh, I have served myself. Mine was in the infantry. Which arm of the service did you belong to?"

"Not the English service at all. I was in the service of Austria."

"Oh, indeed!—Umph! Do you hold a written commission in the service?"

"Why do you ask, sir?"

"Because I am a little curious to know."

"Very well, sir; then I can inform you that there is one of the most evil secrets in the world, for any one who is curious, at the point of my sword; and I shall feel great pleasure in making it fully acquainted with any part of your internal anatomy that you may please to mention, at any time."

"Do you mean that as a threat or a joke?"

"Whichever you please to make of it, sir."

"Then if I were sure that you were a gentleman, instead of suspecting that you are an adventurer, and perhaps something worse, I would chastise your insolence as it deserves."

With this speech, the gentleman turned upon his heel; but Captain Hawk sprang to his feet with flashing eyes,

CAPTAIN HAWK IS SLIGHTLY ANNOYED AT THE PRANKS OF A BOY.

and would have gone after him, had not the young lady whose beauty he had so extravagantly complimented suddenly laid her hand upon his arm.

"Stop—stop!"

"No, I cannot. Another time—I—"

"I order you to stop."

Captain Hawk was awed at the tone in which she spoke, and pausing, he turned and bowed to her, saying—

"If you order me, I have no resource but to obey you; but I wish, for all tha you would be so good as to waive your authority, and let me go for a few minutes only."

"What do you want to do?"

"Well, I hardly know; but I should have knocked that fellow down, I rather think; although it is quite as well that I did not, under the circumstances."

"It is much better," said the young lady. "I command you not to stir any further in this business. Of course, General Gray is mistaken."

"General Gray? Is he a general?"

"He is, and he did not mean to be so rude, I dare say, as you thought him. Let me advise you, colonel, since the words of Jobson has raised a doubt about you, to take some means of satisfying the gentlemen here present of your real position in life, and dispersing the supposition, even, that you can be anything but a gentlaman and an officer."

A deep flush of colour stole over the face of Captain Hawk, and then left him as pale as death itself. The young girl looked at him with alarm, and for the first moment she, too, began to feel just a little suspicious that there was some plot going on, and that poor Jobson was an ill-used man.

"No," said Captain Hawk, as he rose, "I disdain to set myself right in the opinion of those who choose to think ill of me. I will leave this house at once, and never cross its threshold again. I came here as a guest, and I have not received the courtesy of one. But for you, I——Halloa, where is she?"

The young lady had suddenly glided from the side of Captain Hawk, and left the room. With what feelings or opinions regarding him she had left it, he had no means accurately of determining; but he was now not so anxious as he had been to leave the mansion, for he hoped to see her again, and to make a more favourable impression upon her. The fact was, that her exquisite and child-like grace and beauty had made a great impression upon the rather susceptible heart of Captain Hawk.

"I will see her again," he said to himself. "I feel assured that she has an interest in me. The few words of admiration that I uttered to her went direct to her heart. I feel that I almost love her."

The gentleman who had been named as General Gray by the young lady, now kept at the other end of the room to that at which Captain Hawk was, and the conference with the other gentleman and the Marquis of Pembroke seemed to have produced no result, for everything went on comfortably enough. The day began to get on the decline and Captain Hawk made up his mind to leave as soon as there were decided indications of twilight.

He considered that the rest his horse was having in the stables of the marquis—for it had been caught and brought there—was what it wanted, and that it would be much safer at night to go from the place than in the daylight. Where to go, or what to do, he had not determined; but he stood by one of the windows of the mansion watching the changing colours in the winter sky, when some one behind him said—

"Perhaps you will favour us with your company to dinner?"

Hawk turned rapidly, and saw the Marquis of Pembroke.

"I should have great pleasure, my lord," he replied, "but an engagement of importance hastens my departure. Even now I am waiting for—for the night to come."

"The night? Do you prefer the night?"

"At times, my lord, when other and more gentle natures prefer it."

"Oh, an affair of gallantry. That is quite another thing. Well, colonel, we will not detain you, as that is the case; but yet I hope your time has not come yet?"

As the marquis spoke, Captain Hawk saw through the trees on the opposite side of the lawn something that glanced and glittered like steel; but what it was he could not take upon himself to say.

"My lord?"

"Did you speak, colonel?"

"I did. Pray cast your eyes to the trees on the other side of your lawn, and tell me what it is that you see there moving slowly along behind them. I see something, surely, unusual."

The marquis looked steadfastly.

"There is something," he said, "but what it is puzzles me. Captain Rochet, just step here a moment."

"With pleasure," said a young and engaging-looking man, who was of the party.

"What is that moving along slowly on the other side of the trees yonder? There, close by the iron hurdles of the lawn."

The captain shaded his eyes with his hand, and then he said, in a tone that did not admit of the slightest doubt of the fact—

"Infantry!"

"What?"

"A detachment of infantry."

"Soldiers on my estate? Why, what the deuce can they want here, I should like to know? This is a most unprecedented offence. What do you think of it, colonel?—Ah, he is gone! Where is the colonel?"

"Ha!—ha!" cried Jobson, bursting into the room. "He'll be nabbed now!"

CHAPTER XXXIII.

CAPTAIN HAWK MEETS WITH EVIL FORTUNE.

The Marquis of Pembroke and his new guests were not a little amazed at all these strange proceedings, concerning which there were but three persons in the place who could give any information. One of those three was Lord Rholey, the other was Mr. Jobson, and the third was Captain Hawk himself.

Now, it appeared that Mr. Jobson, after the affair of the snuff-box, had felt such an amount of indignation, that when the servants had left him to himself in his chamber, which they would not have done but that he seemed to be pretty quiet, he made up his small mind that he would not rest until he had made yet another effort to bowl out the highwayman.

Dressing himself very carefully again, for, to deceive the servants, he had really undressed and gone to bed, Mr. Jobson managed to slip out of the house by the back way, and to get into a lane which led to the high-road to Hounslow. There he had not waited long before he saw a gamekeeper of the Marquis of Pembroke's, mounted upon a hunter that he had been to the farriers with; and him Mr. Jobson accosted.

"My good fellow," he said, "the Marquis of Pembroke wishes you to ride to the barracks at Hounslow as fast as you can, and give his compliments to the officer in command there, and beg him to send a company of infantry to this place. Tell him that the notorious Captain Hawk, who murdered the chief justice and escaped the other day, is here, and that the marquis don't wish to alarm the ladies until his capture is quite certain."

"Oh, Mr. Jobson, you don't say so!" said the gamekeeper.

"Yes I do, and it will be five guineas in your pocket if you do the errand without any bungling or waste of time."

"Oh, won't I!"

The man had no right to take an order in his master, the Marquis of Pembroke's, name, from any one but his master; but the prospect of the five guineas put an end to all scruples, and off he went at a good pace to the barracks. The officer on duty there could not think of refusing the request of a person such as the Marquis of Pembroke, who was heir-presumptive, too, to one of the oldest dukedoms in England; so a captain's guard was sent at once, with orders to surround the house in such a way, that the escape of any one should be impossible."

Such, then, was the circumstance that to the bewildered eyes of the marquis and his guests, brought a military force on to the estate.

Captain Hawk was not slow in guessing how it was that he had been thus caught in a trap, as it were, and how he owed to his indefatigable enemy, Mr. Jobson, the present most perilous circumstance. There was nothing now for it but a bold push for liberty and life. He yet thought it possible enough that there might be still a means of leaving the premises, if the soldiers had only just arrived, which he hoped was the case; so, retreating from the window, he said at once—

"My lord, I will charge myself with the task of going at once to see what is the meaning of this strange intrusion of the military into your lordship's house. No doubt, there is some good reason."

"Oh, no—no, I will go," said the marquis; but Captain Hawk was much too quick for him. Anticipating that there would be some polite objections to his going, and some other objections that might be more suspicious than polite he left the room so quickly that there was no time to stop him, although several of the gentlemen had a half inclination so to do.

Hawk's idea was to dash down the stairs at once; but he had not got above three steps down, when he saw Jobson in the hall with somebody in a red coat. The fact was, that the moment Jobson had made his triumphant speech in the dining-room, he had left it again, for he did not think that the proximity of Captain Hawk to be quite a safe thing for him now, taking all circumstances into consideration, and he had met one of the officers making his way to the marquis.

Hawk's retreat was, therefore, cut off in that direction. Return to the drawing-room he would not, for that would be now to ensure certain capture, so he landed upon the next flight of stairs that led to the chambers of the mansion.

Captain Hawk may be said now to have had a kind of impression upon his mind that he was all but captured, but still he preserved his presence of mind, so that nothing should escape him which would present to him a chance of releasing himself from the painful circumstances in which he was. He was well armed, and as he reached the next landing—it was the last, too, for the mansion was but of two stories—he drew a pistol from his pocket, and listened attentively over the balustrade to what was going on below

The drawing-room door was opened, and the gentlemen crowded the landing just as the officer and Mr. Jobson reach the top of the stairs.

"What is the meaning of all this?" cried the marquis. "Is my house a barracks? I insist upon knowing what this means."

The officer looked aghast.

"Why, my lord, your express orders——"

"My orders?"

"Allow me to explain. My Lord Pembroke, the man calling himself Colonel Luck is, as I had the honour of telling your lordship before, although your lordship did not do me the honour of believing it, a highwayman; and from a variety of circumstances I am quite convinced that he is no other than Captain Hawk, who murdered the chief justice on Hounslow Heath."

"Oh, no!"

"But I say yes, my lord; and, therefore, I do but do my duty to you, and to the country, and to myself, by causing him to be arrested. I presume, my lord, that he is still in the drawing-room?"

"If this be true, Mr. Jobson," said Lord Pembroke, "we are all here most strangely deceived; but I can't think it."

"Not all deceived, my lord; there is one of your lordship's illustrious guests who is not deceived at all."

"Whom mean you?"

"Lord Rholey."

"Mr. Jobson," said Lord Rholey, "you and I must settle this little affair another time; your conduct is infamous."

"Very good, my lord; you will find me with Lady Rholey at your lordship's town house in Spring Gardens, and her ladyship amusing herself with certain letters that——"

"Hush! hush!" said Lord Rholey "My dear Jobson, how do you do?"

"Better," said Jobson.

"Really, gentlemen," said the marquis, "I think you are all a little mad, for I cannot for the life of me make out what you are all about. If the gentleman styling himself Colonel Luck be an impostor, I am sorry to say he has left the place."

"Left it!" said Jobson; "that is impossible."

"Indeed, he went down stairs just now, and you must have let him pass you as you came up."

"No," said the officer, "no one passed us; besides, there is a soldier on duty at the door, who would let no one pass. He did not come down stairs, my lord, I assure you. He could not have passed this gentleman and me;

and if he had, we should have heard the sentry give an alarm, below."

"Then he is upstairs," said Jobson.

"The devil he is," cried Lord Pembroke. "I will soon have him out if he is. There is no escape from the upper part of the house but by the fire-escapes that are attached to two of the windows, and if he can descend by their ropes, he would pass the drawing-room windows, and alight in the lawn."

"In that case," said the officer, "my men would take him at once; but if you think that he is upstairs, I will order a corporal and a couple of men to come with us, and ferret him out."

"Do so," said Jobson, "do so."

Tho officer called to the corporal and the men in the hall to come up, and Captain Hawk, who, from above, was cognisant of all this, thought that it was now high time for him to look after his safety.

That he would not be taken while he had arms in his hands without a struggle for it, he made up his mind; but still he could not but feel how much better it would be to avoid such a struggle if he possibly could; so he walked hastily and noiselessly along the corridor in which he was, and tried the first door he came to. It was locked. Uttering an execration, he passed on to the second, and the handle, when he turned it, readily opened the door.

"Is that you, Phebe?" said a voice.

"The deuce," thought Captain Hawk, "I am intruding into some lady's dressing-room."

"Phebe, why don't you speak if that is you?" said the voice again. "What an extraordinary girl you are, to come creeping into the room in this way, without speaking. I want to know what is the cause of all that disturbance down stairs."

Captain Hawk now knew by the voice that the speaker was no other than the young lady to whom he paid such rather extravagant compliments to in the drawing-room, and, of coure, he concluded that it was into her dressing room that he had intruded.

The apartment was rather dark towards the end of it next to the door, so Captain Hawk relied upon not being seen, and he quitly closed the door, and fastened it upon the inside.

"Will you speak, Phebe?" said the young lady.

"Pardon me," said Captain Hawk, "I——"

He got no further, before the young lady uttered a cry of surprise and terror, and starting up from before the dressing glass, by which she had been arranging her hair, she cried—

"Oh, who is that? Who was that who spoke? You wicked girl, Phebe, if this be one of your tricks, I declare I will have you sent away this very hour."

"No," said Captain Hawk, "it is no trick of Phebe's. I am Colonel Luck; but I beg of you not to suppose that my intrusion here is for any bad or unjustifiable object. I am pursued—"

"Pursued? For what?"

"Why, the fact is I—I—Oh, miss, I decline to tell you any untruth; and if you can and will afford me your protection, I would rather owe it to your pity, knowing who I really am, than to any other feeling. I am Captain Hawk, the highwayman."

"Gracious Heavens!"

"Nay, do not be alarmed. I hope that, although a highwayman now, I have not forgotten that I was once a gentleman. The fact is, I am hunted. There are those already in the house, who seek my life. If I can escape from them I will; but if I can't, their blood be upon their own heads, for I am well armed, and I am determined to defend myself to the last gasp."

"Oh, what shall I do?"

"Spare the effusion of blood that will ensue. Protect me, and by so doing protect others. It can be of no importance, now, to those who are upon my track whether they take me or not; while to you it will be a cheering reflection that you have saved the lives of several fellow creatures, and done an act of mercy towards me."

"Oh, is it not cruel—very cruel?"

"What is cruel?"

"For you to place me in such a position as this. Your own judgment must show you how I am situated. I must either betray you to those whom you acknowledge as your foes, or I must compromise my own honour by defending you, and saving or trying to save you from them—for, after all, I may not be successful."

"True—alas, too true!"

"And if I am not successful in saving you, I shall have such a slur upon my name and reputation as I dread to think of, and yet done nothing really to aid you."

"You are right—you are right," said Captain Hawk. "Accept my thanks, together with my best respects for the kind words you have spoken to me. I admit that it is far better for me to die, than that your spotless fame should suffer."

"Then what will you do, since you are so convinced upon that point?"

"I will do what I ought to do as regards you, and that is, withdraw myself at once from your chamber. What may occur after that, is contingent upon the proceedings of others, not upon any will of mine."

"Do you really mean what you say?"

"As I live I do."

"Go, then, at once."

"Farewell!"

Captain Hawk, with an alacrity that showed he was fully in earnest, made his way to the door of the chamber, but before he could open it to go out, the young lady called to him, in a voice of emotion—

"Come back—come back!"

"Nay, do not say come back. Why should I return to come between your pure soul and its sense of right?"

The tears coursed each other down her cheeks as she said—

"I will save you. You are generous enough not to press me to do so; but I will save you, and I will rely upon Heaven to preserve me from any evil interpretation of my motives in so doing."

CHAPTER XXXIV.

CAPTAIN HAWK HIDES IN THE YOUNG LADY'S CHAMBER.

There was in the character of Captain Hawk at times, as, no doubt, the reader has already observed, a certain vein of chivalric feeling, which was rather at variance with some of his actions. Such anomalies are, however, anything but unfrequent in such men. The fact is, that with such characters, passion is always at war with principle, and sometimes one gets the advantage and sometimes the other.

There can be very little doubt, however, that if Hawk had had the advantages of careful mental culture in early life, he would have been a very different person to what he was, and his better nature, instead of only breaking out at times through the mists of passion, would have been a pernament and a consistent feeling at all times.

Now, however, one of those occasions had arisen when the better feelings of the man overcame all obstacles. The kindness and the generosity of the young girl, who would run so great a risk of censure to save him, touched his heart; and after a pause, which he found necessary, in order that he might speak with composure, he said to her—

"No. You have convinced and conquered me, and I now feel how very ungenerous it was to ask you to compromise your own character and position, by aiding me in any shape or way."

"Oh, do not speak thus. They will kill you."

"I cannot deny but they will try to do so."

"Then you shall not go."

"Let me go, I pray you. I did look upon you with the eye of admiration for your beauty; but now I know that you possess a mind which is even more beautiful than your face."

"Stay here, but do not speak to me in that way. I will save you, if it be in my power to do so, and Heaven forgive me if I am doing wrong."

"No—no!"

"But I say, yes; for if you go now, and your death should take place, I should for ever look upon myself as your murderess."

The tone of sincerity in which she spoke was not to be doubted, and Captain Hawk hesitated. It was much to escape his enemies if he could. Death was a grievous thing for him to think of; and hunted as he was, like some wild beast, by his fellow-men, there was nothing scarcely that he would not do to baulk them of their prey.

"Listen," he said. "Listen to me."

"I do—I will."

"If you think you can effectually hide me, do so, because then no harm will come to you for doing so; but if you have a doubt about it, let me go, for I will not compromise you upon only the chance of my own rescue from those who would hunt me to the death."

"I can save you."

"Are you sure—are you quite sure?"

"I am. They dare not search this room. They must take my word that you are not here; and under those circumstances I feel that if the question be forced upon me, a falsehood is justifiable."

"How can I ever thank you?—how can I evince to you the grateful feeling that will ever hover around your name?"

"By you silence."

"My silence? How mean you by my silence?"

"I mean, that after you leave this place you should forget that you ever saw me. I mean, that this adventure should sink into oblivion. Be content that you are saved, as you will be, and then never allude to the circumstance."

"Fair Saint! I will obey you."

At this moment the sound of feet and of voices upon the staircase came plainly to the ears of Captain Hawk and the young lady. It was evident that the opinion that he had taken refuge in the upper part of the mansion had gained sufficient ground to induce a search of it.

There was no time to be lost.

"They come," said Hawk.

The young lady turned very pale indeed, and trembled.

"Yes," she said, "I hear them coming, but I will keep faith with you. Creep under this dressing-table. You see that the drapery that covers it reaches nearly to the ground. I will si here opposite to the glass, and be, as it were, arranging my hair, so that no one will suspect that you can possibly be here."

"I see. That will do."

"Quick—oh, quick!"

Some one tapped at the door of the dressing-room, and Captain Hawk found that, indeed, there was no time to lose; so he with considerable dexterity, so as to make no noise, got under the dressing-table. Luckily for him, it was rather a large one, and, as the young lady had said, the drapery with which it was covered reached quite to the floor of the room, and, in fact, some very deep gold fringe that was at the end of the drapery was spread quite upon the floor. If, therefore, the young lady could manage to keep her coolness and presence of mind about her, the danger to Captain Hawk was but very slight indeed, under the circumstances.

Tap! tap! came the demand for admission at the door of the room.

"Are you hidden?" said the young lady, in a whisper.

"I am."

"Hush! Who is there? Who knocks?"

"Miss Egremont," said a voice, "it is I. Can you come out to us a moment? Pray pardon the intrusion."

"Is it the Marquis of Pembroke?"

"Yes, Miss Egremont."

The young lady rose from the chair by the dressing-table, upon which she had thrown herself, and walked towards the door of the room. She opened it at once, and then she saw the Marquis of Pembroke and the officer who had come with the military party, and at a glance, too, that she took rapidly in the direction of the long gallery that constituted the landing, she saw that a couple of soldiers guarded the head of the grand staircase. The officer had his drawn sword in his hand.

"I am really afraid," said the marquis, "that you will hardly be able to pardon the intrusion."

"Oh, yes, easily. But what does it all mean?"

"Simply, my dear Miss Egremont, that one of our guests below, the fellow who was nearly drowned in the Brent, has turned out to be no other than the notorious highwayman, Captain Hawk."

How glad Captain Hawk felt, as he heard these words, that he had not concealed his identity from the young lady.

"Is that possible, my lord?" she said.

"It is, indeed; and what is more, the rascal has made his way up here somewhere, and is hiding in this part of the house. Have you heard any one about the landing?"

"Just now I heard your footsteps coming."

"That is all! You have not been alarmed, then, by any one?"

"Oh, no, not alarmed."

"Confound the fellow," said the officer, "he must be here somewhere, though, for I assure you, my lord, that he could not pass my men without their seeing him. He is in one of the chambers of this part of the house, for a certainty."

"Not a doubt of it," said the marquis. "Allow me again to apologise to you, Miss Egremont, for disturbing you."

The officer bowed, and made an apology likewise, and muttered something about the unpleasant duty he was upon. Miss Egremont bowed and smiled, and went into her room again, and closed the door. She felt as though she could have fainted, if she had not with great courage bourne up against it, as she went towards the dressing-table again. It was some few moments before she could speak, and then she said in a low tone—

"You are saved, I hope."

"Blessings rest upon you," replied Hawk, from under the dressing table.

"Hush! oh, hush! They will not insult me by searching this room, but you must leave as soon as it is at all possible for you to do so with any regard to safety."

"Indeed, and in truth, I will."

"That will do—I am content. I will not hunt you from this place of shelter too soon; that would be to keep the word of promise to your ears, and cheat it to your hopes."

"You are too good to me."

"Hush! not a word. I hear some one coming."

Captain Hawk heard some one coming likewise, and both for his own sake and that of Miss Egremont he was as quiet as a lamb. The sound of rapid feet was heard, and then the door of the chamber was opened sharply, and a young girl came quickly in, crying out—

"Oh, Miss Egremont, what do you think has happened? That handsome Colonel Luck, who was nearly drowned, turns out to be a highwayman."

"Silence, Phebe; you stun me," said Miss Egremont.

"I beg your pardon, miss; I quite forgot I was getting into my old habit of speaking too loud, you see; but I won't do so any more; and you must know that all the house is in an uproar and quite full of soldiers, and they are going to shoot him at once, miss, if they find him, for Mr. Jobson says that that will save a deal of trouble to everybody and expense to the country."

"Indeed?"

"Yes, miss; and I knew you wanted your hair done, and I should have been here before this, only, of course, I wanted to hear all I could, and bring you all the news, you see."

"Yes, that will do."

"And so, you see, miss, the whole house and everybody in it is going to be turned topsy-turvy, to find out the dreadful highwayman; but after all, you know, miss, he is very handsome. I for one should not like to have him killed; should you, now?"

"I have no opinion about it, Phebe."

"Oh, but you know, miss, the good-looking men are really so few, that when one does see one, it makes one long to be married."

"Hold your silly tongue, Phebe. I have frequently told you that I dislike such conversation, and if you continue it, I shall have to look for another maid."

"Oh, pray don't say that, Mr. Egremont; it isn't often that I say anything that I shouldn't, and you know, miss, that a poor serving girl isn't always so much upon her guard as a young lady like you, and I'm afraid that if the highwayman had come to me, and only said 'Phebe, they are going to kill me: will you hide me?' I should have done it."

At these words, a suspicion crossed the mind of Miss Egremont that Phebe knew of the fact of Captain Hawk being hidden in the room; but one glance at the candid face of the young girl disarmed her of that thought, and she replied—

"You will oblige me, Phebe, by saying no more about the subject. It is not one that I feel interested in."

"Oh, very well, miss, I won't say another word, then, about him, though he was good-looking. And now, if you please, I will dress your hair for dinner. How will you have it done miss?"

"Quite plain."

"Very good, Miss Egremont. Perhaps you would like a plait on each side?"

CAPTAIN HAWK HAS A TRIFLING CHAT WITH MIS EGREMONT.

"Yes—yes, anything you like."

"Then I must have some more hair-pins. Let me see: Oh, there are some in the band-box under the dressing-table."

"No."

"Yes [illegible]——"

"Will you attend to me, and be quiet, Phebe? I won't have any pins in my hair to-day, I tell you; let that suffice.

Just do it up in two plain bands, and then go away. I do not intend making any change in my dress at all to-day. Now, be quick, and as I shall not want you any more this evening, you can remain down stairs if you please, Phebe."

"Lor, miss, I never did know you so cross! I hope I haven't been and offended you, Miss Egremont, with any of my nonsense? I am sure if I have, I shall never be able to forgive myself. Have I though, really, miss?"

"No—no; but you will, if you do not be quick and go away."

With this threat hanging over her, Phebe thought it best to say no more, so she rapidly did up her young mistress's hair, and then, with a very quiet show of deference, left the room; but Phebe, when she got outside the door, put herself in a thoughtful attitude.

"What does all this mean?" she said. "Why is she in such a fidget to get rid of me, and why did she shake and tremble in such a way, I wonder? It's very odd. There's something in it, and if there is, my name ain't Phebe Johnson if I don't find it out. Oh, if I can only fix my young lady in anything that she would not like told again, I should, then, never be afraid of her sending me off; and as for perquisites, I should just have as many as I choose to say should be mine. Oh, dear—oh, dear!"

Miss Egremont had opened the door very softly, and suddenly caught Phebe by the arm.

"For what are you waiting here?" she said.

"Waiting here? Miss Egremont, I —that is—Did you say waiting here?"

"I did."

"Oh, you mean then, what am I waiting here for?"

"I do."

"Then I don't know. How should I know, Miss Egremont, what I am waiting here for? Of course, miss, it's for nothing at all. What should I be waiting for, I wonder?"

"Go down stairs, then, to the servants' hall, and remember I don't want you again to-night, so that, until you come up stairs to bed, you will not come up again."

CHAPTER XXXV.

CAPTAIN HAWK DEFEATS PHEBE'S NICE LITTLE PLAN.

When Miss Egremont returned to the dressing-table, after dismissing Phebe in this way, she began to sob as though her heart were breaking. Captain Hawk was much vexed that the affair should have had such an effect upon her, and partially getting from under the table, he said—

"Miss Egremont, I will not—I cannot allow you to be made so miserable by my presence here. I will go at once."

"No, no, no!"

"Yes! but I feel that I ought. It is base of me to owe my safety to your fears. I will go, and in going, permit me to say that I carry with me a sentiment of profound respect, as far as you are concerned, and that I shall ever think of you as one of the most brave and generous, as well as the most charming of your sex."

Upon hearing these words from Captain Hawk, Miss Egremont managed to dry her tears, and to speak with something like composure.

"No," she said, "you must not go now. Having done this much for you, I will not shrink from what there is still to do. I will save you if I can It is naturally repugnant to the feelings of a young girl like myself to see bloodshed, which she might have possibly prevented; so, I say again, you must not think of going."

"But you weep."

"I do weep, for I have reason to believe that my waiting-maid has her suspicions that something unusual is taking place. Nay, I can hardly convince myself but that she suspects you are here."

"You mean the pert girl who was in this room a short time ago?"

"I do. She was even now listening at the door of the chamber. It is not easy to keep her from coming up to this part of the house, as she sleeps in the room immediately opposite to this."

"Heed her not. Should the worst come to the worst, I will adopt some plan of saving you from any evil consequences of having hidden me in this room; and since you say that you would not leave unfinished the act of rare generosity which induced you to give me a shelter, I ask you to let me stay till night, and then when all the mansion have gone to repose, I shall be able with ease to let myself out."

"Be it so, And if I could hope that the memory of this peril would have such an influence over you as to induce you for the future to lead a different life, and to try by some reputable means to live, it would be, after all, a blessed chance."

"For your sake I would do much."

"No—no! Not for my sake, but for your own, I ask you to amend your life; and for the sake, too, of truth, and of justice, and the happiness of others, as well as your own."

Captain Hawk was silent. He knew better than Miss Egremont, that he had already gone too far in the career of crime now to retreat from it; but he felt how profitless was such a discussion with her.

A bell, with a monotous tolling, now sounded through the house, and the first impression of Hawk naturally enough was, that it was an alarm bell; but Miss Egremont told him that it was an announcement that dinner was upon the table.

"I will lock the door of this room," she said, "and take the key with me, for if I do not, the curiosity of Phebe may induce her to visit it while the dinner is in progress, and when she knows it would be inpossible for me to detect her. Farewell!"

"Farewell!" said Captain Hawk. "Do not let any thought of me, or of my possible or probable fate, distress you. All will be well."

The young lady left the room, and Captain Hawk heard her lock the door. There was a great trampling of feet soon in the long corridor, and he heard many voices, and now and then he could distinguish his own name pronounced in tones of aggravation and anger. By getting from under the dressing-table, which he might now do with perfect safety, and placing his ear against the panel of the door, he could hear distinctly enough what was said without, and the voice of the Marquis of Pembroke, which was rather peculiar, struck upon his ears.

The marquis was evidently addressing the officer who had come with the guard from the barracks at Hounslow.

"Sir," he said, "I hope you will favour me with your company at dinner?"

"My lord, I shall be most happy; but is it not a strange and provoking thing that this fellow cannot be found?"

"It is, indeed."

"And we have been into almost every chamber."

"Every one that was not in the actual occupation of the ladies, and you know that it would have been impossible for him to be hidden in any of those rooms, without the ladies being aware of it."

"Oh, quite—quite."

"So it may be said that we have, in fact, searched every room."

The officer placed his hand upon the lock of the chamber in which Captain Hawk was.

"Have we been in here?" he said.

"No, but Miss Egremont was there, and herself assured us."

"Then, my lord, I confess myself puzzled to know what has become of the fellow we have taken such pains to capture."

"And so am I. There must be hiding-places in the house with which he is more familiar with than I am, for really it appears to me as if we had searched all the upper part of it well, And as your men kept a good guard below, he could not have descended the staircase; and there the matter rests enclosed in mystery.

"Mystery, indeed, it is, my lord."

"Well—well. I hear the second dinner-bell, so let us go to the dining-hall, sir. After all, I don't much care, so long as the rascal goes off my premises, whether he is captured or not. It is an uncomfortable piece of business."

The officer and the Marquis of Pembroke left the corridor, and Captain Hawk could just hear the confused sound of their voices as they continued talking on their route down the staircase.

The room was very dark now, and Hawk could barely distinguish the different articles of furniture that were in it. Indeed, the only article that was by its size very distinctly visible, was the large bedstead that was against one of the walls. Hunger, too, in addition to his other discomforts, began to assail Captain Hawk, so that, take it for all in all, his situation was, in truth, none of the most pleasant.

"It may be hours," he muttered, "before she can come here again to release me. How wondrously beautiful she is, to be sure! What eyes she has, and what a heart, gifted with the most extraordinary intelligence and generosity. I thought her, when I spoke to her below in the drawing-room, nothing but a coquette; but now I——Ah! what is that?"

A rattling sound at the lock of the door attracted his observation, and at first his impulse was to hide under the table; but a second thought told him that to all but Miss Egremont herself the door was fast, and, therefore, that he had nothing to fear.

With this idea, which was a just one enough, he crept close up to the door, instead of attempting to hide himself.

The rattling noise at the door still continued.

Captain Hawk placed his eye to the keyhole, but he could see no light. Whoever was there had chosen to come in the dark.

"Drat it!" said a voice. "She has locked the door, and taken away the key."

Captain Hawk had only heard that voice once, but there was no mistaking it It was the voice of Phebe the maid.

"Oh," he thought, "Miss Egremont was right enough when she thought it possible that Phebe might come to search the room in her absence. It is well I am locked in."

"Well," added Phebe, "this is provoking, if ever anything in the world was. The door to be locked up now for the first time, and me been here for three weeks and more! Oh, I'm sure all this means something, that I do. Why was she in such a strange temper, I wonder, all of a sudden, when, as a usual thing, lor bless me, I can turn her round my little finger? and the idea, too, of ordering me not to come up stairs. Oh, a likely thing that, indeed. What can I do now?"

"Bother take you," muttered Captain Hawk, "if you would only choke yourself with your infernal curiosity, it would be the very best thing you could think of doing for me, and for the world in general, I am sure."

"Ah!" cried Phebe, suddenly, with animation. "I have it—I have it. Oh, I shall find it all out now. It's as likely as not, that some of the keys of the other doors will fit this, and if so, won't I try and find out your secret, miss. To be sure I will. Why didn't you trust me with it, eh? Why, my last missis, who was a married lady too, and the wife of an earl, used to let me know all her little intrigues with one and another, and of course she paid me well, and of course I did what was right—that is to say, I helped her as much as I could; and what with what she gave me and the gentlemen gave me, I got a mint of money, till she died, poor thing, and her husband said, he was afraid he should never get another like her. But I'll try the key of my own room first."

Heaven only knows what Phebe expected to find in Miss Egremont's room when she should make her way into it, but curiosity got the better of all fears, and she was, at all events, resolved to make the attempt.

After being absent a few moments, back she came with the key of her own door, and began working away with it in the lock, using all the force she could, as ignorant people will always do with locks, in the absurd fancy that if a key don't fit, strength of wrist will make it do so.

Perhaps a portion of Phebe's failure might be owing to the fact, that Captain Hawk had found a pair of curling irons on the dressing-table, and had pushed the end of them into the lock, meeting Phebe's key and preventing it going far enough to turn at all.

"What a provoking lock!" she exclaimed. "I must try another key. Oh! —oh! Murder! Oh, don't!—oh!"

Captain Hawk was in an agony to find out the cause of these exclamations; but in another moment he heard the voice of Miss Egremont.

"So, Phebe, you are here again?"

"Oh, miss, is it you? Well, I did think, when somebody laid hold of my neck, that it was Old Nick himself."

"Why are you here? Did I not order you to remain down stairs?"

"Yes, you did, Miss Egremont, I will say that of you—that you did. I'm sure that I wouldn't contradict you, no, not for worlds, that I wouldn't, and you so good a young lady, too."

"What are you about here?"

"I thought I would come and put away the toilette things, you see, miss; that was all."

"Phebe, you and I will part to-morrow. You can now go to your own room. I have more than once or twice warned you against this prying propensity of yours, and now it has become so very intolerable that I can endure it no longer. I tell you distinctly that to-morrow you leave my service."

"Leave! What, leave so good a missus!"

"But still, one whose orders you thought were of no consequence. You go from me to-morrow most assuredly."

"Oh, no—no! I could'nt—indeed I couldn't. Here I am, on my two blessed bended knees, and I hopes and I prays as you will keep me."

Miss Egremont made no reply to this appeal, but opening the door with the proper key of it, she walked into the chamber and closed it after her, and secured it on the inside.

Miss Egremont had in her hand a small silver hand-lamp. Captain Hawk had stepped back to the dressing-table, and there he stood, waiting for her to see him. She did not express any surprise at beholding him, but placed the little lamp upon the table and her finger upon her lip, to enjoin him to silence. Miss Egremont had no doubt in the world but that Phebe was at the door of the room.

Captain Hawk fully understood the solicitude she had now for his safety, and for her own reputation, as both were in the greatest danger possible. He bowed, and was profoundly silent.

Miss Egremont then sat down, and trembled excessively for some time; but then she rose and went to the door, and opened it suddenly. She had expected to find Phebe there, but was agreeably disappointed to see that such was not the case. She felt that she could then say to Captain Hawk what she wished; but still she spoke in a whisper, lest the serving maid might be hiding somewhere close at hand. Indeed, the probability was that she occupied at that time her own bed-room, which was across the corridor and directly opposite to that of Miss Egremont. Captain Hawk listened attentively and respectfully to what his fair friend said.

"Under the plea of indisposition, I have left the other ladies and am here," she said. "I hope, now, that as soon as possible you will make an effort to leave the house."

"Indeed, I will."

"That is well. In the course of a couple of hours from this time, I think that the soldiers will be withdrawn, and when they are gone, you have nothing to dread."

"That is true. Of course my death would be certain were I to put myself into collision with a party of soldiers; but as soon as they are off the premises I will take my departure."

"Do so. And now, sir, I——"

Miss Egremont stopped short in what she was going to say, and clasped her hands together in alarm,

"Some one comes," she said; "hide—oh, hide!"

Captain Hawk directly got under the dressing-table, and Miss Egremont arranged the drapery around it so that it should not look as it if had been at all disturbed. She had scarcely done so, and seated herself, when an old lady came into the room, and said—

"Why, my dear, what is the matter with you?"

"I felt rather unwell, aunt, that was all," said Miss Egremont.

"Why, you look unwell," said the old lady. "Come now, I insist upon your going to bed. You will get all right again by morning; but go to bed you must now."

"Oh, no, aunt; I would much rather sit up, indeed I would."

CHAPTER XXXVI.

CAPTAIN HAWK IS ARRESTED.

If Miss Egremont had been cool and collected, instead of exhibiting the amount of flurry that she did, her aunt would probably have made little or no opposition to her sitting up; but, on the contrary, the young lady betrayed so much agitation, that the elder one was only the more confirmed in her opinion of her indisposition, and in the necessity of her going to bed at once.

"Come, now," she said, "I dare say this foolish story of a highwayman being in the house has frightened you, and nothing will do you so much good as a few hours' sleep; your nerves will be then tranquillised, and you will be all right again."

"No—no!"

"But I say, yes—yes. When is it that you have behaved so unkindly to me as to say, 'No—no!' when I recommended any particular course to you? Have I not been a second mother to you?"

"Yes, dear aunt, you have; but—"

"But what?—Oh, nonsense! Call your maid and get yourself undressed as soon as you can, and get into bed."

"My maid has offended me," said Miss Egremont, glad of this small chance of avoiding going to bed. "She has offended me very much, and I will not allow her to attend upon me any more, aunt."

"Well, I think you are quite right to get rid of her. For my part, you know, I never liked the wench, and what you thought was only ignorance and simplicity in her, I had a very different opinion concerning; so I am glad she is going from you. And now I will help you to go to bed myself."

Alas, poor, afflicted Miss Egremont! there was no escape for her now. Her affection for her aunt amounted quite to a reverence, for the old lady had truly observed she had been quite like a second mother to her, and she would not have hurt her feelings for the world by preventing or refusing anything which she insisted upon; so she felt that she must retract.

"Very well, aunt," she said, "if you think I ought, I will go to bed."

"That is right, my dear; get to sleep as soon as you can, my love, and you will awaken quite another thing."

With this, the old lady set to work and soon undressed Miss Egremont, and got her comfortably in bed, little suspecting that Captain Hawk was under the dressing-table, all but a spectator of everything that was taking place.

"Now, my dear," said the aunt, "I will bid you good night at once. I will just light your little night-lamp and then leave you to your repose, which I hope will be sound and healthful. Good night!"

"Good night, aunt."

Miss Egremont could hardly speak, she was in such a state of agitation; and yet could she, after all the kindness she had shown to Captain Hawk, believe that he would try to play the part of a villain towards her? Oh, no—no, surely that was impossible!

The old lady left the room, and then such a stillness reigned in it as one might suppose in some solitude of nature where the foot of man had never yet trodden. There was something startling about that stillness, and while Miss Egremont would not break it, Captain Hawk feared to do so.

He soon, however, recovered from the state of feeling into which he had been thrown, and the idea that he now ought to leave the room came across him in all its intensity. He got out from under the table accordingly, and slowly approached the bed.

"Miss Egremont," he said.

She only answered by her sobs.

"Nay, Miss Egremont, why are you in this state of affliction? Do you feel sorrow that you have aided me thus far?"

"No—no; but go now at once."

"I am, indeed, going."

The light from the little night-lamp shone upon the fair face of Miss Egremont; and as he looked at her, unholy thoughts began to find a place in the brain of Captain Hawk. We know that if that man was the slave of anything it was his own passions; and at the moment, as he continued looking at Miss Egremont, surely a species of insanity must have taken possession of him, to make him forget all that he owed to her.

"Oh, charming girl!" he said, "why are you so beautiful?"

She was alarmed at his tone and manner.

"Oh, go—go at once," she said, "why do you not leave me? You promised that you would go when I should order you to do so. I now order it."

"Yes—yes, I will go. But first let me kiss that cheek—only one kiss, I ask no more."

"No—no! I will alarm the house! Are you, after all, a villain?"

"Nay, that is a harsh word. Why did nature make you so beautiful if your beauty was not to be admired and worshipped? Be but true to yourself, and none need know that my lips have touched your cheek."

"Oh, God!" she cried, "help me now!"

Captain Hawk stretched forth his arm towards her, but he was alarmed at the pallor of her face and the fixed look of her eyes.

"Miss Egremont," he cried, "speak—speak to me. I pray you!"

She was perfectly still.

"By Heavens she has fainted! Now, if I am indeed a villain—No—no! Heaven help me, I am not so bad as that! Farewell—farewell!"

He turned, and hastily made his way to the door of the chamber, and opening it, he made a rush into the corridor, and fell right over some one who had been kneeling at the door.

"Fire! Murder!" cried Phebe.

It was, indeed, that waiting-maid who was trying to listen and to peep by the aid of the key-hole, and who had not had time to get out of his, Captain Hawk's, way when he so rapidly opened the door of the room.

"Confound you!" cried Hawk.

"Help! help! Murder! murder! Fire! Here he is," cried Phebe. "I have him! Hear he is!"

"Silence, on your life!"

Captain Hawk tried to get old of her, but he missed her, and she flew down stairs, and fell from the top to the bottom of the flight, and screaming at a great rate all the way.

Captain Hawk was so enraged that he was inclined to fire one of his pistols after her; but by exerting as much self-command as he could, he prevented himself from so doing. His great object now was to find out if the soldiers had left the place, and he ran half way down the stairs, to see if he could observe any signs of them. He was not long kept in a state of suspense

"Forward!—March!" cried a voice. "You are sure, sergeant, that the men have ball cartridge?"

"Yes, sir."

"It's all up with me now," said Hawk, as he retreated to the corridor again. "I can but sell my life as bravely as possible. Ha! what is this?"

He had trodden upon the key of Phebe's bed-room door, which she had dropped in the corridor upon being surprised by her mistress while she was in the act of trying if it would fit the lock of Miss Egremont's door. That key gave Captain Hawk a new train of thought.

"Let me see," he said: "I have been once in custody and escaped. Why may I not do so again? While there is life there is hope; but if I determine upon my own death, all is lost. It is true, that I might take the lives of some two or three of these soldiers, but what good would that do me? They are but the agents of a system with which they have nothing to do. It would be no revenge whatever. The others would fire upon me, and I should fall—perhaps, too, only hurt grievously, and so be dragged, bleeding, to prison."

Tramp—tramp, came the soldiers up the staircase, and the flash of lights streamed into the corridor.

"Yes," added Captain Hawk, "I am decided. They shall take me, if they find me, and I will not at this juncture aggravate my position by bloodshed, with the feeling that it won't possibly do me any good; but I will be even with you, Miss Phebe, far all your kindness, both to me and to your mistress."

With these words, Captain Hawk retreated into the bed-room of Phebe, the waiting-maid, and closed the door. A light was burning upon the dressing-table, and by its beams he saw that the apartment was a comfortable enough one, and that a large four-post bedstead was in one corner.

Without a moment's hesitation, Hawk got into the bed, and covered the clothes right up to his throat. He then shifted to the other side of the bed, and lay there, so that he gave the appearanec as if two persons had been in the bed, and then he quietly waited the result.

In the course of a few moments there was an immense bustle in the corridor, and Captain Hawk heard the voice of Phebe calling out—

"I tell you I can show you where the highwayman is. I tell you I can give him up, and I will. Oh, the wretch, I should like to see him hanged, that I should. This way, everybody—this way."

"That way?" said the Marquis of Pembroke. "Why, that is the door o Miss Egremont's room."

"To be sure it is, my lord. Do you think that I am as blind as a beetle, and don't know that?"

"But the girl is mad!" said the officer.

"No, Mr. Officer, I ain't mad, though you have got a fine red coat; but I can tell you all, and I don't mind who hears it, that my young misses, Miss Egremont, has discharged me because I didn't approve of her having a fancy highwayman."

"This is too absurd!" said the marquis.

"You will be punished for this, my girl," said Lord Rholey.

"I will take good care of that," said the marquis, angrily. "I am hardly going to hear a young lady, who is my guest, talked of in this way. Oh, madam, I am glad you are here."

These words were addressed to Miss Egremont's aunt, who had just appeared.

"Yes, and so am I," screamed Phebe, "so am I; and I can tell you, my lady, that your niece, Miss Egremont, has got the highwayman in her room now."

"How dare you say such a thing, you hussy?"

"Hussy or not hussy, it's true, ma'am; and all you have to do is to go and look, and there you will find him, I'll eat my head if you don't."

"You vile wretch!" said the aunt, "I will have you prosecuted, if it costs me a thousand pounds."

"Try it, my lady, try it," cried Phebe. "I'm pretty sure that someone kicked me all the way down the stairs and broke my back—at least it's very near broke, and that's much the same thing."

"Is it?" said Lord Rholey.

"Really, this is too absurd," said the Marquis of Pembroke. "Here have we been all startled from our wine by the cries of this girl, that the highwayman was up stairs; and now she tells us an absolutely impossible story about his being in the chamber of Miss Egremont."

"My niece is unwell," said the aunt, "and I myself assisted her into bed an hour ago. I daresay this tumult has terrified the poor child. I will go and see how she is."

"There," cried Phebe, "her door is open."

"Yes, I left it open," said the aunt. "The door happens to have no night bolt, and so I just closed it, as Miss Egremont was abed, before I left the room."

With this, the aunt went into the bedroom, and found Miss Egremont just recovering from the faint into which see had fallen.

"My dear," said the aunt, "here is Phebe will have it that the highwayman is in your room."

"Oh, how wicked," said Miss Egremont. "How wicked of Phebe. I am far from well, aunt; will you stay with me?"

"Certainly, my child; I will be with you again in a moment."

The aunt merely went to the door of the bed-room, to speak to the marquis.

"Nothing in all the world," she said, "can be so wicked as this girl, Phebe, saying what she has said. My niece is really quite ill, and I am going to stay with her; and I assure you all, gentlemen, there is no highwayman in the room."

"Make all our apologies to her," said the marquis, "and tell her that we never for one moment paid the least attention to such a ridiculous fabrication."

"Oh, it's no fabrication," said Phebe; "all I ask is that somebody keeps watch at the door."

"For the protection of the ladies while we search the other rooms," said the officer, "I will place a sentinel at the door; but, I repeat, it is for their protection solely."

"Hoity toity!" said Phebe. "Marry come up! How fine we are, to be sure. Of course, great people with plenty of money never think of doing anything that's wrong, not they."

"Silence!" said the Marquis of Pembroke. "If we are indulged with any more of your insolence, you shall be turned out of the house, late as it is. How dare you give your tongue

MISS EGREMONT IN HER CHAMBER WHERE CAPTAIN HAWK IS CONCEALED.

such unwarrantable licence about your betters?"

This threat had some effect upon Miss Phebe, for she was much more quiet; and when she did speak again, it was in a more subdued tone than she had used before. She knew that when the Marquis of Pembroke said a thing, that he meant it, and would keep his word.

CHAPTER XXXVII.

CAPTAIN HAWK IS ONCE MORE AT BOYES HALL.

SITUATED as he was so very close at hand, it was quite impossible but that Captain Hawk should hear all that was going on in the corridor; and he was well pleased, notwithstanding his own great peril, to find that Phebe got into such general disgrace for her assertions regarding Miss Egremont, towards whom she acted certainly a very base part.

The fact was, that Miss Egremont had been much too indulgent a mistress to the girl, who had presumed too much upon the genuine good temper that she found in her employer to say and do things that were quite outrageous; and now she could not control her anger because Miss Egremont would no longer submit to her caprice and her impertinence.

"What room is this?" said the officer, as he turned to the door of Phebe's chamber.

"Oh, that's my bed-room," she cried, "and there is no reason in the world for any one to go in there. I should never be able to sleep in a room again that a parcel of men had been in; so don't think of going there."

"Nonsense!" said the marquis. "Upon my word, what with the impertinence and the folly combined of this girl, we shall be sick at last. Let us search all the rooms that there are not ladies in."

"But look at me!" cried Phebe. "What am I?"

"Only a female," said the sergeant, as he pushed her on one side; "anything but a wise one into the bargain, I take it. So be so good as to get out of the way."

"You wretch!"

In her rage, Phebe would have made an attempt to scratch the sergeant's face but one of the soldiers laid hold of her round the waist, and fairly lifted her off her feet, notwithstanding all her kicking and struggling to get free, to the great amusement of all the others.

The sergeant approached the door of the bed-room, which had been appropriated to Phebe's use, and turned the handle of the lock.

Now, Captain Hawk had quite made up his mind what to do, and he knew perfectly well that his capture was inevitable if the bed-room was entered at all; so he resolved to pay Miss Phebe for all the ill-nature that had characterised her proceedings with regard to her young mistress, Miss Egremont.

The moment the door was a little way open, Captain Hawk called out—

"Is that you, my darling of a Phebe?"

Everybody heard this, and there was a dead silence, while astonishment sat upon every face.

"Why don't you come in?" added Captain Hawk. "You said you would not be long. What a time you have kept me waiting, you little devil."

The astonishment with which every one (including Phebe herself) heard these words, had reached its height now, and the sergeant called out—

"Hilloa! Who's here?"

"The deuce!" said Captain Hawk. "Who speaks?"

The sergeant made a rush into the room, followed by the officer and the Marquis of Pembroke, and there, sure enough, they saw Captain Hawk, sitting up, and looking very much confused, in Miss Phebe's bed. They laid hands upon him in a moment, and the officer said in stern tones—

"You are our prisoner. Any resistance will be your death."

"Prisoner?"

"Yes. Bind his hands, sergeant."

"Yes, sir."

"Oh, but this is some mistake. Phebe, where are you?—Phebe, have you betrayed me? Oh, you faithless, wicked maid, after protesting that for love of me you would do anything, and promising that you would get me out of the house safely, if I would promise to meet you now and then only. You faithless Phebe! After asking me to hide in your bedroom, too, and saying you would come as soon as you could! Oh, horrid, shameful, traitor of a Phebe, I despise you now!"

"Upon my word, Miss Phebe," said the Marquis, "you are a pretty article."

"Very, indeed," said the officer.

"A most abandoned piece of goods," said Lord Rholey.

"A shameless hussy," said another.

"One of the most awful hypocrites that ever I heard of in all my life," said a gentleman who was present.

"And then to attempt to vilify the character of Miss Egremont too," added the Marquis of Pembroke. "Upon my word, I never did come near such a case of deliberate atrocity."

During the utterance of all these reproaches, the bewildered Phebe could only look from one to the other as they spoke, like a person in a dream. She was too much astounded for some few minutes to speak; but when she did, it was with a shrieking tone that she cried out—

"Oh, what does it all mean?"

"That's what I want to know," said Captain Hawk.

"Oh, am I awake?"

"You are not half wide awake enough to keep secret your own bad conduct, you stupid girl," said the sergeant. "I'm ashamed of you."

"So am I," said Lord Rholey; "and she always pretended to be such a miracle of virtue, too."

"Oh, yes, a perfect paragon," said the marquis.

"Really, gentlemen," said Captain Hawk, "I hope I haven't said anything to make you think that Miss Phebe here is not a very moral and innocent young woman, which I assure you she is."

At this, everybody smiled, and Phebe was in such a way, that, turning upon Captain Hawk, she screamed out—

"Oh, you wretch! I hate the sight of you! Oh, you monster!"

"Oh, well, if you hate the sight of me, there's your key again that you gave me to let myself into your room with. Why did you pretend to be so fond of me if you now hate the sight of me?"

"I pretend to be fond of you?"

"Yes, to be sure."

"Oh, no! oh—oh!"

"Well, how comes he here in your bed?" said Lord Rholey.

"How comes it you are a fool?" said Phebe.

The marquis laughed.

"Come, come, Miss Phebe," he said, "I will trouble you to get out of this house as quickly as you can; it is not so much for your own gross immorality, bad as that is, which induces me to give such an order; but your conduct in trying to blast the good name of your young mistress is too abominable to pass over."

"Much too abominable," said everybody."

"Come—come, Phebe," said Captain Hawk, "you see it is of no use denying it any longer; you know you said you loved me better than either of your last eight men, because I was the biggest. Can you deny that?"

"I'll soon let you know!" cried Phebe, and she made a dash at Captain Hawk, but he adroitly slipped out at the other side of the bed, and left Phebe sprawling upon it, to the great amusement of everyone in the room.

"Let this end," said the Marquis of Pembroke; "it is a most ridiculous proceeding. Is this really Captain Hawk, the highwayman?"

"Yes," shouted Mr. Jobson, "I know it is Captain Hawk."

"Very well, then," said the officer, "I shall order my men to hold him in custody until he can be given up to the civil power. If a constable can be found, I shall be glad."

"There is no single constable who will take charge of him," cried Jobson. He is a most desperate ruffian. Now, my Lord Rholey, are you convinced?"

"Yes, that you are a greater fool than I thought you."

"What is to be done, then?" said the officer. "I can only hold this man, as a felon, a prisoner till the civil power relieves me of him. Can you put him, my lord, into any room of your house for security until a messenger can be sent to London for the officers?"

"Yes, that I can do; and I think, as the hour is so late a one, that it is the best suggestion that can be acted upon. My steward will find some secure place for him until the police arrive, and then they can do as they please in the matter."

This argument was to Captain Hawk the most satisfactory one that could be made, for he had a hope that he might escape from the mansion before the officers arrived: and, indeed, he was not without a suspicion that the marquis would not be sorry if he did so escape.

"Allow me to state," he said, "that you are all mistaken in me; but yet, as I am in the hands of the Marquis of Pembroke, I shall, at least, have the satisfaction of feeling that I shall receive the treatment dictated by the heart and brain of a gentleman."

"But what's to become of me?" cried Phebe.

"If you had your deserts, you would be ducked in one of the fish-ponds," said the marquis; "but as it is, you will be permitted to leave the house without injury. What steps Miss Egremont and her aunt may think proper to take to punish you for your atrocious conduct, is no concern of mine.'

"Why, you idiot!" cried Phebe, "do you believe that I am guilty? No, you can't believe it. I tell you this highwayman came from Miss Egremont's room, and got into my bed."

"There—there, we don't want to hear any more," said Lord Rholey. "Such expressions from the lips of a woman are always very d sgusting."

"Disgusting, you brute! Why you wanted to ki-s me on the stairs only this morning, you mean-looking wretch."

"Oh—oh!" said everybody. "What a dreadful woman this is."

"It's true!" she shouted, "it's true! And you, my Lord Marquis, are no better than you should be, for only the other day you told me I had a pretty chin."

"Oh—oh! Really the woman is mad," said the officer.

"Why, you wretch!" cried Phebe, turning to him, "you began winking at me before you had been in the house ten minutes."

"Poor thing!" said Captain Hawk, "it is quite clear that she is a little out of her mind, and I no longer consider her affection and caresses to me as any compliment."

"Let her be removed and taken care of," said the marquis. "We will try and get her into the country lunatic asylum."

"Yes—yes," said everybody. "That will be best."

This so terrified Phebe, that she made a rush past them all, and reaching the staircase, she flew down it at a great rate, before any one could move to stop her, and disappeared.

"Let her go," said the marquis, "she cannot come to much harm.—Oh, Mr. Leigh, can you place this prisoner anywhere for security, until the police officers come from London to take charge of him?"

"Yes, my lord; he will be quite safe in the muniment-room, along with the armour, and the family portraits and papers."

"Ah! so he will. I did not think of that. It is the strongest room in the mansion, gentlemen, and built to be fire-proof. It is made so to protect the heirlooms of our family, and there they are deposited likewise under the additional protection of iron chests."

"Oh, yes, my lord," added Mr. Leigh the steward. "He will by safer there than in the county jail, I'll warrant, for the door is iron, and the lock is such a one as nobody would think of attempting to pick or to break."

"That will do capitally," said the officer; "and I hope you will consider, my lord, that I am no further responsible for the safe keeping of this Captain Hawk, if it be indeed he."

"That's the question," said Lord Rholey.

"No," cried Jobson. "It's no question—it's——"

"Silence, sir!' said Lord Rholey. 'I desire that you will take yourself off with all convenient speed. It is quite impossible I can have any one as a friend and companion who has made himself so supremely ridiculous as you have lately."

Jobson groaned, for he now found that indeed his patron, Lord Rholey, had made up his mind to do without him. Well he knew that there were many who would be glad enough of the situation he had held for a considerable time, of humble friend to a nobleman with as small a share of brains as Lord Rholey had.

"Oh, my lord," he said, "I beg that your lordship will consider."

"I never considered yet, and I am not going to do so now, Mr. Jobson, to please you," said Lord Rholey, testily.

The marquis bit h s lips to keep himself from laughing outright at this fracas between Lord Rholey and his humble friend; but turning to the sergeant, he said—

"Follow my steward with your prisoner. He will show you where to place him for security."

"Am I to be starved?" said Captain Hawk.

"You will do very well," replied the marquis, "till the officers come. Two hours will, I daresay, bring them here, and then they can use their own discretion as regards you."

CHAPTER XXXVIII.

CAPTAIN HAWK TRIES TO ESCAPE FROM THE STRONG ROOM.

Captain Hawk did not want any food. He only hoped that some servant might be sent to him with some, and that the visit might enable him to do something towards his escape.

In the course of five minutes he was locked up in the muniment-room, as it was called, and in profound darkness, for that room had no windows in it, so that there was not even a night light from the sky within its dreary walls. The door, too, shut so closely, that not a ray of light got through it anywhere but by the key-hole, and that was so weak and inefficient a little pencil of light, that it in nowise detracted from the gloom of the room.

Captain Hawk had a sentinel placed at the door.

"It is not possible they say, that the prisoner can get out," said the sergeant, "but if he should, your duty will be to seize him, and give the alarm to the guard at once; and if he should resist, you will use your arms."

Hawk heard the clash of the soldier's musket as he grounded it upon the stone floor outside the room.

After that all was still for a time.

"I wonder now," thought Captain Hawk, "if Miss Egremont will make any effort to save me?"

We must look upon it as a very special piece of vanity for Hawk to have held any such idea in his head; for, after all, what was he to Miss Egremont? and, to tell the truth, if she had been ever so much inclined, from motives of humanity, to interfere in his behalf, she was really too ill from the fright and excitement she had passed through on his account to leave her bed.

Her aunt was likewise in close attendance upon her.

Captain Hawk was not exactly the sort of man to sit down and despair, even in such an extremity of evil fortune as that which had come over him now; and after a little time he rose, and began feeling cautiously all round the room.

From the glance he had taken of the apartment when first he had been lighted into it, he had seen that some five or six suits of armour hung upon the walls, and now he touched the cold steel breast-plate of one of them.

By feeling slowly up and down this suit of armour, he was able to discover that it was a complete collection of plate armour, and the idea struck him, that it presented to him a faint chance of escape.

"If I had but a light now," he said, "I would endeavour to put on this armour, and by standing close up against the wall with the visor down, who knows but that I may go free? And yet how would they account for my absence? No, I am afraid it would not do; and yet if I only had a light I should like to try it."

As though his wish for the light had been an invocation to bring him one, the door was opened, and the officer and the sergeant appeared. The latter carried a light, a bottle with some wine in it, and a glass, as well as a loaf of bread under his arm.

Silently these thing were placed upon the only table in the room, and then the officer spoke—

"There is no desire upon the part of the Marquis of Pembroke, nor upon that of Lord Rholey, to make your situation worse than it seriously is, so they have sent you some refreshment; and Lord Rholey says, he would like to compare your snuff-box with his, as it attracted the curiosity of Mr. Jobson so much."

Captain Hawk quite understood this message. It was nothing more nor less than a polite request from Lord Rholey for his snuff-box; and so, taking it from his pocket, he handed it to the officer, saying—

"Tell his lordship, I beg his acceptance of this box."

"Very well."

No doubt Lord Rholey had made a confidant of the officer in the business. At least, it seemed so by his manner.

"You will leave me the light?" said Hawk.

"Oh, yes."

"I thank you, sir. It is, after all, something to fall into the hands of a gentleman, let one's situation be ever so unpleasant."

"I wish you had gone away before I reached the house, I am sure," said the officer; "but now my duty compels me to keep you secure. The police are sent for from London, and the sooner they arrive the better I shall be pleased. Good evening to you."

"Good evening," said Captain Hawk. "I have no difficulty, sir, in drawing a line of distinction between your duty and your own feelings."

Once more the prisoner was alone, and now he had what he had so ardently wished for—a light; and he might well be pardoned for the superstitious idea, that the light being brought to him was on account of the fact, that he was by fate to escape from the state of thraldom in which he then was.

People who pass through great dangers, generally pick up such ideas, sooner or later.

There was one thing which he felt particularly easy about, and that was, that he would now meet with no interruption, for some considerable time at least. Although two hours or so had been spoken of as the probable time when the officers might be expected from London, he felt quite sure that it would be much more likely to be double that time.

The light burnt with but a sickly lustre in the damp confined air of the room, but still it was amply sufficient to let Hawk see any object clearly about him. The suit of plate armour that in the dark had attracted his regards, he now saw was a most magnificent coat of mail, indeed; and again the idea of getting it about him came strongly across his imagination.

There was one temptation, too, in his situation to try any hazardous experiment for liberty, and that was, that even if he were discovered, he could but be as before, a prisoner.

"Yes," he said, "I will try it."

It may be supposed that Captain Hawk was no great adept at putting on a suit of armour, for beyond the general kind of knowledge of such matters which every man who has read much has, of course he knew nothing about it. But where there is a will there is a way: so that, after some fumbling and trouble, he managed to get on the greater portion of the armour, and had the satisfaction of finding that it fitted him as if it had been made for him.

The weight of it was prodigious; in fact, it was intended only to be used on horseback, so that Captain Hawk found he could hardly move about with it all upon him.

The visor was of a peculiar make, and when it was closed, it only left a few little holes opposite to each eye and a few more at the mouth to breathe through, otherwise the face was most completely hidden.

"Now," said Captain Hawk, as he closed the visor only partially, but so that with a touch he could clasp it close shut. "Now they may come as soon as they like, and the sooner the better, for I am not so fond of this panoply of steel."

Again strangely it appeared as if the wishes of Captain Hawk gave laws to circumstances, for hardly had these words escaped his lips, than he heard footsteps in the passage outside the door of the room.

"Ah!" he said, "they come, indeed!"

To place himself at once against the wall in the exact spot that had been occupied by the suit of armour was the work of a moment, and then closing the visor, he stood as still as death, waiting the issue of the adventure.

The sound of approaching footsteps became each moment more apparent, and then Captain Hawk heard the sentinel say—

"Who goes there!"

"A friend," said a voice. "Your officer. You can go off duty now; the police from London will take charge of the prisoner."

The soldier marched away to join his comrades in the kitchen of the mansion, where they were making free with the strong ale of the Marquis of Pembroke.

"You have ridden fast?" said a voice.

"Yes, sir," replied another. "The fact is, when we heard it was a likelihood of being Captain Hawk, we did not spare our cattle. It is a great thing to nab him, if we possibly can, sir."

"Well, it seems that this is the very fellow that we have here, then. Pray walk in. Why, hilloa! how is this?"

"How is what, sir?"

"Some one has left the door unfastened."

"You don't mean that, sir?"

"Indeed, but I do."

"Then Captain Hawk has escaped, I'll wager my head. He has given us the slip again, you may depend."

"The deuce he has!"

They all entered the room together, while Captain Hawk was silently cursing his own folly for not having tried the door before he attired himself in the suit of armour. The thought occurred to him that the door had been purposely left open, or rather unlocked, by the officer, when the light and the wine were brought to him, so that he might escape; but he, never suspecting that such a chance was possible, had neglected it.

To be sure, the sentinel would have been rather in the way; and yet, as he took rather a long march down the corridor, he might have been avoided.

This was rather a bitter reflection to Captain Hawk, who so much sighed for feedom.

"It's too true: he is not here."

"No," cried the officer, "of course not!"

"D—n it, what a sell!" said one of them.

"The bird has flown, I'm afraid," said Mr. Leigh, the steward, who was waiting upon the officers. "Well, all I can say is, that I am as sorry as I can possibly be."

"Are there any hiding-places here?"

"Oh, dear, no, not one."

The officers were four in number, and stout, resolute, well-armed men, who were not likely to be trifled with; and it was evident from their manner, that they were terribly vexed at the fact of the disappearance of their prisoner.

Captain Hawk kept perfectly still, which he had less difficulty, no doubt, in doing with the armour upon him, than as if he had been without it, for, to tell the truth, the mere weight of it was enough to keep any one quiet.

Through the little holes opposite to his eyes in the visor, he could see pretty well anything that was straight before the line of vision, but that was all.

"And these are suits of old armour?" said one of the officers.

"Yes, they belong to the family."

"My eye, what guys people must have looked and felt in them!" said another of the officers. "This is rather a fine one, though."

As he spoke, he tapped against the visor of the suit of armour in which Captain Hawk was encased with his knuckles.

"Yes," said the steward, "that is considered to be one of the finest suits in the whole collection, but, you see, gentlemen, that the prisoner is not here, and I can do nothing."

From the cool and serene manner in which the steward took the presumed fact of his escape, Captain Hawk thought still further that it was a planned thing on the part of the marquis and some of his guests to give him the opportunity of escaping; and more than ever he regretted that he had not availed himself of it.

"Well," said one of the officers, "this won't do for us. If he has got out of this room, he may be in the house somewhere, and we must have a good hunt all over it."

"I will speak to the marquis about that."

"Whether you speak to the marquis or not, we must do our duty. We have a warrant that will authorise us to look for our prisoner everywhere that we think it may be likely to find him."

They all left the muniment-room now, but the door was not made fast, and the moment Captain Hawk heard by the decreasing sound of their footsteps that they were some distance off, he slipped out of the room into the corridor, and as well as the weight of his armour would let him, and the necessity of not making a noise, he ran in an opposite direction.

Captain Hawk had not the smallest idea of where the route he was now pursuing would lead him to; but so that it took him away from his foes it was sufficient for the then present moment.

CHAPTER XXXIX.

CAPTAIN HAWK ASTONISHES THE SERVANTS IN THE HALL.

The news of the escape of Captain Hawk from the strong room spread like lightning through the establishment, creating the greatest possible surprise in the minds of all who knew anything of the strength and advantages of that apartment.

Among the servants, the muniment-room had always been considered as a kind of privileged place, which, by some special fiat of providence, was free from the evils and disasters attendant upon all other apartments. It was thought that fire could not touch it—floods could not injure it, and that all the united talents and audacity of all the housebreakers in the world would be in vain to enable them to effect an entry into it.

And now it appeared that one man had found a means of leaving it with the greatest apparent ease.

To be sure, the Marquis of Pembroke winked at Lord Rholey and at the officer of infantry, and they both winked at the Marquis of Pembroke; and all three of these persons had an idea that by leaving the door of the muniment-room only on the latch as had been done, that they had been the means of Captain Hawk's escape.

The reader, however, is aware that such was not the case, inasmuch as Hawk had, unfortunately for him, not been aware of the fact that the door was so left, until it was too late for him to avail himself of the knowledge.

They little expected that he was still in the house, and in a suit of armour too.

There were several motives which induced the Marquis of Pembroke to act as he had done. In the first place, he had a kind of chivalric dislike to the arrest of any one under his roof who had been his guest, even for a short space of time, although under an assumed character; and in the second place, the arrest would involve him in trouble, and attendance at the Old Bailey.

Perhaps this last reason had more weight than the first; but, at all events, the two combined was quite sufficient to induce him to wink at the escape of Hawk.

"I sincerely hope he is gone," said the marquis to Lord Rholey, in a whisper.

"So do I, Pembroke, since I have got back my snuff-box, which, I will say, he returned to me in a very handsome manner."

"Exactly."

From this little bit of dialogue, the reader will not fail to perceive that Lord Rholey had made a confidant of the Marquis of Pembroke, regarding the little adventure that he had had with Captain Hawk.

While all this was going on in the dining-room, whither the gentlemen had repaired, and where they still discussed their claret, Captain Hawk was wandering about a part of the house that was the least frequented of any, looking in vain for some mode of leaving it.

The fact was, that he had tried several doors, and at two of them that he so tried, he had been met by the unwelcome call from some one within the room of "Who's there?"

When he heard that, of course he took himself off as quickly as he could; and at another door that he had tried he had met with a still greater surprise, for as nobody spoke, he opened it and looked in, when he found that there was an old woman in the room darning some stockings, and the moment she saw him she only just uttered the words—"Good gracious!" and slipped off her chair in a swoon.

Captain Hawk was getting desperate.

While, then, he was thus vainly attempting to find some open route by which he might leave the mansion, the officers, who had been so disappointed at not finding him, held a consultation together on the lawn in front of the house.

"He is not far off," said one.

"Do you really think that?" said another.

"Yes, for the best of all possible means, namely, that his horse is in the stable, and that there would have been no difficulty to such a fellow as he is in the world in getting it."

CAPTAIN HAWK IN THE APARTMENT OF MISS EGREMONT.

"That says something."

"It says everything to me. I don't believe that Hawk would have gone without his steed."

"Well, it don't seem likely, now, does it?"

"Not at all," said another. "He is as bold as brass, and them sort of chaps consider their horse as so much a part of themselves, that you may depend he is lurking about the place."

"Then what do you propose?"

"Just this, that we take up our abode in the stable, and there wait for him, for, sooner or later, come there he will."

"By Jove, that is a good idea."

"Yes, but you know very well that it ain't an original one."

"And why not?"

"Didn't I and Joseph Brown take the celebrated pickpocket, Cliff, as he called himself, by finding out that he had a child at nurse at Camberwell, and going and waiting a whole fortnight by the side of the cradle, till at last in he popped, and called out in the coolest manner in all the world—

"'Well, how is the young 'un?'

"'Pretty well, sir,' says I.

"'Why, who are you?' said he with a scared kind of look, and taking two steps to the door again.

"'Lor, sir!' says I, 'don't you know me? You are my prisoner!' and then I was at him, and had him down on his back before you could say 'Jack Robinson,' and the candle upset in the scuffle, before we got the darbies on him, and the baby was rolled under the grate."

"Well—well, we won't dispute about it. Come on to the stable, and there let us keep snug, for, dead or alive, it will be a great thing for us to nab Captain Hawk."

"Ay, will it."

The officers, upon this, made their way to the stable, where Hawk's horse was quietly enjoying an evening's meal of sweet fresh hay, and there they waited with exemplary patience.

We now return to the proceedings of Hawk himself, who was still wandering about the lower part of the house, listening at every door he came to, and encountering not one mode of egress from the mansion, when he wished one in such an emergency.

After a time, he came upon a long stone passage, which had about six windows in its entire length; but as they were upon the ground floor, every one of them was defended by iron bars, so that he could not escape by one of them, which, otherwise, would have been one of the most easy things to do in the world for a man of his activity.

At the farther end of the stone passage, he saw the reflection of a light, which, by its red character, looked like a fire light, and as he neared it, he heard the murmur of voices. Treading as softly as he could in his armour, he approached a door that was just open about an inch or so, and seemed to be placed for the purpose of ventilation.

Hawk peeped through the narrow opening, and saw that the apartment with which the door communicated was the great kitchen of the mansion; and a great kitchen it was—in the full acceptation of the adjective.

The floor of the kitchen was of stone, and it could not be less than some thirty feet square. The height, too, was very unusual for such an apartment. An enormous fire-place had a good roaring fire in it, and it was the light from that that had come out with a ruddy gleam into the passage.

From the roof, by an iron chain, was suspended a lamp, the light from which was quite pallid by the ruddy glow of the fire. The walls were hung round with an immense number of cooking articles, and the greater part of the servants of the establishment were assembled there, enjoying their tea, it being the hour at which they partook of that highly sociable meal.

They looked as comfortable as possible.

"They have lighter hearts," thought Captain Hawk, as he peeped in upon them, "than I shall ever have."

The servants, consisting of some twelve or fifteen persons, went upon the principle, in their conversation, of saving time, by sometimes all talking together; but that was a state of things which did not last long upon the present occasion, as one of the number, who, to judge by his portly aspect, had been long used to the consumption of the good things of this life, suddenly said—

"Well, you may talk as you like about them highwaymen fellows, but in my opinion, mind you, of course it is only my opinion, there's more in his disappearance than meets the eye."

This was a statement that it would have been very difficult indeed to contradict, so the rest only shook their heads, and said that they really shouldn't wonder but there was.

"Yes," added the portly man, who

was the under-butler, "when I saw him first, I said to myself, says I—'That is not a common sort of a person;' and now I want to ask you all a question."

"Yes, Mr. Smithers—yes," sid everybody."

"Hush!"

There was a dead silence in the kitchen.

"I want to ask you all," added Mr. Smithers, "if you ever saw such a wonderful likeness, in you lives, between any two people, as there is or was betweenthat fellow they say is a highwayman and the picture of the old Earl of Pembroke in the long gallery, in armour, that they say was killed by the thingummies in the what-do-you-call-itland."

"Do you mean the Saracens, Mr. Smithers?" said a footman.

"Perhaps I do."

"And the Holy Land?"

"Very likely I do; but that's neither here nor there, as you all know; only I say that, in my opinion, that man was not a man."

"Not a man!" screamed all the female portion of the auditory. "You don't say so?"

"I repeat it. Not a man. What do you think of that, ladies?"

"Why, that it's truly horrid," said a pretty housemaid.

"Exactly."

"Well, but, Mr. Smithers," said the cook, with her eyes as wide open as saucepan lids, "if he ain't a man—what is he?"

"A ghost!"

"A ghost!" cried everybody, and then there was a general movement of chairs closer round the fire. "A ghost!"

"Yes, a ghost; and, in my opinion, mind you, he was neither more nor less than the ghost of the old Earl of Pembroke, as was killed fighting the what-do-you-call-em's in the thingummy land."

"But he was so old," said the pretty housemaid.

"But I suppose, chatter-box, that he was young once, and mightn't it be a ghost of him when he was young?"

"Oh, yes—yes."

"To be sure," said everybody. "To be sure. Mr. Smithers is right enough," and then another movement of the chairs took place, and several looked askance over their shoulders.

"Is that door fast that leads into the stable-yard, and the garden?" said one, glancing to the other end of the room.

"No, it's only on the latch," said another.

"Oh, dear, do fasten it."

"Stuff," said Mr. Smithers, "stuff! Do you fancy, now, that it is any good in the world to fasten a door against a ghost, if he feels inclined to come? Why, he'd as soon pop down the chimney as look at it."

"Oh, dear, Mr. Smithers," said the cook, giving a glance up the spacious flue, "don't say that. I'll forgive everybody everything but meddling with the chimbley, that I will; for if soot falls, and you once get among the blacks, what's to become of your coats, I should like to know?"

"Well," said Mr. Smithers, "I may be wrong—I am not by any means a positive man, and so, I say, that I may be wrong—quite wrong, in a manner of speaking; but, of course, you all know what the old earl did in this very house?"

"Oh, no—no! What?"

"He married."

"Yes—yes?"

"And they do say that he killed his wife, and that was the reason he went to the thingummy land to fight he what-do-you-call-em's; and there's a dreadful story of what happed here the very night he was killed."

CHAPTER XL.

MR. SMITHERS TELLS A DREADFUL ANECDOTE.

Captain Hawk heard all this from his advantageous position outside the door with the greatest ease, and for the last five minutes he had been asking himself in what way the fears of these servants could be made subservient to his means of escape from the mansion.

The mention, by Mr. Smithers, of his supposed ghostly character, made it very tempting for him to carry out such an idea; but when that sapient personage announced a dreadful story, Captain Hawk made up his mind to listen to it, with the hope that it would afford him a hint of action, upon which he might proceed with greater certainly than he otherwise would be able to do.

"Oh, Mr. Smithers," said the cook, "if so be as you has anything dreadful to tell, let me here it at once, for if there's anything in all the world as is my delight, it's horrors."

"And so it's mine," said the pretty housemaid. "Horrors and love is the only two things that in all the world is worth attending to. Don't you think so, Thomas?"

"Oh, dear, no, I like the love," said Thomas, the footman, "without the horrors."

"If," said Mr. Smithers, waving his hand in a very majestic manner. "If you feel inclined to listen to what I have to say, at once say so. If you don't, don't."

"Oh, yes—yes, Mr. Smithers, indeed we do."

"Hem! Very good. It won't take above a couple of minutes to tell, and it's just this, ahem!"

Everybody looked brimful of expectation, and the pretty housemaid got nearer to Thomas, while the cook kept casting furtive glances up the large chimney—for since it had been brought into question, she could not divest her imagination of the terrible supposition that the ghost of the old Marquis of Pembroke, who was killed by the Saracens in the Holy Land, might come into the kitchen that way.

"Listen," said Smithers. "You must know all of you, that on one particular night many years ago, while the wind was howling, and the clouds were going along the sky like mad, and all the weather vanes were screaming, the lights in the house suddenly burnt blue——"

"Blue! Oh, gracious!"

"Silence!"

"Yes—yes, Mr. Smithers; but don't say too much. You left off at blue, sir."

"Well, the awful and mysterious hour of midnight struck twelve——"

"It usually does," said Thomas.

"Sir, if you interrupt me by any such remarks, I will leave you to tell the story yourself, sir."

"But I really don't know it, Mr. Smithers."

"Sir, I didn't say you did; but I say it fearlessly and without the least dread of contradiction, that the man who interrupts me is a humbug!"

Thomas was about to speak, but the pretty housemaid placed her hand over his mouth, and cried "Hush!" so he held his peace, and Mr. Smithers went on with the anecdote, considering that he had struck his auditors with a lowering awe, and upheld his dignity in a proper and efficient manner.

"The lights, as I say, burnt blue, all of them, from the candles in the kitchen to the wax lights in the dining-room all blue, and then a curious noise was heard on the grand staircase; it was a kind of stamp—stamp—stamping noise, as if a horse was coming up; and when the door was opened of the drawing-room, who should they see but the old marquis, in complete armour, coming up the stairs, with his face all over gore, and the blood dripping out of the crevices of his armour, as he came along."

"Oh, how horrid!"

"Yes; but that's not the worst."

"Oh, go on—go on!"

"I'm a-going on. When he got to the top of the stairs, he made a full stop, and he said then, in a dreadful, hollow voice, that sounded as if it came out of six coffins all one in another and then buried in a very deep grave, 'I am here!—I am here!'"

At this moment, Captain Hawk slowly opened the kitchen door, and stalking in, said, in a deep voice that sounded very supernatural from behind his visor—

"I am here!—I am here!"

The servants took but one glance at the figure all clothed in complete steel, and then the roar and the scream that came from all their throats was hideous. Mr. Smithers fell backwards in a coner, chair and all. The pretty housemaid clasped Thomas round the neck, and then fainted away, and the rest made wild rushes into cupboards and under the tables and the dressers, roaring, kicking, screaming, and fainting, in all directions.

"Beware!" said Captain Hawk, "oh beware!—beware!"

He then stalked across the kitchen to the door leading to the stables, which they had mentioned, and which was the very route of all others that he wished to take; and lifting the latch of it, he was out of the kitchen in a moment, to his great satisfaction.

The noise that the servants made in the agony of their fright was sure to speedily alarm the whole house, so that Captain Hawk told himself that he had no time to lose in getting his horse and leaving the house. The armour, though, was now very much in his way, and he paused in a sort of scullery to get off as much of it as he could rapidly disengage from his limbs.

The helmet, and all the most cum brous pieces of the coat of mail, he quickly enough threw from him, and then he left the scullery, closing the door behind him, and found himself at once in the open air, in a small paved court-yard.

One glance showed him a gate, for the stars had come out now, and were sweetly spangling the heavens, spreading a serene and beautiful light after the rain upon the face of the earth.

"That way must lie the stables," said Hawk, and he ran to the gate. It was only on the latch and he was past it in a moment, and then he saw before him the long line of stabling of the mansion.

"I am free now," he said, "if I can but find my horse. This is a delicious feeling now, this calm and cool breath in the open air. Oh, freedom —freedom, what a boon art thou!"

The first portion of the stables he went into had several horses in, which he managed to discern were none of his; but the second door he opened led him to where his horse was, and at his entrance the creature made a sound of congratulation, which Captain Hawk knew in a moment, as it was accustomed to do so upon seeing him after an absence of any length of time.

"Ah, my gallant steed," he said, "we have met again, have we? We will yet have a gallop upon the sweet green meadows this night. Come—come, let me find your gear if I can, and if I can't, why, we must be off without it Oh, for a light!"

"Here's one, Captain Hawk," said a voice.

At the moment, the flash of a lantern, that was suddenly unmasked, was in his eyes, and a couple of strong men sprang upon him, and held his arms tightly.

"Resistance is in vain. Captain Hawk, you are our prisoner. We are London officers, and we know our business."

"Clap the darbies on him," cried another.

"Here you are."

Almost before Captain Hawk could consider where he was, or what had happened to him, he was handcuffed and completely at the mercy of his foes. Then he drew a long breath and made one tremendous and unavailing struggle, after which he was as still as death.

"It won't do, captain. You are nabbed.

"I know it."

"Well, that's all right. We don't want to make you a bit more uncomfortable than we can help, but we have got our duty to do, you see, and we mean to do it. Search him, Western, with me."

With professional tact they searched the pockets of Captain Hawk, and so deprived him of his weapons of offence, and then they very composedly lit a lamp that was in the stable, and proceed to saddle their horses and his likewise.

"Where am I to go?" said Hawk, with a forced calmness in his tone and manner, that did not deceive the officers a bit.

"To London."

"Let me ride my own horse, then."

"No, thank you; one of ours fell lame in coming down here, but it can go at a decent trot, notwithstanding, and you will ride that, captain, as we are in no very particular hurry."

Hawk bit his lip, but made no reply; he felt that these officers did know their business, and that they were not the men to throw away a chance. That he would be conducted to London now, without a likelihood of escape, seemed inevitable.

"You go, Jones," said one, "and let

them know in the house that we have our man."

"No," said Hawk. "It can make no difference to you to come away at once with me. It is useless to make me the gazing stock of the whole household. If you wish to take me to London, start at once."

"Well, I don't mind. What do you say, Western?"

"Oh, I say, come on at once with him. It's no use bothering here with him; we have got him, and that's all we need care about. He has done nothing here, you know, that's worth the mentioning, so just mount and be off."

"Very good."

Captain Hawk felt a little grateful to the officers for sparing him the general gaze and remarks of the house; but he need not have done so, for in complying with his request, they only studied their own convenience, and their own wishes to lodge him in jail as quickly as possible, so that they might go to the Secretary of State's Office, and claim the handsome reward that had been offered for his apprehension.

They mounted him upon the horse that had gone a little lame, so as to deprive him of the chance of giving them a gallop after him, which very likely he would have done if they had let him ride his own steed; and they further secured him, by tying his ankles together with a stout cord, going under the belly of the horse.

"That will do, I think," said one.

"I believe you," laughed another. "You won't give us the slip now, captain, will you?"

Hawk made no reply, and the officers nudged each other, and laughed at the state of dejection that they had got their prisoner to. They rode out of the stable-yard, and had nearly got to the lodge gates of the estate, when they were met by a horseman, who cried out—

"Who goes there?"

"Officers of police with a prisoner," was the ready reply.

"Stop, then, for I am a magistrate. My name is Easthope—you ought to know it."

"If you are Sir William Easthope, sir——"

"I am. Stop at the lodge, here. Who is your prisoner, and what has he done?"

"It is Captain Hawk, sir."

"What, the murderer of Judge Holme?"

"The same, your worship."

"Are you sure of his identity?"

"Oh, yes, your worship, there is no doubt in the world about that. It is all right, sir. He is our man, and no mistake at all in the world, Sir William."

"Prisoner, do you confirm what the officers say?"

"Why should I?" said Hawk.

"Well, there is no reason why you should, certainly; but you well-know, officers, that if you apprehend an escaped prisoner after his committal, and pending his trial, your duty is to take him for examination before the committing magistrate."

"Why, your worship, we are anxious to take him to Newgate. It was Sir John Boyes, of Boyes Hall, who committed him."

"If he will confirm that truth, and admit that he is the person, you can go on with him."

"No," cried Hawk, "my name is Smith."

"Then you must take him to Sir John Boyes' house at once, and I will ride with you. It is, luckily, not out of your way. Mind you, I have no doubt about your being right, but it is as well to do things regular."

"All is right, sir; we will obey your orders, Sir William."

"I shall, perhaps, see *her* again," whispered Hawk.

CHAPTER XLI.

CAPTAIN HAWK HAS TIME TO THINK IN NEWGATE.

There can be no doubt in the world but that the officers would have been much better pleased to have taken Captain Hawk right on to London, although such a course would be a little irregular, and they would have done so, if they had not chanced to encounter his worship "the magistrate."

When, however, he had pointed out

a particular course to them, and they knew at the same time it was the right one, they had no alternative but to obey it.

To be sure, they were rather surprised at the designs of Captain Hawk in the transaction, who for the first time denied, or rather falsified his name, and that, too, with apparently no object—for it did not appear to them that it would do him any good to delay the progress to the metropolis.

They, of course, knew nothing of the powerful attraction there was for Hawk at Boyes Hall. They could not guess, that for the sake of locking only once again into the eyes of the fair May Boyes, that he would consent even to be carried as a felon to that house, where he had been as a guest.

And yet, after all, what a mere chance it was that, even when he got there, he would be permitted to see her who had certainly more than any living person succeeded in changing his vagrant affections. It was by no means necessary that she should make an appearance in the hall; it only wanted for Sir John to say, "That is the man," and then he was at once legally in custody; but yet it was a chance, however remote.

The officers turned towards the hall, and the magistrate accompanied them, for the distance was as nothing.

A remarkable change seemed to come over the aspect of Captain Hawk; for, whereas at his capture he looked apathetic, and, beyond a slight pallor that had crept over his features, there was no change in them, now they were lighted up with a hectic colour, and he was evidently in a state of unusual excitement.

The officers were more wary than before in guarding a prisoner who showed that strange thoughts were passing in his mind; and one of them whispered to him—

"It is your own doing, captain."

"What is my own doing?"

"Why, this going to Boyes Hall. If you had acknowledged who and what you were, you might have gone right on to London with us at once, you know."

"Yes, I know."

"Will you acknowledge now, then, that you are our man?"

"No!"

"Very good. An obstinate man must have his way; but the fact is, that Sir John Boyes is such a donkey that if once we get into his house, there is no knowing when we shall get out of it again."

To this Captain Hawk made no reply, and the officer left his side rather in dudgeon at the little success that his consolatory efforts had had upon the prisoner.

"Yes," thought Captain Hawk, "yes, I may see her. Out of pity to me, or out of the remembrance of her love that once shone brightly and freely in her heart, she may show herself to me, and that will be a something to dream of."

The officers wished to get the magisterial recognition of Captain Hawk over as soon as possible, so they now went on at rather a smart trot, and a turn in the road suddenly brought Boyes Hall, with its Italian garden right in their view.

"Here we are," said one.

A flush spread itself over the face and brow of Hawk; and as he thought of his wretched condition, the idea crossed his mind that, after all, it would have been as well to spare himself the pain, and May Boyes the agony of seeing him again in such a state. Once before she had so seen him, and surely that was suffering enough.

It was too late now, though, to retract, even if he could have brought himself to beg the officers to take him on at once; and so they entered the lodge gates to Boyes Hall.

"Bring your prisoner in slowly," said the magistrate, "and I will ride on to inform Sir John Boyes what is required of him in this matter, so that time will be saved."

"Yes, your worship, we will bring him along."

The magistrate rode hastily to the house; and as Captain Hawk was conducted through the lodge gates, he heard the gardener's wife, who resided there, cry out—

"Lack-a-day, we shall have all our throats cut, for here's that horrid highwayman fellow again! Why don't they hang him at once as an example?"

"Hold your tongue wife," said the

man; "he will be hung soon enough, I'll be bound."

This was the sort of reception that Captain Hawk met with on the threshold, as it were, of that house where he had been ever an honoured guest, but where his name now was a bye-word and a reproach. If such things did not move him, he must have had, indeed, a heart of adamant; but they did move him, only he would not exhibit the extent to which they did so.

And now he seemed as if the very air of the place he was in now was familiar to him, and a death-like sickness came over him at the thought that he might see May much changed by that suffering of the soul, which ever imprints the reward of its agonies upon the face.

He had not thought of that before.

The hall door was reached, and he saw a group of servants curiously looking out for him, as the news had spread that he was coming. But now we must follow the magistrate into the presence of Sir John Boyes, who was at home.

Sir William was pretty well acquainted with some of the peculiarities of Sir John Boyes, as who, indeed, was not, who had ever once been in contact with him? But yet he hoped that upon the present occasion, as it was a mere form to go through, he could not very well make any blunders or interpose any delays.

It did not seem, however, if we may judge by the result, that Sir William knew Sir John Boyes well enough to be able to say exactly what he might do.

Now, when his brother-magistrate was announced to him, Sir John put on an air of the most stately frigidity, and desired that he should be shown into the library, for, said Sir John—

"It looks well to receive people in a library, inasmuch, as in a manner of speaking, it is surrounded by books, which you may have read, and if you have read and understood them, the strong probability is, that they are comprehensible to you."

With this highly euridite speech, Sir John went to the library to meet Sir William.

"Well, Sir John Boyes," cried the other, "I hope I see you well?"

"Why, Sir William—a-hem!—I am as well as such a highly sensitive temperament as mine can be, in a manner of speaking. I hope that I am indebted to something extraordinary for the honour of this visit?"

"Why, you are, Sir John," replied Sir William, smiling as he took out his watch. "I should not have called upon you at this hour, I must confess, if it had not been upon business."

Sir John turned pale as Sir William consulted his chronometer, and then, in a highly confidential tone, he said—

"My dear, sir, is that a family watch?"

"A family watch?"

"Yes, sir. It behoves every person of rank and importance in the country, in my humble opinion, to have a family watch, and I may say that I have one, although, owing to divers little circumstances, in only goes when, in a manner of speaking, it is carried."

"That is not a very lively kind of watch, then, Sir John. I should say, if it were stolen from you it would be no great matter."

"Stolen, sir?"

"Yes; but as that is not the case, I should recommend you to send it to London to be put to rights."

Sir John looked alarmed.

"My good sir," he said, "let us proceed to business. I only spoke of my family watch, to assure you and the world in general that nothing whatever had happened to it, and that, in fact, and in a manner of speaking, it was all right, with the one exception of being broken into pieces."

"That is rather a large exception, Sir John."

"Sir, it may be a large exception, or it may not. We are now, sir, in a room devoted to the ancient authors, with whom it is pleasant to converse, and from whose varied stores of intellect I gather the—the—that is to say, I cull—I mean gather, in a manner of speaking, an insight into cookery."

"Cookery, Sir John?"

"Yes, Sir William, cookery. There is an ancient author over your head."

"The deuce there is!"

"Sit quiet, my dear, sir. I mean on the shelf."

"Well, I only hope he will remain there, that is all."

"Allow me to state, Sir William, that in that ancient author I found out a mode of cooking tomatoes, so that all the flavour went off in an impalpable vapour, and you could not tell the same from turnip water."

EVIL THOUGHTS COME TO HAWK WHILE GAZING ON MISS EGREMONT.

"Allow me to state, then, Sir John, that that ancient author is the greatest idiot I ever heard of."

"Sir, the man who calls an ancient author an idiot, implies that he is an ass."

"Well, he is an ass."

"Very good, Sir William. I beg you to take notice that I did not say he was not, by any means, although I disapprove of calling an ancient author by such an epithet as a general thing; and it seems to me that you might as well pronounce him a donkey."

"Come, Sir John, let's come to business."

"Certainly, sir; but how delightful it is to enjoy so highly classical a conversation as this."

"Oh, stuff, Sir John. The reason of my coming here, is that you may identify a fellow who is in custody at your door, and who denies that he is what he is."

"Indeed, sir?"

"Yes, sir, I allude to Captain Hawk, the murderer and highwayman, who was committed by you for trial, but who, as you are aware, managed to escape from the officers who were conveying him to London. He has been recaptured, and waits for you to identify him."

"Sir, I will do it."

"You will go through that form, then, at once?"

"Sir?"

"I say, I hope you will go through that form at once."

Sir John looked wildly about him, and alarm was visible upon his stolid countenance.

"Sir," he said, "do you want to make game of me in this very room, and surrounded by the ancient authors, or do you not?"

"Good gracious, Sir John, what crotchet have you got in your head now, I wonder? I only ask you to go through a form, and you look at me as if I had proposed something extraordinary to you."

"Allow me to remark," said Sir John Boyes, "that it does seem to me something extraordinary, and that you might as well, sir, ask the representative of all the Boyes' to go through an easy chair or a dining-table as a form; and, moreover, sir, I do not see that there is a form in this apartment."

"Gracious providence, are you mad?"

"No, sir; but allow me to remark, that——"

"Stuff, Sir John! I did not believe that you could be half such a fool. I mean, that you should go through the ceremony of identifying the prisoner, and backing the warrant for his apprehension in due form."

"Then, sir," said Sir John, "I excuse you, so don't make any apologies for your previous blunder."

"Well, that's cool."

"Sir, there is a good fire in the next room. The presence of the ancient authors in this apartment, I often fancy, makes it cool, which is equivalent in my opinion to its being of a low temperature, taking an atmospheric and thermometrical view of the subject."

With this learned speech, which almost astonished himself, Sir John rose and led the way from the library, with the full impression upon his mind that he had made quite an effect with his knowledge and verbosity upon Sir William.

CHAPTER XLII.

CAPTAIN HAWK DOES GET A GLIMPSE OF MAY BOYES.

By the time this little ridiculous interlude between the sapient Sir John Boyes and his brother-magistrate was over, Captain Hawk had been brought to the house, and placed in the very room adjoining the library to which Sir John conducted his friend.

Bitterly did Hawk repent the foolish pertinacity with which he had insisted, as it were, upon being brought to that house, for he met with nothing but glances of contempt and hatred upon all sides; and to a sensitive temper like his, nothing could be very well more galling than to be made a subject of vulgar comment, even by the servants.

Captain Hawk forgot, or he had not chosen even to think, that crime placed him in the social scale far below the very lowest menial in the whole establishment.

His hopes of seeing May decreased each moment; and although he could hardly suppose that the news of his presence would not come to her ears, yet even if she felt disposed to show herself for a moment to the man who had once rejoiced in her love, he did not see how she could very well do it.

They placed him on a chair, and an officer stood on each side of him, for they did not like his looks, and they had a pretty good idea of what he might be as an opponent, even with manacles upon him, provided he got really desperate.

Thus, then, they took care to be ready to fling themselves upon him at a minute's notice, and overpower him. As Sir John Boyes had said, the room was well warmed, and it was well lighted likewise.

"Hem!" said Sir John, as he entered the apartment. "It is a grievous and a troublesome thing to see one man, as I may say, to behold and see one Hawk, the aforesaid prisoner, nevertheless, again in this place."

Poor Sir John was again lapsing into legal phraseology, which he at times would take upon himself to affect.

"Sir John Boyes, if you please, sir," said one of the officers, "if you will be so good as to say at once that this is Captain Hawk, we will take him away at once."

"Si—lence!"

"Certainly, Sir John—certainly."

"Hem!—Ha! Silence in the court. You will understand all of you, that my presence constitutes this a court of justice at once—our person, I should say, being the representative of majesty."

Sir John bowed to himself in the looking-glass at these words.

"Here is the prisoner," said the officer, who took the lead in the affair, and who was most anxious to get out of the highly-troublesome presence of Sir John Boyes.

Upon this Sir John sunk into a chair, and motioning to the other magistrate to take a seat, he said—

"Vagabond!"

Nobody replied to this pleasant title.

"Va abond!" cried Sir John Boyes again. "Let me look at your face, that I may decide, which, by the way, is equivalent to coming to a decision, who and what you are."

Captain Hawk did not speak, but the officers forced him from the chair upon which they had seated him, and brought him tolerably close to Sir John Boyes, who thereupon nodded his head gravely three times, and then said—

"That is the individual."

"That will do, Sir John," said the principal officer. "We will not trouble you any further in this matter, sir."

"Stop."

"Yes, Sir John."

"Oh, you villanous villain!" added Sir John, addressing Captain Hawk, violently. "It appears to me that you are one of those Philistines who, in a manner of speaking, go about in the likeness of hyenas, seeking whom they may devour."

Still Captain Hawk did not speak, and Sir John added, as he raised his arm—

"I may likewise liken this individual to one of those crocodiles, which ancient authors, with whom, by the way, it is pleasant to converse, tell us are to be found in the mud of the Nile."

"Yes, sir," said the officer. "Good evening, Sir John."

"Stop. What prevents me from annihilating that rascal, Captain Hawk, who has made me so nervous, that I often catch myself with some ancient author in my head, turned upside down?"

"If you are not enamoured of this folly," said Captain Hawk to the officers, "I pray you take me hence."

"All's right. Come on."

"What prevents me," added Sir John, getting really in a passion. "What, I say, prevents me from crushing you, reptile as you are?"

Hawk glanced at him, and Sir John quailed beneath that cold, stern glance, and got quite round to the back of his chair.

"Sir John Boyes," said Captain Hawk, in a low, deep-toned voice, every word of which was heard plainly thoughout the apartment, "there are two reasons why you can never come to any serious harm from any hands. The first is your folly, which is so absolute and unconditional, that it would be a slir upon the manhood of any one who should interfere with you. The second is——"

Captain Hawk paused for a moment or two, and then, in a voice that was slightly broken, he added—

"No matter—no matter. Take me from this house."

Sir John was so completely thunderstruck by this speech from the prisoner, that he was silent for several moments, and the officers took, very judiciously, the opportunity of hustling Captain Hawk from the room before he could say anything. They had left their horses in care of one ot their number at the lodge gate, so they, on foot, now hurried Captain Hawk along the gravel path that wound round the well-kept lawn, and led to the lodge.

It will be remembered that the beautiful old Italian garden, with its devices and statues and fountains, was at the back of the hall.

"That's a good job over," said one of the officers.

"Oh, plague take that Sir John Boyes," said another. "I only wonder they don't shut him up in some private mad-house for the rest of his days."

"Hilloa! who goes there?" said a voice.

Captain Hawk started; he knew that voice well. It was that of Ratchley Boyes.

"A prisoner, sir," said the officer who was foremost, "a prisoner, that's all."

"Oh, my father has seen him, I suppose? What has he done?"

"Why, sir, it's Captain Hawk, and we only brought him here to be identified, that was all, sir."

"Captain Hawk!"

The young man advanced, and by the dim night light he looked at him who might be called his old enemy and his old friend. Hawk looked up in Ratchley's face, too, for a moment.

"Alas!" said Ratchley, "and so it has come to this again, Gerald Clifton."

"It has come to this," said Hawk. "Well?"

"Is it well?"

"Go on."

"I have no more o say—and yet I have, too. Gerald Clifton, you will be tried for your life, but you shall not want such assistance as the law allows to be given to the accused; you shall have a skilful advocate, and gold to fee him with. I can do no more."

"I asked nothing."

"No, it is true that you asked nothing, but it is my duty to give without being asked. Farewell! I do not think that we shall meet again."

"We shall!"

Ratchley Boyes turned and walked slowly away without another word, and Captain Hawk would have continued looking after him, but that the officers urged him on again, for they were impatient at the delay that had already taken place at Boyes Hall.

The lodge was now reached in a very few minutes, and there stood one of the servants, with a stable lantern, talking to the officer who had been left in charge of the horses.

"All's right—here they come," said the servant.

"That's the thing," said the officer. "Is it the right one?"

"Oh, yes—yes, of course it is; but, you see, that Sir John Boyes is enough to drive any one mad with his nonsense, that he is."

The servant with the lantern turned aside to laugh, for he did not think it quite the thing to laugh at his master openly, and upon his own premises too.

Hawk had now given up all idea of seeing May Boyes, and he felt a sensation of deep anguish and pain that he should have allowed himself to be brought to the hall, upon so very vague a chance of beholding her. He mounted the horse in silence, and the officers secured him on it as before. The lodge gates were opened.

"Take good care of him," said the lodge-keeper's wife.

"Ay, we will do that."

"Well, mind you do, and there will be plenty will come from here to Tyburn to see him hanged, I promise you."

These words made no sort of impression upon Captain Hawk; he heard them as he heard them not; his thoughts were very differently occupied, indeed, now, than in attending to any of the little passing disagreeables of his position as a prisoner.

His horse walked through the gate, and it was clanged shut after the party in a moment.

"Now for London," said one of the officers.

"Hold!" said a voice.

At the same moment, from amid the gloom of some trees close at hand, there glided a figure wrapped in a cloak. Captain Hawk hung his head upon his breast, and a deep gasping sort of sob came from his lips.

He knew that voice, although it had pronounced but one word.

"Hilloa! What's this?" said the foremost officer. "Get your pistols ready, my men. We don't know what may happen next."

The figure with the cloak darted forward, and stood by the side of the horse upon which Captain Hawk was mounted. The officer flashed the light of the lantern upon that figure, and then they saw that the hood of a cloak was thrown back, and that it concealed the face of a beautiful girl, whose long hair was floating down her shoulders.

That was May Boyes.

The officer shrunk back from before the pale face, that was, if possible, more exquisite in its marble-looking beauty that it had ever been.

"Gerald," she said.

Captain Hawk seemed shaken by some terrible convulsion, but he looked up and their eyes met.

"You came," she said, "to see me."

"I did—God, I did!"

"Look at the wreck!"

"Oh, spare me—spare me!"

He clasped his manacled hands over his face, and she heard the iron that was upon the wrists clank together—she saw by the light of the lantern those bandages of crime, and she shook with a terrible emotion.

"Gerald Clifton, take my pardon."

"No—no! Curse me—curse me!"

"And my blessing."

"No, May! It must not be! Load me with execrations: I deserve them all from your lips."

"No; and you will have my prayers, too. Farewell!"

"Oh, no—no! This is too much!"

She was gone as though she had been suddenly wafted into the air, or as though the earth had swallowed her up from all further observation. This interview had not occupied the space of time that might be comprehended in half a minute; and the officers had been so struck by the marvellous beauty of May, that they had entirely shrunk back, and allowed her to say what she pleased to the prisoner. It was a great relief to them when she was gone.

"Who was she?" said one.

"Stop!" cried Captain Hawk. "You are my captors?"

"Rather so."

"Well, you expect a reward for taking me—I know that; and the reward will be paid to you, whether you bring me in dead or alive."

"It certainly will."

"Then do me the only favour I have asked of you, and the only favour I will ask of living man. Shoot me at once."

"No, captain, that won't suit our book. That may be all very well for you, when you know it is like enough to go hard with you, and when you are just in a kind of fix about that girl who was here, poor thing! But, I tell you, we can't do it. Come on."

Captain Hawk said no more, but he let his head droop upon his chest, and the officer held his horse by the bridle, and so they galloped him to London.

He slept in Newgate that night, and, after all, he did sleep, too.

CHAPTER XLIII

HAWK IS BROUGHT TO TRIAL FOR THE MURDER ON THE HEATH.

There is a principle of elasticity about the minds of some people, which even enables them to rise superior to the cares and troubles of this life, after a little experience of the special annoyance that for the time-being oppresses them.

Some minds, upon the occasion of anything in the shape of a calamity, or any circumstance that gives a severe shock to the nerves, do not take in all the consequences at once. The occurrence has, upon such intellects, a stunning effect, and they suffer much more in the time to come, as the affair, in all its cold, hideous reality, creeps upon them.

There are other persons, again, who see and who suffer from the wound at once. These last are the persons who begin to recover from the effects of any most acute accident, almost at the moment that they suffer from it.

Captain Hawk, or Gerald Clifton, as Ratchley and May Boyes still called him, was one of this latter category. He suffered very acutely, but far from enduringly. It was one sharp pang, and then the wound began to heal. Thus was it, that, notwithstanding he had asked the officer to be kind enough to shoot him at the moment that he was suffering so much remorse at the sight of May Boyes, he was pretty well again by the time he got to Newgate.

Poor May! her sufferings were not of that ephemeral and fleeting character by any means. Such a heart as hers once wounded knew no peace again. It was sad that it should be so, but it was true.

It was an immense congratulation to the police, and to all the people in London who were in any way connected with the adminstration of the law, that Captain Hawk was taken. His being at large was a kind of reproach which they felt growing on them every hour of the day, and which they had no defence to make against; but now that he was caught and in Newgate, they held up their heads again.

At a consultation between all parties concerned, except the prisoner, who was most concerned of all, it was determined to bring him to trial with as much dispatch as possible, for there was still a dread that, by some desperate means, he might escape the arm of justice.

The formal committal from Sir John Boyes was quite sufficient to form an indictment upon, and Captain Hawk was duly informed, that on the following Friday—an ominous day at Newgate to a man accused of a capital offence—he would be put upon his trial.

He made no reply to the communication; but in the course of the day a solicitor called upon him, and said that he had been instructed by a gentleman to take his case in hand.

"I will consider," said Hawk.

"Very well," said the solicitor. "Recollect, that there is not much time, and that, if you mean to give your defence into the able hands that I will place it in, the sooner that it is done the better."

Hawk looked at him for a moment, and then said—

"Is there a chance?"

"There is always a chance. There may be some flaw in the indictment, some informality or mar in the ulterior proceedings that may defect them all, some legal hiatus, in fact, which none but a professional man would discover."

"But otherwise, there is do chance?"

"Well, Mr. a—Hawk, if you confess the act there is no chance, but nobody calls upou you to say that you are guilty. That, permit me to tell you, is contrary to the spirit of the English law."

"Very well, sir; call upon we again, I will consider; and if you see Mr. Ratchley Boyes again, you can tell him that I receive the offer of his kindness in a proper spirit, whether I accept it or not."

"Well, I admit that you have named the gentleman."

"Oh, sir, there is no other who could, and who would do so much for me. So now, farewell. I will see you to-morrow."

With this answer, the attorney was forced to be satisfied for the present; but although in his own mind he felt quite certain that Captain Hawk would be hanged, he yet had no idea of allowing him to step out of the world without professional assistance.

Lawyers feel like physicians upon such subjects: however bad the patien may chance to be, they cannot bear that he should commit so singular an act as to die without consulting them and paying the fee.

During the course of the following morning, the turnkeys at Newgate, made some pounds by showing their prisoner, for the name of Captain Hawk had become rather famous upon the Western-road. These continued intrusions of visitors to his cell were the greatest annoyances that could have been inflicted upon Hawk, and at last he resented them by flinging the wooden bowl, which had been brought to him to wash in, at the next visitor that came.

This energetic conduct put a stop to the disgraceful system that was being carried on.

It was late in the day that the cell-door was opened again, and Ratchley Boyes entered the gloomy place. He had an order from one of the judges to see the prisoner, and the turnkey accordingly locked him in the cell along with Hawk, and left them alone.

This was so unexpected a visit, that Captain Hawk could only look in the face of Ratchley with surprise and silence for a few moments; then he said—

"This is no place for you, sir. Let me advise you to leave the atmosphere of this place to those to whom it is more congenial."

"No, Gerald Clifton. It is congenial to me on account of the errand that brings me here."

"What errand?"

"To try to save you."

Captain Hawk shook his head, and said in a voice that betrayed some emotion—

"Forego the attempt, Ratchley Boyes. It is in vain. I know you too well to suppose that any but the best and noblest feelings brought you here. You would save me if you could, but, perhaps, the best service you could do me, would be to kill me now."

"No, Gerald Clifton, I have a hope that, if you could be only freed from the consequences of this imputed crime, you would, in some other country than this, exert the abilities with which heaven has gifted you in a far different manner to what you have done here."

"No—no!"

"Nay, don't say no to such a hope. It is with it glowing in my heart that I now seek you."

"Ratchley Boyes, what am I to you that you should thus trouble yourself, and deface your fair repute, by crossing the felon's threshold to speak to him? Let me perish, and forget me."

"No. There is one who has not forgotten you, who has urged me to this visit."

"Ah!"

"You guess I allude to my sister. May and I understand each other now. I see there is a flush upon your brow, but you, perhaps, deceive yourself. She did love Gerald Clifton, but she has no place in her heart for Captain Hawk the highwayman."

The fetters in which Hawk was bound made an ominous rattle as he sunk upon a seat.

"Go on," he said. "Go on."

"But," added Ratchley, "she would save you for repentance, and for the hope, that in time you would see the frightful error of you ways; and if you cannot know peace and love upon earth, you might yet receive pardon in Heaven."

"Is that all?"

"Is it not much?—Is it not enough."

"It is more than enough. Tell her that"—Hawk's voice faltered, and he was unable to proceed for a few minutes; then he added—"Tell her that the kindest thing she can do, is to let me die."

"She does not think so; and, therefore, she makes it a request that you will place your case in the hands of the solicitor who called upon you this morning, and, she says, she thinks you will be acquitted."

"Acquitted?"

"Yes; seeing that you are really innocent of the murder, although circumstances are very much against you in the matter."

"She thinks that?"

"She bade me say so to you."

Captain Hawk paced his cell in silence. The fetters went clank, clank, as he did so, and his imagination became entangled in a complete maze of conjectures as to what May meant, and as to how far she really believed what she said, and, likewise, as to what was Ratchley's real opinion upon the subject of his guilt or innocence.

Up to that time, Captain Hawk had not supposed that any one had a doubt regarding the fact of his having committed the murder; but the words that had fallen from Ratchley's lips were almost enough to make him doubt it himself.

"What say you?" said Ratchley, after a pause. "I want your reply."

"I will obey the wishes of May."

"You consent, then, to employ the solicitor, and to leave your case in his hands entirely and completely?"

"I do."

"Then the object of my visit to you is accomplished; and should you be acquitted, you will find me ready at once to forgive and forget the past, and to aid you in leaving England for ever."

"So be it. We shall see. Ratchley, I thank you."

The young man rose, and, turning, walked towards the door; but he did not hold out his hand to Captain Hawk, and the latter felt the slight so keenly, that he was inclined to retract his consent to employ the attorney; but even as the words to do so were upon his lips, he thought of May, and that thought restrained him.

"Be it so," he said.

In another moment, Ratchley was gone.

Captain Hawk now thought that he was free from visitors; but in the course of half-an-hour there came to the cell a man attired in deep black, who, upon being left alone with the prisoner, said—

"Captain Hawk, or Gerald Clifton, call yourself which you may, I have come to make of you a solemn request."

"Well, sir?"

"It is, that, without disguise or equivocation, you will tell me who you really are, your real name, and your parentage, and some of the circumstances of your early life. Hold, sir; I can see that my questions displease you, and you suspect that it is to gratify some idle and morbid curiosity that I came here, or, probably, for some speculative purpose; but such is not the fact. It is for the elucidation of a great fact, which I tremble to think of, that I ask you these questions."

"And the fact, sir?"

"There, sir, you must excuse me. I cannot, I dare not suggest it to you at present. I must have your answers, and then consult others."

"Then, sir, I have no answers to give you."

"But your name is not Hawk?"

"Very good, sir."

"And your name is not Clifton?"

"Very good, sir."

"Is it, then, indeed and in truth your determination to refuse me all answers to my request?"

"It is."

"Then I must tell you who I am."

"It will not make any difference in my views and feelings, sir, towards you, if you tell me twenty times who you are."

"I am the heir at law to all the property of the learned judge, for whose death you are about to be arraigned before a jury of your country."

"Well, sir?"

"I should imagine that my character as such a person would place my motives beyond all doubt or cavil."

"Sir," said Captain Hawk, "you and your motives are nothing to me. I care for neither; and you could not bestow upon me a more acceptable favour than to leave me to myself. I am a prisoner here, and cannot command your absence, inasmuch as, I presume, my jailers have the power to enforce your presence upon me; but, if you are a gentleman, as you affect to be, you will retire."

"Farewell!" said the personage in black; and then summoning the turnkey, he at once left the cell, apparently quite convinced that there was nothing to be got out of Captain Hawk in reply to his questions.

What was the real object of those questions, or to what could they possibly lead or refer, was a matter upon which Hawk could really come to no conclusion, although he worried himself for the next hour with conjectures upon the subject. The most probable idea, and the one that after all had the most hold of his mind, was, that it was desired to get from him information concerning himself, to feed the morbid popular curiosity concerning him through the columns of the newspapers; and if such were the case, he very much rejoiced that he had defeated such a purpose.

"I will give no information to any living being concerning myself," he said. "Let them take my life, and there's an end of me, and all that concerns me and the world."

CHAPTER XLIV.

MAY BOYES HAS AN INTERVIEW WITH A MAN OF LAW.

We can scarcely ask the reader to pity May Boyes: her character is too exalted for so common-place a feeling, and her sufferings lie too deeply to be touched by any ordinary sympathies.

The peace of her mind seemed to have fled for ever; and of all the usual gaiety of her disposition there remained nothing but a shadowy spectre of the past, and the faint remains of a gentle hilarity that would never come again.

Alas, poor May!

Surely it was a greater social crime upon the part of Captain Hawk to rob that young girl of the happiness of her life, and spread such a blight and a desolation over her heart, than at once to strike to death the gray-haired judge upon the heath. And yet one crime is

CAPTAIN HAWK RETURNING LORD RHOLEY'S SNUFF-BOX TO THE OFFICER.

not recognised as such by society at all, while the other is thought worthy of death.

After that brief and sad interview with Hawk by the lodge gate, whither May had stolen forth to meet him, she re-entered the garden with a step that was so uncertain, that she seemed each moment upon the point of falling. The last look of the man she had loved seemed to haunt her, and to weigh heavily upon her heart.

"They will take his life now," she said. "All is over."

Those words, "All is over," seemed to find an echo among the whispering leaves of the tall trees, as they were gently agitated by the wind.

The people at the lodge-gate had seen May; but she was too much beloved by them, and, indeed, by the whole household, for any remark to be made about her, otherwise than in kindness, or for any idle tale to be taken to the house concerning her actions.

May went right round the house towards the terrace at the back, for that was a mode by which she could reach her own room without the necessity of passing through the long passages of the mansion, and so running the chance of meeting some one.

She stood upon the terrace and took a long look at the dusky old garden, and tears came unbidden to her eyes It was upon that spot that she had heard Gerald Clifton, when she thought him all that ought to command admiration and respect, first tell her that he loved her. It was upon that spot that she had, by a glance at his eyes, told him that she loved him, as surely man was never loved before by woman.

Alas! How full of sad and painful recollections that spot was!

The wind among the trees still seemed to whisper those three words, "All is over! all is over!"

She shuddered as she listened.

"Are there spirits," she said, "in the thin air who listen to the wailings of human hearts, and sympathise with their sorrows? If there be such, let them sigh for me!"

She turned from a contemplation of the terrace and the garden, and tottered to her chamber. Her first act was to close the door and lock it, and then she strove to think.

Heaven only knows what dreary, dreadful thoughts passed through the heart of May during the succeeding hours. She must have suffered very deeply, indeed; but she came to a resolution.

What that resolution was we shall not be long in perceiving. It had the effect of substituting action in the place of despair, and so far it was a specially good thing for May Boyes.

The time was not once at which she or any other of the female inhabitants of Boyes Hall were in the habit of leaving the house; but now she rose above all the little minor conventionalities of life. The object she had in view was superior to them all. Yet she was very desirious that she might not be seen by any of the family, for disliking the very shadow of a falsehood as she did, she much preferred avoiding a question, to returning an untrue reply to one.

The object was to save the life of Captain Hawk.

Now, it happened, that not very far across the fields from Boyes Hall, an attorney, of the name of Bolton, had taken up his residence at an old country house that had been for a long time in a state of neglect, and which, no doubt, he had very advantageously possessed himself of. This man May had seen twice, and she knew him to be a man of intellect, and of a certain amount of gentlemanly manners and habits, that made him anything but repugnant. It was to him that May Boyes, notwithstanding the unseasonable hour, was determined to go at once.

Wrapping herself up in the darkest-coloured cloak she could find in her wardrobe, she stood by the door of her chamber, and listened attentively to hear if any sounds in the house disclosed that Sir John was up or not. She well knew that Philippa and Lady Boyes would not dream of retiring to rest till Sir John did.

All was profoundly still, and May concluded that surely they had all gone to bed, and that, perhaps, finding her room door locked, they had fancied she had retired, and so had not made noise enough to disturb her for the mere slight object of bidding her good-night.

"It is well," she said. "I shall pay this visit unobserved by any one, and I shall be able to save him for repentance."

This idea, fallacious as it was, that if Captain Hawk could only be saved from the consequences of his great crime upon Hounslow Heath, that he would forthwith repent, had evidently taken a strong hold of poor May Boyes, while, in reality, Hawk had as little of the repenting cast in his disposition as could very well exist.

She knew that by unbarring the shutters of one of the long windows that opened on to the terrace, she could easily get out of the house; and although it might possibly be dangerous to leave a window, which served so well the purposes of a door, unguarded at such an hour, yet she was not disposed to forego her enterprise from such considerations as those.

From the terrace she could easly descend to the garden, and then leaving it by a door in the wall, the key of which was always hidden in a spot close at hand, well-known to the family, she could get across the two or three meadows which separated her from the lane in which was the front of the house in the occupation of Mr. Bolton, the attorney.

All this was straightforward and easy enough, provided May Boyes had the will to persevere in it; and it was not likely that she would falter now in an affair that sat so near to her heart.

With a perfectly noiseless step she eached the ball-room, with the long French windows that opened upon the terrace. She was not quite successful in removing the shutters without noise, for the iron bar that held them close slipped from her hand, and made a clanging sound against the side of the wall.

May listened for the next five minutes with a throbbing heart, and a terrible anxiety to discover if the noise had disturbed any of the household; and then, as the profound stillness in the house continued, she became satisfied that it had not done so, and that she might proceed in safety.

"All is well," she said. "All is well."

In another moment she had passed out of the house by the open window, and was upon the terrace.

It was not a difficult matter to close the window from the outside, although there were no means of fastening it; but May placed a flower-pot, with a tall rhododendron in it, against the lower part of the window-frame, and that held t close.

These simple arrangements did not consume many minutes, and then drawing the sad-coloured cloak closely around her, for the night air was cold and damp, she descended the few steps of the terrace, and fled rapidly through the garden. Every spot of that garden was familiar to May Boyes, and she took the nearest route to the door in the wall, through which she was to get into the open fields. The key was in its accustomed place, but the lock and the key both were thick with rust, and it was as much as the delicate small hands of May could do to get the door open. She wounded her hand in the effort; but the lock did yield at last, and she was satisfied. She closed the door and locked it on the outer side, and then concealing the key beneath some weeds, close to the foot of the wall, she turned towards the meadows, and looked to observe if any lights were in Mr. Bolton's house.

All was darkness.

This was something of a disappointment; but, with the words "I must and will see him," May Boyes walked rapidly over the meadows, through the tall damp grass, which, in the course of a few minutes, soaked her feet with cold dew.

Little heeding such inconveniences, which at another time would have attracted her attention, and awakened her fears for her health, for May was by no means of such a robust constitution that she could withstand such influences, she ran on until she reached the stile that led to the lane.

There she paused a moment to recover her breath; and as she did so, she fancied she heard a footstep behind her.

This was an alarm she had not expected, for although there was a path across the meadows from the lane, it only led to Boyes Hall, and, therefore, was never used but by the family and household, and by persons who were going direct to the hall, and who might prefer that route to any other. To find that any one was there, was, consequently, a source of renewed alarm.

When May paused, the footstep ceased, and that impressed her still more vividly with the idea that some one was following and watching her.

But what could she do? She was far from inclined to forego her plan upon such an account, and, after all, it might be some vagrant tramp prowling about the fields, as was common enough, or a poacher, possibly, on the look-out for a hare.

Dismissing from her mind, then, as well as she could, the apprehensions which the footsteps had suggested to her, she went rapidly down the lane, and reaching the gate that protected the lawn of Mr. Bolton's house, she rang at the bell.

Up to this moment the resolution of May had not failed her; but as the sound of the bell came upon her ears, and she felt that she had gone too far to retreat, the awkwardness of the mission she had gone upon came much more full across her mind than it had yet done.

How should she address herself to the solicitor?—How explain to him that it was on behalf of a highwayman, and a murderer, she had come out at such an hour to enlist his services?

In these indeed inexpressibly painful thoughts, the appearance of a servant with a lantern, coming down to the gate from the house, warned May that she must at once give up her project, or be firm in it.

"Who is there?" said the man. "Did anybody ring?"

"Yes," said May, "I wish to see Mr. Bolton, on businsss of importance."

"Who are you, ma'am?"

"Tell him a lady wishes to see him on professional business. Open the gate at once."

There was a tone of great command about the manner in which May uttered these words, that induced an instant effect, and the gate was opened by the man, and the lantern held very respectfully, so at to guide the visitor up the path to the house.

"Has Mr. Bolton retired for the night?"

"Oh, dear, no, ma'am—that is, miss, I mean."

The man had caught a glimpse of the sweet, pale face of May Boyes.

She was shown into the lawyer's study, while the servant, after another ineffectual attempt to get her to tell him a name to announce to his master, went without one, and merely with the say, that it was a lady who wished to see Mr. Bolton on business.

Much wondering who the lady could be who at such a time of night, and out of town, too, come to him, Mr. Bolton hastily repaired to his study, not without some suspicion that a trick was being played off upon him, which might end in the abstraction of some of his portable goods and chattels.

A lamp was burning tolerably brightly upon the table in the study, and May sat in such a position, that if the cloak and the bonnet she wore had not very much shaded her face, the attorney must have recognised her in a moment; but he did not do so.

"Madam," he said, "my name is Bolton. I understand that you have some business with me?"

"I have, sir," said May, and she turned her fair face towards him, and let the fold of the cloak fall that partially concealed it.

"Miss May Boyes!" cried the solicitor. "Is it possible?"

"It is too true, sir, that you see me here."

"I am delighted to see you, and so will Mrs. Bolton. I will call her at once, and ——"

"No, sir; I come on business. I have to ask you—that is, I ——"

"Pray calm yourself; you are agitated."

"God knows that I am! Oh! Mr. Bolton, call up all the charity of your heart—all the candour that you are possessed of, and put upon my conduct the fairest construction that you can, for I have come to ask you to interest yourself in the defence of Gerald Clifton upon his trial."

"What! Hawk, the murderer?—the—the robber—the assassin! You astound me, Miss Boyes. I am all amazement!"

CHAPTER XLV.

HAWK FINDS A STRONG CASE IN HIS FAVOUR MOST UNEXPECTEDLY.

Mr. Bolton, the solicitor, might well be all amazement to find no less a personage than May Boyes interesting herself in the fate of one with whom he could scarcely conceive it to be possible she could have any feelings in common; and after the declaration that she had made, he might well look at her, as he did, with a growing mistrust in his mind of her intellect.

Poor May had already said more than she had thought it possible her strength would ever have enabled her to say; and now, with a feeling as though she were nearly choking, she looked in the countenance of Mr. Bolton, to read there, if it were possible for her so to do, his sentiments upon the painful and interesting occasion.

The lawyer at length broke the silence that was as embarrassing to him as it was to her, by saying, in a tone of surprise, although it was, likewise, one of kindness—

"Miss May Boyes, I am very much, indeed, your senior in years, and I daresay all that you have heard of me has induced you to believe that I am what some folks will have it there cannot be in the world—namely, an honest lawyer?"

"Oh, yes! yes! Mr. Bolton; well I know the high estimation in which you are held by all who know you, Do you think, sir, that if I had not known that, or if I had doubted the correctness of popular opinion upon that point, I would have thus thrown myself upon your generosity and kindly consideration?"

Mr. Bolton bowed slightly, for he felt that the fair young creature before him had, indeed, paid him a high compliment by coming to him as she had done.

"Well, Miss Boyes," he said, "let us understand each other; and remember that, although I make no pretence to be a father-confessor, and although there is nothing in all the world that I am ever so loth to receive as confidences that I can do without, I beg you to consider that all you may say to me shall be considered to be most strictly confidential, and will go no further. Of that I hope you feel assured?"

"I do, indeed, Mr. Bolton. If I had had the shadow of a doubt, I assure you, sir, I had not been here to trouble you upon this dreadful occasion."

"Very well. Now, my dear girl, go on, and let me know exactly what you want me to do in this affair of Captain Hawk's, or Gerald Clifton, whichever the fellow's real name may happen to be."

It was distressing to May to hear the man whom she had once loved spoken of in such a tone; but she took no notice of it, and in a low, sweet voice she responded to the inquiry of the solicitor.

"Sir, I have said that I wish you professionally to undertake the defence of Gerald Clifton, who is now in custody, and who will, doubtless, be tried for—for ——"

"Murder!"

"Yes! yes! that is the word; but, alas! alas! I could not utter it!"

May covered her sweet face with her hands, and sobbed.

"Yes," added the attorney, "he will, without a doubt, my dear Miss Boyes, be put upon his trial for the murder of Judge Holmes; and you may depend that he will be found guilty of that truly dreadful deed."

"Oh, no! no!"

The lawyer shook his head, and laying his hand kindly upon that of May's, he said—

"Allow me to say, my dear girl, that you know nothing of these things, and that it is just as it ought to be, that you should know nothing of them."

"But I do, Mr. Bolton; indeed, and in truth, I do know of them; and if you will undertake the defence of Gerald Clifton, he will be saved."

"In good truth, May Boyes, you overrate my humble powers very considerably if you think for a moment that I can step between the law and the consequences of such a crime as the person you speak of has committed. It will be impossible, in the face of the evidence against him, to save him. The facts are too strong to wrestle with."

"Sir, you do not know—pardon me for saying so—but, indeed, and in truth, you do not know what I know of the affair. I wish but for you to tell me you will, as a professional man, undertake the defence of the accused. You do not commit yourself in any way by doing so. Oh! Mr. Bolton, let me hear the welcome sound of 'Yes' from your your lips!"

"I do not know why I need hesitate. The utmost that a professional man can do, Miss Boyes, in such a case as this, is, to see that it is upon clear and legal evidence that his client is committed, and that no injustice is done him."

"Yes! yes! that is all!"

"Well, then, I will undertake to act as his solicitor in the matter; and I will call upon Sir John Boyes to confer with him about it the very first thing in the morning."

"Oh, no! no! no!"

"No?"

"Certainly not, Mr. Bolton. If you act at all for Gerald Clifton, you must act independently of all at Boyes Hall. Do you think that I have come here at such an hour as this, and upon such an errand, to have it blazoned to my father in the morning? Oh, no, Mr. Bolton. Of all men else, I would not have him know it."

Mr. Bolton looked grave.

"Sir—sir, do not retract your consent. From me take your instructions—to me look for your charges."

"No, Miss Boyes, that will I not. If I undertake this affair, it will be with the idea that I am obliging you in some way; and you must permit me to have that gratifiation, which I should lose entirely if I were to be paid for what I do. But now, in sober seriousness, as you are somewhat recovered from the state of agitation you were in, tell me how you think it possible that I, or any one else, can do anything to avert the consequences of his crimes from the head of this unhappy, but guilty young man?"

"By proving what I believe in law you call an *alibi*, sir."

"An *alibi*?"

"Yes; that is, I believe, bringing forward proof that the accused was in another place, and otherwise occupied at the time the alleged crime was committed."

How pale and death-like May Boyes looked as she spoke, and yet how beautiful and how full of determination! Mr. Bolton looked at her with a surprise that he could not have concealed if he would; and then he said—

"There is something more in this than meets the eye, Miss Boyes."

"Well, sir, and if there is?"

"Why, then, I think I ought to know it."

"No, Mr. Bolton, you ought not, I distinctly say, that if an *alibi* be proved by the advisers of Gerald Clifton, he will be free. Is it not so? Is that the law, Mr. Bolton?"

"It is the law and the equity, too, Miss Boyes. No jury could possibly commit a man in the face of a distinct *alibi*."

"Well, sir, that is what I want to prove, and that is what you will, I hope, assist me in satisfactorily proving."

Mr. Bolton now looked more amazed than ever.

"Miss May Boyes," he said, and there was a coldness and rigidity in his tones that rather alarmed May, "when you came here you were pleased to pay me some compliments upon my character which I appreciated very highly, for we always appreciate compliments highly from those whom we respect; and now allow me to ask you how I could possibly receive those compliments as other than gross pieces of irony if I were to lend myself to what you propose?"

"Lend yourself, sir!"

"Yes, Miss Boyes; lend myself! You wish me, as I understand you, to stoop so low as to get up a case of *alibi*, which can only be done by suborning witnesses, for the purpose of rescuing this Captain Hawk from the just consequences of his odious crimes."

"Oh, sir! no! no!"

"No?"

"Not a whit, sir. You completely and entirely mistake me, Mr. Bolton."

"Then, what in the name of all that's incomprehensible is it that you do want me to do, Miss Boyes?"

"Simply to take the necessary steps for enabling those who can, and who upon oath must prove the *alibi*, to do so"

"You astound me! You don't mean to say that it can be proved—that it is a fact—a *bona fide alibi?* You don't mean for one moment to say that you can prove that?"

"I do."

"Why, then, you would intimate that he did not do the deed that all the world, with the exception of yourself, is ready to swear that he is guilty of?"

"The world, sir, should be very cautious, indeed, how it swears to the guilt of any human being. If you will, merely in a professional capacity, act in this matter, I will give you a list of the witnesses who can be found to prove the *alibi* for Gerald Clifton."

Mr. Bolton drew a long breath, and looked at May for some few moments in alarm: then he said in a low tone—

"By Heavens you are the most extraordinary girl I ever came near, Miss Boyes. There is no one who will more rejoice than I, if it should be satisfactorily proved that this young man, indifferent as his character is, did not commit this crime; but do I really understand you, that there are people who will come forward and swear that he was elsewhere at the time?"

"Oh, yes. They will swear it, if they swear to what they saw and what they know, sir."

"Then he did not do it?"

May Boyes was pale before, but now her very lips turned white, and in a low, faint voice, she muttered—

"Sir, there are witnesses who will prove the *alibi*."

The attorney sunk back upon his chair, for he had risen to shade the light with his hand, and to look into the face of the young girl. He was completely bewildered, and, notwithstanding all his experience, and all the clearness of his intellect, he found himself in a complete maze as regarded the affair that May Boyes had placed before him. She waited now in perfect anxiety for the next words that he should speak. They were as follows—

"My dear Miss Boyes, will you give me a few hours to think of this?"

"Yes, sir."

"Very well; then I will write to you early in the morning, without fail."

"Do so, Mr. Bolton; for if you do not, I must go to some stranger, who, not knowing me, will mistake my motive and judge me harshly. I need not say that until I know your answer, I shall be very, very wretched, for this affair sits next to my heart. Oh, sir, may you be guided to do that which I ask of you, for it must be done."

"Stay—stay, I am determined. Once for all, I will do it."

May burst into tears, and Mr. Bolton reconducted her to her seat, from which she had risen to go. After having thus determined, the attorney did not dream of going back from his word; but in the succeeding hours he learnt from May the various particulars which would suffice to prove the *alibi* for Captain Hawk.

Need we say, that in giving him the particulars, she only referred to the ride she had herself taken, when, disguised in his habiliments, she had shown herself at different places and to different people for the express purpose of saving him from the consequences of that night of crime in which he was engaged? As his double, she had got it up, trusting, if it were only believed, it would be certain to save him. But she only told the lawyer where the testimony was to be had, and the facts in corroboration of it, that could be sworn to. She carefully kept her own secret.

"Then, Miss Boyes," he said, "if all this is as you have told it to me, he is to all intents and purposes innocent."

"Well, sir, it is so."

"No man could commit a murder upon Hounslow Heath and be galloping down Oxford Street at the same time I am perfectly astounded at the discrepancy of evidence that you lay before me. I suppose I had better see him to-morrow morning the first thing?"

"No—no, see no one. Let it suffice that upon his trial he plead not guilty, and that you act for him, and see that the people and the facts are all brought forward. You need not see him at all: you will oblige me by not seeing him, Mr. Bolton. I am your client."

"Very good—very good, be it so. I will in the morning place in the hands of one of the leading counsel at the counsel bar the facts you have acquainted me with to-night, and the people you have named and described shall be all promptly communicated with."

"That will do, sir. My utmost will then be done. Farewell, Mr. Bolton, and such thanks as a very, very sad heart indeed can render to you, pray accept from mine."

May Boys now rose to go, but the attorney would see her a part of the way across the meadows; and while doing so, he strove by a little artful cross-questioning to elicit from her something more about the affair than he knew; but in such an attempt he was foiled; for the fact was, that what May Boyes had to conceal was so broad and clear, that she ran no risk in consequence. There were no little facts to embarrass her. Her secret was a massive and tangible one, so there was no chance of any slip of the tongue at all hinting at it.

Mr. Bolton bade her good-night and parted from her, just as wise as he was when he stepped across the threshold of his own door with her. May succeeded in reaching her own chamber without attracting the notice of any one, and Mr. Bolton sat up for an hour or two engaged in recounting what she had told to him; after which he came to the conclusion that if all she had said could be proved, the conviction of Captain Hawk for the murder of the judge upon the heath would be out of the queston.

We do not seek to justify May in the course that she now was pursuing; it was a mere subversion of public justice; but then it must be recollected how she had loved Gerald Clifton, and, alas! how she loved him still; and although she told herself, and she believed, that he never could be anything to her but an object of pity, yet she hoped that if he had time and life to do it in, he might yet, by deep repentance, win the pardon of Heaven for his grievous crimes, and not go from the world in the full flush of youth without a hope of mercy, even where mercy is so infinite.

CHAPTER XLVI.

CAPTAIN HAWK GIVES HIMSELF UP TO DESPAIR IN HIS CELL.

The judicial proceedings necessary to convict Captain Hawk, *alias* Gerald Clifton for the murder of Mr. Justice Holmes, were brief and common-place enough, and in a very short time he found his affairs in that kind of order which promised very speedily to bring him in due course of law to the scaffold.

The officials of Newgate looked upon him as a doomed man. There was a most suspicious gratitude about their manner to him, which showed that they looked upon him as one with whom it was just as well to be upon kindly terms for the short time that he had to encumber the earth with his living presence.

Nothing could be more irksome to such a temperament as Hawk's than this kind of civility from his jailers. If they had stormed, and raved, and cursed at him, he could have made a noise at them in return; but to be treated as the certain sacrifice, and thought not even worth the contradicting or quarrelling with, was to him maddening.

There was in his bosom such a slumbering tempest of passion, that at a word or a look it would have exploded, and possibly hurled him to destruction in its progress.

More than once the terrible idea came across him that he should go mad; and if anything more than another is calculated to produce the mad wreck of reason, such a thought is the most likely.

But it was in the dark and silent hours of the night that he suffered the most. Then, when the one half of the world slept—then, when those whose consciences were not corrupted by crime and injustice, could lie down and calmly sleep off the fatigue of the past day—then was it that Gerald Clifton, with fetters upon his limbs, and within the dark and gloomy cold walls of his cell in Newgate, felt compelled to give the reins to thought, and to think of what he was and of what he might have been.

Let those who fancy that criminality and recklessness have their pleasures, likewise believe that they have their hours of despair—let those who, with a recklessness of the time that is to come, lay up ample stores for future agony, tremble at the ill that they do to others: but still more tremble at the ill they do to themselves; for so sure as that they live and breathe, the day will come when awakened conscience will goad them to desperation.

Gerald Clifton so suffered in his gloomy cell.

There was a kind of low seat in the cell. It was more like a chair without the back to it than anything else. Upon that Gerald Clifton sat. There was a kind of shelf attached to the wall about four feet from the floor, and a mattrass upon it, and a coarse prison rug, or quilt. That was his bed. A small kind of bracket in one corner—for it was not large enough to dignify by the name of a shelf—just sufficed to hold a wooden bowl, in which was some

CAPTAIN HAWK ALARMS THE SERVANTS OF THE MARQUIS OF PEMBROKE.

water, and a coarse loaf of prison bread.

Captain Hawk need not certainly have lived upon prison fare; but he had haughtily rejected all the overtures of the turnkeys to get him more luxurious provisions from out of doors, which they would have been glad to do for a consideration.

High up—close to the roof, in fact, and about three feet beyond his reach—there was a small opening in the wall.

That was the cell window. It was crossed and re-crossed by iron bars, so that even in the daytime it only let in the dim light from the prison yard in little square patches; but now he could see nothing of the night sky even, and as he was in complete darkness, all perception of the shape, size, or the different objects in his cell, had vanished from him completely.

The cell, by-the-by, was just twelve feet in length, and six feet in width—not a great deal larger than a coffin; but yet quite large enough for him. That was all the space, just then, society could spare to the man who had committed, or who was supposed to have committed, a murder.

But the authorities had no right exactly to put Captain Hawk into such a cell as that. As yet, he was only suspected. No man was guilty until the jury of his fellow-men had declared that he was. But then they dreaded that such a man as Hawk—bold, daring, educated, and fertile in resources, and in that power which is the will of knowledge, and which is unknown to ordinary felons and desperadoes—might attempt something in the way of escape.

It was for that reason that they departed a little from the ordinary rule, and paid him the rather equivocal compliment of placing him in the strongest portion of the prison, and in one of the cells which were only used for the condemned and the refractory.

He could, amid the silence of that place, hear the clock of St. Sepulchre's strike the hours. To be sure, the sounds came to him in a dull, muffled kind of way through the grating across the window of his cell; but he did hear them.

Captain Hawk counted slowly twelve o'clock.

What an awful stillness seemed to reign in the world, now, to him, after that hour had struck! To be sure, there was a strange humming noise, if noise it could be at all called, in the air, that he could not understand. It was the subdued expression of the roar and racket of active existence in the great city around him.

That sound only seemed to make his solitude more complete and deadening.

And now, in a few minutes after the hour of midnight, came the inspection of the cells that was always made, and which was to last until the morning. It was necessary to see that every prisoner was safe at that hour, for then the night-watch went on duty, and was answerable for what might happen until seven o'clock in the morning that was to come.

Captain Hawk heard the footsteps of men in the stone passage outside his cell, and then he heard the bar taken down from the door.

"What do they want?" he gasped. "What do they want with me at such an hour as this? Why do they come here?"

He heard the rattling of a huge chain as it was removed from its hold, and his heart beat quickly.

"Are they coming to take me out to death at such a time as this?" he said. Oh, no—no. I am nearly mad to think so."

The lock was shot back, and the cell door creaked upon its massive hinges. At that time the might and the multiplicity of the fastenings of the doors in the old jail of Newgate were considered to be the only means of protection; but now there is a greater reliance upon the exertions of mechanical skill and the accurate working of hard metals.

A flash of light from a lantern found its way into the cell. Captain Hawk rose from the low chair, and looked eagerly to the door.

"Hilloa!" said a voice.

He did not reply.

A couple of turnkeys entered the cell, and another followed with a light ladder over his shoulder.

"What is all this?" cried Hawk. "What do you mean?"

"Oh, not much," laughed one of the men; "it's our last visit, that's all."

"Last visit?"

"Yes, before the night-watch comes on, captain."

"Oh—oh, that is it."

The prisoner sunk back upon his chair again, and the fetters that were upon his limbs clanked together as he did so.

The man with the ladder now placed it against the wall under the little opening, that might, by a good stretch of courtesy, be called a window, and ascending it, he, with a slightly made hammer, that he had in his hand, rang the bars, to detect by the sound if they had been tampered with or not.

"All's right," he said.

The next operation was to sound or ring the fetters that were upon the person of Captain Hawk in the same way; and as they all returned a clear sound, the officers were satisfied, and nodded their acquiescence to the "All right?" of the man who had that duty to do.

"Good night, captain."

"Good night."

"Nothing wanted, I suppose?"

"Oh, yes, a light—a light!"

"Agin the rules."

Hawk's head sunk upon his breast, and he was silent.

"Perhaps he'd like a saw and a chisel, and a hammer or two, or a jemmy," said another of the men, and then he indulged in a loud laugh at what he considered amazing wit.

The door of the cell was slammed shut again, and the various fastenings put up with care, and then the darkness seemed to drop down upon Captain Hawk with double intensity, and to wrap him up as if it were a shroud of the most impenetrable blackness.

"They are gone," he said, "and I am alone again!"

With his arms folded over his chest, and his eyes closed, for it was better to keep them so than to pierce the intense darkness of the cell, he sat for an hour, and the clock of the old church struck one.

Captain Hawk started.

"One," he said; "the first hour of the coming day. Well, let it come! I am lost!—Oh, God—oh, God!"

For a long time after this he was silent, but his mind was upon the rack. The events of his past career were all before him. Troop—troop past him came all the people that he had ever known; and in his imagination they passed before his gaze in their familiar aspects as he had seen them; the dead, though, now appeared to mingle with the living.

He saw May Boyes looking so pale and wan—he saw the bleeding corpse of the judge, whose white hair was clotted in gore; and he sprang up, crying in a loud voice—

"Off—off, spirit—why do you come here? Meet me, if you will and must accuse me, in the open face of day, before the judgment seat, and in the presence of my fellow-men, not here—not here!"

The effort to rise and to speak had dispelled the half dreamy state into which he had fallen, and the visions, which were the results of a distempered fancy, vanished from before his eyes.

"Gone—gone!" he said, "they are all gone. Thank God for that! Courage—courage! Am I a man that I thus give way to such childish fears? Have I had the courage to commit crime, and not the courage to face its consequences? Oh, no—no; this is childish weakness. I will be more myself. Gerald Clifton—Gerald Clifton, arouse yourself, and, at least, meet with courage the fate you have more than once told yourself you would look upon unflinchingly. But do they think to make me a spectacle for the gaping crowd? Do they think that I will be the show for them, upon the scaffold? No!—By Heaven, no!"

He now paced the cell with strides that compelled him to turn each moment, and this continued to and fro movement induced a giddiness that compelled him very shortly to stop it. He then leant against the wall, and remained for a time in deep thought. Then he spoke again.

"What will be the end of all this?" he said. "Death!—yes, death! That will, and must be the end. They will commit me of the judge's murder. Well, I am guilty. And they will bring me back here while they build the scaffold, and then——Why, then, they may take out a corpse to deck it if they like, but the living Gerald Clifton they do not take."

It seemed to him, just then, an exquisite relief, that he had made up his mind to outvie all his other crimes by the last one of self-murder. The means by which he was to lay violent hands upon himself, he had not yet considered; but when a determined man makes his mind up for death, it is hard to say that any species of caution or surveillance upon the part of those about him can suffice to frustrate so simple, and yet so decisive and desperate a resolve.

"Yes," he added, "they will think to make a rare show of me on some Monday morning, but they shall not. That is settled!"

After a time, then, during which his thoughts was busy with a thousand disjointed things, he suddenly started, and in a low voice, spoke again—

"They rang the bars of yonder crevice that they call a window. Did they suppose it to be possible that I could tamper with them? And my fetters, too. They seemed to think that there was some danger of my releasing myself from them. What is their dread is my hope. Is it possible, then, that during the long and dreary hours of the night, I can make one effort for freedom?"

This was an idea which, when once it was awakened, was not at all likely to slumber again in such a mind as Captain Hawk's; and no wonder, then, that it grew upon him, until by the time he heard the church clock strike two, it became an all-engrossing and maddening idea.

Yet, what was he to do? There he was, in a cell alone—fettered, and without a weapon, or a tool of any sort with which he might hope to make his way to freedom.

With a deep sigh over the consciousness that there was no hope in the idea of an escape, he cast himself upon the mattrass which formed his resting-place. An expression of pain escaped him: something in the mattrass had wounded him slightly in the side, and he sprang to the floor of the cell again.

"What is that?" he said. "Are these the usual modes of treating prisoners here? I am slightly wounded."

He felt the mattrass carefully, and by degrees he found that the hurt he had received arose from something that was within it. To turn the corner of it and to grasp a file about six inches in length, and of triangular shape, and with a fine chisel-like end to it, was the work of a moment.

"Ah!" he cried "this is indeed a weapon that may show me the way to freedom, through my prison walls, or through the gates of death."

There could be no doubt but that this file had been hidden in the mattrass by some other prisoner who had meditated effecting an escape from Newgate, and who had been prevented from doing so either by his removal to death upon the scaffold, or to banishment, before he could make use of the means which some associate from without had, no doubt, took no small pains to provide him with.

CHAPTER XLVII.

CAPTAIN HAWK MAKES ONE DESPERATE EFFORT FOR FREEDOM.

THE possession of that little piece of iron, of intrinsic value not one shilling, altered the whole current of Captain Hawk's reflections. No longer did he feel that he was alike abandoned by man and by Heaven; but with the faint hope that began to glow in his breast, that he might by a possibility achieve his freedom, he began to think that there was yet in the great world much that was worth the living for.

"Yes—yes," he said with fresh eagerness, "others before me have contrived, by dint of perseverance, and their own indomitable energy, to bid this prison adieu, and why should not I do so? I have heard of men, who, with but the weak assistance of a rusted nail have escaped from their fetters, and once again breathed in freedom; am I, then, to be daunted, and to think myself less than they?"

The file that he held in his grasp appeared to him as though it were the master-key of Newgate. He was just moving towards the mattrass in order to make a more thorough examination of it, to discover if there were any other tools concealed within it, when a weak flash of light came on to the roof of the cell through the cross-barred window, and he heard a voice say, "All's well!" That was the night-watchman going his rounds, and passing with his lantern the cell in which Hawk was confined. In the course of a few moments he was far off—the sound of his voice died away

—the momentary flash of faint light was gone, and all was darkness and stillness once again.

"So far so good," said Hawk. "It will be some time before he gets round to this spot, and now to work."

It appeared to him that the best and most direct way of proceeding, would be to endeavour to get through the window of the cell, if he could only succeed in removing the iron bars that crossed it; but his fetters, in the first instance, demanded all his attention, for not only did they very naturally hinder his few movements, but even if he should get into the prison yard, he would be all but powerless with them upon his limbs.

Captain Hawk now sat down upon the low chair, and began vigorously to file away at the fetters. The clock of St. Sepulchre's struck two, the clock of St. Sepulchre's struck three, before he fairly got rid of the fetters; but then they fell from him, and he felt wonderfully released as they rattled to the stone floor of the cell.

The probability is, that if he had had a light to work by, he would have been much better able to file off the fetters; but as it was, he was compelled to do the best he could, although he lost time.

"Now for the bars of the window," he said, as he carried the chair to the wall, with the hope, that by standing upon it he should be able to reach the bars; but he found that, even then, he was a good eight inches from even the lower part of them.

"Foiled, am I?" he muttered. "Can I not get any further towards liberty? Oh, yes, I can—I can."

He doubled up the mattrass as well as he could into four, and then flinging it upon the chair, after tying it with the quilt, he found that by standing upon it, he was right up to the window of the cell, so that he could look through it into the court-yard below.

How drear and dark that place looked! There was not the least vestige of a light to be seen, and with a throbbing heart, for he was full of hope, now, Captain Hawk began to try the saw upon the iron bars of the window. To his great satisfaction, he found that the iron of which they were composed was much softer than that which had made up his fetters, and the keen file bit into it with an ease, that was to him infinitely delightful.

Suddenly he heard the tramp of feet, and a light glanced in his eyes. He stooped below the level of the grating in a moment.

Tramp! tramp! came a party of some five or six men across the yard. One of them carried a lantern. The light came, as before, through the window on to the top of the cell.

"Halt!" cried a voice, and the footsteps ceased.

Then there was a solitary footfall, and a strange light glanced on the roof of the cell, and then some voice that had cried "halt!" said—

"All right, watchman?"

"Yes, sir; not a mouse stirring."

"Very good, relieve the watch."

There was a little tramping to and fro, and then a voice said—

"We shall have rain soon."

"It is beginning a little now," said another; "but yet the wind is rising; don't you hear it whistling round the walls? There will only be a shower, that is all."

"Likely enough," said another.

"March!" said the man who was in authority, and then Captain Hawk heard the regular tramp of the watch leaving the spot. Still there was a faint reflection of light upon the ceiling of the cell. It came from the lantern of the new watchman, who, after looking about him for a few moments, slowly moved off, saying as he did so, in the same monotonous tone that his predecessor had used—

"All's well! All's well!"

"I am alone again," said Hawk.

It was still, however, some five minutes or so before he could feel sufficient composure to begin to work again, but the thought that it must be near four o'clock, and that the night was slipping fast from him, renewed him to the necessity of being more active, and he again applied the saw to the iron bars of the window.

Now he heard, indeed, that a gusty kind of wind was rising, for ever and anon it howled past the grating of the cell, and then died away in the distance in low moaning cadences.

"It will smother the faint noise of the saw against the iron bars," said Captain Hawk.

He felt thankful for that wind, and when a dashing spot or two of rain made its way between the bars of the grating, and fell upon his face, he was thankful for them, too, for they refreshed him greatly, and felt like something from the outer world encouraging him to proceed.

"I will succeed," he said, "or perish in the attempt so to do."

One—two – three—four, struck the clock again, and Captain Hawk only just felt that the file had got through one of the iron bars. He took hold of the end that was now loose, and pulled with all his might. The strength that he had was very great, and either the whole of the cross bars shook, or he fancied it.

The idea of getting rid of the obstruction to his freedom in a mass, was, indeed, most cheering, and Captain Hawk paused a moment before he made another effort, so that he might be certain the watchman of the yard was not close at hand to him.

All was still—still as the very grave, and then, summoning all his strength, he brought such a pressure to bear upon the iron bars, that they cracked again, and, finally, several of them broke with a loud snap.

Alarmed at the unexpected noise, Hawk shrunk down below the level of the little orifice, and for the space of abut five minutes he did not move or speak.

If the night-watch had been near the spot he must have heard the sound, but, fortunately for Hawk, he was far away just then, although he had turned his face in that direction, and was coming. A few minutes more, and that faint light that came from the lantern on to the roof of the cell again showed itself.

"All's well!" said the watchman, and he passed on.

"I am safe for another half hour," thought Captain Hawk.

Not to be precipitate, he waited until, by the nicest attention, he could not hear any sound of the watchman's feet, or his voice, and then he rose from his crouching posture, and again commenced operations upon the iron bars.

This time Hawk intended to make sure of his object, if it were possible for his unaided strength to accomplish it at all. He got a good hold of the bars that were already broken, and then he made the effort, and was successful. He had the whole of the grating in such a state, that he could all but lift it bodily from its place at the little window.

The next thing he did was carefully to conceal the file about him, and then he did remove the grating, and looked fairly out into the yard. It was not an easy thing, though, to get through so small a space as that which was open to him. To be sure, it was large enough for him to pass through, but then he had no means of doing so but by going head foremost, and in that case he might be killed or bruised by his fall upon the stones of the yard.

After a little thought upon this awkward contingency, he got down from the chair and the mattrass, and tore the rug of his bed into long strips, and then coiled them up together. He then tied one end to a portion of the bracket in the wall that supported the little shelf, on which was his poor fare, and the other end he let down from the window.

It touched the stones of the yard below.

"If I can keep a clinging hold to this," he thought, "it will save me, and I shall reach the ground in safety. What am I to do, though, when once there? Ah, that is the question."

That was, indeed, the question; but it was not one that Captain Hawk had it in his power to answer just then, or he would have gladly enough done so. All he could do was to release himself from his cell, and then trust to the chapter of accidents for expediting his progress out of Newgate.

Having thus completed, as well as he was able, the preparations for leaving the cell with safety, he listened for a few minutes to ascertain that the watch man was not approaching, and being quite satisfied of that fact, he at once commenced operations.

It was not an easy thing to get through the little orifice in the wall, but by dint of powerfully grasping the lower ledge of it he did succeed, and kept hold, too, of the rug at the same time. When his feet got through, he fairly turned over, executing an involuntary kind of somerset; but he did not hurt himself in the least, because he kept a good hold of the rug.

"Safe so far," he said, as he rapidly recovered himself, and stood in the prison yard. Alas! the high walls of Newgate were yet between him and liberty.

As he stood gazing around him now, the thought struck him, and a very sensible one it was, too, that he ought not by any means to leave the rug hanging from the window of the cell; for although the absence of the wire grating might not be noticed in the darkness, that would surely be seen or stumbled over by the watchman.

Captain Hawk caught up the rug, and cast it into the cell by the window, and then he turned to discover if he could the extent of the yard that he was in, and to calculate his chances of escape from it.

So unprecedentedly dark was the place, and the descending rain so confused the outline of all objects, that, as regarded any idea of space, he might as well have been on Salisbury Plain as in a confined yard of Newgate, so little could he see about him to define any of the limits of the place he was now in.

"There is but one resource," he said, "and that will be to follow the wall and see where it leads me to. I may possibly find some means of surmounting it."

Creeping along close by the wall, now, he went for some time until he heard the watchman's voice cry, "All's well!" Then an idea struck Captain Hawk, which certainly had its courage to recommend it if not much else.

"Yes," he said, "I shall now get out of the prison. The watchman could aid me, no doubt, and perfect my escape, if he would do so. His life is far more precious to him than the detention of a prisoner in Newgate, and so I must convince him that he will lose it if he aid me not."

With the full determination, then, of making an attack upon the watchman, Captain Hawk slunk close to an angle of the wall, where there was a sort of buttress for strengthening it, and awaited the approach of the man.

In the course of a few minutes the lantern shed its faint light around, and was reflected from the moist paving stones. The monotonous drawling voice of the man, who seemed half asleep, repeated the usual "All's well!" and little did he suspect that in a little time all would be anything but well with him.

Like a crouching tiger ready for a spring, Hawk awaited the moment when it would be advisable to make it. The watchman was attired in a large white coat, that had a broad black belt round it, from which hung a villanous-looking cutlass, such as is used on ship-board for boarding the enemy. Upon his arm he rather carelessly held a short carbine. Those were all the arms that the man had, and his duty was to fire the carbine as a signal to the authorities of the prison if he saw or heard anything to give him the assurance or the strong suspicion that something was amiss.

The man came sleepily on. His neck and chin were muffled up in a handkerchief, and his hat was drawn down as low upon his face as it very well could be, to shield him from the rain.

"All's well—all's well."

In another moment he was opposite to Captain Hawk; but the bold highwayman let him get on yet another pace, and then, with a bound that there was no resisting, he rushed upon him, and caught him by the back of the neck with his left hand, while he seized the carbine with his right, and in a low, but distinct voice, said in his ear—

"Make the least resistance or noise, and you are a dead man! If your life is worth anything to you, preserve it by your silence. If worth nothing, lose it, and it will suit me better to kill you than to let you live."

"Oh, Lord!" said the watchman.

—

CHAPTER XLVII.

CAPTAIN HAWK FAILS IN HIS ATTEMPTED ESCAPE FROM NEWGATE.

The fact that the night watchman did not, upon the moment that he was laid hold of by Captain Hawk, raise an alarm, or begin a struggle with his assailant, was sufficient to convince Hawk that he would not do so at all. Reflection would be sure to bring with it the love of self-preservation. It was impulse alone that would have led the man to risk his life.

"For Heaven's sake tell me who you are?" said the man, who could not turn his head either way, owing to the vice-like grasp which his assailant had of his neck.

"Captain Hawk!" was the brief reply.

"Oh, Lord!" said the watchman again. "I'm a dead man!"

"No, you are wrong there, my good fellow. I never take life if I can possibly avoid it. Do not fancy that you are in any danger even, unless you create it for yourself."

"Create it for myself?" said the somewhat puzzled watchman. "I haven't got myself by the throat, captain."

"No; but I have you; and I now tell you that if you are quiet, and make no alarm, but behave yourself like a reasonable man, and give me what aid you can to escape, you will not only be uninjured by me, but I will take care it shall be such a good night's work to you, that if you were to stay here all your life you would not save as much as I shall give you at once."

"But, captain——"

"Well?"

"They will hang me if I help you out of the stone-jug."

"Stuff! they cannot. Besides, if you keep the secret, you may be sure that I will, and who is to know?"

"Oh, dear—oh, dear."

"Have you determined? Make up your mind quickly, my man."

"Yes, I—that is, of course."

"You will aid me?"

"As much as I can; but I don't see, indeed, captain, how I am to get you out of the prison. You know I am not the only guard in it; and these walls round about us now, are not the outer walls. But I'll do what I can, if you will be so good as not to do me any harm; for I assure you I ain't a bit tired of my life yet, though it isn't one of the best."

"Very well; we understand each other now, I hope. Give me the cutlass."

Captain Hawk had already possessed himself of the carbine, and now he took the cutlass likewise from the watchman, and girded it round his own waist.

"Hark you, Mr. Watchman," he said, "if you——"

"Oh! don't speak so loud, sir."

"Thank you for the hint. I will not. But I was going to give you a word or two of advice and caution. If you attempt to leave me, recollect that I shall at once consider that as an act of treachery, and I will fire the carbine after you; and I assure you that I am a very good shot, indeed, and very seldom miss my aim. You know best whether it is loaded with anything dangerous or not."

"A couple of bullets, captain, as I'm a sinner."

"Very good. If you have a fancy for them slipping into your back, well and good, my man; but if not, you will play me no tricks."

The watchman shook with fear.

"Oh, dear, captain," he said, "I don't want to do anything wrong, I'm sure. I'm but a poor fellow. I merely get a matter of eighteen shillings a week here, for being the night-watchman, and that ain't worth a man giving his life for."

"Certainly not. Now, how am I to get out of the yard?"

The watchman groaned.

"What's the matter with you now?"

"Oh, captain, if so be as you don't manage to get away, don't turn round and say it's me, for I will do the very best I can, I assure you; and don't you take a poor fellow's life just because he can't do better than he can."

"There is reason in what you say. Do your best, and I shall not blame you, or be hasty to condemn you. Only, recollect, that there is no time to lose now, and so be quick: you ought to know something about Newgate.

Come, which way are we now to go?"

"There's only one chance, Sir Captain."

"What is that?"

"Why, that you may get to the lobby, and so out. The man on the lock will be most likely taking his pipe and his pot; and it you make a dash at him, you may frighten him as you have me."

"Can you take me to the lobby?"

HAWK IS PUT ON HIS TRIAL AT THE OLD BAILEY.

"I think I can. If there's no bolts but what's on this side of a couple of doors, I know I can, captain."

"Lead on, then, at once, or the morning will be upon us before we can stir from this place. Lead on; and if I escape from these walls, you shall be well paid."

"Have you got the money with you, captain?"

"No; but I will take care that you have it."

"Humph!"

"Do you doubt me?"

"Oh, dear, no, captain. I wouldn't doubt you for all the world, and you with that carbine in your hand—not I. I will do all I can, and trust to you for the recompense. This is the way. Keep close to me, and I will do what can be done."

Captain Hawk had his suspicions of this man. The manner in which he had said "Humph!" upon finding that the captain had not the money at once by him, awakened the utmost fears of Hawk; but it would be as useless as it would be indiscreet now to pause for the purpose of entering into a contention with the man as to whether he meant to betray him or not; so he followed the watchman in silence for some moments, but with a determination to shoot him with the carbine as soon as he should be assured that he was playing a double game, and doing anything that was at variance with his agreement. The watchman kept quite close to the wall as he proceeded; and every now and then he said. "All's well." That was for the purpose of preventing any of the officials of the prison who might be wakeful from supposing that anything was amiss by not hearing that fruitless cry.

After a time. they came to a low arched door, against which the rain was beating and spattering. The watchman examined it for a moment or two, and then he said—

"It's open, captain. Come on. If there's only another one open, we shall get to the lobby easy enough."

The heart of Captain Hawk beat wildly now with the hope that, after all, he might be in another half hour in freedom, and a mile or two from the dreary old walls of Newgate. That the man who was on the lock, as it was technically called, would make some resistance, and, probably, have to be killed or disabled in the struggle, was likely enough; but a man who is escaping from a prison which he well knows will surely, in the regular course of things, yield him up to the scaffold, is not very likely to be nice about the sacrifice of a life, especially when that is the life of one of his jailers.

We have had reason enough, too, to know that Captain Hawk was never very particular upon that subject at all.

"Don't speak above a whisper," said the watchman. "There may or there may not be some one in the passages."

"Thank you for the caution. Go on."

The door that the watchman had opened led into one of those long and gloomy, apparently interminable and noiseless, passages, which in prisons and fortresses are always to be found in abundance. After about three minutes' walking, they reached another door, and the watchman held up his lantern, as he said—

"Is it bolted, captain?"

"Yes, on this side."

"Then it ain't on the other, and we shall get it open easy. This is the way, captain. Let me go a little way to see that all is right. Don't you come, though, yet, captain; for, you see, sometimes they put a watch in the passage beyond here, though not always —It's just as the whim takes the governor."

Captain Hawk stopped for a moment, and the watchman went on; but he did not seem inclined to call for Hawk to follow him.

"Hist!" said Hawk. "Hilloa! Is all safe?"

The watchman returned slowly.

"Back—back!" he said, "Back: there is some one coming."

"Ah!"

Upon the impulse of the moment, Captain Hawk drew back a step, but it was but a step; and then the watchman, throwing down his lantern, made a vigorous effort to slam the door sh[illegible] in his face, and bolt it. But for the fact that the point of one of Captain Hawk's feet was close to the door-post, the watchman would have succeeded in his object: but at it was, he utterly failed; and finding that such was the case, he turned and fled, crying out in wildly alarming accents—

"Help! help! Prison break—prison break! Help! help! Captain Hawk is breaking prison!"

Hawk uttered a malediction upon the head of the man, and levelling the carbice, he fired at once after him.

The report of the weapon in the narrow passage was absolutely deafening for the moment; and then there was a yell, and all was still.

What an ominous stillness that was! How well Captain Hawk knew that in a very few moments it would be broken to some purpose!

"All is lost!" he said—"lost through the treachery of that man, who, I hope, has paid with his life for his villany. All is lost; but let this night be to me the last that I pass in this world. I will not yield. They shall kill me now, and a much better death it is to die with arms in my hands, and surrounded by my foes, than be dragged out to meet it upon a public scaffold. I will not yield to them!"

With this determination, Captain Hawk drew the cutlass from its sheath, and stood upon the defensive in that narrow passage. Truly, it would have been a most hazardous thing for any one to have attempted to interfere with him at that moment of desperation.

As he thus stood, he could hear how the alarm was spreading over the whole building. In the course of a few moments the silence that had seemed to be so profound, after the echoes of the discharge of the carbine had passed away, was broken by a strange humming sound, as though a hive of bees was disturbed. He heard doors shut violently, and he heard the tramp of feet, and then he heard a bell begin to ring in a strange manner at intervals.

That was the alarm bell of the prison, and was to put all the officials, both within and without the walls, upon the alert.

It struck Captain Hawk, then, that he had it in his power to prevent any one from approaching him by the way that the watchman had gone by bolting the door close to which he was. To be sure, the lantern had either gone out when the watchman had cast it down, or the concussion of the air, consequent upon the discharge of the carbine, had put it out: so that Captain Hawk was in the most intense darkness that could be conceived. But yet in so small a place there could be no difficulty in finding the door, and he soon had it bolted. He then tried to retrace his steps to the yard, for there was something terrible and choking in the idea of being attacked by overpowering numbers in that narrow passage, and being slaughtered there in the close pent-up atmosphere, and in the dark, too.

To be sure, it was night outside in the yard; but the night of the open air, with the fresh cool rain, was nothing in comparison to the night in that dismal passage.

Captain Hawk knew that there was nothing in the way to impede him; so he ran to the door that opened to the yard, and pushed it aside, and emerged into the open air. The rain was now coming down in torrents.

Clang! clang—clang! clang! went the alarm bell, and once or twice he thought that the flash of lights came across his eyes. He went into the yard, and there he stood with the cutlass in his right hand, and feeling more like some caged wild animal than anything human: or he felt at that moment like some poor victim of the gladiatorial shows of old Rome, who is caged up by stone walls, and given a sword to aid him in a fight with some lion or fierce tiger, who will soon be let roaring and famished into the arena.

"They will kill me, but I shall not die unrevenged. Some of them will fall with me," he said. "Farewell, May! I did love you; but now farewell for ever—for ever!"

The very pronunciation of the name of May unmanned him for a moment, but it was only for a moment; and then, when he saw at some distance along the yard lights approaching, he was himself again.

A strong party of men was advancing, with several lanterns fixed upon poles, so that they showed a tolerable light around them. The men who carried the lights, kept in the rear of the others, who were well armed.

"Come on," cried Captain Hawk, for now he felt that further concealment was useless and in vain, and that all idea of an escape from Newgate with the inefficient means at his disposal was at an end.

"There he is," cried half a dozen voices.

"He is armed," said one of them.

"Yes," cried Captain Hawk, "I am armed. Which of you is most in love with death? Let him come forward."

"Captain Hawk, this is very bad conduct, indeed," said a voice, "and very foolish conduct. You are not tried yet."

"I care not. I am a prisoner, and I cannot breathe in Newgate. Come on—come on."

"Nevertheless, you must manage to do so a little longer," said another voice, and in a moment Captain Hawk felt a pair of arms from some one behind him twined round him like iron manacles. "All's right. Disarm him."

There was one brief struggle. Hawk and a couple of officers rolled together upon the wet stones of the yard, and then he was overpowered, and a prisoner once more with fetters upon his limbs.

CHAPTER XLVIII.

MAY BOYES PASSES A SAD AND FEARFUL TIME.

We must consider that the condition that May Boyes was in now, was an artificial one. She was in that state of excitement—and it was likely to continue, too, until the trial of Captain Hawk—that all she did, and all she said, were not the natural impulses of her disposition. The circumstances in which that gentle and beautiful being was then, had produced what, probably, physiologists would call a state of partial insanity.

After the step she had taken in getting the aid of Mr. Bolton to conduct the defence of Captain Hawk, and after the manner in which she had furnished him with the particulars of the case which was to prove an alibi, she had done all that she could do in the matter; and if she could have sufficiently calmed herself to pure and quiet reflection, she would gladly have done so; but that was impossible.

There was a wild feverish look about her eyes, and at every little sound she would start as though she were perpetually in dread of some impending danger. She was now very pale, too, was poor May Boyes, save and except a spot upon each cheek, which was of too pure a red to be the sign of a healthful face.

It was Ratchley Boyes who with most agony looked upon these symptoms of the mind preying upon the body—a contest concerning the issue of which there never can be any doubt; for so surely as the stronger will become victor, in the long run, over the weaker, will mortal agony destroy the bodily structure, and send it to the grave.

Alas, poor May! It was sad, indeed, that one so young and so beautiful should come to such a fate; but if ever there were certain signs of a breaking heart in this world, those signs were exhibited in the fading face of May Boyes.

Ratchley met her in the old garden, as she was walking alone, with her hands clasped, upon the morning following her agitating interview with Mr. Bolton, the attroney.

Ratchley came suddenly upon her at the turn of one of the old walks, and upon his appearance she uttered a slight cry, and would have fallen, but that he supported her. What a dreadful state was that when every trivial circumstance so deeply affected her!

For a few moments Ratchley looked at her in silence, and then, in a voice of mournful import, he said—

"May—dear May, what is the meaning of all this? You are ill—very ill."

"Oh, no—no. Much to do yet—"

"What do you mean?"

"Nothing—nothing. Oh, do not ask me what I mean, or what I am, Ratchley. Will you be kind to me?"

"Upon my honour and soul I will."

"Then leave me, brother, and never look at me or think of me. That is the kindest thing that you can do. Oh, forget me."

"May, you know that you ask that which is impossible—your heart tells you that much, and, therefore, you should not ask it. Come, lean upon my arm, and let us walk in the garden. Why do you tremble so, dear May?"

"Do I tremble?"

"And your hand is as cold—as cold as marble."

"So is my heart."

"Nay, do not say that. You were ever won't to have so warm and gentle a heart, that you were the love of all of us, whether we chose to award it to you or not. Why, you were the gayest of the gay—your laugh was the ready echo of the joy of your heart, and your step as light as that of some nymph of the woods and groves, such as we read of in old mythology."

"I shall never laugh again."

"Nay, you must not say that; your young heart has, I know, received a cruel blow, but it is not crushed."

"It is—it is."

"No, May, your reason will come to your aid—your faith in God will come to your aid—you will consider and believe that you would not be here in the great world if it were not that your creator expected of you some duties, and feeling that you will not neglect them. We have all our mission, May; and it is but an ungenerous and a wicked thing to say we will not perform it."

"Brother," said May, "you torture me."

"Torture you, by speaking in the kindliest spirit that I can to you?"

"Yes, because I know that you are right—because I know that you have all the reason, all the argument with you, and that I have none; and yet, for all that, I am so desolate that I have but one wish in the world."

"And that?"

"Is to die."

"Oh, May, it is a grief, indeed, to hear you speak thus. Do you know your own age? You are as yet on the threshold of life. Well, you had a warm, confiding, unsuspecting heart, and you gave it to a villain—you have got it back again, the better for the experience that you have now had of what the most smiling face in the world may hide. Have you no pride—have you no power of self-resignation, that you allow yourself to be beaten down at once, and crushed by one mistake? Oh, May—May, this is not what I should have expected from you."

A transient flush of colour mounted the pale brow of May for a moment, and then it was gone again. She shook as she spoke to him in reply.—

"Leave me, Ratchley, leave me. Do not urge me more now. I will not say, for I do not know, what time may do for me."

"That is well said, sister—there is hope in that. You know that in me you have a real friend as well as an attached brother; but I do not think, May, that I have yet all your confidence."

"You have not, Ratchley: no one has."

"So I surmised. But will you not trust me?"

She shook her head mournfully, and then in a sad tone she said—

"You will not ask me, if I implore you not to do so?"

"I will not."

"Ah, that is good and kind of you, Ratchley. And now I have a request to make to you. It is one that trembles on my lips, and I do not think that if you had spoken to me less kindly than you have that I could have asked it."

"It is granted, May, before it is asked."

"Nay, but you must hear it first, brother. I will not bind you by such a promise as that—you must hear it first."

"Name it, dear May."

"I am going to—to the trial of Gerald Clifton."

"You going?"

"Yes. Alone, if you will not take me; but—but you will take me? Under your protection, and with the thought—that thought will keep me calm—that you will stand between me and all blame and all observation, I wish to go. Oh, brother Ratchley! do not say me nay in this, I implore you do not. You will take me to Gerald Clifton's trial?"

As she spoke these words, her feelings overcame her for the moment, and she burst into such an agony of tears, that the latter part of the sentence was all but unintelligible to Ratchley.

"Calm yourself," he said gently; "you shall go."

"You will take me—you really will?

Oh. Ratchley, you are not merely saying so much to appease me as you would to a child ? You really mean to take me ?"

"I have promised, and I will perform my promise, May, if you do not alter your mind. I do not mean to say but that I would much rather you did not go; but as you so earnestly wish it, I think the refusing you would be worse than the taking you; so of the two evils I prefer the latter, and give you my word that I will take you."

"It is very good and very kind of you, brother."

"Say no more about that. You know that our father will have to go, as he is a witness on the trial, on account of that most impudent and audacious robbery of his watch that was perpetrated by Captain Hawk."

"Yes—yes."

May turned aside her head ; she could not meet the harsh gaze of her brother while he spoke of that act which she knew to be her own---for it will be in the recollection of the reader how May herself had personated Hawk and taken Sir John's watch, and told him to take note of the exact time at which she did so.

"But, Ratchley,' she said, "I do not want our father to know that I am there.'

"Well, that can be easily managed. You shall go to London with me. Leave to me, May, all the minor details of the matter, and be satisfied with my assurance, that if you still wish to go, which I hope you will not, upon the morning of the trial you shall go."

"I am satisfied, brother."

"Well, I think you ought, in return for that ready acquiescence upon my part in an act that my judgment really disapproves of, promise me that you will make an effort to shake off the sad feelings that affect you, and try to be more yourself."

"I will--I will."

"That is well. Already you look better, my dear May, than you did when we met a little time ago. And now let us come into the house, and you see if you cannot withdraw your mind from too serious a contemplation of the past and dread of the future by engaging in some of your ordinary occupations."

May shook her head sadly, but she would not now refuse anything that Ratchly suggested. She felt that in promising to take her to the trial she had received at his hands a great kindness indeed, inasmuch as she knew well that it was against his judgment that he did so promise.

Ratchley had said that Sir John Boyes had to go to the trial, which was strictly true, for he had spoken so much about his family watch that it was thought desirable he should be put into the witness box for the purpose of saying a little more.

To be sure, Sir John would have been delighted to have escaped the ordeal of a cross-examination from an Old Bailey counsel; but it was not to be done, and a personage like him was the last, he felt, to resist the call of the court when he was fairly summoned to attend it.

What increased the perplexity of poor Sir John still greater, was the fact that he was alone in the world as regarded any confidence. He had not a soul to whom he could speak upon the subject, or whose advice he would like to take concerning it.

There was Mr. Bolton, the attorney, to be sure, who would have given his good advice, no doubt ; but then, Sir John thought himself so very important a personage, in comparison with Mr. Bolton, that he would have thought it something of a condescension to ask him what the time of day was ; and, therefore, poor Sir John Boyes was condemned to silence and the old authors, who, by-the-bye, as little enlightened him, as they have ever enlightened anybody else upon any subject of particular consequence.

The day for the trial came round with startling speed, and on the evening preceding it, Mr. Bolton sent the following letter to May :—

"My dear Miss May Boyes,—I have submitted to experienced counsel the extraordinary statements you did me the honour to make to me regarding the innocence of Captain Hawk, the highwayman, of the alleged murder of Judge Holmes. I enclose you a brief note that I have received from the gentleman to whom I entrusted your communication. I need not say that its contents not a little surprised me.

"Of course, having undertaken the defence of the prisoner, I will do all that can be done for him; but in my own mind I am still in a complete maze how to understand the extraordinary conflicting statements regarding him.

"Believe me to be, my dear Miss May Boyes, yours ever,

"CHARLES BOLTON."

The note that was enclosed in this was as follows:—

"Dear Bolton,—If the witnesses appear, and swear to what they say they can swear, Captain Hawk, or whatever the fellow's name may be, must be acquitted. No jury can convict in the face of such an *alibi*. It puzzles me as much as it does you.

"I am, dear Bolton, yours truly,

"JOHN EVELEIGH."

The moment May Boyes had read these two notes, she consigned them to the flames, and then pressing her hands against her heart, she said—

"He will be saved. Yes, he will be saved. And when he is free he shall know all; and if there remains one spark of goodness in his disposition, he will feel that the time for reflection and a new life has begun. To me he can be nothing but the object of my pity; and it is in another land, where we can never meet, that Gerald Clifton should hope to be all that he is not here—an honest and a worthy man."

After this, May sought Ratchley, and touching him lightly upon the arm, she said—

"Brother—to-morrow!

Ratchley nodded.

"I understand you, May, and will keep my word. You are better than you were, sister?"

"I am better. Your kindness has done that. I think that if you had been harsh with me, and had thwarted me in my wish for to-morrow, I should have gone mad."

Ratchley shuddered as he heard her speak.

"Do not mention that word, May," he said. "We will see how you are when twelve months have passed away. I have been thinking over this sad affair, and I wish to heaven that some means could be found of saving Clifton."

"Brother?"

"Yes, May? Why do you pause and look at me so earnestly?"

"Are you sincere in the wish you just now uttered regarding him?"

"I am, indeed."

"Then I will venture upon a prophecy to you. Nay, now, do not look upon me as though you thought me already crazed, for, indeed, and in truth I do not think I am. My prophecy is, that Gerald Clifton will be acquitted to-morrow of the charge of murder."

Ratchley did look at her with undisguised anguish, and then he uttered the one word—"Impossible."

CHAPTER XLIX.

CAPTAIN HAWK IS PUT UPON HIS TRIAL FOR THE MURDER.

THE conduct of May was to Ratchley a perfect mystery. Not having the least suspicion that she, of all people in the world, had taken any means for the purpose of saving the criminal from the just punishment of his grievous crimes, the confidence that she expressed of his acquittal was to him perfectly enigmatical.

"Oh, sister," he said, "tell me, and tell me truly, now, have you any knowledge that I have not upon this subject? Has any mad scheme of escape been reported to you? If so, let me beg of you to tell it to me."

"No, brother, none."

It will be seen that May did not exactly answer her brother with that ingenuousness which was, in truth, a part of her character. She caught at the last of his words, feeling that then she could reply in the negative to the whole; the first part of his question, it will be noticed, she evaded altogether.

Ratchley was not very inquisitorial, or accustomed to cross-examinations, so he did not notice this evasion, but left his sister, satisfied that she had engaged in no mad project for the liberation of Hawk, and fully believing that she had not the full and free use of her ordinary judgment when speaking of him.

"Time," he said to himself, "will do for May what all the argument in the world would fail to accomplish now. It will unite her to the present, and enable her to review those events which have cast a transient cloud over her young life with a cooler and better judgment; but now it is in vain to harass by words that find no echo in her heart."

The night preceding the trial of Captain Hawk was an anxious one to almost every member of the household at Boyes Hall, and to none more so than to Sir John Boyes, who, feeling the necessity of appearing at the trial, was yet in such a state of mental distraction regarding what he should say if questioned about the family watch, that he tossed and tumbled to and fro, and it was early morning before he got to sleep.

It would have been much better for Sir John, though, had he not slept at all than to have encountered the dreams that he did during the brief hour or two that he did lapse into that condition; for in that fretful sleep there came such dreams as made it a misery unspeakable.

He thought that whole troops—long processions, so to speak—of gigantic watches, each as tall and round as a mill-wheel, came rolling over him, and crushing him to fragments, and they were all wound and going, too, so that the terrible noise they made with their unearthly ticking was enough to drive him mad of itself, without any further incitement to such a state. At last his own family watch—the time-keeper of all the Boyes'—that fiend of a watch which had done him so much mischief already, and which bid fair to do so much more—appeared to come before him, swelled out to a monstrous size—a leviathan of a watch.

At this sight, Sir John tried to scream out; but his faculties, as is commonly the case under such circumstances, appeared to be bound up in ribs of steel, and the great Sir John Boyes, of Boyes Hall, could not utter the feeblest whisper. On came the family watch, then, until it toppled over right on to his chest, and there it lay, with the weight as if a house were upon him, and it ticked at such an awful rate, that Sir John felt every nerve in his body shaking and quivering with the concussions given him by the machinery of that awful watch.

And now it seemed to the poor victim as though hours, and days, and weeks, passed wearily by him in this agony, till the watch at last began to creep up to his face, and finally plumped down on to his mouth. The pangs of suffocation were upon Sir John Boyes, and by a mighty effort he shook off the incubus of a nightmare, and sat up in his bed.

The demon watch and the dreadful dream vanished together, and Sir John Boyes drew a long breath as he looked around him with exquisite relief.

"So it's only a dream, after all!" he gasped—"only a dream; and I, Sir John Boyes, of Boyes Hall, have been victimised by a dream, which is as much as to say that—that—yes, that's it."

The chamber was light now, for the day had begun; but it was only the faint light of early dawn. Yet how delightful it appeared to Sir John Boyes after all that he had suffered during the short time that his perplexing dream had lasted!

"It strikes me forcibly," he said, "that I will get up, which is much the same thing as rising. I only wish I had not to go to this most disagreeable and uncomfortable trial, that's all. My nerves—descended as they are from an exceedingly ancient race—really are not accustomed to such scenes as vulgar trials."

Tap! tap! came at the chamber door; and Sir John, after a few minutes' consideration, during which a faint idea came across his mind that there might be something more in his dream than met the eye, and that the demon watch might have returned, ventured to say—

"Who's there?"

"It is I, father," replied Ratchley.

"Oh, my son, Ratchley, the heir to all the Boyes? What do you want?"

"I only wished to let you know, father, that as it was rather late, and we had to be in London very early, it was time to rise."

"Humph! Very good. I shall be in the parlour devoted to breakfast in a very short time, indeed, my son. You haven't seen such a thing as a family watch on the stairs?"

"A what, father?"

"Well—well. It don't matter at all, my son. I shall soon be down in my ancestral breakfast-room, where I shall expect to find the family coffee in a state of preparation, and the toast of all the Boyeses properly buttered."

The style of conversation of Sir John Boyes was too well known to the family to create any surprise, and so

MAY BOYES ENGAGES MR. BOLTON TO DEFEND CAPTAIN HAWK.

Ratchley, without even a smile upon his countenance, went to the breakfast-room, where he found May already arrived, and sitting looking like a ghost.

"Alone, May?" said Ratchley.

"Philippa will be here soon," said May. "Mamma is not well enough to rise this morning. I have been to her room."

The poor girl spoke in a subdued

tone, that sufficiently showed the state of her mind, and made Ratchley conclude, what was indeed the truth, that she had had no rest on the preceding night.

"Alas! sister," he said, "I fear that you have but ill-prepared yourself for the trials and the fatigues of to-day.'

"Do not say that, Ratchley; I am equal to anything. Indeed I am."

"Well, be it as you wish. You will take some breakfast, and when our father comes down I will broach to him the question of taking you, which I think will be the best way of managing it, after all. If he should refuse to do so, though, I will keep my word with you, and go you shall."

"Thanks, Ratchley. You are very kind to me."

How fearfully sad was the tone in which she spoke! It went to the heart of Ratchley, giving him a pang that for some moments prevented him from replying to her, and forcing him to go to the window to conceal his agitation.

Philippa now entered the room, and in a few moments Sir John made his appearance, looking all the worse for his bad night's rest."

"Hem!" said Sir John. "Ratchley, my son, you will order the family coach, for it is fit and proper that I should proceed to London in a manner becoming the only gentleman in the county who can tell who was his great-grandfather's uncle fifty times correctly."

"Yes, father, I will do so. May wants to go with us."

Sir John dropped a small triangular piece of toast that he had been conveying to his illustrious mouth, as he repeated the words—

"May want's to go with us!" And then he added, "Perhaps, I may be permitted to say in the bosom of my own family, that I am astonished."

"Yes, father," said Ratchley. "I do not wonder that you are so; but, I assure you, that the heroes of antiquity were very much in the habit of taking their daughters with them upon public occasions; and it is told of a certain Earl of Cressey, that he never dispersed justice without having his daughter, Madora, at his side; and that her beauty, combined with his dignity, made up a picture that delighted the people."

Sir John placed his finger by the side of his forehead, as he said—

"There is something in that, my son Ratchley—there is something in that. Where did you ascertain that singular fact?"

"From an old manuscript, sir, in the College Library at Oxford."

"We will consider then. May?"

"Yes, father."

"We will take you up to London. If it be satisfactorily settled that the great men of antiquity—the ancient worthies, as one may call them—used to do such things, it behoves us, who are, in a manner of speaking—that is to say, who are—a ——"

"Modern worthies," said Ratchley, "a great man of the modern days."

"Exactly. That is my very meaning, Ratchley. You have, with singular aptitude, hit upon my very meaning, and, therefore, that is all settled."

After this, there could be no doubt whatever of May being permitted to accompany her brother and father to London; and although she regretted as much as Ratchley could the necessity of playing thus upon the foibles of Sir John, yet, after all, it was better to procure his consent than to go without it, even though the means might be, from children to their father, a little questionable.

May and her brother were alone for a little time, while Sir John retired to dress for the journey, and then it was that she thanked Ratchley for seconding her so far.

"My dear May," he said, "I have thought the matter over in every way, and I am quite convinced that the reality of anything that may occur, or of any real suffering you may endure, will fall far short of what your imagination would picture to you, were you to remain here shut up in Boyes Hall while those events were going on in London, in which it would be folly to say that you are not largely interested; therefore, it is now with all the good will in the world I take you."

In the course of another quarter of an hour the old lumbering family-coach of the Boyeses was at the gates of the hall, and Sir John was quite ready to go to town. Philippa remained to attend upon Lady Boyes, who was really very much indisposed, so that the party consisted just of the brother and sister and Sir John himself.

The servants were in, what Sir John called, their state liveries, and looked so grim and stiff that it was quite a wonder that they could move at all, and the old horses, with large rosettes in their heads, were the pictures of animal formality.

Sir John Boyes, whenever he went out in the family coach, was additionally grand and pompous, poor man ; and when he seated himself on the seat of honour in the vehicle, with Ratchley and May on the seat opposite to him, and felt himself surrounded by the faded tapestry lining of the old vehicle, and just caught sight of the rich old woven cloth and the skirts of the coachman's coat through the front window, he felt, indeed, that he was somebody.

"We will proceed," he said, "or, in other words, go on."

Off went the coach, swaying to and fro in a very alarming fashion, and Sir John, with a placid smile, was conveyed to London, quite forgetting for a whole hour all his perplexities about the family watch, and only wondering what a sensation he and his equipage would create in the Old Bailey.

Truly, Sir John might, with much greater truth and likelihood, have calculated upon the sensation that his beautiful daughter, May, would create, for about her charms there could be no second opinion, while, as regarded the family coach of the Boyeses, it was very doubtful if the people would not laugh.

The fresh morning air now imparted to the pale face of poor May such a sweet and delicate colour, that it was delightful to look upon it ; and even Sir John could not help glancing now and then at her, and drawing deductions in his own mind highly favourable to the greatness of the Boyeses.

Ratchley endeavoured to amuse the mind of May, as well as he could, by making casual remarks about indifferent subjects, for he guessed how heavy was her heart ; and she did, being in the presence of her father, and truly estimating, with grateful feelings, the kind intention of Ratchley, contrive to assure him, without betraying much incoherence ; and in this way they reached London.

As they neared the Old Bailey, Sir John correctly settled the family diamond ring upon his finger, so that it would show to the greatest advantage, and put on such an air of what he considered dignity, that poor Ratchley was in an agony for fear he should commit himself in some way, so as to draw down upon him the ridicule of the mob, which, of all passions, is in a London mob most easily excited."

With such a swinging to and fro, as was quite alarming, the family coach stopped at the Old Bailey.

"Sir John Boyes!" announced the footman, and the name was uttered by several of the officials of the courts. "Way for Sir John Boyes!" cried an officer. "Way for Sir John Boyes's carriage!"

Sir John smiled with quite a benign look, and, with all the condescension of a monarch, he alighted, and stepped within the gloomy building before him, followed by Ratchley and May.

CHAPTER L.

THE TRIAL BEGINS.

PROBABLY never, in the history of judicial investigations, had so intense an excitement been created as that which now filled the public mind with clamorous curiosity, regarding the trial of that bold, bad man, who, like a moral pestilence, had spread a blight around him, dealing the destruction of those who trusted him not, and that worse destruction of spirit to those who did trust and love him.

No fabled hero of romance could have stood for the time so high in popular estimation ; probably, this is not the word which would have been proper to apply to the feelings with which people regarded the man, for no doubt general consent would have prolaimed him a ruffian of the first class ; but then to the imagination of almost all persons, the bold and daring acts of such men, not the less bold and daring because they are criminal, have about them such a dash of romance as to become irresistibly and delusively delightful.

Sober, pains-taking, plodding folks rather look at the physical stamina which will induce a highwayman to stop the belated traveller, than at that far more ennobling moral courage which would have induced him to procure a living by honester and less precarious means.

Thus was it that Captain Hawk appeared to most persons something in the shape of a bold and brave adventurer, who was only in a critical position because he had been beaten by the society against which he had waged war.

And then, in these cases, the great mass of mankind are but speculators; their feelings, wishes, and interests have no connection with the event which calls upon their curiosity; of course, but very few of the dense population of England had been robbed by Captain Hawk, and probably still fewer were called upon to decide his fate judicially; and hence was it that the greater number of persons felt neither anger nor concern, but simply watched the little episcopal drama with that kind of interest with which we sit to see the scene depicted by able actors.

His portrait adorned shop-windows. Many who slaved from morning to night for a bare subsistence, thought, with a sigh, over the merrier roving life of the knight of the road, and looked upon him in their hearts as a kind of hero, who had shaken off the trammels of tyrant custom, and carved for himself a new path to pleasure, well worthy of imitation. Songs were sung to his honour; the startling anecdotes of a hundred highwaymen, by flood and field, were all appended to his name; and, like many a hero, he was enveloped in a cloud of laurels, but very few of which he could lay legitimate claim to.

But the multitude must have its idol, and why not a highwayman as well as, if not in preference to, many a character of greater cunning, but of less desert, who has held the highest niche of fame in the temple of popular opinion?

The distinction, then, likewise, between the two great classes of society—the rich and the poor—was then far more marked than it is at present; there was much real arrogance on the one side, and much affected humility on the other; while, on both, there was dislike and suspicion.

Hence all the sympathies of the lower classes, and those who had nothing to lose, went with such a man as Captain Hawk, who, of course, took nothing from them; and one or two stray acts of generosity, in which he had taken from the rich and given to the poor, made him appear to their imagination rather like a knight-errant in the cause of virtue than a depredator.

In the glitter of the few guineas which were cast from the highwayman's pouch to a wandering beggar by the way-side, the crime by which he had obtained the means of being so lavish of his bounty was forgotten.

The public press—which must write to live, as well as live to write—then, as now, found it necessary, in some measure, to pander to popular taste, and something daily about the popular highwayman was generally found to be a palatable food for gossip.

There was a mystery about who and what he was; a thousand suppositions were rife with regard to his origin; and mode of life. The absurd stories that got into circulation concerning him were truly ludicrous—some would make him out to be the illegitimate scion of some noble stock; and others again, not satisfied with vague hints of that description, would have it that royalty itself was to blame for the introduction of such a species of crime and audacity to the world.

The authorities, too, had passed rather an uncomfortable time of it, for am impression han got among them to the effect, that Captain Hawk had ways and means of escaping, which it was difficult to fathom, and that he possessed friends who would make efforts to save him that might go the length of actual violence. No doubt the daring manner in which he had once eluded the officers had to establish such a feeling upon their parts.

Of course, to save themselves from the charge of culpable negligence in the case of their prisoner, the officers had made up a good story, and no wonder, therefore, that the sheriff and the governor of Newgate both passed hours of anxiety while they had Captain

Hawk in their possession; and in every stranger that came to the prison, they were prepared to see the commencement of some desperate attempt to aid the prisoner to escape.

If, however, any such intention was entertained, it was completely unknown to Captain Hawk, who had been by far too strictly taken care of during his residence in Newgate to be able to make any such hostile arrangements.

In the then defective state of the police arrangement, still such an idea was an extremely natural one, and based upon actual experience. There had been, at different times, powerful attempts made by well-organised masses of people to take from the custody of the officials notorious offenders.

In some cases these attempts had resulted in success, although not in many, so that the police were certainly justified, not by fear, but for common prudence, in taking as good care of Captain Hawk as it was possible to do

It was very strange, but no less strange than true, that the very circumstances which certainly made his crimes more serious than they would otherwise have been, namely, the boldness and cleverness with which they were perpetrated, seemed to point him out as a special object of esteem.

People dilated upon the skill with which he had, at various times, eluded capture, and upon the boldness with which he had robbed this one or that one, under circumstances of unusual difficulty.

The crime, too, of which he was now accused, did not happen to the popular eye to present any peculiar features of condemnation. In the first place, all persons who are in any way connected with the administration of the laws are unpopular; and Judge Holme was peculiarly so, inasmuch as his whole course as a judge had been marked by an unmitigated severity against evil-doers.

No one could accuse him of being any other than an upright judge, but, at the same time, everybody knew that he could not be called a merciful one. Nobody loved him, and his death, even at the hands of a murderer, did not tend to awaken any amount of sympathy.

Some people even went so far as to say that Judge Holmes had his own obstinacy to thank for what had occurred—forgetting that he was past thanking anything or anybody—for that he knew Captain Hawk meant to rob him, and either ought to have travelled with such an escort as to make the attempt futile, or have let himself be robbed, and not interposed a useless resistance.

They declared it would be as much murder to hang Hawk, as it was in him to shoot the judge; and, consequently well might the authorities look forward with alarm to what might occur when the highwayman was declared guilty, and condemned to death, as without a doubt he must be on the evidence which would be produced against him.

In those days — we believe there are still many noodles who call them the good old days—the hanging a man was a matter of very minor importance to what it is now; and, when we come to consider that the individual who had been murdered by Captain Hawk was a judge, it is not to be supposed that the rest of the legal fraternity felt towards him any very tender feelings.

If ever a man's doom befor his trial was fixed, Hawk's was.

And now the eventful morning arrived on which he was to be placed at the bar of justice; and great, indeed, was the throng and excitement throughout the precincts of the court.

The witnesses had been, over night, accommodated within Newgate; for, otherwise, it was feared that those who were known to have adverse evidence to give against the prisoner, would scarcely be permitted by the mob without to enter the court; or, if they were, it would only be as a result of a victory obtained by the officials, so that there would have been a petty war carried on all day.

The likelihood, however, of this was obviated, as we say, by the witnesses being lodged in Newgate.

Poor Sir John was in a most serious state of alarm and perturbation, and, from the singular replies he made even to the most trivial questions, it was quite evident that his evidence would be of a very remarkable character, and probably far from easy to understand.

Indeed, it was pretty clear that it was only by the family coach of the Boyeses being for a few moments mistaken for the sheriff's carriage, that that illustrious Sir John was permitted to enter the building appropriated to justice so quietly as he had. He likewise though, had in the presence of May a friend that surely would have induced respect even among the rude spirits of an English mob; and we are inclined to think that Sir John would have been perfectly safe from any insult, so long as his beautiful child was upon his arm.

Several of the servants of the Hall had been subpœnaed by the prosecution as well as by the defence, although it was difficult to imagine what they could be brought to say in favour of the prisoner, which should have any effect against the mass of evidence tending to convict him of a crime concerning which there can be no extenuation.

But we give full credit to Captain Hawk's attorney for knowing what he is about.

The trial took place on a Friday, then, as a matter of course, in consequence of the charge being one which affected the life of the accused; because if found guilty, and sentenced to suffer the extreme penalty of the law, Sunday being a *dies non* in law, it gave him another day to live before the sentence was carried into effect, which the law declared should be in twenty-four hours after conviction.

The court sat at an earlier hour than usual, as the trial was expected to be a protracted one, so that by about ten minutes past eight all things were in readiness, and the judge had taken his seat, having by his side the lord mayor, and several personages of rank, who had come, from motives of curiosity, to hear the proceedings. The moment the doors of the court were opened, the throng that rushed in and filled up every avenue and corner into which any human being could, by any possibility, be thrust, was prodigious.

In vain was some sort of order endeavoured to be maintained. The officers and other official personages of the court were carried along by the mob, like chaff before the wind, and it was then half an hour before the proceedings could be commenced.

It is doubtful if even then—such was the struggle to get into the court—anything like order would have been obtained, had not the judge himself suggested to those who had succeeded in getting in, the propriety of assisting the officers in preventing the mod from without endeavouring to force an entrance.

This had some effect, and those who were nearest to the door fought with the foremost of those without, who were striving to effect the possibility of making a given space hold more persons than could stand upon it.

At length, at about a quarter before ten, some appearance of silence and tranquillity was apparent, and the business of the court commenced.

Let us, however, before the prisoner is placed at the bar, take a brief notice of the persons most interesting to the reader, who are already accommodated with seats in the court of justice.

In rather an obscure corner, but quite intent upon all that was passing, sat Mr. Bolton, who had been so strangely retained by May to conduct the defence of Captain Hawk—that defence which was to come upon the apprehension of the prisoner himself with all the suddenness of a surprise, and all the mistification of a dream—that defence of which he knew nothing, but of which May knew so much—so much more, indeed, than she intended any other human being should ever know in this world.

Mr. Bolton was eagerly watching for some opportunity of speaking to May, and he had not long to wait for it.

There was poor Sir John, with looks of comical agony, his thoughts most painfully intent upon the family watch, and the incidents connected therewith, revolving in his mind what he should say, and what he should not, in order to get as handsomely out of the chronometrical entanglement as he well could.

The only difficulty he eventually experienced was, that none of the questions he imagined would have been put, were put at all, and that he forgot all his projected answers to what were put

Ratchley, too, was there, pale and anxious, ever and anon casting sad and uneasy glances upon his sister's face, agitated almost beyond his powers of self-control. His arm was still suspended by a sling, and there was about his whole appearance the traces of recent severe indisposition.

And there sat May; but, oh! what pen can hope to describe the world of impassioned thoughts that sat upon her face. She was more beautiful than death, but just as sad to look upon—the seal of the destroyer seemed to be set upon every feature—the brain, overwrought, was preying upon itself; her very lips were of a marble hue—her eyes looked dark and lustrous, but the lustre was not of this world—it looked as if, for a time, they had borrowed some sparkling light from kindred stars; her hands were clasped painfully, rigidly; and ever and anon those pale lips moved slightly, as if uttering some sound, which it was necessary so to utter, in order to give a double assurance to some mental aspiration.

Ratchley leaned forward to catch those words, and he heard them faintly uttered; they simply consisted of—

"He will be saved yet—he will be saved yet!"

Her eyes wandered not from that one spot which had been indicated to her as that on which the prisoner would stand. There was bent all her energies—she heard nothing, she saw nothing, but that one vacant place, too soon to be filled by the man brought there by his fellow man to be accused of great crimes—of awful lapses from righteousness, while yet, yes, yet he was her heart's idol.

It was but for a moment, as a person passed close to her face, hiding the object of her gaze from her fixed and concentrated observation, that she looked in the face of the intruder.

"'Tis all done—'tis all done?" she said in a strange hysterical manner, as she leaned forward in a moment.

"Yes," said Mr. Bolton, for it was to that gentleman she spoke,—"yes, all is done as you would wish, and every witness is, to the best of my belief, here. It is a wonderful case."

"Yes—oh, yes, so wonderful."

"It is, indeed, Miss Boyes. I have placed it in good hands as concerns its conduction, which you will not fail to see as it proceeds."

"How can I thank you?"

"By silence."

"Silence, Mr. Bolton? How mean you?"

"Why, to tell the truth, Miss May, I don't like being mixed up in these cases; and although I beg you to understand that I have done all that could be done in this, yet it is out of my line of practice, and would do me no good to be talked of; so all I ask of you is silence."

"I will obey you, sir."

"Thank you, Miss May. But don't think now that I say this in unkindness to you, for if all was to do over again, I would do it gladly."

"Oh, no—no, I will not think anything, but that you have been to me very kind and good, indeed, Mr. Bolton."

"That will do, my dear Miss May. The prisoner will be acquitted."

CHAPTER LI.

THE TRIAL OF CAPTAIN HAWK PROCEEDS, AND GROWS IN INTEREST.

Mr. Bolton left the spot, and May relapsed into her former attitude, and again Ratchley heard her mutter those words which alone seemed to stand between her and mental alienation—

"He will be saved yet—he will be saved yet!"

"Oh! May—May," he said, "why did you come here? You will never—never, sister, be able to go through this scene."

"Yes, Ratchley," said May; "you shall see how well I can enact my part. Watch me—watch me well!"

"Eh?" said Sir John, behind; "who says anything about a watch? Is it the family watch of all the Boyeses you mean? because I have a particular desire, in a manner of speaking, that it shouldn't be mentioned. The fact is, my dear, that watch, as you're well aware, is just at the present moment a kind of a—a—precisely—I hope I make myself quite understood, when I say that—that—that—just so."

"Yes, father," said Ratchley.

"Very good," said Sir John. "Ratchley, how do you feel? Something, do you know, strikes me that there are a great number of common people who never had grandfathers in this court. How do you feel, my son, Ratchley?"

"Much as usual, father. The air is oppressive."

"It is—it is; it's really terrific to think, when people of distinction—a-hem!—and representatives of old families, have to come to any of these exhibitions, that the common herd, the canaille—the—a—the—the—the—are not kept out."

"Hush—hush—hush!" said May.

"Hush, indeed!" exclaimed Sir John. "I believe, in a manner of speaking, it is not often that I make a remark, but when I do, there are not many people who take upon themselves to say, hush! Ratchley, my dear?"

"Yes, father."

"The next time you speak to me, say Sir John—say Sir John, in order that that fat old gentleman behind may know who I am. Call me 'mister,' and ask me the time of day! My dears, call me Sir John. It is just as well people should know when they are in distinguished company, that they may comport themselves with that kind of—of—sort of—of—a—a—yes."

But we had nearly forgotten that there was still another member of the family, or, at all events, of the establishment of the Boyeses in court. Sir John had been determined that, by some means or other, his dignity should be kept up; and having on his establishment a very tall serving-man, he ordered him to dress himself in the state livery of the Boyeses and push himself in on that eventful morning, and then he could tell everybody that he was one of Sir John's servants, and that there was Sir John, the gentleman with the commanding physiognomy, and the Roman nose.

This little manœuvre would have succeeded in attracting some attention, doubtless, had not the serving-man been despoiled of his coat in his efforts to get into the court at all, so that the appearance he presented inside was that of a big, awkward-looking brute, attired in yellow plush breeches, and not a very clean shirt, while a waistcoat of some indescribable pattern, with coach-trimming borders, hung in shreds and patches about him.

Alas! poor Sir John Boyes! It was a sad thing to contemplate, that the more he tried to keep up the dignity of the family, the more ludicrous things would occur to pull down that dignity. The malignant fates surely had some sort of spite against Sir John.

With a sigh, he saw how the very artful manœuvre of the serving-man had failed, and he turned his august attention to the more public proceedings of the court.

The judge's manœuvre, in getting the people inside to resist the people who were out, was, as we before remarked, sufficiently successful to induce something like the appearance of order, and all the preparations appeared to be complete for the commencement of the business of the day.

Every one knew now that the prisoner would, in a few moments, appear at the bar. All felt conscious that he was even now upon his way through those gloomy passages that led from the prison to the court. Yes, he comes, he comes; there is a stir among the multitude, an uneasy shifting of position, and a straining of every eye; those who knew him by sight looked for him, perhaps, with a far greater interest than those who had never set eyes upon him before.

But, oh! what was all that interest and expectation concentrated, and then multiplied a thousandfold, compared with the feelings that swept across the breast of May Boyes, as she, too, felt that the man who was her destiny—and such, indeed, he was—would in another minute meet her gaze?

She did not tremble; she told herself she would not shrink; but with such a gaze as some forlorn wretch might cast upon the wreck of all hope, she looked towards that one spot in which she had centred all her regard, but never with such a fearful interest as now.

He comes—he comes! there is a footstep. The flooring slopes downward from the dock, and his head alone is visible for a moment ; another stride, and more of him is seen ; another, and he stands before the multitude, Captain Hawk, the knight of the road—the idol of the people, the bold, bad man, with blood upon his hands.

A strange, gasping sort of sob came from the lips of May, and she clasped the wrists of Ratchley with a force that

RATCHLEY AND MAY BOYES AT THE TRIAL OF CAPTAIN HAWK.

made the latter utter a short cry of pain.

"May—May," said Ratchley, "for God's sake be calm!"

"I am very calm. I am—very calm. He does not see me yet."

The tall form of the highwayman, as he stood at the bar, not undivested of the graceful bearing which had been always remarkable in him, produced an evident and favourable effect upon the multitude. He was actually greeted with some such a murmur of applause as might succeed the appearance of some favourite actor.

Ought not such a scene to suffice to enable those who are ever upon the hunt for pcpular applause, to estimate it at its real standard? But, no—there will be still people who will hang upon the very breath of the multitude, and find their greatest gratification in the life applause of a crowd that would be equally well pleased at the holiday of the execution. But let us now look at Captain Hawk, the brigand—the murderer—the deceiver of May Boyes—the polished ruffian. There he was, looking more like some highly appreciated martyr to some very holy cause, than what he really was.

He expected that he came there merely to go through the form of a trial, for he knew how the facts were against him, and death appeared to stalk with him into that court, and there to keep him company.

And in personal appearance he was, indeed, wonderfully gifted to ensnare the minds of the unthinking. The white light cast by the looking-glass upon his face did him no harm; it only imparted a kind of spirituality to the almost feminebeauty of his features. He was pale, but his eye had lost none of its brilliancy; his lips were compressed, and their nearly bloodless appearance seemed to arise from that compression than from any other cause; not a muscle seemed to quiver, and yet some thought the attitude in which he stood was one of studied ease, rather than a natural one.

His dress was costly, but it was divested of those professional insignia which marked him too well when out on his marauding expeditions for what he really was. He wore a coat of silvery-grey cloth, trimmed with white lace; there were no ornaments about him, and his apparel rather merited the appellation of rich on account of the costly quality of its material than for any meretricious gaud.

It was no wonder that, coming from the darkness of the cell and its solitude, through the few gloomy passages, into light, and before such a throng of persons, he should be unable to distinguish, for a few moments, even the most familiar faces from those most strange to him.

He seemed, as no doubt was really the case, more intent upon making a favourable impression for himself than upon observing anything or anybody before him.

The murmur of applause, which the judge did not attempt to check, and the criers could not, for it was done and over too suddenly, satisfied him, and then his keen eye could be seen running over the faces before him, as if to pick out from that human mass enemies from friends.

It was a moment or two before he saw the Boyes family, and then his glance evidently first fell upon Sir John, to whom he made a courteous bow.

"D—n his impudence!" said Sir John; "in a manner of speaking, people of distinction have come to a pretty pass."

Then it was evident that he saw May; a flush of colour came across his face, and he shook and recoiled from the front of the dock the whole length of his arm, which clutched it convulsively; his lips moved, and no one knew what sound they would have uttered; but she, who was love's own prescience, knew well that it was her name that came like an echo from his heart.

And now it was that Rachley Boyes looked earnestly in the face of his sister to try if he could resolve the doubt that still lingered in his mind regarding her feelings towards the man who was there before his fellows to answer with his life for the evil that he had done.

"Is it pity, or is it love?" said Ratchley to himself, and as he saw the now death-like features of May's face, he added—"She will never smile again. Her young life is clouded for ever."

"May?" he said.

"Not now—oh, not now!" murmured May.

Ratchley understood her. Her soul was too preoccupied to speak to him, and she wished him to let her be with the companionship of her own thoughts.

The short intervals of silence in which the few words were spoken which we have occasionally recorded, and during which some of the incidents occurred, were much less, in amount of time, than it takes us to present these circumstances to our readers.

Probably, from the moment that Captain Hawk first made his appearance in court, to that when the clerk of the arraigns rose to gabble over the unintelligible jargon called the indictment, did not exceed, at the most, two or three minutes.

But in two or three minutes a heart may be broken, or a kingdom lost.

The indictment charged the prisoner, by a number of aliases, with having, to the disturbance of good order, the violation of peace of the king, and contrary to law, slain, murdered, and taken away the life wrongously of George Holme, knight, and one of his majesty's judges, on the king's highway, in defiance of peace.

There were several counts to the indictment, one of which charged him with an aggravated assault, and another with a highway robbery; but the first and most serious charge, of course, stood foremost; and to any one who knew anything of the circumstances, it seemed but too probable that the jury would not at all be troubled about the others.

Perhaps, if anybody had throughout made up in his mind to the issue of the affair, it was the prisoner himself.

He could have very little doubt, if any, as to the termination of the judicial inquiry; and whether from the first he had intended to take the life of Judge Holme or not, remained as a point for his conscience to dilate upon, and in no way affected the serious charge brought against him, or its still more serious results.

The indictment being concluded, the prisoner was asked to plead.

All eyes were turned upon him, and every ear was upon the stretch to catch the first sound of his voice.

The lips of Captain Hawk moved, but no sound came from them. It seemed as if the lie that he was then to utter would not come forth, and as though there was a struggle between the faint hope that something might arise yet to save him if he did not abandon himself, and that feeling of reckless, bold defiance which prompted him in the face of all—judge, jury, witnesses, and spectators—to avow his crime, and boldly abide the consequences.

"Prisoner at the bar," said the clerk, "what say you,—Guilty, or Not guilty?"

The words again died away in silence. Captain Hawk clenched tightly the front of the bar, and then, with an evident reluctance he spoke—

"Not guilty!"

The farce was then gone through of asking him how he would be tried, and the appropriate answer was returned, so that the proceedings may be said to be fairly commenced.

The crown prosecuted, and the attorney-general rose to state the case to the jury.

A breathless silence pervaded the court, the jury looked particularly anxious, as well as most of those spectators who held distinguished places, on account of their rank or otherwise.

From this general appearance of interest we may except the judge, who leaned back on his seat with half-closed eyes, as if he considered that a mere *pro forma* part of the proceedings was taking place, and that all his duty consisted in keeping quiet, and allowing them to proceed.

In truth, the duty of opening such a case to a jury was but a nominal one, unless the advocate thought it necessary, which was frequently the case, when there was no political animus to dilate on the facts.

We shall perceive, however, that his majesty's attorney-general upon this occasion did consider that something more was necessary than a brief summary of evidence, and his reason for so considering will appear in the course of his address.

Oh, what an agonising time that was now for May Boyes! How intently she fixed her gaze upon the man whom she had once thought the essence of truth and chivalry, and whom she had at last discovered to be such an impostor.

Hawk, too, saw her, and he shook, and his lips quivered as he looked upon that pale face, which he had made so pale.

Sir John thought the pause that ensued was a very good opportunity for making a slight effort to draw attention to himself, so he rose, and taking out his snuff-box, he regaled himself with a pinch, and in such a manner, too, as to exhibit the family diamond ring to great advantage, and then, for fear everybody should not have noticed it and him, he uttered such a sonorous and protracted sneeze, that the court echoed again with it, and the very judge upon the bench looked in alarm to the quarter from whence the sound came.

"Silence!" said the usher of the court, "silence! hush!"

"Person!" said Sir John Boyes to the usher of the court. "Person! did you say 'hush!' and 'silence!' to me? A-chew! a—a—a-chew!"

Sir John Boyes was resolved to assert his right as a free and independent Englishman, to sneeze as often as he liked; and, amid the suffused laughter of the spectators, he sneezed three times more, till the judge said—

"Officers, you will turn any one out who wilfully disturbs the proceedings of the court."

"Allow me to state," said Sir John, "that——"

"For Henven's sake, make that maniac sit down," said the judge.

Ratchley took hold of the skirts of his father's coat and forced him into his seat, but when Sir John looked round to see who had taken such an atrocious liberty with him, Ratchley looked so calm and innocent, that he escaped suspicion, and Sir John pitched upon an elderly, corpulent gentleman as the guilty party.

"Wretch!" said Sir John, "why did you do that? Wait till the trial is over, then I will tell you who I am."

"I know," said the fat man; "an idiot."

"Silence! silence! silence! in the court. Hush! hush!"

CHAPTER LII.

THE ATTORNEY-GENERAL DOES NOT SPARE CAPTAIN HAWK.

All was still now in the court of justice, and we feel that we can call our criminal courts really courts of justice, for every effort is there made to do strict justice to all; and if there be a failure, it is either a mistake or that there is no one inclined to pay for the prosecution. Some of these days, however, we shall have a public prosecutor in this country, which may be just afforded out of the fifty millions of taxation.

But now even Sir John was silent. He had been called a maniac by the judge, and an idiot by the corpulent gentleman behind him; and, so with a full conviction that some convulsion of nature must surely happen after two such events, he watched with a grim complacency to see it.

The judge he rather pitied than otherwise, for he made up his mind that that once eminent and learned individual had gone mad, and that, probably, before the trial was over he would in some very pnblic and unmistakable way exhibit signs of the state of his unhappy mind.

May looked more like a corpse than a living being, and the face of the accused was now of a deathlike paleness.

We linger feelingly upon the crisis which we believe to be approaching as regards those persons in whose fortune we feel ourselves to be so largely interested.

We know the sequel of these events has yet been but dimly shadowed forth to the reader. We know what the single-hearted, the beautiful, and the constant, has yet to suffer; and most of all for thee, May Boyes, do we feel acutely, because we love thee, even for thy very faults. The light that has betrayed thee is light from Heaven. It is through thy best and gentlest feelings that thou hast erred; and beautiful and entitled to admiration art thou, even for thy profound affection and clinging tenderness to one who is far from meriting even the smallest portion of thy esteem.

But let us look again around that crowded court, let us look among the multitude of faces upturned towards the judge, and those who sat with him upon the bench, as some remark fell from his lips, and then again turn with eager attention to the dock, where the celebrated prisoner now stands. Let us look, we say, among them for those familiar faces which have become to us as household charms, as subjects of deep contemplation, or of painful regret, and we shall see how they stand out, as it were, like living, breathing pictures of the past, reminding us of a thousand little incidents in the progress of our story, which else might have merged into forgetfulness like some forgotten dream.

There was not a soul in that crowded court that believed the man who stood at the bar would be in life by that hour on the following Monday morning, so clear appeared to be the story of his terrible guilt.

And even the attorney-general shut up the papers that he had been hastily consulting, and there was a stillness as of the grave in the court. The attention of the jury seemed to be intently, painfully alive to what should transpire, and even the old palsied barristers of the court looked for once in the way deeply interested.

The attorney-general rose, and after a moment's pause commenced as follows:

"Gentle men of the jury, it will be an ungracious as well as an invidious task, for any one appearing before you in the capacity in which I now stand, to do, under ordinary circumstances, much more than as briefly as consistant with perspicuity, place before you the facts presumed to be supported by evidence which will be submitted to your examination, concerning the guilt of the pris oner at the bar.

"But, gentlemen of the jury, there are circumstances connected with this case which take it out of the ordinary rout ineof criminal jurisprudence; strong and marked circumstances, gentlemen of the jury, which induces me, notwithstanding, Heaven knows, I come here without an animus against the unhappy man before you, to become a little discursive with regard to the peculiar character of his offence, and to press upon your attention the great moral and social circumstances which are likely to arise from your decision, after duly and judiciously weighing the evidence against the prisoner.

"Far, very far be it from me, gentlemen of the jury, to attempt to aggravate any one fragment of guilt which may be placed to the charge of the unhappy individual arraigned before you. No, gentlemen of the jury, unfortunately for him, and unfortunately for society, his guilt, according to the instructions I have received, will be but too apparent, and his punishment, according to the law of the land, is not at all ambiguous.

"And when, gentlemen of the jury, we find that an individual is in such a position as to be convicted of an offence as must bring with it the extreme penalty of the law, we may, without doing him a personal injury, for the sake of that society whose social bonds he has broken, and for reverence to that Heaven whose holiest ordinances he has outraged, say somewhat more concerning the character of his offence, than may be considered absolutely necessary in describing the measure of his guilt. Gentlemen, the mere fact that it is one of the judges of the land, one of those placed in authority to administer the laws, who is presumed to have met his death at the hands of the prisoner at the bar, although it cannot and should not add to the punishment of the prisoner, yet imparts a character to the particular act, deserving of the deepest and most serious contemplation of all thinking men.

"It is likewise notorious that the prisoner is one, if not at the head, of a class of offenders, who seem, in the popular eye, to be almost invested with the attributes of heroes.

"Gentlemen of the jury, I say emphatically it is time that in a civilised country like this—a country making rapid strides in the arts, and sciences, and in everything that shall make it great among the nations of the earth—I say, it is time, gentlemen, that in a country such as this, the mantle of invulnerability, and the halo of romance should be stripped from such characters as the prisoner at the bar, and that they should be held up to the public contemplation in their real colours, as robbers, disturbers of the public peace, and the greatest enemies of good policy and industry.

"I do not make these observations with special reference to the prisoner at the bar, but I do make them as regards the class of men of which I consider him a melancholy example—a class, which in a few years will be completely extinct in this country, and concerning whom our successors shall think, and speak, and write as things of tradition, while they wonder that in any community such lawless personages should be suffered to exist.

This philosophical mode of conducting the prosecution seemed to have an immense effect upon the jury, and they looked at the attorney-general as though they felt his words were positively prophetic, and that it would be impossible to gainsay them.

"These men, gentlemen of the jury, are those who, with ill-regulated minds, and restless spirits, want the energy and honesty to be industrious, and, at the same time, have a rapacious longing for the luxuries of existence,

"These are the men, gentlemen of the jury, who look to results solely, and who, casting aside all the suggestions of a better conscience, are satisfied, through any dirty or miry ways, to attain the goal of their ambition; despicable alike in mind as in manners, like moral pestilences, or rank weeds in the garden of society, they flourish, and occupy the space which would be devoted to goodlier purposes.

"You will, I am quite certain, gentlemen of the jury. give me credit for speaking in good faith, when I again assure you, that I, of all this close assembly of persons, should be the very last to wish to do an injustice to the prisoner at the bar, or to punish him more than he ought to be punished, as a mere individual commiting some social offence, because he is one of a very offensive class which commits heinous offences.

"No, gentlemen; all I wish is, that the majesty of the law should be clearly and definitely vindicated; and that the honest, the laborious, and the right-thinking and right-living classes should be protected.

"Is it not monstrous, that, in a highly civilised country like this, every spot of which is well known and properly estimated, it should ever happen that any individual should not be able to pursue his lawful and meritorious calling in peace?

"But, gentlemen of the jury, not to delay you longer with anything of an introductory character, allow me at once now to proceed to a description of the actual case, and a statement, as concise as I can make it, of the transactions which have this day placed the prisoner at the bar of justice.

"He is, by the indictment, which has been read to him by the clerk of the arraigns, accused of the crime of murder, and the circumstances attendant upon that crime are of such a nature as to make it one of the most cold-blooded, premeditated deeds which, of the complexion, has ever been committed.

"In the course of his judicial career, Judge Holme had rendered himself peculiarly obnoxious to evil doers. I say peculiarly obnoxious, for he did his duty; and, of course, you will readily understand, gentlemen of the jury, how a judge who shows a strong and marked disposition to administer the laws firmly becomes in bad odour with persons of the prisoner's class. If a judge were to be a favourite with such persons, we might reasonably suspect that he administered the laws laxly; but his being, as Judge Holme, peculiarly disliked, was, perhaps, one of the greatest compliments that could be bestowed upon that learned individual.

"He, in consequence, then, of the very efficiency with which he discharged the duties which the Crown had, in its wisdom, entrusted to him, became a frequent subject of conversation among that class of persons, whose vicious courses he was making such great exertions to suppress.

"Foremost, then, gentlemen, among those persons, was Captain Hawk, as he chooses to call himself, the prisoner at the bar. He, gentlemen of the jury, carried his indignation against this upright and indefatigable judge so far, and likewise his own audacity to such lengths, that he made a boast of his intention of robbing the judge, as he came home from the Oxford assizes.

"This I shall be able to prove to u in evidence as we proceed; and one ould upon a hasty view of this case, ive supposed that the very fact of the isoner at the bar having made that oast, would be he means of preventig him from carrying it into effect.

"Any one would have imagined the reat which had been uttered against im would be just the sort of thing to revent him, rather than to induce him o surround himself with any extraordinary safeguards.

"With a contempt of the danger hat awaited him, as he had a great ontempt for all danger, this gentleman ravelled with only one servant from Oxford after the assizes.

"That servant, likewise, fell a victim to, it is believed, the prisoner at the bar: and there was another man servant of the judge's, who followed his master from Oxford, but who was not present at the catastrophe, although he has evidence of an important character to give on his trial.

"Gentlemen, there is no doubt whatever about the locality in which this deed was committed. It was done on Hounslow Heath, and at that part of the heath lying the farthest from London, and, consequently, the nearest to the Oxford road; nor can there be much doubt as to the time of the commission of the deed. It was done some time between the hours of ten and eleven on the evening named in the indictment.

"The judge left Oxford in time to arrive at about ten o'clock in the neighbourhood of Hounslow; and we may fairly assume, therefore, that before eleven the deed was done. Of the actual circumstances attendant upon the horrible catastrophe, we can, of course, say nothing, since the only person who can know what these circumstances were, is the prisoner at the bar, and he is not likely to be communicative upon such a subject.

"How he and his victim met, and how they parted, is a matter of which we must be in ignorance, except so far as we know that the judge was left dead, and that his murderer left the spot living. I shall be able, however, gentlemen of the jury, to bring before you evidence which shall so connect the prisoner at the bar with the crime which is laid to his charge, that you will feel convinced that he, and none but he, could have committed it.

"I have no doubt whatever but that you will be told, with much solemnity, what a very circumstantial case this is, and begged to consider how possible it may be, from merely circumstantial evidence, to take the life of a fellow-creature wrongfully. But, gentlemen, you must consider, that the most careful secrecy generally surrounds the greatest crimes. You must consider, more especially, that in cases of murder, there are seldom, indeed, more persons present than the murderer and his victim—in this case there were; but it came to the same thing, for the only other person who was present fell likewise a victim to the prisoner at the bar.

"If, then, we were to pause when evidence, apparently of an extremely conclusive, although circumstantial nature, was brought before us, before we could declare a man guilty, I do think that we should be holding out a strong inducement to the crime of murder, which destroys in very many cases the only evidence of some minor offence."

At this juncture, the pressure of the crowd without, and the resistance of the crowd within the court, produced a scene of confusion that beggars all description, and which compelled the attorney-general to pause in his address to the jury.

The massive doors of the court appeared as though they were, by the action of the two forces, being lifted off their hinges, and the judge consulted with the Lord Mayor, in evident concern, as to what was to be done.

"There is no resource, my lord," said the Lord Mayor, "but to get a strong force on the outside, and begin taking a few of them off to the watch-houses in the neighbourhood. They are mostly thieves, and that proceeding will alarm the remainder."

"May I trust to your kindness," said the judge, "to carry out that admirable suggestion?"

"Oh, certainly, my lord."

The Lord Mayor left the bench, and the attorney-general proceeded—

"I shall place before you, gentlemen

of the jury, in due order, the facts upon which I base my conclusion of the guilt of the prisoner.

"In the first place, I prove him to be Captain Hawk, the famous, or if I were to say the infamous highwayman, perhaps I should be nearer to the mark. Then I shall prove to you that he made more than once a boast that he would rob Judge Holme as he came home from the Oxford assizes, and that such a boast, coming from such a quarter, was much built upon by his comrades and general associates.

"Then, gentlemen, I shall prove to you, that the prisoner was some time waiting in the immediate vicinity of Hounslow Heath, no doubt in order to await the conclusion of the assizes—always a matter of some uncertainty—so that he should not be out of the way when the time came for the commission of the crime to which he had pledged himself.

"He actually, with an amount of assurance such as may well cause you some surprise, managed to become a guest at the house of a gentleman of great respectability, on the borders of the heath. Under the assumed name of Gerald Clifton, he continued to partake of the hospitality of Sir John Boyes, who will this day, from the witness-box, identify the prisoner at the bar as the young man in whom he took a friendly interest, when he believed him to be Gerald Clifton.

"Now, although, gentlemen, Sir John Boyes is no conjurer——"

"Hilloa!" cried Sir John; "what do you mean by that? Am I to sit here and be insulted? I can tell you, sir, that the Boyeses came in with the Conqueror. Ha!"

There was a general laugh, and the judge looked angry.

"Silence—silence!" cried the usher of the court, and in a few moments order was restored; but Sir John still was on his feet, and, by his gesticulations, seemed about to say something more, and would have done so, had not Ratchley pulled him down into his seat again by the lappet of his coat, saying, in a voice of remonstrance—

"Father—father, let them say what they like; they only wish to draw you out, I am sure."

"Draw me out?"

"Yes; to hear what you will say."

"Oh—ah! I understand; it is not every day they get here, in a manner of speaking, the representative of an ancient family. Ah! no wonder when they do they wish to draw him out, so that—a—a—yes."

"Exactly, father."

"Really, gentlemen of the jury," continued the attorney-general, "I had no idea of offending Sir John Boyes, who came in with the Conqueror, although I suppose, in the crowd, since he came in, he has lost that celebrated individual."

This sally produced a laugh, in which even the judge joined; but Sir John Boyes did not at all seem to enjoy the joke, and no doubt, but for Ratchley, he would have risen again.

"However, gentlemen," continued the attorney-general, "if Sir John Boyes feels himself at all offended, I have no objection in the world to soothe his wounded feelings by admitting that he is a conjurer."

The jury smiled, and the judge coughed in his handkerchief to save himself from laughing.

"Then," added the counsel, "I shall be able to prove to you the identity of Gerald Clifton with Captain Hawk, the celebrated highwayman. I shall be able to show you that he was seen, in his assumed character of Gerald Clifton, at Boyes' Hall, up to a certain hour; and that then, disappearing from the hall, he was seen upon the Heath, as Captain Hawk, the highwayman. By evidence it will be seen that he was on the Oxford-road, evidently waiting for some one, and who could that one have been but Judge Holme?

"After that it will be found that he was apprehended close to the spot where the murder was committed, and that he scarcely made an attempt to deny the deed which he now declares himself not guilty of when arraigned before you.

"I admit that all the evidence is circumstantial; but if we show that a deed is committed, and we know that the deed must have resulted from some human agency, and we then show that no one but a certain individual was in circumstances to commit it, it is as good as if we saw him do it with our own eyes, and so had ocular demonstration to his guilt.

"This is the case as regards the prisoner at the bar. If he did not murder Judge Holme, who did? I ask you, gentlemen of the jury, most emphatically, who did?"

A loud cheer now from outside the court, and then a terrible confusion

THE EXAMINATION OF MATTHEW CLARKE.

of voices, announced that the Lord Mayor, with the approval of the Learned Judge upon the bench, was, at all events, making but short work of the plan which had been suggested for getting rid of the mob without.

Some one close to the door o the court must have been positively aggravated by that course of conduct upon the part of the chief magistrate of the City of London, for heavy and repeated blows with a stick upon its upper panels effectually put a stop to the business that was transacting within.

"This is too bad," said the judge.

A loud shout then proclaimed that some party had obtained a victory, and in the course of a few minutes it was found that the mob had been signally defeated, and that the outside of the court was clear.

CHAPTER LIII.

SOME STRANGE WITNESSES ARE EXAMINED FOR THE PROSECUTION.

PERHAPS the attorney-general was not at all sorry that the riotous conduct of the people gave him a little breathing time. He continued his address to the jury, with renewed vigour, as follows:—

"I have but very little more now to say, gentlemen. The defence is in very good and very eloquent hands, but you will think for yourselves, and compare facts with facts; and, as regards the minor indictments which are this day preferred against the prisoner, since they are all contingent upon his greater offence, they could only become of consequence if, by any legal quibble, this notorious malefactor should escape the hands of justice.

"It, however, would appear to me so wonderfully improbable anything should, in the course of this investigation, come out, which should throw any reasonable doubt on your minds of the guilt of the prisoner, but I should be one of the very first persons to implore you to give him the full benefit of such a doubt; for no one more than myself would shrink from the conviction of any man, except upon the very clearest presu mption of his guilt."

The attorney-general sat down. He had concluded all he wished to say, in opening the case to the jury.

It was quite evident that he considered he had so strong a case against Captain Hawk, that his escape was a matter of impossibility; and that now a very short time, indeed, would suffice to make that individual a matter of history, by his being hanged, and so put out of the world. In fact, this was the general expectation, and a hope of extricating him, whom truth compels us to call a bold, bad man, from his present awkward circumstances, reigned but in a very few breasts indeed.

The whole trial was only regarded as food for curiosity by the legal persons present. The conviction of the prisoner they looked upon as a thing of course.

But for all this, there was, in the address of the attorney-general, too much of the spirit of partizanship against a fallen man. He spoke by far too confident of the guilt of the prisoner, who, has he had not yet been convicted, was certainly, according to the policy of the English law, entitled to be considered innocent.

The animus, however, of a counsel against a prisoner was not likely to do him much harm, for it would either be so far covered up as not to show itself sufficiently, and so would not affect the jury, or it would be so apparent that even they would be able, with their small amount of apprehension on such matters, to see that it was prejudice; and give it little weight accordingly.

The judge, likewise, who then considered himself as counsel for the prisoner, would have prevented any such injustice being done him, even had there existed the will to do so.

In calling a witness, and in submitting him to an examination, it was impossible but that he should say something which might be considered a remark, so from one thing the criminal lawyer had got to another, until at last the counsel for the accused, as they do at the present, were allowed to say what they liked, and to revel in the realms of fiction to the full extent of their own fancy so to do.

The eyes of May had repeatedly sought those of Mr. Bolton, to whom she had given so much reliance, and upon the expression of whose very countenance she seemed to think hung the fate of Hawk. It was only once or twice, though, that the attorney would look her way, for he had a kind of presentiment that her eyes were upon him.

When he did look at her, he executed a slight nod, which he meant to go for "All's right; never mind what the attorney-general is saying," although poor May, in her agitation, hardly took it in that sense, for, to the truth, she was fearfully alarmed at the able manner in which the attorney-general had stated the case for the prosecution.

It is necessary, however, that we should mention now, that Mr. Bolton, in pursuance of the opinion that he had broached to May, namely, that it would do his professional character no good to seem to be very intimately mixed up in the defence of Captain Hawk, had, after mature deliberation, engaged Mr. Pump, who already had shown a tact in the conduction of the case before Sir John Boyes. A very liberal fee to that gentleman had induced him to exert the whole of his abilities in favour of Hawk.

Little did he (Captain Hawk) suspect what consultations had been held upon his account, and what pains had been taken to arrange the evidence which it was confidently thought would acquit him of the crime which he knew too well he had committed.

When Mr. Pump come to find out what that evidence was, and to communicate with the witnesses, he was himself thoroughly astounded at its force; and although he could not but fancy that there was some mystery in the whole affair, yet, with that partizanship that a lawyer cannot help to a certain extent feeling for a client in right or wrong, he was not a little pleased that he had an opportunity of meeting Mr. Attorney-General with so strong a case in opposition to *his* strong case.

We shall see how thoroughly astounded the law officers of the crown were at the turn affairs were likely soon to take, and what a bewilderment came over both judge and jury contingent upon the evidence during the progress of this most remarkable trial.

Mr. Pump, to whom had been entrusted the preparation for the defence of the prisoner, was just about the last man to throw away a chance of any sort or description whatever; so he had instructed counsel to make an objection to the indictment, which then might be done either when that document was read, or after the case had been opened, which process might be considered as an extended reading of the indictment.

This gentleman now rose, and said, while the eyes of the whole court were fixed intently upon him—

"My lord, I have a technical objection to make to the indictment, which, in the event of the conviction of the prisoner—a circumstance, by-the-by, almost impossible, innocent as he is—I have respectfully to request your lordship to notice."

"What is it?" said the judge.

"A misdescription of the party said to have been murdered by the prisoner at the bar."

"In what way?"

"The name, my lord."

"Very well, I will make a note of it. But I think I understand to what you allude, and I fear the court, if such be the case, cannot go with you."

"With all submission to your lordship, I——"

"Not now—not now, if you please."

The counsel sat down. He had done all that the point required—that is, he had raised it agreeably to his instructions, and he was satisfied, although a prisoner's counsel will always parley with the judge, if the latter will let him, or, indeed, with any one else, because he considers that it will be a hard case, indeed, if, during such a parley, he cannot put in something favourable to his client, whether it be, as the novelists say, "founded on fact" or not.

The first witness who was called answered to the name of Matthew Clarke, and there was some little trouble experienced before he could be got at, as he was wedged in among the crowd in a manner which looked rather as if he had been trying to make his escape from the court, than remain in it.

He was as thorough a specimen of a ruffian as ever could be exhibited, and some little appearance of his being attired in what doubtless he considered his holiday costume, made him look ten times worse.

"Matthew Clarke," shouted the proper officer, repeatedly, before this fellow made his appearance; and when he did so, and stepped into the witness-box, a low hiss came from the crowd in the court, as if he had been recognised by a number of the body.

"If," said the judge, "officers, you can lay your hands upon any one whom you can swear adopted such a means as I have just heard of intimidating a witness, I will instantly commit him, and have him indicted for the offence, as surely as I am a living man."

These words, uttered with a sincerity that no one for a moment could doubt, for they carried it in their tone, produced an instant silence, and the witness, who had shrunk a little, and looked cowed, glanced around him with more confidence, but he carefully avoided meeting the eyes of Captain Hawk.

The attorney-general rose. and said, "What is your name?"

"Matthew Clarke."

"Do you know personally the prisoner at the bar?"

"Yes."

"You will please to look at him."

"Oh, I know him, without looking at him again. I have looked at him."

"Witness," said the judge, "how dare you stand there, and swear you know the prisoner at the bar without looking at him? How do you know what prisoner may be at the bar this moment?"

Thus admonished, the witness slowly turned and looked at Hawk, and then he shrank from before the withering gaze of contempt that rested upon his face.

"Do you know him?" said the attorney-general.

"Yes—yes."

"State what you know of him."

"He is commonly called Captain Hawk. I don't know his real name. He is the well-known highwayman."

"Did you ever hear of his going by the name of Clifton?"

"Not of myself; but Bill Hammond told me he was called by the gentlefolks, Gerald Clifton."

"Where were you on the night of the murder?"

"In London."

"You have no doubt whatever of the identity of the prisoner at the bar, I presume?"

"Doubt! No, I know him a good deal too well for that."

"Very good; you may go down, unless my learned friend has anything to say to you."

"Only one word," said Hawk's counsel, and rising, he fixed his eyes upon the face of the witness for full a minute's space before he spoke. Then, in a loud voice, he said—

"What has the prisoner at the bar done to you? Speak, sir—upon your oath, I say, what has the prisoner at the bar done to you?"

The fellow quailed before the counsel, and, as if he could not help himself, he said—

"He struck me with his riding-whip. He—he——"

"You may go down. I have done with you. The prisoner for some good cause horsewhipped you, and you come here, then, to swear anything you can to be revenged upon him. Go down, sir, directly; I will not humiliate myself, and insult the jury, by asking such a man another question."

A slight smile—so slight that it was scarcely observable—passed across the features of the attorney-general, while the judge looked as calm and solid as if nobody had raised his voice above a whisper.

But this little episode was intended for the jury, and was not, of course, expected to have any effect upon any of the professional persons present, beyond one of curious calculation as to the tact, or otherwise, with which it was done.

While all this was going on, Captain Hawk remained in one attitude, and that was one in which, so long as he maintained it, it was very difficult, indeed, to see his face at all, as it was partially hidden by his left hand. But although he seemed to look at the witnesses that were placed in the front of the dock, his mental gaze was in reality fixed upon May Boyes.

While he thought that their eyes might meet—while he thought that she was looking at him—he did not give more than a casual glance in that direction; but now that her whole attention seemed to be directed to the counsel who was retained for him, he knew not how, although, perhaps, he guessed, he wished to glance at her.

Did he repent him of the wreck he had made? Let us hope that even then, with death, as he thought, hovering near him, he did so, and told himself that, if the time were to come over again, he would do differently from what he had.

"Any water?" whispered the jailer to Captain Hawk.

He started at the voice, and looked the man in the face.

"Did you speak to me?" he said.

"Yes, captain; I said, any water. You can have some, you know, if you like. It's always allowed to prisoners on trial, if they wants it."

"No, thank you."

The jailer stepped a pace back again, and then Hawk's counsel said something to the counsel for the prosecution, which was replied to with a smile.

"Call William Hammond," said the attorney-general.

William Hammond was called, but, like the spirits of Glendower, he came not when he was called for, and after a time it was quite clear that this witness for the prosecution did not intend to put in an appearance at all.

All this told for the defence, and Hawk's counsel took care to mutter something about people's conscience coming over them at the last moment, sufficiently loud for some of the jury to hear, by which he meant to imply that the aforesaid William Hammond was to have come and done something formidable in the perjury line, but had repented of the same.

"My lord," said the attorney-general, "I am afraid the witnesses for the prosecution are intimidated by the lawless associates of the prisoner."

"Show that," said the judge, "and I will show those persons that the arm of the law is quite long enough to reach them."

"I am not just now, my lord, in a position to bring parties before you, but I shall be, without doubt. I now call John Foster."

John Foster was close at hand, and easily found. He looked like some decent sort of mechanic.

"What are you, John Foster?" said the attorney-general.

"I am a saddler, residing at Oxford. Have been a resident there for twelve years, and have many customers among the collegians—among the rest, Mr. Ratchley Boyes. Know that gentleman well by sight, as well as a friend of his, of the name of Clifton. Have heard the last named person called Mr. Gerald Clifton. The prisoner now at the bar of this court is the individual called Gerald Clifton, Will swear to that distinctly. Have seen him more than a hundred times."

The attorney-general was done with this witness, but the prisoner's counsel seemed quite resolved that he would let no one escape, so he rose and said—

"Well, Mr. Foster, you have sworn very confidently to the prisoner at the bar being the same person whom you knew at Oxford—as a Mr. Gerald Clifton."

"Yes."

"Well, you will, I have no doubt, feel regret, because you are a respectable man, and, I am sure, would scorn on any consideration, to perjure yourself, to find that you were actually mistaken?"

"Well, I should!"

"Very good. You may go down."

Everybody looked terribly puzzled to know what the counsel wanted to prove by this. Perhaps, in proportion to its obscurity, they considered that it was profound; but certainly Mr. Foster, who seemed a simple-minded man enough, left the witness-box, looking very much bewildered, and rather uneasy.

"Gentlemen of the jury," said the attorney-general, "the next witness whom I shall call before you, is named John Sargent, and was the confidential domestic of the late lamented Judge Holme."

This witness was attired in deep mourning, and when he was placed in the witness-box, everybody felt that now there would come something like a distinct narrative of how the murder was done.

"Your name is John Sargent?"

"It is."

"You were the confidential servant of the late Judge Holme?"

"I was."

"Please, then, to state to the jury as fully and distinctly as you can, the circumstances attendant upon the death of your master."

There was a pause of some moments' duration, and then this man commenced, with considerable clearness, his narrative.

"The judge, my master," he said, "spoke to me at Oxford about some family affairs, before he left there; and then he spoke about the highwayman who was reported to have said he would rob him before he got to his house in London."

"Were these family affairs strictly of a private nature?" said the attorney-general.

"Why, in a manner they were, rather, and I don't know, sir, how far I ought to go on concerning such questions. There are secrets in all families, gentlemen, and the judge had his, I can assure you."

There was a pause now, during which the attorney-general whispered to his colleague, and you might have heard a pin drop in the crowded court.

CHAPTER LIV.

CAPTAIN HAWK BECOMES MORE AND MORE ASTONISHED.

The attorney general, after the pause had subsisted, for three or four minutes, glaned at the judge, as he said—

"I merely ask the witness this question, gentlemen of the jury, because we have found, by such experience as enforces upon the most sceptical mind the truth of the phenomenon, that many persons, previous to death, feel a kind of conviction, or a presentiment, that the end of their mortal career is at hand, and make such arrangements connected with their worldly affairs as such a state may warrant."

"I don't know now that there is any necessity," said the judge's servant, "for keeping what my master said a secret, but it has nothing to do with the case."

"Then there can be no use in stating it," said the judge.

"Well, then, go on with the regular narrative."

"I answered the judge, when he spoke of the highwayman, and advised him to take some precautions against the expected attack, but he would not do so.'

"Were you with him on his journey to town?"

"I was not. The servant who accompanied him was named Gowers, and was killed on the heath. I was on horseback, and having been left by my master at Oxford, to execute some commissions there for him, I did not expect to reach London until some time after his arrival."

"Was that the case?"

"No; it appears that, in consequence of the darkness of some portion of the night, and my losing my way upon the heath, I passed him; but I turned again upon believing, in consequence of inquiries I made of persons coming down the road, convincing me that the judge's carriage had not passed, and I again struck upon the heath."

"When was that?"

"As nearly as I can guess——"

"We cannot have guessing. Can you, or can you not, swear to us what was the hour when you, for the second time that night, were upon Hounslow Heath?"

"It struck eleven soon after I was there."

"You are quite clear of that?"

"Oh, quite. I cannot be mistaken on such a point."

"Go on, then."

"I struck across the heath in what I considered would be the direction of the Oxford-road, and as I did so my heart misgave me that all was not right, and I longed to meet my master. After I had gone some distance, I fancied I heard some sounds indicative of strife, and I spurred forwards."

"Were those sounds voices?"

"Yes; and I thought I heard wheels and horses' feet. I redoubled my speed, and then suddenly a horseman crossed my path."

"Was he coming fast?"

"No; at a gentle sort of trot, merely,"

"Describe him."

"He wore a scarlet coat, and a hat looped up with some jewel, as it looked to me, His cravat struck me as being rich looking, and the horse he rode was a dark bay. He reined in a moment when he saw me, and then he clapped spurs to his steed, I suppose, for the animal gave a great bound, as if suddenly urged painfully, and in another moment he passed me."

"Did you see his face?"

"Plainly."

"Look at the prisoner at the bar."

The witness turned and looked steadfastly at Hawk, and the eyes of every one in the court took the same direction.

"Was that the person you met, in the way you have described; upon Hounslow Heath?"

At this home question to the witness, every eye sought his, and the intense attention of every one in court, to his expected reply, became peculiarly painful.

That this witness was a cautious man, there could be little doubt, and he felt the truly awful situation in which he was placed, for circumstances looked so at that moment as if upon what he should next say hung the life of the man who stood at that bar arraigned for murder.

If that witness at that moment had chose to express a doubt—had thought proper, having a close regard for his oath, to say—"No, I do not think that is the man," no jury could, with safety, have convicted the prisoner.

There was something awful and confusing to a man of simple habits and ideas, whose life had passed off with laudable gratitude, to find himself suddenly thrust into such a position.

The witness was silent.

"I ask you again, upon your oath," said the counsel, "was that the man? Look well at the prisoner at the bar."

"Prisoner," said the judge, "do not hide your face from the witness."

"Hide my face?" cried Captain Hawk, suddenly turning a full front to the witness. "Who says that?"

It was quite evident that the attitude he had assumed was an accidental one, and not for the purpose of concealing his face.

"That will do," said the judge.

"Now, witness," said the attorney-general again. "Now that you can have no possible difficulty in looking well at the prisoner, I again ask you—Was that the man?"

The witness spoke at last.

"To the best of my belief, yes."

"Will you swear to his identity?"

"I will. There surely cannot be two people so much alike."

"What followed?"

"Not knowing, of course, what had happened, I rode on, and found my master murdered on the heath. Gowers, the man who had gone with him, was dying, too, and all he said was—'Stop him—stop him! he is yet in sight.'"

"You gave an alarm?"

"I rather think I did; but the fact was, I became so ill from nervousness and horror, that I could not guide my horse, and I was thrown, and struck my head so forcibly, that it was broad daylight when I recovered, and then I crawled to the nearest habitation, and found that the dead body of my master had been taken to Boyes Hall."

"And that, then, is all you know of these circumstances?"

"That is all."

As the witness spoke these words, the jury looked at each other, as if they would have said—"And enough, too!"

"My learned brother," remarked the attorney-general, "for the defence, may have some questions to ask you."

Hawk's counsel rose, and said, quite solemnly—

"You are quite clear that it was eleven o'clock you heard strike after you came upon the heath?"

"I counted every stroke."

"And from all you saw, when you came up to the spot where your master lay, it was quite clear to you, I presume, that the murder had been freshly committed?"

"There is no doubt upon my mind, whatever, that the man I met was coming from the commission of the deed."

"That will do. I have no more questions to ask of you."

Everybody looked a little amazed at this rather brief cross-examination of a principal witness, and the more especially, too, as that cross-examination seemed only to have for its object the bringing out, in yet stronger language, what the witness had already deposed to, and the whole of which seemed to be so very much againet the prisoner.

The next witness called was a man who, at ten o'clock, had been passed on the Oxford-road by Judge Holme's carriage, which he knew, and which then was more than three quarters of an hour's drive, at the rate he was going, from Hounslow; so that there was abundant evidence to prove that the deed of blood must have been committed some time between ten and eleven, but much nearer to the latter hour than the former.

Hawk's counsel again questioned this witness as to the exactness of the time, and that was all he seemed desirous of doing.

Then followed some evidence which had been detailed at the inquest, and the statement of the officer who had captured Captain Hawk in the immediate scene of the murder. After this, Sir John Boyes was called.

The moment his name was announced, he gave a groan, for now he made sure that he was about to be terribly pestered on account of the extraordinary proceedings connected with the most mysterious abstraction, and then the most mysterious return, of the family watch, which had given him so much uneasiness.

He was sworn, and the attorney-general, in a conciliatory voice, said to him—

"Sir John Boyes, I am quite sure that you have not done me the injustice in your mind of supposing for one moment that, in the few remarks which fell from me during my address to the jury, I intended in any way to attack you, or to cast a slur upon the illustrious name you bear?"

"Ahem!" said Sir John, "I am satisfied."

"Will you then, Sir John, oblige me by looking at the prisoner at the bar?"

"I have hardly," said Sir John, "been doing anything else for two hours."

"Will you look again, Sir John?"

"Very good."

"Is he the person who partook of the hospitality of Boyes Hall under the name of Gerald Clifton?"

"Yes."

"You can swear unhesitatingly to that?"

"Of course I can."

"What were his habits while residing at the Hall?"

Sir John took out the family snuff-box, and was upon the point of indulging himself with a pinch before he answered the question; but the attorney-general called out in rather a startling voice—

"Stop!"

Sir John Boyes very nearly let the snuff-box drop, and then he said—

"Stop who?"

"My dear Sir John, allow me to suggest, that, as snuff appears, from the sample we had of it a little time since, to have a very powerful effect upon your olfactory organ, you defer the pinch till you have time to sneeze, without interrupting rather important business."

"Allow me to remark, sir," said Sir John, "that I do not think I am treated in this court as becomes the representative of an ancient family."

"I am sorry to hear you say that, Sir John," said the attorney-general. "I think that the vast crowd of people here present for the purpose of seeing you, ought to satisfy you that your name is duly appreciated."

"Seeing me?"

"Yes, Sir John; and I don't think I could have given the attention to these proceedings that I have, if I had not known that I should speak in the presence of so astute a critic, and so distinguished a personage as yourself."

"Mr. Attorney-General," said Sir John, as he returned his snuff-box to his pocket, "I can only say, that you fill your situation with singular ability, which is as much as to say that you a—that is, in a manner of speaking, very good."

"Thank you, Sir John. And now, what were the habits of the prisoner at the bar, during the time he was under you illustrious roof?"

"His habits? Oh, he always drank three bottles of the best wine."

"But what did he do of an evening?"

"That I cannot tell, for he generally went out after dinner, and we never saw anything more of him till breakfast time."

"Did not this singular proceeding excite your astonishment and suspicion?"

"Well, it did; but then, you see, in a manner of speaking, I go to sleep myself after dinner, and in the evening I converse with ancient authors in my library; so, taking one thing with another, I—I—a—exactly."

"Nothing can be clearer, Sir John; I have nothing more to trouble you about."

Sir John drew a long breath of relief, and was congratulating himself that the watch business would not come to light, when the counsel for Captain Hawk rose, and then his heart died within him.

"I have to request, Sir John Boyes,

CAPTAIN HAWK SWOONS ON DISCOVERING IN JUDGE HOLME HIS FATHER.

that you will not leave the court," he said; "I believe that you have had a subpœna as a witness for the defence?"

"I have."

"This is strange and irregular," said the attorney-general. "Why cannot my learned friend, now that the witness is in the box, examine him?"

"Because it is not time," said

Hawk's counsel. "It may be unusual for the defence to summon one of the witnesses for the prosecution, but it may be done, and it confers upon me the right of calling upon Sir John when I please."

"Certainly, certainly," said the judge.

Sir John was relieved for a time, and returned to his seat.

The next witness was a countryman, who gave his name as Jervis, and he deposed as follows:—

"I was walking on the Oxford-road, about three miles on the other side of Hounslow and towards London, when I was overtaken by a horseman, who came up at a trot, and said to me—'Hilloa, my friend, have you seen a coach pass?' 'No,' said I. 'Thank you,' he said, and he trotted on. After a time I met him again, and he appeared to be waiting for the coach he mentioned."

"Can you describe the man whom you so met?"

"Yes; he wore a scarlet coat—a handsome lace cravat. He looked tall in the saddle, and rode a dark bay horse."

"Can you swear that the prisoner at the bar is the man?"

"I should not like to swear it, but he's wonderfully like him."

"What time was this?"

"At half-past nine. I looked at my watch. It's always right. It's a family watch."

"The idea," muttered Sir John, "of common people having family watches. What will the world come to?"

"That will do," said the attorney-general.

Hawk's counsel declined asking any questions of this witness.

A groom of Sir John Boyes was now called, who said that at about half-past eight o'clock on the evening in question, Gerald Clifton rode from the Hall, and he was confident he came not back again.

Of this witness no questions were asked, and now there was a slight pause, after which the attorney-general said—

"Gentlemen of the jury, that is the case for the prosecution."

Captain Hawk's counsel rose on the moment, and never had mortal man a more confident look, as he said, in a loud clear voice that was heard distinctly in every corner of the crowded court—

"Gentlemen of the jury, it is my cheering and delightful task to prove to you the innocence of the prisoner at the bar, of this heavy and grievous offence against the laws of God and of man, that which he stands most unjustly charged with before you."

The very counsel at the bar looked at each other, as much as to say—"Well, that's cool, at all events," for not one of those learned gentlemen entertained the least doubt about the guilt of the prisoner, and they looked upon his conviction as a thing of course, after the powerful amount of evidence, circumstantial though it was, which was brought forward to connect him with the terrible and murderous deed.

The attorney-general shook his head, and looked as if he would have said—

"My learned brother, you are going a little too far."

But nothing daunted by the general surprise with which his declaration had been received, the counsel continued—

"Gentlemen of the jury,

"The case now before you is, to my mind, one of the most remarkable which has ever been brought to the cognizance of this court. It is a case resting solely upon circumstantial evidence, but that circumstantial evidence appears to be of so strong a character, as to leave no room whatever for a doubt of any reasonable description concerning the guilt of the prisoner.

"He and the person passing by the name of Gerald Clifton to the family of Sir John Boyes, are sworn to be one and the same person; and, moreover, he is sworn to be the celebrated highwayman, known popularly as Captain Hawk.

"Gentlemen, we will admit all that. It is Gerald Clifton, alias Captain Hawk, who stands at the bar; but he is guiltless of the crime for which he stands here accused, and such being the case, whatever else he may have done, or whatever may be his notions of morality, he is as much entitled to an acquittal at your hands as if he were one of the most useful, as well as one of the most virtuous and distinguished ornaments of society.

"Gentlemen, so far from shrinking in any way from the case, and from the array of evidence which the learned gentleman who has conducted the prosecution considered it his duty to lay before you, I glory in that case and those facts, inasmuch as from them I shall be able to prove the innocence of the prisoner at the bar.

"As the case of my learned friend stands, it is this—

"Captain Hawk, the highwayman by repute, and the prisoner at the bar, for I admit him to be that personage, introduced himself as Gerald Clifton to the family of Sir John Boyes, with what object is not stated, nor does it matter as regards this truly singular case. At eight o'clock on the evening in question, that evening on which Judge Holme was returning from the Oxford assizes, he, Clifton, left Boyes Hall. At half-past he was met on the Oxford-road by a witness, who will not actually swear to the identity of the prisoner at the bar with the person whom he so met. At ten o'clock the judge's carriage is seen proceeding towards Hounslow, and somewhere between ten and eleven the deed must have been committed.

"Thus we have Captain Hawk's time pretty well accounted for from eight o'clock in the evening until eleven, when he passed the witness, John Sargent. This, with all deference to my learned friend, I understand to be a fair and comprehensive statement of his case.

"Gentlemen of the jury, it is a very perfect case—a very capital case—a very clear case—with one exception, and that is, that the prisoner at the bar is not the man who was met on the Oxford-road—not the man who attacked the judge, and not the man who passed John Sargent on the night of the murder as the clock struck eleven.

"Gentlemen of the jury, I say this most advisedly. There never was, and I do think I shall not be going too far if I say there never will be a more perfect *alibi* proved in a court of justice than I shall this day prove for the unjustly accused prisoner at the bar."

Everybody looked amazed, and not among the least so was Captain Hawk, who gazed upon the face of his counsel with a fixed expression of wonder and incredulity that was obse ved by many in court; and which tended among such to induce an opinion that the counsel would surely break down in so daring a defence.

"Gentlemen," he continued, "I will now give you a true version of what occurred on that eventful evening, as regards the prisoner at the bar.

"His motive in introducing himself to the family of Sir John Boyes, by the name of Gerald Clifton, was a good one. He lamented the course of life which he was leading, and he thought that if he could awaken an interest sufficiently strong in that family to warrant him in doing so with safety, he would one day tell them who and what he was, and bespeak Sir John's good offices to release him from a course of existence not in accordance with his real wishes.

"But now to the charge."

The excitement now, and the surprise of every one in the crowded court, with the exception of May Boyes and those to whom she had entrusted the defence of Captain Hawk, was beyond all description.

Hawk himself looked like a man in a dream, so confounded was he at what he thought the unblushing assurance of the counsel who had his case in hand.

CHAPTER LV.

THE UNSWERABLE DEFENCE ASTONISHES THE JURY.

After a pause of a few seconds, the advocate continued—

"The prisoner was pressed for money—very much pressed for money, not for his own purposes, but for the necessities of another, whom he felt bound to by ties he would not and could not break. On the evening in question he resolved—and luckily for him that he did so—that he would ride to London, and endeavour, among some persons who knew him in the metropolis to raise the sum he wanted.

"So urgent was the necessity, that

he felt desperate, and there can be but little doubt of the fact, that if a good opportunity had presented itself on that evening, he would not have scrupled, by some robbery, to take what he wanted.

"After leaving Boyes Hall, he went to the Talbot Inn, where he was known as Gerald Clifton. He remained there for some time, and he did ask the landlady to lend him some money, which she would have done had she had it in her house.

"He was, however, disappointed; he got none, and he returned to Boyes Hall. He tied his horse to a gate, and made his way on to a terrace, which was along one side of the mansion, and which is accessible from the library window. It was now fast, and he saw Sir John Boyes sitting in his library, reading. He lingered for a time asking himself if he should attempt to borrow the sum of money he wanted of Sir John or not,

"He determined upon not doing so; but, with a recklessness of character which belongs to him, and an almost boyish spirit of mischief, he then, attired as he was in his highwayman costume—for mark you, gentlemen of the jury, he had consumed some time in going to a hut upon the heath, and changing the ordinary dress of Gerald Clifton for the more startling and dashing attire of the knight of the road—opened one of the windows, and stepped in to Sir John's library.

"His intention was merely to startle the old gentleman, but upon seeing how paralysed he was by the sudden and most unexpected visit, he laid hands on Sir John's watch, which lay before him, merely in a frolic, and took it away.

"It was then half-past ten, the very time when one of the witnesses deposes to have seen Captain Hawk on the Oxford-road, some three miles or so from Hounslow.

"Gentlemen of the jury, he then left Boyes Hall, mounted his horse, and rode to London. At one minute to eleven I have a witness who deposed to seeing him some miles on the London-road, and at eleven you have the evidence of John Sargent, that he saw a man upon the heath, who, no doubt, was the murderer of Judge Holme.

"And now, gentlemen of the jury, I can prove to you that the prisoner now at the bar was at Tyburn-gate at ten minutes past eleven; at a public-house in Oxford-street, at a little over the quarter-past that hour, where he drank some wine, and was seen by half-a-dozen persons, after which he rode off in the direction of Holborn.

"Gentlemen of the jury, I need follow his movements no further. The man who took the watch of Sir John Boyes from him in the library at Boyes Hall at half-past ten, or earlier a little, as indeed it was, could not be at the same time, or nearly so, three miles on the Oxford-road trotting to and fro, and asking people if they had seen a carriage pass. The man who, a little before eleven, was miles away, could not, at a quarter before that hour, stop Judge Holme, and then at eleven pass John Sargent on the heath, and be then at Tyburn-gate at ten minutes past eleven.

"Moreover, I have a witness, a public officer, of the name of Long, who can depose unhesitatingly to seeing a person on the heath in all respects resembling the prisoner, and whom he believed to be Captain Hawk, at half-past nine, and to dodging him about till ten, at which hour he warned a young female, whom he met on horseback, of the proximity of the highwayman.

"Thus you will see, gentlemen of the jury, what a mass of contradictions is brought before you on this subject, and now it will become evident to you that although Judge Holme has been stopped on Hounslow Heath, and most foully murdered, that dreadful deed has not been done by the prisoner at the bar.

"You will bear in mind, gentlemen of the jury, that no question is raised with regard to the identity of the prisoner at the bar with the Gerald Clifton who was the guest of Sir John Boyes. The groom of Sir John, one of the witnesses for the prosecution, has proved to you that Gerald Clifton left Boyes Hall at eight; and now, gentlemen of the jury, it is my duty to trace his proceedings on that evening till eleven."

The first witness now called was

Peter Butts, the landlord of the Talbot, and he said—

"Mr. Gerald Clifton was at my house on the night of the murder till quite nine. He trotted off across the heath."

The attorney-general, who had listened with evident wonder to the line of defence taken up, rose, and said to this witness—

"In what direction did he trot off?"

"Towards the Oxford-road."

"Do you recognise in the person at the bar Gerald Clifton?"

"Oh, to be sure."

"What do yo mean by quite nine?"

"About five minutes or so past. He seemed queer in his mind, and drank hard."

Long, the officer, who had had so bad a reception from Sir John Boyes, was then called, and he deposed to seeing Captain Hawk upon the heath at half-past nine, and dogged him about till ten, when he warned a young girl, whom he met on horseback, of the vicinity of that noted highwayman.

Then Sir John Boyes was recalled.

The moment Sir John heard his name again pronounced, he gave a groan, for now he suspected that the watch affair was at last coming out; he had only been saved up for the express purpose of dumbfoundering him at last, when he least expected it.

He sat still for a few moments, but the crier of the court again pronounced his name, and as all eyes were turned upon him, he had no resource but to rise, which he did, and addresssing the judge, he said—

"Really, my lord, a—a—in a manner of speaking, you know, I have said all I want to say."

"But we will trouble you, Sir John Boyes," said the counsel for Captain Hawk, "to add something to the testimony, which, in the sacred cause of truth and justice, we know that you will be the last man in the world to shrink from."

This was attacking poor Sir John on his weak point. Alas! that such a great man should have a weak point; but so it was, and, candidly speaking, we really cannot help it. He walked to the witness-box, muttering as he did so that, at all events, there were some lawyers who seemed to know what was due to rank and illustrious descent.

The ceremony of swearing Sir John, as it had been done on the occasion of his examination for the prisoner, was not again necessary, and the judge told him to take notice of the facts.

"Now, Sir John Boyes," commenced the counsel of Captain Hawk, "from a gentleman of your rank and station, and high character, any remark is of importance, and your testimony in favour of the prisoner at the bar will consequently be of the very greatest vital importance."

"A-hem!" coughed Sir John.

"Now, sir, how did you pass your time on the evening in which this alleged murder was committed, with which the prisoner at the bar stands charged?"

"Why, a-hem!—after coffee with my Lady Boyes, I retired to converse with the ancient authors."

"Where?"

"In my library. I assure the court that I consider,"

"Certainly, certainly. But be so good, Sir John, before you bestow those remarks upon things in general, which I know will be listened to by everybody in this court with the greatest satisfaction, to tell us what occurred while you were there reading the works of the ancient authors?"

"What occurred?—a—a-hem!"

"Yes; what occurred?"

"Why—a—a--my family watch; I suppose you want to know about my family watch?"

"Yes, Sir John."

"Then the fact is, that while I was reading one of the ancient authors, a most singular circumstance occurred. The window of the library was opened, and a man came in. He walked up to me, and he took away my family watch. That's a fact."

"And what did you do?"

"Oh, what did I do? What would you have done?"

"Well, Sir John, if you really wish to know what I should have done, I should have said to myself--What is a family watch compared to the life of a fellow-creature? I will not rise up and smash this fellow as I might, but I will let him take the watch, at the same time that I will give him such a look, as shall haunt him while he lives, and which may awaken the pangs of conscience sufficiently to induce him to return the watch."

"Yes, yes," cried Sir John; "that's just what I did; you are a remarkably clever man, sir; and I can only say that I shall be very happy at any time to see you at Boyes Hall."

"Many thanks, Sir John. I feel the honour."

Sir John looked round him with quite a triumphant expression of countenance. Here he was, by the ingenuity of the counsel, relieved from his great difficulty, namely, how to explain why he had allowed himself to be robbed in his own house by one man—he, the illustrious descendant of all the Boyeses—those Boyeses who had fought at Agincourt, at Cressey, and at Poictiers. It was a wonderful relief to find an argument placed in his mouth which converted what looked like pusilanimity into magnanimity. Sir John was wonderfully pleased.

"Now, sir," added the counsel, "you will be so good as to tell the jury at what hour precisely this occurrence happened."

"At half-past ten o'clock."

"Are you certain?"

"Yes. The unhappy individual, to whom I really showed, I consider, more consideration than he deserved, called my attention to the time."

"There can be no doubt; and you swear to the fact?"

"Oh, yes—certainly."

"That will do, Sir John; I regret to have troubled you at such length, but the jury will perceive, from this most important testimony, that the accused person could not have been upon the Oxford-road and in Sir John Boyes's library at one and the same time."

The attorney-general now rose, before Sir John quitted the box, and he said to him,—

"Sir John Boyes, did you know that the prisoner at the bar was the person who took your watch?"

"Why, no; I could not swear to that."

"Then it might have been some one else, while the prisoner at the bar, of course, for all you know, might have been elsewhere?"

"Why, it was like him, but I cannot swear it was the man."

"Very well; I have no further questions to ask of you."

The next witness that was called for the defence was a man named John Lee, and he was the waggoner that had been stopped by May Boyes on her route to London, while she was personating Captain Hawk, with the intention of saving him from the consequences of whatever crimes he may commit on that eventful night, although she little suspected that the one he would commit would at all approach in enormity that of murder.

This man stated as follows:—

"It wanted about ten minutes to eleven, when I first heard the sound of horses feet, and in a few minutes more the waggon was stopped by Captain Hawk, the great highwayman. He asked me if there was anybody worth robbing in the waggon, and I told him as there wasn't, and he asked me what o'clock it were, and I told him what o'clock it were."

"Which way did he ride?"

"Towards London."

"You are certain it had not struck eleven?"

"Quite. Oh, blese you, yes—quite."

"You may now tell the jury if the prisoner at the bar is the person who stopped you on the highway."

"Well, he hadn't that coat on."

"No; but do you think he is the man?"

"Well, I do."

"Very well; you may go down now."

"Wait a moment," said the attorney-general. "John Lee, will you swear that the prisoner at the bar was the man who stopped you? Remember, you are on your solemn oath, and that the life of a fellow-creature is in the balance. I repeat, will you, as a man of conscience, swear that the prisoner at the bar is the same person who stopped your waggon in the manner you have related to the jury?"

The waggoner listened to this appeal with some appearance of terror, and then he looked hard at the prisoner for some time, after which he shook his head and said,—

"No, no, I couldn't swear."

"You cannot conscientiously swear that he is the man?"

"I cannot."

"That will do."

Down sat the attorney-general. The course he was now pursuing was, to the legal persons present, quite sufficiently apparent. It was impossible he could successfully contend against the weight of evidence which was brought forward to prove that, on the night in question, there must have been two persons with all the costume, and all the outward appearance of Captain Hawk, one of whom had no doubt committed the murder on the heath, while the other had been galloping about on the London road, with various objects apparently. Therefore, his whole object now was to prove, that the prisoner at the bar was the one of those two who had committed the murder, and hence he got an advantage, when any witness for the defence could not, or would not, swear to the prisoner at the bar as being the party concerning whom he could depose something, because, by the defence, the prisoner was admitted to be Captain Hawk, and it was he whom the indictment named as the murderer.

But the strongest evidence was yet to come, and the next witness called was named Anthony Bell.

He was a good-humoured, rough-looking fellow, and, in answer to the questions of the counsel, he stated as follows:

"I know Captain Hawk, the celebrated highwayman, well by sight. The prisoner at the bar is Captain Hawk. I could swear to him among a thousand people. I keep Tyburn-gate. I recollect well the night when it was said that Captain Hawk had murdered Judge Holme. I was at the gate on that night. I have not been absent from the gate half-a-dozen nights for as many years."

"What occurred on that night?"

"Two gentlemen stopped to speak to me."

"What time was that?"

"About eleven."

"Not later?"

"Not above a minute or two."

"Well, go on."

"Two gentlemen were talking to me, when somebody on horseback came sharp down the road. I called out to my boy to shut the gate, for I thought it was a trick, and then I saw it was Captain Hawk, and I let him through."

"Now, are you quite sure about the identity?"

"About who? Do you mean the gate?"

"No, no; I mean, are you quite sure that the man whom you let through the gate was Captain Hawk?"

"Do you think I'm a fool? Of course I is."

"No, my friend, I think you are far from a fool; I only wished that the jury should hear you say so, as emphatically as possible, that, on your oath, the man on horseback, who was permitted to pass through the gate at Tyburn-toll, free, was Captain Hawk."

"Oh, very well. It was."

"And the prisoner at the bar?"

"Ah, to be sure; and he knows it. Ask him."

"We cannot do that, but your evidence is sufficient. How long do you suppose it would take a fleet horse to reach Tyburn-gate from the spot where the dead body of Judge Holme was found?"

"I have been to the spot on Hounslow Heath, and I mean to say that, if a good horse did it in something like forty minutes, he'd be an out-and-outer."

"Did the horse ridden by Captain Hawk look distressed?"

"No; and, from what I saw of the animal, it could not have come the distance under half as much time again."

"Which way did he go?"

"To London direct; and I saw no more of him that night."

"But he might have gone back again, and, by making a round, avoid Tyburn-gate?"

"Oh, yes; to be sure."

"You perceive, gentlemen of the jury, that nothing can be made of the fact, that Captain Hawk was taken in the morning in the neighbourhood of Hounslow, because you hear he could have gone back again by another route; but, as he left too soon to commit murder, and went back too late, I wonder how on earth he can be connected with the deed in any way."

"My learned friend," said the attorney-general, "just does as he likes. At one moment he questions a witness and at another he endeavours to sway the jury; but I can see before me, in the jury-box, countenances, the intelligence depicted in which forbids the hope that any conclusion but one highly favourable to the ends of justice will be arrived at, notwithstanding the eloquence of my learned friend."

"It is," said Hawk's counsel, "upon that very intelligence, and which, like my learned friend, I have noticed, that I rely. I have done with you, Anthony Bell."

It was quite evident now that, notwithstanding all his tact and long experience in the courts, that the attorney-general was losing temper a little, and he darted an angry glance at the witnesses.

CHAPTER LVI.

THE ATTORNEY-GENERAL FINDS CROSS-EXAMINATION RATHER A FAILURE.

"I repeat," said Hawk's counsel, "that I have done with you, Anthony Bell, and you can go down, so far as I am concerned.

"Very good."

"Stop," said the attorney-general. "Anthony Bell, pray do not be in such a hurry."

"I ain't in a hurry. Like you, sir, I'm paid for my time."

"Come, sir, we want none of your low wit here. Are you the owner of Tyburn-gate?"

"The owner?"

"Yes. Do the proceeds of the gate belong to you?"

"To be sure not; my master has the coppers."

"And he relies upon your honesty to pay over to him the amount of tolls receivable at the gate?"

"Oh, dear, no."

"No!"

"No—not a bit of it. He says to me, 'Anthony Bell,' says he, 'I believes,' says he, 'as you goes halves with me—confound you! but the fellow I had afore you was worser, so give us hold of what you have got.' You see by that 'ere, that he don't trust my honesty at all."

"Are you in the habit of letting persons through the gate for nothing?"

"I should think not."

"Then, perhaps, you confine such a delicate compliment to gentlemen of the road, and think it particularly due to your acquaintance, Captain Hawk?"

"He ain't no acquaintance o' mine."

"Then how do you know him so well?"

"'Cos he often passed the gate, and people have pointed him out to me."

"Oh, people who were acquaintances of his and likewise of yours?"

"Yes."

"Well, I thought we should come at that. He is a friend of yours, I suppose?"

"Well—yes."

"And so you would do him a good turn if you could. Now, who are your dear friends who know Captain Hawk so well that they were able to point him out to you as the celebrated highwayman?"

"Bow-street officers, and one of 'em Mr. Long; and as for why I let him through the gate for nothing, it was because, only a little time before, he threw me a guinea, and said, 'That'll do for my tolls till it's used up,' and it ain't half used up yet."

The attorney-general looked vexed. He had made positively nothing of his cross-examination of this man, and so he had the prudence to give it up, and to sit down with what appearance of contentment he might.

"Call George Lucombe," said Hawk's counsel; and a man, with an amazingly fat face, and a sleek, greasy-looking head, made his appearance.

He deposed as follows.—

"I am the landlord of the Goat and Boots public-house in Oxford-street. On the evening of the murder, Captain Hawk rode up to the door of my house, and ordered some wine. I brought it out to him myself in a flagon. He drank it, and threw the drainings at me. He always does. It was then a little after eleven only. Can't say for five minutes, but I am certain it was not the quarter past. I should take the Goat and Boots to be nigh nine miles from the spot on which Judge Holme was murdered. I have been there. The prisoner at the bar is Captain Hawk. I swear he is; and, likewise, that he is the same person who stopped at my house and had the flagon of wine on the night in question."

The attorney-general cross-examined this witness.

"Is not yours a thieves' house?"

"No; we would not have a lawyer within the doors."

There was a laugh, which the judge

RATCHLEY ENDEAVOURING TO CONSOLE HIS SISTER, MAY.

suppressed, and then the attorney-general continued—

"You know what an *alibi* is?"

"Yes,"

"What is it?"

"Showing as you wasn't where somebody else says as you was."

"Exactly. Captain Hawk is very popular, is he not?"

"Yes; he's uncommon *populous*."

'Well then, of course, you and others of his friends would do for him what you could, especially in so serious a matter as the present?"

"In course he would."

"Even to getting up an *alibi?*"

"There wasn't no occasion, 'cos, you see, it's true. We may be no great good, some of us, but we ain't so bad as to come into a court of justice, and to make out black is white and white is black, for a few guineas, like you lawyers do; but it's always the way, if a man or woman is a bad 'un, they never is easy till they have tried to make out everybody else a little bit worser, if they can."

"My learned friend's witnesses for the defence," said the attorney-general, "have been well taken care of. They are adepts. I have no more questions to ask of you."

"That is the case for the defence," said Captain Hawk's counsel; "and, if the learned counsel for the prosecution now addresses the jury, I shall claim the courtesy, if not the right of a reply, which is usually accorded to the prisoner's counsel."

CHAPTER LVII.

THE VERDICT, AND ITS RESULTS.

THERE was now a most anxious pause of some moments' duration. The attorney-general seemed to be considering whether he should leave the case to the jury just where it was, or attempt yet to make something of it.

The threat of a reply by the counsel for the defence was not to be, in so complicated a case, entirely disregarded, and yet there were some things which he wished to say that he would like to have unsaid.

But, probably, the most interesting spectacle in the court was the countenance of the prisoner.

As witness after witness came up to depose to circumstances in his favour, of which he was profoundly ignorant, he changed completely from the calm, haughty demeanour, which he had at first assumed, to one expressive of intense interest and unbounded astonishment.

The address of his own counsel for the defence had been listened to by him with the sort of interest which a man might be supposed to feel in a well-told romance; and how he intended to give the least semblance of truth to his statements certainly got the better of Hawk entirely to conceive

But when witness after witness came forward with their well-concocted chain of evidence in his favour, he began to think that he must have dreamt the murder, and that what they stated must be true.

It was Sir John Boyes's evidence, however, which completed his mystification. The story of the family watch with which Sir John connected him, came upon him with the greatest surprise. He was lost in amazement, and more than once uneasily shifted his position, and whispered to himself—

"Is all this real, or is the murder on the heath a vision?"

May Boyes kept her eyes fixed upon his face, and she saw the mental struggle. She dreaded some ebullition of feeling, and it was a relief to her when the last witness for the ingenious defence had been examined, and had said his say, so that there were, at all events, no more surprises for Captain Hawk.

The attorney-general suddenly decided in his own mind that he would address the jury, and he rose, amid the most profound stillness in the court.

"Gentlemen of the jury, I rise to address you again upon one of the most extraordinary cases that ever, in the whole course of my professional experience, I met with.

"The defence has partaken of a character which more than ever calls upon you to exercise the most calm and deliberate judgment, when you come to consider of the important facts connected with the equally important charge against the prisoner at the bar.

"Heaven forbid, gentlemen of the jury, that I, or any other advocate practising here, should, with a spirit of partisanship, endeavour to procure a conviction. Far better it is that ten guilty men should escape the punishment awarded by the laws of their country to the crimes which they may have committed, than that one innocent man should suffer wrongfully.

"You will, therefore, I am sure, gentlemen of the jury, in the observations which I feel it now to be my duty to address to you, do me the justice to believe that I am actuated solely by a strong desire that the truth should become apparent, and that the right should triumph, and public justice and public morality be vindicated.

"Gentlemen, it appears to me, and I think it will be evident to you, that the case for the defence leads to one of two conclusions. Either the witnesses who have this day appeared before you to prove an *alibi* for the prisoner at the bar, are most awfully and deeply perjured; or that, on the night named in the indictment as that on which the lamented Judge Holme met his death, there were two persons abroad, alike in dress, alike in figure, alike mounted, and alike in habits and pursuits, either of whom may be sworn to as Captain Hawk, the well known highwayman.

"Now, gentlemen of the jury, it is not a pleasant thing to accuse a number of witnesses of such gross and deliberate perjury as would lay to their charge, if the former of these suppositions were the one adopted. I shall leave it to you, gentlemen, from what you have heard and seen of those witnesses, to form your own conclusion, merely drawing the attention to one remarkable fact in the chain of evidence, which is this:—

"The only two witnesses whose evidence we can, and must, I think, all agree to receive, as above all suspicion, are Sir John Boyes, and the waggoner, John Lee.

"Now, gentlemen, you cannot have failed to notice that these are the only two witnesses who will not positively swear to the identity of the prisoner at the bar with the person whom they describe as having the appearance popularly believed to be presented by Captain Hawk, the noted highwayman.

"This is an important fact, gentlemen of the jury, and I doubt not but you will allow it to have its full weight. But while it is an important fact in the way in which I have put it to you, it likewise goes to prove that, on the evening in question, there were two persons, alike in costume and general appearance, abroad, one of whom murdered Judge Holme, while the other took a canter to London, passing on his route the waggoner, John Lee, the toll-bar man, Anthony Bell, and stopping at the Goat and Boots, a notorious thieves' house in Oxford-road, where we lose sight of him.

"And why, gentlemen of the jury, do we lose sight of him there? Simply because the object of his ride was concluded—namely, to get up, for such an occasion as this, an *alibi* for the prisoner.

"Gentlemen of the jury, I give up the point about there not being two persons of similar costumes and appearance abroad on that night—I believe there were. I do honestly believe that, if such additional testimony had been, in the judgment of my learned friend, necessary for the defence, he could have got many more most respectable and undeniable witnesses to prove that such a person rode to London within the hours named, although I do not believe that one of those disinterested persons would have sworn in this court, that the prisoner now at the bar was that person.

"We find Richard the Third, gentlemen of the jury, exclaiming at the battle of Bosworth—

'"There be six Richmonds in the field to-day.'

And so, gentlemen, I think we may safely say that there were two highwaymen on the road that night.

"And now, gentlemen of the jury, ask yourselves, if you please, if it would not have been one of the easiest things in the world for the prisoner at the bar to have dressed some confederate in the costume he himself usually wore, and despatched him to London, while he himself remained behind to do the deed of blood with which he stands charged.

"This would have been a very simple device; and when we consider that it is sworn that the person at the bar—ay, and none other but he—made the threat and the boast about his intention of attacking Judge Holme, I think the circumstance affords us a strong argument for believing, without doing him an injustice, that he is the man.

"It was night, and a dark night, too, when the fictitious Captain Hawk, be he whom he may, rode to London, so that his disguise was favoured; and then, again, why did he not come back again? Why did he not return through

Tyburn-gate to Hounslow, for by so doing, he would have bettered the evidence in his favour, I contend, in so far as he would have made a second appearance, which would have added probability to the first.

"But no, gentlemen. There was—admitting for one moment that Anthony Bell spoke the truth, and really was taken in, amazingly cunning fellow as he is, by the mock Captain Hawk—the probability that by a second appearance he might be discovered; besides, the real and the sham captain might both have been taken, which would have been an awkward enough circumstance, as one or other of them would have had his civility severely taxed about taking precedence at Tyburn.

"But, gentlemen of the jury, such was, you may safely come to the conclusion, not the case, and he who rode to London, remained in London.

"And, besides, did this sham Captain Hawk betray no anxiety to establish the object of his mission? Did he ride heedlessly? Not so. He asks Sir John Boyes the time of night, and he makes him particulary remark it—and wherefore? Because he may be evidence.

"He then asks the waggoner, John Lee, the hour, and for the same reason. This clever personage betrayed himself as he rode on, gentlemen, and the plot, ingenious though it was, is, I think, by the evidence which you have this day heard, as clear as the sun at noonday,

"Gentlemen, I leave the case in your hands. God forbid an injustice should be done to any one, but, in the name of the law, I call upon you to vindicate the majesty of justice, and to punish the evil-doer."

The attorney-general sat down. He had evidently made a strong and, for the prisoner, unfavourable impression upon the mind of every one in court, by what he had said; but upon no heart did his words fall with more appalling force than they did upon that of May Boyes.

She, and she only, knew, while others might suspect, that he had hit upon the truth, and, with her own soul depending upon the issue, she now waited the result of the fearful trial.

Captain Hawk's counsel was entitled to a reply, and he at once, upon the attorney-general resuming his seat, rose to avail himself of it.

"Gentlemen of the jury," he said, "the learned attorney-general has found it totally impossible, with any show of probability, to contend against the witnesses for the defence. He is forced to admit what must be apparent to any one here present, and what we stated, and fully admitted from the first, that, on the night in question, that there were two individuals alike in costume, and general appearance, abroad. That happens to be precisely the part taken up for the defence, and my learned friend has now felicitously quoted from Shakspere, the angry expression of disappointment from Richard the Third, when he says,—

"'There be six Richmonds in the field to-day.

But my learned friend forgot to add, that when he applied that quotation to two highwaymen, he should, with King Richard, have remarked, that he had 'not the right one;' and then I could have admired the quotation more, because, unquestionably, there wers two highwaymen; but my learned friend has 'not the right one.'

"Gentlemen of the jury, I am quite certain, that, although it is unquestionably my duty to draw your attention to certain conclusions, which the evidence you have this day heard forces upon our attention, yet those conclusions are such as must have presented themselves to your minds before now.

"The fact of there being, on the most sad and eventful night when the much-lamented Judge Holme came by his decease, two persons on and about the heath at Hounslow, is a matter which we all admit, and, likewise, that one of these persons went to London, while the other remained at Hounslow to commit a murder, is a fact on which we do not all join issue. But when my learned friend goes so far as to say that the prisoner at the bar is he who remained on the heath, and not he who went to London, I must confess that he seems to me to draw a most unwarrantable and cruel conclusion from the evidence which has this day been brought before you.

"And, gentlemen of the jury, upon what does my learned friend found that assumption? Why, first, upon the fact, that some of the witnesses who do not know the person of Captain Hawk intimately, cannot, in the hurry and the confusion of a moment, conscientiously say that he is the prisoner at the bar, and the same man, who, under extraordinary circumstances, they came in contact with; while others who do know him well, by sight, have, of course, no such hesitation, but are enabled at once to swear to a fact so important to the interest of the prisoner.

"Really, gentlemen of the jury, this is too bad. Is it upon what people *don't* know, and upon what they *cannot* swear to, that we are called upon to take the life of a fellow-creature, or upon what they *do* know, and what they *can* swear to?

"But, gentlemen, I rest with confidence upon your judgment. The veritable narrative that I gave you at the commencement of this inquiry, when the statement for the defence began, remains untouched.

"The prisoner at the bar is Captain Hawk, the celebrated highwayman, if you will—perhaps the term notorious would be better. But we have no right to find a man guilty of that of which he is wrongfully accused, because he may be guilty of other things, bad enough, perhaps, of themselves, but of which, at that time, he is not accused at all. We have no right to find Captain Hawk guilty of the murder of Judge Holme, because he has committed some highway robberies.

"Then, gentlemen, as I told you before, the person at the bar is Captain Hawk, and he personated the gentleman known so favourably to the Boyes' family as Gerald Clifton. He did make the boast that he would rob Judge Holme as he came home from the Oxford assizes; and the very fact that he did so, was, and ought to be, a sufficient proof that he never intended to attempt such an act.

"It was a foolish thing to make that boast, for I look upon it that it is a circumstance which more than any other has pointed the finger of suspicion against him, and made men tell themselves that he, in all human probability, was the murderer, although he is so perfectly innocent.

"But yet, gentlemen, while I admit the bad effects of that most indiscreet boast, and that it should never have been made, I think that upon a little examination of this subject, you will agree with me that it is not without its importance as a part of the defence of the prisoner at the bar.

"That boast was sufficiently notorious among those lawless persons with whom the prisoner associated himself, and among them it was likewise sufficiently notorious that Captain Hawk only intended it as a jest, and really was endeavouring to withdraw himself from the disreputable course of life he had for some time unhappily pursued.

"This, I say, was well enough known; and the mode of dress of Captain Hawk was likewise well remembered. What so easy, then, that some lawless person should say to himself—'Under the prestige of Captain Hawk's name, and attired like unto him, so that the guilt shall fall upon his head, I will essay this adventure, and see what is to be got by robbing Judge Holme?'

"This, gentlemen of the jury, to my apprehension, has been the case. The real murderer has yet escaped the hands of justice. No doubt terrified, after he had, in consequence of the resistance offered to him, committed the heinous offence of murder, at the act, he fled; while Captain Hawk, quickly returning to Hounslow, after his ride to London, and forgetting all about Judge Holme, and, indeed, not knowing that he was then returning from the assizes, is seized and accused of the desperate and most indefensible deed.

"I do not mean to say, gentlemen of the jury, but that the officers who took Captain Hawk, as well as those who determined upon his prosecution, were justified, until the singular circumstances are explained, which made him seem guilty, in a manner compatible with his innocence. But now they are so explained, and I confidently expect at your hands an acquittal."

The counsel for the defence sat down; and it was evident that his address for the prisoner had already produced a great effect in his favour with the jury.

All that now remained was, the summing up of the judge; and, although, in ordinary cases, counsel can pretty well guess which way that summing up will go, yet, such was the great complexity of this trial, that the most experienced of them were puzzled and confounded.

The judge turned over his notes for some moments; and then, amid the most breathless stillness in the crowded court, he said—

"Gentlemen of the jury, I regret that you have heard more oratory both for the prosecution and for the defence in this case, than ought to creep into criminal jurisprudence, where facts, and facts alone, ought to have any weight. You must dismiss from your minds all the verbiage in which this case has been dressed. You have nothing to do with whether there be highwaymen or not, or whether their existence be a great social evil or not. All you have to consider is, that a certain man is placed before you accused of murder, and to determine, according to your consciences, to the best of your ability, whether or not the evidence of an accusatory character brought against him, is sufficient to establish his guilt.

"The prisoner stands charged with the murder of Judge Holme: on the particular night named in the indictment, he, or some one like him in dress and appearance, is met on the Oxford-road, at a time when he, or some other person of similar dress and outward bearing, is robbing Sir John Boyes of a watch. Again, such a person is seen at eleven o'clock, by the witness Sargent, upon Hounslow-heath; while such a person is likewise seen by the witness, John Lee, at the same hour, some miles off.

"These facts, gentlemen of the jury, are quite sufficient to establish in the mind of any reasonable man the supposition, that on the night in question there were two persons similary attired, and so similar in general appearance, as to involve the question regarding their separate acts in a vast amount of mystification.

"A charge more circumstantially supported, and more circumstantially rebutted, never came before me; and instead of, as is usual in cases of this nature, the evidence being all on one side, and denied simply upon the other, all the evidence, in all its main points, is admitted on both sides; but a directly contrary inference drawn from it."

At this moment, one of the jury rose, and in a voice of alarm addressed the jury, saying—

"Please you, my lord, Mr. Jones says he will eat his boots sooner than bring him in guilty, and I have had but a very light breakfast, and so—"

"Sir," cried the judge, "this is very irregular. Sit down, sir. It is quite clear that you are unfit for a juryman, when you make such remarks as that. Your conduct is scandalous."

The abashed juryman sat down, and, amid a general titter in the court, the judge resumed his address.

CHAPTER LVIII.

EVERYTHING GOES IN FAVOUR OF CAPTAIN HAWK.

For a moment or two it seemed as if the judge had confused his notes, but that was only for a moment or two, and then he commenced as follows:—

"Now, gentlemen of the jury, the learned counsel for the prosecution may be right in his supposition that the prisoner at the bar, being the man who had made a boast that he would rob Judge Holme as he came from the Oxford assizes, determined to fulfil that boast; and, to do so at the least possible risk, he got up all this mystification by attiring some confederate in costume similar to his own, and sending him on the road to London, while he, Hawk, himself, committed the crime of which he stands charged.

"But you will recollect that this is a supposition, and that it is unsupported by a breath of evidence.

"On the contrary, then, for the defence, it is urged that Captain Hawk, as he is termed, rode to London on account of pecuniary difficulties, and never so much as wasted a thought upon Judge Holme. And in support of this, we have him sworn to by those who ought to know him best, and who we cannot take upon ourselves to say are foresworn.

"Gentlemen of the jury, the secrets

of all men's hearts are known to Heaven only, and human judgment, even at the best, is a weak and fallible thing. Whether the prisoner at the bar be guilty or not guilty of the dreadful crime with which he stands charged, is known to himself and to his Creator. But, if he be innocent, it would be an awful thing for us to condemn him.

"My learned brother has remarked that it is better ten guilty men should escape the penalties of their crimes, than that one innocent man should suffer wrongously, and that is a sentiment which I am disposed to echo.

"I do not, looking at this case in all its bearings, then, gentlemen, think it would be safe to convict the prisoner at the bar of the murder of Judge Holme. It would not be safe, as regards the administration of justice and public policy. There is strong doubt, and, according to the humane bearing of the laws of this realm, we are bound, I think, to give the accused man the benefit of such strong doubt.

"But, if, gentlemen of the jury, you conscientiously think that the evidence you have heard be sufficient to satisfy you of the guilt of the prisoner, you will fearlessly, and without the reproach of any honest man, return a verdict according. If, however, on the contrary, you have any doubts, and any feelings regarding the complexity of the case, which would prevent you from bringing in a verdict of guilty, you will find it to be your duty to acquit the prisoner now at the bar."

This summing up of the judge settled the question, and every one who heard it looked upon the prisoner as virtually acquitted.

There could not have been a summing up more strongly in favour of the prisoner, and the attorney-general looked by no means surprised at it. Perhaps he had already, from what had been done for the defence, given up the case in his own mind as a hopeless one regarding the prosecution.

May Boyes now shook so excessively that her agitation was painfully manifest to all near her, and her brother, Ratchley, as he held her hand clasped in one of his own, implored her to be calm.

"I will—I will," she said. "He is saved, and why, then, should I not be calm?"

The strange manner in which he had been rescued from death—that death which, in his owd mind, he must have looked upon as almost certain—could not but have a great and remarkable effect upon Captain Hawk.

All the insolent assumption of demeanour which he had put on had gone, and was completely absorbed in the intense interest he felt in the proceedings, which took him far more by surprise than they could possibly take any one else. He looked in the face of the judge as he spoke with the air of a man who is credulous about how his sense of hearing is serving him; and, when he found that there was so strong a disposition of a favourable nature towards him, he trembled more probably than he would have done had he been condemned to death; for in that case, pride would have supported him, while now such a feeling was completely swallowed up in the rush of new emotions which came over him.

How such a defence, so complete, so well knit together, and so powerful, had been got up for him, baffled all his conjectures.

He could have understood about the evidence of the man at the turnpike, because he knew that, before he took to that line of life, he had levied contributions upon the public in a very different way; and he could have understood how the landlord of the Goat and Boots migh not have been over particular concerning an oath or two; but the evidence of Sir John Boyes it was that puzzled him, and gave to the whole affair, as concerned his mind, a dream-like and unreal aspect.

Once or twice it did come across him that May Boyes might make some exertions to save him; but when he come to remember how impossible it would have been for her or any one else to have suborned Sir John, he was compelled to give up the supposition in despair.

It was not until the judge had finished his summing up that it occurred to Captain Hawk that he had been haunted on the heath and terrified on that night, by some mysterious horseman; and, when that thought did cross his mind, a cold perspiration broke out upon his brow, and he said to himself—

"There is something more than human in all this!"

The jury did not request to leave the box. The fattest man had, of course, been chosen to be foreman; and, as the majority of them were, as juries usually are, about as pig-headed and stupid animals as any one could find, it was a great relief to be told by the judge what to do.

One proposed a verdict of "Guilty, but we don't think he did it;" but that ingenious idea was negatived, and, after about ten minutes, they turned around in their box, and faced the court.

The clerk of the arraigns then rose, and said—

"Gentlemen of the jury, are you agreed upon your verdict?"

"We *is*," said the foreman.

"Do you find the prisoner at the bar guilty or not guilty?"

There was a silence of about a minute's duration. It was an anxious one, notwithstanding every one felt what the verdict would be, and then the foreman said—

"Not Guilty!"

CHAPTER LIX.

THE ESCAPE AND THE PURSUIT.

This verdict, although so well expected by all who heard it, that it could not be in any way a surprise, yet seemed to cause much feeling and commotion in the court.

There was an evident inclination to applaud on the parts of some of the persons present; while vexation sat on the countenance of the attorney-general, which he scarcely attempted to conceal. Probably he felt, like many others in court, that the prisoner must have owed his escape to some juggling, which, just then, it was beyond the bounds of human ingenuity to find out sufficiently to enable the prosecution to triumph over it.

And the worst of the affair was, that the prisoner now, having been once tried for the murder of Judge Holme, could not be again indicted for that offence, if the most conclusive evidence of his guilt that it was possible to conceive were to be discovered, it being contrary altogether to the practice of English law to try a man twice, under any circumstances whatever, for the same offence.

The counsel for Hawk immediately rose, and addressing the attorney-general, he said—

"I presume that, after the verdict just delivered by the jury, the prosecution will not feel disposed to proceed with the other indictments against the prisoner, resting as they do upon similar evidence."

The attorney-general nodded, and threw himself back in his seat.

"Then, my lord," said Hawk's counsel, "I have to pray for the immediate discharge from custody of the prisoner at the bar, who now stands before us as an innocent man, accused of nothing whatever."

"Such an application," said the judge, "is very proper, and not such as the court will resist. Prisoner at the bar, you have had here a most patient trial—a trial from which you hvea emerged unscathed—Heaven, and your own conscience, can alone decide whether deservedly so or not; but human judgment, bearing in mind its fallibility, has not considered itself justified in convicting you of the heavy crime laid to your charge, upon the evidence which has been this day adduced against you.

"I sincerely hope that this day's proceedings will operate upon you as a serious warning. I do, from the very bottom of my heart, indulge a hope that these proceedings will induce you to alter your mode of life, and endeavour to turn such talents as you may possess into some channel where honest industry will enable you to earn a creditable livelihood.

"Although you have this day, by a jury who have taken a most single-minded, merciful, and upright view of the case brought before them, been acquitted of the heinous crime of murder, yet quite enough is known and ad mitted to convince us that you lead a most lawless life.

"You are one of those persons, so emphatically spoken of by the learned counsel who has conducted this prosecution, who, disdaining the ordinary industrial arts, and those legitimate channels by which people may do something for society in exchange for their support, resort to a pernicious course

CAPTAIN HAWK NEAR HAMPSTEAD, LISTENING FOR HIS PURSUERS.

of life, which they endeavour to surround with a false lustre, because they carry it on boldly.

"By the admission of your counsel, you are a highwayman; and he strove only to obtain some doubtful credit for you because you were that, and not a murderer. Well, you may not be a murderer—God forbid that I should say you are; but you must, if you have any power of reflection at all, feel that your course of life is extremely likely to make you one.

"You should ponder over this, and ponder well. Your present escape should be a source to you of the deepest reflection; and if, upon a careful consideration of the great danger you have this day escaped, you should, as I sincerely hope you may, come to a conclusion that you have been pursuing a course frightfully at variance with your interest, both in this world, and in that which is to come, and in which you have carved so unenviable a reputation, whatever you may have thought of it, you will be able to look back upon this day as a subject for congratulation rather than of annoyance or regret.

"It would be a dreadful thing for me, sitting here as I do, to take upon myself to say that there has been any juggling or chicanery in this affair. I am bound to administer the law as I find it, and to look to facts as they appear before me, and, therefore, am I bound to consider you as entirely innocent of the crime with which you have been charged this day. Those who have given evidence each way, must settle that evidence with their own consciences, and with their creator."

How strangely the mind of the judge was wavering upon the subject of the guilt or innocence of Captain Hawk yet. It was quite a singular study of human nature, to see how the extraordinary features of that case had thrown him out of his routine of thought.

"Your counsel has very properly," continued the judge, playing rather nervously with the paper before him, as though he thought that, after all, he was doing what was not right. "Your counsel has very properly, in the due discharge of his duty, after what has taken place here, asked for your discharge from custody, and it is not in letter neither is it in the spirit of the laws of this nation, that any individual should be held in custody after a jury of his peers have found him innocent of the offence for which he was brought before them to be tried."

Hawk bowed slightly at this point to the judge, and looked anxiously towards the door of the court, as if he would have said—"Open it to me, and let me go; I am no longer your prisoner."

"Therefore," added the judge, "I give you your liberty, and I direct the officers of the court to let you go."

The judge looked earnestly at him, and inclined his head to listen to what he had to say.

"My Lord, as the jury has declared me innocent, and as your lordship, in your justice and wisdom, has declared that I may not be detained, I beg to know if I am not entitled to the property that the officers of police took violently from me at the time of my capture."

"You are so entitled. What was that property?"

"My horse is all I ask for, and my arms."

The judge looked at the Lord Mayor, and then at the sheriff, and the sheriff looked a little confused as he rubbed his hands one over the other.

"Where is the horse?" said the judge. "If we do justice here, let us do it completely and not by halves."

The sheriff whispered something to the Lord Mayor, and the Lord Mayor shook his head and whispered something to the judge, who thereupon said—

"The sheriff has placed the horse in his stables for safety. In ten minutes it will be at the door of the court at the disposal of the late prisoner at the bar."

"Ten minutes, my lord?" said the sheriff—"I—I—that is—I will send it to him."

"Oh, no," said the judge. "Let him have it at once, Mr. Sheriff, if you please. Do not leave the shadow of a reprisal upon any of us in this most strange and unaccountable business. Let him have his horse at once."

"And my arms?" said Hawk.

"It is illegal to carry arms," said the judge. "Do not ask for them. Go forth, sir, like a peaceable citizen, and Heaven send that you may prove to be one in the time that is to come."

Captain Hawk saw the policy of not pressing for his arms, and he merely bowed to the judge, in reply to the remarks of that functionary. The most comical thing, though, was to see the looks of the jail fuctionaries, who, now, felt themselves obliged to give up the man whom they had looked upon as doomed, and of whom they had thought to make all the profit they were accustomed to make in a hundred underhand ways in such cases.

The head turnkey rubbed his nose violently, and, in a whisper, the under turnkey said—

"Is it all real, Bill, or is it only a kind of a what-do-you-call-it—a vision?"

"I ain't a vision," said Bill. "We shall have to let him go, and no sort of mistake at all, no how, Joe. We is done brown this time, rather."

CHAPTER LX.

CAPTAIN HAWK HAS SOME NARROW ESCAPES IN THE STREETS.

The turnkeys might be astonished, and the officials of Newgate might be loath to give up what they considered their vested interests in such a man as Captain Hawk. The judge, even, upon the bench, might feel a little bewildered at the turn affairs had taked; and the attorney-general might knit his brows, and bite his neither lip in a vain attempt to puzzle out the how and why Captain Hawk had escaped the meshes of the law; but none could be so full of amazement upon that account, as Captain Hawk himself was. It was with the greatest difficulty he subdued the expression of his intense astonishment at the turn things had taken.

There he was, acquitted by virtue of an overwhelming mass of testimony in his favour of the crime laid to his charge, and which no one knew so well as he himself that he was really guilty of.

"Have all these people perjured themselves on my account," thought Hawk, "and if so, what powerful and mysterious agency has been at work among them to induce them so to do?"

Strange to say, he did not once suspect that May Boyes was the good genius who had worked for him so strenously, and who had snatched him from that death, which else, nothing in this world could have saved him from: and yet, he ought to have suspected that no other feeling than the abounding love of woman could have worked such a seeming miracle.

"The prisoner is at liberty," said the judge, who, probably, saw that the officials rather hesitated in the matter.

The head turnkey of Newgate ventured to speak—

"My lord, if your lordship pleases—"

"Well?" said the judge.

"Is—is—he—that is, my lord, is it really true that Captain Hawk, my lord, is to be let go now, my lord?"

"The prisoner is acquitted, and he is free."

"There's—the—the jail fees."

"Having," said Hawk, "been acquitted by the jury of the charge laid against me in this court, I ask the court if I can be legally detained?"

"No," said the judge, "you are free."

In a moment more, Captain Hawk was pressing on towards the door of the court, and then a voice whispered in his ear—

"Your horse is at the door, captain."

"Ah, my old friend Joe?"

"Yes, captain, the same. All's right."

"So it seems, Joe."

Hawk had the greatest anxiety to get out of the court, and to mount and be off. He saw a knot of officers whispering together, and he could well guess that he was the subject of their discourse. Well he knew that nothing would be easier than to get up some charge against him, if they so chose; and, indeed, had it not seemed to be a fact past all kind of doubt that he would be convicted of the murder of Judge Holme, there would have been a count or two in the indictment, charging him with minor offences; but the prosecutors had been by far too sanguine.

"Make way!" cried several voices; "make way for Captain Hawk! Clear away from the door, there—make way! Don't join the man up so! This way, captain! This is the route!"

Hawk could only advance slowly to the door of the court; but the moment he got there, before he could descend the short flight of steps, there arose a tremendous cheer of congratulation at his escape; for all the light-fingered gentry of London had there assembled to hear the trial, and they considered the escape of Hawk as something like a personal triumph to themselves.

Strange to say, too, notwithstanding the evidence and the apparently triumphant *alibi* that Captain Hawk's counsel had been able to set up for him so successfully, they all fully believed that he had committed the offence for which he had been put upon his trial.

It was only some unusal chances, they considered, that had got him off; and the name of the attorney and of the barrister engaged in the proceedings was cherished as a thing worth knowing.

"This way, captain," cried one. "Never mind the beaks, now."

"It's the grabs as will be after him," said another. "Bother the beaks."

"Where's my horse?" cried Hawk.

"Here," shouted a hundred voices. "Here, in the blessed Old Bailey."

Hawk shouldered his way down the stone staircase as quickly as he could, and crossing the vestibule, he emerged into the open air.

Oh, what a delightful feeling it was that came over Hawk, now that he found once more the canopy of Heaven above him, and felt that he was a free man, even if it were but for the brief space of some hours. Was it not something to know that he might fight for his life, now, if he were attacked, and he thought that if he could but get clear of the interminable streets of London, how happy he might be. Captain Hawk thought the streets of London then interminable.—What would he have thought of them now?

There, close to the curb-stone, stood his horse, fully accoutred for the road, and, as the shadows of the evening now were casting themselves rapidly over all things, Hawk looked at the sea of uplifted faces before him with a strange feeling, as though he were so hemmed in by a living multitude that escape would be out of the question.

There was another roaring shout now from more than two thousand throats, as the people saw Hawk lay his hand upon the gallant steed that then awaited him. In another moment he was in the saddle, and then, from that more elevated position, he was able to see more clearly around him, and to wonder how his possible or probable fate could attract such a dense mass of people.

A hand was suddenly laid upon his arm.

"Captain Hawk," said a voice.

"Ha!" cried Hawk, "so soon; would you drag me to jail again. No, I will die first."

A groan of execration burst from the crowd; but the person who excited all this indignation had no such hostile intentions towards Hawk, and he only said, as he pushed a little canvass bag into his hand—

"Here is gold. It is sent to you by one who prays you to fly and to repent."

"Repent! did you say?"

"Yes, she—that is, the person—"

"Ah, yes, you have told me who it is, now. Tell her that I cannot take money from her; but, at the same time, assure her that I am not without means."

"Do take it."

"No. It is from May Boyes—I mean Miss May Boyes."

"That I know nothing about," said the man. "I am the clerk to your attorney, and he gave me this money to bring to you, and told me to urge you to accept it. I hope that you will do so."

"No—Farewell."

Hawk now turned his horse's head in the direction of Snow Hill; but he found that it was impossible to proceed beyond a walk, and what was still more perplexing and fraught with danger to him, was the fact that the mob, as if actuated by one impulse, moved along with him; so that the same people were by his side, and he appeared but to be the centre of that slowly moving mass of heads.

A kind of groaning scream burst suddenly from many lips, and Captain Hawk hastily turned his head to know the reason of it, for it came from the Old Bailey, at the top of which he now was.

Upon the steps of the debtor's door of the prison of Newgate he saw a man standing without a hat, and in the street immediately below, were some six or eight mounted men, and some horses without riders, which were, even as he, Hawk, looked, rapidly mounted. He saw the man without the hat point towards him, and then waive his arm, and then the mob gave another shout of scorn and derision.

"What is it?" cried Hawk.

"The sheriff has offered two hundred pounds reward for your apprehension, as soon as you are out of the bounds of the city," said one, sufficiently near Captain Hawk to make himself heard.

"Ah, indeed! and they are officers?"

"Yes, those mounted men there, and there's more of them a coming as fast as they can get the police-horses out."

"Police-horses," said Captain Hawk, with a smile, as he patted the neck of his steed, and knew that he could leave them all far behind him, if he had but common fair play. "Well, eight or ten to one is long odds. We must have a race for it."

"Take the north road," said a man close to him. "You will find it the best for you; they expect you at Tyburn Gate. They have sent off some horsemen to come upon you at unawares there?"

"Thank you, friend. You can do me a great favour if you like."

"What is it?"

"There's a gunsmith's on Snow Hill. Take these guineas and buy me a pair of pistols, a flask, and some powder and balls. You need not say who they are for, you know."

"Certainly not, captain. Though I is a prig, I knows what honour is, blow me."

The fellow took the gold that Captain Hawk gave him, and then worked his way through the crowd like an eel.

"He will play me false, I suppose," thought Hawk, "but it don't much matter. I must get out of this throng, though."

Raising himself in his stirrups, he now cried out in a loud, clear voice—

"My good friends, if you wish me to get clear of the Philistines, and to have a chance of my life, and I think you do——"

"Hurrah! Hurrah!" roared the crowd.

"I say, I think you do," added Hawk, waiting until the roaring shout had in some measure subsided, "you open a lane for me to pass among you now at once."

"And close it up behind," added a voice, in such stentorian accents that it produced a general laugh. Captain Hawk nodded, as much as to say—

"Yes, that is what I would have added, but my kind friend has said it for me."

This suggestion, which was the only practical one for the escape of Captain Hawk, was eagerly embraced by the people, and an opening was made in the crowd, as if by magic, for him to pass through, while it closed up behind him like the temporarily parted waves of the sea, in the wake of some ship rushing onwards to its destination.

The officers at once saw that by this means their prey would escape them, and as the sheriff had taken upon himself the responsibility of ordering Hawk's recapture, and had offered a handsome reward for him, the officers did not feel disposed very readily to submit to any course of proceedings which might have the effect of letting him slip through their fingers.

When the mob closed upon them in this manner, they formed themselves into a compact body, and tried to charge through the multitude towards Snow Hill; but such a manœuvre was easier to conceive than to execute, for, although, those closest to the police might give way, they only fell upon others, who did not know very well what the increased pressure was about, and so resisted it at once.

Under these circumstances, all that the officers succeeded in doing was to get along about twenty feet, and then to compact the mob so closely, that they could not get out of the way if they wished.

In vain the officers swore, and spurred their horses on—in vain the mob roared and shouted, until at last one of the officers, drawing his cutlass, cut open the head of a man who had laid hold of the rein of his horse.

This was at once the signal for a general outbreak of popular indignation against the police.

"Down with them!" cried many voices. "Down with the cut-throats!

Down with the butchers! Upset them. Don't hurt the cattle, but down with the men!"

Groans, yells, catcalls, shrieks, and every other species of noise that a wild and excited mob could give utterance to, now filled the air, and, no doubt, the fact of the rapidly increasing darkness, which rendered individuals less likely to be recognised, gave the mob a degree of confidence which in daylight it would hardly have had.

The officers began to see that their situation was anything but a safe, or pleasant one. He who might be said to be in command of the little party was an experienced man, and he knew that nothing now could save them from being severely ill-used by such a mob as was about them, and, perhaps, killed, but some vigorous movement, at once.

"We must cut our way onwards, or leave our bodies in the mire," he said. "Draw your cutlasses, men. Charge after me, and don't be nice about it. It is our only chance for our lives."

The rest of the party were pretty much of the same opinion, and in an instant every man had his cutlass in his hand. They spurred on their horses, and slashing right and left, with a brutality that even the perilous circumstances they were in hardly justified, they began to make some way through the dense crowd opposed to them.

This sudden and energetic proceeding of the officers produced a temporary panic among the crowd, which was just what they hoped, and expected; and they no sooner saw this temporary success of the expedient, than they became more and more savage, and cut and slashed at the people like demons. The oaths, shrieks, shouts, and great tumult that now arose beggars all possible description, and the little body of officers marched their path through death and wounds towards Snow Hill.

They were not destined to get there, just yet, though.

CHAPTER LXI.

CAPTAIN HAWK TAKES TO THE NORTH ROAD AT A CANTER.

During this time, while so fearful a scene was being enacted in the Old Bailey, Captain Hawk had fairly succeeded in turning his horse's head towards Holborn, and, indeed, he was making very rapid way down Snow Hill, when he heard the shrieks and the shouts behind, and all the wild tumult of the battle that was going on between the people and the police.

For a moment his heart smote him that so much misery and bloodshed should be upon his account; and with glowing cheeks, and flashing eyes, he turned his horses' head in the direction of the Old Bailey again.

"What is all this?" he said.

"You can't do any good, captain," said a voice. "It is the police cutting down the people; but they deserve it if they like to put up with it. They might eat them, if they like, for there's enough of them."

A moment's thought convinced Hawk how utterly futile any effort of his would be in such a *fracas* as that which was proceeding; and, indeed, as he was the inciting cause of it, the best thing he could possibly do to check it was to get out of the way as quickly as possible.

With this intent, he went down Snow Hill where the crowd was much more straggling and open at a canter. In the excitement of the moment he had quite forgot the man and the pistols; but a voice suddenly called out to him as he was passing on—

"Captain—captain! here they are."

Captain Hawk turned his head, and the man who had so candidly avowed himself to be a pickpocket, rushed up to the side of his horse, and handed him a pair of highly-finished pistols, and a pouch containing powder and bullets.

"They are both loaded, captain," said the man. "I got the old fool of a gunmaker to put a charge into each of them."

"I wish I had time to thank you," said Hawk; "but perhaps we may meet again some day, my friend."

"Oh, don't mention it, captain. All's right."

"Stop! stop!" cried the gunmaker, rushing out of his shop. "Oh, stop!'

"What for—eh? I paid you."

"Yes; but you said the pistols were for the sheriff. I didn't go for to come to think to sell pistols to a highwayman! That's Captain Hawk."

"Go to the deuce with you!"

"And I loaded 'em, too, and rammed 'em down so nice and tight."

"All the better. Did I pay you?"

"Yes; but——"

"Hold your row, then," said the confessed prig, as he dashed a handful of not the most salubrious mud right in the face of the gunsmith.

While this was going on, Hawk had trotted up Holborn Hill, after carefully placing the pistols in the holsters of his saddle. The *fracas* in the Old Bailey came upon his ears still, and he gradually increased his pace, patting his steed upon the neck as he did so, for he intended to give the creature a gallop of a good ten miles into the country before he stopped.

It was a strange thing to see Captain Hawk, perfectly well known to be a highwayman, going now along Holborn, and the people upon each side of the way stopping to look at him, but not one raising a hand against him, or even dreaming of an attempt to follow him; while several of the poorer class actually gave him a cheer as he passed. What cared they for his criminal reputation. He, and such as he, did not rob them on the highways.

There was, at the time we write, a little public-house called The Old Bowl, at the corner of Brook-street Holborn, and as Hawk reached that, he drew up, and called out—

"Hilloa! Any good wine here? There used to be."

"Bravo!" cried a disorderly kind of throng that was rapidly increasing in numbers each moment. "Bravo! Long live the captain!"

The landlord of the house bustled out in a moment.

"What is it? Bless me, what is it?"

"Wine, and the best," cried Hawk. "The old silver flagon."

"Oh, lor, it's the captain!"

"Quick, I say — quick! There's bloodhounds upon my path!"

"Ah, captain! you may call them that," said a squalid-looking woman. "They shot my husband, the wretches!"

"What for?"

"Suspicions of—of rob—rob—robbing," sobbed the woman, "and now I am starving, and my poor child, too."

"I wish I had more to give you," said Hawk, as he threw the woman several guineas.

"Here's the wine, captain," cried the landlord, as he rushed out with a silver flagon, that held about a pint. Hawk took it in his hand, and holding it for a moment at arms length, he cried—

"Here's good luck to you all."

"Thank you, captain — thank you. Bravo! Hurrah for the captain!"

Hawk tossed off the wine, and as he let the last drop or two pour from the flagon to the road, he cried—

"A pot of the old ale in a punch bowl!"

"Bless us, yes," cried the landlord, as he flew into his house again. "A pot of old ale in the punch-bowl! Quick—quick! A pot of old ale!—that's right. Here it is, captain, nothing but cream on it. Oh, lor, this is the stuff."

"Give it to the horse."

The landlord held the bowl to the horses mouth, and the pot of old ale disappeared as if it had jumped down the creature's throat by some necromancy; and the mob, which was rapidly increasing, shouted their gratification, and really thought the bold, dashing highwayman, the finest fellow under the sun.

"Anything else, captain?" said the landlord, wiping his brow with his apron.

"Nothing. Thank you."

"All's right."

"The police!" shouted a voice, "Here they come! Off with you, captain."

"Oh, indeed," said Hawk, "I hope they are well mounted."

Bending himself low in the saddle, Hawk passed his hand slowly down the neck of his horse, and then he gave a strange chirruping sort of whistle, and the creature laid its ears back upon its neck for an instant, and then, like an arrow from a bow, off it went.

The pace was tremendous. Holborn was left behind. The long straggling thoroughfare of the Tottenham-court-road was passed in a few seconds; and then the path was bordered by fields upon each side, until the little hamlet, for such it was then, of Camden Town was reached. Hawk took the left-hand road, leading to Hampstead; and by the time he had fairly cleared the hill, and reached the George public-house, all idea of pursuing him was out of the question.

Captain Hawk, however, did not pause, but starting up Red Lion Hill, to the dismay of some dozen or two pigs, which were basking in the mud, he rattled through Hampstead, where the lamps were alight; but they only sufficed to render the darkness more puzzling. Three minutes more, and Hawk was upon the old Heath.

Then he paused a few moments, and again patted the neck of his horse. Not a hair was turned, and yet the speed had been something truly terrific, and the hills had been all against them.

"Well done," said Hawk.

The horse snorted and danced its head, as if delighted by the praises, and the caresses of its master. How well Hawk knew the power of kindness upon animals; and how very few persons know it, that have to do with them; although it is one of those natural facts that those who run may read.

For the space of about five minutes, Captain Hawk now sat as motionless upon his horse, as though he had been a statue, and listened intently. Not the least sound of coming pursuers reached his ears; and after thoroughly satisfying himself of that fact, he said—

"They have given it up, and the most prudent thing they could do, too. By Heaven I should not have been over nice in the use of these pistols. But we won't wait here, my gallant steed. We are yet a little too near to the smoke of the great city. Ah, who would have taken upon him last night, at this hour, to say that I should be now well mounted and well armed upon Hampstead Heath? such are the mutations of life. Well, be it so. I am the sport of some destiny that evidently don't consult me in the disposal of its gifts—I have no time to think now—On—on.

Leaving, now, Captain Hawk to proceed whither his fancy might direct him, we will take a brief glance at how the tumult in the Old Bailey proceeded and ended.

We left the officers making a wild and determined attack upon the people with their cutlasses, an attack which the quicker seemed to secure its success, because, upon their parts, the most sanguinary, until at last, for its very brutality and indiscriminate slaughter, it utterly failed.

A woman, with a child in her arms, was there. Was ever a mob collected, for any earthly purpose or object, without a woman with a child in her arms in the midst of it? Well, a woman with a child—a mere infant, happened to come in the way of the blood-thirsty officers, and the foremost of them, with one blow of his cutlass, sent her reeling and shrieking to the earth, with her face covered with blood.

This was more than the mob would or could bear. With a yell, like demons, they rushed upon the officers and did what would have saved them from all the ugly cuts they got before—namely, closed upon them, and in an instant they were disarmed. Two only of them, owing to the horses upon which they were mounted going about mad with the excitement of the scene, and the blows they received, carried off their riders in safety into Smithfield, where they fell exhausted. The others were dragged to the ground, and trampled to death by thousauds of feet.

A line was made for the terrified horses to escape, and they fled riderless into the city.

The shouts and imprecations of the mob were now so truly terrific that the authorites of Newgate hastily armed all the turnkeys, and put the prison in as great a state of defence as upon the spur of the moment they possibly could. The houses all along the Old Bailey, opposite to Newgate, were broken openfor arms, and the cry out was "Burn the stone-jug," nowever absurd it might seem to attempt to visit a stone-jug with such a fate.

The time for lighting the street-lamps had long since passed, but, of course, while such a tumult raged, no attempt was made to perform that usual service; but yet the mob got soon, from an oil-shop in the Old Bailey which they broke into, provided with a number of links, which, when lighted and held up aloft, cast a strange flickering glare upon the sea of angry faces below them.

CAPTAIN HAWK DURING THE ADDRESS TO HIM FROM THE JUDGE.

"The sheriff! The sheriff!" cried some hundreds of voices—"Death to the sheriff!"

They well remembered that it was the sheriff who had instigated the whole proceedings, by awakening the cupidity of the officers with the offer of two hundred pounds reward for the capture of Captain Hawk, and there can be no doubt but that if that functionary had not been snugly ensconced within the strong walls of Newgate, that night would have witnessed the end of his term of office.

"Burn the prison! Down with Newgate!" was still the favourite shout, when it was found that the obnoxious sheriff was not to be got at, and a wild rush was made up the little steps leading to the vestibule of the prison.

Of course, the effort to force the strong door there was utterly futile; but an attack upon that portion of the building called the governor's house, certainly produced more results.

In a moment every window in that part of Newgate was smashed to atoms, and it appeared rather doubtful whether the door of the governor's residence would stand the strokes of a pick-axe, which was now used by one of the mob upon it with prodigious power.

"Pull him out! Out with the sheriff! We will burn the sheriff and the governor. Down with Newgate! Set it alight! Hurrah for Hawk! Down with the police!"

Such are only a few of the wild shouts of the multitude, when, from the end of the Old Bailey leading upon Ludgate-hill, there arose a cry from some hundred voices, which rose above all other sounds, of—

"The soldiers! The soldiers!"

This shout made the mob pause. The most resolute among them knew perfectly well that they stood no chance whatever in a contest with the military, and all that seemed to remain now, was to ascertain if the cry were a false alarm of the enemy, or the real truth.

All doubt upon the subject was in the course of the next minute put an end to, by the appearance of the foremost men of a troop of horse, at the corner of the Old Bailey by Ludgate-hill.

A man had been despatched through the prison, by a secret way to the back of it, and so round by St. Paul's Churchyard, and by Ludgate-hill and the Strand, to the Horse-guards, carrying a note from the recorder of London and the sheriff, to the effect, that the civil power could not cope with the mob that was threatening the peace of the city.

A troop of horse had been the immediate response, and, now, the mob felt that there was nothing for it but flight.

It was quite evident that the officer in command of the military had no wish to come into contact with the populace, for the word was given to advance only at a trot up the Old Bailey; and it was a strange thing to see how the links were cast down—how all cries and shouts ceased—and how the dense mob melted away, like wax before a fire, as the troop of horse, occupying the whole width of the carriage-way, trotted up the Old Bailey.

In two minutes there was not a soul to be seen opposite Newgate but the horse-guards, who halted in close column when in the middle of the way.

CHAPTER LXII.

CAPTAIN HAWK BEGINS TO COMPREHEND HOW HE WAS SAVED.

Having thus disposed of the memorable riot in the Old Bailey, upon which occasion no less a number than seven persons came to a shocking death, we again take up our position by the side of Captain Hawk, as he slowly walked his horse down the northern slope of Hampstead-heath.

Amid the busy and the intense excitement of the events of that day, Captain Hawk had only had time to wonder, but none to reflect, concerning the wonderful and, to him, totally inexplicable manner in which he had been saved from death, which he had, himself, looked forward to as the certain result of his trial.

Now he began to ask himself, how it had possibly happened that people, of apparently fair enough repute, had thought proper to come forward, for the sake of proving an *alibi* for him, and deliberately perjure themselves by so doing; for he knew that all they said had not the shadow of a foundation.

"It is more than strange," he said. "What on earth can be the meaning of it? I know well that money, freely and judiciously bestowed in London, will purchase evidence; but I never heard of anything got up with such admirable tact as this was. It looked so like the truth that it staggered even myself as I listened to it."

Captain Hawk did not suspect, as

yet, that the witnesses were all, in their own ideas, the witnesses of truth; although, in reality, they were so awfully mistaken.

"Yes," he added. "It is a mystery, which I shall never feel satisfied about, until I have cleared. Hark! what is that? Surely, I heard a horse's feet upon the heath, behind me."

There was nothing at all remarkable in the fact of a horseman being upon the heath; but, to the guilty soul of Hawk, it was an alarm. Oh, what a wretched state of existence that must be to any human being, when the mear tread of a fellow-creature's foot, or the sound of the horse's hoofs of a mounted man, brings a fancy of dread.

Too well Hawk knew that he was the enemy of all men, and that the hearts of all men were roused against him; for, although in the face of the law he had been acquitted of the specific guilt laid to his charge, he knew his own position, and that he was still obnoxious to those laws, both human and divine, which he had so frequently outraged.

Captain Hawk brought his horse to a pause, and, bending low upon the saddle, he listened intently for the sound that had disturbed him. In a few moments he heard it again.

"It is a horse," he said; "but why should I fly from one man only? Pshaw! have I turned coward since I stood at the bar of the Old Bailey?"

With this impression, he placed his hand upon one of the pistols that he had procured upon Snow-hill, and which were in the holsters of his saddle, and drawing to the side of the road, he resolved to let the coming traveller pass him.

It was strange, that at that moment no idea of stopping the horseman and robbing him came across the mind of Hawk. It would seem as if recent events had had the effect of throwing his mind off his professional pursuits.

The horseman came rapidly on, and was within about half-a-dozen yards of him, when, suddenly drawing up, he cried out in a voice that proclaimed he was very young indeed—

"Hilloa! Who are you?"

Upon this, Captain Hawk rode calmly out into the middle of the road, and confronted him, saying—

"You have young and sharp eyes, sir, to see me in the dark here."

"Yes, thank you, I have pretty good eyes. But are you Captain Hawk, the highwayman, who was acquitted of murder at the Old Bailey to-day?"

This question was asked in such a cool, easy manner, that Hawk was completely astounded at it, coming as it did from one who was by his voice little more than a mere lad.

"Why don't you answer me?" said the stranger, again. "I hope you are not afraid to say Yes, for I am quite alone; but if you really can say No with truth, I must ride on yet a little further."

"Who are you that asks the information?"

"Ah! that is almost an answer in the affirmative, I think. You are Captain Hawk? Is it not so?"

"Well?"

"Oh, I am as glad as possible that I have overtaken you; but you were sure to take this road, so I thought sooner or later I should come up with you."

"In the name of all that's abominable," said Hawk, "what do you want with me? and who are you?"

"There's no occasion to get into a passion about it. I have a letter for you, that is all."

"A letter for me?"

"Yes. I suppose you can read?"

"Insolence! How dare you? Pshaw! I should but disgrace myself by touching a boy. But come, sir, you may push my patience too far, and then you will bitterly repent too late of your folly."

"I did not come here to quarrel with you, captain, but to deliver to you a letter from one who has amply paid me for my labour."

"Oh, you are well paid for this insolence?"

"Oh, yes, capitally paid. I was richly rewarded by a faint smile, and a softly murmured—'Thank you;' and after that I would have followed you to the world's end to give you the letter, and fought you afterwards, if you thought proper. But here is the letter. By Heaven, I thought I had lost it at the moment; but here it is. Why don't you come and take it of me?"

Captain Hawk was completely confounded at the cool courage of the youth who could speak to him in such a style, and he hesitated for a moment before he could make up his mind to advance towards the outstretched hand of the young stranger, in which he saw something faintly; but whether it was a letter or a pistol, it was hard to say amid the positive darkness of the night.

"Are you afraid?" said the lad.

"Afraid, did you say?"

"Yes, to be sure, I did. I think, after I venture my life on a lonely road with you, you might as well feel tolerably assured that you have nothing to fear."

"It is not fear, boy, but surprise, that actuates me, and makes me seem to hesitate. Fear and I are strangers to each other, and I can be brave enough even to let you go unpunished for your heedless speech. But, in the name of all that is gracious and truthful, tell me who you bring this letter from?"

The young lad hesitated for a few moments; and then, in a low voice, he said—

"She said nothing about secrecy; and the letter itself, of course, will explain all, I suppose?"

"She? Did you say she?"

"Yes, I did."

"Then you mean May—that is, you mean the younger Miss Boyes?"

"I do."

"Give me the letter—oh, give it to me. Excuse me for any harsh words I have said to you. I knew you not. You are her messenger, and I knew you not. Oh, boy, why did you not banish at once all suspicion of you or your intentions from my mind by coming with her name upon your lips?"

"I don't like coming to a highwayman with the name of an honourable young lady upon my lips."

"Hush!—oh, hush! Say nothing now, I beg of you, which shall weaken the impression of kindness I bear towards you. And so she gave you this for me? She bade you follow me with it?"

"She did."

"And who are you? Tell me that, in order that I may remember who it is that has done so much kindness to me."

"It was for her I did it. My name is Bolton. I am the son of Mr. Bolton, the solicitor. We reside close to Boyes Hall, and Miss May knows me very well, so she knew that she had but to bid me go upon any business or message for her, and if I had life it would be done. Now, sir, I have delivered to you the letter, and we have nothing more to say to each other, I presume; so I will bid you good evening, and ride back to Boyes Hall at once."

"And you will see her there?"

"In good truth I hope so."

"And—and—you——"

"Well, sir, what would you say?"

"Just what I can gather from your manner, that you love May Boyes. Ah! that start confirms me in the thought. You are young, very young; but a few short years, now, will cover that defect. No doubt your prospects are good, and your name is a stainless one. You love her with all your heart and soul, is it not so, and you would make her your wife?—Speak, is it not so?"

"Oh, yes—yes! Heaven bless her!"

"Amen!" Captain Hawk seemed to be half choked when he tried to speak again; but he said, in a low tone—"Cherish that love, boy, and it will be the solace and the joy of all your life—cherish it, and you will find it the sunshine of your existence to the latest space of human life. Go back to her, and tell her what I said to you—say that I have but one thought regarding her, and that is, that she may be very, very happy in the time that is to come! Farewell!—farewell!"

"Stay—stay!"

"What would you now?"

The lad rode close up to the side of Hawk, and laying his hand upon his arm—how it shook as he so laid it!—and striving, even amid the darkness, to look into his face, he said in a tremulous voice—

"And did you love her?"

"I did.

"And—and she—she——"

Hawk discerned what was passing in the mind of the young lover; and for the moment he felt inclined, in the triumph of his passion, to cry out—"She loved me, and loves me still!" but before the words could pass his lips, a better feeling, for once, came to the heart of the bold, bad man, and he said in a very low tone—

"Be at ease, boy. Knowing something of me, and what I might have been, she pitied me; but she did not love me. Are you satisfied?"

"I am—I am! No one could be loved by May Boyes, and have the heart to deny it. Oh, no—no! Go, sir, now; I thank you—I thank you from my heart. Go now—that is, I will go. Farewell!"

Captain Hawk did not speak, but crushing up the letter in his hand, he just touched the bridle of his horse, and was off at a gallop.

It took a ride of some three miles to enable Hawk to compose his mind a little, after what had happened. More than once he felt inclined to turn his horse's head, and ride back after young Bolton, and yell in his ears the unwelcome intelligence that he, Hawk, had been beloved by May Boyes, if pride had succeeded in conquering the passion now; but he as often checked the ungenerous impulse to act in such a fashion, and rode on, until he got some distance past Finchley Common.

The rain that was falling now very fast, began to attract the attention of Hawk; and he pulled up beneath a row of trees by the way-side.

"The letter," he said—"yes, the letter from May. It is here; but where shall I find light to read it by?"

As he spoke, he glanced around him, and saw at some distance through the trees a faint gleam of light. The probability was, that it came from the window of some mansion close at hand; but yet, inclined as he was to try if he could get light and shelter, Captain Hawk crossed the road, to examine if there were any path to lead him in the direction of the light. It was just then, that a strange pattering sound came upon the ground a long way off; and he paused to listen to it.

"Some horsemen upon the road tonight," he said. "Curses on them! Am I yet to be hunted by them, after all that has already happened? One would think, now, that the scene in the Old Bailey was enough to occupy them, without their galloping after me into the open country."

By the character of the sound, which now each moment increased in intensity, Captain Hawk guessed that it was a party of some five or six persons, that was rapidly coming up to the spot where he was by Finchley Common. Of course, he had no possible means of knowing if they were friends or foes; but the probability was that they were the latter, and, consequently, it became of great importance to him to find some place of shelter from them as speedily as possible.

The light he had seen might or might not lead to some hospitable roof; but, at all events, he determined to risk it, and seeing dimly only, but yet sufficiently distinctly, a white gate by the road-side, he dismounted, and essayed to open it; but he found that it was secured by a heavy padlock.

This was rather a disappointment; but after a little search, he found a block of stone embedded in the ground close by one of the gate-posts, to aid in its support, and by hammering at that with his heel, he managed to loosen it, and then, lifting it in both hands, he in a moment smashed the padlock, and the gate was open to him.

He had then only just time to lead his horse through the gate and to close it, when the party of mounted men that he had heard upon the road, reached the spot.

"Halt!" cried a voice, and the tone was so military, that, for the moment, Captain Hawk thought that they must be soldiers who were after him. A few moments, though sufficed to convince him that such was not the case.

"What say you now, comrades?" added the voice, "to going in twos up and down the cross-roads?"

"Well, perhaps it will be best," said another. "Of course, nothing is easier for him to get out of our way while we all keep together here on the high road, for I don't see myself how he is to help eluding us if he keeps the most ordinary look out."

"Very well, then, we will separate, and only recollect that it will be a great object to bring him in alive; but if that cannot be done, why, the next best thing is to shoot him. Come on; there's a lane or two a little above here."

"All's right, sir."

CHAPTER LXIII.

CAPTAIN HAWK BRINGS COMFORT TO A DISTRESSED FAMILY.

Captain Hawk did not doubt for a moment but that he was the person alluded to, who was to be brought in alive if possible, but shot as the next best thing to do if that could not conveniently be accomplished, and he congratulated himself upon the shelter he had obtained just in time.

The men rode on at rather a sharp trot, and then Hawk said, bitterly—

"I have the lives of two of you in my hands, at all events, and it would have gone hard indeed with me if I had not availed myself of the privilege of taking them. It is strange that for the doubtful advantage of a few pounds, armed men will encounter the risk of death or of severe wounds."

Captain Hawk forgot when he made that reflection that a man in the army will encounter death or mutilation for a much less sum, as we know that gentlemen of education will mount a scaling ladder or storm a bank for the small sum of three shillings and eightpence a day, while what are called common soldiers will follow for the odd eightpence.

Knowing such facts Captain Hawk ought not to have felt the least surprise at the officers of the police risking their lives in coming after him, for there was by this time a very handsome reward offered indeed.

The fact was, that although the judge on the bench at the Old Bailey had thought proper to take rather a chivalrous idea of the law, and to insist upon Captain Hawk being allowed to leave the court unmolested, the magistracy of the police of London had taken a very different idea of the affair; and when it had got perfectly well known that Hawk was free and off northward, they offered a handsome reward at once for him, and armed parties began, in quite an amateur-like spirit, to scour the country in search of him.

It became, now, a matter of serious concern with Captain Hawk to know what on earth he should do next. The night was getting to be a very bad one, and he knew of no place to go to with any certainty of obtaining shelter. The roads were evidently patrolled by his foes; and should he defeat one party of them, the probability was that the noise of that conflict would bring upon him another.

"This is awkward," he said, "and, moreover, here I am without the means even of reading this letter, which I am dying with anxiety to see the contents of."

With the bridle of his horse still over his arm, he glanced in the direction of the house, in the ground of which he undoubtedly was, and to his consternation he saw some men rapidly advancing towards him with lighted lanterns.

By that light he saw that he was in a sort of meadow, and that there was a white gate at the other extremity of it, very similar to the one that he had broken down at the side of the road. It was through that gate that the persons with lanterns were making their way.

"By Heaven, this is malapropos indeed," said Hawk. "I must to the road again. The people may know nothing of me, but it will not do to have a contest with them for trespassing."

Hawk had his foot in the stirrup, and was about to mount, when he heard the voice of a female say—

"Now, Gregory you will go right down to the vale, for the lieutenant can't be expected to know his way well, as he was never here before. It's very kind of him to come at all."

"Yes, missus," said a voice in reply; "but how shall I know him?"

"Why, Gregory, if you see a gentleman on horseback, you must stop him, you know, and say—'Are you the lieutenant'?"

"Lor, mum, he will think as I'm a highwayman, safe."

"Nonsense! You will say—'Are you Lieutenant Dundas?' and when he says—'Yes,' you can say—'This way, sir,' and bring him to the house."

"But if he don't say, yes, missus, what am I to say then?"

"Nothing, stupid."

"Oh, lor, but he mightn't think that civil. You may depend, missus, he'll think that's a sell."

"A what?"

"A sell, missus. What do you suppose anybody would think at being met on the highway, and being asked, 'Are you Lieutenant Dundas?' and then when he said—'No,' to say to him—'Nothing special?' I shall get my head broke, to a moral certainty, missus."

"Oh, dear—oh, dear, was ever any one troubled by such stupidity! I didn't mean you to say that. I want you to say no more, you idiot."

"Lor, missus, that's worse, a great deal."

"Oh, grant me patience! Here, John, do you understand?"

"Yes, ma'am."

"Then you go at once, and let Gregory remain here, do."

"But you'll know him, ma'am, when he does come, I supposes, and it will be all right?"

"Why, bless the man, how should I know him, when he's a strange officer, coming from London, to tell me how George gets on, that's all? Didn't I write to him to ask him to come, on particular business, and didn't he write to say he would, and, of course, he will come."

"But didn't you tell him, ma'am, what you wanted him for?"

"To be sure not. I was afraid he would only send a letter if I did, and then I should not have been able to ask him one half the things that I, of course, want to ask him."

"Oh, lor!"

"Why, what's the matter, John? What are you laughing at now?"

"Why, ma'am, I was a thinking that the officer might be in a great rage, you see, at being sent for all this way about nothing but George."

"If he has the feelings of a man, he won't. George is my nephew, and that ought to be sufficient for him, I think; so go into the road at once, do you hear, and take care this lantern don't go out."

"All's right, ma'am."

To this little dialogue Captain Hawk had listened with the greatest attention, and the idea struck him at once that, after all, he might do very much worse than personate the officer who had been sent for by the lady, and who, it was very unlikely indeed, would make his appearance so far from town, on such a night, too. If he did decide upon such a course, it was necessary that he should do so quickly, for he was close to the gate through which they were coming, and the only difficulty he had, was concerning the name of the lady, which, not having been yet mentioned by the servants, he had no means of knowing.

Difficult as it was, though, this was to be overcome by prudence, and so Captain Hawk made up his mind not to be detained from availing himself of the certain good of a shelter for the night, because it might be attended by uncertain dangers.

"Hilloa!" he called out so suddenly that the man who had the lantern dropped it, and the old lady immediately fell into the hedge.

"Who's that?" said John.

"The Lord have mercy upon us," said Gregory. "If it should be some highwayman now?"

"Hilloa!" cried Captain Hawk, again. "I'm afraid I have lost my way here. You with the lantern, just come forward, here, and tell me where I am."

"Why, you are in one of Mrs. Crawley's fields, whoever you are," said John, who was much the most courageous of the two servants belonging to the lady.

This was just what Hawk wanted.

"Mrs. Crawley?" he said. "How strange. Why, that is the lady who I wish to see. Ask her if she expects a Lieutenant Dundas."

"Dundas!" cried the lady. "Oh, my head—my back! Oh—oh, he is here! My dear sir, walk in."

"Thank you, madam, here I am."

"Pray sit down, sir, if you please. I insist upon your sitting down."

"I am afraid, madam, the meadow is rather damp."

"Oh, dear—oh, dear, where is my poor brains, to be sure, I am so confused. I thought we were in the drawing-room. Here, Gregory, you hold the lantern—John, you open the gate, and how do you do, sir?"

"Pretty well, thank you, madam. How are you?"

"So—so, sir; only so—so. The rheumatic pain still continues, I am sorry to say, round the small of my back. Where have you got with the lantern, John?—oh, there you are. This way, sir, if you please. Oh, dear me, and so you are really come? Well, who would have thought it! But you soldiers are so gallant, really."

"It would ill become a soldier, and a gentleman, madam, when a lady requests him to call upon her, for him to refuse to do so. Here I am, and if your servants will be so good as to take charge of my horse, I daresay he will be thankful for their kind attention to him."

"To be sure. John—that is, Gregory—no, I mean John—where are you? Take the officer's horse directly, you two wretches—no, not both of you. One of you come here and keep on holding the lantern. Well, Lieutenant Dundas, and how are you?"

"Pretty well, madam," replied Hawk, for the second time to this very interesting question. "I am pretty well, how are you?"

"Tolerable, if it wasn't for the rheumatism."

"I'm sorry to hear you are so afflicted, madam."

"Well, so am I, do you know. This way, major, if you please—that is, I mean captain—dear me, no, I mean lieutenant; but, I believe, it's all the same?"

"Pretty much so in this instance, madam."

"Ah, I thought it was. I had a great-uncle who was a general, or a corporal, or something of that sort, in the army."

"Had you, indeed?"

"Yes. But I can't take upon myself to say what it was, but its much the same, I suppose, sir?"

"Oh, yes there is a differance, slightly; but to a philosophic mind it is much the same whether a man be a general or a corporal."

"That's just my idea, sir, and so here we are across the lawn, and I do hope you will make yourself as comfortable as possible. Thomasina!—Thomasina!—where are you I wonder? Here Gregory—John—no, Jane or Mary, I mean, go and tell my niece, Thomasina, that the lieutenant she said wouldn't come, has come. Ah, go and tell her that, and tell her if she wants to hear all about her brother George, she must come down stairs this minute."

There was a handsome flight of stone-steps leading to the house from the lawn, and the lady preceded Captain Hawk up them, and through a large hall, and into about as comfortable a dining-room as he ever in all his life had seen.

"Welcome, colonel," she said. "Welcome—I mean, ensign—no, lieutenant. Well, it don't matter. Perhaps you won't mind my calling you anything of that sort that comes uppermost, knowing that I mean you all the time?"

"Centainly, madam; please yourself. Call me field-marshal, if you like."

"Well, that's very kind of you, and if you have any wish to be one, I only hope you may some of these days, though I don't know what it is exactly; but it don't sound very well, and, perhaps, in my ignorance of such things, I am only offending you?"

"No, not at all, my dear madam. Allow me to assure you, that it is no insult at all to be made a field-marshal."

"But wouldn't you rather, now, be promoted to be a corporal?"

"It's quite a matter of taste, madam, but I don't think I should."

"Really now!—Well, will you have something to eat? John—no, I mean Mary—where are you, Mary? Oh, there you are. Well, have you told Thomasina that the general is here?"

"Yes, madam."

"And what does she say?"

"She presents her compliments to him, and will be down directly."

"Then let us have tea, and do you bring a tray for the corporal, with a couple of cold fowls and ham."

MAY BOYES.

"This will do," thought Captain Hawk, as he placed his hair a little in order, and spruced himself up as well as he could, in expectation that Thomasina would be worth looking at.

"Now, my dear major, you will sit down by the fire and enjoy yourself, and make yourself quite at home, and let me assure you, that we shall be always glad to see you. It's true that since the death of poor Mr. Crawley, I don't see much company; but still, you will always find a hearty welcome here."

"What more could any one wish for madam?"

"Well, it's very kind of you, Mr. Marshal of the Fields, to say that, of course; but here comes my niece, Thomasina, and the sister of our George, you know."

Captain Hawk rose as the door of the apartment opened, and a young girl of not more than sixteen years of age entered the room. Hawk looked at her with much delight. He thought that he had never seen any one so truly and so purely beautiful, no, not even May Boyes; but then there was no sort of comparison to be drawn between them, they were so widely different in all respects.

Thomasina was a head above May Boyes; she had none of that dignity of beauty which May Boyes possessed, and which struck with awe the beholder, as well as dazzling his eyes. The features of Thomasina were all of the gentle quietest kind. There was the fair auburn hair, the rich colour upon the cheek, the soft blue eye; but it was the charming aspect of guileless innocence that pervaded the whole face, that made it such a delight to look upon, and which quite fascinated the gaze of Captain Hawk.

This young creature advanced timidly into the room, and her aunt introduced her with her utmost volubility to Captain Hawk.

"My dear, this is the colonel—I mean the corporal—that is to say, oh, yes, the major, who has come so kindly to tell us all about George, you know,"

The young lady executed a curtsey that would not have disgraced a palace, and a flush overspread her face, as she said—

"Sir, I know not how to welcome you, or what to say to you. The conduct of my aunt in writing to you is so—so strange."

"Oh, not at all," said Captain Hawk. "I am sure, I have reason to be glad that she thought of adopting such a course, since it has procured me the happiness I now enjoy."

There is no doubt but that Thomasina fully understood this compliment as it was intended by Captain Hawk, but she made no reply to it, and the aunt immediately said—

"Dear me, Thomasina, I don't see anything extraordinary in the affair."

"Oh, yes, aunt, there is indeed!"

"Well, I will be judged by the corporal"

"Corporal, aunt? The gentleman is not a corporal"

"Oh, he says it's all the same, and I can just call him what I like, and so I don't see any harm in writing to him. The army is in Flanders. Well, I see by the newspapers that this gentleman has come home from there, and, of course, I wrote to him to ask him about our George, and here he is."

"Nothing can possibly be more rational, or to the purpose," said Hawk.

CHAPTER LXIV.

CAPTAIN HAWK MAKES RATHER A PRECIPITATE RETREAT FROM MRS. CRAWLEY'S.

THE fair Thomasina looked a little reproachfully at Hawk, for she thought he was amusing himself at the expense of her aunt, who, despite all her foibles, she loved very dearly from her excellent heart.

Captain Hawk saw the look, and he took care when he spoke to the old lady again to throw into his manner as much kindness and consideration as possible.

The tea was served most elegantly; and a couple of cold fowls, and a Westphalia ham, with a bottle of rare old Madeira, being put at the disposal of Hawk, he managed, notwithstanding that his eyes would travel to the sweet face of Thomasina very often, to make an excellent repast.

It showed great forbearance upon the part of the aunt as well as the young lady not to question him until he had satisfied his hunger; but when they saw that nothing remained of the two fowls but the bones, and that there was rather a tremendous gap in the Westphalia ham, they no longer thought it necessary to be so any more, and the old lady said—

"Now, general, will you be so good as to tell us all about our George?"

"Did you know him, sir?" said Thomasina.

"Perfectly well," said Hawk. "Hem! A very nice young man, and I can even now trace a resemblance to his sister."

"As like as two peas," said Mrs. Crawley.

"Oh, no, aunt."

"Oh, but I say yes, my dear. Of course, George is taller than you are, though he is not a giant; but you are very much shorter. Well, colonel, and how is he?"

"Perfectly well, madam, and only sighing to be back again to those dear relations whom he has left in England."

"How good of him!" replied Thomasina.

"How like him," said the aunt.

"Yes, madam," added Hawk, who in the midst of all the untruths he was now indulging in, found one excuse to himself in the fact that he was diffusing real happiness for a time. "Yes, madam, he is very much esteemed in his regiment indeed; and I will say that there is no young man for whom I entertain a more sincere and cordial respect than I do for him."

"You are too good, sir," said Thomasina, as the tears came to her eyes. "I am sure we can never thank you sufficiently."

"I am more than repaid by hearing you say so."

"Well, but," said Mrs. Crawley, "has he been in any battles, major?"

"Oh, yes, in several engagements."

"Engagements? I do hope that he won't think of making any engagements till I have seen the party. He is much too young to think of engagements yet, I am sure."

"Aunt," said Thomasina, laughing, "you don't understand the lieutenant; he means battles with the enemy."

"Ah! dear me," said Mrs. Crawley, casting up her eyes, and inspired by a sudden thought, "it was old port that was your poor dear uncle's greatest enemy, and that gave him the gout in his stomach at last. Oh, how time does creep on, and on, and on. Excuse me, captain."

"Don't mention it, madam. But I very much fear, now, that I am intruding upon both of you."

"Oh, no—no—no, not at all. I am quite sure that Thomasina is as well pleased as I am with your charming company."

"The gentleman is entitled to our most respectful gratitude, aunt, for being so kind as to come here, no doubt at personal inconvenience to himself, just to gratify us; but, sir, if you please, I should like very much to ask you one question."

"I shall answer it with pleasure."

"Well, sir,"—here Thomasina looked carefully and anxiously in the face of Captain Hawk, and her voice slightly trembled, as she added—"how is poor George's eye, sir?"

"His eye?"

"Yes, his left eye, poor fellow."

"Oh, his left eye, poor fellow—that is his—not his right eye, of course, but his left eye, poor fellow."

"Yes, I ought to have recollected to have asked you that at once," said Mrs. Crawley. "How is his eye?"

"Why, a—that is to say, as to his eye—his left eye?"

"Yes—yes," they both said, together.

"Well, ladies, I am happy to tell you that it is as well as can be expected."

"Oh!" they both said.

"Yes, I can assure you, ladies, of that fact—his left eye is as well as we can all hope or expect."

"That is very satisfactory," said Thomasina. "Did he ever mention to you how it happened, sir?"

"No—he only smiled when he spoke of it, but never mentioned it."

"How generous of him. I did it."

"You, Miss Thomasina? You did it?"

"I did, Lieutenant Dundas. I assure you, I did. It was quite an accident; but I threw a hard ball into his left eye. Oh—oh, poor George."

The feelings of the young lady appeared to be completely overpowering her, and by way of giving her some satisfaction, Captain Hawk immediately said—

"I can assure you, that by the care of the surgeon of the regiment, a wonderful change has taken place, and you will be surprised when you see his eye."

"Shall I, indeed, sir?"

"You will, I assure you; and I am very happy to be able to say so much to you upon the subject."

The aunt now, after a conference with a servant that seemed to premise that something was wrong in some part of the house, rose and left the room, and Captain Hawk found himself alone with Thomasina. The young lady appeared for a moment to feel the awkwardness of being left to keep up a conversation with one who was all but an entire stranger to her, and she said, in a low voice—

"I wish George had troubled you with a letter for us, sir."

"A letter?" said Captain Hawk, and then, with the mere sound of the word, there rushed across his recollection the letter he had had from May Boyes, and which he had, in the hurry of getting through the gate by the meadow, thrust in a very crumpled up condition into his pocket. "A letter? Oh, yes, I wish he had written with all my heart."

"But he did not?"

"No—he had no idea, probably, that I should be honoured by an invitation to the house."

"Ah, sir, you are good enough to put the matter in that light. But you must have been very much surprised, sir, at receiving a note from my aunt, asking you, a perfect stranger, to the house?"

"Oh, no. The fact is, I could see in a moment the kind and guileless feelings that dictated it, and so—so—"

Captain Hawk was truly vexed that to this young and lovely girl he was compelled to act such a part of deceit, and to involve himself in such a complete mesh of untruths. He began stammering, and speaking in such a manner, that she could not possibly help seeing there was something the matter with him, when the door was suddenly opened, and the footman appeared, with a silver salver in his hand, upon which lay a card.

"What is it, Gregory?" said Thomasina.

"A gentleman, if you please, miss, to see missus."

"Indeed? Who can it me? Is that his card?"

"Yes, miss."

The fair Thomasina took the card, and to the consternation of Hawk, and her own surprise, she read upon it the name of—

"Lieutenant Dundas, 61st foot."

Thomasina looked at Captain Hawk, and Captain Hawk looked at Thomasina, and then she said—

"Oh, sir, how is this—what am I to think?"

"About what, Miss Thomasina?"

"Look at this card, sir—your name is on it. There must be some imosture here. Where is my aunt, Gregory?"

"Here, miss."

The aunt entered the room by another door, and, as she did, she said—

"Dear me, what is it? I hope no visitors, Gregory? Is that anyone's card, I wonder? Let me look at it. I did hope, general, that we should have had the pleasure of your company, to talk about our poor dear George, all alone. Why, bless me, what is this? 'Lieutenant Dundas, 61st foot!' What does it mean? Gregory, who gave you this?"

"Gentleman in reception room, missus."

"A gentleman? Why, this is the general, the corporal I mean," pointing to Hawk, who bowed, and then finding that Thomasina was looking very pale and frightened, he thought that he ought to say something, and in a cool, determined voice, he said—

"I had hoped, ladies, not to be compelled to call your attention to a little fact that may alarm you, but which I hope you will think much less of, on account of my presence here to protect you. Gregory, you can stay outside the door for a few moments, but be at hand."

"Yes, sir."

"Allow me, then, now that we are alone, to tell you, ladies, that having mislaid the letter you were kind enough to send to me, I heard that it was picked up by the notorious Captain Hawk, the highwayman."

Both the ladies screamed.

"Hush! for the love of Heaven—hush! and hear me out. I say it was picked up after his acquittal of the murder of Judge Holme, by the notorious Captain Hawk, and I came here at great speed, distressing my horse to do so, for fear the rascal should take it into his head to personate me, and bring, perhaps, a gang of thieves to rob the house, and possibly murder the inmates."

Mrs. Crawley fell to the floor, and propped herself up against a chair, and the beautiful and gentle Thomasina looked very pale.

"I intended, I assure you, to stay here all night, to protecc you," added

Captain Hawk, "but I did not intend to say anything to you of it, if no alarm took place; but now I cannot doubt but that this is the man."

"The highwayman?" said Mrs. Crawley

"The same."

"But how did he get your card?" said Thomasina.

"Easily. I keep my cards in my pocket-book, and it was that I lost, with your aunt's letter in it, and other papers of importance to me, and I have no doubt but that the man now below has it."

"Oh, corporal," said Mrs. Crawley, "you will protect us? Our reliance is upon you and Providence, you know. Oh, the villain, why didn't they hang him at the old what's-its-name—Bailey, I mean, and so rid society of him? What shall I do? My dear Thomasina, little did I expect that your aunt's house would prove to you a dreadful place. Only tell us what to do, major, and we will do it at once. Shall we—oh, corporal, shall we get up the chimney?"

"I don't think that there is the slightest occasion, madam. It is quite possible that the fellow may have a gang at his heels hidden about the shrubberies, and if so, we must be very cautious what we are about. Indeed, I should advise that you have him up here at once, and say as little as possible about George to him; but leave me to speak to him, and to fathom his intentions if I possibly can do so. Of course, you may rely upon my protection, for I am well armed."

"Oh, don't let us have any fighting here," said the aunt. "I will send down word that I am not at home."

"That will do," said Thomasina, "if Gregory has not already said you were within. Gregory—Gregory!"

"Yes, miss," said Gregory, popping his head in at the door, from his close proximity to which, it appeared pretty evident that he had heard everything that had been said. Indeed, the alarmed expression of Gregory's countenance was a pretty good guarantee of that fact.

"Did you tell the gentleman below Gregory, that aunt was at home?"

"Yes, miss, I did."

"Then show him up," said Captain Hawk.

Gregory disappeared to execute the order, and Hawk said, rapidly—

"Let me beg of you both to be cool and collected. Leave this all to me. It is a most fortunate thing that I am here to meet this fellow, or there is no knowing how far his insolence might carry him. I beg that you will not be under any alarm."

"Oh, sir," said Thomasina, "we cannot help being alarmed."

"No, Corporal Dundas, we cannot help it," said Mrs. Crawley; "but let what will happen, I do hope that—oh, dear, here he is."

Gregory then opened the door, and announced—

"The gentleman from down below, if you please, miss. Oh, dear—oh, dear!"

A rather corpulent man, rather below the middle size, and in an undress military uniform, entered the room. From the expression of his face, it was pretty clear that the lieutenant was rather fond of the bottle; but yet there was about his clear, ample brow, and full gray eye, an expression of great good-humour. He bowed rather low to the ladies, and rather sharply to Captain Hawk, and then he said—

"I had the honour to receive a note from Mrs. Crawley, and as a request from a lady amounts to a command, I am here according to your orders, if you please, ladies."

They both curtsied to him, and Captain Hawk, in his blandest accents, said—

"Pray be seated, sir—pray take a seat, captain."

"Captain? I wish I were. I am only lieutenant, sir, although I am well aware that those of that rank often assume the name of captain."

"I am quite sure you ought to be a captain," said Hawk, placing an emphasis upon the word, and looking at Mrs. Crawley, who laughed slightly. "I hope you are quite well, sir? Will you allow me to offer you some rather choice Madeira?"

"Thank you—thank you. A friend of the family, I presume, sir?"

"Oh, yes. I hope so."

"Decidedly so," said Mrs. Crawley.

"Hem! We often see *hawks* about the place."

"Aunt?" said Thomasina, and she shook her head deprecatingly.

"Hawks?" said the lieutenant; "I daresay you do, ma'am, and sparrows for them to pounce upon, too. But of all the sweet birds that ever with unflagging wing skim the blue vault of Heaven, there is none to my mind like the gentle timid dove, who, with one look, wins your heart for ever."

The liutenant accompanied these words by such a wicked glance of adimration of the fair Thomasina, that there was no possibility of mistaking their obvious meaning as applying to her. I was quite a speech for the lieutenant to make.

CHAPTER LXV.

THE PERPLEXITIES AT THE VILLA STILL CONTINUE, AND END RATHER ODDLY.

"Perhaps," said Mrs. Crawley, "you would like to take some refreshment, sir?"

"Well, madam, I don't mind if I do. It is a good distance out here, I assure you; but I apprehend you have few visitors."

"Oh, dear me, yes, we have many, and some of them, I hope, apprehend as well as most folks."

"Hem!" said Captain Hawk, for he saw that Mrs. Crawley was going a little too far in her play upon words, and was likely to produce a denouement too soon. The fair Thomasina shook her pretty little head again at her aunt, and took the opportunity, as she crept close to Hawk for protection, of whispering—

"Aunt is so very indiscreet."

"Rather so," said Hawk.

"But oh, sir, what shall we do?"

"Hush — hush! Don't seem to notice him."

"I won't—I won't!"

Such refreshment as the larder afforded was now placed before the lieutenant, and after an apology for eating in the presence of the ladies, while they only indulged themselves with tea, he added—

"In the ups and downs of a soldier's life, madam, there are many occasions when we are glad to steal——"

"Steal!" cried Mrs. Crawley. "Oh, dear, there's no doubt of that, I fear."

"None in the least," said Thomasina; "None in the least, I'm afraid."

"Ah," said Hawk, "it's a bad habit."

"Why, what do you all mean?" cried the lieutenant, throwing down his knife and fork. "I mean, that we are obliged to steal a brief five minutes from our duties to snatch a meal, and then think ourselves lucky."

"No doubt, sir," said Hawk. "These ladies, I'm sure, meant nothing at all of a disrespectful character to your cloth."

"Oh, no doubt of that. Besides, a soldier never can do anything but laugh at a little badinage from the ladies. All I can say is, that I have known occasions when I should have been transported——"

"Sir," said Mrs. Crawley, "that I have no doubt is true, and I can only hope the occasion may arise again."

"So do I," said Thomasina. "So do I."

"Allow me," said Captain Hawk, "to share in the general sentiment; and the sooner the occasion arises the better it will be for society at large, I am quite certain."

"Why, what the deuce do you all mean?" cried the lieutenant, who was of rather a fiery and testy disposition. "What is the meaning of it all? Cannot a man say that during his campaigns he would have been often transported with pleasure to get such a drop of Madeira as this, without you all catching him up in the middle of his sentence in this odd way?"

"Pray excuse us, capt—that is to say, lieutenant," said Mrs. Crawley; "we—we didn't mean that, as it's only a joke."

"Oh, well, a joke is a joke, ma'am: and, of course, as your guest and a soldier, I must allow you to joke upon me as much as you like; but to one who had not seen such severe trials as I have——"

"Trials?" cried Mrs. Crawley; "then you have been tried?"

"Severely tried, madam."

"Well, and how came you to get off?"

"Off?"

"Hem!" said Captain Hawk, and Thomasina again shook her head at her aunt, while the lieutenant looked from one to the other, with his wine in his hand, in astonishment, not unmingled with some degree of apprehension that he had got into a lunatic asylum.

"There you go again, all of you," he cried. "Upon my life, madam, if you want to hear anything about your nephew, you must write to some other officer than me."

"Oh, yes," said Captain Hawk, who was anxious, after all, nothing should really prevent Mrs. Crawley and Thomasina from procuring authentic information. "Oh, yes, sir; this lady is, I assure you, very anxious to hear of him."

"And so am I," said Thomasina.

"Very good; then I can only inform you that he is the greatest scamp I ever knew, and a disgrace to the regiment, out of which he will be packed as soon as possible, you may depend."

"What, my nephew?" screamed Mrs. Crawley.

"My brother?" bellowed Thomasina.

"You don't say so?" said Captain Hawk, coolly.

"Yes, I do," added the lieutenant, whose odd reception had had the effect of bringing forth all the irascibility of his temper—"yes, I do; and it was that very fact that induced me to come here."

"Oh, indeed!"

"To be sure, madam. I thought, you see"—here he made a curious kind of grin—"I thought that it required somebody to break the intelligence to you in a milder way."

"You certainly, sir," said Captain Hawk, "are well adapted for such a delicate affair, for I must say the mild way in which you have broken the news is quite extraordinary."

"Oh, sir, if it meets with your approbation, that is quite another thing," added the lieutenant. "I hope you are a gentleman, sir?"

"One great proof of it," said Captain Hawk, "is, that I keep my temper."

The lieutenant coloured up at this remark; but Mrs. Crawley rose and left the room, saying as she did so—

"Excuse me, gentlemen. I shall not be long gone."

"Oh, don't mention it, madam," cried the lieutenant. "I'm sure the gentleman has something to say to me."

Upon this, Thomasina, too, rose, and Captain Hawk showed her to the door, squeezing her hand very gently and gallantly as he did so—an attention which she replied to by a slight flush of colour and a smile, for the fair Thomasina was really a pretty girl, and there can be no doubt in the world but that she was fully aware of that fact; for, somehow, if the glass of a pretty girl does not convince her of such a state of things, she is sure to encounter some one who will open her eyes to the pleasing intelligence.

"Now, sir," said the lieutenant, when he and Captain Hawk were alone—"now, sir."

"Well, sir?" said Hawk.

"Perhaps you have no objection to repeat what you said?"

"What was it?"

"Oh, some stuff about a gentleman keeping his temper."

"I am quite sure you know it; therefore, I need not repeat it. It seems to have made impression enough upon you."

"Impression? What do you mean, sir?"

"Just what I say."

"Well, sir, your tongue is sharp enough; and if your sword is as sharp, you can have no objection to cross it with mine."

"Do you mean a duel?"

"Yes, sir, I do."

"Oh, then I decline."

"You—decline?"

"To be sure I do. I am not at all offended. On the contrary, I have been rather amused with you than otherwise, and I am certainly not going to run you through the body on that account."

"Well, of all the cool pieces of insolence that I ever heard of, this beats them. Now, sir, I distinctly challenge you to meet me in the morning at the back of Montague House, and in a very few minutes I will convince you that my acquaintance is not quite so amusing as you now seem to imagine it."

"But I am not at all offended."

"Take that, then," said the lieutenant, as he threw a glass of wine into Captain Hawk's face.

"Hark you, sir," said Hawk; "I will meet you at six o'clock at the back of Montague House, since you are so anxious for a duel with me; but you have adopted a mode of forcing me to this meeting which the result of the meeting, be it what it may, cannot expiate; therefore, I will settle that part of the business now."

With one stride, Hawk crossed to where the lieutenant was sitting, and seizing his nose between his fingers with his right hand, he took up the decanter of Madeira with his left, and with one blow smashed it over his countenance.

"Murder!" said the lieutenant.

The door at this moment opened, and Mrs. Crawley called out in a loud voice—

"They are coming—they are coming! All's right now. They are coming, my dear sir—they are coming!"

"Who?" cried Hawk.

"The officers of police, to be sure. I am quite certain this wretch is Captain Hawk, the highwayman, so I asked them to come in and take him, and there are several of them who say they know him quite well."

"The d—l they do," said Hawk.

A confused tumult of people ascending the great staircase now came upon Hawk's ear. The lieutenant was trying to rid himself of the Madeira, and the broken glass that hung about his face, and cursing and swearing in the most awful manner that can be conceived as he did so. Thomasina stood in an attitude of alarm at the door.

"Here they are!" cried Mrs. Crawley, with quite an air of exultation. "Here they are! Come up—this way—he is here!"

"The d—l he is!" said the lieutenant.

"Good night," said Captain Hawk, and opening one of the French windows of the drawing-room he at once passed out into the balcony that was beyond. Now, upon coming to the house, dark as it was, he had managed to see that the balcony of the drawing-room and of the lower apartments, where it formed a sort veranda, were all in one, and formed quite a feature in front of the mansion, and it had struck him how very easy it would be either to ascend or descend by the aid of the trellis-work.

That knowledge now stood him in good stead.

If Captain Hawk, though, had had any idea that the officers would have failed to recognise him, he would not have left his rather snug quarters at Mrs. Crawley's for that night, but he was well aware that recent events had made his person so well known to the whole of the police, that the idea of their hesitating a moment between him and the lieutenant was quite out of the question.

Escape, then, was all that was left him to think of.

It was strange, now, that the moment he stepped on the balcony and felt that he was about to leave that house, the letter that he had in his pocket, still unread, from May Boyes, came to his recollection. Was it the bright eyes of the poor Thomasina that had obliterated the thought of that letter, which he had at the time of its reception been so very anxious to read? We have no good idea of the constancy of Captain Hawk.

The night was finer than it had been, clouds were drifting over the sky, but no rain was falling. There was a delightful springy freshness in the air, too, that Captain Hawk inhaled with pleasure. He took but one glance through the window, which he had closed after him, and saw that the alarm was no false one, for some half dozen men, whom he knew, by that kind of tact which persons in his profession so soon acquire, to be officers, made their appearance quickly.

"That will do," said Hawk.

In another moment he had vaulted over the iron rail of the balcony, keeping a good hold with his hands, and then he began to descend with the ease and agility of a squirrel.

There was no difficulty whatever in reaching the ground, for there were so many footholds that it was quite as convenient a mode of descent as though a ladder had been there placed.

"That is all right," said Hawk. "Now let me see: I did notice which way the stables lay. Oh, yes, to the right here."

Hastily crossing the lawn, he very nearly disabled him self by rather heedlessly running against some iron hurdles that fenced it in, and which, not expecting at the moment, he did not look for.

CAPTAIN HAWK BRINGS STRANGE NEWS TO MRS. CRAWLEY OF HER SON.

Rather a hasty malediction escaped him, but he did not relax in his speed, but crossing the hurdles, he made his way through a gate towards the stables.

Of course, without his horse, Captain Hawk felt that he was nothing, and it would be indeed a dear price to pay for his few hours' shelter, and the refreshment he had had, if he should be compelled in consequence to leave his gallant steed with the enemy. The mere thought of the possibility of such a thing was agonising to him.

Suddenly a dog rushed at him. It was one of those small pestering dogs that there is no such thing as getting rid of. It barked and yelped around him, and it was in vain that Hawk make fruitless attempts to settle its career by a kick. The little dog knew better than to come in the way of the heavy boot; but he kept up an unceasing attack upon him, and then a man's voice called out—

"Hilloa!—who's there?"

"Quick—my horse," cried Hawk. "Mrs. Crawley is in danger, and I have friends close at hand. Get me out my horse at once, my good fellow."

"What, be you, the—what do you call 'em?"

"Yes—yes. I am the—what do you call 'em. Be quick, do."

"Oh, then, you're the sojer as was with Master George?"

"Yes. My horse. Quick—quick."

"And you knew'd him?"

"Of course I did. Come now, my good fellow, my horse, if you please."

"Ha!—ha!"

"What do you mean by that?"

"Wasn't he a rum un?"

Captain Hawk made a rush at the fellow, and clapping a pistol to his face, he said—

"Hark, you. I am not accustomed to be trifled with. I cannot take upon myself to say whether this is stupidity, or what you think your wit; but in either case, if you don't get out my horse this minute I'll scatter your brains over the yard here. Do you understand that?"

"Oh, lor, to be sure I do. This way, sir."

It was surprising now to see the alarmed alacrity with which Captain Hawk's steed was brought out, and the saddle put upon him by this man, whose countenance, as he placed a stable lantern so that some of its beams fell upon it, showed the state of dreadful fear he was in.

"It's all ready, sir," he said. "It's all ready, if you please, sir."

"Very well. Don't trifle with a man who is in a hurry another time, my friend. And now you will get a guinea by showing me the shortest way to the main road, and be quick about it."

"It's this way, sir, across the lawn. The horse's feet won't hurt."

Captain Hawk rather hesitated about crossing the lawn, which was in such close proximity to the mansion; but not liking to get up any suspicion in the mind of the man that he was only intent upon escape, he cried—

"Very well; lead the way."

The man hastily pulled down a hurdle, so that there was no necessity for taking a jump in the dark over them, and Captain Hawk walked his horse after him over the lawn. He had not hardly got half-way, though, when several voices cried out from the windows and balcony—

"There he goes! There he goes!"

At the same moment there was the sharp report of a couple of pistols, and one of the bullets struck Hawk's hat.

Drawing one of his pistols, he levelled at random at the balcony, but at the moment he heard the voice of Thomasina, saying—

"No—no, you shall not kill him! It is murder, and must not be done here. Aunt, I call upon you to stop them."

Hawk returned the pistol to his saddle, as he said—

"By Heavens! I might have shot her. I am so rejoiced she spoke."

CHAPTER LXVI.

CAPTAIN HAWK IS CHASED, AND ESCAPES BY A BOLD MANŒUVRE.

THE man who had up to this attended upon him from the stables, now, upon finding that there was some danger, and that pistol-shots were flying about him rather more plentiful than seemed to him at all desirable, turned and fled, so that Captain Hawk was alone, and left to his own chances and resources.

It was well for him that, with an idea that it was possible he might have to make rather a hurried escape from the house, he had paid so much attention to the route he had come upon entering it.

Casting his eyes about him, he saw a

remarkably beautiful cedar tree at one end of the lawn, and he knew that he had, upon entering the grounds, had that upon his left hand; therefore, of course, in leaving, it was necessary that it should turn it on the right.

"That will do," he said. "Forward!"

Bang went another pistol-shot, now, and from the manner in which his horse started Captain Hawk was afraid that the creature had been hit by the bullet; but that seemed to be not the case, for the horse recovered again on the moment, and went on at a bound. The fact was, as Captain Hawk afterwards discovered, the bullet had just touched the tip of the horse's ear.

After getting quite clear of the lawn, Hawk knew that there was a white gate to come to, and he just managed to see it before him. Urging his horse at it, he made the creature, who probably saw the gate clearer than his master did, leap it in good style.

"There he goes!" cried a voice.

"Confound you," muttered Hawk.

"It's a good five hundred pounds now for you all!" cried the voice again. "I see him."

The voice came from a man in a large elder tree close at hand, and Hawk fired a pistol right into the thickest portion of it.

"Do you feel him as well as see him," he said, "busy-body?"

The howl that followed the discharge of the pistol might be either pain or fright, Hawk did not stop to inquire which, but galloped over the meadow in a few seconds, and cleared the other gate into the road, just as he heard the sounds of horses feet after him.

Turning to look who were his pursuers, he saw in the dim night light a man on some light-coloured horse coming on at a gallop.

"Surrender!" cried the man. "Surrender while you have life to do so, Hawk. It is useless to resist. I have made up my mind to have you, so you are as good as nabbed."

"Cool that, rather," said Hawk.

Rapidly dismounting, he dragged from the hedge a long white-looking stick, and placing his hat upon it, he stuck it through the topmost bar of the gate, so that it stuck up about a yard above it. Hawk knew well that there was not a horse in the world who would jump the gate with such an object before his eyes to baulk him.

"Come on, now, my friend!" cried Hawk. "You seem well mounted. Leap the gate, if you can do it."

"That is soon done," said the officer.

Putting his horse at full speed to the gate, he thought to go over it quite easy, but the creature reared when he was tolerably close to it, and nearly fell right over on his back. The horseman uttered a shout of rage, and put him at it again, but with the same result.

"I don't know that I need wait for you," said Captain Hawk; "you can't do it, so I have the pleasure of bidding you good night."

"Stop!"

"What for, pray."

"I am Mr. Arthur Lamb. Do you know me, knave?"

"Yes, you are a man I have heard of as an amateur constable in London—a man who, having a good business if he had chosen to attend to it, and a respectable one too, became so enamoured of thief-taking, that he neglects everything for that fancy."

"Yes, I'm the fellow, and there you go."

Crack! went one of Mr. Lamb's pistols, and the bullet whistled so close to Captain Hawk's head, that he felt the current of air it made.

Hawk had but one pistol loaded now, and he felt rather loth to throw it away upon Mr. Lamb.

"Villain," he said, "what is my life or death to you? I could now kill you, but I spare you with the hope that it will awaken your mercy, not to me, for I ask it not of you, and can defend myself, but to some other who is not so well provided, and who may fall into you clutches."

With these words, Captain Hawk turned his horse's head towards the country, and went off at a gallop.

It was with the greatest difficulty that Captain Hawk succeeded in controlling his inclination to shoot Lamb; but he was glad he had succeeded in doing so; and after going a couple of miles and hearing no pursuit after him, he drew rein, and while he suffered his horse to crop some short sweet grass that was upon the road-side, he reloaded the pistol he had discharged.

"Am I free of those fellows at last?" he said, as he listened attentively, and heard no sound save the faint notes of some bird, who thus gave notice of the approach of the dawn, although to the less fine senses of man, there was as yet no indication of it.

He alighted to tighten the girth of his saddle, which the stable-man had not in his fright been very particular about; and then as he regained the saddle, he heard a crackling sound among some brush-wood a short distance from him, over a hedge to the left of the road.

Hawk passed his hand gently down the neck of his horse, as he said—"Hush!" and the animal stood stock still as though it had been cut out of stone.

The noise continued, and then he heard a voice. It was the detestable voice of Lamb. It had a peculiar croak in it, which when once heard, there was no such thing as ever forgetting again.

"Don't you see," he said, "that by getting right through Lord Hargrove's property we come out upon the high road, and save a good mile. He won't keep up the speed he went off at, and I'll be bound that we shall come upon him at some road-side inn or another."

"Indeed," thought Hawk.

"Do you think so, Mr. Lamb?" said another voice.

"To be sure I do. Now, come on, and don't say much, unless I speak to you. Here are six of us, with good cattle, and one thing we do know, that he is not close at hand."

"Yes, Mr. Lamb; but how came you to miss him at the gate?"

"Well, I might have shot him if I had liked, but something came over me to spare him, so I said to him—'Now, Captain Hawk, remember, I spare your life, and I hope it will, if you escape the officers, make you have some mercy upon any one whom you may meet, and who may not be able to defend himself as I am.'"

"And what did he say?"

"Oh, he just rode off, that's all."

"Impudent impostor," muttered Captain Hawk to himself. "This shall not go unpunished, if I can possibly punish it."

Hawk was now in rather a difficulty. If he remained where he was, of course there was every chance that he would soon be seen by the party in pursuit of him, and if he galloped off, the first sound of his horse's feet would let them know where he was. Still, the latter course was the best, for, after all, they had to extricate themselves from the sort of plantation in which they were, and they had to gain the road and to mount, all of which would take up some time.

"Oh, I shall be a good mile ahead of them," said Hawk, "and a mile is a long way in a chase."

Raising himself in his stirrups, then, he called out in a loud voice that, no doubt, considerably startled the advancing party—

"Lamb!—Lamb!"

"Who's that?" said Lamb. "Stand clear, my men. There's somebody here who calls out Lamb. Who can it be?"

"Arthur Lamb!"

"Yes—who are you?"

"Oh, I only wished to say that the account you pretended to give of the meeting and the parley with Captain Hawk at the gate is a lie. It was he who spared you, and not you who spared him. That's all. Good night, Lamb."

"The devil!" said Lamb.

In another moment the clatter of the hoofs of Hawk's horse proclaimed him gone, and then the measured, steady tread of the creature's feet upon the road, showed to the officers that it was a long and sturdy gallop they would have to take after him.

Hawk hardly knew where he was, he had got so far in a part of the neighbourhood of London where he was not much in the habit of exploring; but he fancied that in the darkness he soon saw houses, and he felt quite certain that the morning was close at hand, for the tall trees and the hedges seemed to stand out from the darkness as though there were a halo of faint light encircling each of them. After a time, Hawk heard a boy whistling in a meadow, and he drew up, and called over the hedge to him—

"Hilloa, my lad, where does this road lead to?"

"Hodly, right on," said the boy.

"Thank you."

Hawk now knew pretty well whereabouts he was, and as the morning was so close at hand, he thought he would look out for a place of rest and shelter for himself and horse before it fairly broke. He did not think that the pursuit after him, led by such a man as Lamb, would be very active now, for he knew how great an objection the officers who considered themselves regularly in the bus'ness had even to associating themselves with him, who was but a kind of amateur and interloper.

"They will rather lose me," said Hawk, "than catch me, with him in their company, I feel convinced: so I have not much to fear, at all events."

There was a little rise in the ground now, which, if there had been light enough, would have enabled him to see for a considerable distance around him; but, as yet, the dawn was not sufficiently advanced, and a few hundred yards from his eyes there was nothing but an undistinguishable mass of trees, and sky, and fields.

Close to him, though, on his right hand, there was a narrow lane, and he was at a loss for a few minutes to know why it was that his horse seemed to have such a partiality for that lane, and to be inclined to go into it, whether he, Captain Hawk, would or no.

By listening attentively, though, he heard the trickling sound of water, and then he understood what his horse wanted.

"Ah, my good friend," he said, as he patted the animal on the neck. "They gave you nothing to drink where you were put up last, I find. I wonder if you had even a mouthful of hay? I suspect not, though."

Hawk dismounted, now, and led his horse down the narrow green lane, and as he went, the pleasant murmur of the little streamlet that was there came each moment more and more plainly upon his ears. The lane was most impenetrably dark, for it was so overgrown with vegetation, that, no doubt, even at noon-day in summer, it was a cool and shadowy retreat· so that it was not likely that at such a dim and early hour in the morning it could be other than blackness itself.

It seemed to Hawk as though he were actually feeling his way.

The horse was much more confidential in his progress than his master, and it is an undoubted fact that all animals have a greater power of concentrating their vision than human beings have, and that they can, therefore, see better in the dark than we can. Captain Hawk's steed exemplified this by all but leading his master to the banks of the little stream, and then Hawk heard the creature drinking.

"I should have no objection to a draught of the water myself," he said, "if I could only see first of all what it is like; but I don't exactly seem to relish the idea of trying it in the dark."

Captain Hawk, if he could only have got over the idea of the thing, might well have ventured after his horse had drank at the little streamlet, for he might, with perfect safety, have made sure that it was sweet and wholesome, or the horse would have taken none.

The feeling, though, of safety in such a place was very great, and Hawk at once made up his mind to stay there till there was a little more light and animation upon the face of nature, so that he might see where he nearly was, and shape his after course accordingly. By feeling about with his hands a little he found a grassy bank, upon which he sat down, keeping the bridle of his steed upon his arm; and thus as he was so close to the ground, he was in a favourable position for learning if any one should come to disturb the serenity of the scene.

Not a sound but the ripple of the stream now reached him, and now and then the crisp grass yielding to the teeth of his horse.

"Oh, for the light of day," said Hawk, as he took May's letter from his pocket, and held it in vain before his eyes. The superscription even, which might be supposed to be in bold characters, was quite invisible.

"Well," he said, "I must wait for day and for danger, for I fancy they will come to me together."

A drowsy feeling began to steal over

him. No doubt the fatigue he had gone through, and the monotonous ripple of the stream at his feet, tended to produce the irresistible feeling of fatigue that came across him now. It was in vain that he tried to battle against it.

Gradually the highwayman's head drooped upon his breast. May's letter fell from his nerveless grasp, and nearly tumbled into the stream. In another moment, Captain Hawk was fast asleep.

Now, indeed, was the time, if his enemies could but have guessed, to come upon him and lead him to prison, and possibly to death; but there he slept calmly and safely, and for the space of three hours no one came along that secret lane to disturb him.

The birds warbled up in the trees and the hedges—and the butterfly shook the dew from its wings, and prepared for another day of sunshine and delight. The wild bee hummed past his ears, and the lowing of cattle in the meadows, came with a faint echo up the old lane.

The rest of Captain Hawk was dreamless, no doubt, until near its termination, and then he thought that he was in the grasp of the officers, and that one of them had hold of his arm, with a grasp that he tried in vain to shake off. The excitement of that dream aroused him, and he fancied that his horse had laid down to rest, although the end of the bridle was still around his master's arm, and that it was in misery that he pulled at it so forcibly as almost to drag Captain Hawk over on to his back.

Through the interstices of the leaves of the old trees, which mingled their topmost branches together overhead, the daylight came streaming down upon the little rivulet, lighting it up with sparkling beauty, and those mild and tempered rays, too, fell upon Captain Hawk and upon his horse, and upon the grass, and the tall weeds, and upon many a wild flower that there grew in fragrance and in beauty, all unseen by the eye of vulgar curiosity.

In truth, it was a sweet and sylvanic kind of scene that was about the highwayman, and one that might well have awakened in his heart very different emotions from those that were in accordance with his wild profession.

If one might judge by the looks of Hawk, at that moment, it would seem as if he had a recollection that there was a time when he was something very different from what the world now reputed him.

With the letter in his hand, he looked into the little stream, and a strange passion crossed his face, that for a moment seemed perfectly demoniac, and then melted down, as it were, to an aspect of great tenderness.

"Poor May!" he said. "Alas, poor May!"

CHAPTER LXVII.

MR. LAMB BRINGS HIS CAREER TO AN END, AND HAWK READS MAY'S LETTER.

OTHER people were roused to action, though, by the dawn of that sweet morning, as well as Captain Hawk the highwayman, and among those other people was Mr. Lamb.

Now, it so happened that that redoubtable worthy had found out how unwilling the officers were to follow him, and he attributed it to the great uncertainty there was of discovering Captain Hawk amid the darkness of such a night.

"I don't think," he said, addressing the officer—"I don't think that you have any very bright hopes of discovering the fellow, just now, notwithstanding all our skill and perseverance."

"Certainly not, sir," replied one of the officers. "You may depend upon it, now that we have missed him, that one of two things has taken place."

"Ah, indeed! and what may they be?"

"Why, he has either gone right away off, and won't stop for five hundred miles, or——"

"Five hundred miles, do you say?"

"Yes, sir, the deuce a one less, or else he is hiding somewhere about here. Now, if he has gone off so far as I have mentioned, perhaps you wouldn't like to go after him, sir?"

"Oh, dear no. Five hundred miles? Oh, no."

"Then, if he is hiding anywhere about here, sir, there's nothing would please him so much as our poking about all the night hunting for him, 'cos, you see, sir, then he would know quite well that we and our cattle would be all done up by the morning, while he would be as fresh, perhaps, as a daisy, and off he would go, laughing at us, while we were fit for nothing better than to go to bed, and our horses to be put up in the first stable that would take them in."

"Well—a-hem!" said Mr. Lamb, "there is something in that."

"A great deal, sir."

"Well, I won't deny but that there may be a great deal, but what do you advise, my men, under these rather harassing and uncomfortable circumstances?"

"Why, sir, of course it is great presumption of us to offer you any sort of advice, considering all your experience."

"Oh, no—no—say on."

"And all your cleverness, sir."

"Oh, don't mention it. Go on, my good man, with what you were about to say. I am a plain man—a very plain man, indeed."

"Well then, sir, we think it is better to put up for the night, as near here as possible, and then when we are all quite fresh in the morning, renew the hunt for Captain Hawk."

"Not a bad idea that," said Mr. Lamb. "We will do it. It strikes me, do you know, that he has either gone far off, or that he is hiding close at hand."

The officers laughed, but they did not think proper to remind Mr. Lamb that that idea was the one that they had only just given to him, which probably it would not have struck him at all, so they let him take what credit for it he could or he chose, and then they set about looking for a halting place for the night.

A road-side inn, the sign-board of which promised in the most specious manner, "Good Entertainment for Man and Beast," was soon found, and the whole party came to a halt, and Mr. Lamb was soon snugly ensconced in the parlour, talking of his great exploits in the thief-taking line, and of how he fully meant to apprehend Captain Hawk in the morning.

The officers, when they found that Lamb was in full talk, quietly dropped off one by one, and getting out their horses, left him at the inn all alone in his glory, and pushed on in pursuit, as they hoped and believed, of Hawk.

They little suspected, though, that, after all, Mr. Lamb was nearer to the prey they so ardently desired to entrap than they were, or they would not have laughed among themselves quite so heartily at the joke of leaving him behind so cleverly as they considered they had done.

In due time, Mr. Lamb retired to rest, leaving orders that he should be called the very first thing in the morning, as soon as there was light enough to see to dress.

The boots at the inn obeyed him to the letter, by nearly pulling him out of bed at such an hour, that he felt full of shivering at the idea of rising; nevertheless he did so, and descended to the lower part of the house, when he soon found out the trick that had been played him by the officers.

Full of indignation, then, and very cold, for there was no fire as yet even in the kitchen of the inn, Mr. Lamb sallied out for a walk, and his good, or ill luck, whichever it may be really termed, took him along the meadow that was on one side of the very lane in which Captain Hawk had passed the night, in company with his gallant steed; and at the very time that Hawk had the letter from May Boyes in his hand, and was lost in the strange reverie that had come over him, Mr. Lamb was glaring at him, as if fascinated, through the branches of a bramble bush.

Terrified at the idea of encountering such a man as Captain Hawk single-handed, and yet delighted at the idea of having himself found him, after being deserted by the officers, Mr. Lamb left the spot cautiously upon his hands and knees, and succeeded in getting back to the inn.

With such a rush that he at once knocked the landlady down flat in the passage, Mr. Lamb made his way into the inn, and shouted out—

"Pitchforks! pitchforks and blunderbusses! Pistols, and knives, and scythes! How many men are there here?"

"Murder!" screamed the landlady, for hearing mention made of such murderous implements, and in such a tone of voice, too, she thought nothing less than she was in the hands of some maniac, who was calling aloud for weapons with which to cut her to pieces. "Help! murder!" she screamed, and she kept up such a drumming with her heels upon the passage floor, that one might suppose a regiment of soldiers had taken possession of the house, and was beating to arms.

The landlord made a rush down the stairs — the ostler flew from the stables—the barmaid screamed; and amid all the din and confusion, Mr. Lamb still roared out—

"A blunderbuss! Who has a blunderbuss?"

The ostler seized him by the throat, and the landlord caught him by one arm.

"Oh, you willin!" said the ostler. "You have killed missus."

"Has he, really, though?" said the landlord. "What a very—Hem! What an inconsiderate man, to be sure!"

"I ain't dead," cried the landlady—"I ain't dead at all."

"Oh, missus, more you isn't!" said the ostler.

"Oh, dear me," sighed the landlord, "I thought there was no such luc—I mean, I thought I was not such an unhappy man as that dreadful bereavement would make me."

"You are all mistaken," cried Mr Lamb. "I don't want to kill the landlady nor anybody else; but if you will all come with me, I will show you where you may lay hold at once of Captain Hawk, the highwayman."

"Captain Hawk?" cried everybody.

"Yes; for whom, dead or alive, there is now a reward of no less a sum than three hundred guineas down!"

"Down!" cried everybody.

"On—the—nail."

The landlady gathered herself to her feet—the landlord ran into the bar parlour and brought out an old musket—the ostler flew to the stable-yard, and returned with a hay-fork—and the barmaid armed herself with a cheese-knife.

"Where is he?" they all cried in chorus—"where is he?"

"Hush!" said Mr. Lamb.

You might then have heard a pin drop, so still was every one, for they expected some disclosure of the fearful proximity of Captain Hawk, and they did not know whether their lives were worth a minute's purchase or not.

"Hush! Be still!"

"We is," said the ostler.

"Silence!—silence!"

"I are," said the barmaid.

"Where is he?" whispered the landlord.

"In the lane."

"The lane!" said everybody in chorus, as nicely as if they had been trained to say it so.

"Yes, a little way down the lane yonder. He don't at all suspect anything. I rather think he is half asleep."

"Catch a weasel asleep," said the ostler.

"But I tell you he is, for I went as close to him as close could be, and he never saw me. He is either asleep, or he is in what you may call a brown study."

"Dear me," said the barmaid, "I thought you said he was in the lane."

"Silence! Come with me, all of you, and when I shoot him you can all rush upon him and seize the body."

"What body?" said every one, drawing back a pace or two.

"Why, his, to be sure, when I have shot him dead."

"Oh!"

"Is he handsome?" said the barmaid.

"Why, yes, to tell the truth, he is about as good-looking a fellow as ever you saw, or as ever you are likely to see."

The barmaid put away the cheese-knife.

"Is he strong?" said the landlord.

"Well, they say he is."

"Then I—that is—no—I rather think I can't go."

"Will he fight?" said the ostler.

"Fight? Won't he. He don't know what fear is, they say."

"Then I do—I've got my stable to look to."

"What, will none of you come?"

"Thank you, no," said the landlord. "You go and put a bullet into his head, and come and tell us you have done so, and then we will all go and help you to carry the body; but what's a part of three hundred guineas to one, if one's head is nearly knocked off one's shoulder, I should like to know?"

"Or one's chesteses has a bullet in it," said the ostler.

MAY'S MESSENGER DELIVERS HER NOTE TO CAPTAIN HAWK.

"Or one's front teeth knocked out," said the barmaid, who was in the habit of making a very lavish display of hers when she opened her mouth.

"I'm afraid you are a set of cowards," said Mr. Lamb. "I only wish I had had my pistols with me when I saw him, I could have popped him off as easy as possible, and I've half a mind to go the same way now, and have a shy at him."

"Ah, do," said the landlord; "go,

sir, and then you will have all the glory, you know, to yourself."

"And all the money," said the ostler.

"And all the danger," said the barmaid, "for I daresay he will shoot you, Mr. What's-your-name, a great deal sooner than you will shoot him, and then how nice you will look, to be sure, won't you?"

"I don't care. I'll go and try; and if he sees me, I'll pretend I was looking for mushrooms in the meadow, or water-cresses by the side of the little stream, and he can but rob me of what I have in my pockets, and I'll take good care that that is not much."

With this valorous resolve, Mr. Lamb looked to the priming of his pistols, and he actually set off alone, with the full intention, not of attempting the capture of Captain Hawk, but of shooting him in a cowardly manner from behind a hedge, and then he could make up what story he liked afterwards, he considered, about the fight he would pretend to have had with the strong and determined highwayman.

It is not to be wondered at now, that this adventure had, to the imagination of Mr. Lamb, a most enticing and seductive appearance. There he was alone, and if he could bring in the dead body of Hawk, and claim the reward and the honour, he felt that his name would be made for ever in the line of business for which he had such a *penchant*.

Vanity, cupidity, and anger against the officers who had deserted him at the inn, all conspired to lead him on, and to blind him to the positive dangers of an enterprise, which, under any other less exciting circumstances, he would have most decidedly have shrunk from, for there was no real courage in Mr. Lamb. If there had been, it would be the capture, and not the assassination of Captain Hawk, that he would have aimed at accomplishing upon that, to him, eventful morning.

Not more than a quarter of an hour had elapsed since Mr. Lamb had made the announcement at the inn of the proximity of the dreaded and celebrated highwayman. The lane was not above five minutes' walk from the house, and when Lamb started to carry out his project, everybody at the inn waited in breathless eagerness for some sound indicative of the completion of the enterprise that he went upon.

To be sure, it did. when they come to think of it, seem a dastardly thing for a man to creep behind a hedge for the purpose of shooting down another, as if he had been a wild beast; but no one made that remark, although, no doubt, the sentiment was naturally present in every bosom.

While these thoughts and feelings were each moment becoming more and more apparent at the inn, Mr. Lamb had reached the stile which led into the meadow from which he had espied Captain Hawk in so wild and uneasy an attitude by the banks of the pretty little streamlet in the lane.

More than once Lamb paused and faltered in his resolution; and the dread of a failure, and it's possible consequences, came across his mind with fearful intensity; but as often the brighter side of the picture presented itself to him, and he fancied he saw the three hundred guineas all glittering before him, and heard the sheriff saying—

"Well, done. Mr. Lamb."

Urged onwards by these considerations, he stooped down among the tall grass, and crept noiselessly towards the spot in the hedge from which he had looked upon the highwayman only so short a time before, and with a desperate kind of resolution now, he held valiantly enough on his way to death or victory.

CHAPTER LXVIII.

CAPTAIN HAWK TAKES A RAPID RIDE TO HOUNSLOW HEATH.

THERE was rather a dense white mist upon the meadow, so that the approaching enemy was well-enough concealed from Captain Hawk, who sat still by the banks of the stream, little suspecting the very imminent danger to which he was about to be exposed from a foe whom he would have held in utter contempt.

We will follow the proceedings of Mr. Lamb.

As he moved the hedge, a tremor came over him, which he began to fear would be fatal to him, as it might, if he could not shake it off, have the effect of bewildering his aim with a pistol at Captain Hawk, and to fire at him and miss him, would be worse than letting him alone completely, so far as he, Lamb, was concerned.

The dew, too, was on the grass in such abundance, that before he had got a third of the way to the hedge, his nether garments were completely soaked, and his feet and legs were as cold as—as charity, we will say, and Heaven knows that that is cold enough.

The teeth of Mr. Lamb began to chatter; for his blood by no means circulated with its wonted briskness through his veins; and by the time he was within a few paces of the hedge, he would have given five of the expected three hundred guineas for a good glass of hot brandy-and-water—ay, that he would; and, perhaps, more than five of them.

Making a painful effort to keep his teeth quiet, for they were very much inclined to play like a pair of castanets, he got a little closer, and finally dropped, quietly enough, into a kind of water-course that was close to the hedge.

Like a snake cautiously leaving its covert, Mr. Lamb now raised his head just a little, and peered through the hedge. There sat Captain Hawk.

Quite a flush of expectation, now that he had it all his own way, came over Lamb, and he drew the pistol that came nearest to his hand carefully from his breast pocket.

Captain Hawk was slowly breaking the seal of the letter from May Boyes; and Lamb heard him quite distinctly say—

"I don't know why I seem to dread reading this letter; and yet it must be read."

The excitement, now, of the moment had had the effect of making the blood of the amateur thief-taker circulate a little more freely; and he fully believed that the life of Captain Hawk, the great highwayman, was in his hands.

One thing was quite evident, and that was, that Hawk had not the shadow of a suspicion that an enemy, armed for his destruction, was so near at hand; for he spread open the letter with all the unconcern regarding every other object but it that can possibly be conceived.

"Alas, poor, poor, May!" he said.

"May?" thought Mr. Lamb. "Dear me, it is June. What does he mean by May, I wonder?"

"Do you, or do you not love me still?" added Hawk.

"Oh, indeed," thought Lamb, as he placed his finger upon the trigger of the pistol, and shutting one eye, took a deliberate aim right in the face of Captain Hawk. "It don't much matter to you, my fine fellow, I rather think, now, whether anybody loves you or not, for your last hour has come. Last hour, do I say? It is your last minute."

"Yes," added Hawk, as his eyes wandered down the page of letter-paper before him. "How well I know that character."

Mr. Lamb knew that one of his pistols was rather hard to pull at the trigger, so he placed two fingers upon it, for he was determined not to fail; and then, just as Captain Hawk held the letter a little closer to his face, to commence the perusal of it in earnest, Mr. Lamb pulled the trigger of his pistol.

Snap! it went, and the pan was only half thrown up by the lock, but the powder did not explode.

Hawk uttered an exclamation, and half rose; but before he could entirely get to his feet, Mr. Lamb, with more presence of mind than any one would have been inclined to give him credit for, pulled back the lock again, and again fired at Hawk; and that time the pistol went off.

"Ha!—ha! I have him!" cried Lamb. "I have blown his head off! Ha!—ha! there he goes!"

"Not at all," said Hawk "It is only my hat; and as for myself, I only slipped in rising upon the wet grass."

"Help!" roared Mr Lamb—"help!"

Hawk took a pistol from his pocket, and levelled it through the hedge in a moment.

"Be quite my dear sir," he said, "you have had your shot, and it is my turn now. If I miss you, I give you my word of honour, you shall have another chance at me."

"Oh, no—no!" cried Lamb. "The devil, no! I was only trying to get some water-cresses to pickle—I mean mushrooms, upon my honour. Murder! Help!—Murder! Fire!"

"I am going to fire," said Hawk. "Can't you be quiet?"

"No—no! Certainly not! Oh, don't—don't! Oh—oh!"

Mr. Lamb now adopted a very curious mode of trying to escape the just vengeance of Captain Hawk, and that was by throwing himself flat upon the meadow, and actually rolling away from the hedge at a great rate.

"Confound the fellow," said Hawk. "I shall miss him now, if I don't mind."

Crack! went the pistol, and with a shout of agony, Mr. Lamb ceased his rolling, and lay quite still upon his back.

"That will do," said Hawk. "He well deserved it. The cowardly rascal, to try to take a man's life from behind a hedge in such a fashion; and a close touch, too, it was. Humph! a couple of bullets right through my hat. By Jove, they must have travelled within a hair's breadth of my skull."

Captain Hawk felt that after the firing and the outcry that had been raised by Mr. Lamb, that lane was no longer a safe abiding place for him, and he put his horse into trim for the road again as quickly as he could, for he had taken the bit from the animal's mouth, in order to enable it to feed all the easier.

Reloading the pistol that he had discharged, then, and placing it in the breast of his waistcoat, so that he could lay hold of it at a moment's notice, Captain Hawk sprang to his saddle, and then being elevated above the hedge, he took a long look over the meadows, as well as he could see for the white mist which still rolled in clouds over the surface.

The only sign of anything human that he saw, was the body of Mr. Lamb, still lying upon its back, precisely as it had rolled after the successful shot that he, Hawk, had sent after it.

"Confound the fool," muttered Hawk, "what did he force me to take his life for?"

It was evident that he, Hawk, was very much annoyed at the necessity that had compelled him, in self-preservation, to fire at Mr. Lamb; but certainly if ever a return shot was, in this world, justifiable, that which had laid the amateur thief-taker upon his back in the meadow was one.

"It's of no use wasting time in idle regrets," said Hawk. "I must be off at once now, for there is no knowing what associates that mad-headed fool may have."

Feeling, then, satisfied that he had May's letter quite safe in one of his pockets, Hawk trotted up the lane towards the high road, and when he reached it, he looked to the right and to the left, with the conviction that he should soon see some enemies.

"No one?" said Hawk. "Can it be possible that this fellow was alone in his enterprise? Did he think himself a match for me? It looks like it."

A trot of a couple of minutes now brought Hawk to the inn, and then he drew up, and called out in a loud voice—

"Hilloa! House—house—house!"

The landlord came to the door with a large dish-cover in his hand, which he kept holding up as a kind of shield between him and Hawk, and moving about in the most ludicrous manner, as he cried out in a lugubrious tone of voice—

"Don't, now—don't. It wasn't any of us. We told him not to go. Oh, don't!"

"Don't what?"

"Don't be a shooting of us, Mr. Hawk. We know you, sir, if you please, and assure you we didn't have anything to do with it. Good-morning, sir. How are you?"

"I suppose you allude," said Hawk, "to the idiot, who lies dead in yonder meadow?"

"Yes, to the idiot. God bless my soul, is he a corpus?"

"A glass of ale!"

"A what, sir? A glass of ale has he turned to?"

"Fool! What do you mean? I order you to bring me a glass of ale. Come, be quick."

"Oh, dear, yes, sir. Wife, a glass of ale for the highwayman—dear me, no, I mean the gentleman."

"A glass of ale, Ann," said the landlady to the barmaid. "A glass of the old ale for the mur—bless my heart, I mean the good-looking gentleman on the brown horse."

"He is good-looking," said the barmaid, as she drew the ale, and brought it out to Captain Hawk.

"And his 'oss is a good 'un," said the ostler.

"Oh, but, sir, if you please," said the landlord, looking very pale. "Is he a corpus? I do so want to know."

"Wherefore?"

"Why, you see, sir, the inquest will be held here, and the jury are sure to drink a pot of ale apiece, at the very least, to say nothing of the coroner, who they do say takes brandy-and-water till he can't take any more."

Captain Hawk drank the ale, and then he said—

"If you were to ask me if a man who came skulking behind a hedge to murder me, has received the reward of his folly, I can tell you, that I have every reason to believe he has."

"The reward!" cried the landlady. "Oh, good, Mr. Highwayman, you don't mean to say he will get the reward, after all?"

"If he does," said Hawk, "it will be in another world. Good morning to you all."

With this Captain Hawk trotted off a little way, but a thought struck him that he should like to know who it was with whom he had had the contest in the lane, and he hastily returned, and cried out to the landlord, who stood at the door of the inn, looking the picture of consternation—

"Who was it that assaulted me in the lane? You seem to know all about it here."

"Oh, sir, it was Mr. Lamb, and we told him not to go all for to kill you, if you please, Mr. High——Oh, dear, I mean, sir. But, you see, he would do it."

"You mean to say he would try and sacrifice his own worthless life in the horrid attempt to murder me? for murder it would have been if ever there was a murder done in this world. You call him Lamb, but the part he acted was that of a tiger or a fox."

"And a goose, sir, if you please," said the barmaid.

"Just so," said Hawk.

Once more he turned his horse's head from the door of the inn, and galloped off at a rate that soon left it and its wondering and terrified inhabitants far enough behind him.

The morning had now made considerable progress, and the birds were singing merrily from the trees and bushes that lined the road, while each moment the sunshine was getting broader and more powerful, and the mists that had obscured the low-lying ground had completely cleared away and vanished before the light and heat of the suns rays.

Captain Hawk halted, and took from his pocket May's letter. His hand trembled, as he held it, and he read as follows—

"Boyes Hall.

"Gerald Clifton,—You are saved from the death which all but myself considered as your inevitable doom. To you, doubtless, it is still a mystery as regards the how that you were so saved. Let it continue one. My first request of you is, by the memory of happier days, that you will not attempt to penetrate that mystery.

"Yes, Gerald Clifton—for by that name, as being one more associated with your character as a gentleman, I prefer addressing you—you are free; but it is for you to make a use of that freedom which shall really make it a good act, or an abuse of it, which shall make the regret and pain of the being who procured it for you.

"There is a future in this world even for you, Gerald Clifton. You are young, and although, in the sight of God and man, your crimes are great, let us hope and believe that much may yet be done to entitle you to mercy, where mercy is infinite.

"This is no time to carp at words, or to be nice and chary about sentences. I loved you. You will perceive that I speak in the past tense. Let that be significant to you. I loved a gentleman, and a man of honour, named Gerald Clifton. I can have no feelings in common with Hawk, the highwayman

"Repent!—repent! Let prayer and repentance go some way towards making your peace with Heaven—let your future life be different from the past; and that you may earn the mercy of your Creator, and so disarm his sterner justice, will be ever the prayer of "M. B."

Captain Hawk read this letter twice, and then the blood slowly mounted to his cheeks and brow.

"She loves me not," he said.

With a sudden rush, the blood retreated to his heart again, leaving him ghastly pale; and then he burst into a wild laugh, as he crumbled the letter up in his hand and cried—

"Yes, she loves me still. Far easier would it be to quench the fire of a volcano than to put out the love that has once warmed such a heart as that of May Boyes. Were she to swear to the contrary, I would still say that she loves me still. In the past tense does she speak?—That past will be ever present to her, and she will strive in vain to forget it."

He thrust the letter into the breast of his apparel, and giving the horse an impetus forward, he galloped on at frantic speed for about a mile; then suddenly drawing up, he said—

"So, she would dismiss me with a sermon, would she? But no, she shall not. I love her now as I never loved her. I will go to Boyes Hall to-night!"

Animated by this resolve, Captain Hawk felt that nothing human could stop him in carrying it out, and he tested the powers of his steed at a fearful rate.

Perhaps he would hardly have liked even then to confess to himself how deeply May Boyes' letter had affected him. Those expressions in which she had spoken of the impossibility of one such as she was thinking of such as he was, had rankled in his heart.

"I will see her," he cried. "Yes, I will see her, if I die for the attempt! I will see her, and show her that she loves me still."

CHAPTER LXIX.

MAY BOYES GIVES CAPTAIN HAWK SOME GOOD AND GENTLE ADVICE.

It certainly was pride and mortified vanity that now actuated the proceedings of Captain Hawk, more than any other feeling. We doubt if even they had not had the effect of for a time overcoming the affection which, to tell the honest truth, he really had for May Boyes.

If ever he had loved any one with a passion approaching to what true love should be, that one was May; and if anything is more hard to learn than another, it certainly is that kind of scorn from the object of one's affection, which takes the shape that it had done from May to Captain Hawk.

"Alas!" he cried, "she thinks herself far above me, does she? She thinks that she would only demean herself by entertaining even a lingering feeling of regret for Hawk the highwayman; and she will delude herself with the thought that she has shaken herself free from the infection of my love; but I will prove to her the contrary before the dawn of another day."

If Hawk had but paused to contemplate the difficulties and the dangers of the enterprise upon which he was bound, surely even he would have paused before persevering so madly in it; but he did not pause.

On—on he went across the country at a rapid pace, making his way as though he were riding a steeple-chase, and was bound to overcome every obstacle in his way, rather than go round it, towards Boyes Hall.

In a little time his horse began to partake of the wild spirit of its master, and the creature darted onwards, with distended nostrils and flashing eyes, at a prodigious pace.

How long it took him to reach Ealing Common, Captain Hawk had not the slightest idea, nor will we detain the reader from the scene that took place at Boyes Hall upon that night by any details of the minor proceedings of Captain Hawk. Let it suffice that we point him out to the reader at the hour of midnight, half hidden in a little cluster of trees that were in the immediate vicinity of Boyes Hall.

Certainly by this time a little reflection had come to the aid of the highwayman. We do not mean to say that he had given up his design of having an interview with May; but he had cooled down concerning it so far that, while he did not waver in the least in the resolve, he was better able to consider the best mode of carrying it out.

Before, however, we proceed to detail wha means Captain Hawk took to compass his views, we will take a peep into the interior of Boyes Hall, and see in what condition the family, with which we are by this time so well acquainted, has been left, by the really extraordinary events of the trial at the Old Bailey, which had terminated so contrary to all expectation in the acquittal of Captain Hawk.

To say that poor Sir John Boyes was thoroughly and completely astounded by the events of the day in London, is to say but little regarding the real state of that gentleman's faculties. He had doubts, not only concerning his own material existence, but concerning the fact that there was such a place as Boyes Hall at all, or such a person in the world as Captain Hawk, the highwayman.

At supper, Sir John was unusually sententious.

"I would only wish to remark," he said, "concerning the seeming circumstances that have taken place at the Old Bailey, if there is an Old Bailey, that I shall never again have sufficient faith in events to take upon myself to say what will be and what will not be, for after the most careful thought upon this extraordinary——"

"A little of the breast, if you please father," said Ratchley.

Sir John paused, and looked first at the cold capon before him, and then at his son.

"For May I asked," said Ratchley.

"Are you aware," said Sir John, as he directed a circle in the air with the carving-knife, as though he were a necromancer, and was making some spell for the enchantment of the family. "Are you aware of who I am?"

"Oh, yes, father."

"Then, sir, I am a goose!"

They all looked at Sir John.

"I repeat, I am a goose—if——"

"Oh!" said everybody.

"If I allow anybody to interrupt me, while I am making a remark; for when I make a remark, I may say that it really amounts to an observation."

"I beg your pardon," said Ratchley. "I only——"

"Si—lence!"

"Very good, father."

"What was I saying, Philippa, my child, when the male scion of our house endeavoured to convert me into a goose?"

"Something about the acquittal of the highwayman, father."

"True—true. I was about to say that after careful thought, and some slight remembrance of what the old author's think and say about such things, that acquitting such a man as Captain Hawk, or Gerald Clifton, whichever may be his name, is equivalent to letting him off."

"Just so, father," said Ratchley.

"Call Anthony."

"I am here, Sir John," said the butler, making a very low bow sideways from Sir John's chair—"I am here, quite at your service, Sir John."

"Oh, very good," said Sir John, giving Anthony a crack on the top of the head with the knob of silver at the end of the carving-fork, as he gave his left arm a flourish.

"Oh, lor!" said Anthony—"oh!"

"What is the matter?"

"Why, Sir John, you—you rather hit me with the handle of the carving-fork, you see, Sir John, and it ain't very soft."

"Never mind."

"Thank you, Sir John. It's raised a bump."

"I believe, when I say never mind, if there were twenty bumps, why, there is an end of the business. It was an accident, Anthony. But I was about, as you are an old and valued servant, Anthony——"

"Yes, Sir John."

"Si—lence! I was about to ask you a question."

Anthony rubbed the bump on his head, and bowed again; but he took good care to keep a sharp eye on the carving-fork, as, for all he knew to the contrary, the prongs might come next, and they would be anything but pleasant.

"Anthony," added Sir John, "am I awake?"

"Awake, Sir John? Oh, dear, yes, sir, if you please."

"Then you do not think, Anthony, that the proceedings of this day are a dream?"

"Oh, dear, no, Sir John."

"Very good."

Sir John rose with great dignity, and waving his hand, he said—

"Those who have a desire to go to bed may do so now, as soon as to them it shall seem proper. I am about now to retire into that *sanctum sanctorum*, the library, where, in a state of learned leisure, I may be permitted to consult the old authors with regard to the remarkable circumstances that have occurred touching this highwayman, Captain Hawk, and things in general."

Nobody was in the least inclined to stop Sir John Boyes, so he left the apartment, fully impressed with the idea that he had made a sensation in the family, and convinced every one of the profundity of his intellectual acquirements.

Happy Sir John Boyes! What a dreadful thing it would be for you to be just a little wiser than you are—what an unhappy wretch might you become if that excellent conceit were to be by any means taken from you! Let us hope that such will never be the case in this world.

Ratchley Boyes seemed to have upon his mind an uneasy kind of suspicion that May was in some way or another connected with the mystery of the acquittal of Captain Hawk; and yet it was quite impossible that he could come to any positive conclusion upon that subject, so he was condemned to all the torturing suspense which a vexatious suspicion is sure to get up in the mind.

As for May herself, she looked calm and unimpassioned. The great excitement that she had laboured under, and which had lent the glow of a transcient colour to her cheeks for the last few days was over, and nothing now was more likely than that she would subside into a state of dreamy indifference to the world and its concerns.

Such a state of mind, if indeed May Boyes were doomed to relapse into it, was just that which in all probability might end in a kind of religious mania.

Let us hope that superstition, with its benumbing influence, will not succeed in the destruction of that pure and beautiful young spirit!

"I will watch my sister," said Ratchley to himself, "I will watch her with the eye of Argus. It is a thousand pities that that bold bad man is again let loose upon the society to which he has already done such grievous wrong, and so, feeling that the remembrance of him may not be yet extinct in the mind of my sister, I shall but do my duty to her and to myself by watching her well."

May had no idea that such suspicions existed in the mind of her brother, or she would have trembled at the possibility of another collision between him and Captain Hawk. It was well that she had no such thought, for she had sorrows enough to contend against without that as an additional one.

Ratchley had to engage Philippa in the self-imposed task of keeping watch upon the actions of May; and although he found her by no means averse to doing so, yet he found likewise that in some way the whole train of events had taken such a hold of her imagination, that she was too terrified to be very useful or vigilant.

"Ratchley," she said, "I don't know how it is, but I have a dreadful fear that May's mind is not what it used to be."

Ratchley shuddered.

"You don't mean, Philippa, that—that—you cannot mean that you think her senses in any way shattered?"

Philippa only answered by her tears.

This was a new affliction for Ratchley; but, notwithstanding the prognostications of Philippa and his fears, such was not the case. May Boyes might, and, no doubt, did suffer much, but her vigorous intellect remained yet intact and perfect.

HAWK, ON LEAVING NEWGATE, WARNED OF THE ATTEMPT TO RECAPTURE HIM.

CHAPTER LXX.

CAPTAIN HAWK INVADES BOYES HALL IN THE DEAD OF THE NIGHT.

Passing now over a short space of time, and the various events that had occurred to Captain Hawk from the period when he left the bar of the Old Bailey, acquitted of the heinous offence laid to his charge, to that moment when he paused by the cluster of trees close to Boyes Hall, we once more turn attention to him and to his proceedings.

The night had turned dark and stormy, and a cold wind was blowing from the north, bringing with it now and then, as it encountered clouds from the south, that with an undercurrent of air swept across the country, a sufficiently low temperature to convert their contents from rain to a kind of sleet, that was most penetrating and distressing.

The wind itself, too, whistled mournfully among the old trees, as though it would warn Captain Hawk, who had taken shelter among them, to forego the enterprise upon which he had come to that well remembered spot.

In vain, though, did the elements attempt to place any barrier to the passions of that bold, bad spirit; he felt his pride and his self-love wounded, and he could not make up his mind to leave the spot.

Suddenly he heard a footfall among the trees a few paces from where he was, and he bent his head low upon the saddle of his horse to listen more accurately to the sound.

It was quite clear that some one was approaching, with very cautious steps, the spot upon which he, Hawk, had come to a halt, so he moved closer to the huge trunk of an old chestnut-tree that was within a few paces of him, and he placed his hand upon one of his pistols.

Hawk then heard a voice, which gave utterance to an oath or two, and then said—

"I wonder, now, if any of the people about the old crib they call Boyes Hall can tell me which way the captain has gone? Bother take him, I didn't think I cared half enough for him, after all, to come hunting for him in this way, but still I should like to know what's become of him, for they say the troopers were hard upon his track after he left the Bailey."

Captain Hawk knew that voice from the first. It belonged to his confederate at the hut, whither he now and then repaired to rest both himself and his horse, and where the reader has already been a witness to some strange scenes.

It is hard to say whether Hawk was at all touched or not by the rough kind of devotion which this man had towards him. If he were, he was very successful in effectually concealing such a weakness, for that, no doubt, was what he would, to himself, have called it.

"If I could only, now,' added the man, "fall in with any of the servants, late though it is, I daresay I should be able to get some news of him. Ah, he's a bad one, but still I don't see why I should desert him, when all the world turns its back upon him; and I won't, neither."

Hawk was debating in his own mind whether this man was likely to be an assistance or an hindrance to him in what he was about to attempt; but at length he decided that it was much more likely, inasmuch as he had him entirely under his own control, that he would be the former, so he called out to him in a low, but clearly defined voice—

"What would you with me? I am here."

"Oh, lor!" cried the man, "that's the captain, as sure as fate."

"Silence!"

"Yes, captain; but how are you? Well, I am glad to see you—that is to say, I don't see you, but I have heard you. Couldn't you swear a little, to let a fellow be quite sure that it's you, captain?"

"Go to the devil!"

"That's right. Go it—come it again, captain! Why, you are all right, after all. Well, this is a comfort. It does one's heart good, now, to be sworn at a little in the old way. I did think that the troopers had been just one too many for you, captain, especially after such a narrow squeak as I heard you had of it at the Old Bailey. How are you?"

"Hold your row. I am here, and as usual. Let that suffice for you. How came you here?"

"To look for you."

"Pshaw! You might have been better employed. Are you armed?"

"Rather."

"Then mind my horse. I am going to Boyes Hall, and it will be better that I go on foot. Do not stir from this place upon any account. I will come to you as soon as I conveniently can."

"To Boyes Hall, captain?"

"Yes—and why not? When did I give you the liberty of questioning my actions? If I choose to visit her—if I choose to risk my neck again—to—to——"

"Ah, captain, I thought as much. You won't let that young creature alone when you might. Come, now, don't get into a passion with me. It ain't no sort of good, and you know that as well as I do. You have but one real friend in the world, and that is the one as is talking to you now, and I say to you, you have done mischief enough already at Boyes Hall."

"Villain!"

"Go it. I mean to have my say, for all that. You can have yours afterwards. I don't suppose but what you will take your own course, in spite of all I can say to you, and the more's the pity; but do be a little human."

"Are you mad?"

"Oh, dear, no—a long way off; but I have seen a something of this affair, and I have heard a good deal more, and I tell you it isn't a manly thing to try to make a wreck of a young creature who, if she falls at all, falls because she loves you, and so ought to be saved, in a way of speaking, by you on that very account. She is a young lady—mild and gentle. I have seen her—she is like some young flower that's been out in a frosty night—she will never be herself again; and so I say, captain, let her be—let her be!"

Twice Hawk opened his mouth to speak—and they were words of passion that he meant to utter—but he could not do so. There is, after all, something so sacred in truth, that however unpalatable it may be, it bears down all opposition; and so, with all the will to be violent and cruel, Captain Hawk found that if he tried to assume the appearance of passion, it would be quite a failure with him.

"Stop," he said, in a low voice. "Say no more. I will now answer you. Say no more."

"That's right, captain. I won't. I only want you to know that it is in good feeling to you, as well as to the poor young thing in yonder great house, that I do speak."

"That is enough."

"Then you ain't going to blow up like a powder magazine?"

"No—no."

"You ain't saving yourself up to come out with a burst that will be enough to take a fellow's head off?"

"I am not. You hear me speak, and by my voice you can gather that I am quite calm and collected. Is it not so?"

"It sounds so."

"And it is. Now, I am not at all angry with you for what you have said, and I will satisfy you by telling you, that it is to bid a last farewell to May Boyes that I am here to-night. It is to tell her, that as regards me she is free as air; and that, for the time that is to come, she must think of me no more. That is my errand. Does that explanation of its motive satisfy you, my old friend?"

"It does."

"Then once more we understand each other. You have said, that you believe yourself the only real friend I have in all the world. I believe it likewise."

"We won't say any more about that, captain."

"Oh, yes, but we will. I want to let you know, once and for all, that I don't quite forget all your devotion to me. I know well, that I am, at times, wild and hasty in what I say and do, but—"

"Now, I won't hear another word, captain."

"Well—well, I—"

"Don't, now don't. I am very sorry I spoke at all to you about it, and the fact is, I shan't feel quite satisfied that all's right between us again till you have pretty well d——d me, and, perhaps thrown something at my head."

Captain Hawk smiled sadly, and if his faithful, though rough follower could have seen that smile, he would have seen one of those captivating graces that had so largely helped to ensnare the heart of poor May Boyes; for nothing could be sweeter, or more full of tender softness, than the smile of Captain Hawk.

How strange it was, that with such graces as one would think only compatible with the higher attributes of human nature, he should be what he was!

"Very well," he said. "Wait for me here. If you should hear the discharge of a pistol-shot, try to make your way in the direction it comes from, for it will be a signal from me to you that I want the horse—you understand that?"

"Perfectly."

"Good-night, then, till we meet again."

Hawk had dismounted, and for the last few moments he had been, by the touch, carefully examining a very small, but exquisitely made pair of pistols which he had with him, and which would, if occasion required, both go into one waistcoat-pocket. He well knew that such arms were of little use at any distance, but in a house, or in any close encounter, they were certainly to be depended upon, as they never missed fire.

Of course, we need hardly say that at that time the most highly-finished fire-arms were on the old flint and steel principle, as the percussion cap, with all its manifold advantages, was not, as the song says, invented "till arter that;" so that the weapons of Captain Hawk were upon that, now, old-fashioned construction.

For the rest, he had found them concealed in the hollow of a tree close to that spot, where, closely wrapped up in a skin of chamois leather, he had left them previous to his arrest for the murder of Judge Holme.

The grounds of Boyes Hall, although not by any means extensive, were exceedingly diversified, so that there was abundance of opportunity for any one not well acquainted with their intricacies to lose his way in them. In the case of Hawk, however, such a contingency was not at all likely to arise, as during his visits to the Hall as its honoured guest, Gerald Clifton, he had made quite a study of the place.

There was not a tree—a shrub—a rustic seat, or a shady arch, or a statue in the gardens that was to him unknown; so he vaulted over the oak fence with the most perfect conviction that he should find no difficulty either in approaching or in retreating from the old mansion.

All was profoundly still in the gardens, and not a light was perceptible from any window of the house.

CHAPTER LXXI.

CAPTAIN HAWK AUDACIOUSLY BREAKS INTO BOYES HALL IN THE NIGHT.

The reader is already, from the various incidents of the story, perfectly well acquainted with the premises which called Sir John Boyes master. The terrace which ran along the garden front of the house, and from which a view of the whole of the ornamental portion of the grounds could be obtained, has been more than once mentioned.

It was towards this terrace that Hawk now made his stealthy way through the garden.

He knew perfectly well the situation of the sleeping room that was appropriated to the use of May Boyes, and although it did not actually open on to the terrace, yet he thought that the easiest mode of obtaining an entrance to the mansion would be at that part of it, as there were some seven or eight long windows reaching from the ceilings of a couple of the principal rooms right down to the marble flooring of the terrace.

Once only as he approached the house Hawk thought that he saw the flash of a light past one of the windows, but he had his doubts whether he was not deceived in thinking that it was a light, as often in intense darkness, when the imagination is excited, such gleams of seeming light will appear momentarily before the eyes, having no other origin than in a disturbed brain.

"It was surely nothing," said Hawk, as he continued his course, and soon ascended the steps of the terrace, and stood crouchingly among the rarer plants which were ranged upon it opposite to the long windows already mentioned.

After now listening with most intense attention for about five minutes, with his ear close to one of the windows, Hawk made up his mind that nothing indicative of life was stirring within the house; so, he at once, after coming to that conclusion, proceeded to endeavour to effect an entrance to one of the rooms opening from, or upon the terrace.

"I have two missions here," he told

himself. "The one is to ask May if she can explain to me the mystery of the evidence which came forward to my rescue at the trial; and the other is to leave her free for ever from all remembrance of our attachment. If she can scorn me, it is fitting that I should return to her the allegiance of her love."

No doubt, Hawk fully believed that such were the objects of his going to Boyes Hall; but it is no uncommon thing for people to grossly deceive themselves with regard to their own impulses of action; and in this particular, Captain Hawk was undergoing that species of self-deception without a doubt.

By the aid of a diamond ring which he wore, he succeeded in cutting away a large pane of glass from one of the windows, expecting to find but little opposition from the shutters within; but in that he was disappointed; for the moment he shook the shutters, ever so lightly, a bell, which was attached to it by a spring, began to ring, and he started back in alarm.

"Curses on it!" he muttered, as the bell ceased its light tones, for it had only been gently shaken. "Curses on it, what is the meaning of this extraordinary caution? I never heard of such before, when I have slept at the hall."

Captain Hawk, if he had given the matter a little reflection, would, no doubt, have come to the conclusion that he had himself to thank for the extraordinary precaution taken at Boyes Hall to keep off midnight depredators. It was the fear of his exploits, and the talk of the murder of Judge Holme, which had sufficiently alarmed Lady Boyes to induce her to order that all the long disused precautions should be taken for the protection of the mansion that its resources afforded.

Hence was it that doors were double locked, that for years had not been locked at all—windows were barred across that had been innocent of such suspicious appendages for Heaven knows how long; and the old butler had found that bells were adapted to be hung at the backs of the shutters of the windows opening on to the terrace; and so, after a long hunt in a huge lumber-room, the bells were found, and duly restored to use.

Captain Hawk was rather nonplussed at such an unexpected state of things.

"Can they have any suspicions," he whispered, "that I might pay a visit to the hall? Oh, no—no. That is too wild a supposition. Of all places else, they might well suppose that I should avoid this, where I am so well known, that if even any domestic were to see me, my destruction would be certain."

After a little thought, Hawk resolved all the unusual fastenings of Boyes Hall to the true reason—namely, the recent alarm which his own exploits had created in the neighbourhood; but such an assurance was very far from facilitating his progress.

That any attempt now to enter by one of those windows would be fatal to concealment, he could not but feel; so he gave up that part of his project.

"I must try another plan," he said. "There is a balcony to the window of May's apartment, and there can be but little difficulty in climbing to it. It is by that window that I must seek her, and I will do so if it involve the loss of my life."

Captain Hawk spoke of the attempt involving the loss of his life, because he had made up his mind that he would not be taken alive, and that if affairs got really desperate, he would resist to such an extent as must either save him by the dispersion of his foes, or kill him by their perseverance in the attempt to make a prisoner of him. It was only the strong passions that had brought him to that house that could at all have engendered such feelings as these were.

Hastily, then, leaving the terrace, he made his way round the northern angle of the mansion; and treading rather recklessly through flower-beds that were in his direct route, he soon gained that clump of rich vegetation from the shadow of which, upon a former occasion, he had looked up to the chamber of May Boyes, and seen that piece of beauty and innocence in some of the anguish which her acquaintance with him had entailed upon a heart that should have known as yet nothing but sunshine.

The profound stillness of the mansion and its grounds would have been something appalling to one less used to the solitudes of nature at all hours than Captain Hawk. It seemed as though the very air had become stagnated, and as though even insect life had ceased while that man trod the soft leafy glades of the garden upon his sinful errand.

It was a sinful errand, inasmuch as it was to add further disquietude to a soul already sufficiently oppressed by him, and by his acts.

A very few minutes now sufficed to enable Hawk to reach that portion of the old garden which was immediately below the window of May's apartment.

The balcony, although it was one of considerable size, could hardly be seen in the darkness, and it was only after looking at it very intently for awhile that a dim and wavy outline of it could be seen against the house.

"Yes," muttered Hawk. "This is the spot. Yonder is the window from which I saw her upon a former occasion, and be it my task now to clamber to her presence."

Beneath the balcony, and straggling right up to it, was a rose-tree of great beauty and ancient growth. The long young green stems of the plant intwined themselves within the balustrade of the balcony, but the older wood was firmly fastened to the wall, and was of considerable thickness.

The only chance that Captain Hawk had of reaching the balcony was by the aid of the rose-tree.

Deeply he congratulated himself that the small noise the bell attached to the shutters he had moved had failed to have the effect of alarming any one in the house.

The soft stillness was quite sufficient to convince him that there was no suspicion of such a presence as his in the place; and he cautiously now began to try the strength of the rose-tree to bear him.

There was one awkward discovery, though, that Hawk soon made, and that was, that every rose has its thorns, for when he tried to secure a hold of the ancient tree, he got his hands lacerated after a fashion that was anything but agreeable.

By the aid of a thick pair of riding gloves that he had with him, he got over this difficulty to some extent, however; and finding that the thick stem of the tree would bear his weight with ease, he cautiously climbed until he got a clutch at the balcony.

After that, his course was easy enough.

The highwayman was young and agile, and to get a good hold with even one hand was to set the question at rest as regarded drawing himself up into the balcony. With great ease and dexterity he vaulted now over the balustrade, and safely alighted close to the window of the room in which, if no changes had taken place, May Boyes slept, or where she lay without sleeping, as she was of late but too apt to do; for gentle sleep,

"Nature's great comforter,"

will not visit the eyelids of the wretched.

Now it was that Hawk felt would be required all his caution, and all his dexterity. If, upon the first impulse, May Boyes were to raise an alarm, the pobability is, that he would be captured, or, at all events, he would have to effect a hasty and an inglorious retreat at once.

If, however, he could make her aware of his presence, and get over the first moment of her surprise without a scream, he flattered himself that then he would have nothing to fear.

We shall see how far the calculations of Captain Hawk were verified by the facts as they occurred.

The window, as was the case with all those of the mansion that opened upon balconies, or on the terrace of the garden, was a French one; so that it was likely, upon its hinges, to open with much less noise than as if a harsh, and, perhaps, musical sash had to be lifted.

And now, carefully, Hawk looked and felt for the fastening of one of the glass doors, as they might be called; and by a gentle violence he soon found that nothing would suffice to enable him to open the window but to get his hand within it; and that could only be done by the removal of one of the squares of glass in the lower part of it.

The diamond ring that the highwayman wore now came in again handily, and the brittle matter yielded to the touch of the harder substance. With a slight clatter, falling faintly upon his boots, and partly upon the flooring of the balcony. the greater part of one of the panes of glass dropped from the fame-work.

Hawk listened, with an attention that was positively painful, to hear if that noise had the effect of alarming May Boyes; but all continued still.

"She sleeps!" he said.

In another moment he had slipped his hand through the broken pane of glass, and unfastened the window, noiselessly.

CHAPTER LXXII.

CAPTAIN HAWK IS IN GREAT DANGER, IN BOYES HALL, BUT IS SAVED.

The Venetian blind attached, within, to the window was still between him and the room.

Captain Hawk conjectured, and not without reason, too, that any attempt to move that blind would be attended by a noise, which would have the effect of startling May, provided she was really sleeping in that apartment.

"Would it not be better," he said, "to call to her in a tone of voice, which while it sufficed to awaken her, would not have the effect of creating alarm?"

This seemed to be a rational course; and yet the dread of arousing her suddenly, before, perhaps, she could have any opportunity of knowing who it was that, at such an hour, disturbed her slumbers, made him pause before he could possibly make up his mind to such a rational course, and apparently the best that he could, under the circumstances, pursue, as it seemed to be at the moment.

At length, with an increasing conviction that that would be the safest course, after slightly touching the blind, and finding that it was inclined to make all the noise that might be anticipated from it, Captain Hawk ventured, in a low, but distinct whisper, for he wanted her to recognise his tones, to say—

"May—May Boyes!"

There was no reply to the call, nor the least noise within the chamber to lead to the impression that the tones of his voice had fallen upon the ears of the sleeper.

The maddening idea, now, took possession of Captain Hawk, that it was just possible May might not be sleeping in that apartment, and that all the pains, and all the anxieties he had taken, and endured, might be in vain upon the occasion. This idea was just one of those that, as soon as it was at all started, was sure to increase, in likelihood, with each passing moment; so that his anxiety, and his dread that such might be the fact, induced him to disregard all noise that the Venetian blind might make, and to move it at once for the purpose of making his way into the chamber.

We do not mean to say that he removed the blind recklessly. On the contrary, he was as cautious with it as he could possibly be; but yet it would rattle a little.

Despite the rattling, however, Captain Hawk stepped into the chamber of the mansion, which he believed to be in the occupation of May Boyes.

Upon finding his way, then, right into the room, he made a discovery, which before he had not noticed, and that was the existance of a night-lamp in the room; but it was placed behind a screen, so that a broad black shadow was cast all over the apartment, and it was only by a ring of white light upon the ceiling above the lamp that he, Hawk, could see that it was there at all.

That circumstance, however, at once put an end to any doubts he might have had regarding the fact of whether the chamber were occupied or not. There only now remained for him to ascertain if the occupant was May Boyes or any other of the family at the hall.

Now Captain Hawk could hear distinctly the low, regular breathing of some one who slept in the old fashioned bed that was in the centre of the room, and his own breath came only by sudden and agitated starts from his lips as a whirl of fears and hopes crossed his mind regarding the sort of reception that May Boyes would give to him at such an hour, and in such a place.

"If she really loves me still," he thought, "she can forget and forgive anything; but if she loves me not, here is an offence which will at once anger her and efface all tender recollection or regret concerning me from her mind."

Which did Hawk wish should be the case? Oh, if he had not the generosity to wish for the happiness of May and for the securing to her of that peace of mind he had robbed her of, the latter would have been the state of things he would have wished for; but as it was he was not so generous.

No, Captain Hawk yet clung to the hope that, despite all that had happened—despite the fact that he knew must be so well known, now, beyond all dispute to May, that he was a highwayman—despite her strong suspicion, if she did not entertain it as a fact, that he was a murderer, she would not be able to obliterate her former affection for him, but would yet yield to a love which he had some reason to believe, from former experiences, would overcome all reason, and set all propobility at defiance.

Then there was the hope that lay at the bottom of the heart of Captain Hawk, and yet he had formed no precise designs for the future. The probability is that if he had felt assured she loved him still he would never have come upon his present perilous and indefinable expedition.

Of such incongruous thoughts and feelings, and of such apparent contradictions is human passions composed that difficulty and danger appear to be the essential conditions of the love of some persons, and with ease and safety that specious kind of love vanishes at once.

All in the house was so profoundly still that there could be no question at all of the fact that every one had retired for the night, so that even, in the event of an alarm, it was hardly to be supposed that a bold, active spirit like Captain Hawk's would not have ample time to carry itself out of danger.

With this feeling he got more calm and composed.

"Now," he whispered to himself, "now to ascertain beyond a doubt that it is May who sleeps on yonder bed."

So intensely shadowy was the bed, in consequence of the old heavy brocade curtains being nearly all drawn close, that, although Captain Hawk had crept noiselessly to the side of it, and actually saw that some one lay sleeping, he could only see the dim outline of a form, and could by no means take upon himself to say that it was May's.

"I must have the light," he whispered.

This was perilous, but still it was the only course that he could consistently pursue, if he meant at all to persevere in his object; so he strode lightly to the screen, behind which was the light, and soon possessed himself of the little lamp, with which he again approached the side of the antique bedstead upon which the sleeper lay.

Hawk shaded the lamp with his left hand as he approached, so that no sudden effect should be produced upon the eyes of the sleeper before he should be able to look upon those eyes, and assure himself to whom they belonged.

The soft, low breathing continued, now, to assure him that, as yet, there was no alarm, and he held the light between the curtains, so that it shed a subdued gleam upon the bed, and there lay May Boyes.

Yes, one glance was sufficient for Captain Hawk to recognise that once joyous, but still beautiful face; but the beauty was of a different aspect to what it had been only one short year before that time.

Then the bloom of health had rested upon those cheeks, and the soul's pure serenity and joy sparkled in the eyes. Now poor May was wan and pale, and even as she slept the long lashes of her sweet eyes were damp with tears.

The light did not awaken her as Hawk held it.

One arm was without the bedclothes, lying like a piece of pure marble in its stillness, and the little hand was half open only. Suddenly she moved slightly.

Hawk shaded the light again, and all was still as before.

It was at that moment that a thought did cross him, that it would be better, and nobler, far, of him to leave that fair, and, as yet, innocent girl to the griefs she had already had, than to add to them by his ill-timed presence; and he did move two steps from the side of the bed. He had turned his head

THE LIEUTENANT IRRITATES HAWK TO FIGHT A DUEL.

aside, and then he looked again, and as he saw the sweet, pale face, and the classically chisseled lips, he felt enraptured more than ever he had been with the rare and exquisite beauty of the young creature, of whose happiness he had made such a wreck.

"By Heavens," he whispered, "she is matchless!"

He must have uttered the words in

something above a whisper, for as the last one passed his lips, May uttered a long-drawn sigh, and just as Hawk shaded the light again with his hand, she opened her eyes.

Now, although by shading his light he kept the glare of it from her face, he sent it all on his own, and when May looked up she could not but see the countenance of Captain Hawk clearly and distinctly before her.

"May," he said, in an accent of despairing affection. "May—my own beautiful May! It is I—your Gerald Clifton—loving you as he ever loved you!"

May half rose up in the bed, and clasping her hands together, she uttered one piercing shriek, that it was quite out of the question to suppose could do otherwise than awake every soul in the mansion.

"D———n!" cried Hawk.

Another shriek from May ran into the echo of the former one, and Hawk absolutely reeled before the stunning, ringing cadence of those sounds.

"Hold, by Heaven!" he cried. "You wish to murder me, May?"

"A dream—a dream!" she cried. "A horrible vision!"

"No--I tell you, no. It is I, Gerald Clifton! I came to ask you to forgive me all the past, and to promise to leave you for ever if you did so; and for the future to learn to love virtue for your sake; but by the alarm you have given you have killed me."

"Oh, no—no!"

"But I say, yes. You have done so, and Heaven only knows who else may fall in the encounter that will now take place in this room. Do you not hear me?"

"I do. Fly, wretched man—fly and leave this place—I charge you at once; Do not let your blood be upon the heads of my kindred!"

"I cannot. I must defend myself."

"Would you do more murder?"

"If goaded to desperation I will turn upon my foes—Now I hear them coming!"

A confused rushing of feet, and banging of doors through the mansion was come plainly upon Captain Hawk's ears.

"Lost—lost!" cried May.

"Who is lost?" said Hawk, catching at the hope that she must turn, and that it was for him she wept so bitterly.

"I am lost," she said. "Who will suppose that even you could be so wicked as to come here without my cognisance? It is I who am lost. Oh, wretched man! Was it not enough that you converted my youth into a barren solitude, that you made me the victim of an attachment that—oh, God! what am I saying? Surely I can die—I can die!"

The noise in the mansion increased each moment, and the trampling of feet came nearer.

"Listen to me," said Hawk. "I came here upon a desperate errand; but I would give the world now to be outside the house. I do not speak for my own sake, May, but for yours. I did not mind the matter as I now mind it; but it is in your power to save my life—perhaps the life of your father, and of your brother, and your own good name. The secret of my presence may lie in our own hands, if you please that it should so remain."

"No—no. They come, and you will not leave me? Oh, what have I done, gracious Heaven, that I should suffer so much misery?"

"Peace—peace. It is not possible, May, that I can escape by the way I came to this room. I will get behind yonder screen, and you have but to say that a dream caused you to cry out, and beg them to leave you to repose again, and all will be well—I swear to you that so soon as the house is quieted again I will leave it. Can you not believe me?"

"Oh, Heaven! direct me."

"She hesitates," thought Captain Hawk, "and it is done."

Without another word he dashed behind the screen, having placed the light upon a little table by the side of the bed; and just as he did so there came a violent knocking at the door of the chamber.

"May! May!" cried a voice, "open the door! Was it you who screamed? May! May! Speak to me!"

That was the voice of Ratchley Boyes.

Poor May was too bewildered and

agitated to reply, and Ratchley hammered frantically at the door.

"My son," said a voice, "allow the representative of all the Boyeses, who by-the-bye, is very cold about the legs in the draught upon the landing, to call through the key-hole."

"Curses," thought Captain Hawk, "Sir John Boyes is there likewise."

CHAPTER LXXIII.

MAY SCREENS HAWK, WHO MAKES AN UNGENEROUS RETURN FOR KINDNESS.

"MAY!" cried her brother. "If you do not speak I will have the door down in another moment."

"I can hear!" said May.

"Thank God, she lives!" said Ratchley. "Stand aside, father, while I rush against the door with all my might and strength. It will, probably, give way if I do so."

"No—no," said May. "I will open the door."

Tremblingly she arose, and throwing around her a chintz morning wrapper, she stepped across the floor, and lifted the bolt of the door.

"Oh, come—come," she said, "father—brother! Thank God, you have both come."

"Sister, May, what is the matter?" said Ratchley, as with a drawn sword in his hand, he made his way into the room. Sir John Boyes, with his wig on the hind part before, bobbed about in the door-way, with a tall silver candlestick in his hand, in which a wax candle had been hastily lighted.

May sobbed bitterly.

"My child," said Sir John, "allow me to remark that there was a noise, and that my son Ratchley, here, has made me carry the light, and that my legs—I may say, the legs of one of the oldest baronets, as regards the title, I mean in the knightdom."

"Silence, father," said Ratchley. "Let May tell us the cause of the alarm. Speak, May."

"A dream!"

"A dream?"

"A dream!" gasped Sir John, as he sank into an old arm chair. "A dream? I did think that the family of the Boyeses was spared such vulgar things as dreams; I am surprised that what may be called the ancient aristocracy of a country should——"

"Stop, father. Are you sure, May, that it was but a dream?"

As he spoke, Ratchley's eyes glared rather fiercely round the room, and he grasped his sword menacingly.

"Oh, yes——"

"Unhand me, May. I will search—"

"No—no! I have but one request to make to you—Yes, I have, two."

"Two requests?" said Sir John, "as in a manner of speaking——"

"Yes, father. For Heaven's sake be quiet. Let us hear what May has to say to us."

"The one request is that you, brother, and you, father, will forgive me for causing this alarm, and the other is, that you will at once leave me to myself."

"You don't say so," said Sir John. "Well, we graciously forgive; and, as regards leaving you alone, we— "

"Yes, father, we will get Phillipa to stay with poor May; and this is only some frightful dream, after all, my dear sister?"

"Only some frightful dream?" repeated May with a shudder. "Oh, leave me now, brother, I pray you, I implore you to leave me!"

But why do you look so wildly about you, May? You seem still under the influence of the vision that has so much disturbed your slumbers?"

"And my slumbers," said Sir John.

"Oh, no—no It is not so. Do not fancy that—do not fancy anything but what I tell you; I say, it is a dream, and nothing but a dream. Do not doubt me. Oh go—go—go!"

The vehemence of her manner, the distraction of her tones, and the way in which she clung to his arm, all tended to surprise poor Ratchley, and to make him think that there was more in the affair than met the eye or ear, or that May was still labouring under a species of nightmare, notwithstanding she was up, and, apparently, wide enough awake.

"But, my dear May—" he began.

"You do not love me."

"Not love you?"

"No—no. No one loves me. If you

loved me, you would go at once from this room, when I so much implore you to do so."

"Well, May, we will go; but you see, your conduct amazes your father. I will tap at the door of Phillipa's chamber, and send her to you, so that you shall not be alone."

"Oh, no—no! Do not—do not—you will kill me!"

"Kill you?"

"Yes, by this seeming kindness. All I ask of you is, that you should go, and go at once."

"My dear, there is a draught," said Sir John, "and the legs of the representative of your family suffer—"

"There is, indeed, a draught," said Ratchley; "and, if I mistake not, it comes in some degree from yonder window."

"No!" shouted May—no!"

"Nay, permit me. Well, you shall come with me, since you will cling to my arm so pertinaciously. Now, you see, May, that you have left your window open, and I daresay your dream might be accounted for by the flapping of the blind, or, perchance, the presence of a bat or owl."

"Oh, yes, it must have been as you say, brother, a bat or an owl."

"But how imprudent of you, May, to go to rest with your window swinging open."

"Oh, very—very," said May. "Oh, yes, you are quite right, brother. Will you close it for me?"

As he closed the window, Ratchley muttered to himself—"There is more in this affair than meets the eye, and I will do my best to unravel the mystery." Then, having closed the French window, he turned to his sister, and said aloud—

"This is strange," said Ratchley—"very strange, indeed, May. But let me implore you to alter your determination, and to allow Philippa to remain with you."

"Oh, no—no. Do you wish to drive me mad?"

"Did she say mad?" cried Sir John.

"I did, father."

"Well, I can only say that to have one's feet so cold is quite enough to excite the brain of any one, and I wonder that I am not mad; for the old authors say that you ought to keep your feet warm, and your head cool; but I am, in a manner of speaking, *vice versa*, which is equivalent to being the other way."

"Yes, father," said Ratchley. "And now, I think, as May so particularly wishes it, that we ought to leave her to herself. You hear, father, that she says it was only a dream, and no doubt she is very sorry for having disturbed us for nothing."

"She cannot possibly be one half so sorry as I am," said Sir John, as he made his way majestically to the door of the apartment. "Come away, then, my son; and as for you, May, I beg to give you, as the head of the noble Boyes family, a little advice for your future guidance—"

"Another time, father," said Ratchley.

"My son and heir to my titles and estates," said Sir John, drawing himself up with great dignity, "I very much grieve to observe that you have shown an irreverend disposition to interrupt me upon several occasions, when words of wisdom were flowing from my lips."

"Well, father, I beg your pardon. We will leave May alone."

"May Boyes," said Sir John, who was determined not to be baulked of his speech by any one—"May Boyes—youngest scion of an illustrious house, and female specimen of its varied attractions—of its varied attractions, I may say—allow me to observe, that to dream otherwise than in a highly serene and aristocratic and gentle manner, is most subversive of natural dignity, and, in a manner of speaking, low—that is to say, decidedly vulgar."

"Yes, father," said Ratchley; "and——"

"Silence, son and heir!"

"I attend to you, father," said May.

"It is well. And now permit me to observe—Good night—good night. We for the present pardon you for dreaming."

"You are very kind, father. Good night."

"Ah!" said Sir John, as holding the candlestick some foot or so above his illustrious head, he walked into the corridor—"Ah! I may barely say youngest scion of an illustrious house, and female specimen of its varied attractions. Ratchley?"

"Yes, father."

"I hope you fully appreciate the happy expression?"

"What happy expression, father?"

"Goodness gracious!"

"Oh, sir, what is the matter?"

"Nothing. But is it possible that you did not hear me mention May as the female specimen of the varied attractions of our illustrious house?"

"Oh, yes, father."

"That, then, is the happy expression."

With this explanation, Sir John waved his hand graciously, and folding his dressing-gown around him as though it had been some robe of state, he started off to his sleeping chamber again, leaving Ratchley in the dark to make his way to his own room as best he might. But Ratchley was not at all sorry to get rid of the company of Sir John, for he wished to be alone, and at liberty to act as he thought it his duty to do for the good of his sister, May, whom he strongly suspected had some better cause than a troubled dream for calling out in the way she had done.

It had so happened that Ratchley had been reading in his room, and had only thrown off a portion of his clothing when the piercing shrieks of May had burst upon his ears, so that he was ready for any adventure that might present itself to him; and after a little thought he made his way to his apartment again.

When there, Ratchley opened an old escritoir and took from it a pair of beautifully wrought pistols, and carefully loaded them. Then fastening his sword-belt on, he put his hat well upon his head, and stepped down the grand staircase to the hall.

"I do not like the idea of that open window of May's room," he said to himself; "she gave no explanation of it at all. It was I who helped her out of the difficulty, because I did not wish our father to question her; but I was far from satisfied myself, and I am no nearer being satisfied now."

The plan of operation that Ratchley had determined upon was very simple. It was to go to the garden of the hall, and wait beneath May's window and take his chance of what might happen.

It is not to be thought for one moment that Ratchley had any unworthy suspicions concerning his sister. He knew May too well for that, but he did think it was just possible that her firm and gentle spirit might be acted upon by some impulses and some fallacious reasonings which it was his duty to protect her from the consequences of.

"If there be any wrong done, or doing," he said, "she is the victim. If there be any snare, it is she who has to be preserved from its effect, and it is my duty so to preserve her. Yes, sister May, I will save you from the wickedness of others, and, if needs be, I will save you from the weakness of yourself."

CHAPTER LXXIII.

A CONTEST TAKES PLACE BETWEEN CAPTAIN HAWK AND RATCHLEY BOYES.

If the grounds of Boyes Hall were well known to Captain Hawk by his having been a visitor several times to the place, and taking the trouble to make himself perfectly well acquainted with it, how much better must they have been known to Ratchley, who was born and bred amid the shades of the old trees, and who had first learnt to walk tottering from one old trunk to the other.

At any hour, by night or by day, Ratchley could have placed his hand upon any tree in the place without the smallest glance at it, and told you what it was, and all its peculiarities.

In the course of a very few minutes, now, the young man was beneath the window of May's apartment, and then he regretted that he had closed it, inasmuch as that circumstance would, no doubt, prevent him from hearing if anything that he ought to hear took place in the apartment.

As it was, he took up a station with his back against a tree at some little distance off, and kept his eyes fixed upon the window.

Had there been any other species of blind to the window but so conspicuous a one as a Venetian, no doubt Ratchley would have had, sooner than he did get it, evidence that his sister, May, was not alone. But we must not anticipate events; and it is necessary to leave Ratchley where he is, in order to return to the chamber of the innocent and agitated May.

Perhaps if the young girl had been asked the question if her conduct in screening Captain Hawk had arisen more from a desire to save him than from a desire to prevent a collision between him and Ratchley, which might be fatal to the latter, and if she had had all the wish in the world to reply with the most perfect truth to the inquiry, she would have found it difficult to do so at that period of violent feeling and restive agitation.

Now, however, that she had got her father and brother from the room, she could truly have said, in the face of all the world, and called upon Heaven itself to attest the truth of the sentiment, that she had but one wish with regard to Hawk, and that was, that he should immediately leave that chamber.

Yet, when she felt that she was alone in that chamber with him, she felt all the small amount of courage that had supported her during the agitating scene she had gone through passing away from her, and she reeled towards a chair, as she cried—

"Leave me! Oh, leave me now, if you have one particle of heart or of manhood in you!"

Hawk stepped out from behind the screen.

The light fell full upon his face, as he appeared now before the terrified eyes of May Boyes, and she saw how preternaturally pale he was, even to his very lips, which were bloodless, and apparently curved inwards with emotion.

There was a wild and terrible flashing of his eyes, too, as he glanced at the young girl, which was truly terrible to behold at such a time.

"May," he said—"May Boyes," and then he paused as if he would fain have spoken more; but his labouring breathing stopped him from so doing.

May gathered courage.

"Leave me, sir," she said. "I have saved you from the, perhaps, just vengeance of those who came here to protect me, and now, I say, leave me."

"Leave you?"

"I command you to leave me, sir!"

"May, hear me."

"No. Not a word. Already am I guilty of much imprudence by hearing you so far as I have, and by conniving for a moment at your pres nce here. Your course is free and open to you to leave this room by the route that you entered it. Go!"

"I will go. I will leave you as I found you in peace and in honour; but do not send me away thus, as if you doubted either my intentions, or your own courage and virtue."

"I doubt nothing, sir. I only say, go."

"Sir, do you call me? Ah! where is the familiar and well-remembered 'Gerald' that used to come so softly and sweetly from your lips? Am I then grown so hateful to you?"

"You will grow hateful to me. Oh, go—go!"

"I am going. Do not look at me with such eyes. You are ill, May—I know that you are. Your looks proclaim it—I speak to you now as one who was once a dear friend."

"No—no—I am only sick at sight of thee!"

"Can this be possible?"

"God, he will not go! I tell you, sir, your death and my death, that may come to better men than yourself, that may be contingent upon your staying here, be upon your own head."

"Hush—oh, hush! you will alarm the house again."

"I *will* alarm the house again. Oh, rash fool that I was not to declare at once to my brother the presence of this man! No—no. He is not a man—he is some fiend who has special power to drive me mad for some great fault that I have committed—some unknown sin against Heaven, that thus I am to be punished for!"

"I cannot leave you thus," said Captain Hawk, in a low, gloomy voice. "If I leave you thus, you or I will go mad—perhaps both of us."

"You shall leave me, then!"

"I will not.'

May advanced two steps towards him; but Hawk, with an affectation of coolness—it could not possibly be the reality of the feeling—crossed his arms upon his chest, and looked her full in the face.

"No, May Boyes," he said, "I will not and cannot leave you in this frame of mind. I have no bad intention in coming here to-night—I had no forethought of evil to you, or to any one. I am here, it is true, in your chamber; but if I fly with your reproaches ringing in my ears, you will think that you have rid yourself of a guilty wretch, who came full of thoughts of crime and wickedness, but who was terrified away. I will not go under such a delusion!"

May staggered to her seat again.

"No," added Hawk, "if it cost me my life. There is a conventional impropriety in my being here. I know that well; but that is all. I meet you here; and now with the same respect I treat you as if it were in the broad blaze of a mid-day sun.'"

"No—no!"

"Yes, I say—yes. If it please you to summon your furious and impassioned brother again to this apartment, let him come. I know one great source of your anxiety is that I may injure him; but I tell you, May Boyes, that your opinion of me dead is so much more dear to me, and more delightful to my soul, than your shuddering scorn while living, that I will not defend myself against Ratchley, and he may now come and murder me before your eyes. Will that satisfy you?"

"Oh, no—no!"

"What then? What would you have me do? Would you have me add to my other sins in your eye that of cowardice? No, May, I can die, but I cannot leave you with the impression that I came here like a thief in the night, and being baulked by your firmness in my purpose, skulked away again in shame and in confusion. No, that would be worse than death."

May looked at him fixeed; and then, in a low wailing voice, she spoke, saying—

"Speak, then, Gerald Clifton, since it must be so. In the name of all that is good and gracious, why come you here?"

"I will tell you May—I—I—will tell you"—he was evidently much agitated—"You wrote to me."

"I did."

"And the letter maddened me."

"Alas! it was meant to calm, to soothe, to do good to the lost spirit."

"It maddened me, for it spoke of all our affection as of a dream which had passed away, never to return again. It spoke of me as of one so low, so debased, that I might never more lift my eyes to the radiance of your beauty. It crushed my heart!"

He clasped his hands over his face, and was violently agitated.

"Poor, weak, lost man," said May. "I did not mean to crush thy heart; but it is true that you are not the Gerald Clifton to whom I gave my young, earnest affection. No, you are another; and so I did seek to crush all idea that you might still madly cherish that I was weak enough to think of you as once I thought."

"Oh, no—no!"

"It is the truth."

"Then you—you do not love me now?"

"Love *you?* The robber—the murderer!"

"Oh, peace—peace! The law has said that I did not do the deed of which I am accused."

May waved her hand and pointed with her forefinger in his face; he cowed before her, and then she said faintly—

"But you know that you are guilty!"

"No—no, you do not know it—the evidence!"

"Was but a trick—a juggle. Go now, Gerald Clifton, go and strive to make your peace with offended Heaven. It was to give you time to repent that you were spared."

"That I was spared! Who spared me?"

"I did."

"You?"

"Yes, I spared you. It was my work. Now you know the truth. Go at once, and do not blast me by your presence. It will be a joy to me if in time to come I hear no more of your crimes; but if I do, I shall not regret giving a wretch the opportunity of leading a better life before he went to his last account, although he madly cast that opportunity from him. Go now, I say. We do not know each other more."

Hawk felt goaded to despair.

"Ha!" he cried, "is this the woman's love that we hear so much about in tale and song? The love which, when once awakened shall exist for ever? Is this the constancy of a young heart to its own idol? May Boyes, I tell you that I love you still."

"Hence—oh, hence!"

"It is you who are changed not I. I was always, at least always while you knew me, what I am."

"But you were a wretch, like other assassins."

"Assassins?"

"Yes; you are worse than an ordinary assassin who uses his hired poniard, for that one only stabs the heart of his victim, but you stab the peace—the very soul. Oh, hence—hence! Do not make me say that I hate you."

"You dare not say it."

"Ah, dare I not? Villain!"

"Oh, pardon—pardon me, May—May, I know not what I say. Let me at least go from you with one kind word—one good and gentle wish."

He flung himself upon his knees at her feet, and clasped his hands together in an agony of supplication.

May shrunk back.

"No—no," he added. "I know that I am wrong—I know that I am guilty, but not from your lips did I expect to hear my utter condemnation."

"Go—oh, go!"

"Yes, I will go, but I go now without a hope—I go with my mind full of despair—I go not to repentance, for by your scorn you have destroyed all such gentle and humble thoughts, but I go to crush the fiend, remorse, by the excitement of foul crime."

"No! Oh, say not that."

"It is the truth."

"Gerald Clifton?"

"Ah, that tone is of the old stamp; you do not utterly cast me off—you do not loathe me?"

"God forbid that I should loathe any of his creatures; but if you wish me to think more gently of you in the time to come, you will not leave this place in the spirit that you just now invoked."

"And will you think more gently of me if I leave you in a different spirit? if I promise you that in the time to come I will do battle with the promptings of my evil genius?"

"Oh, yes—yes, Heaven has mercy and hope for the greatest criminal, and why should I, one of its miserably weak creatures, have less mercy?"

"Farewell," he said, rising. "I may not hope that you can say as yet a gentler word than that to me. Farewell. I will not ask you to think of me sometimes, but I will live in the hope yet of looking into those eyes, which to me are glimpses of Heaven itself."

"Go—go."

"I go. May Heaven bless and reward you for the few kind words that you have spoken."

"Farewell!"

"You have spoken those words to the heart you might have broken, and so am I deeply thankful. The secret of this midnight visit now belongs to only you and me. It will never pass my lips—it need never pass yours."

May shuddered, and still she said, faintly, "Go."

Captain Hawk thought truly enough that he could not back out of his wild and perilous adventure upon better terms with May than the present; so he at once gave her a proof of the sincerity of his convictions that she would listen to no more protestations from him, if not of the sincerity of all he said, by going towards the window, and opening it. He turned towards her yet for a moment before he stepped on to the balcony, and said in a low, soft, musical voice—

"Dear one, farewell!"

"Farewell!" she said; and then she fell fainting to the floor of the chamber; but, luckily, Hawk did not see her so fall, and he stepped on to the balcony, and prepared to effect his descent to the garden by the route he had come.

It was then that, with a heart beating with rage, Ratchley saw him.

RATCHLEY SEEKING THE BODY OF HAWK IN THE GARDENS.

CHAPTER LXXIV.

CAPTAIN HAWK, ALTHOUGH WOUNDED, REACHES THE HUT UPON THE HEATH.

If Ratchley Boyes had entered at the moment he saw Captain Hawk, or Gerald Clifton, whichever name he may be called, he would have sprung forward, and there and then, before he descended from the window of May's apartment, defied him to the combat; but the young man had reflection enough left to him in his anger to feel that Hawk might escape him if he were to be aware that he, Ratchley, was waiting for him in the garden below.

Here Ratchley waited until he saw him climb over the balustrade of the balcony and slowly effect his descent.

"Oh," said Ratchley to himself, "what hinders me from shooting him as he leaves that chamber, and as I am abundantly justified in doing, considering all things? Why is it that my hand rises not against that man who to us in this once peaceful house has been more than a midnight assassain?"

Ratchley asked such questions of himself; but he could, if he had dived into the recesses of his own heart, have found an answer to them.

If he had not known who it was who was then escaping from the chamber, he might have fired at him; but with the knowledge that it was the man against whom he had so deep and just a cause for quarrel, a strange feeling stayed his hand.

To Ratchley's nice sense of honour it would have seemed like a murder to shoot Captain Hawk while he was in so defenceless a condition as clinging to the vegetation, by the aid of which he had managed to reach to the window of May's room, and was now with an equal fecility descending.

But Ratchley's suspense need only sustain itself for a few moments. Captain Hawk sprang to the ground, and as he did so, he said—

"She is mine—she is mine yet!"

Those words came to the ears of Ratchley, and added the last taunt to the rage that was swelling in his bosom. The reader can easily conceive that they were calculated to convey an imputation that he, Captain Hawk, could not with truth make against the honour of May, and which, in all candour, he did not intend to make.

The meaning that Hawk attached to them was simply, that he had seen, or fancied he had seen, sufficient symptoms of relenting towards him in the heart of May to come to the opinion that, notwithstanding all that had taken place, she loved him still in the secret recesses of her innermost heart.

To Ratchley the words brought a thrill of agony, as they seemed to imply the fact of the utmost success of a favoured lover.

"Now for Joe and my horse, and then for the road," said Hawk, as he advanced a few steps along the garden path.

In another minute, Ratchley was before him.

"Hold!" he said.

"Ah!" cried Hawk, as he stepped back and placed his hand upon the stock of a pistol that he had ready primed and loaded. "Who dares to intercept my progress?"

"I," said Ratchley.

"Ratchley, by all that is damnable!"

"Yes, villain. It is Ratchley, to you discomfiture."

Well?"

"Thief! murderer! midnight robber! assassin——"

"Go on. Has the polite and elegant Ratchley Boyes any other choice epithets to lavish upon his quondam friend, Gerald Clifton? If so, utter them; I am patient."

"Perjured villain—insidious monster, that like an envenomed reptile, crawls into the confidence of our unsuspecting bosom but to be warmed and then to sting it."

"Good—very good. You are rather happy in your comparisons, but as I am pressed for time, I will bid you good-night."

"Will you?"

"Oh, yes. At some other time I may, perhaps, feel disposed to listen to your fine eloquence, but now I am otherwise engaged."

"If you stir from here, I will blow your brains out."

"Beware!"

"Beware, say you? It is you who should beware, villain that you are."

"Ratchley Boyes, with you I am somewhat more patient than I am with most men; but there is a limit to that patience. Beware how you pass it. Stand from my path."

"No, coward, I will not."

"Coward?"

"Yes, all thieves are cowards. You know, that with the loss of honour courage goes—of course you are a coward."

"Fool! Goad me not to do a deed I should in cooler moments repent me of."

"Now, would not any one suppose," said Ratchley, "that this rascal is the injured brother, and that I was the person whom he had seen descend from the window of his sister's chamber?"

"If that is what is annoying you, I

can tell you that your suspicions are as unworthy as they are wrong."

"Indeed?"

"I went not there for any criminality with May. I leave her chamber with honour. Now, sir, let me pass."

"No, liar!"

"Dare you repeat that word?"

"Yes, a thousand times, if it will make you man enough to fight. Liar!—liar!"

"Enough. Your blood be upon your own head."

"No, upon your soul be it if I fall, and let it, along with my sister's dishonour, weigh you down to perdition. I stand here. Take your place where you will, and give the signal to fire, and I will obey it. I feel that by giving you the treatment only due to a gentleman, thus in some measure I compromise my own honour; but I will waive that objection, and this shall be a duel, and not an act of expiatory vengeance, as it well might be."

"Ratchley Boyes," said Hawk, as he stamped with excitement and impatient anger upon the greensward, "you know not what you say. You are mad—mad, I say."

"Perchance so. Take your place, sir."

"You have in your head a crotchet concerning your sister's dishonour, for which you would sacrifice your life. I swear to you that May is, for me, as pure as any angel."

"Mind, I shoot you where you are."

"You will, then, force this contest upon me?"

"I will."

"Your act be it, then, and not mine, come what may of it."

"Take your choice, sir."

"Choice of what?"

"Of these pistols. They are both loaded well."

"Keep your arms. I have my own with me, and since you will have it, the sooner this is over the better. I spared you once, Ratchley, but the time for such weakness has gone past. I do not let the same snake bite me twice"

"Take your place, sir."

"Ha—ha! on my soul, but this is rich. You throw away a life from pique and not from principle. But be it so. That is your business, not mine, fool that you are. You know that when I choose to hit my mark, it is hit."

"Shall I fire now?"

Without another word Captain Hawk turned upon his heel and strode ten paces from Ratchley, and then turning, he stuck his heel into the soft turf, as he cried out—

"Will this satisfy you?"

"If it does you—certainly."

"Are you ready?"

"Quite."

"Fire, then, and curses on your obstinacy that has made me do a deed—ah—God!"

The pistols were discharged simultaneously, and Hawk fell upon his back upon the grass.

Ratchley walked up to him, and by the pale night-light, looked down upon him as he there lay.

"Wretched man," said Ratchley, "so this is your end, after all? To fall by my hand! Rather would I that some other than I had stricken you. But as it is done, I will not regret the death of a felon."

"Curses on the chance!" muttered Hawk, as he made an unavailing attempt to rise. "Curses—oh, such bitter curses!"

"Wretched man, is this a time to utter maledictions?"

"Ay, the deepest."

"Do you not fear?"

"Fear! Ha—ha! I never feared, and if this be my last moment I am not now going to begin. May the bitterest maledictions of an undying hate pursue you, Ratchley Boyes—may you know no peace—no joy—may doubt and horror clog your soul—may you——"

"Hilloa!" cried a voice from one of the windows of the mansion. "I heard shots, and I may say that they suggest to my mind the idea of the discharge of fire-arms. Who is there? Hilloa!

A shrill scream came then upon the night air.

"Father, I am here," cried Ratchley. "Ring up the servants. It is I."

"Who is I?"

"Ratchley. Don't you know my voice?"

"The heir presumptive to the dignity of the Boyeses in the garden in the middle of the night," said Sir John, "firing pistol shots? I don't recollect any precedent for such a course in the annals of antiquity. Murder! Murder! Help!"

"What is the matter, father?"

"I don't know—yes I do. It's this infernal window that has no counterpoise to it, has come down, and is confining the representative of majesty and of all the Boyeses to the window-sill. I am nearly decapitated already, as his blessed majesty Charles the what's-his-name was."

"Never mind."

"Never mind, did you say? Go to the deuce, sir—go to the—murder—help! I can't stand this sort of thing. Hilloa!"

Ratchley now moved to the front door of the mansion, and made a vigorous appeal to the bell that was there, and which had the effect of completing the alarm of the servants who had all jumped up from their beds at the sound of the firing in the garden.

Lady Boyes missing Sir John, ran out of her chamber, calling aloud to him, and Philippa was silenced by her extreme terror, and with all the inclination in the world to scream aloud, could not find breath to do so.

Now, it happened that, in order to reach the window out of which he had looked, and which was one at the end of a corridor, poor Sir John had mounted on a stool with three legs, which just elevated him about six inches from the floor, and enabled him to crane his long body and neck out at the window.

Lady Boyes, in her agitation, calling loudly upon Sir John, rushed past the spot, and kicked the stool from Sir John's feet, so that there he hung at the window, and doubtless, if he had not managed just to tip the floor with the points of his toes, and so partially support himself, the representative of the Boyeses would have come by a very original and untimely end, indeed, upon that eventful night.

"Murder!" he cried. "Assassination—ass—ass—assination! Murder! Help!—Murder!"

Some of the armed servants, who had hastily procured lights, released Sir John, and down he fell to the floor, just as Ratchley, who had been let into the house, rushed up the grand staircase.

Lady Boyes now ran against everybody, and cried out that Sir John was murdered; and Philippa, who had recovered sufficiently to add to the general uproar by screaming, did not omit to do so.

"For Heaven's sake," cried Ratchley, "be silent, all of you."

"Fire!" cried one. "Thieves!" shouted another. "Help!" bellowed three or four, who were not in need of help at all; and poor Sir John sat upon the floor in a brocade morning gown, with his eyes nearly starting out of his head, partly by fright, and partly by semi-strangulation.

CHAPTER LXXV.

CAPTAIN HAWK RATHER MYSTERIOUSLY DISAPPEARS FROM THE GARDEN.

"Father! father!" cried Ratchley, "what is the meaning of all this? Let me beg of you to say!"

"Ah!—Oh!" said Sir John.

"Are you hurt?"

"Ah!—oh!"

"What has happened to him? Can any one here tell me? Surely he is dreaming."

"Sir John had his head out at the window that had no weight to it," said one of the servants, "and it is possible enough, Master Ratchley, that it came down on his hand."

"Was that it, father?"

"Ah!—Oh!"

Seeing that there was nothing in the shape of a rational account to be got from Sir John of the disaster that had happened to him, Ratchley turned to a couple of the men servants, and said—

"Follow me. Get a lantern, one of you, so that we may have light in the garden, for there lies there a wounded, or a dead man, I do not at this moment know which."

"Oh, my son Ratchley, you are not hurt?"

"Not a bit, mother; but some one else is, I expect, so do not delay me. Humanity is a sacred duty, even to our worst foes."

"Foes? Ah, who is it that you speak of?"

"A midnight robber!"

"Thieves!" said Sir John. "Oh—oh, I knew it."

"Mother," added Ratchley, in a whisper, "and you Philippa, go to May's chamber, and save her from—from—"

"From what, my son?"

"Oh, from what?" said Philippa.

Ratchley held his hand over his eyes for a moment, and he was too deeply affected to speak. Then he added—

"God, I know not! It may be from herself, poor victim; but go to her—go to her at once, and ask me no more, I pray you."

"Here's the lantern, Master Ratchley."

"Thanks—thanks. Follow me."

Ratchley hastily descended the grand staircase, followed by the two serving men, who were not a little curious to know where their young master was about to lead them at such an hour of the night, and who it was who had suffered from the pistol-shots they had heard distinctly fired so short a time since in the garden.

Ratchley did not hasten to the spot upon which he had left Captain Hawk. He felt no pleasure in the idea of the sight that might meet his gaze when he should reach it; but with slow and melancholy strides he led the way.

The servant with the lantern followed close behind him, holding it up so that the rays fell upon the path before Ratchley, showing him the way that he had to go.

The other man—who felt rather timid on the occasion, and who had snatched a loaded gun out of the hall as he passed through it—kept at a little distance.

"Oh, Master Ratchley, what is it?" said the servant with the lantern. "I hopes as it ain't nothing very horrid?"

"Oh, no—no."

"Not a ghost, Master Ratchley?"

"Certainly not."

"That's a comfort. I ain't no good at ghosts, you see, sir. Any mortal man I don't mind; but when you come to spirits, oh, dear, they is ever so much one too many for me."

"You need fear nothing."

"Thank you, Master Ratchley, I am glad to hear that, not, sir, that I'm at all afraid of ghosts or anything else, not I."

"Oh, lor! what's that you say, Gregory?" cried the other man. "Did you say ghosts? Come, now, do tell us."

"Ah, Humphrey, you are a coward."

"Oh, dear, I know it, and I own it. Pray, Master Ratchley is there any danger? Oh, do say, Master Ratchley, if you please!"

"If either of you," said Ratchley, sternly, "object to accompanying me, say so at once. I did not command your services at such an hour as this, I only requested them. But give me the lantern and go both of you back to your beds, if you are too cowardly to follow me."

"Oh, no, sir; we will come."

"Oh, yes, yes; I didn't mean that, sir."

"Follow in silence, then. I have enough to engage my mind, Heaven knows, without having it disturbed by your folly."

Thus rebuked, the servants followed Ratchley in silence, and when they turned an angle of the house they observed that he faltered in his walk for a moment, and then heard him say—

"This is folly, indeed. What do I dread?

'The sleeping and the dead are but as pictures.'

I will face him even in his gore."

At that word gore, the hair of Gregory's head very nearly stood upon an end, and he shook the lantern so, that the shadows of the trees and the flowering shrubs about the spot danced again, as though instinct with a strange life.

Ratchley was by far too much occupied now with his own thoughts to pay any attention to either Gregory or Humphrey, and he reached what he thought was the spot upon which he had left Captain Hawk wounded, to all seeming, mortally.

He was gone!

Ratchley started, and then said to himself—

"I am confused and mistaken. This is not the place—yet it must be. There is the old cedar tree—there the little fountain. It is the spot, but *he* has vanished."

"Who, sir—oh, sir, who!"

"Silence! Give me the light?"

"Y—e—s, Master Ratchley. But did you say vanished? 'Cos, you see, sir, that is what ghosts do, you know, sir, and if so be anything was here, and now isn't, and is gone off in a vanish, a ghost it was and a ghost it were, you know, sir."

"Silence! I say—I will not hear more."

The tone in which Ratchley now spoke awed Gregory into silence, and without another word, he let his young master take the lantern from him.

Ratchley then carefully looked upon the grass, and in a few moments he saw the spot where Captain Hawk had dug his heel into the soft turf when he had cried out that it was time to fire. Close to that lay, sparkling in the light, a little pool of blood.

"It is the place," said Ratchley.

The mysterious disappearance of Hawk now quite took possession of the young man's imagination, and he stood irresolute, and full of strange thoughts, while the servants gazed upon him with astonishment.

"Gone—gone!" he said.

"Ye—e—s," gasped Gregory, more from the desire to say something, than from any comprehension of what his master referred to by that solemnly pronounced word, "Gone."

"Hark ye, both of you."

"Yes, Master Ratchley."

"Go back to the house, and if you are questioned about me, say that I shall soon return."

"If you please, sir, we will."

"Go—go at once."

Now, no doubt, both Gregory and Humphrey would have succeeded in effecting a very orderly and perfectly successful retreat, but for one very trivial circumstance that occurred, and showed what disastrous effects will ensue from trivial circumstances, in spite of all human knowledge and precautions.

It happened that an owl slept in the cedar tree to which Ratchley had alluded, and it happened, likewise, that a ray of the lantern went right into the owl's face, to his great discomfiture, so, after winking a great many times, out he flew bewildered by the light, and uttering a loud hoot, dashed right into the face of the unfortunate, and already sufficiently terrified Humphrey.

With a roar that might have been heard for a mile round the spot, Humphrey fell flat upon his back.

"Murder!" shouted Gregory, and down he threw the lantern.

"Fire!" yelled Humphrey, and as he still held the gun in his grasp, he pulled the trigger, and off it went with a stunning report, and shot the unfortunate owl, who had been the cause of all the mischief, dead upon the spot.

Ratchley could not, for the life of him make out what had happened to both the men, for Gregory, after throwing down the lantern, had fallen on Humphrey in his frantic and ill-directed efforts to escape from the spot at once, and there they both lay roaring upon the grass, and unable to get away from each other.

"Idiots!" cried Ratchley, "what is the meaning of all this folly? Do you wish to drive me mad between you?"

"Oh, lor, sir! Oh, we couldn't help it—indeed we couldn't," said Gregory; "and, besides, Master Ratchley, it wasn't me. It was all Humphrey's doings."

"But a ghost all over feathers came plump in my face," said Humphrey, "and what was I to do then, I wonder?"

"Be off, both of you, at once. No sooner has one alarm subsided, which had a real cause for it, than you raise another which had no foundation but your own folly. How dared you fire the gun you had with you?"

"Oh, Master Ratchley, I only just pulled the trigger, and then, if you'll believe me, sir, off it went of itself."

"What a night this is," said Ratchley to himself; and then turning to the still trembling servants, he added—"Go to the house, both of you, and explain that this new alarm is nothing. No doubt the gun-shot has been heard, and has awakened all the fears of those in the house again. Go—go quickly, and explain the cause of it."

"Yes, sir—yes, Master Ratchley. But you ain't a going to stay all alone by yourself, sir, here?"

"I am."

"What, with no end of ghosts,

sir? Oh, you can't mean it surely, Master Ratchley! And only to think of the ghost with feathers on his face. Oh, dear—oh, dear, I shall never survive the shock."

"Go—go!"

The tone in which Ratchley now spoke had its effect, and the two servants made their way with speed to the house, not a little glad, to tell the truth, to get under its roof again; for notwithstanding all their affected sympathy for the lonly condition of Ratchley in the garden, where they thought him exposed to various dangers of the supernatural world, they were glad enough to leave him.

When Ratchley found himself alone, although he was in the dark, he glanced around him again, to assure himself that he was not mistaken regarding the spot upon which the singular duel had been fought beweeu him and Captain Hawk.

He felt only the more assured of the fact that he was upon the right spot, now that the lantern was gone; for inasmuch as it was in the dark that he had met and encountered Captain Hawk, and marked the spot with reference to the dim outlines of surrounding objects, he now saw that the same aspects were familiar to him, and that there could be no rational doubt upon the subject.

But Hawk was gone.

There was the mystery. A man who had apparently been so badly wounded that even in the presence of his worst enemy he had not been able to rise to his feet, had suddenly disappeared in the most inexplicable way that could be imagined.

A dim idea crossed the mind of Ratchley for a moment that Captain Hawk might only have been pretending to be wounded, in order to put an end to the fight; but when he came to recollect that the light of the lantern had revealed to him a pool of blood upon the grass, that idea vanished.

Such a course of conduct, too, was at variance with the character of Captain Hawk.

The more Ratchley thought the matter over, the more puzzled he became to account for it.

"What can be the meaning of it?" he said. "Are the terrors and the mysteries of this night not over? By Heaven! I will not leave a spot of the garden unsearched. I may find the villain yet in hiding somewhere."

CHAPTER LXXVI.

CAPTAIN HAWK WRITES A LETTER TO MAY, WHO FORMS A RESOLUTION.

WHILE Ratchley, by the now dim light of the coming dawn, is searching the old garden, every inch of which he knew so well, we will account to the reader for the sudden and mysterious disappearance of Captain Hawk from the spot where Ratchley had left him wounded.

The report of Ratchley's pistol had taken effect in the side of the highwayman, and his own impression was that the wound was fatal, for when he attempted to rise, the most acute pain that ever in his life he had felt prevented him.

"It is over with me at last," he reasoned, when he was alone. "All is past now, and this is the end of the mad desire to see you once again, May Boyes. Farewell—farewell, for ever and ever!"

With a shudder, Captain Hawk closed his eyes, and fancied that death was hovering over him, for a deadly faintness crept over his faculties, and there he lay as firmly convinced that he was faintly breathing his last as ever any human being was.

Something like a voice close at hand had the effect of rousing him for a moment; and then he heard the tones that he knew so well of the man of the hut to whom he had left the care of his horse, saying—

"I'm sure I heard pistol-shots. I wonder where the captain is? I hope nothing has gone amiss with him at last."

The desire not to die in that place came strongly over the faultering faculties of Hawk, and by a great effort he managed to cry out—

"I am here!—I am here!"

The man heard him, and was by his side in a moment.

"Oh, lor! You don't mean to say this is you?"

"Joe—Joe!"

"Have they winged you at last?"

"Done for me, Joe. I am—hit. It is all over now; but—but——"

"Well, now, this is hard. Bother it, captain! how come you to let 'em do this sort of thing?"

"Joe — I — closer — I can't speak loud. Stoop."

"Yes, I hears you."

"Don't let me die here."

"How can I help it, captain? Lord bless you, I am sorry enough for you; but I ain't one of the snivelling sort, you see. Oh, dear! it's a lonely sort of a cove I shall feel when you is gone. I knows as you are a bad 'un; but I was used to you, and everythink—Well, I never! I didn't go for to think it would have come to this, no how."

"Joe—Joe!"

"Yes, captain? What do you bring it in now?"

"Peace! Listen to me."

"Cut along."

"I don't want to die here. Do you understand me? You may do me a last service, Joe, and not the least of the many for which I have not thanked you, but for which I thank you now."

"What is it?"

"Drag me from this place, and hide me anywhere, so that they may not find me. I would not that one of the family occupying this place should look upon me in death. Do this much, and I can make you rich."

"You don't mean it?"

"Yes, I do. You know the old chestnut-tree close to the hut—the one with the bark so plentifully pealed off?"

"Yes, I knows it."

"Dig at its roots, and take what you can find."

"Oh, indeed? I tell you what it is, now, captain—if so be as I had wanted to take your tin, I'd have took it before now, for I happened to know that you put it there; but I ain't one half sich a wagabone as you seem to think me; so, I tell you, I won't have it—no, not one farden on it, except so be as you does really kick the bucket, you know, captain, and then it will be no good to you, you see—eh?"

Hawk did not reply.

"Eh? Did you speak—eh?"

All was still.

"Gone," said Joe. "Oh, lor! and this is the—the finish and the end, and the—oh, lor! poor fellow. He was a rum 'un in his time, and if nobody else is sorry for him, I is. Yes, I, Joe, is. Ah, well, groaning and piping of one's eye never yet brought a dead man to life again, so it ain't of no use. But let me see; he didn't want no how to be feft here. Well, come along, captain. It shan't be said as Joe didn't do the last thing as you asked of him."

Joe had amazing strength, and stooping over the insensible form of Captain Hawk, he lifted it off the ground, and flung it over his shoulder, and he bolted off through the garden as if he were not carrying any very great weight, although Hawk was by no means a very light burthen.

It appears that Joe, hearing the shots fired, one of which had, to all appearance, proved so fatal to Hawk, had tied the bridle of his horse to a tree, and had made his way into the garden by pulling down a rotten paling in a part of the enclosure.

His object now was to reach that same spot again, and so emerge with the body of the captain.

The garden of Boyes Hall was quite an unknown region to Joe, and he found some difficulty in pitching upon the route by which, guided as he had been by the sound of the fire-arms, he had made his way to the spot upon which the duel had been fought.

After traversing several paths, and rather desperately making a short cut or two to nowhere over several flower-beds, Joe stopped, for he was thoroughly bewildered and lost in the intricacies of the garden.

"Confound it," he said, "people ought to put up direction posts in places like this here. I have gone out of my way, that's for certain, and I shall be running against something soon, if I don't mind."

Joe considered a little, and then he struck upon an idea.

"All's right," he said. "I'll get right on over everything and through everything but the trees till I reach the paling, and then by following it I must, in course of time, come to the place I got in at."

This was certainly the most rational course that Joe could pursue in the difficulty he was placed in, so off he started in as straight a line as he could after taking a glance round him, and feeling satisfied that he was not by any mistake making his way towards the house, which would have been fatal to his purpose.

A rather sharp progress of about

MR. LAMB FINDS HIMSELF MISTAKEN IN THE CAPTURE OF HAWK.

three minutes' duration, to the great detriment of several clumps of flowers, through which Joe strode without any mercy, brought him to the paling which divided a portion of the old garden from the open country.

"All's right, now," he said, "and I know which way to turn, too, for there is that little fountain concern that I passed as I came in. All's right."

Joe ran along by the side of the paling till he came to where he had broken in, and then he carefully got through again with Captain Hawk, and found the horse waiting patiently for him.

"Now, captain," said Joe, "dead or alive, I have done what you asked me to do. I have taken you away from that place, and they won't find you. But let me see what next is to be done. Oh, I have it! Take him to the hut, in course."

Joe was beginning now to feel that it was not a very light weight that he had upon his shoulders, and it was a great relief to him to place the body of Captain Hawk on the horse.

"Eugh!" he said, as he gave himself a stretch. "I'd rather carry you a week than a fortnight certainly; but now we shall do capital. Come on, old chap, you won't be troubled to gallop with your master any more, I take it; and if I don't think proper to go on the road myself, I suppose I'd better take you to some country fair and get what I can for you."

The horse to whom these words were addressed, was perfectly well acquainted with Joe, and gave him a friendly push with his nose.

"What, you don't want to be sold?"

The horse pushed him again.

"You don't want to part with old Joe? Well you shan't, then. Come, now, is you satisfied now, old fellow?"

Joe quite pleased himself with the idea that the horse understood him, and taking the bridle in his hand he led the animal, with its insensible master upon its back, in the direction of the hut.

A soft misty rain began to fall before Joe got to the miserable-looking hovel in which he resided, so that both he and Captain Hawk were tolerably wet before the horse was led under the shelter of a little shed attached to the hut.

The morning, though, had really made a considerable advance by that time, and although some drifting clouds from the south-west made the sky not so light as it would have been, yet there was sufficient of the young daylight to enable Joe to see well about him.

He now felt terribly perplexed to know what to do with the body of Captain Hawk.

It will be seen that Joe did not for a moment doubt the apparent fact of the death of his imperious master.

"Well," said Joe, "here we is certainly, but what to be at now we is here, I hardly know. I suppose I shall have to bury him. Oh, dear!"

Joe went to a little mound in the neighbourhood of the hut and looked carefully over the fields and lanes in the neighbourhood, but he could see no one, so that he was tolerably satisfied that he should not be interrupted.

With a heavy heart, for, strange to say, the man loved the harsh and cruel Captain Hawk, as some nature's have a tendency to love those who tyrannise over them, he proceeded to lift the body off the horse and to convey it into the hut.

"Lie there, old master," said Joe, as he placed the body carefully upon the little pallet bed that was in one corner of the little room which served him, Joe, for "kitchen and parlour and hall." "Lie there, Captain, while I attend to the horse."

Joe then went out to the steed, and shaking down some litter, and throwing half a truss of hay before the horse, he took off his head gear and left him to amuse himself, quite satisfied that he would not stray from the place.

Joe, then, as he crept back to the room in which he had left Hawk's body, said to himself—

"I will bury him in the garden, and nobody will know of it but me. Yes, I will pop him quietly underground there, and folks will wonder for a time what has become of him. Oh, dear—oh, dear! I shan't be over fond of this place, I take it, when all this job is settled."

Joe now drew aside a little curtain that shaded the window, and he could then see the face of Captain Hawk more plainly. It was smeared with blood as though a gory hand had been drawn across it, and that was indeed the fact, for it was one of his own hands, soaked in the blood from his wound, that he had, while lying upon the ground in the garden at Boyes Hall, drawn across his face.

"Ah, there he is," said Joe. "There he is. Well, it's a pity; but, after all, it's better than Newgate and the noose of the hangman—oh, a good deal better. He always used to say that when he did go he hoped as he should go like—Ah, what's that?"

The clatter of a horse's feet at a hard trot came plainly upon Joe's ears at that moment.

Springing to the window of the hut, he looked out, but he could see no one, although the sound came each moment more and more plainly upon his ears,

"Confound it, I hope nobody is coming here," he muttered; "and yet who should come here? It's out of everybody's way. No—nobody can come here, except in a fog or something of that sort, when they have lost their way; but it's light enough now for anybody to see where they are going."

The sound of the horse's feet came nearer and nearer.

"By Jove," cried Joe; "somebody is coming, though, and no mistake at all. Who the d—l is it?"

"Hilloa!" cried a voice.

Joe hurried to the door of the hut, and sprang out on to the saturated pathway of the lane. A man in a cloak, which hung around him in heavy folds, saturated with rain, drew up about twenty paces from him, and called out—

"Does this road lead to Hanger Hill?"

"It ain't a road," said Joe.

"Well, this lane, then, since you are so very particular."

"No, it don't."

"Where does it lead to, then?"

"Don't know. Your best plan, though, is to turn your horse's head whence you came from, for I don't want visitors, I can tell you."

"But, my good fellow, I want to get the nearest way to my destination. My name is Hill—I am Mr. Hill the surgeon, whom you may, perhaps, have heard of."

"A surgeon?" cried Joe. "A doctor, you mean? Ah, a doctor!"

CHAPTER LXXVII.

JOE FINDS OUT THAT HE HAS MADE A SLIGHT MISTAKE.

As Joe spoke, he approached the surgeon so rapidly, that that gentleman might very well be excused for the supposition that came over him at the moment that Joe had some peculiar spite against doctors, and meant to avenge it upon him.

"Keep off," he cried. "I am armed."

"Oh, curse your arms!" said Joe. "I don't want them; I want you to come and look at a dead body."

"A dead body?"

"Yes. Come in. It ain't the proper sort of thing to put any one under ground till some doctor has said it is all right to do so; so come in and take a look at it. I'll pay you."

"But what is the use of my looking at a dead body?"

"Don't ask me what is the use, because I don't know, but I beg of you to do so. There's no harm meant to you. I am here alone with the dead, I tell you, sir, and I pray you to come into the hut and have a look at him; but if you should just chance to know him, when you see him, perhaps you won't mind keeping that knowledge to yourself, for it would do nobody any good to know, and might do some harm."

"Gentlemen of my profession," said the surgeon, whose curiosity was now awakened, "are always confidential. I will say nothing, you may depend, be the dead man whom he may."

"Come in, then. It's a guinea, ain't it, as you ought to have?"

"Oh, never mind that."

"But I do mind it, I tell you, and I mean to say that you shall have it, too."

"But, my good man——"

"I ain't a good man, so don't be saying things as isn't right, I beg of you, but come along after me. I'll tie your horse by the bridle to the low limb of this tree. Ah," muttered Joe, as he tied up the doctor's horse, "*his* horse has been tied here many a time, but it won't never be tied here no more, I take it, no how."

"Well, my friend," said the surgeon, "now where is the body?"

"I ain't your friend, but the body is nigh by here, sir. You shan't go and say as you hadn't your guinea, and so that you have a right to tell who you saw here, and all that sort of thing."

"Well, well, you shall have your own way. I will take the guinea, and, as you say, then this will be a regular professional visit."

"Just so. Come in."

The surgeon stooped as he entered the hut, for the door was so low that he would have struck his hat off if he had not done so, and, in fact, Joe had, from long use, got so much into the habit of stooping to enter his hut, that he paid that compliment to all doors whatever, let the height of them be what it might, and let him be in any building whatever.

"Now," said the surgeon, "where is he?"

"There," said Joe, and he drew from off the couch a counterpane that he had thrown over the dead body of Captain Hawk.

"Indeed."

"What makes you say, indeed?"

"Because I see that this is a death caused by violence."

"Oh, yes, it was violence," said Joe.

The surgeon looked in the face of the body, and then he looked at Joe, and nodded his head, as he said—

"Yes, I know him."

"The d—l you do! Who is he, then?"

"Hawk, the highwayman."

"That's the verdict. It's the captain, sure enough, and there's the last of him. Now, Mr. Doctor, Hawk and me is very old friends, and I want you see, to give him christian burial in the garden, so I don't want the grabs, or the beaks, or the big wigs, to know anything about it."

"I shall not mention it. Place that blind on one side, Mr. a—I don't know your name."

"Call me Joe."

"Very good. Now, where is he hurt?"

"Don't know."

"You don't know?"

"Not I. You ought to know, being a doctor. But all I know is that he has kicked the blessed bucket, and there he is."

"Well, we will see."

The surgeon speedily loosened the clothing over the chest of Captain Hawk, and then laid his ear flat over the region of the heart.

"Lor!" said Joe, "does you expect as there's anything a moving in the inside of him, doctor?"

The surgeon made a movement with his hand indicative of his wish for silence, and Joe remained as if he were transfixed in the attitude he chanced to be in till the doctor lifted up his head again.

"Well?" said Joe. "Well?"

"It's a slight mistake."

"What's a slight mistake?"

"He is not dead."

"Not dead? The captain alive and kicking still? You don't mean that?"

"He is alive, certainly, if not kicking, Mr. Joe, and if you had given him that christian burial in the garden you mentioned, you would have done him great injustice. There is plenty of life in him yet. I see that the wound is in the head."

"Oh, lor—oh, lor!" said Joe, "what a thing it is to be a doctor. I suppose it was your coming in that put a little life in him, sir, again?"

The doctor shook his head.

"They do say of us, Joe," he said, "that our appearance often puts life out of people; but I don't think your friend, here, can be in a very bad state. Hold him up in this way, if you can."

"All right. I have him."

"Now, have you any vinegar in the house?"

"In the teacup on that shelf yonder."

"That will do."

"The devil! What do you mean by that?"

The teacup was three-parts full of vinegar of rather a pungent quality, and without the smallest hesitation, the surgeon flung it with all his force right into the face of Captain Hawk.

The effect of this mode of treatment was very speedily apparent. There was a nervous twitching of the muscles of the face, and then Captain Hawk opened his eyes.

"Hurrah!" cried Joe.

"Silence!" said the doctor, sternly. "Do you think a man just recovering from a state of insensibility wants that savage kind of noise bellowed in his ears? Be silent, if you please."

"I begs yer parding," said Joe. "It comed rather natural, you see, doctor, at that 'ere moment."

"Hush—hush!"

Captain Hawk looked rather wildly about him, and then he drew a long breath and gave a slight shudder, as he said—

"Ah!"

"Oh, lor!" said Joe. "He says somethink. Don't you think a glass of good strong brandy now would——"

"No."

"Oh, wery good. I only mentioned it. No offence, I hopes, in course, only I always finds that the kind of physic as agrees with my blessed constitution best of all."

"Will you be quiet?"

"To be sure I will. Lor, how he does look about him, to be sure."

"Well, Captain Hawk," said the surgeon. "How are you now?"

Hawk put his hand up to his head and moaned.

"Ah, no doubt your head aches, but that will go off. Now let me see what is really the matter. Humph! Here is the track of a bullet along the head, and, no doubt, it stunned you. Why, there is only a scalp wound, after all. Are you no better?"

"No," said Hawk. "My head!"

"Now, Mr. Joe?"

"Here I is."

"Just get some of that brandy you spoke of."

"With all the pleasure in life."

"And place a table-spoonful in a quart of cold water."

"Good gracious, won't that be rather weak, Mr. Doctor, don't you think? A table-spoonful in a quart of water! Oh, my eye, there will be cold without, with a vengeance. Oh—oh! you don't mean it, sir?"

"Yes, I do. You must then soak a few towels in it, and place them round your friend's head, and as fast as one gets warm you must replace it by a cool one. I don't see that I can do anything more for him, but if I can, I will call as I go by the end of this lane to-morrow about the same time as this. Do you understand me?"

"To be sure I does. It ain't to drink, after all. Well, to be sure, I didn't think as anybody in his senses would make such grog as that, nohow—a spoonful of brandy to a quart of water! Oh, dear—oh, dear!"

"Where am I?" said Hawk.

"Here, to be sure," said Joe.

That assurance did not seem to convey any very clear impression to the still rather bewildered faculties of Captain Hawk. It was something like a person calling out—"I," in answer to the inquiry of "Who is there?" After a pause of a moment or two, he said—

"Where is Ratchley?"

"Who?" said Joe.

"Ratchley Boyes. I did not hit him! No—no! I know all now—I fell, myself, at his fire. He hit me. Ah, yes, I must have fainted. It was in the old garden, to be sure. I was mad to agree to fight him; for to hit or to miss him were equally bad. Ah, Joe, is that you? Yes—yes. This is the hut in the lane. I recollect all now, and I know where I am."

"It's a wonderful, out-and-out cure," said Joe, "as ever was, doctor; and if ever I go dead, won't I send for you—that's all. Oh, my eye, it was a near go, when you comes to think of it."

One thing was quite evident, and that was, that Captain Hawk had, after all, sustained but little actual injury from Ratchley's pistol-shot beyond the shock, which had deprived him of consciousness for the time, and gave him the semblance of death.

Joe made the surgeon take his fee, and got a promise from him that he would call on the morrow, and then that gentleman took his leave.

Captain Hawk, with one of the towels soaked in the brandy and water round his head, lay upon his back, on the rather hard couch in the outer room of the hut.

Joe approached him carefully.

"Captain?"

"Well, Joe?"

"How are you now, captain?"

"Better. But how came I here? Tell me all about it, Joe. I know where I was, and I know where I am;

but I don't know how I came here, at all."

"Then I'll soon tell you, captain. You see, I heard pistol-shots in the old garden, and I thought to myself that some mischief was going on, so I made what haste I could to the spot, and there I found you."

"Ah, I see it all now."

"In course you do. I thought that somebody had done for you at last; but whether or no, it struck me you would rather not be left there."

"You were right."

"Well, I just took you up, and carried you off."

"You don't mean to tell me, Joe, that you carried me all the way from the garden of Boyes Hall to this place?"

"Oh, dear, no. There was the horse. He did that part of the business after I had got you through the paling, and I intended to bury you in the garden in a little while, for I didn't like the idea of the traps or the beaks getting hold on you, dead or alive."

"Thank you; but it's a good thing you thought of sending for the surgeon, Joe."

"I didn't."

"You didn't? Then how came he here?"

"I met him in the lane. He was asking his way, and he told me he was a doctor; so I thought I would just take him here, and get him to give a look at you before I covered you up."

"Which you would have done promptly?"

"Rather."

"Then it appears from all this, Joe, that I have had a narrow escape of being buried alive, after all?"

"Well, I don't know," said Joe, as he looked a little puzzled at this proposition. "Perhaps you might have sneezed, or winked with one eye, or something of that sort, afore it was all over."

"Or I might not."

"Well, you might not."

"Joe, I thank you for the care you have taken of me, and most of all from my heart do I thank you for removing me from the garden at Boyes Hall. I would rather have been buried alive here than found there by Ratchley Boyes, when he should have returned with his servants."

"Ah! that's all right, then?"

"It is. But are we alone here?"

"I understand you, captain. *She* has not come back."

"Well, I can't help it. This hut, poor and wretched as it is, was in some sort a refuge for her, poor thing; but if she deserts it, well and good, it is her own act; so I will say no more about her. Look to the horse, Joe; and now I feel as if I could go to sleep."

"All's right," said Joe.

With great care, this rough man then covered Captain Hawk with the large and warm counterpane; and then drawing the blind of the little casement close again, so that too much light should not make its way into the apartment to disturb the rest of the highwayman, he left the room, and went to look after the horse, which he had never expected would again bear the weight of its master.

* * * *

We now leave Captain Hawk to sleep off the effect of the slight wound he had received, and repair again to Boyes Hall.

The most active search of the gardens and grounds had failed to give to Ratchley any idea as to what had become of his late opponent; and when the daylight fairly came, the young man was still in the open air, pacing the lawn with an aspect of deep thought.

The question that was uppermost in the mind of Ratchley was, "Is Hawk dead or alive?"

To all appearance, the shot had taken full effect; and reasoning without the fact that the seeming dead body had disappeared so mysteriously, Ratchley Boyes would have said certainly that Hawk had at last received his death wound; but if so, where was he?

Had Ratchley not possessed the ample knowledge that he did of the character of Hawk, he might have started another proposition with regard to the affair, and that was, that in falling as he had, and lying so still, he was only counterfeiting death.

This was not a tenable proposition, though, considering the disposition of the man, which was such as totally to put to flight the idea of any such subterfuge upon his part.

Wearied and troubled by useless thought, Ratchley at last repaired to the breakfast room of Boyes Hall.

From his sister Philippa, who soon appeared there, he heard that poor May had passed the remainder of the night in a succession of fainting fits, the first one of which had been produced by the pistol-shots, that had convinced her there was a contest going on in the garden.

"And now, brother," said Philippa, "was it, indeed, Gerald Clifton who disturbed us all to such an extent?"

"Yes, sister, it was he, and none other."

"Oh, is it not sad to think that he could subject us to so much persecution, after all that we have already suffered for his sake?"

"It is, indeed; but I do think that we shall hear no more of him now. The grave will not give up its dead to vex us."

"You really think he is no more?"

"That is my impression, Philippa, I assure you."

Philippa trembled, as she said—

"Will it be at all prudent to tell May as much, do you think, brother?"

A flush of colour came to the cheek of Ratchley as he replied rather tartly,

"Yes, I think that, prudent or not prudent, she ought to know. If May can so disgrace her name and family by still harbouring feelings of interest or affection for such a man, the sooner they are quenched for ever by a knowledge of his death the better."

"Hush! here is our father."

"Hem!' said Sir John, as he entered the room. "Hem! I regret to say that I, in a manner of speaking, am not in that highly salubrious condition this morning as I ought to be—I say, as I—ought—to—be—Ha!"

"I regret to hear it, sir," said Ratchley.

"Hem! Ha! You regret to here it?"

"I do, sir."

"Very good. Hand me an egg, then."

"Yes, sir."

"Hem! When a window shuts suddenly upon the neck of an illustrious individual, it follows generally that it gives a jar."

"A what, father?" said Philippa; "a window—a jar?"

"Daughter Philippa, allow me to observe that you interrupted me."

"Yes, father; but I—"

"Ah—ah—silence! Silence! I speak."

Sir John waited until the silence had continued for a sufficiently long space to assure him that it was quite respectful; and then, with a wave of his hand, which he had taken care to adorn with some of the princely rings, he added—

"The window gave a jar to my nervous system. The jar I spoke of was not a piece of earthenware with a spout and a handle; but it was a—a kind of mental jar, I meant."

"Yes, father."

"Then don't interrupt me another time, daughter. If you were a small child, which you are not, for the Boyes' family are inclined to be rather extensive, I should request Lady Boyes to punish you; but, as it is, we will say no more about it."

"Thank you, father."

"Si—lence!"

Ratchley, despite all the vexations and troubles that were pressing upon his mind, was compelled to go to the window, and affect to looking out, to conceal the smile that would come to his lips at the pomposity of Sir John, which no circumstances seemed to be sufficient to repress.

Lady Boyes did not appear at breakfast, in consequence, as Sir John said, of indisposition, which, he added, was equivalent to not being very well.

After the breakfast, Sir John sunk into the recesses of a most easy chair, and looking sternly at Ratchley, he said—

"Sir!"

Ratchley rather started at this mode of address; but he slightly inclined his head, and then Sir John continued.

"The father, sir, is no more."

"The who, sir?"

"The father, I say, Ratchley Boyes, Esquire, the father is no more."

"I really, sir, do not quite comprehend."

"Ah! I did not expect that the pure sentiments of a delicate judgment would be quite comprehended; but allow me to state, that I have sent my compliments to Sir William Dodd."

"Oh, indeed, sir!"

"Yes, with a request that as he is in the commission of the peace, he will step over here, and aid me to take your deposition. We then, as two magistrates, will put you, Ratchley Boyes, Esquire, on your oath, and in that proceeding the father is no more."

"Oh, I quite understand you now, sir."

"Of course."

"You mean, that when you act in your official capacity as a magistrate, you no longer consider that you are to look to me as your son, but just as any other individual having a statement to make?"

"That is just what I said."

"Exactly, father. I quite understand; but don't you think—"

"No, sir, I don't"

"Pray hear me, father. Don't you think that it would be rather inconsistent to make a judicial affair of the matter?"

"No, sir, the magistrate does not."

"Very well, sir, of course you will have to give evidence yourself, and it is very likely that poor May will be compelled to appear."

"Hem! Ha! But a—a, that is, in good sober truth, Ratchley, who was it you shot in the garden?"

"The witness, father," said Ratchley, "is not upon his oath. The son is no more."

"How dare you, sir?"

"Oh, father, let us both be rational. It was Hawk, the highwayman, who fell, I think, by my hand, and I really think that the least said about the matter is the best. We cannot tell what injurious reports may get into circulation about the affair, even to the injury of poor May's honour. I am very sorry, father, you have sent for Sir William Dodd. You see, the whole matter may get into the newspapers, and we shall then never hear the the last of it."

"Bless me, I did not think. The magistrate is no more, and the father speaks now. I—really, in a manner of speaking—"

"Sir William Dodd!" announced a servant.

Sir John looked puzzled.

"Allow me, father, to speak to Sir William."

"Very good. The father lives again, and he allows the son to act. The magistrate and the witness dissipate—puff!—into thin air—I may say into thin air—hem!"

"Request Sir William Dodd to come here," said Ratchley.

The servant departed upon his errand, and in the course of a few moments, Sir William Dodd, a hale, hearty, country gentleman, made his appearance.

"Hey-day, Sir John," he cried, "what's amiss, that you should send man and horse after me in such a hurry?"

"The witness, Sir William," said Sir John, "that is, the father—no—I mean the magistrate—that is to say the son—God bless me, what do I mean?"

"Ha! ha!" laughed Sir William, "of course you don't know."

"Hem! I am afraid just at the present moment that I do not; but my son here, Ratchley Boyes, Esquire, will tell you all about it. He knows, my dear sir, and I will listen. Ha! I will listen, and if anything occurs to me regarding the opinions of ancient authors, I will let you know."

"Thank you, Sir John," said Sir William Dodd, "I am very much obliged indeed, though I have no great opinion of ancient authors myself."

"What, Sir William?"

"I say I have no great opinion myself of the ancient authors."

"Good gracious!"

"Ah, you may say good gracious, Sir John, as much as you like, but that is my opinion, my dear sir, and so I say it."

Sir John groaned, but he said no more just then, and Ratchley, who had not been sorry for the little time that had been given to him by his father and Sir William, had arranged in his own mind what he had to say to the magistrate, now that he had been sent for, since it would be difficult to send him away now without entering into something like an explanation with him.

"I am afraid, sir," said Ratchley, "that we have sent for you upon very insufficient grounds indeed."

"Oh, don't mention that," said Sir William, in an undertone to Ratchley. "I am by this time pretty well used to the rather odd vagaries of my old and trusted friend, Sir John, not in-

CAPTAIN HAWK WAITING THE APPEARANCE OF MAY BOYES.

tending any offence, of course, to you, Ratchley."

"None is taken, Sir William, I assure you; but the fact is, that last night there was a man in the garden, and I am afraid I have shot him."

"Indeed!"

"Yes, Sir William, I have some reason to believe that I fired at him and shot him, but I don't know that the shot is mortal."

"Where is he?"

"That, Sir William, is the most mysterious part of the affair. I left him lying upon the lawn apparently dead, while I went to call the servants, and when I got back, along with them, to the spot, he was gone."

"Then you did not kill him, after all?"

"Well, I really don't know; but, I may say, from the glimpse I had of him, that to the best of my belief it was no other than Captain Hawk, the highwayman."

"Ah, indeed?"

"Yes, Sir William, and so we thought that your advice would be valuable in the matter, so that we might know what to do."

"My good friend, you can do nothing."

"You think so?"

"Well, ask yourself what you can do. You find a man in your garden—you fire at him, and then he disappears, and so there is an end of the affair. You can do nothing more, that I can see, in the matter."

"Well, then," said Ratchley, "we need not say any more about it."

CHAPTER LXXVIII.

MAY HAS A STORMY INTERVIEW WITH HER BROTHER RATCHLEY.

The conclusion to which Sir William Dodd had been, in a manner of speaking, compelled to come to was just the one that Ratchley Boyes had wished to bring about.

As the magistrate was there, it was absolutely necessary to say something to him, and that something Ratchley wished to be conclusive.

In the course of the next half hour Sir William left Boyes Hall, after having had a dispute with Sir John about the merits of the cookery of the ancients compared with that of the moderns.

"Sir William Dodd," said Sir John, as he stalked into the library, and slightly touched his forehead, "is decidedly weak here."

"Sir John Boyes," said Sir William, as he mounted his horse at the gate of Boyes Hall, "is an ass."

With these highly satisfactory opinions, then, of each other, the two gentlemen had separated.

Ratchley had just taken his gun and was going a ramble with it and his dog, when Philippa came to him.

"Brother," she said, "May is up; she says she is quite well, only she insists upon an interview with you."

"I expected she would—I may say that I feared she would; but I am quite prepared to speak to her."

"Oh, brother, be mindful of what you say to her!"

"I will—I will."

"But I mean, that she is really ill and weak."

"I know she is weak; but, from my soul, Philippa, I hope she is not weak enough to have any regrets about that scoundrel, Hawk?"

"Alas—alas!"

"You know she has?"

"No—I know nothing. She will hardly speak to me at all, and it seems as if I would be the last person she would take into her confidence. I don't know how it is, but such is the case."

"Where is she?"

"In the cedar-parlour."

"I will go to her at once, then."

"Oh, Ratchley, be patient and forbearing with her. You know not the mischief that an angry word might produce. If she be weak, you should be strong enough to pity her."

"You are right, Philippa—you are right, and I am not angry that you have spoken to me in this way. I will be cautious of how I tell her that which she ought to know, and which, for her peace of mind, she must know."

It will be seen that there was, after all, with all his good feeling, something of the autocrat about Ratchley. The fact was, that the puerility of his father had early invested the young man with a kind of authority in the family, which otherwise he would not have possessed, and hence was it that he got into the habit of speaking with too much the air of a master of the house to his sisters, and to every one in it except Sir John.

Yet Ratchley loved May.

The reader has seen too many actions of his affection for her to leave any doubt upon that point; and if in what he is about to say to her he shall for a moment appear to be harsh and unfeeling, it will only be from the fact, that his heart is truly wounded at her condition, and that he loves her honour as well as he loves himself.

The cedar-parlour at Boyes Hall was one of the choicest small rooms of the mansion. It was panelled with cedar, which always imparted to the air of the apartment the faint odour of that wood, although it was some three hundred years old.

Ratchley felt that it would require all his courage to go through with the interview that May had sought with him; and as he went along a corridor towards the cedar-parlour, he more than once felt a dread of the approaching scene.

"It is my duty," he said, "and I will go through with it. There is no one else to tell her that which she ought to know, namely—that all thought, all idea of that man, Hawk, ought to be banished for ever from her mind, and that his death blots him from the world and its affairs."

Ratchley paused a moment at the door of the apartment, and then he tapped gently at it.

"Come in," said a faint voice.

He opened the door and entered the room gently. May was seated by the open window, which looked into a very retired part of the garden; but Ratchley was rather startled to see what, if he had given a thought to the locality, he must have known at once namely—that through an opening among the trees the exact spot of his encounter with Captain Hawk could be seen.

At the first flush of this fact, it seemed as if May had chosen that room, and that window, with the knowledge of such a fact; but a moment's consideration convinced Ratchley that the coincidence was only accidental, after all.

It was not possible that May could have any knowledge of the spot upon which Hawk had been left lying apparently in death, and weltering in his blood.

Ratchley felt faint at heart when he looked at his sister.

Never before had poor May looked so pale and wan as she did now. Not a vestige of colour remained in her face.

She saw that Ratchley was looking fixedly at her.

"Close the door, Ratchley," she said.

He did so.

"Oh, sister May, you are too unwell to speak to me upon the subject which, I know, is uppermost in your mind. Let me beg of you to retire to your own chamber, and endeavour by rest to restore yourself to something like your former self."

"No."

"Nay—I entreat you. You cannot see yourself, and, therefore, cannot tell how pale and sad you look."

"My mirror is faithful," said May, "and I have looked in it. Shall I tell you what I think, Ratchley?"

"Yes—I hope I am entitled to your confidence."

"Then, brother, I think that it is you who desired this interview more than I do. Is not that the truth? Tell me at once, and let me feel that I can and ought to believe you, or it will argue ill for what more we have to say to each other."

"It is something of the truth, but not all," said Ratchley, sadly. "I felt for you all that I uttered."

"Think no more of me then, except so far as regards what I shall say to you."

"Be it so."

"You will answer me truly that which I shall ask of you?"

"I will. Your requisition that I should so do makes the task that my conscience had set me to perform all the easier."

May was silent for a moment or two, and then she said—

"You had a contest with Gerald Clifton?"

"With Hawk, the highwayman and murderer I had, and likewise saw——"

"Oh, peace, brother—peace. Answer me first."

"Nay, sister, it is you who should answer me. How came that bold, bad man in your chamber? That is the question that you should answer to me—to your father, to your mother—to your sister—to all the world that loves truth and honour."

The colour slowly rose to May's cheeks, as she said—

"Do *you* suspect *me*?"

"No."

"That is well."

"No, May, I do not suspect you. I only ask for information. Will you answer me?"

"I will. As Heaven is my judge, I know not, except it was by climbing the balcony, how that man reached my chamber."

"I blush to ask you. Did you know of his coming?"

"And I breathe shame to hear you, and answer you—No."

"I believe you, May; but—but—"

"Say on," said May, faintly.

"You screamed, no doubt, at his appearance, and it was after that that I saw him leave your chamber. What became of him in the interim?"

May was silent.

"Oh, sister, answer me that."

"I will not."

Ratchley staggered to a seat, so completely prostrated was he by this all but admission upon the part of May that she had connived at the concealment of Hawk in her chamber, for where else could he be concealed than there?

"No—no!" exclaimed Ratchley, after a pause. "I cannot yet reconcile my mind to what seems so frightful a fact. You will not answer me, because you are affected at the question, or at my manner of putting it."

"As you please."

"But when you know, as I can assure you, that I do not insinuate aught to your prejudice by what I say, you will answer it."

"I will not."

"May—May, I implore you not to force me to the conclusion that the question I have put is one that you could answer if you would."

"I will not answer."

"Sister, are you mad?"

"God help me, I hope not."

"You will drive me mad. Was I ever deficient in love for you? Did I ever treat you otherwise than as one very dear to me, indeed? Have I not even done wrong by showing ever too marked a preference for you as my favourite sister?"

"Yes, Ratchley."

"By the memory of all that love, then that I have ever felt for you, and which I feel none the less now, I implore you to answer me the question I have proposed to you."

"No."

"You will not? You still persist?"

"I will not. I still persist."

"Wretched girl!"

"Ay, how true that is, brother Ratchley. I am a very wretched girl."

"You make yourself such by this obstinacy which amounts to criminality."

"As you please, brother, but I suppose now that I have refused to answer you the question you put to me, you consider yourself absolved from your promise to answer those I wish to put to you?"

"Perhaps not."

"Then I will put them."

"Do so," said Ratchley, with a sort of savageness in his tone. "Perhaps I shall have some pleasure in replying to you."

"Even that is possible."

"Nay, sister, I meant not that. Let those words pass as though they had not been uttered. They were but an ebullition of temper. I cannot at all times command my feelings as I would wish."

"Alas! nor I, nor any one."

"Let me know your question, then, May, and I will answer it as quickly as I can, but I will answer it truly. I will not, at the risk of your fortune, peace, and honour, tamper with the truth. What I know, you shall know."

"That is all that I can ask—it is all that I dare ask of you, brother. The question I would put to you trembles on my lips. I feel faint and ill, and I seem as if the world were stepping from me."

"Retire to your chamber."

"No—no!"

"Let me ring for assistance, then. Your sister will come to you."

"Oh, no—no! If you would not kill me quite, you will let this interview take its course. It need not be broken off now, Ratchley. All that there is to say between you and me must now be said."

"Be it so."

"Then—then when you had a contest with Gerald Clifton——"

"With Hawk, the highwayman."

"Peace, brother! This is no time to jangle about names. Let it suffice that you know well who I mean."

"Be it so. Go on."

"How did you and he separate? You, I perceive, are unhurt."

"True, sister. You ask a plain question, and you shall have the plain truth. I prepare you for a shock. I regret that it will be one, not for the fact, but for the effect. In plain language, then, I killed the ruffian!"

May, with a shriek, fell from her chair to the floor.

CHAPTER LXXIX.

CAPTAIN HAWK RECOVERS, AND MAKES A STRANGE RESOLUTION.

Captain Hawk slept for eight hours upon the rude couch in the hut, and Joe began to have serious apprehensions, notwithstanding all that the surgeon had said to him to the contrary, that it was a sleep which would be eternal.

Some twenty times he crept up to the side of the couch to listen if he could for a certainty catch the sound of the breathing of Hawk; and when he did so, he crept away again, somewhat satisfied; but at last he got rather desperate at the prolonged sleep.

"When the deuce," said Joe, "is he going to wake up, I wonder? Why, it's now getting towards the evening."

"Joe!"

"Oh, lor! there he is. Coming. Yes, here I is. How are you, now, captain?"

"Better still."

"That's all right, then. Why, this brush ain't hurt you, I suppose, then, captain, at all to speak of?"

"Oh, no. I have been thinking."

"Sleeping you mean, captain?"

"No; for the last hour I have been thinking deeply."

"I only wish you had said so, for I have been in a regular trembling for just about that space of time, thinking that you didn't intend all for to wake up agin in this here world."

"No fear of that."

"But what have you been thinking about, captain?"

"About making a great change."

"A great change?—a great change? What the deuce does he mean by that? You don't mean, captain, that you is a-going to turn religious?"

"That would be a great change, indeed, Joe. But I don't mean that; I mean in our mode of life."

"Oh, that's it. D—n it, he's going to try to get a honest living, as they calls it. Oh, dear! that will never last long. I suppose that rap on the head has put him a little out of sorts. Well, captain, what is the change to be, arter all?"

"I intend to try life in London as a man of fashion."

"Oh, lor!"

"Have you any objection?"

"None in the least. It can't make no difference to me. The rain will come in at the roof of this blessed place all the same, I take it, and the chimney will smoke, and so I don't see what difference it can make to me, captain, what you do in London, or anywhere else, so long as you come to the little old crib now and then as you used to do."

"You misunderstand me, Joe."

"Do I, captain?"

"Yes, most completely. I mean to take you with me."

"Me?"

"To be sure. I feel now that I can truly say, without the shadow of a doubt, that you are much attached to me. You have many times done me good service, Joe, and I cannot help thinking that the gloom and the solitude of this place must at times be very irksome to you."

Joe looked about him for a few moments, and then he said—

"Well, it ain't to say the most lively place in all the world, captain, to be sure."

"Of course not. I shall plunge, perhaps, into some of the follies of the town, Joe, and you will see more of life in one month than you would see here in a whole year."

"Very likely; but—but——"

"Go on. What would you say?"

"Oh, you are such a one for getting

into a passion with a fellow, that I hardly like to say what I was going to say; but if you will be a little patient, and hear a fellow out, I don't mind saying it."

"Go on. What is it? I promise to hear you with patience."

"Well then, captain, where is the money to come from?"

"If that is all your concern, Joe, I can put your mind at rest about it easily by the assurance that I have plenty."

"The deuce you have?"

"Yes. Anticipating that some evil day might come, when a rapid flight from England might possibly be necessary, I have from time to time laid by large sums, and I know where to lay my hand upon an amount that will last us some time; and when that is gone, I will find some mode of replenishing our purses."

"Not a doubt of that, captain."

"Well, is all agreed?"

"Yes, captain. I don't mean to say but that I do rather like the old crib. It's more dull to others than it is to me."

"I daresay it is, Joe."

"I have got used to the old broken-down den, and I like it in my way. But, however, if you are going, captain, why it's no use a-thinking about it. I'll go, too; and there's one thing, I can come back to it when I like, if other matters don't go on agreeable in London."

"That you certainly can, Joe."

"Agreed then, captain. Only bear in mind you are not to fly into a passion, and be ready to snap one's head off, if one should say to you some day, 'I want to go back to the old hut in the country.'"

"Far from it, Joe. I pledge you my word that as soon as you express such a wish, and that you really mean it, and then——"

"Hilloa!" cried a voice from outside the hut.

Joe started, and Captain Hawk half rose from the little miserable couch on which he lay.

"Who is that?" he said.

"Don't know," said Joe; "but I'll soon see."

"Hilloa!" cried the voice again.

"Go—go. Keep them amused while I rise."

"But you ain't able."

"Tush! I have ridden fifty miles sometimes in no better a condition than I am in now for the journey. Where is the horse?"

"In the shed."

"Very good. Is he all right for the road?"

"Yes, captain; but if you be off, am I to wait here for you, or to follow you to London?"

"Follow me, Joe. Come to the Royal Hotel in Pall Mall, within a few doors of St. James's Palace, and ask for Colonel Green!"

"Colonel Green? Well, that's a rum 'un. You ain't Green, captain, whatever else you may be. Hoi! They are coming it rather!"

A furious knocking at the door of the hut now interrupted the colloquy, and a voice called out—

"Is there a blacksmith about this neighbourhood?"

"Blacksmith!" said Joe. "What next? You be off, captain. I don't like the sound of that fellow's voice at all. It isn't natural. You be off. Don't mount, and hold the horse's head down, captain, till you get past all the shrubbery before you show yourself. Colonel Green, at the Royal Hotel, Pall Mall? That's it, I think."

"It is. Good day."

Captain Hawk glided from the room just as a heavy blow with a hammer split the door of the hut right down the middle, and disclosed have a dozen well-armed men at the entrance.

"Resist," said a voice, "and you are a dead man."

"Oh, don't mention it," said Joe. "What's the row now?"

They rushed into the hut, and seized him.

"Now, my fine fellow," said one, "we have you."

"Yes," said Joe; "but I can't return the compliment, for you are about as ugly a piece of human nature as I ever saw."

"Blow out his brains, if he tries any treachery!"

"Treachery?" said Joe. "Well, a lot of fellows come with some talk about a blacksmith, and then they break the door of a man's house in two, and collar him without asking his leave in the least, and then they talk about treachery. Cool, that ! "

"Search the place," cried the man. "We will unearth the fox."

"Oh, lor!" said Joe. "It's a fox, arter all."

"Silence!"

"Oh, certainly. Is there anything else I can do to oblige you?"

"Do you see that?" cried the man, showing a constable's staff.

"Yes."

"Well, perhaps, my fine fellow, you know what it is. Well, if you don't mind what you are about, we will just knock you on the head."

"You don't say so? Is it legal to take a man into custody, and then knock him on the head, old ugly?"

The other officers could not for the life of them help laughing at the imperturbable coolness of Joe as he spoke to their chief, who very likely, if he had thought he would be seconded by his men, would really have done Joe a mischief. As it was, he was forced to content himself with an unlimited amount of cursing.

"Go it," said Joe. "You'll get ill very soon, old gentleman."

The party of officers, for such they were, searched the hut carefully, but, of course, without the least success; and then the chief turned to Joe, and affecting quite a smiling face, he said—

"Come, now, old fellow, I don't see why you and I should fall out, after all."

"Oh," said Joe.

"No, I don't see it a bit. We are both men of business, of course, and will do the best we can for ourselves—Eh?"

"Ah, very likely. At all events, you will; so that's enough for you, you know."

"Ha! ha! you are a wag."

"Well, I really didn't know it."

"Oh, yes, you are; and now—let me see. I must give you five pounds."

"You don't say so?"

"Yes, five pounds in gold—that is to say, five guineas, you know—ah!—and then you will just give us a hint where to pitch upon Captain Hawk, the highwayman, and all will be right."

"So it will."

"You will tell us?"

"All I know I will."

"Well, out with it—now for it."

"Well, nothing."

"Nothing? What the deuce do you mean by 'Well, nothing'—eh? Come, come, you stand in a very ticklish situation, and if you are not very careful you will sleep in Newgate to-night."

"Ha! ha!"

"You laugh at that, do you? Wery well—we shall see. You shall sleep in prison to-night, as safe as you are born."

"No, I won't."

"But I say you shall."

"But I say I won't—I'll keep awake!"

The officers burst into a loud laugh at this, and their chief stamped about the hut like a madman.

"Take this fellow into custody," he cried. "The magistrates have certain and precise information that Hawk has been in this place. He was seen here by one who knows him well."

"The doctor!" thought Joe.

"And," added the officer, "although that one who saw him was but a boy, yet he is too sharp a one to be easily deceived, and there can be no doubt but that he was right."

"It wasn't the doctor," thought Joe, "arter all."

"Now, hark you, fellow!" added the constable.

"Drive on," said Joe.

"If you don't at once give me such information regarding Hawk, the highwayman, as shall enable me to go and capture him, I will take you to London, and lodge you in jail, and the magistrates will commit you as an accomplice in Hawk's robberies."

"Come along, then."

"You won't tell?"

"Got nothing to tell, or else wouldn't I? Of course. Do you think I could resist such a very insinuating old buffer as you is?"

"Take him away! Take him away!"

"We have searched the place, sir," said one of the officers; "but there's nothing here. There's the fresh marks of a horse's feet, though, close at hand."

"Ah, then, he has escaped! The villain!"

"Well," said Joe, "that was villanous; for if he was here at all, the idea of not staying for you, sets him up as a first-rate villain, off-hand, I should say; but if you will take me with you, gentlemen, of course, I can't help it; but I don't exactly think that you will find it turn out agreeable."

"Ha! ha! We will take our chance of that, my man. Now, comrades, we have done all the good we can here. Let us be off."

CHAPTER LXXX.

JOE GIVES THE OFFICERS SOME TROUBLE ON THE ROAD TO LONDON.

To tell the truth, the officers felt rather puzzled to know what to do with Joe. They did not like to leave him, and they did not like to take him with them.

In the former case, they felt pretty well sure that he and Captain Hawk would soon join company again, and have a laugh at them; and in the latter, they did not feel quite at ease as to what the magistrates might say to them for taking a man into custody without a charge.

They consulted a little.

"Come, now," said Joe, "don't be laying your heads together plotting mischief in that sort of way. If you are going, you——"

"Silence!"

"Well, that's a good 'un. Here a fellow is in his own little bit of a crib, and he is told he mustn't so much as speak."

"This conduct will be worse for you, my fine fellow."

"You don't say so?"

"We will take him," said the chief officer. "Clap the darbies on him."

Two of the constables seized Joe, and placed, with professional dexterity, a pair of handcuffs on his wrists, to which he made no sort of opposition, for he well knew how perfectly useless it would be to do so.

"Now then," he said, "perhaps as you have taken a fellow into custody, and clapped his wrists into this fix, you won't mind saying what it is for?"

"Hiding and assisting in the escape of a felon."

"Prove it."

"Oh, leave us alone for that. We will prove it."

"Oh," said Joe, "now I understand you; of course, what one of you says, another will swear to, and so on. Well, in that way, you can prove anything you like; so it's no use saying anything further about it."

"Come on—come on."

The officers were quite convinced that if Captain Hawk had been there at all, he had escaped them; but they were not quite sure of the fact of his recent presence in the hut; so that, after all, their capture of Joe was rather a bit of ill-natured spite, just because they had failed in their object than anything else.

Joe felt that this was the case; but, at the same time, he knew what terrible latitude of action was given by a lax magistracy to the officers, and he had no hope whatever of getting any justice done him in London, notwithstanding he felt that the officers were in no position to make any substantial charge against him.

There was another hope, though, that animated Joe, and that was, that Captain Hawk, in the extremity of his fortunes, would not desert him, and the sequel showed that that hope was well founded enough.

The officers were well mounted; and one of them took Joe behind him, he being fastened to his waist by a leathern belt; and as Joe's hands were secured in the handcuffs, it was quite out of his power to make even an attempt to escape, the consequences of which would revert upon himself in the long run.

"Now, my men," said the chief officer, "the sooner we lodge this rascal in jail, the better."

"Yes; that's all right," said the others.

"Yes, to be sure," said Joe; "and as soon as I get to London, I can send for my family solicitor, and then you will all get nicely trounced for taking an innocent man into custody."

"We will take our chance, old fellow."

"Well, now, I tell you what I will

do, without going any further, if you like."

"Ah!" said the chief officer, with a grin of self-gratification, "I thought we should bring this fellow to terms at last, when he found we didn't mean to stand any nonsense."

"Well, it's for you to accept or reject it at once," said Joe.

"Out with it. What is it?"

MR. LAMA ATTEMPTS THE LIFE OF HAWK WHILE READING MAY'S LETTER.

"You want Captain Hawk?"

"We do—we do."

"Well, then, if you leave me alone, I assure you the first time I should happen to have him pointed out to me, for I don't happen to know the gent myself, I will let him know as much."

"Confound you!"

"Why, what can I do more?"

"On—on. Give him a knock on

the head, Jenkins, if he don't hold his tongue. Ride on."

"Well—well," said Joe, after they had gone another half mile, "I was only joking up to now; but the fact is, this sort of thing neither suits you, gentlemen, nor me. It don't do you any good, and it don't do me any good, and I'm quite sure that as men of sense, every one of you will be glad of getting well out of this adventure."

'What have you got to say now?"

"Well, here I am, and you can't get any good out of me, you know, and you have got my family lawyer in perspective in London, who, for the sake of making a good bill, will stick to you all like a leech on account of the false imprisonment."

"Gammon!"

"Ah, you may call it gammon, if you like, but I can tell you all that you will find it to be something remarkably different, indeed. Now, I tell you what I will do."

"Well, what is it?"

"I'll let you off for five pounds a piece."

"Curse you!" cried the man behind whom Joe was riding, and he gave him a poke or two with his elbow, but Joe took care to return the compliment by kicking the man's legs, which was all he could do in the way of retaliation, so that quite a fight was got up between them, in the midst of which a horseman slowly emerged from a gateway communicating with the lodge of an estate close at hand.

The horseman was a man of advanced age. His hair was quite white and floated from under his broad shovel hat in wavy masses. His clothing proclaimed him a clergyman, but the horse he rode was a beautiful animal, and looked hardly staid and sober enough for such a clerical and elderly rider.

"Here's some gentleman," said the chief officer. "Be quiet, will you. Don't be kicking up a racket. It may be some country magistrate, too, for all we know to the contrary."

Joe left off kicking the officer, and the officer left off punching Joe in the ribs with his elbow, and then Joe glanced at the old clergyman, and the moment he did so, he cried out—

"Oh, my eye!"

"What now?" said the chief officer.

"I only said, 'Oh, my eye!' This wagabone of a fellow that you have put me behind wants to be the death of me. He ain't satisfied with punching all the breath out of my body with his elbow, but he has poked something in my eye now."

"I didn't," said the officer.

"You did, you wretch."

"Peace," said the chief of the party, and then touching his hat to the clergyman, he was about to ride on, when that gentleman said in a weak, tremulous voice—

"Stop—stop, my men. What is all this, eh? What is it?"

"We are Bow-street officers, sir."

"Oh, all right, then, and very proper. And this is some very bad member of society, no doubt. Yes—yes?"

"I ain't,' said Joe.

"What does he say?"

"He says, sir, as he isn't, but we know he is. He is the companion of Captain Hawk, the highwayman."

"What, of that bold, bad man, who ought to have been hanged long ago if the law had been satisfied? Dear me—dear me! I am Archdeacon Hensell, and a magistrate of the county."

"Yes, sir—yes, your honour. I thought he was some nob," whispered the officer to one of his companions. "We shouldn't have took this fellow, if you please, sir, but he knows where Captain Hawk is, and he won't tell."

"Shocking—shocking," said the archdeacon, and then riding up to Joe, he said in a solemn tone—

"Man—man, do you not know that it is a duty you owe to your fellow-men to give them such information of law-breakers as they require? These officers are trying to do their duty, and you are neglecting yours. Do you know where this Captain Hawk is?"

"Rather!" said Joe.

"What does he mean by rather?"

"He means a few," said one of the officers.

"A few? Dear me, what a strange phraseology. I cannot understand it."

"I mean, that I do know, old stick-in-the-mud," said Joe, "and so there's an end of it, but I mean, at the same time, that I don't intend to tell."

"But you must, young man."

"I shan't. Make me if you can."

"Oh, young man—young man, I am very much afraid you are on the high-road to the gallows, and that after that you will go where you little expect. I fear that you are one of those who cannot expect mercy here or forgiveness hereafter."

"Don't frighten a cove."

"You are a lost sinner; you are as a sheep that has strayed from the fold, and who, thinking that there are fairer and richer pastures in some other valley, finds itself suddenly at the brink of a precipice, beneath which there is nothing but a bubbling, seething lake of burning brimstone, and from which comes the shrieks of the condemned."

"Oh, lor!" said Joe.

"You are frightening him, I do think, reverend sir," whispered the chief officer. "Press him hard, for it would be a great thing to find out where Hawk is hidden, if it can possibly be done."

"So it would. Hark you, young man, I am a magistrate, and, as I understand that there is no very specific charge against you, I will undertake, if you lead us to where Captain Hawk, the highwayman, can be captured, to let you go free yourself. But we will not be tampered with. We must have Hawk before we let you go."

"Certainly, reverend sir," said the chief officer, "that's the way to put it."

"I don't know what to say," said Joe, "nor I don't know what to do."

"Do what is right."

"Well, I will; but—but——"

"What would you say, wretched man?"

"Do you really think, sir, that old what-do-you-call-him is likely to get hold of me in the long run?"

"I have no doubt about it."

"Oh, lor!—oh, lor! Here's a nice mess I'm in; officers a pulling at me and a frightening me in this here world, and the old gentleman a grabbing at me in the next."

"That is your fate, unless——"

"Oh, is there a chance, sir?"

"Yes, there is a chance. If you from this time try to do what's right, and begin by letting the officers of justice know where the man is whom they very properly, as far as they are concerned, wish to capture, you will have a fair chance of saving yourself from the dreadful fate that otherwise awaits you."

"I will do it, then."

"What," said the chief officer, "will you tell us where Captain Hawk is?"

"Yes, I will tell this gentleman. I will do more than that, too, for I will take you all to where you can lay hands on him, if you like."

"That is the very thing."

"If the gent as is a parson will ride a little on ahead with me, I will tell him all about it."

"That will do," said the archdeacon; and then taking the chief officer a little upon one side, he whispered to him—"I have frightened this man out of the truth, and I have no doubt but that now, if I keep up the impression that I have made upon him, he will show you where you can find the criminal you are in search of. I regret, though, that my engagements will not permit me to go further with you."

"I am sorry for that, too, sir."

"Well, it can't be helped. Let me ride with him a little in advance, and I will keep up the impression for as long a period as my time will permit me. Keep the handcuffs on him, but take your man on one of his comrades' horses, and don't be far behind us, for he looks rather a ruffian, and I am too old to receive with impunity even a chance blow from him."

"Oh, we will keep an eye on him, sir. It's all right. He can just hold the horse in with his hands in the darbies, and that's all."

"In the what?"

"Beg pardon, sir—the handcuffs I mean."

"Oh—ah! Dear me, what a strange name to give them."

The arrangement which had been proposed by the archdeacon was carried into effect, and Joe was upon the officer's horse alone.

"Now, fellow," said the archdeacon, "I can ride a little way with you. Which is the direction that the man is to be found in?"

"Captain Hawk, sir?"

"Yes—yes, the notorious criminal, Hawk."

"Right away there, sir, whence we came from."

"Very well. Now, you will ride by my side, and you may depend upon it that, much as I dislike the idea of bloodshed, I shall order the officers to fire upon you if you attempt any escape or ony violence whatever, and I hope, now, that for your own sake, both here and hereafter, you will act seemly and honestly in the matter."

"Ah, sir, it was that there brimstone all a bubbling and a boiling, as you spoke of, that gave me a turn."

"He's a poor wretch, after all," said the chief officer. "Let us keep back a little. The old gent will frighten him out of his wits."

"He's half done that already," said one of the officers.

"Yes," said another. "He seems all of a shake. I didn't think by his manner at the hut, now, that he was the sort of fellow that would be so easily talked over."

"Well," added the chief officer, with a philosophical look, "you see these persons have a way of doing it that other people haven't. They look at you in such a kind of manner, that it seems to go right through you. When the old gent spoke about all that lot of brimstone, I saw the fellow give quite a sort of shiver."

"So did I."

"Well, it's a good thing we met with him."

"But, I say," said one, "what's a harchdeacon?"

"Oh, an archdeacon? Why, he's a kind of a—a sort of, you know well enough, what an archdeacon is."

"I'll be banged if I do."

"Then, I don't; but it's some sort of top sawyer of a parson, you see, and no doubt it's a d——d good thing."

"Leave the parsons alone for that. You may be quite sure of its being a good thing, if they think it worth while to have anything to do with it. But what a horse he has."

"Yes; it's a beauty."

"And look at his seat in the saddle. I should say that old gent, now, has been a first-rate rider in his time. No doubt he goes after the hounds, now. There's lots of parsons as does, I have heard, though it don't sound like saving folks' souls, that, does it, somehow?"

CHAPTER LXXXI.

THE ARCHDEACON UNDERGOES A STRANGE METAMORPHOSIS.

The archdeacon certainly was superbly mounted; and he as certainly had the look that the officers so much commented upon, and which made them say that some parsons had a way of looking like hunters, as he did.

Perhaps Joe had his own opinion of the archdeacon from the first moment that he joined the party; and, perhaps, the reader had likewise; and, in all human probability, their two opinions would not be far off from agreeing with each other.

We shall soon see.

"Now, my good man," said the archdeacon to Joe, as they rode a little in advance of the officers. "My good man, what is required of you is, in the name of providence, to tell where Captain Hawk, the famous, and I may say atrocious, or rather infamous highwayman is hidden?"

"Oh, lor!" said Joe.

"That is what I require of you, young man."

"Good again," said Joe.

"Hem!" said the archdeacon, raising his voice, so that the officers should hear him. "It is a very simple thing that is required of you, young man, indeed. All you have to do, is to take us to the place of concealment of that man, and so save yourself both in this world and in the next."

"You don't say so?" said Joe. "Well, I think I had better do it, I admit, sir."

"Of course you had."

The archdeacon turned slightly in his saddle, and motioned the officers to keep off, which they did; and then in a low tone, he said—

"Joe, can you ride well with the darbies on you?"

"Rather, captain."

"Did you know me?" added Captain Hawk, for it was indeed no other than that daring personage, upon his own magnificent horse, which, after once seeing, no one could mistake. "Did you know me?"

"Well, I'm blessed if I did at first. But in course I knew the horse, and then I knew you."

"Exactly. Now, Joe, the only chance of escape, is by a gallop for it. You are well acquainted with the nature of the ground hereabouts, and must lead the officers where we shall have a fair start."

"Trust me for that, captain. And so you wouldn't desert poor Joe, after all, captain?"

"Phaw!"

"Ah, you may say that; but I shan't forget it, I can tell you, captain, no, not if——"

"Peace—peace! there is no need of anything of that sort between you and me, Joe. We both do the best we can; and the worst policy in the world for us to pursue, would be to desert or play the traitor with each other. I know I can confide in you, and it would be a hard thing if you could not do as much in me."

"Yes, but——"

"There, that will do; give all your attention, Joe, to what we have to do. The road must be well traversed."

"It shall, captain. This ain't a bad horse that I ride, and it seems to be tolerably fresh."

"It is a right good one, Joe; and there is one thing that I don't forget, and that is, that no one can get so much out of a horse as you, in the way of a leap or a dashing gallop for a mile or two; therefore, I am easy about that if we get a fair start."

"Well, captain, so am I. But these bracelets that they have put upon me, take half the life out of me."

"That can't be helped."

"Don't you think you could gammon them to take them off, captain? Oh, if you only could, I should feel like twice the man I am. Can you do that?"

"No. It would only excite needless suspicion. It must not be attempted, Joe. We are increasing our distance each minute from the officers, and it is just as well to let well alone."

"That's true."

"I will leave it to you, then, entirely to select the spot where the start is to be made."

"Very good, captain. About a mile on ahead, just as we are going, there is a little lane that is only wide enough to let a couple of horsemen go abreast in it."

"Rather a bad place to be fired at, Joe, by the officers, who will not scruple to use their pistols."

"Yes, captain; but I don't intend to start there. At the end of that lane there is a gate that shuts rather awkwardly with a spring. Now, I tell you what will be the plan. When we get close at hand to the gate, you must dismount, and open it, and we must go through. A good hard push will then close fast the spring in such a way, that nothing but stronger tools than they have with them can open it, unless they know the dodge of lifting it off its hinges, and they won't think of that in a hurry."

"Good."

"Well, captain, that will give us a start."

"What is beyond the gate?"

"Why, a great straggling field, of about forty acres, and there's a stream running along one side of it, and winding away ever so far, quite cutting that part of the country in two. That we must jump."

"Very well; and then?"

"Why then, captain, we get into a high-road again, which would take us right off to Guildford, if we went on it for a few miles; but there's loads of places to stop at, if we are so inclined, on the road, right and left."

"That might do."

"I think as it will, captain."

"Well, so do I. Only as you know the peculiarities of the gate you speak of, I think that you had better take it in hand, Joe."

"Ah, captain, I would in a minute, but you forget these confounded darbies that I have on me."

"Ah, I did at the moment. Well, Joe, I will manage the gate; and now all we have to do is to jog on."

"Hadn't you better, captain, say something to the officers? for I just saw, as I turned the corner of my eye round to the men, that they were a laying of their heads together in a kind of a talk, and it may be that they think things ain't quite right."

"Yes—I will speak to them."

Captain Hawk paused, and turned his horse's head towards the officers, and beckoned to the chief constable, who rode up to him, and then Hawk said to him—

"The fellow not only says he is prepared to take us to where Captain Hawk is hidden, but he promises to make other important revelations regarding his career, and I promise him a free pardon from the secretary of state if he does so; but he wants a witness to the promise, so you now hear me make it to him."

"Yes, sir," said the officer.

"If you," added Hawk, turning to Joe, "make such revelations as shall clear up the mystery connected with the murder of Judge Holme, so as to convict Hawk, the highwayman, of it, I pledge you my word that, up to that date, you shall have a free pardon, from the secretary of state, for all offences whatever."

"That seems fair enough," said Joe, who was quite delighted with the coolness and tact with which Captain Hawk deceived the chief officer.

"Yes," said the officer, "I am a witness to that."

"Then the prisoner is so far satisfied," said Hawk.

"Oh, well, yes," replied Joe. "I am, as you say, sir, so far satisfied, and I will tell all I know."

Hawk bent forward to the officer, and whispered to him—

"Keep your men back. This fellow is, I find, very superstitious, and I expect before we have gone another mile to frighten him into a revelation of matters that the authorities very much wish to know. Keep a good distance off, though, for he is nervously alive to the fact that he may be overheard."

"Just so, sir. I will."

The officer rode back to his comrades, and imparted what the archdeacon had said, to which they listened with evident interest, and one of them said—

"Well, if that parson frightens him into clearing up that affair of the murder, it will be one good thing done, for that has bothered us all."

"Ay," said another, "it has."

"Yes," added the chief officer, "there is not a constable or a magistrate in the kingdom that does not fully believe Captain Hawk did the murder, and yet nobody can make out how he got up such a famous *alibi*."

"It was a famous *alibi*; and I tell you what my wife says about it. She says that Captain Hawk is well acquainted with old Nick, and that he went and showed himself in the likeness of Hawk to all the people who came and got up the *alibi* for him, while he was on the common murdering Judge Holme."

"There is something in that," said another of the officers.

"Stop a bit," said the chief officer. "By Jove, that gives me an idea."

"Does it, sir?"

"Yes, it does. By Jove, yes, and a good one, too."

"What is it, sir?"

"Why, just at present, I think I will keep it to myself, you see, as it may not, after all, turn out to be any good; but I will think it over."

"I say, though, what a way off that parson is getting with that fellow; I hope all's right."

"Right? To be sure it is. Ain't the fellow handcuffed? What harm can he do the parson?"

"Well, none; but yet, I—I don't somehow——"

"You don't somehow what?"

"Well, if I must say it, I don't exactly like that parson's looks. My wife has an idea that the devil and Captain Hawk are as thick as thieves, you see, and what, suppose that should be him?"

"Who? The captain?"

"No; the other gent."

"What stuff! How can you talk in that way? Hilloa! Where the deuce have they got to now? They have turned down some lane, and are out of our sight. Come on, comrades, I don't exactly intend to lose sight of our prisoner for all the parsons in the world. Come on—come on."

The officers, who had been letting their horses go at quite a gentle walk, now all broken into a trot, and from a trot to a kind of half-gallop, which soon brought them to the corner of the lane down which Captain Hawk and Joe had turned to the left of the high road.

When Hawk and Joe had gone on again, after the few minutes of trifling conversation that the former had had with the chief officer, they both had increased the speed of their horses, but in so careful a manner, that while the officers were talking away themselves, the distance between the two parties had materially increased in extent.

This was just what Captain Hawk wanted, for well he knew that every pace he was further from the officers multiplied his chances of escape amazingly.

"Joe," he said, "is the lane near at hand?"

"Yes, captain; quite close now. Oh, sir, how you did gammon that fellow, to be sure, captain! Well, I never! You have got a face to say things as I couldn't say for the life of me. But that comes of being a gentleman."

Captain Hawk made no reply to this rather original compliment to his gentility, and they trotted quietly on till Joe, seeing a house that was at the corner of the lane, drew Hawk's attention to it, by saying—

"We are close on it now, captain."

"That is all right," said Hawk, as glancing behind him he saw that they had nearly doubled their distance from the officers. "As soon as we get into the lane, Joe, let us make speed, for we shall be out of their sight."

"Yes, captain, and out of their hearing, too, for the lane is so shaded both in summer and winter, that it almost always is wet and miry, so that the horses' feet won't make much sound in going over it."

"That is fortunate. Now for it!"

They turned into the lane, as the officers had seen, and went some twenty paces or so down it as solemnly as might be; but then they set their horses to a gallop each of them, and it so happened that they did so at the same moment that the officers had commenced making speed; so that neither party could be said to lose any time from the moment that Captain Hawk and Joe had turned into the narrow old lane.

Captain Hawk and Joe, though, made the greatest speed, for they got to a hard gallop as quickly as they could, and in a few minutes reached the gate that Joe had spoken of.

Just as they got to that part the officers reached the commencement of the lane.

"Now, captain," said Joe, "there's the gate. It's all right."

"I will open it," said Hawk; and hastily dismounting, he got the gate open, and led both horses through it.

"Pull it far back, captain, and then dash it shut with all the force you can, and you will get it past the spring, and if that don't puzzle them a bit I don't know what will."

Captain Hawk understood perfectly what Joe meant him to do; and indeed, if the gate could only be forced by a sudden jerk past the piece of spring steel that it partially closed upon, and which stopped it from banging against the post, there was no mode of opening it but by lifting it off its hinges, or absolutely breaking it down, and either way would take some time both in thought and in execution.

With a swing that was enough to send the gate and its support all to smash together, Captain Hawk shut it.

"Done," said Joe. "It's done, now, captain. Oh, if I could only get rid of these darbies, I should feel as comfortable as possible, now; but I can't—d—n it, I can't, so there's no use in growling over them."

"Not a bit," said Hawk, as he remounted. "I will rid you of them as soon as I can."

CHAPTER LXXXII.

CAPTAIN HAWK AND JOE EFFECT THEIR ESCAPE, AND GO TO LONDON.

At such a mad gallop that their cattle were perfectly terrified at it, the officers now came down the lane, for they began, now, to have the most serious doubts concerning the good faith of the pretended archdeacon, and the idea of being so egregiously taken in was gall and wormwood to them all, and drove them nearly frantic.

Yet it was not quite certain. There was still a hope in the mind of the chief officer that all might be right; but it was a hope that each moment got fainter and fainter.

They reached the gate.

"Where are they, sir?" cried one of the men.

"D—n them! I don't see them at all. Open the gate, one of you. They could not get over the hedge."

"Not a bit of it, sir. There they go."

"Where—where?"

"There, over the hillock, yonder. Now they are gone again."

The officers all rose in their stirrups, and took a last, long look at the archdeacon and their prisoner as they rose to the top of a little grassy eminence, some half a mile off, and appeared for an instant upon its summit, and then disappeared over it.

"Gone!" said the chief officer.

"Gone!" said the others.

"And the reward?" said one.

"Is changed into ridicule," said another.

"Curses!" cried the chief officer. "I will pursue them, if it cost me my life. We can raise the country after them wherever we go. The description of them is easy, and they connot be mistaken. By Jove! I never was so thoroughly done in all my life. Open the gate, Roberts. Why the deuce don't you open the gate?"

"Because I can't."

"You can't, idiot?"

"Try yourself and be hanged to it," said the man, sulkily giving up the attempt. "It's fast, and in some diabolical manner, too, that I don't at all understand. A man is not an idiot 'cos he can't open a gate that won't open at all."

"This is Captain Hawk's doings, for a thousand pounds," said the chief officer, as he dismounted, and soon saw what was the matter with the gate; and then going to the hinges, he cried—"It is all right. A couple of you give it a good lift, and it will come off its hinges. That's the way to do it. A little higher. Now for it. There it goes, and be hanged to it."

The gate was thrown down, and in another moment the officers were in the meadow beyond it, and going in a straggling company on the route that they had seen the archdeacon and their prisoner take.

In their over haste, though, these men now felt how utterly hopeless was any attempt to come up with men so well mounted as their prisoner and Captain Hawk was; for now they made up their minds that the pretended archdeacon was no other than that personage, and, probably, they would not have gone upon the wild-goose chase before them now if it had not been some relief to their chagrin.

After scouring the country for a mile or two, and seeing nothing of the fugitives, the chief officer pulled up, and in a dolorous voice, he said to his comrades—

"It's no go!"

"Not a bit of a go," said one of them.

"Well, here we are, all in the same mess; and I tell you, my good fellows, nobody knows what has happened but ourselves, and if we keep on our errand, nobody can have the laugh of us. It ain't at all likely that Captain Hawk will ever say anything about it, if we don't."

"There is good sense in that," said one of the men. "I don't like anybody to have a laugh at me no more than my neighbours."

"And I generally quarrel if anybody sets to a grinning at me," said another, rather sneeringly.

"Very well, then," said the chief officer; "let it be quite understood among us all that we keep the thing to ourselves."

"Agreed—agreed!"

"Well, that's a comfort; and mind, now, I stand brandy-and-water all round when we get to London."

"That'll do. Hurrah!"

The officers seemed by this general offer of the brandy-and-water to be as much consoled as if they had, after all, caught Captain Hawk and his man, Joe, and one of them said—

"After all, we may have him another time, you know, and then we can have a good laugh, if we like, at how we were jilted to-day."

"To be sure we can."

With this, they sought the first high-road they could get to, and took their route to London, pretending to be much better pleased than they were in reality; for they felt their disappointment rather keenly, and the chief of them would have freely given his share of the reward only to have had the pleasure of getting a good grasp of the

CAPTAIN HAWK IN THE GARDEN OF BOYES HALL.

collar of the mock archdeacon; but that was not at all a likely thing to ensue.

We now return to Captain Hawk and Joe.

At the first flush of the affair, any one would be apt to think that the appearance of Captain Hawk and Joe upon the summit of a hillock, where they would be likely enough to be seen by their enemies, whenthey might have gone round it on the low land, was an unwise thing upon their parts; but it was only a little manœuvre of Joe's.

After getting across the first meadow or two, he said to Captain Hawk, who was a little behind him—

"They ain't got through the gate, captain, and I tell you what we can do, if you want to go to London."

"What, Joe? I do want to go to London."

"At once, captain?"

"Yes, Joe—at once."

"Very good; then the best way will be to crawl on the top of one of the little grass hillocks, so as to let the officers see us, and then we can turn short to the left, and a mile of country past, we shall get into the high-road again."

"What road?"

"The Guildford road, captain; and if you don't think that the daylight is rather against you, I should say there will be no sort of difficulty in getting to London in two hours' time from now."

"Let it be so, then. I like that better than your first plan of operation, Joe."

"Very good, then; here goes. Oh, la! Oh, dear!"

"What's the matter?"

"These blessed darbies, captain. If I could only get rid of them, I should feel like the Joe as was, instead of feeling like the Joe as is. They seem, captain, do you know, as if they eat me up."

"Never mind, Joe. As soon as we see a blacksmith's place I will make short work of the handcuffs; but as it is, I have no means of relieving you of them, and any ill-directed, awkward attempts to do so, could only end in hurting your hands, without accomplishing the object."

"That's true, captain. Then I must just grin, and bear it."

Joe might grin, and he did so; but it was anything but a grin of mirth; and he did not bear the handcuffs with anything like the philosophy that one would have expected from his character; but then it must be admitted that such a state of things brought with them a feeling of such total helplessness to a strong, hearty man, that he might well be excused for any sort of impatience he might feel under the infliction.

The grassy promontory was passed, and then they struck across a few fields exactly at right angles to the course they had been pursuing, which, as Joe had predicted, brought them out in the high-road to London.

"A gallop now, Joe," said Captain Hawk, "will be everything. Can you manage your horse well with your hands in that condition?"

"Oh, yes, captain, tolerably. It ain't pleasant; but I can do it."

"Come on, then."

They did not put their horses to an absolute gallop, for to have done that would, probably, have attracted more attention on the road than they would have liked, but they got such a capital canter out of them that, after all, it was very little inferior to a gallop.

They reached a straggling lot of houses to the right of the road, and Joe heard the clank of a smith's hammer.

"Hip—hip—hurrah!" he cried.

"Are you mad?" said Captain Hawk, sharply drawing up, and looking with surprise at his follower.

"No—but I shall be soon if I don't get rid of these darbies. Only listen to that sound, captain. What is it?"

"Ah! the clank of a smith's hammer, is it not Joe?"

"To be sure it is."

"Then you shall be free, my good fellow. I had really quite forgotten your state of bondage. I see the ruddy glare of a forge light. Come on, Joe. By fair means or by foul, we will procure the services of this smith for you."

"Thank you, captain. It's the most particular thing I can ask of you just now. If I can get my hands at liberty, I shall not know how to contain myself; and I do think, if they knew how these darbies have served me out for the last hour or so, they would be quite satisfied that they had had their revenge out of me. I'd take my chance of a bullet or two, with great pleasure, rather than be cooped up in this way."

Captain Hawk trotted up to the door of a curious-looking smithy that was by the road side, and he saw a great bulky-looking lad hammering away at a red-hot horse shoe, and singing at his work.

"When nought goes right in the 'versal world,
And everything goes wrong—
When you can't eat your witta nor drink your beer,
Nor anyways push along—
The wery best thing for a chap to do
Is to *blew* up the fire like blazes,
And clip (bang, bang!) at a red-hot shoe,
'Till the——"

"Ah!" said the fellow, stopping his work, and dashing the perspiration with the back of his hand from his brow. "There it is. I can't find no good rhyme as comes in well to blazes."

"Hilloa!" cried Captain Hawk.

"Eh? Who are you?"

"Your friend, young fellow. I'll give you a rhyme.

"The very best thing for a chap to do
Is to blow up the fire like blazes,
And to clip away at a red hot shoe,
'Till he finds a rhyme that amazes!"

"Dang it, yes," said the young smith; "that's it."

"To be sure it is. Are you the owner of the smithy?"

"No. Master is."

"Who are you, then?"

"Oh, I'm his little boy, you see."

The little boy stood about six feet three, and was stout in proportion.

"Ah!" said Hawk, "so I see; you are a promising youth, and quite a poet; but I want you to do a little job for me, my fine fellow, if you have a few minutes to spare."

"All's right, sir. What is it?"

"Only a trifle."

"Horse cast a shoe?"

"No. Take those off."

Joe leant from his horse, and held his manacled hands towards the young smith.

There was a dead silence for a few moments, during which the smith rubbed his chin with his hammer, and then he said—

"Humph! Take them off?"

"Yes."

"The handcuffs?"

"Just so."

"Who are you, and how came they on?"

"Hark you, my friend," said Captain Hawk. "It don't matter how they came on. All I have got to say is, that on they are, and off we want 'em; and I don't think you are the sort of fellow to say no to such a job. We are what we are; but if you won't do it, I leave you to your own thoughts, that when you could do a kind thing you wouldn't, for fear it mightn't turn out the best for you in the end. You are not the man I took you for, I see."

"Yes, I am. Stay a bit. I'll do it."

"You will?"

"To be sure, I will."

The young smith darted into the smithy, and then, in a moment or two, returned with a bundle of picklocks.

"Hold still," he said. "Hold still and steady for a moment. It will soon be done. I know how to manage it."

"Hold hard, there!" cried a voice from the smithy. "What are you about, you boy, there?"

"Who is that?" said Hawk.

"The old man."

"The old man? Who is the old man?"

"Master."

"Ah, then, he will interfere?"

"Perhaps."

Click went the lock of the handcuffs, and they fell to the ground. Joe immediately put his hands to his mouth, and crowed loudly in imitation of a cock so capitally, that the young smith, although he started back at the suddenness of the sound, gave a slap to his thigh, as he called out—

"Dang it, that's good!"

"Confound you all, what is the meaning of this, I say?" cried the blacksmith again, advancing with a threatening look to the 'little boy.' "What have you been about?"

"Nothing, master."

"Ah, what have we here?"

The handcuffs had attracted his attention, and he picked them up from the ground, where they had fallen when released from the wrists of Joe.

"If you don't know, old fellow," said Joe, "what they are, I only hope that your ignorance will be enlightened some day by being intimately acquainted with 'em; so now good-day. You may keep 'em agin you want 'em, old file."

"Stop—stop!"

"Oh, how likely," said Joe.

"I must take you all into custody, for I think you are no better than you should be."

"Come after us, then," said Captain Hawk. "Of course we will wait for you in the Old Bailey. You will find a good walk do you good."

CHAPTER LXXXIII.

CAPTAIN HAWK SETTLES HIMSELF COMFORTABLY IN THE METROPOLIS.

Joe and Captain Hawk trotted off, and as they glanced round at the smith they saw him belabouring the broad back of the "little boy" with a thick stick, while the latter was cutting the most extraordinary capers under the punishment.

"Is that young fellow a downright fool," said Joe to Captain Hawk, "or is his precious faculties only regularly bamboozled with his poetry and stuff?"

"A little of both, Joe," said Hawk, "I think."

"Very likely, captain. I never knowd any good come of poetry and all that sort of thing. Did you, sir?"

"Never."

"To be sure not. I was in service once with a poet; but, lor bless you, he didn't get on no how."

"Well, Joe, you shall give me a little of your experiences at another opportunity, but at present you will be so good as to listen to me, for it is necessary that I should tell you what I mean to do in London when we shall get there. Are you attending to me?"

"Yes, captain; in course I is."

"What are you laughing at, then?"

"Oh, I am only having a quiet kind of a laugh, you see, captain, to myself, at the idea of having got rid of these darbies so very comfortably. I feel quite myself again, now, and as if I could jump over the moon if I had only a run long enough to give me a good spring."

Hawk smiled at this comment of Joe's, and then he added, in a calm, serious voice—

"Joe, I think that the road is getting vulgar."

"Eh?"

"The road is getting vulgar, I say."

"Oh!"

"Plague take you, don't you understand me? I mean that I don't think picking up a living on the highway is very gentlemanly, and so I shall, for the present, at all events, leave it."

"Wery good, captain."

"People without education or manners, and with nothing but brutality, now, steal a horse, and with all the swaggering impudence in the world come upon the highway, and so they bring discredit upon a genteel profession, and make society condemn us altogether as a low set."

"There's something in that, captain."

"I know there is; and, therefore, Joe, I mean for the present—mind I say for the present, for something may happen, possibly enough, to induce me to alter my determination—to go to London, and try what can be done among the aristocracy in a genteel and light sort of way."

"Oh, I know," said Joe. "I understand."

"Well, I'm glad you do."

"You means a little swindling?"

"What?"

"Eh? Don't you?"

"If you use that word again I will knock your stupid head off."

"Oh, very good. I ain't no scholard, you see, captain, so I don't know the perlite way of speaking of things, but you see, 'atween you and me and the post, I didn't think as we needed to have minced the matter much; but howsomdever, in course, I'll call things just what you please."

"You had better keep a strict guard over your stupid tongue," said Hawk, biting his lip with vexation.

"Very good," said Joe.

"I mean," added Hawk, "to mingle with the highest and noblest of the land."

"Are they always found together, captain?" said Joe.

Hawk laughed outright at this.

"Joe," he said, "you are no fool. They are not always found together; and, indeed, I might take upon myself, Joe, to say that they are very seldom found together; for a man may be noble without being great, and great without being noble. Nobility, and the nickname that it gives to people, is the servility of little minds. When once the barrier is passed that separates the commonality from the nobility, you soon perceive of what really common and vulgar materials great people, as they are called and considered, are made of."

"That's my idea, captain."

"It is a true one, Joe."

"But what do you mean to do, captain, when you gets among such a rummy lot, eh?"

"I mean to make money by play."

"Oh, cheating."

"Cheating?"

"Well—well, captain, don't be in a rage. I thought, in course, that you meant cheating, for I never did hear of any good being done by play, as they call it, that wasn't done by cheating."

Captain Hawk was silent for a time. Perhaps he began to repent of bringing such a shrewd observer as Joe with him to London; but when he came to reflect upon the real affection which the kind-hearted creature had for him, he concluded, and rightly too, that Joe's tested good services would be exerted all in his power, and so would be a great acquisition to him in many an adventure that might occur.

"Joe," he said after rather a long pause, "I have no doubt that you and I will get on very well together, but we need not discuss too minutely what names are even given to my proceedings in London. For the present, let it suffice for me to tell you what I want you to do, and what we are to be about immediately upon our arrival in the great metropolis."

"Exactly," said Joe. "Go on, captain."

"Then, in the first place, Joe, we will both alter our appearances as much as possible."

"Very good."

"I shall proceed, in the first instance, to a livery-stable, and put up our horses, and then to some tailor's, where ready-made apparel is kept, and do all we can to alter our outward appearances. Yes, Joe; I shall put you into a suit of rich, but not gaudy, livery. Have you any objection?"

"Not the least. Anything for a bit of fun."

"Very well. I shall then dress myself in the first style of fashion, and then, hiring a coach, we will go to a hotel and put up, and I shall leave it to you, when you are questioned, as, of course, you will be, to give out that my wealth is incalculable, and that you rather suspect I am one of the Austrian royal family."

"Oh, lor!"

"Do you understand all that?"

"Yes. But why do you want to be a foreigner? Pah! You know what a set they are."

"Because I must give myself a title, and an English one would soon be found not of the true sort—you understand, Joe?—while, if I call myself Count something,' all will be well, and it will be quite impossible for any one to find out that that is a delusion, because all foreign countships are delusions."

"Exactly, captain. What next?"

"You will then intimate that I am here upon some secret mission of vast importance, and you can say that I hired you at Dover."

"Wery good; but if, among all these abominable lies, I forget one, I shall be in a mess, I suppose?"

"Lies?"

"Oh, begs your pardon, I—I—didn't mean lies."

"Uttering misrepresentations to mislead the curiosity of people who have no right to inquire should not be called lies, Joe."

"Sartinly not, captain."

"Then don't call them such again."

"Wery good. But will it matter much, captain, if I forget one or two of the misrepresentations?"

"No."

"Then my mind is easy about that, and I think I know all that you want of me, captain."

"I think you do, Joe; and here we are entering Oxford Street; so now you will be so good as to mind what you are about, and do not let any indiscreet word escape you, and above all, Joe, mind and resist the temptation of revealing anything; for if you do not while you are making a friend or or two, you may be thwarting me of the means of making hundreds."

"All's right, captain."

Hawk now put up the horses at the first livery-stables he came to, and walking, then, down Oxford Road, as it was then called, till he got to Bond Street, he entered that emporium of fashion, as it was then, and not as it is now, the resort of ancient tradesmen, who know not the present requirements of the age, and faded dandies, who strive, like elderly mothers, to flutter round the flame of their past successes.

Bond Street was at that time in its glory, for there was not such another street in London, and Captain Hawk knew well that he would have no difficulty in suiting himself with whatever he wanted there.

Arriving at a fashionable tailor's, Hawk walked in with the air of a man who knew his welcome, and the proprietor of the shop bowed to the very floor.

"Here is my servant," said Captain Hawk. "I want him fitted at once with a suit of livery. Price is no object, provided the goods be of the finest quality, and the colour crimson."

"Yes, sir—yes, sir; certainly."

Joe looked over Captain Hawk's head, and beckoned to the tailor; and when he had that individual close to him, he whispered—

"Don't say, Sir."

"Eh? Not Sir?"

"No."

"Why not? What shall I say?"

"He's a count, and the Emperor of Austria's cousin."

"You—don't—say—so?"

"I—do—say—so."

"Oh!"

"Ah!"

The tailor approached Captain Hawk again, and made another bow, as he said—

"Allow me, your royal highness, to thank your royal highness humbly for your royal highness's great kindness in patronising this shop."

"Ah!" said Captain Hawk, "who told you I was the—But no matter: you will be so good as only to know me as Count Arnault."

"Count Arnault!" said the tailor, bowing low again, and then, in a loud voice, he shrieked out—"Simmins?"

"Yes, sir," squeaked a miserable specimen of humanity from a perch near the roof, where a desk was placed.

"Enter the name of the Count Arnault upon a fresh leaf of the day-book, Simmins."

"Yes, sir."

"And, Simmins?"

"Yes, sir?"

"Enter the name of the Count Arnault upon a fresh leaf of the ledger, Simmins."

"Yes, sir."

"Now, your royal highness—I mean count—I shall be only too happy to execute your illustrious commands."

In the course of half an hour, Joe was gorgeously fitted out in a livery of fine crimson cloth, bound with silver lace, and Captain Hawk himself had purchased three rich suits of fashionable clothing, in one of which he attired himself at the tailor's, and really looked most aristocratic and magnificent.

The only thing that annoyed the tailor was the fact of Captain Hawk taking out a pocket-book full of notes, and saying—

"How much is there to pay?"

"Allow me the honour of having the illustrious name of Count Arnault upon my books?" said the tailor.

"No—I pay now. I might leave England for the Imperial Court at an hour's notice, and then you don't expect that I am to remember that I owe something to a tailor?"

"Oh, dear—oh, dear! It's thirty-seven pounds, fourteen shillings, and fivepence."

"Take that fifty-pound-note. I daresay I shall want some other articles, and if I do I will send for them."

"But the change, noble sir?"

Joe winked at the tailor, and pulling him by the sleeve, whispered—

"He never takes change!"

"The deuce he don't!"

"Never. Money is nothing to him. He can get it by the shovelful!"

"You don't mean that? There he goes! He's gone! Go after him, my dear friend, and—and take this for yourself."

The tailor pushed a five-pound note into Joe's hand, and then, advising him to run after his master as quickly as he could, he stood rubbing his hands together in great glee, and standing, congratulating himself upon his prospects in general, upon his door-step.

"I shall be a sheriff," he said. "Yes, there is nothing in all the world that I can see to hinder me from becoming a sheriff. Let me see: I will employ two or three hundred starving tailors, and I will sweat 'em. Ah, that's the plan—I will sweat 'em—that's the way to be a sheriff now-a-days. Ha! ha! I'll do it nicely. Let me consider. If I employ a hundred tailors, and give them nine shillings a week each, for the first week, and then take off a shilling from each of their wages the next week, I save five pounds—ah, five pounds sure to me, and only one shilling a week to them. Why, they would be the greatest brutes in the world to say a word against it! Trimmins, I say! Trimmins?"

"Yes, sir," said a meek-looking man.

"Put an advertisement in the *Times*, Trimmins, stating that we are the only tailors in the world that are worth employing, and take eighteenpence a week off everybodys wages."

"Oh, lor, sir, mine too?"

"O course, Trimmins. Be off with you, sir! You have a wife and eight children, and I know you cannot give up your situation. Ah, I shall certainly be a sheriff!"

While the tailor was thus delighting his soul with the idea of honours and rewards in prospect, Captain Hawk wended his way to a fashionable hotel in Burlington Street, closely followed by Joe in his splendid livery.

CHAPTER LXXXIV.

CAPTAIN HAWK GOES TO AN ENTERTAINMENT IN SPRING GARDENS.

Now, if anybody of less imposing appearance than Captain Hawk had tried the kind of game that he thought of carrying out, it would probably have been a failure; but it must be recollected, that he had many advantages.

In the first place, nature had done a great deal for Hawk, in giving him the exterior of a gentleman. He had about him that indescribable air of aristocratic birth and breeding, which none but the English gentleman can possess. His hands were as delicate and beautifully framed as those of some young girl, and the hand is one of the great distinguishing features between the high and the low.

There was an expression, too, upon his face, which, although it was compounded of much wickedness, was yet what would be called decidedly aristocratic, so that at a glance you would say, "That may be, and probably is, an unscrupulous, bad man; but he belongs to a class of society that for generations has been surrounded by all the luxuries and appliances of wealth."

Add to all this the fact, that Captain Hawk had received a first-rate education—that is to say, the kind of education which would have fitted him for the bar, whither it was intended that he should have taken those talents which we have seen became so perverted by his vices and his follies to vile uses.

When such a man thus is carefully dressed, and with that taste and tact which such a man would be likely to dress in, we cannot but admit that he is very likely to look like a gentleman, in the eyes even of the best judges.

Upon reaching, then, the hotel where he had determined to take up his abode, he was received with a condescension such as at once convinced him of the general character of the landlord and the waiters: for Hawk knew that he looked like a gentleman, and, therefore, it would have been a violation of moral judgment to have taken him for anything else.

Hawk saw a flight of stairs before him, and judging that, as is a matter of course in English establishments, the best rooms were upon the first floor, he ascended the stairs with all the coolness in the world. A door was half open on the landing, and led to a magnificent suit of four rooms, in one of which Hawk sat down.

The landlord made his appearance, and executed a low bow.

"Oh, are you the—a landlord?" said Hawk.

"I have the honour, sir, to receive you into my house."

"These rooms engaged ?"

"No, sir."

"Very good. They will do for me for the present."

The landlord bowed again.

"Perhaps you would like to know who I am ? Well, it is natural. I am an Austrian noble."

Another bow.

"And if you want a reference, the Prince Regent will oblige me, I have no doubt, if you call upon him, and say that the count is with you. The Count from Threw, you can say. He may not tell you exactly who I am, for perhaps he would hardly think himself justified, but he will tell you that what I choose to say I am, why, I am. Will that do ?"

"Perfectly, my lord—perfectly. I shall not, for one moment, think of troubling the prince. Oh, dear, no. I am abundantly satisfied. Your lordship's appearance is enough for me."

"Very well. I shall reside here, then, and I shall leave all minor arrangements to you. I have but one servant with me. Of course, he will attend upon me. After that, I leave all to you. It is not my intention to order dinners, but you will lay the table with what you like. If anything thereon suits me, I eat ; if not, I leave it alone."

The landlord bowed again.

"Will that do?"

"Perfectly, my lord. I am only too happy to have the honour of your lordship's patronage. May I humbly inquire at what hours your lordship would like the separate meals of the day served?"

"I don't know."

The landlord bowed again.

"He don't know," he said to himself. "He is evidently a very great man. I must speak to the servant, that is quite clear, and I must bribe him, too, and get as much information out of him as possible. Hem! My lord—my lord ?"

"Speak."

"Shall I have the honour of taking any commands from your lordship at this present moment ?"

"A glass of spring water, and a shall piece of toasted bread."

The landlord retired from the room in a moment to execute this monstrous order for his illustrious guest. Captain Hawk looked after him with a smile of scorn, as he said—

"Now, how easy a thing it is to fool these people. By Heaven, I can manage them as I could twist a piece of plastic clay to any shape I chose between may finger and thumb. Well, this sort of life, I think, will suit me for a time in London. I get tired of vagabonding after a while. Ah, here is a paper of the day, too. Let me see what fashionable intelligence we have."

The *St. James's Chronicle* was at that time the fashionable paper, and Captain Hawk having comfortably bestowed himself upon a sofa—ay, as comfortably as if there were not a price upon his head, and as if some of the most vigilant officers of the police were not cudgelling their brains for some plan to capture him—and proceeded to entertain himself with the newspaper.

"Let me see," he said. "I must now take good care to make myself thoroughly *au fait* at all the fashionable doings in London. By Jove, I have been for so long rusticating that I feel almost like a fish out of water."

The paper contained the usual amount of frivolous and foolish gossiping matters that fashionable newspapers usually contain.

There was an account of Lady Fiddlefaddle's entertainment—how the Countess Rouge's *soiree* was put off because the Duchess of Brazenface was going to have a rout on the same night, and then, too, there were obscure accounts regarding approaching marriages in high life, such as—

"We understand that Lord Finikin, the only son and heir of the Duke of Blunderers, will shortly lead to the hymeneal altar the young, lovely, and accomplished Lady Clara Phiffs, youngest daughter of the great Phiffs of Toady Hall."

"Bah!" said Captain Hawk, as he dropped the paper from his hands. "How puerile and disgusting all this is. After all, the road is better. Well—well, I want a change, so I will mingle with this class of people for awhile, however much I may in my heart despise them."

He did indeed despise them, as all right-thinking honest-hearted men and women must do.

Take the example.

The young and lovely and accomplished Lady Clara Phiffs, of Toady Hall, who was mentioned in the newspaper paragraph that Captain

HAWK IN THE CHAMBER OF MAY BOYES.

Hawk had read, was a faded, crabbed, bilious old maid, of thirty-eight years of age, who, after making the most horrible exertions to get married for nearly twenty London seasons, had at length purchased—yes, purchased, with eighteen thousand pounds, which had been left her, a ruined debauchee and gambler, who was the Lord Finikin.

These are the sort of people that fashionable newspapers delight to honour—for whom those delicate little paragraphs about hymeneal altars are penned in the present *Morning Post*, and copied with a *naive* simplicity into the great, stormy, vulgar *Times*.

We cannot help saying with Captain Hawk upon this occasion—"Bah!"

There came a tap at the door of the apartment in which Hawk had placed himself.

"Come in."

It was Joe who made his appearance.

"Oh, is that you?"

"Yes, captain. I——"

"Shut the door."

"Oh, lor, I was near forgetting; but I just came to say that I had had all sorts of questions asked about you, captain, down stairs, and that I had crammed the waiters above a bit, rather."

"What did you tell them?"

"Oh, I stuck to that story about Austria, and all that sort of thing, but as I couldn't think of the name you said you was to be called, I just said you were the count, and then I shook my head, as much as to say, I won't tell you count who."

"Call me Count Astral. I have thought that will be a better name than the former, Joe."

"Very good."

"But what I want you to insinuate is, that that is not my name, but that I am one of the Austrian royal family, you understand."

"Oh, yes, I understand. Catch a weasel asleep, captain—count I mean. Oh, lor, I'm afraid I shall be calling you captain when I oughtn't."

"I'm afraid so too, Joe."

"Well, I'll try not, count. There, I got that out famous."

"So you did. And now, once for all, Joe, let me beg of you to understand that I am a member of the royal family of Austria, and that I am here upon a secret mission, of a political and domestic nature."

"A political and domestic nature? Oh!"

"You comprehend me?"

"In course I does."

"Very good, Joe. Now I—"

"Somebody a-coming," said Joe.

The landlord himself brought in the water and the piece of toast, that had been the order of Captain Hawk, or Count Astral, as during his stay in London it will be most correct for the most part to call him.

"I have the honour, your highness, to bring you the water and the toast you were so good as to order."

"Very well, but I prefer not to be addressed according to my rank here."

"Oh—ah!"

"Do not call me highness."

"I have the honor of hearing your high—hem!—your gracious commands, my lord—hem!"

"I intend to call myself Count Astral while in this country. Do you hear me?"

"Certainly, my Lord Count Astroy."

"No, idiot! Astral."

"I am an idiot—oh dear me! Count Astral. That is it. Yes, my lord?"

"You will quite understand, though, that that is only an assumed title."

"Quite, your high—I beg a thousand pardons—quite, your lordship. It is very usual for great foreigners to adopt travelling names."

"Just so. My Astral estates give me the title, though, when I choose to assume it. But I now want you to find me a respectable messenger who can leave for me a few cards."

"Certainly, your lordship; my son will have great pleasure, and feel deeply the honour conferred upon him."

"Very good. Get me some plain cards, that he may write my name and title upon, and send him to me."

The landlord backed himself out of the august presence of the count with great reverence; and in the course of ten minutes a tall, spooney-looking youth, of about sixteen years of age, with his mouth wide open, and a profusion of lank flaxen hair, made his appearance.

"Who are you?" said the count.

"Alfred, if you please, your majesty."

"Oh the landlord's son?"

"Yes, your grace."

"Very good. What have you there?"

"The cards, your worship."

"Sit down then, and write upon some half dozen of them, 'The Count Astral, Vienna.'"

"Yes, my lord."

"D—n the fellow!" muttered Hawk, "what title will he give me next? What an idiot he does look, to be sure. What on earth can be the use of such a fellow as that in this world? I can't help looking at him."

CHAPTER LXXXV.

CAPTAIN HAWK FINDS ACCEPTANCE IN FASHIONABLE SOCIETY.

The landlord's son wrote upon six of the plain cards the words—

"The Count Astral, Vienna."

"It's done, your worship," he said.

"Very good. Now I want you to take one of these cards to the Prince of Wales, at Carlton House. That is, you leave it at the door."

"Yes, noble sir."

"Another you take to the prime minister at Spring Gardens, and a third you leave for the king, at St. James's Palace."

"Oh, lor!"

"What's the matter now?"

"Nothing, your honour. I was only a-thinking that—that it was quite a great honour."

"Pho! pho! Go now. By the bye, are you the only son of your father?"

"Yes, your worship. Father says, that if there were two of us with such abilities, we should be setting the Thames on fire some day."

"Indeed! And what does your cleverness consist of, or in?"

"I play the flute, noble sir."

"I thought as much. I never knew a fool that did not. You may go now."

"Yes, your worshipful worship."

"Was there ever such a goose as that?" said Hawk, as he look up the *St. James's Chronicle* again.

"Why, you see," said Joe, "he's useful, such a follow as that, in his way, I dare say; for if there wasn't fools in this world, there would be no wise men."

"How so, Joe?"

"Just because, captain—I mean, count, you wouldn't know 'em from the others."

"Well," laughed Hawk, "there is some truth in that, Joe. Everything in this world is comparative. But let me see—What have we here? Humph! Ha!"

He read from the paper—

"We understand that the party this evening at the Marchioness of Poodleton's, in Spring Gardens, will be the most *recherche* entertainment of the season, and that the *elite* of the *beau-monde* is expected to grace the saloons of her ladyship."

"Oh, lor!" said Joe, "what does all that mean? They shouldn't abuse people in the newspapers in that way, captain."

"Abuse people? What do you mean, Joe?"

"Why, all those hard words is genteel swearing, I take it. Ain't they, captain?"

Captain Hawk roared with laughter at this mistake of Joe's; and when he could speak, he said—

"Oh, Joe, you could not have said a more rich thing than that if you had tried it. But no matter. I intend to go to this grand party to-night."

"You, captain?"

"Yes, to be sure; and why not?"

"Oh, lor! how will you get them to invite you?"

Hawk laughed, as he replied—

"I will not wait for that little ceremony, Joe. I will go without; and when I get there, which assuredly I shall, it will go hard with me but I succeed in forming some noticeable acquaintance with some of the really accidental visitors. Now, Joe, I will give you a list of things that I want you to get me for this night's work."

"Do, captain, and don't forget a jemmy."

"A what?"

"A small jemmy, captain—one of them that goes into one's pocket. They is uncommon handy."

"And do you think that I am going to condescend to anything one half so vulgar as robbery?"

"Oh, lor! ain't you?"

"Certainly not, Joe. I do not mean to say but that, in a polite way, I may borrow a diamond snuff-box, or possibly a necklace, or a few bracelets from the ladies, if they should be worth the taking; but I shall use more polished weapons than a jemmy, I assure you."

"But I've seed a jemmy," said Joe, "polished up to that degree, that you might have seed your face in it, captain."

Count Astral only smiled, and then made out the list of things that Joe was to get him. They consisted of perfumes, soaps, essences, gloves, lace, muffles and cravats, and various little matters connected with the toilette.

"There, Joe," he said, "go and get those. Here is plenty of money, and don't scruple to give a high price for them all."

"Oh, my eye!" said Joe, "I never did hear of such things. Pray, sir, what is 'Essence de Vanilles?'"

"Be off with you. They will give it to you at the perfumer's, and that is all you need care about it."

Joe, holding up his hands, and nodding his head, left the room. He began to have rather an idea that his master, the count, was going a little out of his senses.

When he was gone, Hawk paced the magnificent apartment to and fro for some time, and then he said—

"Yes, I will try a campaign, as in in good truth it may well be called, in London. All the world is my enemy, and so I plunder whom I can. By some lucky chance, I may possibly make enough to get out of this mode of life; and if I do, I will go to the continent, and live at ease, and forget May Boyes."

He sank into a chair with a deep sigh, and for the space of about three minutes he did not speak. It was then, in a low, soft voice, he said—

"Ah, can I forget her?"

That was a question which his heart answered for him at once in the negative, for the fact was that never had he loved May half so well as he loved her now that there was both difficulty and danger in the way of even looking upon her.

It is incidental to the whole human race, and most particularly is it so to lovers, that the estimation of an object increases just in proportion as the difficulty in the way of its possession increases; and so it was with Captain Hawk to a great extent.

While he was a visitor at Boyes Hall, and when twenty times a day he could look into the sweet face of May Boyes, it did not seem to him so great a treat or so precious a state of things that he should be able to do so; but now that he dare not, for peril of his very life, show himself there, it appeared to be the greatest thing upon earth to him if he could but have held her hand in his for one minute, and had the privilege of addressing her for that short space of time.

Alas! how perverse is human nature. Always grasping after the unattainable, and disregarding the good that is in its power. But so it ever has been, so it is, and so it ever most surely will be.

The landlord's son, of course, before going with the cards to their various destinations, took good care to spread the news of those destinations to everybody in the hotel, and then off he started.

Now, it looked a bold and hazardous thing to send him upon such a mission, but, in reality, it was no such thing, for the cards, at all the places he took them to, were, by the well-bred domestics, received with the greatest civility. What else could they do?

"The Count Astral, Vienna?" said the porter at the Prince of Wales's. "Very good, that will do," and the card was duly deposited in a small basket, to be taken along with others to the prince's secretary.

"By Jove," said the landlord's son, "they know him there, for even the porter says, 'that will do.'"

At the prime-minister's the card was received with the same civility, as a matter of course, and at the palace a gentleman usher took it, and said—

"Who is the Count Astral?"

"Don't know," said the landlord's son; "but he belongs to the royal family of Austria."

"Oh, very good. It's all right."

Fully impressed, then, with an idea that it was in good truth all right, the landlord's son came back to report the success of his mission, and then Captain

Hawk resolved upon doing a very impertinent thing.

He knew well that even should he succeed in obtaining admission to the *fete* at the Marchioness of Poodleton's that evening, although nothing might be said to him on that occasion, that some inquiry might be made on the following morning as to who and what he was.

It was to meet that inquiry that Captain Hawk now thought of a plan that he thought would do so, although it required all the impudence in the world to carry it out.

That plan was to make a call upon the secretary of state for foreign affairs.

Now, Hawk did not care one straw what sort of rebuff he might meet with at the office of the secretary. He knew that he would be treated with courtesy, even if he were all but turned out of the place; but he knew, too, that having been there at all, the expenditure of a trifle would suffice to get the fact recorded in the very newspaper that he held in his hand—the fashionable *St. James's Chronicle.*

If he attained that end, why it would answer all his purpose, and that was his object.

If Hawk had not been pretty well supplied with ready money, he would have felt some difficulty in the matter; but it happened that he was in a very good state as regarded that essential; and after receiving the report of the landlord's son about the cards, he desired that the landlord himself might be sent for.

With a profusion of bows, that individual made his appearance before his illustrious guest.

"Hark you, sir," said Hawk. "If any one should come from the Austrian Embassy for me, say that I decline giving them an audience."

"Yes, my lord. Your lordship declines giving them an audience? Certainly, my lord count."

"And, landlord, I want you to send me some person to whom I can give directions concerning the equipage that I want during my stay in London. I suppose you can find somebody who will meet my wants in that particular?"

"Most certainly, my lord."

"Go and do so, then."

In the course of half-an-hour Captain Hawk had made an agreement, for one month, with a livery stable-keeper, for the hire of a carriage, a pair of horses, and a coachman and two footmen in liveries that he specified; and as he paid a handsome sum in advance, the arrangement was perfectly satisfactory, and the livery stable-keeper handed the landlord of the hotel a liberal douceur for the recommendation.

Thus far, then, all things went on snugly with Captain Hawk, and nothing was more unlikely than that in the Austrian nobleman any one would imagine Hawk, the highwayman, who was so recently tried at the Old Bailey for his life.

CHAPTER LXXXVI.

CAPTAIN HAWK VISITS THE SECRETARY OF STATE FOR FOREIGN AFFAIRS.

The carriage that Hawk had ordered was punctually at the door of the hotel at the hour that it had been promised by the livery stable-keeper.

It was quite a gorgeous turn-out, and the footmen and the coachman in their liveries looked as if they had belonged to an Austrian prince all their lives, and really thought something particular of it.

What will not money do in London?

Joe had faithfully enough executed his mission and the Count Astral descended to the hall of the hotel in an elegant full-dress, with a lace pocket-handkerchief in his hand that had cost no less a sum than five guineas.

The landlord, and all the disengaged waiters of the establishment, were in the hall to do honour to the illustrious personage who was going out. A little crowd collected on the pavement outside.

"Who is it?" said one. "Oh, who is it?"

"I don't know," said another; "but it's some devilish great man, you may depend."

"The King of Austria, I do think,"

said one of the waiters, in a confidental tone.

This got wind among the crowd, and the people were ready to knock each other down to get a good view of such a wonderful specimen of humanity as a king.

Only tell an English crowd that there is a king to be seen, or a queen, and they go mad directly.

The waiters all bowed very low, and with a stately kind of affability, Captain Hawk slightly inclined his head, and entered his carriage.

"Bravo!" cried the people. "Hurrah!"

"Stand back!" said the footmen—"stand back!"

Joe approached the carriage door, and touched his hat, and the count said to him—

"To the secretary of state for foreign affairs."

"To the secretary of state about his own affairs," said Joe to the coachman.

"What?" said the coachman.

"Oh, you stupid," said one of the footmen. "He means Lord North's, in Privy Gardens, coachman."

"Oh! Ah! The *furrin* secretary?"

"Yes—yes."

"Hurrah!" cried the mob again, and it was each moment increasing in number.

The carriage then drove off, and Joe was glad to dart into the hotel to avoid the questions that were poured in upon him on all sides.

There was one person, however, who would not take a denial, but with a note-book in one hand, and a pencil in the other, he made his way into the hall of the hotel, and said—

"I report for the *St. James's Chronicle*. Who is it?—who is it? Of course, we will give the name of the hotel in full."

"Then, sir," said the landlord, "you can say, among the fashionable arrivals—'At Muggins's Hotel, the Prince Astral and suite.'"

"On a secret commission," said Joe.

"Mission, I suppose you mean?" said the reporter

"Very good. Have it your own way.'

"And he has gone now to the secretary of state for foreign affairs?" said the reporter, hastily pocketing his notes. "I will run there, and try and find out how long his audience lasts, and what else I can about him."

Off set the reporter at the top of his speed after the carriage of——Captain Hawk, the highwayman!

During the short drive to the office of Lord North, who then filled the office of foreign secretary of state in this country, Captain Hawk had made up his mind what to say when he got there; so that when the carriage drew up, with a dash and a rattle, at the door, he was quite prepared for whatever might happen in the ordinary course of things.

The sight of so well-appointed a vehicle had quite an effect upon the officials at the secretary of state's office, and the doors were flung open, as Hawk descended from his vehicle.

"Lord North within?" he said.

"Yes, sir."

Without another word, Hawk tendered his card.

"This way, my lord," said the servant, as he glanced at the card, and then continued his mode of addressing Captain Hawk, who followed him into a well-appointed room, in which he was requested to take a seat.

In the course of a few moments a gentleman made his appearance; and after bowing to Hawk, said, respectfully—

"Lord North presents his compliments, and begs to say, that as he has not the honour of knowing the Count Astral, perhaps I, as his private secretary, might be favoured with a message.'

"I expected," said Hawk, "that his lordship would by this time have received private letters from the consul at Vienna, which would have possessed him of the object of my visit."

"I fear not."

"That is rather awkward. I am afraid the courier, then, has miscarried in some way. I came post, and with extraordinary speed."

"I will mention all this to his lordship, if you please, count?"

"You will greatly oblige me, sir."

The private secretary left Hawk, and

was away about ten minutes, and then he returned, and said—

"His lordship has received no letter, but is quite willing, in a non-official capacity, to see you, count, and to learn from you any statement you may do him the honour to make."

"I am greatly obliged," said Captain Hawk, rising, "but the fact is, I am in this country in quite a private capacity, and upon a mission not at all political, and I do not wish to come into contact with an embassy; so I would rather wait until the emperor's letter comes, although I am greatly impressed with the courtesy of Lord North."

"Then the Emperor of Austria has written to his lordship?"

"Certainly, so he informed me, and the courier was sent six hours before I left Vienna. There is a letter to the king, and one to Lord North. It is very provoking."

"It is, count."

"Something must have happend to the courier."

"It is possible enough, count; but under these circumstances, I must say, that I cannot see any impropriety in your seeing the minister. You can explain the object of your journey, and the letter may come to hand in the course of the day."

"Well, I think I—yet—no—no. The subject matter of my mission is so—so important to the royal family, that—that—and yet——"

"I will take you at once to his lordship, count."

"Why, the fact is, I am not the Count Astral, and yet I am."

"You are, and you are not?"

"Exactly. Astral is the name of one of my estates, and my higher title makes it——I am half disposed, sir, to tell you who I really am; and yet, the emperor begged me to be careful."

"As you please, prince," said the secretary.

"Well—well, I will come again. I will wait till the letter comes."

"Humph!" said the secretary to himself. "How quickly he took the title [illegible] him. This is one of the P[illegible] house of Austria." Then he [illegible] aloud—"I assure you that Lord North would deeply regret missing the pleasure of seeing you."

"And so do I."

"Then pray allow me—"

"No—no. Good morning. Tell Lord North that I will come to him again, and that, in the meantime, I highly appreciate his courtesy, and that of his most talented and distinguished secretary, whom I shall live in hope of meeting some day at the court of Vienna."

With these words, Captain Hawk executed a superb bow, and walked to the door.

The secretary did the honours by following him to his carriage-door bareheaded, and so off went Captain Hawk, having succeeded to a miracle in his visit to the secretary of state for foreign affairs, and leaving behind him an admirable impression.

The secretary looked after the carriage with a puzzled air, and the porter looked at the secretary, and then a clerk arrived, and looked at them both.

"Who was that, Mr. Secretary?" said the clerk.

"One of the princes of the Austrian royal family, I believe, and a most gentlemanly fellow he is too."

"Been to see North, I suppose?"

"No, plague take it, he would not see him, because certain papers and credentials had not arrived from the court at Vienna. I am afraid I have done wrong, though, in letting him go. He calls himself Count Astral."

"A travelling title."

"Oh, yes. He said so."

It was at this moment that the reporter for the *St. James's Chronicle* made his appearance at the door, and as the private secretary and the clerk retired from the hall, the porter gave a nod to the collector of fashionable intelligence, for they were very well acquainted.

"Hilloa, Mr. Smith," he said, "you seem in a hurry."

"I am—I am. Have you had a Count Astral here?"

"Yes."

"And has he gone?"

"Just now."

"The deuce! I am too late. But at all events I can put down that the

Count Astral had a private audience of Lord North, of half an hour's duration."

"No doubt about it. But I can tell you a secret."

"You can?"

"Hem! Why, yes, I can."

"About this Count Astral?"

The porter nodded.

"Then, my good fellow, I am authorised by one of the proprietors to offer you half a guinea."

"A whole one you mean, Mr. Smith."

"Well—well, what is the secret?"

"Money down."

"There it is then. Dear me, I hope it is worth it, or the proprietors will give me a precious talking to for giving it to you, I assure you. Well, what is it?"

"That Count What's-his-name is one of the princes of the Austrian royal family."

"You don't mean it?"

"I—do."

"Well, but how do you know? Are you sure of it? That's the question. Are you sure, or is it only an idea?"

"Mr. Smith, I never had an idea in all my life."

"By Jove! I believe you there."

"I heard our private secretary say it, and if that is not enough, I don't know what is."

"It is enough. A thousand thanks. I can dish the whole affair up into quite a nice little paragraph, and it will sound quite romantic, too. I must be off to the office at once. Who knows but that the proprietors may think a second edition imperatively called for by the most extraordinary, most authentic and highly-interesting intelligence? I will be off at once. Ha! ha! they would look a long way before they found such a reporter as I am."

"And the secretary of state for foreign affairs," said the official of the hall of Lord North's house, "would go a long way before he found a porter like me."

Mr. Smith rushed off to his office, and the porter shut the door.

CHAPTER LXXXVIII

SHOWS WHAT AN EXCELLENT RECEPTION CAPTAIN HAWK GOT FROM LADY POODLETON.

The proprietors of the *St. James's Chronicle* did think it highly expedient to publish a second edition, which, as the first had not sold, came in very handy.

In that second edition appeared the following delectable little paragraph:—

"We may state, that we are in possession of the facts connected with an important movement in the political and domestic states of Au——ia. We forbear to mention the name of the continental state; but we may say that its capital is V——a. It appears that a prince of the blood royal is now in London, and has had an interview, of a deeply interesting character, with Lord N——h at the F——n Off——e."

This paragraph set all the old women and restless fools who doat upon the small doings of the aristocracy thinking to the extent of their capacities.

In the Court Intelligence, too, appeared the following little paragraph, which just happened to suit the views of Captain Hawk:—

"Count Astral, from Vienna, had an interview with Lord North at the office of foreign affairs this day, upon subjects of deep importance to the courts of Austria and St. James's."

"That will do," said Hawk, as he read this paragraph; and then he summoned Joe.

"Here ye is," said Joe. "How do you find yourself—eh? D—n all the world! Tow—row—row!"

Hawk looked at him, and the conviction that Joe was tipsy came across him too firmly to be for a moment doubted.

"Joe?"

"Yes. Here you are—

"'Oh, the road—the road is a tidy shop,
When travellers come apace.
Oh, then's the time for a gallant knight,
With the crape upon his face.
Heigho!—heigho! sir traveller stop—
Heigho!'"

Captain Hawk rose, and catching

Joe by the collar, he said, as he forced him into a chair—

"Utter another word till I bid you, and I will blow your brains out!"

Joe had just sense enough left to feel quite certain that when Captain Hawk said such a thing as that, he thoroughly meant it; so he sat quite still, staring at his master, and with a slight suspicion in his own mind that

CAPTAIN HAWK WOUNDED BY RATCHLEY BOYES.

he had been making too free with glasses of brandy-and-water in the bar of the hotel below.

The count rang the bell.

A waiter made his appearance.

"Send the landlord here."

"Yes, my lord"

The landlord came into the room almost double with humility, for he had just finished reading not only the announcement in the *St. James's Chronicle* of Count Astral having had an interview with Lord North; but he had seen and conned over the mysterious paragraph, which he had no difficulty at all in his own mind in associating with his illustrious visitor.

"Did your lordship do me the honour to say that I was wanted?"

"Yes. You see that fellow?"

"With all due deference, I do, my lord."

"Well, I picked him up in this country, and employed him from pure charity, as he said he had been robbed of all he had by a highwayman of the name of—of what was the name? Tut—tut, oh, Hawk."

"Captain Hawk, my lord."

"Ah, yes."

"A most notorious rogue, and as ugly a fellow as ever was, my lord. We have all heard of him."

"Well, and the return this knave makes to me is to get drunk. Now, landlord, understand me—if you serve him with another drop of anything but water, unless with my express permission, I at once leave the house."

"Oh, my lord, he shall not have so much as the drains of a glass to save his life."

"Very well; now bring me some brandy."

"Brandy, my lord?"

"Yes. Are you deaf?"

"Oh, dear no, only I—that is, I could hardly think—I mean it seemed so—oh, dear, I will get it directly."

"What's the row?" said Joe.

"Nothing particular," said Captain Hawk, as he quietly awaited the return of the landlord with a bottle of bandy. Then pouring out a glass full—it was about half-a-pint—Captain Hawk held it to Joe, saying—

"Drink"

"Eh?"

"Drink, I say."

"Oh, won't I. Here's your health Mr. Count—captain—Oh, dear, I—here you is.'

Joe drank about a fourth of the brandy and his face got very red.

"More!" cried Hawk.

He drank another fourth, and his eyes seemed as if they were about to burst out of their sockets.

"More!" cried Hawk again, in such an imperious voice, that again Joe put the glass to his lips, but yet there was some left in it, and Captain Hawk just took it from him in time to save it from falling to the floor and being dashed to pieces.

"That will do," said Hawk, as he flung what remained of the brandy into Joe's face. Overcome then completely by the dose of the ardent spirit that he had taken, Joe slipped off the chair and fell insensible to the floor.

"Oh, dear," said the landlord, "I'm afraid that he is, in a manner of speaking, dead drunk."

"Yes," said the sham count. "That is his punishment. He will not feel very well when he awakens from this state, and until then let him lie there."

As he spoke, Hawk, by a great exercise of strength, stooped over the miserable form of Joe, and flung him into a corner of the room as if he had been so much rubbish. The landlord looked rather alarmed.

"Good gracious," he thought, "that's the way they serve 'em in Austria, I suppose."

"What is the time?" said Hawk.

"Ten, my lord."

"Very well; is the carriage in waiting?"

"It is, my lord."

The count was full dressed, and rising, he pointed to the prostrate form of Joe, as he said—

"Let him lie there till I return. I am going to the Marchioness of Poodleton's entertainment."

The landlord flung all the doors open as the count slowly took his way to his carriage. The two hall-footmen had blazing flambeaus in their hands, as was then the fashion, and a little crowd had collected to see who it was that was about to get into the handsome chariot at the door of the hotel.

The count got into the carriage.

"Where to, my lord?"

"To the Marchioness of Poodleton's rout."

"Yes, my lord. The Marchioness of Poodleton's rout, coachman!"

Off went the horses at a brisk trot, [illegible] footmen ran one on each side of [illegible] blazing torches, which at that [illegible] was considered the very height of fashion to do, and which, to tell the truth, was highly necessary, considering the very defective state in which the lighting of London was then in.

"Now, impudence, assist me," said Captain Hawk. "I must make my way without a card of invite to the house that I am going to; but that I suspect will, after all, not be very difficult to do."

As the carriage neared Spring Gardens, the count began to notice all the signs of a grand entertainment going on, for the street was nearly blocked up by carriages, and there was such a swearing among the coachmen and lackeys, and rushing to and fro on the part of the footmen, that it was nothing but a scene of riot and confusion.

"Ah," said Hawk, "this is as favourable to me. No one will be able to question my pretensions to admission amid such a tumult as this."

The count's coachman managed to get next to a splendid chariot, from which he saw four gentlemen alight, and the idea then struck the count that a more favourable opportunity could not occur for him to reach the house unquestioned.

He sprang from his carriage at once, therefore, and walked forward along with the four gentlemen, one of whom exhibited a card, which was received with a low bow by a servant out of livery, and then he said—

"Pray walk up, your grace."

"Oh," thought the count, "I am in good company, it seems, as far as titles go."

They all ascended the grand staircase of the house, and Captain Hawk followed, being evidently taken for one of the party by the servants of the place.

At the top of the stairs they paused, and their names were asked and answered.

"The Duke of Queenstorom."

"Lord Alfred Moneytop."

"The Marquis of Swindlehem."

"General Grainger."

"Count Astral," said Captain Hawk, in a low tone of voice to the gentleman usher, who, with all the power of his lungs, then shouted out—

"The Count Astral!"

The sound of that name apeared to excite a feeling of very great interest in the minds of all present, and as Captain Hawk walked boldly into the grand saloon, which was brilliantly lighted and crowded with company, he heard some one say—

"By Jove! that is the Austrian who is mentioned in the second edition of the *Chronicle*."

"The very same," said another.

"Is it the Archduke Charles?"

"Very likely."

"Very likely, indeed," thought Captain Hawk. "I will be anything you like, gentlemen."

Amid the blaze of light and the flash of jewels, and the gaze of some three or four hundred pairs of eyes, any one who did not possess the consummate assurance that Captain Hawk did, might well have been somewhat abashed; but such was far from being the case with him, and it is highly probable that a consciousness that his exterior was perfect, and could stand any amount of scrutiny, contributed in no small degree to produce that feeling of perfect confidence in himself and in his own resources, which he felt upon this rather ticklish occasion in his life.

CHAPTER LXXXIX.

CAPTAIN HAWK GETS ON ADMIRABLY AT THE ENTERTAINMENT.

Captain Hawk walked quite leisurely along the brilliant saloon, and he soon stopped the ladies from gazing at him in too marked a manner by bowing very profoundly to every one who did so.

"Quite a gentleman, at all events," said a voice close to him. "He is used to it."

"Of course," said another. "Receptions occur continually at Vienna, and there they carry *politesse* a long way."

"Gentlemen," said a fussy sort of individual, "I have found it out. He is the emperor's youngest brother."

"So I thought."

"Very good, indeed," thought Captain Hawk. "As long as they

consider me the youngest brother, even of an emperor, I shall be eminently admired, no doubt."

An elderly gentleman now advanced to Captain Hawk, and bowing, he said with a bland smile—

"Allow me, your highness, to thank you, in the name of the marchioness and myself, for the kindness of this visit."

"I presume," said Hawk, with a gracious smile, "that I have the pleasure of addressing the Marquis of Poodleton."

The marquis bowed.

"I assure you, marquis," added Hawk, "it is quite a gratification to me to pay my respects to the countess upon this occasion, and to you."

"Oh, your highness is so good as to allude to the countess's uncle, who was ambassador at your court some years since."

Captain Hawk bowed and smiled.

"May I have the honour of introducing the countess to your highness?"

"Nay, rather, my lord, let me have both the honour and the pleasure of being introduced to the countess. I am here only as the Count Astral."

"Your highness is too good."

"Oh, no—no."

"Yes, I must really say it. Your highness is indeed by far too good and kind. This way, your highness."

The stupid old Marquis of Poodleton went on a little before, and when he reached his lady he whispered rapidly—

"It is the Archduke Charles!"

"I knew it."

"Hush! He don't want it known. He distinctly alluded to your uncle. It is a remembrance of his mission to Vienna that brought him here to-night to pay his respects to you."

"Oh, how kind—how——"

"Hem! He is here. Allow me, your royal highness, to——"

"Nay, my dear marquis, you will do the Count Astral a favour by introducing him to the Marchioness of Poodleton."

Quite a little circle gathered now round Captain Hawk and the host and hostess of the house, so that it was really something like his, Hawk's, holding a kind of court; and, to tell the truth, he did the trick very neatly indeed, and looked the grandee to perfection.

Then whispers ran through the rooms that it was the Archduke Charles of Austria who was there, under the incognito of Count Astral; and prodigious was the crushing and squeezing among the ladies to get a sight of him.

Some of the rather extensive old dowagers used the lateral portion of their corporealities as battering-rams to make a way through the throng, and in the course of another ten minutes Hawk was quite the centre of all the attraction.

"I regret this," he said.

"Oh, your highness," said the marquis, "really if you regret it, it is so distressing."

"It is indeed," said the marchioness. "And does your highness recollect my uncle, Lord Croftus?"

"But dimly. And yet I do recollect that we in Vienna heard much of the beauty of one, who now seems to set time at defiance, and to be but in the spring-tide of her charms."

Captain Hawk bowed low at the end of this elegantly-enough worded, but really rather powerful compliment; but when is the incense of flattery too strong for the ears of a lady of a certain age? The marchioness was enchanted, and gave herself so many airs, that it was quite awful to behold.

"Oh, Angelina," said a young lady to her sister, "that poor Marchioness of Poodleton will go into hysteric."

"What is it all about, Dora?"

"It is that Austrian prince, who is paying some of his foreign compliments, that mean nothing, and which have quite intoxicated the old woman."

"He! he!" laughed the marchioness, "you are really too gallant, your royal highness."

"Not at all. I have rather, when at home, a character for bluntness, and for speaking my mind."

"Allow me," interposed the Marquis of Poodleton, who had rushed off, quite breathless, to fetch something that he held in his hand. "Allow me, your royal highness, to ask if you recollect the diamond snuff-box which was presented to the marchioness's uncle, by your august brother, the Emperor of Austria."

"Let me see it, marquis. Oh, yes—gold is it not, and set with brilliants?"

"It is, your highness. But there is a portrait in the inside of the lid."

"Ah, yes!"

"Well, your highness, we never knew whose portrait it was, although we guess it to be one of your sisters."

"No—no."

"No?"

"Oh, dear, no. It is the portrait of a cousin of the empress's. She is dead now."

"Dead! In—deed!"

"Ah!" said Hawk—"ah—yes! One of these diamonds is loose in the setting. No—yes—it is loose."

"Is it, indeed? I will have it seen to to-morrow morning the very first thing. I—"

"No, marquis—no, madam. You will allow me to get it put to rights for you. I will take no denial. There, now, it is of no use saying another word about it."

Captain Hawk coolly put the diamond snuff-box into his pocket.

"But the idea," said the marchioness, "of the prince being troubled with it. Oh, the idea!"

"Shocking!" said the marquis.

"Now, if I hear another word, I will keep the box, and never let you have it back again, except you give me, in exchange, that ring on your ladyship's finger."

"If you would graciously accept this ring," said the marchioness, "I should only be too happy."

"No," whispered the marquis—"no—hem! Cost six hundred pounds. Oh, dear, no."

"Madam," said Captain Hawk, "I can refuse you nothing," and he took the ring, and placed it on his own finger. "You must allow me to send you in return a suite of diamonds that belonged to one of our family, and which was presented by the Emperor of Russia to us as a token of esteem. They are but trifles, for the court jeweller only valued them in his inventory at about eight thousand pounds of English money."

"Oh—oh!" said the marchioness and the marquis both at once, and the ring and the snuff-box were no longer thought of for a moment.

It was at this juncture that a young lady approached the countess, and said, in a low tone—

"Introduce me, do!"

"Well, your royal highness, allow me to introduce—"

"Your youngest sister, I daresay," said Hawk.

"Oh, gracious, no. My daughter."

"Your daughter? Is it possible that you so young—(the marchioness was fifty-two)—could—Oh, really, madam!"

The marchioness was in ecstasies, and duly introduced to the Count Astral her daughter, Matilda, who executed a curtsey to the highwayman which looked as if it would never be over.

"Shall we dance to-night?" said Hawk.

"The sets are now forming, your highness," said the marchioness, and then Hawk just took the tips of the gloved fingers of Matilda in his hand, and said—

"May I hope for the honour of so fair a partner, Lady Matilda?"

"With pleasure."

"Oh, dear!" exclaimed an old maid of some forty-eight—"oh, dear! Those Poodletons are quite resolved that no other girl shall have a chance with the prince but their own. It is really too abominable, that it is."

Somebody was bowing so low to Captain Hawk, that, as he was leading Lady Matilda to the dance, he nearly fell over him, and, as it was, he all but knocked his wig right off.

"Really, sir, I beg pardon," said Hawk.

"It is I, your highness, who should do that—it is I. But, perhaps Lady Matilda will do me the kindness of introducing me to your highness?"

"Lord North," said Lady Matilda.

"Oh, the foreign secretary?" said Hawk.

"The same, your highness. Allow me to say how very sorry I am that I missed the pleasure of seeing you when you favoured me with a call this morning. I am very much afraid that my secretary did not quite understand—"

"Nay, my lord, I met with nothing but the greatest courtesy from your secretary. It was my own wish to leave without seeing your lordship. But as you now have my letters—"

"I beg pardon, I am sorry to say that they have not yet come to hand."

Captain Hawk pretended to bite his lip with vexation, as he said—

"Then the courier is dead."

"He must have miscarried, your highness. But do not let that vex you. Your highness will perhaps let me see you in the morning. I will pay my respects to you."

"No—no. Not till you get the emperor's letters, my lord, I cannot think of it."

"I bow to your highness's decision."

Lord North then sidled away. The band struck up a delicious dance now, and Captain Hawk, smiling upon the really beautiful girl by his side as in good truth few could smile, said—

"Now, shall we both be quite natural and human, and enjoy this dance?"

"Oh, yes—yes."

"What a delightful person," thought Lady Matilda, "this Austrian prince is."

"Upon my life," thought Hawk, "this is a fine girl. But I will not trifle with her; I will make up to some of the old rich ones, wh , no doubt, are to be found in these rooms in abundance."

Hawk danced c[illegible]tally, and he really enjoyed the invigo[illegible]ing exercise with so fair a partner as the Lady Matilda.

CHAPTER XC.

CAPTAIN HAWK MAKES THE ACQUAINTANCE OF LADY SNEERLEY.

Many were the envious looks cast upon Matilda Poodleton by disengaged ladies while she danced with the prince; but she heeded them not, for she was drinking in deep draughts of love as she glanced into the handsome face of her partner, and bright visions of the future were fluttering about the heart of the young girl.

The marchioness and the marquis were in ecstasies. Never had they given such an entertainment, and never to their minds had anything gone off so enchantingly. They had not, as they ought to have done, stopped to make any inquiries regarding the Austrian prince, but they themselves lent a currency to his pretensions by roundly asserting that they not only knew that he was the Archduke Charles, but more than hinting that they knew he was coming to England, and what he was coming for.

The dance being over, Captain Hawk led Lady Matilda to her seat, and then taking a chair by the side of the marchioness, he said, in quite a gay tone of voice—

"I should like to know some of your English aristocrats. Will you be so good, quite confidentially, to tell me something about them?"

"Oh, yes—yes, with pleasure."

"Who is that young man, then, with the rather vacant expression of countenance yonder, with a star on his breast?"

"Oh, that is the Prince of Prussia."

"A fool?"

"Oh, prince, how very satirical you are! Well, he is a—a—rather a fool. But you won't let it go any further?"

"Not for the world. Who is that lady with the red head-dress, sitting on the couch yonder?"

"Oh, the wretch!"

"Well, she looks one."

"She is one, prince. Really, her conduct is disgraceful; and but that she is related to the queen, you see, and so is in the best society, I would not on any account have tolerated her in the house. She is an old maid."

"You don't say so?"

"Oh, yes; at least—he! he!—she says she is."

"That is quite another thing."

"Oh, prince, what a wicked wit you have, to be sure; you quite make me blush."

"Through your paint, then, it must be," said Captain Hawk to himself.

"Ah," added the marchioness, "she is immensely rich, and is trying to get a young husband. Her name is Deliva—the Countess de Deliva she calls herself; but they do say that she was once a Mrs. Jenkins."

"Oh!"

"Yes But you won't let that go any further?"

"Certainly not. But how came she related to the queen, then?"

"Why, you see, prince, the late Jenkins was a rich man, and so he might marry which of the German princesses he pleased, provided he would support all her family; and he did marry the cousin—you know all the German petty princesses are cousins—of Queen Charlotte."

"I understand; and, now I think of it, the emperor has said something to me of the same sort."

"Then he had it from my uncle."

"He said as much."

"I have no doubt of it. Oh, prince, if my uncle had but been alive! But he is dead, poor dear man."

"What a pity!"

"He would have known you, prince."

"Would he? Well, I am sorry he is dead, then. It would be so really delightful to have somebody here who would know me."

"So it would. But they might steal—"

"Eh?—steal?"

"You from us."

"Oh—ah, to be sure. But I beg to assure you that I shall be quite, in a manner of speaking—"

"Transported, I hope."

"The devil!"

"To see the Austrian ambassador, who will be here immediately, I expect, for I have sent a special messenger to invite him here to-night, quite on your account, prince."

"Then allow me, madam, to say, that you have done a very imprudent thing; for the last words of the emperor to me were, 'Now, Charles, don't see or exchange one word with our ambassador, as your mission is a state secret from him, and you must not know him, nor he you, if it can be helped.'"

"Good gracious, what can I do?"

"I don't know. But I must leave you, madam."

"Oh, I shall faint."

"And so shall I," said Lady Matilda.

"Don't think of such a thing," said Captain Hawk, "I beg of you. Ladies, I will, if you please, take—"

"Count Killmanseggilic, the Austrian ambassador, and suite," cried the major-domo at the saloon door.

"D—n his suite," said Captain Hawk.

The marchioness uttered a faint scream, and Lady Deliva, who had been scanning Captain Hawk with her eyes, thought that this was a good opportunity of introducing her faded charms to his notice, and she rushed forward with a vinaigrette, which she held under the nose of the marchioness, and made her sneeze dreadfully.

"Oh, get away," said the marchioness.

"My dear marchioness," said Lady Deliva, "I really thought that you were ill. Allow me to apologise, prince, for this intrusion. I really—I—oh, prince, I—"

"There needs no apology," whispered Captain Hawk, "from Lady Deliva. I am enchanted to make her acquaintance, and consider the moment in which I do so the happiest of my life!"

"Oh—oh, prince—oh!"

"Ma, that vineger has taken the skin off your nose," said Lady Matilda to her mother.

"No, my dear, it is only the enamel that I have on my face, that is all."

"Oh, to be sure; I forgot that, ma."

Lady Deliva sunk into a chair in such a flutter of delight, that she let Captain Hawk alone for a few moments, and he had time to whisper to the marchioness,

"Madam, I must not see the Austrian ambassador. Can you take me secretly out of the public rooms, so that I may not encounter him?"

"Oh, yes, if it must be so."

"Madam, if I see him, there are circumstances that will cause me to draw my sword, and run him through the body."

"Oh, gracious! Come this way. Matilda, my love, you come likewise. Oh, what a flutter I am in, to be sure! Circumstances that will cause you to run the ambassador through the body! Oh, gracious me! But of course he would be a most ill-mannered wretch to object to such a thing from a prince."

"Very," said Captain Hawk; "and yet, madam, I am afraid he would do so."

"Do you, indeed? This way—this way."

The marchioness raised a curtain, and led Captain Hawk at once from the grand saloon through a dimly lighted room, and through another door that conducted at once to a well and elegantly furnished boudoir.

"This, prince, is my own room, as I call it. There's no one but myself and Matilda can intrude."

"Then, I fear that my presence here is most remarkably intrusive, my dear madam."

"Oh, not at all."

"Not—at—all," said Lady Matilda, with a sigh.

"Confound this girl," thought Hawk, "she is smitten already either with me or my supposed rank. But I suppose it is the latter, after all. Oh, if she did but know who I was in reality!"

"Now, prince, let me beg of you to take a little refreshment," said the marchioness.

"Oh, no," replied Hawk. "Indeed, I am in want of nothing, while I have the pleasure of your society. But I find that I have given a deal of trouble, and perhaps placed you both in an awkward position."

"Not at all. I will just go and give some orders, prince, and trespass upon you, in the meantime, to remain with my dear and only child, Matilda, who is a blessing to her mother, and who has always refused every offer. Ah, now, my dear, mind that some day your young and innocent heart is not enslaved never to be free again."

"Nay, but, madam—"

The marchioness left the boudoir, for, although she heard the prince beg her to stay, she would not listen to the request, but was quite resolved he should have an opportunity, if he would but have the kindness to embrace it, to say as tender things to Lady Matilda as he might.

"Hem!" said Hawk, "and your name is Matilda?"

"Yes, prince."

"Ah! call me not prince."

"What should I call you then?"

"Would you mind calling me Charles?"

"That would not be proper, considering your rank and—and—the—the—the—"

"The what, fair one?"

"The very early character of our acquaintance."

"Ah, but if the prince chooses to waive his prerogative, there is no harm done; and as for the early character of our acquaintance, there are people whom we know better in one half hour, than we can know others if we had a lifetime in which to try to do so."

"Ah, how true!"

"May I hope, that we shall know each other well? Ah, Lady Matilda, I came to England upon such a mission, that I feel I ought to tell it to you."

"To me?"

"Yes, dear girl."

"Oh, prince—really!"

"But are you not a dear girl?"

She only looked at him with an arch smile.

"Pa says I am, for I cost him more than he likes to expend upon me. He complains that I am always wanting something."

"Can that be possible? Why does he not purchase for you jewels that you ought to wear, and not such a necklace as this, Lady Matilda?"

"Oh, it cost three hundred pounds."

"A mere trifle. I must change it for you. I will take it and get you another instead. We must add another mite to the price, and then see what the jeweller will do for us."

"Oh, how generous! How princely!" said the unsuspecting Matilda, who had not the slightest idea of the impossition that was being practised upon her.

"Not at all," said Hawk, as he pocketed the necklace, which he had so adroitly taken from the neck of Lady Matilda.

"But, you said, prince, that you would tell me why you came to England. Will you, indeed make such confidence with me?"

"With pleasure. I came for a wife!"

"A wife?"

"Yes, in good truth, that is my sole object."

"It is one in every way worthy of you."

"Is it indeed!" thought Captain Hawk. "Hem! You are pleased to be very kind and complimentary, my lady; but I hope and trust that my secret, for I assure you that it is one, will go no further."

CONSULTATION BETWEEN MR. BOLTON AND JOHN EVELEIGH.

"Oh, not for worlds!"

Lady Matilda looked unutterable things; and Captain Hawk, if he had not before been in such an enviable possition, was most certainly then at the very height of popularity.

Of course, he well knew that the pretended secret of his presence in England would soon be blazed about the fashionable world.

CHAPTER XCI.

THE LADY DELIVA SENDS A NOTE TO THE MOCK PRINCE OF AUSTRIA.

THE rooms now of Lady Poodleton to use the language of the *St. James's Chronicle,* blazed with rank and fashion; and certainly if her ladyship's object was to collect a crowd, and to make everybody very uncomfortable, indeed, there could not possibly have been a better way of accomplishing it.

Hawk, though, had some idea of retiring early.

"I will leave soon," he thought, "and then her ladyship will have time in my absence to spread this nice little piece of intelligence regarding my matrimonial intentions in coming to England. Oh, how strangely willing people ever are to be deceived, when the deception favours their own views!"

It was not quite such an easy thing,

though, as one might suppose it to be, to get away from Lady Poodleton's party, for that lady kept an eye upon the Austrian prince, and made Lady Matilda do the same.

"I am watched," thought Hawk; "but I will take the first opportunity I can of giving your generous ladyship the slip."

Watching, then, for an opening in the crowd, which took place as a pompous man in the Windsor uniform was announced as the Duke of Puddenbrains, Captain Hawk made his way to the door of the grand saloon; but he there unfortunately trod upon the toe of a gentleman, who raised quite a shout, as he said—

"This d——d Austrian, or whatever he is, can know nothing of corns, or he would tread lighter."

"Sir, I am very sorry," said Hawk.

"Oh, go to the devil, sir, with your sorrow. You ought to be more careful."

"Indeed, sir, I beg your pardon."

"Bah!"

"Did you address that to me, sir?"

"If you like to take it, I did," said the other.

"Do you know who I am, sir?"

"No, nor do I care, that is one thing. I am Colonel Hamilton. Perhaps, after that information, you would rather not know anything further of me, young gentleman?"

"I don't need to know anything further," said Hawk. "I know quite enough; although, until this moment, I never heard your name mentioned."

"Indeed?"

"Just so, sir; and I know that you are a bully and a coward."

"S'death, sir! I——"

"Oh, sir, be quiet, or I shall have to put you out at the window."

"What is it?—what is it?" cried half a dozen persons pressing round them. "What is the matter? What is it?"

"Nothing," said Colonel Hamilton; "only this gentleman inquired after a friend of mine, that is all. Pray, gentlemen, be so good as to keep off. Sir," bowing to Captain Hawk, "I am delighted to make your acquaintance—very delighted, indeed."

"The pleasure is by no means wanted," said Hawk.

The colonel bowed, and smiled, and sidled away, and was in a few moments lost to Hawk's observation in the fashionable throng with which he was surrounded.

"A strange fellow that," said Hawk to himself. "At first he seemed inclined to pick a quarrel, and then he goes off looking as pleased as possible the moment I take the only means in my power of obliging him."

"Your highness?" said a voice in Hawk's ear.

He turned rapidly, and saw a sallow-looking man bowing in a very courtly manner close to him.

"Did you address me, sir?" said Hawk.

"I had that honour. Would your highness inform me when I might have the honour of calling upon you to-morrow?"

"I don't receive visitors, sir."

"Ah, indeed? But upon this occasion"—here the sallow-faced man came quite close to Hawk—"and as the friend of Colonel Hamilton, I am quite sure you will break through your resolve."

"The friend of Colonel Hamilton?"

"Yes, your highness. No doubt your highness has already had some little affairs of honour?"

"Oh, I understand you, sir."

"I could expect no less from your highness."

"You mean, that I am to fight Colonel Hamilton, because I trod upon his toe? Is that it?"

The sallow-faced man only bowed and grinned.

"Tell him, then, that I shall shoot him, or run him through the body, whichever he may happen to prefer, with all the pleasure in life, and you will find me at Muggins's Hotel."

"You are very good—very good, your highness. I have the honour to bid you adieu."

"And I the pleasure," said Hawk.

"Ah! demme!" said a voice, "that is rich. Ah — a-chew! a-chew! Devilish strong snuff this, demme!"

An exquisite of the style shape of fashion of that period was close to Hawk and handed him his box, out of which Hawk took a pinch of snuff, saying as he did so—

"I am sorry not to have the pleasure of knowing you, sir."

"Oh—ah, don't — demme!—don't mention that. Sink me! Ah, all the men upon town know me. I am Lord Noddie."

"Oh, Lord Noddie?"

"Yes, that's the a—the title. Ah, demme!"

"It is much graced, my lord, by its possessor."

Captain Hawk bowed slightly as he uttered this compliment, and Lord Noddie made a very low salaam—so low, indeed, that he had suddenly to clap his hand on the top of his head to keep his wig from falling off.

"Demme! that's good. Ah, count—I hear you call yourself Count Astral?"

"I do, my lord."

"Ah, I should esteem it quite—demme!—an honour if you would allow me to—demme!—be your friend upon this little occasion."

Hawk smiled.

"You allude to the challenge I am threatened with from Colonel Hamilton?"

"Ah, yes. Step aside. Demme! I will tell you. Of course, count, you don't know the fellow; but I do. He is a confirmed duellist, and one of the most successful, too. Demme! they do say he has killed eight men, and now nobody will fight with him, and he is quite rejoiced that he has picked you up."

"Indeed!"

"Yes; ah, that's it. But if your highness will allow me—demme! as I feel rather used-up, and want a little a—excitement—something to make me a—a—I don't know how to explain it; but, perhaps, I should say alive—you will oblige me by allowing me the honour of aiding upon the little interesting occasion of your settlement."

"My settlement, my lord?"

"Pardon the absurd word; but, ah! demme! I assure you I will see you disposed of in the most gentlemanly way."

"I am infinitely obliged to you."

"Don't mention it—pray don't."

"I won't, then; but as I fully intend to settle the colonel, I hope that phase of the affair will not in any way interfere with your enjoyment?"

"Oh, no—not at all."

"Thank you. I feel how very obliging your lordship is. May I hope that you will do me the honour of breakfasting with me?"

"Yos—yos. Demme! yos. Baron Salter will call."

"Who is Baron Salter?"

"The ill-looking fellow who spoke to you just now. You will pardon me, count; but—demme!—when one sees the baron whisper to any one, of course it can be only a message from the colonel; so I could not help knowing it, demme! It looks rude; but it can't be helped."

"Make no apologies, Lord Noddie, I beg of you. Being as I am in London without credentials, and desirous as I am of being unknown except to the few to whom I shall have the pleasure to discover myself when those credentials come, I take it as a singular favour on the part of your lordship to offer me your assistance upon this little occasion, and hope for the future pleasure of your acquaintance."

"The—demme! the future—ah!"

"I hope you see no objection, my lord?"

"None in life—oh, none in life, provided the colonel is so good as to give me and yourself the opportunity of breakfasting together more than once. What is your hour, count?"

"I will make it yours."

"Eleven, then. You stay at Muggins's?"

"I do."

"Then I shall do myself the honour of attending you."

They bowed again, and Hawk made his way partially down the staircase, when a page thrust a note, done up in a three cornered shape, into his hand, and then disappeared in a moment.

"What next," thought Hawk, and pausing in a recess on the staircase that was filled with rare evergreens, he opened the note and read—

"His highness is requested by a lady to step into the conservatory."

"Oh," said Hawk, "am I? I suppose this is the entrance to it. To be sure it is. Well, I will see what the gods have in store for me to-night yet."

Half-a-dozen steps took him through a pair of glass doors, into a small conservatory, but no one was there, although a white glove lay upon one of the seats, as if to intimate that its owner was near at hand.

The music from the grand saloon only penetrated into this place in a dim and uncertain manner, so as to fill the air with soft sounds.

A chandelier, the ground-glass globes of which were tinted green, shed a soft and sweet light upon the rare plants that were there collected, and the air, too, was laden with perfume, so as to feel rather sickly.

Hawk lifted the glove and looked at it.

"This should fit a young hand," he said.

As he spoke, there was a rustling of silk close to him, and from among a group of Provence rose-trees in full blossom, there issued a young lady of great personal attractions, carrying one glove in her hand. At sight of Captain Hawk she paused, and started, and then drew back.

"Permit me to hope," he said "that my presence does not terrify you."

"Oh, no, sir; but—I came for my glove."

"It is here."

"I thank you, sir."

She curtsied and was retiring, when Hawk said—

"Allow me to hope that, although the invitation that brought me here was brief, the pleasure of this interview will be a little further prolonged."

"Invitation, sir?"

"Yes, this note."

"Oh, sir, it was not I. I wrote no note."

"A thousand pardons. I am, unhappily, then mistaken. I did hope, and yet, if it be any offence, I will no longer hope it, that this billet came from you."

"This is dreadful," said the young lady.

"Dreadful, say you? How so?"

"Oh, sir, I do not know you, nor do you know me; but is it not truly dreadful that any gentleman should think me capable of writing to him?"

"Well," said Captain Hawk, "if you say it is dreadful, why dreadful be it; but yet, permit me to remark, that much depends upon the honour——"

"Of the lady?"

"No, not so much as upon the honour of the gentleman."

"Ah, that is true. But I left a glove here, and that was what brought me to this place again."

"It is here. Ah, my dear young lady, let me hope that you will permit me to know what name to attach to her who, in my dreams, will henceforward be a divinity, and who will occupy all my waking hours by the thought of her wondrous beauty."

This was what Joe would have called "pitching it rather strong." The young lady looked rather confused.

"My name," she said, "is—is——"

"Sweet saint, tell it to me."

"Is Maria."

"Henceforward I will hold that name in reverence."

"Sir, you are so very—that is, so gallant, that—that I really cannot help feeling that the accident which has brought me back to this place in search of my lost glove is one that—that——"

"That you will never regret?"

"Nay, I did not say that."

"But you thought it."

"This is very unfair, sir, to speculate upon my thoughts. But I must now leave you, sir, with thanks for the many kind compliments you have been pleased to pay to one who, however, is too well acquainted with her own deficiencies to imagine for a moment that she deserves them."

With these words, which were very smoothly and elegantly spoken, the young lady bowed and retired from the conservatory, leaving Captain Hawk rather smitten with her youth and beauty.

"By Jove," he said, "there are none in the saloons to compare with her. She is, in good truth, a charming creature. Ah, she has left her glove here. Was that accident, now, or intention?"

That was a question which Captain Hawk found it impossible to answer satisfactorily; but he took the glove in his hand, and looked at it carefully, when he saw that there was some writing on the inside of it, and after some trouble he deciphered the words:

"M. A., Shrubland House, Kensington."

"Ha! ha!" he said, "so that is the address of the charmer. Now, after all, is this but a planned thing, or is it all accidental? Well, I don't care. I will have some amusement among these butterflies of fashion, somehow, if they have among them to pay in the end rather dearly for it."

He waited for a few minutes longer in the conservatory, but no one came to him; and although from that circumstance he might suspect that, after all, Miss Maria might be the real person who had written the little billet to him yet it was not conclusive evidence to that effect.

It was just possible that some one else had indicted it, and had come to keep the appointment, but seeing him with the young lady, had gone off again in anger or in fear.

Captain Hawk found it as difficult as all men ever find it to believe that youth and beauty can be associated with other than fair and virtuous, and sincere qualities. Perhaps he, as many have, will find occasion to alter his mind upon that particular.

There was now no great difficulty in descending the grand staircase, and when he reached the hall, he said to the first lackey he saw—

"Order Count Astral's carriage."

The hall and the street in a few moments resounded with the shouts of "Count Astral's carriage stops the way!"

CHAPTER XCII.

CAPTAIN HAWK FINDS ENOUGH ON HIS HANDS IN A DUEL AND AN INTRIGUE.

The carriage was in waiting, and Joe, tolerably sober, for he had recovered pretty well from the extra quantity of liquor he had taken, was ready to attend upon the captain with all due respect.

The drive to the hotel was short; and just as a neighbouring church clock was striking four in the morning, Captain Hawk entered his temporary home.

Hawk felt that if he was to carry on this sort of life that he had begun now, he must husband his resources, so he immediately retired to rest, giving orders that he should not be aroused until ten the next morning; and then with the facility that he had in so doing, he banished from his mind all excitements that would have disturbed him, and fell fast asleep in the magnificent bed prepared for him at the hotel.

* * * *

"Ten o'clock, if you pleases!"

"What?" cried Hawk, as he looked up, and found the daylight streaming into the apartment. "Ten o'clock so soon?"

"Not a bit sooner than usual, captain" said Joe. "Oh, murder!"

"You villain!" said Hawk, as he threw a pillow at him, "I only wish it had been a something hard enough to hurt your head."

"Why, what have I done, now?" said Joe.

"Called me captain."

"Oh, lor! Well, that was a blunder. Count—ah, that's it—count, I admit that that was rather a little blunder."

"And I suppose it was equally one to get drunk last night—eh?"

"Drunk?"

"Yes, drunk. Oh, you need not look so astonished. It is a fact, for all that. And now I tell you what it is, Master Joe—if you make such another mistake, I will shoot you. You are very well aware that when I make a threat it is not by any means an idle one, and that I am just the sort of man to keep my word."

"You is," said Joe.

"Good. You can keep what I have just now said, then, in remembrance."

"Very good, count; we will say no more about it, then, just now, if you please. It's never worth while to make a row about things as is past and gone in this here world. Lor bless you, there's sure to be quite enough of things a-coming to make disagreeables about. I forgives you."

"You must," muttered Hawk, as he rapidly dressed himself.

"Sir, did you speak?"

"Go to the landlord, and say that I expect Lord Noddie to breakfast with me, and that, therefore, he is to lay the table for two."

"Very good. Lord Noddie? Oh, my eye! what a name. Lord Noddie? Well, I never! Where did you pick him up, cap—no, I mean, count."

"It is well you do. Wait a moment."

"Yes, count, I—Oh, don't!"

Smash! came the wash-hand basin, with a tolerable amount of soapy water in it, at the head of Joe.

"Take that for your insolence and carelessness."

"Now you have done it," said Joe, as he looked at the stream of water all down the front of his livery. "Well, it don't matter to me. The tailor will suffer, in course. I'll see to the breakfast, count, and am much obliged to you for all favours past, present, and a-coming."

With these words, Joe left the apartment, and if he had not done so with some alacrity, the propability is that some other portable article of the toilette would have come at his head. Captain Hawk looked after him in silence for a few moments, and then he said—

"Confound that fellow! I very much fear that he will play some trick yet with his forgetfulness and his love of the bottle; and, but that I know he is as faithful to me as any one might ever wish, I would get rid of him. He is at once a perpetual danger and a perpetual safeguard; so, I suppose, I must put up with the evil of the one for the sake of the good of the other."

This was strictly true as regarded Joe, whose attachment to Hawk was so great that he would not for one half moment have hesitated to place himself in the way of certain death to shield his master. And yet, what did he get in return for such generous, or rather foolish devotion?—Abuse!

Well, there are natures in this world that will comprehend nothing but kicks, and that you spoil absolutely by real kindness, but which you may attach to you to any extent by downright selfishness and ill usage.

Joe must have been one of those natures surely.

Captain Hawk was quick at his toilette, and before the appointed time of meeting Lord Noddie, he repaired to the breakfast room, attired in a magnificent dressing-gown of quilted satin, that the confiding tailor had sent him home, and felt uncommonly grateful that he had got the order for it.

It was not trifles that commonly excited the wonder or the admiration of Captain Hawk; but the breakfast table at the hotel certainly, for a moment or two, rather amazed him by its magnificence.

The table was covered with one glitter of gold and silver plate. The fact was, that the landlord of the hotel was determined to retain his royal and illustrious guest at all hazards, in order to get the better in the way of fashion, if he could, of a rival establishment; and with that view he had gone to a fashionable silversmith's, and bargained for the loan of such an assortment of rich goods for the use of the Austrian Prince, as no other house of public entertainment could at all pretend to.

"This is the thing, indeed," said Hawk.

"Rather," said Joe, who was regarding the table with looks of envy.

"Silence!"

"Hem! Count—I say, count?"

"Say it."

"There's lots of little things here as would go into a fellow's pocket. I suppose, you have no objection to a fellow—

Hawk took a pistol from his pocket, and deliberately prepared it for use; but Joe bolted out of the room as if he had been shot out of a cannon, and in so doing, ran against some one on the landing, and they both rolled down three or four stairs together.

"Demme! what's this?" said a voice. "Consume me, if I am not dislocated. Ah—demme! Murder!"

It was no other than my Lord Noddie, whom the landlord himself was showing, with all due ceremony, to the count's breakfast room.

"I could not help it," said Joe.

"Demme! you brute!

"Oh—oh!" said the landlord. "I am so—so very sorry. The idea of your lordship encountering such an accident in my house."

"D—n your house."

"Yes, my lord, if you please."

"And dem this fellow!"

"Exactly," said Joe.

Both Joe and the landlord now bowed to the Lord Noddie, who was rather anxiously rubbing the back of his head, which had come into serious contact with the edge of one of the stairs.

"You infernal villain!" he said to Joe.

"I is," said Joe.

"Where is my excellent friend, the count?"

"This way, my lord," said the landlord, "this way. May I hope that your lordship, if you are hurt, will never mind it?"

"And go on never minding," added Joe, "till your head don't ache no more; then you will be as comfortable as bricks."

"A couple of dem rascals!" muttered the Lord Noddie. "I do believe, if such a thing were possible with a nobleman, they are making game of me. I do, indeed."

The landlord then opened the door of the breakfast room, and in quite a soft and delicate voice, cried out—

"My Lord Noddie!"

Captain Hawk looked round with a smile.

"Ah, my lord, I hope you are well?"

"Demme, yes, I am pretty well. How is it with your lordship?"

"Quite well, thank you. Pray be seated. We do not stand upon ceremony here in London, so we beg you will be seated."

"Demme, yes. Ah! Anything in this way, prince?"

Lord Noddie offered his snuff-box.

"Thank you, not before breakfast. You are the most punctual of men, my dear Lord Noddie. Did you stay late at Lady Poodleton's?"

"Demme, no!"

"Nor did I. By the by, where is a place called Kensington?"

"Kensington? Oh, ah, it is a suburb of this city, close to the old palace. There are some human beings there, I believe."

"Do you know a house called Shrubland."

"Shrub—land? Demme, no! Some citizen's horrid home, perhaps. There are common people, my dear prince, everywhere. Demme, not that I totally despise them. Oh, no, I used to do so—ah! I used to do so, and to wonder at providence for permitting them to live."

"Common people?"

"Yos! yos! Demme! Common people. But I changed my opinion. A little cream, allow me to hand you, prince?"

"Thank you. But how came you to change your opinion about common people, my Lord Noddie?"

"Just this way. I was making the remark, demme! to the prime minister, that it was something wrong that there should be vulgar and common people in the world, and he took hold of me by the fifth button of my waiscoat, and demme! says he, 'Noddie, my dear boy, you are right in the abstract—quite right in the abstract, my dear boy,' says he, 'but—but,' says he—some dry toast?"

"Thank you. But what did he say?"

"'Why, Noddie, my boy,' says he, 'the common people and the vulgar kind,' says he—demme! some cream?"

"No thank, you."

"'He! he! my boy, Noddie,' says he, 'the common people pay the taxes, and we spend 'em,' demme! says he."

"How true."

"So it struck me upon a little consideration; and ever since then, you see, count, I modified my opinion, and think that, after all, providence creates nothing in vain, and that even common people and vulgar working men and tradesmen, and all that sort of thing, have their appointed use, for they pay the taxes, demme, and we spend 'em."

"Capital," said Hawk, "capital!"

"I suppose that never struck you before?"

"Never; at least, if I had a slight idea of it before, it never came to my mind in so forcible a shape, my dear Noddie."

The door of the breakfast-room was gently opened, and the landlord, in a soft tone, as if it were quite a liberty to take to speak at all in the presence of so illustrious a person as his guest, said, as he bowed low to the floor—

"An individual calling himself Baron

Salter, if your highness pleases, has called, and says that he much desires speech of your highness."

"Tell him to wait."

"Yes, demme!" added Lord Noddie, "tell him to wait."

"I shall have that honour," said the landlord, as he withdrew and shut the door as if it were made of very thin glass indeed.

"And were you amused last night?" said Hawk.

"Demme, no."

"No?"

"Not at all. I have never been amused since I was a child, and then it was rather a swindle, for I didn't know any better, demme!"

"Ha—ha! Upon my word, Noddie, that is good."

"Eh?"

"I say that is rich. But I suppose it will be as well to see this rascal who is below, after all, will it not?"

"Demme, yes!"

"Order him up."

Lord Noddie was quite in raptures at the cool manner in which the Prince of Austria treated the ambassador from fighting Colonel Hamilton, as he was called, and he rang the bell with quite an air. The fact was, that Colonel Hamilton was the pest of society, and every one wished that somebody should be fortunate enough to put him out of it and the world at the same time.

"Send the baron up!"

Baron Salter, the sallow, insidious-looking man who had spoken to Captain Hawk at the entertainment, entered the room. There was a slight flush of colour upon his countenance as he entered, for the manner in which he had been told to wait had by no means improved his temper.

"Well, sir?" said Hawk.

"Do I speak to Count Astral?"

"You do, sir."

"Then allow me to remark——"

"I will not, sir, unless your remark is one that I ought to hear," said Captain Hawk, in a voice of thunder.

Lord Noddie applauded by tapping an empty egg-shell with a golden spoon.

"Count Astral, I came here on behalf of my friend, Colonel Hamilton, and I was merely going to say that it is not usual for one gentleman, without good reason, to keep another gentleman waiting in the hall of a hotel."

"Who are you, sir?"

"Baron Salter."

"Baron of what or where? Who granted you your barony? Of what state do you hold it?—Not of Austria!"

"Good," said Lord Noddie.

The baron's countenance turned livid with rage and fear, as he said—

"My title, count, has nothing to do with the affair."

"Yes, but it has, for how do I know but that both you and your principal may be nothing better than a couple of adventurers, swindlers, sharpers, or even highwaymen, eh?"

"Sir?"

"Well, sir?"

"By G—d, you shall answer for this!"

"I will, sir, answer for it. And now to come to your errand. What is it? I will waive the question of your rather questionable title, and think of that by-and-bye. Now, sir, what do you want with me? Speak out, Baron Salter, with a query attached to the barony—speak out, sir."

"Demme! this is capital," said Lord Noddie. "I couldn't have done it!"

CHAPTER XCIII.

CAPTAIN HAWK AGREES TO FIGHT COLONEL HAMILTON AT THE BACK OF MONTAGUE HOUSE.

Whether or not Captain Hawk, in his address to the friend of Colonel Hamilton, had hit the right nail on the head, and the barony of Baron Salter was not a title that could be said of a doubtful story even, to be founded on facts, remains to be seen; but certain it is, he had raised such a world of indignation in the breast of the baron, that it was with the greatest difficulty that illustrious individual could control himself sufficiently to declare his errand.

"Count Astral," he said, "I have the honour to appear here as the friend of Colonel Hamilton."

"Stop," said Hawk, "stop a moment. Lord Noddie?"

"Your highness?"

"Is that man, Hamilton, a colonel in the English service or not?"

"He is."

"Oh, very good; then it is only his friend, the baron, who is at all a doubtful character, after all."

The baron bit his lips.

"Count Astral," he added, "I bring

HATCHLEY INFORMS SIR WILLIAM DODD OF THE DUEL IN THE GARDEN.

you a challenge on the part of my friend, Colonel Hamilton, and it is usual in such cases to treat the bearer of such a document with some degree of courtesy."

"Pray be seated, then, sir. I want to do just what is usual. My friend, Lord Noddie, here will arrange with you the particulars of this little meeting, and whatever he agrees to I will answer for. Don't mind me, gentlemen; I will read the paper while you settle the matter."

Captain Hawk very coolly took up

the newspaper to read, while Lord Noddie and Baron Salter consulted together in a low tone. At length, Lord Noddie said—

"Count, it is agreed that you and the colonel are to meet in the meadows at the back of Montague House this evening at one hour before sunset."

"Very good."

"You can bring your own pistols if you like, gentlemen," said the baron.

"Oh, no," said Hawk. "I don't fight with pistols."

"Not with pistols, count?"

"Certainly not. As the challenged party, I have the choice of weapons, and I say swords."

"But swords are quite out of fashion now, count. All gentlemen now fight with pistols in England, I do assure you."

"Then, sir, I will set an example to the contrary. You can tell your principal that as I trod upon his toe, I will, to further satisfy him, run him through the body at the hour appointed; and if he has any affairs to settle he had better do so as soon as possible."

"But, count, I really am not sure of whether the colonel would like to fight with swords or not upon this occasion."

"He shall, sir."

"Shall?"

"Yes, sir. Since he has mooted the subject of fighting, he shall fight me, and he shall fight with swords, too. I now will take no denial. If he had left me alone, I should not have descended so low as to interfere with him, for I hear that he is a bully, and, consequently, a blackguard; but since he has thought proper to interfere with me, he shall take the consequences of so doing."

"Very well, sir."

The baron rose and bowed.

"Is all that settled, then, demme!" said Lord Noddie.

"I must consult the colonel."

"What, sir!" cried Hawk. "Do you have the impudence to come here and challenge me, and then, because you cannot be allowed to dictate the weapons you should use in the encounter, attempt to back out of the affair? I tell you if Colonel Hamilton does not meet me at the place and hour appointed, I will not sleep till I have found him out, and punished him for his audacity."

"Good again, demme!" said Lord Noddie.

"Then, count, in the name of Colonel Hamilton, I accept the terms proposed," said the baron, with a low bow.

"Very good, sir. I will be there."

Captain Hawk took up the newspaper again with all the coolness in the world, and commenced reading, and the baron bowed himself out of the room, cursing in his inmost heart the errand that he had been sent upon by his friend, the colonel.

"'Pon soul," said Lord Noddie, "you did that capitally, count. Why, Hamilton will be half frightened to death, demme! before night."

"These bullies are always curs at heart," said Hawk. "It is but a bit of acting to cow a craven disposition. Of that I feel quite assured. But do not let me trespass upon your valuable time, Lord Noddie, now. We shall meet when and where you please in the evening."

"I will do myself both the honour and the pleasure of calling for your highness, and I doubt not but that this duel will be the world's talk for the next—let me see—the next eight days."

"That's a long time," said Hawk, smiling.

"Demme! it is."

Lord Noddie rose to go, and as he reached the door of the room, Joe appeared with a silver tray, upon which lay a note.

"For me?" said Hawk.

"Yes, count."

"Good day," said Lord Noddie, "good day, count. I will be with you in good time."

"Good day, my lord. Believe me, I am much obliged by your kind services upon this occasion."

"Demme! don't mention that."

Lord Noddie left, and Captain Hawk opened the note, which had at the top of it the word "Confidential," and then proceeded as follows—

"If the Prince of Austria really meant what he seemed to mean, and really felt what he appeared to feel, the Lady Deliva will be only too happy to see him this evening at eight, to chocolate.

"St. James's Street."

Hawk laughed.

"Upon my word," he said, "I am getting on in the fashionable world, rather. Young and old seem alike to be smitten with the idea of allying themselves to the House of Austria. Here have I not been in the fashionable world of London yet quite twenty-four hours, and I have one duel and two intrigues, if not three, on my hands; and I have insulted a doubtful baron and made friends with a fool."

"Ha—ha!" laughed Joe.

"Silence!"

"Oh, well, I only laughed, that's all; but I am as sober as a judge."

"I see that you are sober, Joe, and I am willing to forget the past, if you will be careful for the time that is to come."

"Won't I!"

"Very good. I am going to fight a duel this evening at six o'clock. I believe the sun don't set till about seven, now, does it?"

"Quite seven, count."

"Very well. You will come with me, and that Lord Noddie will be there likewise; so hold yourself in readiness at half-past five to follow me to the fields at the back of Montague House."

"All's right, count; that's where all the nobs fight now-a-days, they say."

"I know it. In the meantime, though, I want you to go to Kensington and find out for me a house or villa called Shrubland House."

"Exactly. I'll find it."

"And, as you go, take a note to Lady Deliva's, in St. James's Street. I don't know the number; but a little inquiry will find it for you, no doubt."

"All's right, cap—count I mean. Oh, lor!"

Captain Hawk took no notice of this little slip of the tongue upon the part of Joe; but he wrote the following note to Lady Deliva:—

"The Count Astral presents his admiration, and will be with Lady Deliva at the hour appointed. Till then, he is as one shut out of Paradise."

Joe took the precious epistle, and departed on his two errands, while Captain Hawk reclined back in his easy chair, and, with half-shut eyes, contemplated his prospects, as they just then appeared.

"Let me see," he said. "I shall kill this Colonel Hamilton, I daresay, or so badly wound the rascal, that he will be out of everybody's way for a long time to come, and then I must take chocolate with Lady Deliva, from whom I hope to be able to make much profit. She shall fill my purse, and I don't care if I spend a little of her money upon Maria at Shrubland House, or upon any other young and fair creature who may attract the eye of an Austrian Prince! Oh, what fools these fashionable folks are! They pride themselves upon the fact, or rather the pretended fact, that exterior is nothing to them, and yet how they are deceived by me almost solely on that ground. Well, well, I will carry on this game till I can carry it on no longer, and then to the road again. It will be delightful to be mounted on my gallant steed, and out on the road, after all this soft and silky life of fashion."

Captain Hawk warmed himself by a canter in the park till it was time to go to the hotel and dine, which he did at four o'clock, that being the fashionable hour of the day then for partaking of that meal.

Joe had been very diligent in his inquiries, and made his appearance before Hawk with some news.

"I took the letter to Lady Devil," said Joe.

"Deliva! not Devil."

"Well, it's much the same, count, ain't it?"

"It is a woman, and, therefore, it is much the same, Joe. It don't matter. Well, go on."

"After that, I went to Kensington to look for Shrubland House."

"And you found it?"

"Well, not exactly."

"Not exactly? What do you mean by that, rascal? You found it, or you did not?"

"Just so, count."

"There is no middle course in the matter that I am at all aware of. Go on."

"Well, captain, I first of all went to the World's End ——"

"The what?"

"The World's End; capital ale they sell there—not that I took above a thimbleful of it, of course; but still I could find that it was rather the right sort of thing."

"Well—well?"

"Very good. They couldn't tell me anything about Shrubland House, so then I went to Noah's Ark."

"Tut—tut!"

"And there I had a slight taste of their ale; but it wasn't quite up to the scratch, as I told the landlord, so I went off at once and stalked into the Frying-Pan and Extinguisher."

"You rascal! it seems to me that you have just been making a tour through all the taverns between here and Kensington. Is it not so?"

"Oh, no—no."

"What, then? Tell me in a word, have you got any information respecting the place I sent you to look for, or have you not?"

"To be sure I have."

"Out with it, then. What is it?"

"Why, at the Running Hound, I can assure you, captain—I mean, count—that they have got some old October ale that ——"

"You knave—you villain! Did you find Shrubland House?"

"No; I ——"

"Get out of the room, then, you sot. I do from my heart believe that you are now drunk, but have the skill to conceal the fact in some way. Get out of the room this instant, you scoundrel, or I shall be tempted to do you a serious mischief, I tell you. Get out—get out!"

Joe thought it prudent to make a rather precipitate retreat, which he did upon the spur of the moment, or, no doubt, the captain would have managed to throw some of the dinner equipage at his head, without being at all particular as to the consequences of so doing, or the amount of injury he might inflict.

"Oh," said Joe, as he withdrew outside the door, "oh, he gets rather worser and worser in his temper as he gets older. I don't know who will be able to live with him next, I'm sure."

Captain Hawk soon concluded his dinner, for he knew that he had much to do that evening, and he wanted to keep himself light and active for the coming encounter with Captain Hamilton—not that he had any dread of what might be the result of that encounter, but he did not wish to throw a chance away, as, of course, he could not tell whether or not the colonel might be expert at the use of the sword.

The presumption was that such was not the case, or the wily Baron Salter would not have shown so decided a predilection for the pistol as he did.

Lord Noddie was true to his appointment, and entered the captain's room at half-past five, rather plainly dressed, and covered up above that again in a large coverlet cloak, such as were then very fashionable.

Captain Hawk welcomed him with all that grace of manner, which, in a different position of life to that which he had chosen to occupy, would have been a theme of admiration, and which was so completely lost in the, career of the highwayman.

"My dear Noddie," he said, "I am extremely obliged to you, for I really did not wish to go to our embassy, and pull our ambassador out at his time of life to second me in this duel; and if I had, you know, he would have thought himself bound to follow me to the field."

"No doubt of it. Demme! I am very much gratified, indeed, prince, that I have been enabled to be of any service to you."

"It is a very great service, I can assure you."

"Well, we will say no more about that, then, if you please, prince. But are you provided with swords?"

"Only the one I wear; and that is one that you will by an inspection, I think, agree with me may be fully depended upon."

"Very good, then; let us be off at once."

"Is it time?"

"Why, scarcely. But, then, it is so much better in these little affairs to be too soon than too late, you know."

"It is. I am ready."

Captain Hawk was very much pleased to see that, now there was some real business to do, Lord Noddie was not by any means so fantastical in his behaviour and manner as he had been when nothing called for special attention from him, beyond the ordinary affairs of every-day existence; and he left the hotel with him on foot.

Joe was in the hall, and at a sign from Hawk followed them.

CHAPTER XCIV.

DESCRIBES THE DUEL AT THE BACK OF MONTAGUE HOUSE.

At the period of which we write, Montague House, which is now pulled down to make way for the present building devoted to the purposes of the British Museum, stood quite at the extremity of the town in that direction.

The streets and squares which stretch out northward of that spot were not then dreamt of; and some very beautiful meadows, adorned in their hedgerows with very stately trees, were to be found at the back of Montague House.

The house itself was a large brick building, faced on the edges with stone, and was sold to the nation, for the purpose of holding the treasures of the Museum, for a large sum of money, by its owner. It was, however, soon found to be inadequate to its purpose, as every thing in this country is soon found to be after it is paid for; and the present building, which looks more like a workhouse or a hospital than a fine public building, was erected on its site.

It was the custom, then, for the bloods and gallants, as they called themselves, of the town, to fight duels in the fields at the back of Montague House; and to such an extent did duelling get, that in the subsequent reign some very stringent examples had to be made for the purpose of in some measure repressing it.

The Colonel Hamilton with whom Captain Hawk was going to fight, was one of the most celebrated—or, we might rather say, infamous, for surely such a reputation was of an infamous character—duellists of the period. He had come out of so many encounters with success, that no one liked to fight with him, so he went through society insulting whom he pleased, and defying all men.

His meeting with Captain Hawk was one of those incidents in his career which, no doubt, fate had reserved for him, and which generally, sooner or later, puts an end to the vicious existence of such pests of society.

Of course, now-a-days, it would be quite out of the question that any such man as Colonel Hamilton could exist long. The force of public opinion and the strong arm of the law would soon put him down. But then it was not by any means so easy to do so.

If Captain Hawk was well pleased to see that, with all his oddities and affectations, Lord Noddie had still that constitutional courage which belongs to all Englishmen, Lord Noddie was no less delighted to find that his friend, the prince, as he thought him, considered no more about going to fight a duel than sitting down to dinner.

"I suppose this rascal will come?" said Hawk.

"Demme! yes, unless the swords frighten him a little."

"If he comes not, you must instruct me where I shall be likely to find him, for I shall have to horsewhip him."

"That I will do with pleasure."

Joe kept at a respectful enough distance from Captain Hawk, but yet he knew very well what was about to take place, and that a duel was on the *tapis*. Perhaps if he had not had the very high opinion of Captain Hawk that he really had, he, Joe, might have felt some degree of uneasiness at the fact that one whom he served so faithfully, and upon whose life his own continued prosperity so much depended, should be exposed to the chances of a duel.

But Joe, along with admiration of Captain Hawk, as on might say it was the natural result of it, had unbounded confidence in his skill and in his courage; and if the humble follower had been put upon his oath upon the subject, and had really felt desirous to say just what he really thought, he must have stated in the most unhesitating manner, that he thought the captain, as he called him, a fair match for any two people.

With such an opinion, then, of the prowess of his master, it is no wonder that Joe followed him and Lord Noddie to the meadows at the back of Montague House with all the composure in the world.

"You will," said Lord Noddie, as they came to a turning that led right into the fields from Bloomsbury. "You will, demme! be entitled to a piece of plate from the ladies, if you put the colonel out of the way."

"Why?"

"Because I say it. Because it will be a good thing."

"Why from the ladies?"

"Because, demme! he has put out of the world more pretty fellows than enough, and they all hate him, the dears, one and all, demme! they do."

"I will try to deserve it, then, my Lord Noddie, you may depend."

"Do so."

They went through a gate, and so on right into Bloomsbury Fields, and as the evening was fine and they had a great extent of open country before them, sweetly tinged by the fading sunlight, Captain Hawk could not but pause to admire the scene that bloomed in beauty around him.

Such a prospect so near to the great city has not been to be seen for a very long time. The building projects of the Bedford family, which erected the squares and streets to the north of the British Museum, entirely covered up the fine fields of Bloomsbury.

Captain Hawk was looking to the north-west, so that he had a greater prospect over all the open country towards the Edgeware Road, across the swampy meadows that now constitute the Regent's Park, and to the right the route to Hampstead and Highgate, then private villages, which still retain their old rusticity, was distinctly visible.

The fields looked fresh and fair. A few lowing kine were lazily returning to their sheds. The tinkle of the sheep bell came from somewhere about where Euston Square, south, now stands, and the gnats,

"A busy rout,"

were playing their last game at "touch" by the side of a sweet-smelling hawthorn hedge.

To the left were the garden walls of old Montague House, and at some distance further on was an unfinished building, which the then Duke of Bedford was building for a town residence.

"This is a fine scene," said Hawk.

"Demme! yes," said Lord Noddie, as he indulged himself with a pinch of snuff, "to them who like it."

"And do not you, my friend?"

"No. Demme! no."

"Why, what can you see to object to in it?"

"My dear count, it is really too—too—in a manner of speaking, it is a—a—demme!"

"That is a lucid description of what it is, I must confess; but I suppose you would say that you are so old a denizen of the town that you have lost taste for the simple beauties of the dear old country?"

"Ah, demme! yes. I never had much affection for a cow or a pig, or a sheep. The lowing of the oxen, the squeaking of the pigs, and the baa! of the lambs never struck me as being half so musical as the warbling of some pretty little signora at Ranelagh, demme!"

"But my dear friend, the flowers?"

"Ah, demme! the artificial ones are better."

"Better?"

"Yes, they don't fade: and if you like to sprinkle a rose with any essence you please, you get a pleasing floricultural variety—demme!"

"But the sunlight——"

"Wax candles for me before all the world."

"The trees—the grass—the hedgerows—Oh, my lord, do not tell me that your taste is so vitiated that you have lost all enjoyment of such natural delights."

"Demme, it's no loss. I never had it."

"Yes, my lord—oh, it is born with us. Time and circumstance may change our tastes, as it changes us in all other particulars; but still it is a loss not to be able to return to the country and live natural for a little time. Now—"

"Demme!—Murder!"

"What is the matter?"

"There! This is one of your enjoyments. I only tried to give a rap with my glass to something that was buzzing round my head, and it immediately lit upon my nose and has given me a sting, and raised this red bump. Oh, oh!—what will Lady Pompositie say when she sees my nose look so positively red and vulgar?"

"It's only a wasp," said Hawk.

"That's all," said Joe.

"Only—all! Well, I suppose it is. I didn't expect it was an eagle hardly. Oh, ye gods! that I, Lord Noddie, should venture into the fields, and be stung by a wasp. It will be, if it ever becomes known, and I sincerely trust you will keep the secret, my dear count, the subject of a week's raillery in the fashionable world. There will be half a dozen epigrammatic affairs contingent upon the circumstance, and I shall be exposed to all the sarcastic wit of Lady Sphitefool."

"You may depend upon my secrecy."

"A thousand thanks. I wonder what will remove the pain and the swelling?"

"A little stone-blue," said Joe.

"A little who?"

"It isn't a little who, my lord. A little stone-blue, I said. It is what the women use to colour their ruffs and laces with. You have only to take it and rub it on your nose, and it will ease the smart."

"Blue! But, my good friend, will it impart a—demme!—a blue colour to my nose?"

"Why, yes, it may."

"Curse me, then, if the remedy is not worse than the disease! Demme! I would rather be excused. Stone-blue! Crush me, count, if I like the idea!"

"Many medicines are worse than the disease they propose to contest with. But who have we here?"

"Ah, our men, by Jove!"

From a distant corner of the meadow three persons approached, and Captain Hawk saw that the foremost one was the Baron Salter, who had borne him the malicious message from his rascally employer, Colonel Hamilton.

The colonel himself followed, and appeared to be in quite a gay and easy conversation with the gentlemen who were with him.

"Who is that with my friend, the colonel?" said Hawk.

"'Pon my life," replied Lord Noddie, "I don't know; but I suppose it is same one who has a—come—demme!—to see a—the sport."

"Very likely."

"It don't matter. With your man we make three, so we can't object to the presence of a third party on the other side."

"I have no objection in the least," said Hawk. "Half London may turn out to Bloomsbury fields to see this little affair if they like."

"Exactly. But here they are."

As the party approached, Colonel Hamilton paused and allowed Baron Salter and the gentleman, who was a stranger to Hawk, to come on without him. Upon this Hawk stepped aside and permitted Lord Noddie to meet them, and then he heard Noddie exclaim—

"Ah, doctor, is that you?"

"At your service," replied the strange gentleman, executing a low bow and giving his hat a very courtly flourish before he replaced it upon the little powdered wig he wore.

From this Hawk concluded that Colonel Hamilton had thought it advisable to have surgical assistance upon the spot. Such a course was not at all unusual in the desperate duels that were fought at that time of day.

The Baron Salter now bowed to Lord Noddie and Lord Noddie bowed to Baron Salter, and then the latter said—

"Good evening, my lord."

"Good evening," responded Lord Noddie. "Demme!"

"My principal has taken the liberty to bring Doctor Hodge."

"Exactly. I am very glad to see him."

"Hem!"

"Ha!"

"Well," added the baron, "I have succeeded."

"In what?"

"In what I hardly thought, my lord, I should succeed, and that is, in inducing the colonel to arrange this little affair."

"I thought it was arranged," said Lord Noddie, coolly helping himself to a pinch of snuff. "Demme, I thought we all came here just because it was all duly arranged."

"Your lordship misunderstands me."

"Oh, go on, then."

Clap went down the lid of the snuff-box just as the baron was about to dip his fingers in to take a pinch. He looked as black as a thunder-cloud at Lord Noddie and muttered something which sounded like a threat, upon which Lord Noddie just lightly touched the handle of his sword and said—

"Baron, I can present you with something a little more pungent than snuff if you feel at all inclined for it, demme!"

"My lord, I really do not comprehend."

"Oh, I think you do."

"I hope that nothing will occur to disturb the good understanding that subsists between your lordship and your humble servant."

"There is no understanding at all, baron. What I want to see is the duel over and settled in a gentlemanly way. The sun is fast setting, and my principal is quite ready; methinks yours seems to hang back a little."

"Not so, my lord, I assure you; but I was about to say that I had, after in-[illegible]ible pains, succeeded in inducing the colonel to say that he is not at all desirous of pushing this affair any further."

"You don't say so?"

"I do, my lord."

"Oh! What, will the redoubtable Colonel Hamilton, the crack duellist, back out of an affair like this? Oh, it is not possible! The man only lives in society upon his repute as a bully and a ruffian; and if he should commit an act that is not in character with such a reputation, he will be repudiated at once. Demme! that he will."

"We do not meet here to quarrel, my lord."

"Perhaps we do."

"Then your lordship has no objection to my repeating what you have just said to the colonel, I presume?"

"None in life. But, my dear baron, you know upon that event I shall have to fight him, and if such be the case, I will fight you first."

"Me?"

"Yes. I will now give you a contingent challenge. If Colonel Hamilton challenges me, I challenge you. Do you understand that? Demme!"

"I do, my lord."

"Very good; then, if your man is ready, mine is."

"Stop, my lord. I was going to say that, with a wish to spare the life of a prince of the blood royal of Austria, the colonel will accept a written apology from the count."

"Indeed!"

"Yes. I repeat, it was with the greatest difficulty I got him to consent to such an urgent request; but as he has consented, of course he will keep his word. What do you, as a gentleman and a friend of the count's, say to that, my lord? I pray you to consider that his life is now in your hands."

"How very kind you are, to be sure!"

"Oh, my lord, it is my duty to be kind. I would be kind enough to cut your throat, if I only had the opportunity to do it," muttered the baron to himself.

"What did you say?"

"Oh, my lord, nothing — nothing but a congratulation, I assure you, my lord."

CHAPTER XCV.

GIVES AN ACCOUNT OF HOW A DUEL WAS FOUGHT IN BYGONE TIMES.

Lord Noddie looked at the baron, and shook his head.

"I am pretty sure—demme!" he said—"I am pretty sure that you are a rogue; but but if I were d——d sure, which, perhaps, I shall be some day, I would kick you!"

"Kick—me?"

"Yes."

"Oh—oh! Colonel — colonel, this is dreadful! Colonel, I say! If you please, step this way."

"What is it?" said the colonel, stalking up to where Lord Noddie and the baron had been settling the particulars of the duel—"what is it, my dear baron? You look excited."

"And well I may be."

"As how—as how?"

"I believe, colonel, I may take upon my myself to say, that in all the duels you have fought, you have fought them with gentlemen."

"Assuredly. What of that?"

"Why, colonel, as your friend—as having the honour to be your friend

MAY LISTENING TO THE RETREATING FOOTSTEPS OF HAWK FROM THE HALL.

upon this little interesting occasion—and I beg to assure you, colonel, that I consider it to be a very high honour, indeed, to be so—I say, as your friend—hem! ha!—as the a—a the a—friend——"

"Pray come to the point," said Lord Noddie.

"My lord," said the colonel, looking uncommonly fierce, "allow me to listen to my friend, if I pleaseto do so. I rather think that what the baron is now saying, or about to say, is addressed to me, and not to your lordship."

"Allow me to suggest, colonel," said Lord Noddle, as he indulged himself with a pinch of snuff—"allow me to suggest——"

"No, my lord, I will not."

"But you shall!"

"Shall, my lord?—shall? Is that a word for any man in his right senses to say to me? Confusion and perdition!"

"I say you shall. I came here with the expectation of meeting a man who would, at all events, fight a duel he had provoked in the ordinary way that such affairs were managed by gentlemen. Colonel, you have chosen a man for your second who don't know his business."

"Not know my business?" said the baron. "I beg to say that I have seen more throats cut than——"

"Silence," said the colonel. "Well, my lord, since you have something to suggest that you say I shall listen to, what it is?"

"Just that you have no business interfering in the conference between the two seconds upon this occasion."

The colonel bowed.

"You are very right, my lord."

"I know it, colonel."

"That," said the baron, "I, too, admit. But this case is, I beg to assure you, colonel, quite exceptional. The sort of language that Lord Noddie has used to me is such that, in the exercise of my duties as your second, colonel, I will withdraw you from the ground."

"But, my dear baron, I——"

"Nay, now, colonel, allow me to act in this matter, as I have the most undoubted right to do so. You have placed your honour in my hands, you know, colonel."

"Yes, but——"

"If you please, allow me. You have placed your honour in my hands, and, therefore, I am to judge what is best to preserve it; so I say that whether the other party makes an apology or not, this duel is not to take place under the circumstances."

"Well, if that be your decision, baron, I submit."

"Oh—oh!" cried Lord Noddie, "you submit, do you, colonel? You submit to the dictation of this creature, who would lick the dust off your boots, if you bid him—you submit to this jackall—this terrible villain, who, not having the courage to be a rogue on his own account, is forced to be the journeyman to a master in the craft!"

"Death and the devil, sir!" cried the colonel, "what do you mean by that?"

"Just what I say, colonel. Nothing else, I assure you, and I here say that you shall fight."

"Shall fight?"

"You shall fight. You comprehend that, I suppose? I rather think it is very plain English that, demme!"

"Then—I—will."

"Very good."

"Baron—baron, I say!"

"Yes, colonel—yes: your humble servant, colonel."

"Unlock the pistol-case—unlock the pistol-case directly, baron. If we are to fight—ha! ha!—let us do so at once. Ha! ha! I rather think I shall make a dissension in the royal circle of the House of Austria. Ha! ha!"

"Stop a bit," said Lord Noddie, as he indulged in another pinch of snuff, "stop a bit."

"Wherefore, sir?"

"We fight with swords."

"Oh, absurd," cried the colonel,—"absurd."

"Very absurd, indeed," cried the baron. "Allow me, my lord, to assure you that fighting with swords is quite—quite Gothic, I may say, in a manner of speaking, quite out of the fashion, and has never been resorted to since the genteeler weapon, the pistol, has been in use among gentlemen."

"We fight with swords."

"Really, this is too absurd," said the colonel; "but, if I may be allowed to make a suggestion, I would say, let us have a shot at each other first, and if nothing comes of that I am then willing to engage the count with swords."

"Nothing can be fairer," said the baron, holding up his hands, and affecting to be quite in an ecstasy of admiration at the great candour of the colonel. "Nothing can be fairer."

"We don't consent," said Lord Noddie.

"Not consent?"

"Oh, dear, no. We fight with swords. The count has accepted the colonel's challenge, and, as the challenged party, he has a right to name the weapons. Certainly, so long as he keeps he exercise of that right within the range of those weapons known to gentlemen, he is fairly entitled to it; so he intends to fight with swords; but if that should be non-effective I will take upon myself to say, in his name, that he will afterwards fight with pistols."

"Oh, oh—nonsense."

"Did you address that little observation to me, baron?"

"No, my lord."

"Oh, very well; if you had—but no matter. Ah, here is the count, who, naturally enough, is impatient."

Captain Hawk had heard and seen enough of what was going on to quite well understand that there was considerable reluctance upon the part of the colonel and his friend, the baron, to come to the scratch, and he now resolved to put an end to all parley upon the subject by a few energetic words.

"Pray, my Lord Noddie," he said, "what is amiss? I have several appointments this evening, and really shall be late."

"It simply amounts to the fact that they don't want to fight," said Lord Noddie, quite calmly.

"Not want to fight? After bringing me here, too, at some inconvenience? Oh, impossible."

"Quite so, count," said the baron; "but the fact is, we would rather not fight with swords, that is all."

"And why not, sir?"

"Oh, why—we—a—a—that is, we are not in the habit of fighting with that weapon, and all gentlemen now use the pistol, I assure you, count."

"Oh, no, baron."

"Nay, allow me to assure you——"

"Allow me to say that I have not the smallest doubt of your assurance; but here I came to fight—here I came, too, to fight with swords, and when I get to the ground upon such an errand I will fight; and if there be any backing out of this affair now, either upon the part of the principal or his second, I will horsewhip both of them."

The baron made a spring back like a galvanised frog, and a crimson tinge of rage came over the face of the colonel, as he observed—

"You shall not be disappointed, count. By Heaven, I would fight you with swords—with scythes—with anything rather than not have your blood."

"Thank you, colonel. Now, my Lord Noddie, I presume that there will be no further difficulty in this matter at all?"

"None. Demme!"

The preparations for the conflict now proceeded rapidly. Lord Noddie requested to know if the colonel would use his own sword or one that he, Lord Noddie, had brought with him, and the answer was that he preferred his own; but Lord Noddie would have it measured against Captain Hawk's, for he saw that it was longer by a few inches; not that he cared about that, but he wished the fact to be established, in case a lie should be told even upon that trivial point after the duel was over.

Hawk took off his coat and waistcoat, and laid his shirt-collar back, and rolled up his sleeves. The colonel buttoned his coat right up to the throat, and then Lord Noddie said to the baron—

"Won't the colonel strip, demme!"

The baron replied—

"No. He is so very susceptible to cold, that he prefers the disadvantage of fighting with his coat on."

"Dress again, count," said Lord Noddie. "Don't leave them anything to say after this little affair is over."

Upon this, Captain Hawk put on his clothes again, and buttoned his coat up to the chin in the same manner that the colonel had buttoned his. He then drew his sword, and made such a rapid evolution with it around him, that in the rich sunset it looked like a gleam of fire more than anything else; and when he finished, by laying hold of the point with his thumb and finger and jumping over it to and fro several times, the colonel's face assumed quite a ghastly hue, and the baron really shook.

"Are you ready?" said Lord Noddie.

"Quite," said Hawk.

"And you, gentlemen, are you quite ready?"

"Oh, yes," said the baron, shaking as he spoke, "we—we accept the apology."

"What apology?"

"Silence, baron," said the colonel. "I accept no apology now."

"None has been tendered," said Lord Noddie, as he drew his sword, and switched it with a whistling sound in the air. "Now, baron, if you please."

"If—I—please?"

"Yes, to be sure. I feel quite certain that I have hurt your feelings through the little discussion we have had sufficiently to induce you to be glad of the opportunity of crossing swords with me; and as we may do so upon this occasion without any further preliminaries, why, here am I."

"Oh, dear no, my dear Lord Noddie, I assure you."

"Of what?"

"That you have not hurt my feelings in the least, and I quite feel—that—that, in fact, I know your lordship did not mean any offence."

"Oh, but I did."

"Then I forgive your lordship."

"Well, baron, I am sorry to say that you hurt my feelings, and that I cannot forgive you; so, if you will not fight upon your own account, you must upon mine. There is no escape for you, demme!"

The baron slowly drew his sword, for he, indeed, saw that there was no escape for him. He looked imploringly at the colonel, but that personage was too much engaged with his own affairs to pay any attention to him, the baron. He then looked at Lord Noddie, and in the calm, assured countenance of that odd mixture of foppery and courage he saw but little hope.

"Oh, fool—fool that I am!" he thought, "to come here as the second of the colonel in this affair. I feel that this is my last hour in this world. Oh, if I could but see a good chance of running away now."

CHAPTER XCVI.

THE DUEL TAKES PLACE, AND HAS SOME RATHER SINGULAR RESULTS.

The poor baron looked the picture of misery as he stood opposed to Lord Noddie.

As for the colonel, he was a man of real angry passions, and the turn the affair had taken had roused them all into activity, so that he was in something of the frame of mind that would have induced him to fight with anybody just then, and with any weapon.

Captain Hawk was as cool and as collected as any man could possibly be; and in the easy, graceful attitude he assumed, the colonel might well have read the fact that he had opposed to him a man who was a perfect master of the weapon he had in his hand.

"What!" said the colonel, "do you fight, baron?"

"Yes, colonel."

"Wonders will never cease!"

"My Lord Noddie!" cried Hawk, "I beg that you will not think it necessary to draw in my cause upon this occasion."

"Oh, no, demme! this is quite a little private affair between the worthy baron and myself, I assure you."

"That is quite another affair. I wish you, my lord, all the *bon fortune* that I am quite sure you so eminently deserve."

"Many thanks, count—many thanks. Now, baron, if you please, are you quite ready? for really I feel that to keep you any longer out of the society of your ancestors is only tantalising you; and as, no doubt, they are all to be found in a certain warm place down below, I feel quite satisfied that you will join them."

"Now, colonel," said Captain Hawk, with quite an easy air. "Have at you!"

There was a clash of swords, and Hawk and the colonel stood face to face with each other. Up to that moment neither of them could have any precise idea as to the amount of skill that his opponent possessed with the sword; but Captain Hawk, who knew his own powers with that weapon, was better pleased to find, after a pass or two, that the colonel was a really good fencer, than as if he had discovered him to be but a tyro in the use of that weapon.

It was the skill of the colonel that was fatal to him.

If Hawk had found that he fought at random, but with courage, he would not have been able to bring himself to take his life; but as it was, he felt that it was something like a fair fight.

Their swords rang together, and several times sparks were emitted by the rapidity with which the blades crossed each other, while there were deep indentations in the turf upon which they stood, where the combatants necessarily dug their heels into it to steady themselves.

They were well matched as to height these two men, for the colonel was a tall man, and Hawk was one likewise, so that in no very particular way could either be said to have an advantage over the other.

The fight continued for about two minutes, and then the colonel in making a furious lunge at Hawk, slipped, and fell on to one knee.

Nothing would have been easier at that moment than for Hawk to have run him through the body; but, on the contrary, he drew back, and turning the point of his sword, he said—

"Rise, colonel; the grass is slippery."

The colonel rose, and without a word of thanks, or betraying that he in any way appreciated the chivalric courtesy of his antagonist, he commenced the combat again.

Captain Hawk felt so disgusted with the fellow, that he now fought more warily than he had done before, and calmly waited for some opportunity of giving him a home thrust that would put an end to the affair at once.

Captain Hawk had not very long to wait for such an opportunity occurring. The colonel, after a display of some really capital fencing, suddenly made a feint by attempting to thrust at the eyes of his antagonist, and then stepping to one side, he adroitly made a thrust at him to run him through, but his sword caught in the cuff of Hawk's coat and ripped the sleeve up to the elbow. Hawk then shortened his arm, and made a half turn, and thrust full at the breast of the colonel, saying as he did so—

"The duel is over!"

The thrust was so direct and positive, that Captain Hawk felt the colonel ought to be run through the body, and he fully expected to feel the hilt of his sword striking against his chest, as the only thing which would stop its progress; but what was his surprise, when his sword bent into a half circle, and then broke off within a couple of inches of the hilt, the piece broken off flying into the air as if it had been discharged from a bow, while the colonel only staggered a little from the effect of the thrust, and was as little injured by it as if he had been made of iron.

The truth flashed across the mind of Captain Hawk in a moment. He at once understood why the colonel was so victorious in his duels, and why he had such an objection to fight with swords instead of pistols. The villain wore a breast-plate of steel, that was shot-proof, under his clothes.

Captain Hawk had now but one resource, and that was to prevent the rascal from taking any advantage of his defenceless position, so he rushed upon him before he could do so, and grappled him by the throat with such a clutch, that escape was out of the question.

"Villain! villain!" cried Hawk. "Your career is at an end. I will hold you up to the scorn of the whole world."

"Never!" said the colonel. "You die yourself first."

As he spoke, he dropped his sword, and drew a small stiletto of about six inches in length from the breast of his apparel, and made a desperate effort to assassinate Captain Hawk with it, by plunging it in him; but the great strength of Hawk now stood him in good need and he eluded the blow, but in doing so he was compelled to let go the colonel's throat.

The villain finding himself at liberty, in an evil moment for him, thought that it might be still possible for him to save his life by flight, and he turned and ran towards Montague House.

Captain Hawk picked up the sword that the colonel had dropped, and pursued him.

There were few people who would have stood the remotest chance with Hawk at a race. He was uncommonly fleet of foot; and although the dread of death, which was upon the mind of the colonel, will make a man do wonders, yet there is a limit to all physical exertion. No mortal man can do more than his powers actually warrant, and so, although the colonel put forth all his speed, Hawk gained rapidly upon him.

A bound now brought Hawk within arms-length of him.

"Wretch! die the death you deserve!" cried Hawk. "It is a coward's death, but the only one that is fit for you."

The colonel raised a shriek of dismay, and would have turned to oppose his protected breast to the sword, but before he could do so Hawk was close to him, and had with one lunge of his own weapon run him through the back.

The point of the sword struck against the inner surface of the breast-plate, and the colonel fell.

"That is over," said Hawk.

The wretched man rolled over on to his back, and clutched at the grass frantically, as he made an effort to rise; but it was too much for him, and there he lay, uttering the most awful maledictions upon the hand that had laid him low.

Hawk now looked around for his friend Lord Noddie, to whose proceedings he had not been able to pay any attention, so entirely engaged had he been with the colonel. Noddie was quite calmly walking towards him, followed by Joe and the surgeon, but the baron was nowhere to be seen.

"Noddie has done for the baron," thought Hawk.

This was not the case, as will presently appear.

Nothing in the world—and it is really doubtful, if anything in the next could accomplish such a result—seemed to be sufficient to put Lord Noddie at all out of his way; and so, notwithstanding the really, one would have thought, exciting scene that had taken place in that meadow at the back of old Montague House, he strutted up to Captain Hawk with all his usual indolence.

"Well, count," he said. "How has this little matter ended—eh? How does our old friend the colonel get on?"

"Behold him!"

"What! Down? Demme, colonel, this is the end of it."

"It is as you see," said Captain Hawk. "I only hope there is still sufficient life left in him to enable him to say, that at his last moments he feels repentance for his various villanies, for I here declare to you all, that the lives this man has taken in his various duels were nothing but so many murders!"

"Murders!" said Lord Noddie.

"Yes, my lord, nothing in the world else but murders, as I live, I declare them to be such."

"I don't think, sir," said the surgeon, "that such a sentiment comes with a very good grace from you."

"And why not, sir?"

"Can you ask me why not, when here at your feet lies one who is now dying from your hands? Has not the gentleman fallen in a duel with you? But I can tell you, count, that this affair will have to be investigated before the magistrates."

"Indeed, sir!"

"Yes, count, I saw the whole affair. The colonel dropped his sword and fled. You had no right to pursue and kill him. The duel was over, sir. You might have covered his name with obloquy and contempt, because he did so fly; but I say, sir, that you had no right to follow him and to take his life. It is contrary to the habits of Englishmen."

"The colonel, I suppose, then, is your friend?" said Captain Hawk.

"He was."

"Is his wound mortal?"

"It is so."

"No—no!" gasped the colonel. "Oh, no—not that—not that! Anything but that! Oh, God! I cannot—die! I ought not to die yet!"

"Demme!" said Lord Noddie, "I don't see any ought not in the case, colonel."

"Gentlemen," said Captain Hawk, "it is true that I did in the heat of passion pursue this man, and take his life, for that he is dying I, who have not much skill in such matters, can yet well perceive. I am sorry enough that I did so pursue him and so kill him, I assure you all; but that I am justified in so doing, I contend."

"I appeal to my Lord Noddie," said the surgeon.

"Well," said Noddie, "I will think of it. But yet, upon the first flush of the affair, I should say it would have been better if the count had let him go, as his flight was an evident giving up of the fight."

"Come here," said Captain Hawk. "Gentlemen, come here."

As he spoke, Hawk knelt by the dying man, and ripped open his coat and waistcoat, and tore aside the breast of his shirt.

"Now, gentlemen, you will see the

reason why I followed and took the life of this man. Under ordinary circumstances, I should not have done so; but after he had treacherously striven to take my life—after I found that my sword broke against his breast, and after I could come to no other conclusion than what is evident to you, what else would you have me do?"

They all looked with surprise at the colonel, for his chest was covered by a steel corslet of such exquisite shape and workmanship, that while it was very light, and scarcely added anything to the apparent thickness of the body, was an effectual safeguard against the attack of a sword, or even the passage of a pistol-bullet.

"The villain!" said Lord Noddie.

"I have no more to say," remarked the surgeon. "I give him up. Count, I pray you to pardon what I have said."

"Don't mention it, sir," said Hawk. "I honour you for it. When you thought that wrong had been done, you said so boldly like a man, and as a man should; but now that you see you were mistaken, you as candidly avow it."

"I do, sir—I do."

"And now, gentlemen, I leave you to exonerate me from any charge that may be brought against me in reference to this matter, for you see the utter worthlessness of the man I have slain."

CHAPTER XCVII.

CAPTAIN HAWK ACQUIRES GREAT REPUTATION FROM HIS DUEL WITH THE COLONEL.

This discovery of the baseness of the colonel had more effect upon Lord Noddie than anything else in the whole affair had had, and there was quite a look of anger upon the face of the surgeon as he looked at the body.

"Demme!" said Lord Noddie, with unwonted energy for him, as he took a larger than usual pinch of snuff—"demme! I feel as mad as—as—I don't know what; but I do feel very mad."

"Don't mind it, my lord," said Hawk. "I do hope that in ridding society of this man, I have done it some good service; but you, sir"—to the surgeon—"you must only look upon this wounded man as a patient; and forgetting who and what he is, do the best you can for him."

"I can do nothing. His wound is mortal: he is dying."

The wretched man heard these words, and his glaring eyes rolled fearfully, and his parched lips opened as he uttered a hoarse, strange scream; and then he cried out—

"No—no! Not dying! Who—oh, who says that? I cannot, I will not die yet. It is too horrible for me to think of death. What's this—oh, what's this before my eye? All is changed in colour. The trees—the fields—the sunshine. All—all changed!"

"He is going fast," said the surgeon.

There was a pause of a minute or two, and then the dying man added in a faint tone, for his strength was fast ebbing, and he was not long for this world—

"Go away—away! I tell you you would fight. Don't look at me with those dreadful eyes—oh, don't! It is false—the bullet did not strike me, and then bounced off as it would have done from a rock! I say it did not! Who says it did? I did not stagger with the blow of the bullet, and yet leave the field unhurt. Oh, help!—help! Murder! Do not crowd about me in this way. I see you all—bleeding forms that ye are—pointing at me with your gory fingers! I know you come to drive me mad—mad—mad!"

"This is a fearful end," said Hawk.

"Demme! yes," said Lord Noddie.

"It is nearly over," remarked the surgeon. "See how he pulls up the grass, and tosses it in the air."

"He does—he does."

"Demme! it would be a charity to put him out of his misery."

"He suffers nothing now," said the surgeon.

"There, again!" cried the dying man. "Oh, God! there again! They were gone, but they are come again—a ghastly mob—all that I killed—that I murdered! Yes, murdered is the word. Now—now, baron, be sure you rivet the corslet tightly. It is ball proof. Ha!

ha! It is ball proof! It has been tested ere this. So, this count will fight, will he? Well, let it be at sunset, and let the soft twilight shed upon us before the shots are fired, and then all will be well—all will be quite well. Baron, where are you? Dark—dark—all is dark, now. Dark night, and I am in a sea of blood—blood!"

He strove, now, to rise; but in the effort his spirit fled with one ear-piercing shriek, that made those who watched his awful death start back, and look at each other in dismay.

The sun at that moment sunk below the western horizon, and a sudden gloom came over the field. A cold air, too, with a sighing sound, swept past them, and there they stood for some moments in silence with the dead.

Joe, who had walked up to the spot, was the first to break the stillness, by saying—

"What's to be done with the corpus, count?"

Captain Hawk started, and turned to Lord Noddie.

"My lord," he said, "I will in this affair be entirely guided by what you may think right and proper. As you direct me, I will so proceed. What ought I to do?"

"Nothing, count, that I can see."

"But the dead body—is that to be left here?"

"Yes. I should say yes."

"The dead body," said the surgeon, "is no concern of yours, I should think, count. It is the second of the colonel who ought to take care of that, you know. All you have to do is to leave the field with your friends, and your duty is done."

"Very good, sir. But talking of the second of the colonel, I had quite forgotten the baron in all this affair. What became of him, my Lord Noddie? I had an idea that you and he were about to have a little supplimentary fight upon your own accounts."

"So we were—demme!—but the fact is, that after a threat or two, the baron turned and fled at such speed, that it quite astonished me, for he was over a hedge, and through a ditch, and then out of sight, before I could take a pinch of snuff—Demme!"

"The cowardly rascal! You did not pursue him?"

"I pursue him? Oh, dear no. Demme! I take everything in this world as easy as I can; and as for scampering across the fields after such a man as that, I could not think of it, I beg to assure you, count, for a moment. Oh, dear, no—demme!"

"Like master, like man," said Joe. "There was a precious pair of 'em."

Captain Hawk made a sign to Joe to be silent; for when he began to speak, there was always the risk that he might say too much, and Joe stepped back, and held his peace accordingly.

"And so you think that I may consider this affair as ended, my Lord Noddie?" said Hawk.

"You may, count. You may depend that nobody will move in this matter, and I will myself tell the secretary of state to-morrow morning, demme!—so that the officials of the law will shut their eyes to the affair; and I can only now congratulate you, count, upon the reputation you will enjoy as the person who got rid of—for the good of society—such a man as the colonel."

"Then we will leave this spot."

"Certainly. Come on. Ah, I suspect that the baron will no longer now be visible in the gay world."

They left the spot, after bidding good-by to the surgeon, who still lingered about the field; and Joe, as he looked back at him, shook his head, as he said—

"Ah, it don't want a conjuror to find out what that doctor is about. He wants to grab the body to cut up, that's what he wants. Well, everybody to his taste. Oh, lor! I shouldn't like it, no how."

This supposition of Joe's was the correct one; for no sooner had Captain Hawk and my Lord Noddie got out of sight, than the doctor dragged the body close under a hedge, where it was not likely to be observed, and covered it with some branches he pulled from a hedge, and there he left it.

Now, it was not from any love to the deceased, or tender care for his memory, that the surgeon so acted, for he hurried home, and then waiting until the night had a little advanced, he again repaired to the spot with a chaise and a sack, and a couple of others of his own profession, and they soon had the dead body safely housed in a dissecting-room.

Such was the end of the professed duellist, and a very proper one, too, for such a man; for, as the surgeon remarked—

"This fellow was of no use at all to society while living, and it is, therefore,

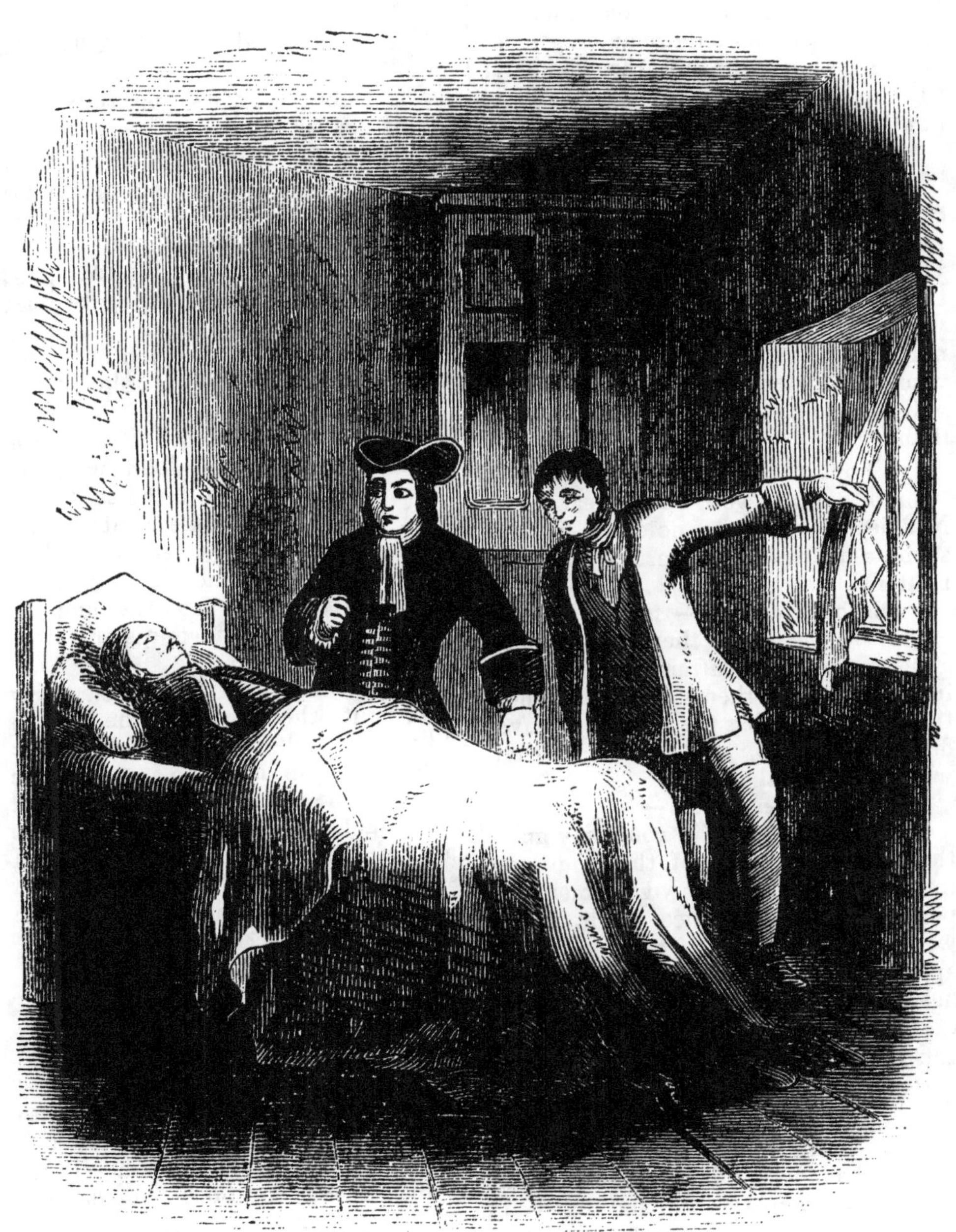

THE SURGEON EXAMINES HAWK IN THE OLD HUT.

a very delightful thing to think that he may be of some service to it now that he is no more."

My Lord Noddie would make Captain Hawk come home with him to take some refreshment after the duel; and although Hawk was by no manner of means unmindful of the fact that he had an appointment upon that evening, the time to keep it had not yet come, and he knew that he had sufficient command over himself not to drink too much wine to forget it.

"Demme!" said Lord Noddie, "this story of the death of the colonel will be one of the best that is upon the *tapis* for the next three months. Demme! it would require an elopement or a seduction of the most racy character to cope with it in public interest at all."

"You think so?" laughed Hawk.

"I know it, my dear count; and I can only say that you will be the lion of the day. The women will adore you. The men who lived in dread of the colonel will in their hearts thank you; and those who are in any way or manner connected with the victims who have fallen by the colonel's hand, will, I have no doubt, seek you out to thank you."

"I hope not," said Captain Hawk; "for I assure you, my dear Lord Noddie, that I have no desire for any such amount of notoriety in the matter."

"Oh, but they will—they will."

"Well, then, if they do, and are gentlemen, I am afraid I shall feel inclined to tell them, that what they thank me for doing they ought to have done themselves, and, perhaps, that will not please them."

"Why, a—demme! I——"

Before Lord Noddie could say another word, the door of the room was flung open, and a crowd of men appeared at the entrance to it. One well-dressed man, of rather superior appearance, lifted his hat from his head, and walked in, saying in reply to the questioning look of Captain Hawk and Lord Noddie—

"Gentlemen, I have to apologize for the troublesome duty that is put upon me; but I have received information that a man has been killed in the fields behind Montague House, and that you were both engaged in the transaction."

"Why, you are Sir John Rose—demme!—the magistrate," said Lord Noddie, "are you not, sir?"

"I am, sir."

Captain Hawk, upon this, did not feel in a very pleasant situation, and he shifted his chair a little, so as to bring his face more into the shade than it had been before.

"Well, Sir John, what do you want? Demme!"

"It will be my duty, sir, to take you into custody."

"Me?"

"Yes, my lord, as you killed the man."

"Oh, not I. It was my friend, the Count Astral."

"Then the count is my prisoner. Jenkins, you will take charge of the count, and take care that you do not forget he is a gentleman."

An officer strode into the room, and fixed a rather scrutinizing gaze upon Captain Hawk.

"Demme!" said Lord Noddie, "who told you of this affair, Sir John?"

"The Baron Salter."

"I thought as much. Well, it was a duel—a fair duel, Sir John, whatever Baron Salter may say to the contrary; and I should think my security for the appearance of Count Astral will be sufficient. The count is a prince of the blood royal of Austria, and you know that the prime minister is my uncle."

"Your word will be sufficient, my lord; but the fact is, the person calling himself Baron Salter who brought the information to my office described the affair as a murder, and never said a word about a duel. He gave me the information in writing, I assure you, my lord."

"Very well—demme! Will he appear to-morrow?"

"So he promised."

"Then we shall attend you, Sir John, you may depend. I go security for the count; and if the baron should really be there, I will make him eat the written statement that he has given of the transaction. Take a glass of wine, Sir John. I am always happy to see in my house so efficient a magistrate, and so accomplished a gentleman."

"My lord, I beg to acknowledge your kindness, and to relieve you and the count from my presence. I suspect I have been very much deceived in this matter; but we will see about that in the morning."

In a few moments more the magistrate and his officers had retired from the house, and the apprehensions of Captain Hawk were, at all events, for the time being, quite at an end.

This affair was well over, as far as Captain Hawk was concerned, for he could not help having the dread all the while the officers and the magistrate were in the room, that some of them might possibly recognise in the Count Astral no other than the well known Captain Hawk, the highwayman.

It is quite surprising, though, how when the mind is led completely in another direction than that of suspicion of any particular identity, or state of things, it will almost reject the evidence of the senses. If the magistrate had thought that Count Astral was the very image of Hawk the highwayman, it is probable enough he would never for a moment have supposed it possible that they could be one and the same person.

Well might Hawk congratulate himself upon the termination of an adventure in the progress of which he had incurred considerable danger, but which, it must be admitted, he had carried out from first to last with the greatest possible address.

He felt that if now he could but go on for a time, without awaking any suspicions as to who and what he was, he might make a rich harvest from the follies and the vanities of those around him.

The time, though, for keeping the appointment that he had made with the Lady Deliva was close at hand, and he was compelled, in order not to go back from his word, to leave even the fascinating society of Lord Noddie.

That sagacious nobleman, though, was of the greatest service to Captain Hawk, as by associating with him he had in some degree become a guarantee of his pretentions to be somebody of very great importance.

CHAPTER XCVIII.

HAWK PROCEEDS TO KEEP HIS APPOINTMENT WITH THE LADY DELIVA.

When Hawk reached the hotel where he put up, he made such changes in his appearance as he thought would be desirable, considering he was going to meet a lady, although it was not a very young nor a very fascinating specimen of the gentle sex.

The object, though, of Hawk was to make the old lady pay handsomely for the pleasure she might feel in the fond fancy that she had at last had the good fortune to accomplish with her faded charms what she had never been able to do with them while they were in their youth, namely, entrap a husband.

We shall soon see how the audacious Captain Hawk progressed with the old lady.

He did not think it at all worth while to take Joe with him upon this adventure, as there was no danger of any sort to be apprehended in the pursuit of such an individual as that ancient mummy, who had shown herself enamoured of him.

It was not at all probable that he would meet with any rival in the field who would insist upon one or both dying for the sake of the Lady Deliva.

"Now," said Hawk to himself, as he proceeded on foot to keep the appointment. "Now, must I set a just and proper value upon my time and conversation, and take good care that I am well paid for both. I only hope the old hag will not be too loving, that is all."

The house of Lady Deliva was one of the most fashionable and extensive of any in the quarter of the town in which she resided, full as that district was of the mansions of the nobility, and celebrated as it was for its expensive character.

It was rather a wonder to Hawk that she could venture to receive a visitor in so public a manner, as to a certain extent his visit was sure to be; but as he had wrapped himself up in a large cloak, he thought it was just possible he might have the good fortune to enter the house without being observed.

The idea of being lampooned afterwards, by any of the small wits of fashionable society, upon an intrigue with the Lady Deliva, was a contingency that presented itself to Captain Hawk in rather uncomfortable colours; and, therefore, he was more intent upon the fact that his present visit should be a secret one, than probably the old lady herself was.

"Confound her," thought Hawk, as he approached her house, "why the deuce did she not name some out-of-the-way place in the suburbs as the appointed spot, instead of here, where I run the chance of being seen by a thousand eyes?"

"Sir! sir!"

Some one touched Captain Hawk on the arm.

Upon turning rapidly, and in some alarm, for it was not very agreeable for a gentleman of Captain Hawk's profession to be touched upon the arm suddenly in the open street, he saw a female attired in a cloak and hood, the latter of which was so far drawn over her face as half to hide it.

"Sir?"

"Well, what do you want?"

"You are a count?"

"Hem! I don't know."

"Oh, yes, you are the Austrian Prince, are you not?"

"Quite a mistake, my good woman. Quite a mistake, I assure you. But if it be alms you want, take that purse of silver and go."

"Oh, no—no. You mistake. Are you not going to pay a visit to a lady?"

"What is that to you? I suppose it is not high treason in London for a gentleman to visit a lady?"

"Certainly not; but if the lady's name begins with a D, I am in her service, and have been looking for you."

"Ah! say you so? Well, it does begin with a D; and it ends with an A."

"That is sufficient. You are the gentleman; and you will be so good as to follow me."

"By your lady's order?"

"Yes; she thinks, and so ought you, that a little secrecy just at first is essential; as she has no desire to make herself the subject of the gossip of the world."

"I admire her discretion," said Captain Hawk; "and confess to you, most admirable of waiting-maids, that I had something of the same idea myself."

"You mistake, sir!"

"Oh, do I—as how?"

"I am not a waiting-maid."

"Then I beg ten thousand pardons; and would seal each of them with a kiss, if I—that is ——"

"If you thought me handsome enough, you mean?"

"Why, you are a witch, I see, instead of a waiting-woman."

"I am the companion, sir, of Lady Deliva."

"Humph! do you like it?"

"Sir?"

"Pray, pardon me; but the question came uppermost."

"Oh, sir, I am very much afraid that you are only about to amuse yourself at the expense of the poor old lady; and if so, I beg that you—will—will ——"

"Will what?"

The female laughed, as she added—

"I hope that you will punish her as she deserves, for thinking at her time of life of the men. There, sir, I have trusted you with enough of my thoughts to risk my situation. But if you are a gentleman, as in good truth I think you are, you will not betray me."

"May I lose my head if I do."

"But will you not be equally candid with me? Will you not tell me if indeed and in truth you have any idea of making a woman of fifty-five years of age your wife or not?"

"Is this a trap or not?" thought Captain Hawk to himself; "or is it real and genuine, now? Well, I will trust this woman, come what may. It is better to run that risk than to make her an enemy."

"Why, to tell you the truth," he said, "I have no desire or intention to publicly inflict any pain upon the Lady Deliva; yet I must own that the love of frolic has more to do with the present affair by a great deal than the one of the lady."

"So I thought."

"You are quite right, there."

"And it serves her right, the old cat! the old wretch! it serves her right! Here have I been putting up with her horrid whims and fancies for I don't know how long, all with the distinct understanding that she would never marry, but die some day, and leave me the bulk of her property; and yet she is constantly upon the look-out for some man who will marry her."

"You don't say so?"

"Yes; and there is but one safeguard,

and that lies in the fact that her pride will not permit her to wed any one that is not a member of the nobility."

"Oh, indeed!"

"Yes, count; and were it not for that feeling in her mind, I have no doubt but that some low, penniless adventurer would, ere this, have possessed himself of her hand and fortune, to squander the latter in extravagances, and to cast the former from him with contempt."

"There can be no doubt."

"Well, well, follow me, count. I am to take you into the house by the garden entrance, which is in St James's Park; and all I hope is, that you will convince the old wretch that if she attempts to inveigle men in this way, she will only expose herself and her pretensions to ridicule and contempt."

"I will follow you," said Captain Hawk; "and of one thing you may be quite assured, namely, that I would not marry the Lady Deliva if she could put me in possession of the fabled wealth of the mines of Golconda."

"I don't suppose you would, count. A handsome man like you, indeed, to wed such an old—Fuff! I hate to think of her."

Captain Hawk laughingly followed the companion, of whose sincerity he now entertained no doubt; for there was a stifled vehemence about her manner when she spoke of the Lady Deliva, which eloquently pourtrayed the detestation in which she held her, and which could not have been by any possibility acted in so life-like a manner even by the most accomplished performer the world ever saw.

The companion, then, as she styled herself, led the way into St. James's Park through the iron gates close to Marlborough-house, and Captain Hawk, not to excite unusual observation, followed her at some little distance, but took care not to lose sight of her.

The house in which the Lady Deliva lived was so situated that it had a portion of its garden close to the park; and at a quiet little nook near the wall of St. James's Palace the companion paused and took a rapid glance about her.

Captain Hawk paused likewise, but he kept an eye upon her movements, for he was now more than ever intent upon carrying out this adventure.

With great rapidity, then, the companion took a small key from a silken bag she had upon her arm, and unlocking a little door in the wall, she glided from the sight of Hawk. The door, however, was held open, so he construed that into a signal for him to follow, which he did at once.

The moment he crossed the threshold of the little doorway the door was closed and locked.

"All's well, thank Heaven," said the woman. "Nobody has seen us thus far, at all events."

"And where are we now?" said Hawk.

"Oh, we are all right now. This is the garden of her ladyship's house. You are sure nobody saw you?"

"I cannot be sure; but I did not observe that any one was at all near the spot."

"That will do—that will do. Thank God, I have a reputation to lose that I am, perhaps, a little more particular about than my lady is about hers. I am not lowly born. My father was a knight."

"Indeed."

"Yes, he went up with an address from the city, and was knighted by the king. He was in a large way of business."

"You don't say so!"

"Oh, yes, sir; and I only hope that, as we are quite alone in this garden, and as nobody can possibly interrupt us or hear a word that passes, you will not take any advantage of a lady in such a situation."

"I should scorn myself if I could do so."

"Hem!"

"Confound her," said Captain Hawk, to himself, "she is just a degree or two worse than her mistress, I declare."

"Hem!" said the companion again.

"I beg to assure you," said Hawk, "that my respect for you is so very great, that I hope you will meet me tomorrow evening on this spot."

"Really! Me meet a man, and alone? Oh, how could you ask such a thing? At what hour?"

"Nine."

"Then, sir, I can tell you that I do

think your conduct to be very bad indeed, and I shall be here punctually, if you tap with your knuckles at the outside of the little door in the wall punctually to the minute, just out of curiosity to hear what in your amazing impudence you will say for yourself."

"Thank you. And now, my good creature, let me go to the old lady at once."

"Ah, the old lady, indeed! I'm sure if I was a man I would as soon go to the old gentleman, and that's the polite name for Old Nick. But come on; this is the way. You will soon find what an old cat she is; and her treatment of Julie is enough to curdle one's blood."

"Who is Julie?"

"Oh, a child that she has the care of, that's all. The poor little infant is the daughter of her brother, and resides in the house; but Lady Deliva don't treat her half so well as she does her fat monkey, as I often tell her."

"It's too bad. But we can make up for it, you know, by being kind to the child."

"Oh, as for that, it is a little self-willed creature enough, and I can't say that I like it at all."

CHAPTER XCIX.

THE LADY DELIVA MAKES CAPTAIN HAWK A RATHER HANDSOME PRESENT.

"A NICE life this poor child Julie, that they talk about, must lead between these two women," thought Hawk, as he followed the companion through the garden to the house.

A flight of stone steps led to a door, the key of which the companion was possessed of, and upon opening which Hawk found a gleam of light come upon his eyes.

"This way," she said; "this way."

"I come," said Hawk; "the light is dazzling rather."

"Oh, sir, you should not say that. When you see my lady you may well be dazzled, for though I say it, perhaps, who may be accused of partiality to her, I will assert that a finer woman is not to be met with in all England."

"What the devil are you at now?" said Hawk.

"Hush!"

The companion gave Hawk a nudge with her elbow, as she then whispered to him—

"Caution! The old cat hears, now, every word that is spoken above a whisper."

"Oh, the deuce she does!"

"Yes; so mind what you are about. Here—this may, sir, if you please. I'm sure you are a fortunate man, that you are."

Captain Hawk took the hint, and said—

"I esteem myself as such; and I must say that I never yet found one woman praise another so much, and with such fervour, as you praise your lady, although I quite agree with you in all that you can possibly say of her."

"Come," thought Hawk, "that is drawing the long bow pretty well, I do think."

"This way, sir—this way. Now, if you please, sir, to open that door, and walk straight on, you will find my lady. Oh, the cat!"

"Thank you—thank you. Upon my life you do it well. Ha! ha!"

"Hush! Oh, hush!"

"I understand."

Captain Hawk opened the door indicatied to him by the companion, and entered a room, which, by its splendour, entirely took him by surprise, and for a moment or two rivetted all his attention.

This room was about twenty feet square, and the ceiling was either actually concave, or so skilfully painted in perspective to look so, that it had all the same effect—the walls were hung with fluted satin, and in the centre, depended from the ceiling, was a chandelier of cut glass, carrying twenty wax lights. The furniture of the room was of white and gold; and upon an ottoman of white satin, covered with gold open-work brocade, sat the old Lady Deliva.

A table in the centre of the room had upon it a cold collation, laid out in the most enticing manner, and composed of the choicest viands.

No wonder that Captain Hawk stood looking about him for a moment or two rather bewildered, notwithstanding all his usual self-possession, to find himself in such a fairy palace as that seemed to be.

Perhaps the Lady Deliva was not displeased to see the effect which her gorgeous house had upon him, although it was at the sacrifice of some few complimentary words to herself.

Hawk, however, was soon alive to the necessity of playing the part that he had to play, and he advanced to the lady.

"Madam," he said, "you see before you one of the most humble and devoted of your slaves."

"Oh, count, you are too gallant."

"That is impossible, Lady Deliva."

"How so, sir?"

"Because the language of gallantry fades before the language of truth, when one speaks with any sincerity of the charms of the Lady Deliva."

As he sopke, Captain Hawk bowed low to the elderly lady, who at such highly complimentary language was in quite a flutter of delight.

"Oh, count, you are really so—so very complimentary."

"Not at all."

"I am afraid you think me very bold?"

"On the contrary, my dear madam, I consider you as the very pattern of modesty."

"Ah, how good of you to say that. Ah, me! my poor heart! I'm afraid that, after all, count, we young ladies are but poor, weak, fragile creatures."

"Young ladies!" thought Captain Hawk. "The lord deliver us from young ladies of fifty-five! My dear madam, you do yourself quite an injustice."

"But, my dear count."

"My dear Lady Devila!"

"Don't you think that it has been very injudicious on my part to allow you to come in this may to my boudoir?"

"Not at all. Some one certainly might have been here so coarse-minded as to lose respect for a lady who was so condescending; but I have made it a rule through life, always to receive any respect and regard from a lady, in proportion as she is kind and confiding to me."

"Oh, indeed!"

"Yes, madam, that is the custom of my country, and I hope and trust you consider it a gallant one."

"Oh, yes—yes. Hem! It is so. But yet, there is no occasion to carry that feeling to far."

"Oh, madam, can it be possible to carry respect too far?"

"Well—well, we will not talk of that. I am a very sensitive being, count, I assure you."

"And so am I."

"I am all soul, in a manner of speaking, and the fervour of my affection I never doubt."

"Nor I."

"Oh, count, I love!"

"So do I."

"Can it really be? Oh, is it possible? No—yes! Oh, my poor, fond, foolish heart, be still! This rapture, perhaps, is too much. Oh, count, I am the soul of modesty and delicacy, and I suffer dreadfully, through not expressing my feeling's; so I must leave you to guess them when I say, that I love you!"

"Madam, the feeling is reciprocal, I assure you."

"Ah, me!"

"Oh, dear!"

The old lady flourished a great ivory fan about at such a rate, that at last she broke it all to pieces, and then she said, upon finding that Captain Hawk would keep upon the other side of the table—

"Count, I beg to assure you that I am completely at my own disposal; completely, I may say."

"How delightful!"

"I have no mamma to speak to—no papa to interfere between me and my choice!"

"I should think not," thought Captain Hawk. "If you had, they would be as old as the patriarchs by this time."

"And my fortune, count, is rather large."

"So is mine, madam. My vast estates in Moldavia are beyond even my own knowledge,"

"Then, my dear count, if, indeed, it be, as you say, you mission in England to get wedded, may I hope that you are suited?"

"I am, if——"

"If what?"

"If you consent, charming Lady Deliva."

"You make me blush, and yet I must own that I do consent."

"Oh, name the happy day! Do not let me linger very long in dire suspense. May I say this day month?"

"Oh, you wicked man, say to-morrow."

"To-morrow!"

"Ah, can it be that you consider that too soon?"

"Only in one way, and that is, that it would be rather a difficult thing for a courier to go from here to Vienna and get back again by to-morrow; and out of compliment to the Emperor of Austria, I must let him know what I have decided upon in the matrimonial way in England."

"Alas! alas!"

"But perhaps this day week?"

"Well, we will say this day week, my dear count!"

"Do so, Lady Deliva, and by that time I shall have got my remittances from the emperor, without which I am without means in London, and I have rejected the advances that our ambassador would have been but too happy to hand to me. The Prince Regent, though, I daresay, will oblige me with a thousand pounds."

"The Prince Regent? Oh, no, count! If he thought you had half the money at disposal, he would come to borrow it of you before you got up in the morning, I assure you."

"You amaze me!"

"And yet it is true, my dear count. You must allow me to supply your wish. Come, now, how much will you have?"

"Oh, no—no! I cannot—really—I cannot think of borrowing money of a lady."

"Then do so without thinking, charming count. I will give you a draft upon my banker for whatever you want."

"This is too kind—too generous!"

"Not upon the terms that *we* are on, count. Oh, no! I certainly do admit that, under any other circumstances——"

"Really, madam, I know not how to respond to this great generosity; but, as you say, under the present circumstances, it would be a species of false delicacy of me to refuse you."

"It would, indeed, count. I assure you that I am quite rich enough to do what I like with money."

"That, to me, is a severe blow."

"A blow?"

"Yes, to my feelings; for with my immense resources I had hoped that when I loved I should have been able to offer to the fond object of my idolatry such a fortune as would have tended to convince her of the true servitude of my heart; but you, Lady Deliva, are above fortune, and can only court it."

"Nay, what does it matter? Ah, count, I am but too much inclined to believe your honest words, without any aid from your fortune."

"You are too good."

"No—no. Pray take some refreshment, my dear count. I have taken the liberty of ordering a little collation to be prepared for you; and while you refresh yourself I will write a draft upon my bankers for any sum that you require."

"Ah, well, I must see whether the agent of my Hungarian mines cannot find some present that is worthy of the acceptance of such a divinity as yourself."

"Shall I say one thousand pounds, my dear count?"

The Lady Deliva had the pen in her hand to sign a draft for the amount, but Captain Hawk, with the most unblushing effrontery, said, after the pretence of a moment's thought—

"Perhaps, my dear Lady Deliva, as it may be yet a fortnight before the courier arrives from Vienna, you had better make it two."

"Two thousand?"

"Yes."

"I will do so. It don't matter a bit, my dear count; and if you had said four thousand pounds, I assure you that it would have been all the same to me."

"The deuce it would," thought Captain Hawk. "Why, this old woman is an inexhaustible mine of wealth, I declare."

"But you know, count, that you will often see me, and if you want more you can ask me, and my resources are at your service always."

THE BLACKSMITH FLOGGING HIS APPRENTICE FOR UNHANDCUFFING JOE.

"Ah!" said Captain Hawk, as he watched her draw the cheque, "can it be possible that I have awakened so much interest in such a tender bosom?"

"You have—you have!"

"Thank you!" Captain Hawk pocketed the cheque with all the easy nonchalance in the world, and then he said—"Oh, what a dreadful thought it is to me that the hour of our separation has come."

"The hour of our separation?"

"Yes, Lady Deliva, I am compelled to see a special courier who is going this very hour to Vienna, or nothing would induce me to tear myself from you."

"Oh, count!"

"Oh, Lady Deliva! oh, I could tear the hair out of my head with the frantic idea that I am not able to stay. But another time when I come here there will be no such hinderance, let us hope."

"Well, I do regret——"

"Regret, Lady Deliva? I do more than regret: I am in that state of madness in consequence, that I really do not know if I shall survive till the morning. I am quite frantic, I assure you. Do I not look a little wild?"

CHAPTER C.

CAPTAIN HAWK HAS AN INTERVIEW WITH THE CHILD JULIE.

As he spoke, Captain Hawk gave his head such a shake, that he brought all his long dark hair over his face, and certainly did look a little wild.

"You do—you do," sobbed Lady Deliva. "But, oh, for my sake, my precious count, preserve your life and your reason."

"I will try—I will try. For your sake I will try. I feel, now, that I have indeed a stake in existence—I feel that I have a something and a somebody to live for. Oh, how cold—how sterile—how dismal—how dreadful and how blank was my existence until this night, when I see my Deliva, and I know that she loves me!"

"Oh, you fascinating man!"

"No—no. It is you who are the fascinating woman—it is you who are the paragon—the phœnix of your sex. Nature after she had fashioned you must have been exhausted, and that is how we see so many ugly girls about now. All the beauty was used up in the manufacture of a Deliva!"

"Well, I must say that you pay the most charming of compliments, count, and with a grace, too, that is all your own. Oh, how easy one may see that you have been nurtured in one of the politest courts in Europe."

"There, Lady Deliva, you speak with the partiality of one who loves."

"Ah, no! But must you go?"

"Indeed and in truth I must, however hard I feel the necessity to be; and that it is so you may guess from the difficulty I find in expressing it. Oh, madam, I am as one who, after being storm-tossed upon the wild ocean of uncertainty, finds a port at last, only to be compelled to leave its dear and friendly shelter at the moment he thought it all his own."

"Delightful man! Oh, say that I shall see you soon again."

"You shall—you shall!"

"Then I will not detain you now."

What a pleasant speech that was for Captain Hawk to hear! The Lady Deliva touched a silver hand-bell, which brought into her presence the companion.

"You will show this gentleman out."

"Yes, my lady. This way, sir, if you please."

Captain Hawk thought by the manner in which Lady Deliva spoke to the companion, as she called herself, that he was right in his conjecture concerning her, and that she was nothing but the waiting-maid, and had given herself the higher title in order to seem to be a little better than she was. That did not concern him, however, and after casting an expressive look at the Lady Deliva, which was returned by the most languishing glance possible, he left the apartment after the waiting-maid.

That prudent individual did not say one word until she was quite certain they were out of ear-shot of her mistress, and then turning to Captain Hawk, she said rapidly—

"Oh, however did you get away so soon?"

"Why, the fact is, I have an engagement."

"A fiddlestick! Nonsense!"

Captain Hawk laughed.

"I see," he said, "you are not quite so credulous as Lady Deliva."

"Certainly not. But I don't blame you—how can I?—for getting away so soon as you could from that odious old cat. Of course, you are quite disgusted with her."

"She is not very charming."

"Very charming, indeed! Oh, the old hag! You can't think how I do hate that old woman."

"Well, perhaps, you have cause so to do; and, now, I will bid you good night, and you may be sure that I will not forget our little delightful and charming engagement."

"Will you not?"

"Oh, honour—honour. Upon my

honour I will keep my word, and upon my word I will respect my honour."

"Well, come this way."

The waiting-woman led the way through a number of rather intricate passages, and Captain Hawk felt quite convinced that he was not being taken the same way out of the premises as he had been brought in, and he said as much to the female who was his guide upon the occasion.

"No," she said; "the fact is, that this is a very old and very extensive house. They say that there is some sort of communication between it and the palace."

"St. James's?"

"Yes; and that such a communication is as old as the reign of King Henry the Eight, when the palace was changed from a hospital to a royal residence."

"I have heard that such a change took place, and that previously to that the palace was a nunnery."

"So it was. But—oh, count!"

"Eh?"

"Oh, count, can it be true?—Can I really flatter my poor heart with the idea that you love me? You have said as much; but really you men are so deceiving. My three husbands each deceived me."

"Three husbands?"

"Ah, yes, I have had three, and bad ones they all were; so I have made up my mind not to marry again; but I don't mean that such a determination should prevent me from loving."

"Certainly not."

"And you, count, are the very *beau ideal* of my fancy. I have often thought that just such a man as you would make this poor weak and susceptible heart believe almost anything."

"You don't say so?"

"I do—I do, indeed. And now, count, as you have in so capital a way got rid of Lady Deliva—as you have satisfied her that you are out of the house, you shall remain and sup with me."

"My dear creature, I really——"

"Nay, now, you shall. I will not admit of any excuses. It is, I know, a great favour upon my part; but when I do love—ah, me!—when I do love, it is not a cold chicken, or a bottle of Burgundy that will stand in the way of my affection. So sup with me you shall, my dear count; and you shall tell me all your adventures, for so elegant a person must have had a great many."

Captain Hawk began to think that he was in a worse situation with the maid than he was with the mistress, and that it would be much more difficult to get rid of the former than the latter. The idea of remaining, though, was so repugnant to his feelings, that he resolved to make an effort to achieve his freedom; so he said—

"I do not deny but that it is likely enough my distaste to the society of Lady Deliva would have induced me to make some sort of excuse to get away from her; but the fact is, what I told her was directly and wholly true."

"What was that?"

"That I had an engagement this evening that must be kept. I am compelled to go."

"The engagement is with a—a—woman?"

"No—no. Indeed it is not. It is with the Austrian Ambassador. A courier from Venice is even now waiting for me before he can start upon his journey, and every hour's delay here is, of course, an hour lost when he gets there; so I beg you will excuse me for this time."

"Can this be possible?"

"I did not think, I must confess, that you would have doubted my word."

"Well—well, I will only keep you a few hours."

"A few hours would be fatal."

"Oh, you cruel man! You—you are cruel!"

"Don't make a fuss. I shall remain in London a considerable time, I assure you, and there will be plenty of opportunities of our meeting; but to-night it must not be. Where are we now? I don't recollect this room as we came in."

"No; it is another."

"Is it the way out to the park?"

"Oh—oh—oh!"

"What the deuce is the matter now? Surely you are a woman of sense; and after having had three husbands, you ought to know that when a man says he has an engagement in the way I have said it, he means to keep it."

She seemed a little alarmed at the tone in which Captain Hawk spoke, and replied to him more readily—

"Well, well, if you must go, you shall, indeed. But only wait here for a few moments while I go for a bottle of wine. You must drink my health before you go."

"That I cannot, upon any account; and I beg that you will dismiss from your mind any doubt of my courtesy towards you, for you may do so with perfect safety."

"I will; indeed I will."

"That is right. Come, come, I don't mind telling you; but the fact is, I have fought a duel before coming here this evening; and that has had the effect of damaging my affairs a little."

"A duel?"

"Oh, yes, at the back of Montague House; and, as I killed my man, you see, it is but proper that I should let the Emperor of Austria know all about it, in order that he may send an autograph note to the Prince Regent to stay proceedings in the matter, in case the relations of the dead man should be disagreeable."

"Oh, Heavens! and you have been in such danger?"

"Danger?"

"Yes. Is not a duel dangerous?"

"Not to me. It is rather that way, I admit, as regards any one who is imprudent enough to fight with me; but I beg you to understand, that there is no danger to me personally."

"Do you always kill them, then?"

"Always. It is a duty I owe to myself, and in many cases a duty I owe to society; for when I go out with a professed duellist, I look upon him as something like a mad dog, and the sooner such are put out of the world the better."

"You are as brave as you are handsome. But I will not detain you now many minutes. Remain, I beg of you, where you are, and I will soon return to you."

With these words the waiting-maid left the room, and Captain Hawk was alone. After a few minutes' thought, he said—

"I wonder why she is so anxious that I should drink a glass of wine before I leave the house? It is rather odd, and just a little suspicious, I think. I have heard of such things as one glass of wine being so got up that it obscured the judgment sufficiently to lead to another. Ha! I must be upon my guard against the waiting-woman."

When this idea took possession of Captain Hawk, he was pretty sure not to forget it; and he walked to the door that she had rather carefully closed upon him.

That door was fast.

"As I suspected," he said. "I am a prisoner!—a prisoner to a woman! Pooh! that is rather too ridiculous! I will soon escape. And yet, what can she get by drugging me? I don't know, but I have a fancy that you are no friend of mine, my sweet waiting-woman!"

The dread that Lady Deliva's companion would not let him go so easily as that befooled lady had done was so strong upon the mind of Captain Hawk, that, after waiting in this apartment for the space of about five minutes, the daring idea seized him that he would make an effort to escape from the place.

"If I never see the old woman again," he thought, "nor the companion either, the two thousand pounds will pay me pretty well; and for her own sake, Lady Deliva will be ashamed to say a word about the transaction, the publication of which would cover her with ridicule only. Yes, I will try to escape before my other inamorato gets back."

With this view Captain Hawk looked anxiously round the room, and saw a small richly moulded door in one corner. He tried it, and found that it yielded to his touch. All beyond it was profound darkness, but yet he thought, from the direction that it opened in, it would be sure to lead him to the garden.

If, indeed, it led to the front of the house, he did not care, so long as it enabled him to escape.

He held the door open for a moment or two, and listened. There was no noise beyond it, but he thought he heard the footsteps of the companion approaching the room from the other entrance to it. Alarmed at these sounds, Hawk let the door shut, and his hand falling upon a small bolt, he at once shot it into its socket.

He was now in rather a narrow passage, as he could ascertain by feeling the wall on each side of him, but all was so profoundly dark that he had not the least notion of where he was going, and he walked on with exceeding caution.

CHAPTER CI.

CAPTAIN HAWK FINDS THE CHILD RATHER INTERESTING, AND ANGERS THE COMPANION.

CAPTAIN HAWK, if he had reflected for a moment—but then, to tell the truth, he was not much given to reflection—might have had a pretty good idea that he was jeapordising the continuance of a state of things that might be of great advantage to him, by his present rather foolish and precipitate proceedings.

In the first place, if it was found out that he was there, playing at hide-and-seek, as it were, in that house, the Lady Deliva would in all probability awaken from her dream of foolish infatuation, and shake him off for ever.

In the next place, he was risking the loss of the good-will of the maid and the confidant, and that, under such circumstances, was a loss of magnitude.

But then, as we say, Captain Hawk did not belong to the careful and reflecting order of mortals, and so long as he was engaged in some sort of adventure that promised to be pleasing in its results, he did not look particularly at the possibilites of what might take place of quite a different kind.

Certainly, none could blame him for the attempt to get rid of the companion to Lady Deliva, for of the two she was rather more disagreeable than Lady Deliva herself, inasmuch as she at all events wanted that ordinary charm of woman, which an educated female is sure to possess, in a very high degree, over one of a different description.

We find, then, that Captain Hawk is in profound darkness, and that he has not the slightest idea with regard to where he is going, or to whither the passage in which he is in will lead him ultimately.

All he congratulated himself upon was the fact that there was a door with a bolt upon it between him and the companion to the Lady Deliva.

"Confound her," thought Hawk, "she may be the Lady Deliva's companion if she likes, but she shall be none of mine."

With this sentiment in his mind, Hawk crept slowly and silently onwards, feeling his way with the greatest possible caution, so that he might not run against any obstruction in the dark.

After he had gone some distance in this manner, he felt that there was a bar to his further progress, for it seemed to him as though he had reached a wall that completely stopped him from getting any further in that direction.

This was an obstacle that rather puzzled him, and he passed his hand slowly all over it, till he found that what he had mistaken for a wall was most unquestionably a door.

After a little time he found a latch to it, but that did not suffice to open it, and he was some time longer in discovering quite at the top of it a small bolt, something similar to the one which he had shot into its socket on the inner side of the door that had led him from the room where he waited for the companion.

It did not take Captain Hawk many moments to move the bolt from its hold, and then to his great joy the door at once yielded to a touch, and gently and noiselessly swung open.

"This will do," he said. "It leads somewhere, at all events, and where I don't really much care, so that it is away from the immediate neighbourhood of those two detestable women."

The hatred that Captain Hawk had to the Lady Deliva and her attendant, was certainly on the increase, and a circumstance was upon the point of taking place, which more than any other was calculated to increase that hatred.

His curiosity was worderfully excited, now, to know where the open door would lead him to, and he stepped forward at a pace that if there had been anything to fall over, to run against, or any staircase to be precipitated down, he would certainly have encountered such calamities without the least power to save himself from their consequences.

This extra want of caution upon the part of Captain Hawk, was by no manner of means habitual to him; but upon this occasion it appeared to be a part of his nature, and on he went, with a rapid and blundering step, as though he was quite resolved to find out and to fall into any accident that might be there prepared for him.

Good luck rather than any merit of his own saved him; and Captain Hawk did very narrowly miss a little staircase that was so precipitous, that if he had fallen down it this veritable history must have come to a very abrupt and sudden conclusion, for there and then he must inevitably have broken his neck.

The old saying that the devil is good to his own, must have proved in this instance to be very strictly true; and so the captain in this instance fairly escaped.

By almost a hair's breadth he missed the staircase, down which, if he had but been precipitated, a grand crash would have been the end of his career.

All unconscious, then, of the danger that he had escaped, Hawk crept on till a voice arrested him.

Yes, a voice arrested him more completely than as if a hand had been laid upon him for such a purpose, inasmuch as the latter he would have resisted, whereas to the magic influence of the former he gave way at once.

The voice was the most magical and gentle that Captain Hawk had ever heard.

"What siren," he said, in a low tone, "can possibly occupy this house? What fair and wondrous being can exist to give utterance to such exquisite tones?"

There could be no doubt but that the voice was a very young one by the rich fulness of its flute-like notes. It was singing, and Captain Hawk stopped entranced to listen to the following words, warbled forth with so much sweetness:—

IF YOU ASK ME WHAT I LOVE.

If you ask me what I love,
What answer would you have?
I love all things so fair and good:
The wood—the sky—the wave;
But most I love the gentle flowers
That bloom so fair and free;
They fill the air with odours sweet,
And I think that they love me—
Ah, yes—ah, yes,
And I think that they love me!

If you ask me why I love,
I answer, 'tis my doom.
I cannot live and cease to love;
I'd rather seek the tomb.
But though I love the flow'rets fair,
The birds are dear and free;
They fill the air with melody,
And I think that they love me—
Ah, yes—ah, yes,
I think that they love me!

The voice ceased, and then there came a few sweetly wild and yet exquisitely musical twanging notes from a guitar, after which all was still as the grave.

For some few minutes Captain Hawk remained so entranced by the sweetness of the melody that he had listened to, that although he was burning with the wish to find out who the songstress was, he did not move hand or foot to do so.

The trance of delight, though, did not last long. Romantic as Captain Hawk was, he had yet a strain of strong poetical courage in his composition.

"I will find out," he said, "from what pretty throat those sounds came, or I will perish in the attempt to do so."

There was no difficulty at all in deciding which direction the tones had come from. They were in advance of where he stood, so all he could do was to proceed onwards and try to find some other door which would lead him to the songstress.

Full of this idea, Captain Hawk moved onwards; but now he was pretty careful to make no noise, for he had a dread that if his footsteps were heard she who had sung so sweetly might take the alarm and adopt some mode of effectually preventing him from gratifying his curiosity regarding her.

Treading, then, as lightly as it was possible that foot could fall, Captain Hawk moved onwards. By extending his arms out on each side of him he found that he was still in a narrow passage, and he did not think he had passed any outlet from it either to the left or to the right.

"All is well," he told himself. "I must surely be nearing the abode of this enchantress."

Suddenly he touched something that yielded before his hands, and another touch at it convinced him that it was velvet. He moved his hand up and down and found that it hung before him in long fluted folds, and so he jumped to the not very unlikely conclusion that it was a curtain.

While he was cautiously feeling this obstruction to his further progress he was quite startled by hearing a voice say—

"Well, the roses live the longest, I delare."

Captain Hawk fairly started back, for the voice appeared to be quite close to him. There was no mistaking the exquisite, fresh, bird-like tones, for they were the same that had warbled forth the song he had listened to with so much delight.

A moment's reflection sufficed, now, to let Captain Hawk feel convinced that the speaker was upon the other side of the velvet curtain at which he had at length arrived.

The idea that he now had but to stretch forth his hand and remove the curtain from before him, and so get a sight of the fair one, was the very thing that prevented him from doing so. Such is the known inconsistency of human nature, that we often hesitate to do that which we have it completely in our power to do, and which we have been sighing to be able to perform.

Perhaps, though, Captain Hawk was a little afraid that too rash a removal of the veil which hid from him the being who had so enchanted him with her voice, might have the effect of destroying the imaginative picture he had drawn to himself of her charms.

If such had indeed been the case, it would be far better that he should remain in a state of imaginary bliss, than be rudely awakened to an unwelcome truth in the matter.

"Yes," said the voice again, "the roses live the longest, after all, although the hyacinth is a long liver too, with its pretty bells."

This young creature, whoever she was, with her sweet voice, was evidently alone, and was communing with her flowers.

Captain Hawk ran his eye all over the curtain that hid her from his sight, with the hope of finding some crevice through which he might take a peep at her; but there was none. A thought then struck him, as necessity is the mother of invention, and as no necessity is so very prolific in that way as love, that he might easily establish for himself a peep-hole by the aid of his pen-knife.

Luckily, as he considered, he had one with him; so, opening one of the bright and sharp blades, he quite noiselessly cut a hole in the velvet curtain, and was able to peep through it without in the least degree desturbing the fair resident of the room.

What Captain Hawk there saw, most certainly deserves a separate chapter, and all we will say in this one was, that he was far—very far indeed from being disappointed.

CHAPTER CII.

THE LADY DELIVA TRIES TO REVENGE HERSELF FOR HAWK'S FAITHLESSNESS.

The room into which Hawk looked through the little slit that he had made in the curtain, was but a small one; but one so prettily and neatly decorated he thought he had never surely see, and should never see again.

The ceiling was domed, and from the centre there hung a little chandelier of pure crystal, carrying twenty lights; but they were all so small, that they looked like stars only.

The room was quite a menagerie of flowers, birds, and elegant nick-nacks of all sorts and kinds, such as might be supposed to be the delight of a young girl. A guitar lay across a table of satin-wood, and a piano was in one corner, with a quantity of music scattered about it. Drawing materials were upon another table, and it was evident that the being who occupied that room, was one in whom were centred all the graces and the arts of the highest civilization.

We have mentioned the process by which Captain Hawk came to a knowledge of the contents of that apartment. He commenced with the living occupant of it, and we terminate with her, because we do not wish, after once mentioning her, to be distracted from her and her proceedings by other objects.

Seated, then, upon a very low ottoman—so low that it was only about six inches from the floor—was a young girl of such exquisite beauty, that Captain Hawk might well be excused for looking at her for a few moments with the impression that she was a being of another world.

The age of the young creature did not appear to be more than fifteen or sixteen at the very utmost. She was dressed very plainly, indeed, in a kind of loose robe of white silk. Her long dark hair hung down her back and shoulders nearly to her waist, and was only confined to her temples slightly by a piece of blue ribbon.

Ornament and decoration upon her she had none.

It might have been that the artificial light lent something to the delicacy of her complexion, and so aided to make up the superlative character of her beauty; but she certainly did look like some nymph who had found her way to that little boudoir from the sky, and was pleasing herself by tending the flowers for its earthly occupant.

"Good Heavens!" said Captain Hawk to himself, "was there ever such a creature in this world?"

The young girl was carefully arranging some flowers in a China vase, and removing such of them as had faded away.

"Ah, yes," she said, "here is a gaudy tulip, and it is quite useless. You are of no further use, Master Tulip. Come, now, make way for this little rose-bud."

"Enchanting creature!" said Captain Hawk.

The young girl looked up with a face of alarm. The fact was that, in his admiration of her, he had spoken rather too loud for prudence; and although she had not heard what he said, yet there had come to her ears the sound of his voice.

"Oh, what was that?" she said. "I could really have thought that some one spoke."

She looked cautiously all round her; and then with a smile, she said—

"Oh, how foolish of me to think such a thing, when I know that I am here quite alone, and my aunt Deliva tells me that I am not fit to take into society, because I am such a poor ignorant young girl, that all the fine people would laugh at me. Well, I don't care; so long as they leave me my birds and my flowers, I can do very well without society.

"But most I love the gentle flowers
That bloom so fair and free;
They fill the air with odours sweet,
And I think that they love me—
Ah, yes—ah, yes,
I think that they love me."

BARCN SALTER DELIVERING HAMILTON'S CHALLENGE TO CAPTAIN HAWK.

There was the sweet voice again in that snatch of song that had so entranced the spirit of Captain Hawk before.

Now, the recollection of what he had heard Lady Deliva and the companion say of some "child" that was in the house, came across his mind, and he no longer doubted but that chance—a blessed chance he thought it—had brought him into the presence of the lovely young being who was so called.

That the Lady Deliva, retaining as she did a vivid desire for adventure and intrigue herself, should hesitate about introducing such a young and fascinating creature into society was natural enough for such a woman. What would she have looked by the side of such a piece of excellence ?

"Well," thought Captain Hawk,

"if I had got nothing by coming here but the sight of this young beauty, I should be most amply rewarded for all my trouble; but I have got well paid in cash besides."

"Heigho!" said the young girl; "and yet, at times, I do wish I had some one to talk to."

"You shall," thought Hawk.

"I am so tired of being quite alone. If the birds and the flowers could speak to me, of course that would be quite a different thing; but they cannot, and there is no pleasure in talking to aunt Deliva, or that disagreeable waiting-woman of hers. Oh, no, I don't like either of them."

"Nor I either," said Hawk.

"Oh, gracious! what was that?"

"D—n it," thought Hawk, "I have unwittingly alarmed her again, pretty creature that she is."

The alarm of the young girl upon this second sound of a voice in such close proximity to her was much greater than it had been in the first instance; for she might fairly attribute it to her imagination, or to some accidental sound in the house that had produced that tone; but a second sound of the same description gave much more ample food for conjecture.

"I have done it now," thought Hawk, "and thoroughly alarmed her; so the best way will be to speak to her at once."

With this resolve, he altered his voice to as soft and consolatory accents as he could speak.

"Be not alarmed. It is a friend who speaks to you. It is one who would shed his last drop of blood in your defence."

"Oh, who is that?"

"Nay, you terrify yourself without reason, Let me assure you that there is no one in all the world who will more carefully shield you from all harm than I would."

"Good Heavens! where are you?"

"I am here behind the velvet curtain; but without your permission so to do, I will not emerge from the place of concealment."

"But who are you?"

"A gentleman."

"Oh, then you must not come here—indeed, you must not."

"But why not?"

"My aunt Deliva has told me, that of all creatures in the world that I need most dread, a gentleman is the worst."

"Ah, your aunt has deceived you."

"No—no."

"But I assure you that she has, indeed, deceived you, or, perhaps, you have to some extent deceived yourself by misunderstanding what she exactly meant."

"No, I don't think that; so go away."

"But let me tell you that what your aunt must have meant was to warn you against sham gentlemen, not real ones. Now, I am a real one."

"Oh, if I thought that, of course it would be quite another thing; but, indeed, she never drew any such distinction to me."

"Then she ought to have done so."

"But how came you where you are? My aunt told me, and so did Margaret, her waiting-woman, that it was quite out of the question any one but themselves could get to this room."

"Accident has befriended me, fair one, and enabled me to have the joy of looking upon you."

"Oh, that you cannot."

"Nay, but I can."

"How so? Is not the curtain between us?"

"Yes, but love can look through a curtain."

"What is this love that you have mentioned several times?"

"Why, don't you know? I thought that in the pretty song that you sung just now it was mentioned."

"Ah, yes, I can very well comprehend how I may love the birds and the sweet flowers; but there is some other sort of love, is there not?"

"There is, dear one."

"Oh, no—don't come here—don't. Indeed, you must not. Oh, how very wrong of you."

Captain Hawk had suddenly drawn aside the curtain, and entered the room, where he knelt at the feet of the young girl, who seemed to be really very much terrified at his presence.

"Pray pardon me," he said, "for this intrusion, but at the same time allow me to beg of you to be under no sort of fear of me. I do not come to injure you by word or look or deed I do love you, and I admire you so much that your very innocence is your safeguard."

"Oh, I am not afraid; but—but——"

"Go on, dear one."

"I wish you would go away."

"Then I obey you."

Captain Hawk rose, and put on a very melancholy look, as he said—

"Believe me, none but a real gentleman would obey you in this precipitate way, and I do so because I would not for a moment have you doubt me. It is a sad thing, though, for me to leave you thus."

"Shall you be very unhappy?"

"Indeed, and in truth I shall."

"Well, then, you may stay a little while."

"May I, though?"

"Oh, yes; but you must be very good, indeed, you know, and if you hear my aunt or the waiting-woman coming, you must go directly, for I don't know what they would say to me or do to me if they thought that I encouraged you here."

"I will be all obedience, I assure you."

"Mind you are. And now, what is your name?"

"Oh, my name? Why, that is Gerald."

Captain Hawk had been so suddenly asked this question, that he gave his real name.

"Gerald! Well, it is not a very ugly name. And what are you, Gerald? I should like to know what you are."

"Simply a gentleman."

"With plenty of money, like my aunt?"

"Yes, just so."

"And you go to all sorts of gay places, and see company, and amuse yourself very much?"

"I do; and if you were with me how much more delightful it would be."

"I don't think my aunt would let me go."

"Nor I either. But what is your name, dear one?"

"Why, my name is Angela, but they don't call me that, and I don't know exactly what my aunt does call me, if ever she speaks of me to other people; but I know that Angela is my real name."

"It is a sweet name, dear Angela, and well becomes you. But how very lonely you must be here."

"Well, I am a little."

"You are not frightened at me now, I hope, are you?"

"Oh, no; what have I to be frightened at? I know that I am quite safe."

CHAPTER CIII.

THE LADY DELIVA'S COMPANION MAKES AN UNWELCOME DISCOVERY.

The tone in which the young creature said that she knew she was quite safe rather puzzled Captain Hawk, for he was rather of a different opinion, and thought that living there alone, as it were, she was anything but safe. Besides, there was about her such complete simplicity and artlessness, that any one with the most ordinary duplicity could deceive her.

"And so, you think yourself quite safe?" said Captain Hawk, as he walked up to her, and took up some of the long tresses of her beautiful hair, and let them fall through his fingers.

"Oh, yes—yes."

"And you are not afraid of me?"

"No. Why should I be afraid of you?"

Captain Hawk placed his arm round her neck, and drew her gently towards him till her lips touched his, and then he kissed her gently, and she made not the slightest resistance.

"Ah, no," she said, "why should I be afraid of you? I am, perhaps, a very foolish and simple girl, and my aunt often says that I know nothing, and, therefore, am not fit for society, and so I please myself by thinking that I have a protector ever near me."

"A protector? Who do you mean?"

"Oh, hush! I feel that the great God, who made us all, the sweet birds, and the flowers, will protect me; and that those who would deceive his innocent and unsuspecting creatures will suffer from his retribution. Here, in this little chamber, the spirit of his love is present, and will protect me."

Captain Hawk withdrew his arm from around the neck of the young girl and shuddered. He felt at that moment as if all strength had left him, and as though a child might have vanquished him.

"Strong—strong in your belief," he said, in a low tone—"more than strong in your innocence. You are indeed safe, Angela."

"Oh, yes, I am safe."

"From all who have the capacity to think, you are safe, my dear girl. I love you still; but it is as a sister I love you."

Captain Hawk rose and paced the room in agitation. He felt that the simple reliance upon the Divinity that actuated that young girl, had made him a convert, and completely vanquished him; and yet, he could hardly imagine how, with his thoughts and opinions, such an effect had been produced upon him in such a moment.

"Ah!" she said, "now you are angry with poor Angela?"

"Oh, no—no."

"Are you really not? Well, then, come and sit by her again, and speak to her of the great world, of which she knows so little."

"Yes, Angela, I will sit by you and speak to you of that great world of which you know so little, and of which it will be a happy thing for you if you never know more."

"Say you so?"

"Yes, my dear Angela; for the fact is, it is a bad world—oh! such a very bad world, that even a knowledge of its wickedness, without any participation in it, is debasing. You are not afraid of me now?"

"Not at all."

"And—and may I kiss you again?"

"If you like."

She leaned her sweet face towards his; but the flush of shame came across the countenance of Captain Hawk, and he felt at that moment that he was playing the unmanly part of taking advantage of a trusting child in knowledge, and all but a child in years.

He could not kiss her.

"Ah, my dear friend," she said, as she flung her arm round his neck, "you seem to be unwell, or else you are angry with poor Angela?"

"No—no."

"And yet you look disturbed."

"I am disturbed, Angela. I must leave you at once and for ever. God bless you, dear girl; but it will be as well that we should never meet again."

"Wretch!" screamed a voice; and in a moment the velvet curtain was torn aside, and the waiting-woman of the Lady Deliva appeared upon the threshold of the room.

"Ah, indeed!" said Captain Hawk.

"Oh!" cried Angela, "I am lost—lost!"

"You monster!" cried the waiting-woman, shaking her clenched hand at Captain Hawk; "you monster!"

"Really, I am at a loss to know the meaning of all this abuse?" he said, as he rose, and calmly confronted the infuriated woman.

It was at that moment that Hawk felt what a joy it was to him that he had respected the innocence of the young girl, who crouched down terrified by his side. Had he played the part of a villain in his interview with her, he could not have confronted the woman with the calm, assured look he wore.

"Well, madam," he added, "what is the matter?"

"The matter?"

"Yes. I ask what is the matter? You burst into this room with rage in your looks, uttering words of contumely and reproach; and I ask you in consequence, what is the matter?"

"Oh, was there ever such assurance!"

"Upon your part do you mean?"

"No, wretch, but upon yours. I now see it all. You had heard of the pretty baby face of this child, and nothing, to be sure, would serve your turn but finding her out. Oh, it is a manly thing, indeed! And you, you little horrid hussy, you will be taken somewhere where you will repent your vile conduct."

"Silence!" said Captain Hawk.

"Silence, indeed! A pretty thing—"

"Silence, woman! Do not profane the ears of this young and innocent being with your vile expressions. She is innocent as yet. God only knows how long she will be, seeing in what keeping she is. But I ask of you, as a woman, to spare her the knowledge even of what you suspect her."

"Suspect her?"

"Yes. I tell you she is as pure and innocent as when I was a hundred miles from this spot. I have been brought here by accident. I have respected the angelic and spotless innocence of this child. Do you do so likewise."

"I am staggered."

"It may appear strange, but it is true."

"True? Ha! ha! Oh, dear, no, it is not at its truth that I am at all staggered, for I don't believe a word of it; but it is at your most wonderful and astonishing assurance."

"And I am much more surprised at yours, I assure you."

"Oh, indeed; are you?"

"Indeed I am; and I desire that you quit the apartment this moment, unless you can behave yourself a little better in it than you have up to this moment shown a disposition to do."

"Oh! oh! oh!"

"Pray what is the matter now, madam?"

"The matter, you specimen of villany and imposture? How can you possibly ask such a question? First you seduce an innocent baby, and then you ask me what is the matter? But I will soon take care that all this is settled."

"Oh, stop—stop!" cried Angela. "Indeed I don't know what you are so angry about."

"Oh, don't you? But I won't say anything more to you, miss. Your aunt will settle with you."

With these words, the waiting-woman flounced out of the room, leaving poor Angela in a state of great alarm; and Captain Hawk himself very much puzzled to know what to do next under the circumstances.

For once, he found himself in the extremely novel position of the protector of innocence against unjust accusations; and no wonder that he did not exactly know how to comport himself under such very new circumstances.

That the waiting-maid had gone to convey the rather astounding news to the Lady Deliva that the Austrian prince had found his way to the chamber of the "child," he could not entertain a doubt; and he had a very tolerable idea, from what he had seen of the Lady Deliva, of the effect that such a piece of intelligence was likely to have upon that lady.

In good truth, Captain Hawk felt himself to be most awkwardly situated.

Poor Angela did nothing now but cry, so that after a little time, he thought that his present duty was to try to console her, and to reassure her mind.

"My dear Angela," he said, "listen to me."

"Yes, yes, I will."

"You have nothing to fear—you have done no wrong, and you should bear in mind that you are not to blame even for my presence here, for I came without your knowledge or invitation.

"Oh, but they won't believe that."

"Well, well, never mind them. Laugh at them."

"I can't. I only wish I could."

"But you must try to do so. Let them say what they like, and do you turn a deaf ear to it all."

"Well, I will try. But they do terrify me so, they say such things, and sometimes my aunt strikes me."

"She had better not do so while I am here. But tell me, have you no other friend but your aunt in all the world?"

"Oh, yes—yes, my poor father."

"Your father? Why, how is this? Is it possible that you have a father living?"

"I hope he is living. But he gave me to my aunt, you see, Mr. Gerald, and so ever since then I have lived here, and not seen him; and he used to be so kind to me, and to love me so dearly, that I have never ceased to wonder that he could give me to my aunt, as he has done."

"What did he say to you about it?"

"Oh, nothing. I was taken out of my bed one night, and placed in a boat on the river, and brought here, and then they told me he had given me to them, you see."

"And did it never, Angela, occur to you to doubt the truth of the statement?"

"Doubt?—the truth of it?"

"Yes. Did it, I say, never occur to you to doubt it?"

"Oh, but people could not be quite so wicked as to tell stories?"

"God bless your innocence! Do you think that that is the extent of wickedness at which people stop appalled?"

"I never tell stories."

"No, Angela, you do not, but you are an exception, I assure you, to a very general rule, and thousands do tell stories in the world; so I have no doubt but that you were forcibly or fraudulently taken away from your father. I cannot think for a moment that he could have consented to part with you, and you are quite a little simpleton to think as much."

"Oh, I am—I am! And now, Gerald, that you tell me people do tell stories, I am sure my aunt and her waiting-maid do."

"No doubt of it."

"But you don't, Gerald?"

"Not to you," said Captain Hawk, faintly.

"Oh, hush! They are coming—I hear the sound of footsteps. Cannot you escape from here, Gerald? They will kill you. Oh try to go away, and forget that you ever saw poor Angela."

"No, Angela, I have no fears; but if I had, I would at any risk stay and defend you. They shall not harm you while I have life to protect you."

CHAPTER CIV.

THE LADY DELIVA BEHAVES WITH GREAT SINGULARITY.

Captain Hawk listened, and he too heard the sound of approaching footsteps in the passage beyond the velvet curtain, which had been so unceremoniously pulled down by the waiting-woman in her anger at the supposed duplicity of Captain Hawk.

"They come," he said.

"Oh, yes, and I do so dread their coming," said Angela. "If you were not here, I should not so much mind."

"Nay, fear nothing. I can defend, I assure you, both you and myself against much greater force than your aunt Deliva can possibly bring against us. Be under no alarm. I beg of you."

"I will strive to be calm."

"Do so, dear Angela—do so."

She flung her arms round him, but he gently disengaged himself from her, whispering to her as he did so, "My dear, dear girl, you will by holding me in this way only anger your aunt still more, and give her occasion to say unkinder things than she otherwise would say.

"Shall I, indeed?"

"Yes—yes. I will keep away from you, and I advise you to say as little as possible."

"I will do just as you wish me, Gerald. Oh, they come—they come, now, and I know my aunt is so violent when she is angry."

Captain Hawk had a pretty good idea that the aunt could be tolerably violent when she was angry, so he stepped a pace or two before the young girl, with a determination, let what might come of it, to protect her from any violence.

The flash of a light in the narrow passage on the other side of the velvet curtain came upon his sight, and then he heard the voice of the waiting-woman say—

"This way, my lady. You will find the prince here, my lady, along with the child."

Strange to say, the tone of voice in which the waiting-woman now spoke was very different from the violent one that she had thought proper to use when in the boudoir of Angela only a short time ago, and Captain Hawk listened to the softened tones in amazement.

If he was surprised at the mild tones of the maid, though, he had still more reason to be surprised at the extraordinary manner in which the mistress took his presence in that part of her mansion, where certainly he was about as intrusive a visitor as it was possible any one could be.

Lady Deliva walked into the room looking as cool and calm as possible. By the light that he was able to see her in, Captain Hawk did not detect that she looked in the smallest degree ruffled.

Surprise at finding a woman of whose strong passions he had heard so much, and whom he could not help feeling that he had really injured, looking so much as if nothing was the matter, fairly stopped his breath, and he could not help gazing at her with a surprise that was manifest in his face.

Lady Deliva herself broke the silence.

"Count," she said, "I hear you have lost your way in my rather intricate house, and I fear that you have been but very indifferently entertained by this child here."

"Madam, I—I——"

"Nay, count, it will be very kind and complimentary upon your part to praise her, but really I beg you will not; I do not like to make children vain of themselves."

Captain Hawk stared at Lady Deliva with open eyes.

"You see, my lady," said the companion, "that Count Astral must have taken the wrong turning, and so got into this room where the child was, without intending it."

"Oh, that is quite sufficiently evident," said the Lady Deliva.

"Yes," said Captain Hawk, "I—a—a—suppose it is so, my dear madam."

"Oh, count, you know it is."

"Yes, I know it—that is to say, I think I——d—n it!"

"Count?"

"Pardon me, madam. It is so very seldom that I utter anything in the shape of an explative, that I hope and trust you will be so good as to look over this one."

"Oh, certainly. My dear child, I hope you have not been talking any of your nonsense to the count."

"Oh, no, aunt."

"On the contrary," said Captain Hawk, "she has spoken to me in the most charming and unaffected manner that you can possibly conceive. She is your niece, I believe, my dear madam?"

"Yes, she is so. But it really distresses me to think that you have by this very malapropos little adventure broken the appointment, to keep which you were compelled to do your feelings the violence to tear yourself away from me only a short time ago."

"Why—a—yes—I have—oh, yes, I am too late."

"Then you can stay?"

"No, I can't stay."

"You can't stay? Oh, my dear count, you are too diffident—you are very much too diffident, I assure you. Allow me to beg that you will quite look upon this house as your own. At least, you will do me the favour to take a cup of coffee?"

"I am afraid that I intrude."

"Not at all. We will have it in this room, along with my charming little child here. I call her mine from the affection that I bear towards her. You will stay, count?"

"I wonder," thought Captain Hawk, "what the devil all this means? Is it, after all, only the faint prelude to some storm that her ladyship will, when least expected, burst out with to the confusion of both the pretty niece and myself? Well, no matter: I will stay and weather it out, and save the young girl from the worst consequences of it."

Captain Hawk, with the idea growing each moment into more strength in his mind that the Lady Deliva was only playing a part, and meant a great deal more than she said, was now resolved that he would not leave the place until he acquired something like a certainty one way or the other.

With an assumed cheerfulness, then, he said to the Lady Deliva—

"I am a great deal too late for the appointment, for the keeping of which, as you say, I was compelled to leave the house, or rather, I should say, to try to leave it, so it will really give me the highest gratification to remain."

"You do me great honour, count, and give me great pleasure."

"And you are not really angry at all then, aunt?" said Angela, in a very low and imploring tone of voice.

"Angry, my child? At what?"

"Oh, nothing, aunt; only I was afraid that perhaps you might, you know, be just a little—a very little—"

"Oh, pho! say no more about it, my dear. I suppose you think that I should be angry with you, because my friend, the count, missed his way in my house, and finding you here, you tried your best to amuse him? Oh, my dear, it was quite your duty, as well as your pleasure, so to do."

Captain Hawk did not like the look that accompanied these words at all; but he kept his suspicions that all was not right to himself, only he resolved to keep such a watch upon the proceedings of the Countess Deliva, that it would not be very easy for her to play any tricks.

"Let her not attempt aught to the injury of Angela," thought Captain Hawk, "or I will take good care it shall be the worst night's work ever she did in her life."

"Come, order coffee for us here," said Lady Deliva to the waiting-woman, who had stood by during all this time, looking as calm, and as composed, and as humble as it was possible for her to look, and as it she had little or nothing to do with what had taken place, or its consequences.

"I will bring your ladyship coffee myself," said the waiting-woman, "for your ladyship would not wish any of the servants to intrude into these rooms."

"True—true; I had forgotten that. Our dear child, count, is quite a little recluse."

"Is she, indeed?"

"Oh, yes; but when she is a little older, I daresay she will make quite a sensation in the world of fashion."

"She certainly will, my lady."

"My dear child, you look rather dull. Come, you shall sing to us while we take our coffee, and perhaps you will surprise the count by your proficiency in music. If so, we must think upon how the count may surprise you in return."

"What does she mean by that?" thought Captain Hawk.

The more he listened to the tones of the Lady Deliva the more did Captain Hawk become convinced that there was some hidden meaning in them, and that all she was saying, under the pretence of being quite pleased and satisfied, was but a grave and subtle piece of irony. This was a conviction which by no manner of means made Captain Hawk feel more comfortable than he had done; and he began to look upon the affair now in the light of a fencing match, during the course of which one or other of the contending parties might give his adversary a mortal stab, and be well enough pleased to do so.

There was only one supposition in his mind that held out the faintest hope that all might yet be well, and that arose from the idea, that it was just possible the waiting-maid had sufficient influence over the Lady Deliva to convince her that the whole affair was a mistake, and that she had adopted that course for the purpose of screening her own conduct in the affair.

This was a supposition which occurred to Hawk's mind as just tolerably likely; but yet he could not take upon himself to say that such was the fact.

"I think the gentleman has heard me sing, aunt," said Angela.

"Oh, has he?"

"Yes, a little," said Captain Hawk; "but far from that satisfying me, it has rather had the effect of inducing an earnest wish to hear you again."

"Certainly," said Lady Deliva. "It will take some little time to get the coffee ready, and during that period we may as well have a song from the child."

"As you please, aunt."

Angela went to the side table, and picked up her guitar, and just ran her hand rapidly along the strings of it, and then she commenced singing in a clear tone of voice, and looking at Captain Hawk as she did so.

CHAPTER CV.

HAWK IS WARNED OF DANGER BY ANGELA.

The song that the young creature sung was very short, and was, in words, as follow:—

BEWARE, BEWARE OF SMILING SKIES.

"Oh, beware of smiling skies—
The storm-cloud lowers near;
Oh, beware of too much sun,
For then is most to fear.
Beware, beware of smiling skies!

HAWK READING THE NEWSPAPER IN THE FASHIONABLE HOTEL.

"There are flowers of radiant hues,
So beautiful to see;
But from their breath comes ready death,
That may be found by thee!
Beware—oh, then, beware!"

She dropped the guitar, and burst into tears.

Captain Hawk sprang to his feet, and the Lady Deliva, clapping her hands together, burst into a peal of laughter, which she had some difficulty in subduing; and when she had done so, she said—

"I really do believe that the child is so terrified at my finding you here, count, that nothing will convince her I do not intend to do something very dreadful to her and to you upon that account. But what can I say to set such fears at rest?"

"Oh, aunt," said Angela, "you do, then, indeed and in truth, forgive both this gentleman and me?"

"I do, indeed, if it will please you to hear me say so; although I must add that I don't see anything to forgive. As yet, there is no harm done. I am quite certain that I can depend upon the honour of the count."

"You can, madam," said Captain Hawk. "Nothing has passed between me and this young lady but what all the world might have looked upon, and none be the worse for it."

"Oh, certainly, of course. Who could doubt it?"

"I am rejoiced, Lady Deliva, that you do not doubt it."

"And I, count, am equally rejoiced to find you rejoiced. Come, you foolish girl, dry your tears, and do not think it at all necessary to liken me to too sunny a sky, or to the South American flowers, whose perfume is fatal to human life."

"Oh, aunt, I—I ——"

"Stuff, girl! It is of no use your denying it. You did, by that extemporaneous ditty, think you were warning the count, did you not?"

"Aunt, I never uttered a falsehood in all my life. I did."

"Ha! ha! Oh, dear—oh, dear! I shall die with laughing! And you, count—for goodness gracious sake, do tell the truth—did you take the warning, now, or did you not?"

"I thought it strange ——"

"That is sufficient. Oh, dear—oh, dear! Margaret, where are you with that coffee? Oh, here you are. What do you think? Here has been our child singing a song to the count, to warn him that I wish to poison him. What do you think of that?"

The waiting-maid had just appeared at the entrance to the room with a little silver tray, on which there were three cups of coffee; and she staggered back so as her mistress spoke, that it was with difficulty she saved the whole tray and its contents from falling.

"Why, you silly creature, what are you about?"

"My foot slipped, madam."

"There, there, put down the coffee. I hope it is the best?"

"The very best, madam."

"Why, then, that will do, capitally. You can wait, if you please, just within there, in case I want you."

"Yes, madam."

"And now, my child, you will join me and the count in a cup of coffee, which, I hope, will have the effect of convincing you that I am not so terrible a being as you did me the honour of supposing me to be. Oh! what a capital anecdote this will make in the saloons of the court! You must positively write me out the song, my dear."

"Yes, aunt—I—will—"

"Why do you tremble?"

"Did I tremble, aunt? I am sure I have no wish to tremble."

"No wish, you foolish child? Of course you have no wish, and no occasion, either. Come, take your coffee."

The Lady Deliva took hold of one of the cups; and the waiting-maid immediately said, "Hem!" upon which the Lady Deliva took the one next to it; and in the most charming manner handed the one that she had previously touched to Captain Hawk.

"There, my dear count," she said, "this you will find such coffee as I don't think is to be found elsewhere in all England. It is, I assure you, made from a recipe of my own; and I feel quite sure that you will never complain of it. Come, drink."

"Shall I sing again, aunt?" said Angela, suddenly coming forward right between Lady Deliva and Captain Hawk, and stretching out her arm behind her towards the latter. In her hand was a little piece of paper, which Hawk took on the moment; and saw written upon it in pencil—

"*Poisoned coffee!*"

To thrust the paper into his bosom after reading it was the work of a moment with Captain Hawk.

"Pray, get out of the way, child," said Lady Deliva, "if you please. I cannot see the count for you."

"Oh, I beg your pardon, aunt. I know I am so very awkward. But shall I sing again?"

"If you like."

"Let me hear a tune on the piano, if

you please," said Captain Hawk. "It looks very invitingly open at yonder end of the room. I presume you play?"

"Oh, yes."

"Then oblige the count at once, do," said Lady Deliva. "Go and play one of your best compositions, child. Count, you don't take your coffee."

"I will, though, madam."

Captain Hawk took the little exquisite china cup in his hand—it did not hold above a couple of tablespoonfuls—and turned towards Angela with it as he said—

"I shall have great pleasure, though, in hearing another song, although there will be no occasion for any warning, now."

Their eyes met for a moment; and Captain Hawk upturned the little coffee cup, and the small quantity that was in it of liquid fell with a noiseless flow to the floor, where the thick carpet absorbed it in a moment.

"Oh, no," said Angela. "I feel quite convinced there is no occasion for any warning now."

When Captain Hawk turned round again, he affected to be taking the coffee cup from his lips, and then he placed it upon the table. A look of positive find-like triumph was upon the countenance of Lady Deliva.

"How do you like that coffee, count?" she said.

"Why," he replied, "the flavour of it is rather new to me; and yet I thought it was a drink with which I was well acquainted."

"Oh, yes; but, as you say, this is of a new flavour entirely. I beg to assure you, count, that it is a flavour of my own preparation. Silence, girl! We don't want to be dinned by your noise."

This rather ungenerous speech was addressed to Angela, who had commenced playing the piano with great skill. She ceased on the moment, and cast rather a terrified glance at her imperious aunt, who leant back in her chair, and looked keenly and curiously at Captain Hawk.

"Confound the old jezebel," thought Hawk; "she is speculating now upon my looks, under the idea that I have taken her poisoned coffee. I wonder how soon, now, it would have taken effect upon me?"

Captain Hawk had an intention of amusing himself a little at the expense of the Lady Deliva by affecting that the coffee had overcome him, and he was rather anxious to know what she would do or say when she should find that such was the case. He could hardly believe that even she would see him die without some compunctious twitchings upon the subject.

In such an idea he showed that he knew little if anything of the wild passions of the woman with whom he had to deal; and the result of his further knowledge of her certainly opened his eyes to a page in the history of human nature, such as he had hardly thought there was to read.

By the manner in which she watched him, he had a pretty good idea that she expected the poison to work rapidly, and he said in a well-affected voice of confusion—

"I think I will leave you now, Lady Deliva. I—don't feel very well just now."

"Inded?" she replied, in a voice of triumph. "So, you do not feel very well, prince?"

"Oh, aunt, is he a prince?" said Angela.

"Hold your tongue, girl, or you shall be punished after a fashion that you will remember for some time to come. What is it to you who or what he is?"

"But, aunt——"

"Silence, I say!"

The look that accompanied these words was such that poor Angela was much too terrified to reply, and she cowered down by the piano in silent terror. She had seen Captain Hawk, though, cast away the coffee that she knew was poisoned, and that was a great consolation to her. He at least was not suffering from the effects of the subtle drug which the Lady Deliva had hoped to be able so easily to administer to him.

"Well, count, how are you now?"

"I can hardly tell. I—think that—"

"That what?"

"I am getting worse."

"Well, there is something in the air of this house that don't agree with some people, and particularly with people who are not very scrupulous about keeping faith with others—you understand? Come, now, count, where did you see this child before you came here to-night?"

"What child?"

"Yonder child, who, no doubt, has told you that her name is Angela."

"I cannot tell. I feel so ill."

"Rise, Sir Count, and follow me."

Captain Hawk did rise; but he took care to do so in such a manner as to make it appear to be quite an effort so to do, and he tottered to the door of the room after the Lady Deliva.

"Beware!" cried Angela.

"Oh, my dear," said the lady, "it is all settled, and I will return to you in an hour, and give you the punishment you deserve, you may depend upon that."

CHAPTER CVI.

ANGELA STILL WARNS CAPTAIN HAWK OF HIS DANGER.

Poor Angela shrank back, and trembled at these words from the Lady Deliva. The poor girl knew too well what they meant, and that her imperious and brutal aunt was quite capable of inflicting upon her a terrible chastisement.

"Oh, no—no!" she said; "spare me!"

"We shall see—we shall see."

"All's—safe—I will protect you," said Captain Hawk, pretending to speak with difficulty, and hoping that Angela would have perspicuity enough to see that he was merely acting a part for the purpose of deceiving her aunt—"I will protect you—if I can."

"Yes, if you can," said the Lady Deliva. "If you can, you may. But come, count, I beg that you will follow me; and if you feel too faint and weak to walk, I will assist you."

"Thank you," said Hawk. "I am to be faint and weak, am I?" he thought. "Well—well, I will keep up that delusion well enough."

Now, Hawk was well armed, and he knew that at any moment he was much more than a match for the Lady Deliva and her waiting-maid, who had apparently taken so little part in all this proceeding, but who had, in reality, mixed, by her mistress's directions, in the coffee the diabolical potion which if he, Hawk, had but taken, would, no doubt, have deprived him of existence.

As the Lady Deliva went out of Angela's room, and passed the waiting-maid in the passage, she whispered to her—

"You did not use enough."

"Oh yes, an over-dose."

"But he dose not suffer much."

"He must have an iron constitution, my lady, to stand what he has taken, I assure you."

"Well, well, he will drop soon. Count, follow me. You do appear to be a little indisposed, but no doubt that will soon go off, and you will be quite well again."

"I hope so," said Captain Hawk, very faintly.

Angela was left sobbing bitterly, and Captain Hawk followed the Lady Deliva along the gloomy passage, while the waiting-maid followed him again.

That these two wicked women had contrived between them the idea of murdering him, because they had found that he utterly disregarded their vicious advances, and attached himself to the beautiful young Angela, was now a proposition past a doubt; but they little suspected how completely they were foiled by the warnings of Angela, and the clever sleight of hand with which Captain Hawk had got rid of the coffee without drinking it.

As the waiting-maid was behind him, Captain Hawk felt the necessity of playing his part well, so he took good care to stumble along the passage in such a manner that more than once he dealt the Lady Deliva quite a severe blow on the back, in his pretended efforts to save himself from falling.

All this she took very well, indeed, as it only tended further to assure her that she was being amply revenged upon him for his slight of her.

After a time they reached the room from which Captain Hawk had strayed, upon the occasion of escaping from the troublesome company of the waiting-maid, and then they paused.

The waiting-woman placed the light that she had carried on the table that was in the centre of this apartment.

"Open the door now," said the Lady Deliva.

"Yes, madam. But is it not a little too soon?"

"Oh, no. How are you now, count?"

Captain Hawk affected to be quite unable to answer her, upon which she said, with all the cool ferocity of one who was accustomed to such deeds—

"He won't live half an hour longer."

"No," said the waiting-maid, "I don't suppose he will; but he may turn violent before his death. You know some of them do."

"Some of them?" thought Captain Hawk. "D—n it, this woman is a wholesale hand at this sort of thing."

"Yes," replied the Lady Deliva. "I know that some of them are apt to do so; but if he should, it don't matter. He can do nothing but knock himself about against the walls a little, you know."

"That is true, my lady."

"Open the door, then, at once."

Upon this the waiting-maid went to a part of the wainscot-wall of the room, where certainly there was no appearance of any door, and touched a spring, when a tall door opened in the panel.

All looked black as night in a dungeon beyond this door, and Captain Hawk, who waited a few moments to consider of whether he would quietly go through it or not, pretended to be forced to fall into a chair for support.

"I think he is going now," said Lady Deliva.

"Very likely, madam."

"Ah! Oh!" said Hawk.

"Upon my word, Margaret, I'm very much afraid you have not given him the dose you say you did. I don't accuse you of wilfully omitting it; but you have given less than you thought."

"Well, madam, there is nothing easier in the world, than putting a knife in his breast if you think that—or into his back."

"Thank you," thought Captain Hawk.

"Well, I don't know," said the Lady Deliva; "it don't much matter whether he is a long time or not in dying; so let us get him into the death chamber, and close it up again."

"Very well, madam. Now, count, will you get up? Come, make an effort to get up. The pretty little Angela is calling you."

"Eh? Oh!" said Captain Hawk.

"That name revives him a little."

"Ah," said the Lady Deliva, "and when we have safety disposed of this all but dead man, and I have had a few hours repose, of which I stand much in need, we will go to Miss Angela, and make her remember this night's proceedings. Oh, I could kill her!"

"Don't think of that, madam. It is much more satisfactory to keep her, and punish her after."

"Yes—yes, it is. Her cries are music to my ears. I will punish her, and she knows it too. She suffers already many pangs in anticipation of what is to come."

"No doubt of that, madam; and she amply deserves so to suffer."

"She does—she does. Now help me to raise the count from his chair, and let us throw him into the room. It is no matter how he falls if we can but get him past the secret panel. All will then be well."

"Quite well, madam."

While they thus conversed in hurried whispers, but still not quite so low as for one word of what they said to escape the observation of Captain Hawk, he had been thinking what it was best to do, and he came to the conclusion that he should go into the room they had opened for his reception. He was the more inclined to do so because the Lady Deliva had spoken of her intention of taking a few hours' rest before she went to inflict some punishment upon Angela. If that had not been the case he would not have allowed either the Lady Deliva or her sweet waiting-maid to leave his sight.

Between them they now managed to hoist him up from the chair and drag him along the floor towards the door that they had opened in the secret panel. He just allowed his feet to touch the ground so as to aid them a little in their endeavours, but he took care to kick them both severely.

"Curses on him!" muttered the Lady Deliva.

"Oh, I could knock his head off!" said the waiting-maid. "I do so hate him, and he has kicked me dreadfully."

"So he has me. Oh, Margaret—Margaret is not this a shocking thing to think that this is the fifth man I have been compelled to dispose of in this way for breaking faith with me?"

"All men are faithless, my lady."

"I begin to think they are, and that it is quite a mercy you and I, in our long stay in India, found out this means of being revenged upon them."

"It is—it is."

Captain Hawk heard all this with mingled feelings of horror at the two hags who thus coolly confessed to five murders, and exulted at the thought that it had been reserved for him to put an end to such a course of iniquity, and to rescue the sweet and fair Angela from such an association.

They dragged him to the open panel in the wall, and in they threw him to the room it opened to.

Captain Hawk pretended to fall down in a heap on to the floor, and then he uttered a deep groan.

"He is gone," said Lady Deliva.

"Dead do you mean, my lady?"

"No, I don't know that he is dead, but I mean that as far as we are concerned and the world in general, he is gone."

"Oh, yes, there is no doubt about that, my lady. But don't you think there will be a f[illegible]?"

"About what?"

"About him, as he is a person of some rank, they say, in his own country. However, that don't matter, so long as he is not traced to this house, and I don't think he can be."

"Certainly not. It is very unlikely that he told any one he was coming here, and if he did, I would simply say that he had not been. But the fact is, men do not leave word where they have gone when they go on such errands as brought him to this house."

"That is true."

"Close the panel."

With a sharp clap shut the panel was closed, and Captain Hawk found himself in the most absolute darkness.

Captain Hawk had really played his part wonderfully well, although it had certainly cost him some trouble to do so. There could be no doubt that the Lady Deliva, and her beautiful waiting-maid, thought him all but a dead man.

How two females could by any possibility conceive such an amount of wickedness, it is hard to understand; and were it not that we know from experience that even that gentle and endearing sex, under some excitements, are capable of such acts, we should hesitate to believe that even the Lady Deliva could be so demoniac as she really was.

Facts are stubborn things, however, and there was Captain Hawk all alone in the room, which was expected by those who placed him there to be his tomb.

As we have said, the darkness was most excessive.

CHAPTER CVII.

CAPTAIN HAWK MANAGES TO THROW A LIGHT UPON A DREADFUL SIGHT.

CAPTAIN HAWK listened to the departing footsteps of the two hags who had thrust him into that secret chamber, as they hastily left the door of it, for the security of which they evidently depended much more upon secrecy than they did upon its strength.

"Gone," said Hawk, as he drew a long breath. "They are gone. Ah, what a dreadful odour, is in this room."

The long breath that he had drawn was anything delicious, for there was some awful peculiarity in the atmosphere of that room, that made it almost choke him, and he gasped again, as he stretched out his hands to get hold of something to support him, for he felt his strength fail him.

"Confound them," he said, "if they have failed with the poisoned coffee, the air of this room is enough to kill any one."

By dint of placing his handkerchief on his mouth, he breathed more freely, for through the thin cambric the foul air was as it were filtered, and much that had loaded it with noxious particles was kept out of the lungs of Captain Hawk.

Still there was evidently so little vitality in the air of the place, that he felt the urgent necessity of getting out of it as quickly as he possibly could, and he accordingly began to feel about him for the door by which he had been conducted to that terribly nauseous abode.

At any risk, Captain Hawk made up his mind that he would leave it, and if he should not be able to find the precise mode of opening the panel, he felt fully confident that by putting his shoulder to it, he should tolerably soon succeed in having it down.

With this object, then, of escape at all hazards from that terrible place, and with his handkerchief clutched in his teeth so as to breathe through it, Captain Hawk trod carefully over the floor, swaying his arm to and fro to touch the wall, and so get to the spot of it where he might find the secret panel.

He soon touched the wall, for the room was, after all, but of small dimensions; and then he crept on, keeping his hands upon the wainscoting till he came to what he thought at first was the door he was in search of.

Captain Hawk was soon convinced that this was a mistake, and that it was the shutter of a window that he had come to.

"Better and better," he said. "I thought that probably enough there was no window to this place, but here is one; and if I don't get it open, and so have some of the fresh cool night air into this room, it is such a window as never yet was made by mortal man."

He felt that nothing was to be done well by hurrying, so he felt very carefully over the shutters until he found the bar that fastened them, and after that his progress was easy.

The bar he got down by main force, as it appeared really to have rusted in its place; and the moment it fell—which, by the by, it did with more noise than it was at all prudent under the circumstances for him to make—the shutters yawned open.

The night happened to be a very dark one, and the window was so begrimed by dirt that he could not see out at all, although he placed his face close to one of the panes.

"It is no matter," he said. "At all events, I will have some air through the window; and if I cannot open it I will smash it."

He felt that by far the better plan was to open the window if he could do so, as that gave him an opportunity of closing the place again, and letting it, to all appearance, wear its usual aspect, whereas, if he had broken one of the panes of glass, it would have been a pretty good hint to the Lady Deliva, if she should look up to the casement from without, that something had taken place in that room not strictly in accordance with her views and intentions.

The window stuck fearfully, so that, in truth, it was anything but an easy matter to open it; nevertheless, after exerting great force to it, Captain Hawk had the satisfaction of feeling it suddenly give way, and he threw it up to half its height.

Oh! how inconceivably delicious the cool night air was as now it came with a rush upon his face! He drank it in as though it had been the most delicious nectar, and so, indeed, it was to him. The sickness and the giddiness which the air of the room had for a time produced, wore off in a moment, and he felt strong and well.

It was so delightful a thing to lean out of the window and to inhale the fresh air, that it was some time before Captain Hawk could pay any attention to anything else whatever. But this extatic feeling changed at last into the calm enjoyment of the fresh air, and he was then able to look about him somewhat.

The first thing that struck him was the fact that the window was all but completely blocked up on the outside by the branches of trees, which had been let grow quite wild right up against it, so that by merely stretching forth his hand he could touch them.

What sort of place it was that the window looked into he had not light enough to see; but he could hardly suppose that it was the garden of the house in which Lady Deliva carried on her unholy practices.

"Oh! for the morning!" he said—"Oh, but for one ray of light to let me see with clearness and precision the secrets of this dreadful place, for I feel conscious that there are secrets connected with it that I am doomed to see, and which will, perhaps, astonish even me."

Once, then, he turned, and looked into the room that was behind him, but all was dark and drear; and, besides, he caught just a sniff of the noxious vapour that was there in abundance; and he was glad to lean out at the window again, to breathe the fresh, cool night air.

As he so leant out, he thought he heard a voice. This was a circumstance of the utmost importance, and Captain Hawk leant from the window and listened with all the intensity he could bring to bear upon the act.

The voice came again upon his ear, and it sounded like one of familiarity. It came nearer and nearer at each moment, and at length was quite close at hand under the tall trees; and he could detect the tones to be those of the Lady Deliva's waiting-woman; but she evidently spoke under great excitement.

"Not sleep?" she said. "Well, is it to be wondered at? I advise that you quit this house at once."

"No—no," replied the Lady Deliva; "oh, God! no!"

"Well, what will you do?"

"I know not. You are as well aware as I am of the fact that I dare not show myself in France. That story of the Chateau of Lunenburgh is still too green to be forgotten."

"Well, but there is Germany open to you."

"No, no; I will yet remain in England some time. Do you know that a soothsayer in India, whose prognostications were never known to fail, told me that it was in England that my destiny was to be fulfilled?"

"I have heard you say so."

"Well, then, torture me no more by this absurd advice to leave it."

"Madam, you are yourself the dupe of the soothsayer, for you seem to think it a sort of obligation upon you to do all you possibly can to carry out his prediction. Does not that strike you as being very absurd?"

"It may be so."

"Oh, madam, it is—it is so. You are safe now—at least you are comparatively safe, and so let me implore you to be wholly so. The day—the dreadful day may come, when you least expect it, when some terrible discoveries [illegible] take place."

"Peace—peace!"

"No. It is my duty to speak to you, and I say, that when possibly you and I least expect it, the secrets of that room of death may be blazoned out to the light of day; and then you will, in the bitterness of your feelings, regret that it is too late to take the advice of one who has always been faithful to you."

"No—no."

"Oh, madam, I say yes. You have been good and kind to me."

"Yes. Have not I made you rich?"

"Yes—yes."

"Have I refused you anything you ever asked of me?"

"No—no."

"Then why come to taunt me? I tell you it is my fate to stay here. You know that my wealth is immense. From my East Indian relatives I inherited a fortune, that even at this moment I scarcely know the extent of."

"Fly, then, from this place."

"The old story. Nothing but flight will serve you."

"Ah, madam, you know that I will not leave you—you know that I am so much attached to you that, much as I wish to leave England, I would not go without you."

"I know that you have bound yourself by such an oath, that even you may well tremble to think of it, to stay here with me—I know that you are well aware that by my gold I could purchase your destruction anywhere, if you were to attempt to leave me. But this is idle. If the consequences of the acts that have been committed in this house are to fall upon my head, they will likewise upon yours."

"I know it—I know it."

"Then be at peace."

"Oh, I wish I could—I wish I could! But, although this is the fifth——"

"Pshaw!"

"I say, this is the fifth murder that has been done by the same means, I never felt so full of fear concerning any of the others as I do about this one; and yet I do not know why it is so. I tremble, madam, in spite of all my efforts not to do so; and it seems as if a voice whispered to me, 'Despair! Your career is nearly at an end. The avenger is abroad!'"

THE WAITERS AT THE HOTEL BOWING HAWK TO HIS CARRIAGE.

"This is idle nonsense," said the Lady Deliva.

"But you, madam, could not sleep."

"I had a dream, as I told you. It was but a dream, though, and from the first moment of awakening my mind recovered from it. I came out here into the fresh air then, as you know I always do when my rest is disturbed by any visions of the night. The day will do as well for me to sleep in as the night, and my rest will not be the less profound with the thought that I have had vengeance upon another faithless one."

"Did you think that this man loved you?"

"I did not care."

"Not care, madam?"

"No. Listen, girl. All I want is

certain civility, and the company of one who will make my solitude less irksome. Perhaps some one might possibly love me a little; but when I find that I am grossly deceived—when I find that it is merely for my money that a few civil nothings were said to me, and then that I am either made the sport of the town, or that even in my own house I find myself forgotten for such a child as Angela, I do feel that I ought to be avenged, and I am."

"You are indeed."

"Well, and properly so. You say there are five who have fallen. Be it so. They all five paid me mock attention. They all five robbed me, and then laughed at me, and so they died."

"Died indeed. Oh, how I shudder as at times I look up at the window of that dreadful room."

CHAPTER CVIII.

CAP AIN HAWK IS IN TIME TO SAVE ANGELA FROM THE RAGE OF LADY DELIVA.

As the waiting-maid pronounced the words with which our last chapter concluded, nothing was more natural than that she should look up at the window of the room to which she alluded.

Captain Hawk, therefore, thought it prudent to draw in his head, for although, secluded as he was, the bougts of the trees seemed quite sufficient to hide him from the sight of the ladies in the garden, to say nothing of the intense darkness of the night, he could not be quite sure of that fact.

There was a silence of several minutes' duration now, or else the Lady Deliva spoke in so low a key that Hawk could not catch the sounds she gave utterance to with his head within the room as it now was.

After a few minutes, though, he ventured again to look out, and then he heard the waiting-maid saying in a low, anxious tone—

"But, my lady, that must be a delusion, I feel assured that it is a delusion; and if I were you I would send Angela far away, and have done with her. You see that it was by her means that this Austrian count was led astray."

"No—no."

"Yes; but, madam, I assure you I heard him speaking to her in such a tone, that there could be no doubt of his feelings towards her. He was quite enslaved by her beauty."

"It has been prophesied that my life is mixed up somehow in hers, and so I dread to kill her."

"Oh, how can it be that you my lady, who are of such a strong and masculine judgment in most things, give way to foolish phrophecies, and lead your attention even to the pretended predictions of human beings like our selves."

"It is of no use addressing me upon that point. I will punish and I will persecute her her; but I will not kill her. Come now to her chamber—you shall assist me. I will have some revenge upon her for the mischief she has done, although, after all, she was only the means of my more rapidly discovering the perfidious heart of the count."

"Well, madam, I have no love for her, and will readily assist you in punishing her as she deserves. Come at once, madam. It will distract your mind from other subjects."

"Confound the hags!" thought Captain Hawk, "they will go and half murder that sweet, quiet Angela, if I do not find some mode of preventing them from so doing. What on earth do they mean to do to her, I wonder? Well, well—I will prevent them, if possible. Ah, there is the faint glow of coming light in the sky. It is the morning."

As Captain Hawk looked over the tree-tops, he could see that the sky was getting each minute a faint glow of light over it; and as it rapidly increased, the twitter of a bird in a tree close at hand convinced him that it was no mistake, but that the morning was really coming.

Captain Hawk now leaned from the window to look for some mode of getting out of the room, so that he might go to the protection of Angela, for the idea that she would be subjected to the revengeful brutality of the Lady Deliva and the waiting maid was one that drove him nearly frantic to think of.

The early dawn had yet not made sufficient progress to enable him to see objects in the room with any degree of distinction, but he saw that there was furniture in it; and as he stepp d across the floor, he thought that there lay some dark object in his path, that he had some difficulty to avoid treading upon.

A sickening sensation came over him at the idea that it might be the corpse of one of the four victims of the passions of the Lady Deliva.

"When light does come," he said, "I shall learn, I expect, some truly terrible secrets connected with this room."

Avoiding, then, as much as possible distracting his mind with other matters, Captain Hawk turned his whole attention towards finding out the secret panel in the wall. Although there was nothing that could possibly be called light in the room, yet the open window and the coming dawn had spread a sort of twilight over the walls, so that he could much easier trace them than he had done before. It was by no means a very good way of proceeding, inasmuch as it incurred the risk of giving alarm; but Captain Hawk found that the only plan to discover which was the movable panel, would be by tapping them with his knuckles in succession.

As good luck would have it, the very second one that he so tapped returned a hollow sound, and he began an eager examination of it with his fingers to find the mode of opening it.

An accident befriended him, for he soon pass d his hand over a small metal nob about the size of a button, and upon pressing it the panel flew open inwards, striking him rather sharply as it did so.

That panel must have closed with great accuracy, for in the room beyond there was a lamp upon the table, and yet not one ray of it had found its way into the apartment where Captain Hawk had been a prisoner. That room was a prettily furnished one, and Hawk had just time to glance around it when he heard approaching footsteps.

The urgency of the moment was such, that, instead of again passing through the panel in the wall to the secret room, which would have been the best mode of proceeding, he simply closed the panel, and then hastily hid himself in the ante-room behind one of the window curtains, which were exceedingly full and handsome, and reached right on to the floor.

Such a place of concealment, if there had been upon the part of the Lady Deliva and her confidant the least idea that any one was there hidden, would have been useless; but Captain Hawk owed his security to the fact that they neither of them could have such an idea.

Scarcely had he fairly hidden himself and arranged the folds of the massive curtain around him than they both entered the room.

The waiting-maid carried a light, and the Lady Deliva had in her hand a rope.

"Oh, there is a lamp here," said the waiting-maid.

"You left it?"

"I did, my lady."

"Are you certain that nothing of the count's was left in the house? What became of his hat?"

"I have hidden it, my lady."

"Well, I leave these minor concerns to you; but the word must be, destroy, not hide."

"Certainly, my lady. Shall we go on?"

"Stop a moment."

The Lady Deliva, with rather a tottering step, approached the panel in the wall, and the impression of Captain Hawk at the moment was that she intended to open it; but such was not her intention. She only placed her ear against it and listened attentively for about half a minute.

"All is still," she said.

"Oh, yes, madam. The poison has done its work long ago, now, you may depend."

"I wonder if the window of this room remains quite secure."

"Assuredly, madam; what can make it otherwise?"

"Nothing—nothing; only I thought just now—but perhaps it was only fancy —I thought that I heard the rattle as of a window-frame shaken by the wind."

"It cannot be, my lady."

"No—no, as you say, it cannot be; and yet how very nervous I feel. I don't know when I have felt so full of all sorts of undefined fears as I do now. What can be the meaning of it?"

"Want of rest and the increasing danger of remaining in this place, my lady. Oh, if I could only persuade you to leave!"

"Hush! no more of that. Let us go now. Where is the rope?"

"Your ladyship has it over your arm."

"Oh, true—true. I did not notice it. Take the light and lead the way, Margaret. At least I will satisfy my vengeance against Angela. She has been for some time enduring the torture of suspense, for, no doubt, she has expected me; and now when she sees me, she will be half dead with fright, for well she knows what she has to expect."

"And serve her right, too," said the waiting-maid.

"Yes—yes. Lead the way."

They both crossed the room and went out at a door on the opposite side of it, leaving the lamp that had been upon the table still burning there.

Captain Hawk in a moment emerged from his place of concealment, and stood listening for some few minutes in silence. Then he strode up to the table and lifted the lamp from it.

"Now is my time," he said, "to find out the precise mode of opening the secret panel from this side."

By the aid of the lamp he soon found a little button of brass in the wall similar to that which by pressure on the other side had opened the panel to let him out of the room. A slight pressure with his thumb now produced a similar result.

"I will leave it open," he said, "so that if after rescuing Angela, which I will do by frightening the Lady Deliva rather than by showing myself if I can, I may get back to this room, which I must before I leave this house make a thorough examination of."

Placing, then, the lamp upon the table as near the exact spot he had taken it from as he could recollect, Captain Hawk went lightly but swiftly after the Lady Deliva and the waiting-maid.

In the fulness of their security, for they did not think that any living soul except themselves and poor Angela were to be found in that portion of the mansion, they left all the doors they passed through open, so that Hawk had no difficulty in following them, and he soon reached either the same velvet curtain past which he had gone upon the former occasion, and which had been put up again in its proper position, or another one so similar to it that it might well be mistaken for it. Then he came to a pause, for he heard voices within the apartment.

In great agitation of mind, for he was fearful that some serious injury might be done to Angela, Captain Hawk now sought for another little hole in the velvet, through which he might peep into the room.

By the aid of his knife, as upon the former occasion, he soon made for himself an orifice in one of the heavy folds of the curtain through which he could peep.

The sight that met his gaze was one that filled him with indignation against the Lady Deliva.

Angela was kneeling upon the floor, and a rope was round her neck, which the Lady Deliva was holding. The poor young girl seemed to be in a terrible state of fear, and the waiting-maid was tying her ancles together with another piece of rope.

"Good heavens," thought Captain Hawk, "they must mean to hang her or to strangle her by these preparations."

Angela was in her night-dress only, and she looked exquisitely beautiful, as with uplifted hands and her eyes streaming with tears, she besought the mercy of the Lady Deliva.

The whole attitude and bearing of the young girl was of the most agonizing description, and it was quite evident, that whatever really were the intentions of the Lady Deliva and the waiting-maid towards her, that she anticipated the very worst fate that could possibly befall her at their hands.

Captain Hawk stood at the curtain for a few moments, irresolutely.

CHAPTER CIX.

THE LADY DELIVA IS A PREY TO SUPERNATURAL FEARS.

PERHAPS it was the beautiful figure and form of Angela that so entranced Captain Hawk, as he there stood at the little opening in the velvet curtain that he had made with his penknife, or perhaps it was that feeling of hesitation which makes us pause while contemplating some scene of terror, to see if our senses are not deceiving us.

It did, indeed, seem to him so very impossible that any one could deliberately injure such a being as Angela, that he might well be forgiven for the doubt of the reality ot what he saw.

The long and beautiful ringlets of the silken hair of the young creature reached to her waist, and as the tears streamed from he eyes they fell upon the thin white robes in which she was enveloped.

"Oh, aunt, aunt," she cried, "have some mercy upon me. Indeed I did not invite that gentleman here."

"Oh, no," said Lady Deliva, "I don't suppose or say for a moment that you did."

"Then what have I done that is wrong?"

"What if I decline saying?"

"Then it is surely unjust as well as cruel to punish me, is it not?"

"Very likely; but whac if I choose to be unjust and cruel both? What then, minx, I ask you? What then, painted doll?"

"Alas, aunt, I do not paint."

"Wretch! I know what you mean by that allusion. You would dare to insinuate that I do."

"Oh, no—no! I did not indeed mean anything of the sort. Is it likely—is it reasonable, that now when I am terrified at the idea of what you may be about to do to me, I should say anything which I might be sure would anger you?"

"Likely or not, you have said it."

"Oh, mercy—mercy."

"Have you tied her ancles together?"

"Yes, my lady," said the waiting-maid.

"Give me, then, that piece of spare rope."

The waiting-maid handed to the Lady Deliva a piece of rope, of about two feet in length, and then the latter said—

"Now you hold the rope that is round her neck, and that will keep her from moving. She cannot kick if you have tied her ancles firmly together."

"Indeed I have, my lady."

"Oh, have mercy upon me, I implore you!" said Angela. "You intend to kill me, I am sure you do. Oh, aunt, aunt, do not take my life! Spare my life, I beg of you. I am too young to die yet, indeed and in truth I am."

"Now," said the Lady Deliva to the attendant.

"Yes, my lady."

Captain Hawk could stand this scene no longer, and just as the waiting-maid laid hold of Angela, and was about to drag her from her knees, he said, in a deep hollow voice—

"Forbear!"

The waiting-maid uttered a shriek of dismay, and the Lady Deliva dropped the piece of rope that she had in her hand, while poor Angela sprang to her feet, and looked about her in as much surprise as alarm, to know where the opportune sound had come from.

"Forbear!" said Captain Hawk again, and then he hastily stepped back, so that he was out of the immediate way of being seen at the curtain, provided they any of them had the courage to move it to look for the origin of the sound

It was some few minutes, though, before any of the party in the little pretty chamber of Angela could recover sufficiently from their surprise to speak at all; and then it was Angela herself who said—

"Oh, aunt, you see that even Heaven interferes to save me, and you will surely be merciful to me now."

"What was it?" said the Lady Deliva, in a strange hoarse whisper—"Oh, what was it?"

The waiting-maid trembled so excessively, that she could not reply to this question of her mistress.

"It was a voice," said Angela.

"What said it?—what said it? Whom did it address?"

"You, aunt, surely."

"Me—me? Oh, no, it did not address me."

"Indeed, aunt, it did, for the voice said 'Forbear!' and that alluded to what you were doing to me, or about to do. So now indeed and in truth you will forbear, will you not?"

"No—no. I must shake off this terror. It is but a delusion. There is some natural and easy explanation of it to be found, I feel assured. I will not be the dupe of my own fears."

As she spoke, the Lady Deliva made a dart forward to the velvet curtain and hastily drew it aside. It was pretty evident that she had expected some rather awful sight to meet her gaze, for it was with a tone of great relief that she uttered the word—

"Nothing!"

"Is there nothing?" said the waiting-maid, now recovering sufficiently to ask the question.

"Nothing—nothing."

"Oh, Heaven! I was afraid——"

"Of what?"

"Alas! I know not. My mind is so full of fears, that I should find it hard to say what I most feared."

"It was nothing. A mere delusion—a fancy. I will not believe that it was a voice."

"A delusion, aunt, and a fancy," said Angela, "may come over the excited senses of one person; but not over those of three at once, and at the same time. That would be too curious a coincidence for human belief. There was a voice, and it said 'Forbear!' twice."

"No! I say, no! Did you hear it?"

"I did, my lady," replied the waiting-maid.

"And what was the object of it? I would ask, what was the object of it? If there be such things as supernatural beings—if it be possible for the disembodied spirit to revisit the world it has flown from, surely the occasion should be a great one."

"It was to save me," said Angela.

"To save you? Fool! I did not intend to kill you."

"But you did intend, aunt, to punish me."

"Why, yes, perhaps I did."

"Ah, then the spirit came to save me."

"No; there is something more in this than I can now understand exactly. A spirit does not come from another world to interfere with the chastisement of a child."

"But I am hardly a child now, aunt."

"Peace! How dare you speak?"

"Let me advise you, my lady," said the waiting-maid. "Give up the present idea of punishing this girl. The daylight will soon be here again, and then a better opportunity can be taken. Let us release her."

"As you please."

"Oh, aunt, I thank you from my heart. Indeed I do."

"Silence! You have nothing to thank me for. Your punishment is but deferred, not given up, I assure you."

"Is it?" thought Captain Hawk. "I will take good care that it is given up, as well as deferred."

The waiting-maid now, with an officiousness that showed how much frightened she had been by the sound of the voice, untied the ancles of the young girl, and took the cord from off her neck; so that she was free again.

"Let us leave this chamber," said Lady Deliva. "Come at once; and as for you, Angela, I leave you yet to reflect upon what you will suffer, for suffer you shall, although you have escaped this time."

Angela made no answer to this; but stood by her little drawing table drying her tears as best she could; and then Captain Hawk thought that it would be but prudent to retreat before the Lady Deliva and her waiting-maid came into the passage in which he was, at the almost certainty of discovering him there, and so getting a ready enough explanation of the mystery of the fearful voice.

The route to the chamber in which they supposed him to be lying in death was but short; and as he had left the panel open for just such an emergency as now had occurred, he passed through it in a moment, and closed it.

Captain Hawk was rather fearful that the sharp snap with which the panel closed might have the effect of startling the Lady Deliva and her waiting-maid; and, indeed, when they reached the room from which the secret panel opened, he found that they had heard something of the little noise.

They both paused, and he heard the Lady Deliva say—

"I tell you I did hear a sound. You must be deaf. It came plainly enough upon my ears."

"What was it, madam?"

"I am afraid to tell myself what it sounded like."

"But tell me."

"Well, then, it was more like the spring of the secret panel than anything else."

"Oh, impossible!"

"So I would fain believe—so I would like to believe that it is impossible."

"It is so. Can the dead rise and open panels? Oh, no—no. There are so very many accidental noises that might assume that character, especially now that your senses are acute from expecting to hear something.

"That is true; but yet—yet——"

"Yet what, my lady?"

"I wish I had courage now to go into that room of death."

"Oh, do not think of it."

"I am afraid to think of it. The very idea of the sights that would there meet my gaze goes far to stop the beating of my heart, and I fear that they would make an impression upon my brain that I should never again be able to rid it of."

"They would, indeed. Let me implore you to pass on. It will drive you mad to stand here and think of entering that dreadful room."

"It will—it will."

The Lady Deliva tottered on after the waiting-maid, who was both full as terrified as her mistress was, only that her terror took a slightly different aspect. The mistress wished, if she could by any possibility have done so, to have found out the cause of the mysterious voice, while the maid had but one idea, and that was to get as speedily as possible out of the immediate proximity of it.

It was rather a relief to Captain Hawk when he found that they had passed on, not that upon reflection he could scarcely think that the Lady Deliva was at all likely to visit that room; but still the mere idea of it was a threat of a disarrangement of his plans.

CHAPTER CX.

CAPTAIN HAWK MAKES SOME AWFUL DISCOVERIES IN THE LADY DELIVA'S HOUSE.

Pending the doubt, if, indeed, it were really one, of whether the Lady Deliva would venture or not into the room where Captain Hawk had taken refuge, he had not had time to look at all about him.

When, however, he felt certain that she had passed on with the sweet and delightful waiting-maid, he was able to turn all his attention to the place in which he found himself.

The morning, during the time that he had been engaged in rescuing Angela from the contemplated cruelty of her aunt, had made considerable progress, and as that room faced the east, it caught more of the early light than it otherwise would have done.

Hawk was quite surprised when he turned from listening at the panel to find how light it was.

And yet a portion of the shutters that he had opened had swung shut, so that there was rather a deep shadow in one part of the apartment, and he hastily advanced to open it. When he had done so, and turned round again, he stood transfixed with horror at the sight that met his gaze in that fearful apartment.

First, as regarded the room itself, it was not above twelve or fourteen feet square at the utmost, and it was rather meanly furnished; but it had another species of furnishing that was really almost too horrible to contemplate.

Lying upon the floor close to Captain Hawk's feet—in fact, he had trodden once upon and once over that loathsome object—lay a dead body in the process of decay, and presenting one of the most horrible spectacles that could be imagined.

The face had fallen in, and the lower jaw had got loose from its articulation, and had fallen upon the breast. The clothes were saturated with the horrible moisture engendered by the decomposition of the soft parts of the body, and crawling out of one of the eyes there was a slimy, shiny-looking insect.

Captain Hawk was certainly not a nervous nor a timid man, but he did shrink from contact with that frightful spectacle with a terror that was vividly depicted upon his face.

That, however, was not the only object of horror in that chamber.

Propped up in a sitting position, in one corner of the room, was another dead body.

This corpse seemed to have stiffened, and partially dried up, as it were, into the attitude it had assumed in death. The face appeared to have a yellow kind of greasy skin drawn over it tightly, without any flesh being beneath it, and the eyes looked like two pieces of bright tin fixed in the great gaping sockets.

"D—n it!" said Hawk, as he turned his eyes away with a shudder, "that is worse than the other."

A couch was in the room, and there lay upon it a mass of something, which, by its shape, there could be no possible mistake about being another dead body.

Captain Hawk had not the remotest desire in the world to approach any closer to it. He was quite content to take all its terrors upon trust for what they were.

And now, as his eyes wandered over the room, he saw, projecting from under the table that was in the centre of it, a pair of boots, and he shuddered as he said—

"By Heaven, that makes four of them!"

Captain Hawk leant upon the window-sill, and asked himself what he should do under the frightful circumstances. It was in vain, though, that he tried to turn his eyes from a contemplation of the frightful objects in the room. They attracted him by a species of horrible fascination that he could not resist, and if he looked from the window for a few moments, with his back towards them, he would suddenly start round as though he fully expected to find them all crowded so close to him.

This was a state of things which would soon have powerfully affected his nervous system, if allowed to continue for any length of time, so he felt the necessity of altering it.

"I cannot stay here," he said. "And yet what on earth am I to do to bring this horrible woman to justice? I dare not appear myself in a court of justice as her accuser of this matter, for there are too many who would be able to point to me and to name me as what I am. No—no, that would not do. I must first make my escape from here, and then think of how to manage her accusation."

With this idea, Captain Hawk measured with his eye the height from the window to the garden below, and he found that it was very considerable, indeed, although where he would fall appeared to be a spot wholly devoted to the dry dead leaves and the refuse of the garden.

After a little time, though, the thought occurred to him that it would be easy enough to descend by the aid of the tree, whose branches all but touched the window.

This was quite conclusive then as regarded the mode by which he was to leave the room. How after that was accomplished he was to get out of the garden unnoticed, was quite another affair, and one that he could come to no decision upon where he was.

"What is to hinder," he said, as he cast another fearful glance at the festering remains of poor mortality that were in the room. "What is to hinder me from giving secret information to the police? Then they can come and take possession of the house, and soon find enough to criminate the Lady Deliva without any help of mine in the matter. Ah, that will be the way."

He gave this idea some more attentive thought before he left the room, and it struck him, lest there might be any mismanagement on the part of the police that would give the Lady Deliva time to effect another disposition of her victims that it would be as well for him to have some sort of evidence of their having been there.

"If I could find anything belongin

HAWK AND MARIA IN THE CONSERVATORY.

to one, or, indeed, each of them, and send that as a token to the police, it would be as well," he said, as he slowly approached the bodies.

The one that was upon the floor first attracted his attention, and he saw something glittering about the dead hand as he looked.

"A ring!" he exclaimed. "The very thing."

It was the very thing, but the idea of stooping to possess himself of it was not at all the very thing.

Captain Hawk, though, was in full dress, and he wore a court sword, so that it served capitally to spare him the pain and the disgust of touching the corpse with his fingers. With the point of his sword he poked the ring away from the dead finger, and then picked it up.

From the look of it he thought that

it was a gem of some rather considerable value, and so he thought that in the hands of the police it would, in all probability, be a capital means of identifying that body.

Advancing, then, to the one that sat up by the wall in so awful a manner, he looked to see if there was anything about it that would serve as a memorial of its presence there.

When he came to make a minute investigation of this body, he found that it was in a military uniform, which only in some instances had rotted and fallen from the pestiferous limbs.

A gorget, or the half moon shaped piece of silver that officers of a certain rank used to wear round the neck, rested upon the breast of the corpse. It was very black with tarnish; but a touch from the point of Captain Hawk's sword not only disengaged the gorget, but gave a slight impulse to the body; so that, with a rattle of the old bones, it fell forward upon its face in a heap on the floor.

Captain Hawk started back out of its way, as well he might, without any disparagement of his courage.

This was altogether a sickening task that he had set himself; but he was so intent upon getting together evidence that would have the effect of convicting Dady Deliva, that, notwithstanding all his repugnance to it, he carried it out.

From one of the other corpses he took a diamond knee-buckle, and from the last one he took the only portable thing he could find, which was the sword; but he broke the blade off, and only preserved the hilt, upon which there was a coronet engraved, and a cipher, which would, no doubt, lead to its satisfactory identification.

Thus, there was nothing that Captain Hawk had possessed himself of that was very heavy, while everything was very much to the purpose, and likely to be such as in the hands of the police would lead to a full discovery of what had been the violence of the Lady Deliva's jealous rage.

The next object, then, of Hawk's was to get from the place without being seen; so that the murderess should have no opportunity of escape before the arm of justice could reach her.

Approaching the window, he found that he could in the easiest manner in the world get on to a very thick branch of the tree; and it was with no small gratification that he bade adieu to the chamber of death, in which he had passed so much time.

He took the precaution, as he could easily do it from the the branch of the tree, to shut the window; so that if by daylight the Lady Deliva should take a look up there, she would not be able to say that the window had been touched, inasmuch as from the height that it was from the ground, and the dazzling nature of the glass, it would be very difficult for her to take upon herself to say that the shutters were open.

However, Captain Hawk ventured that, and rapidly descended from the tree.

When he touched the ground, which at the foot of the tree was a beautiful green sward, he stopped and listened for some few minutes, in order to discover if any one was in the garden or not.

All was still.

Captain Hawk now advanced in as direct a line as he could from the house through the trees; but he had not gone very far before he heard a footfall, and he paused and hid behind the trunk of a large tree, when in a few moments he saw a man with a wheelbarrow full of dead leaves, which he seemed to be taking in the very direction that he, Captain Hawk, had so recently come from.

To let this man pass him was the easiest thing in the world; and when he had got a considerable distance off, Hawk ran on again through the garden, seeking for some outlet from it.

After this there was no great difficulty in getting through the garden; and Captain Hawk reached a low wall, which he could, by standing upon the exposed roots of an old tree, just look over. That wall bounded the garden of the Lady Deliva's house in that direction from the Green Park.

"Free at last!" thought Hawk, as he made a spring at the wall, and caught the top of it.

To a young man of his strength and activity it was but the work of a moment to surmount the wall and to spring into the park on the other side of it.

At that lonely hour no one was about, so that he could not only congratulate himself upon his escape from the Lady Deliva and her machinations, but likewise on the perfect secrecy of the whole transaction so long as he chose.

CHAPTER CXI

CAPTAIN HAWK DENOUNCES THE LADY DELIVA TO THE MAGISTRACY.

THE night of anxiety and excitement that Captain Hawk had passed told a little even upon his iron constitution; and had he consulted his own feelings he would have at once sought repose.

He felt, though, that the knowledge he possessed of the frightful secrets of the Lady Deliva's house was such that he dared not keep it to himself. The danger, too, that the young girl was in formed to him a powerful motive to immediate action.

Still, he walked hastily across the park in the direction of his hotel, for the scramble through the garden and over the wall had not impaired his apparel; and he felt that however urgent might be the necessity of some immediate course of action upon his part regarding the guilt of the Lady Deliva, it must be, for his own sake, carefully considered in all its bearings.

The reader can easily conceive that Hawk did not by any means covet an interview with the magistracy of London upon any subject; for that he would be recognised as the man so recently tried for the murder of Judge Holme, was so clear a fact, that he shrunk naturally enough from making so great a sacrifice as his personal liberty, and perhaps his life even, for the sake of getting the better of the Lady Deliva, and surrendering her up to justice.

Hawk felt that what was to be done must be done in some way without compromising himself, and there was the difficulty of the whole transaction—a difficulty which he turned over in his mind carefully as he proceeded to the hotel.

When he reached the door of that establishment, the first person he saw was Joe, with a look of great anxiety upon his face. The moment Joe saw the captain, though, his whole expression changed; and while a broad grin came over his features, he cried out—

"Why, odds bobs, there you are again!"

"What do you mean?"

"Mean, captain? Why, I—oh, I mean, my lord—I mean that I thought you were nabbed to a certainty."

"You have no busines to think. Stay where you are; I shall have need to send you on a message soon, I dare say."

"All's right. Any luck with the petticoats?"

"Hold your noise, idiot!"

Hawk entered the hotel, and made his way to the brilliant suite of rooms that he had taken. He flung himself into a seat, and drew a long breath of exquisite relief as he did so, for he felt that he had never been nearer death than he had been on that night that, with all it's wild excitements and terrors, had just passed away.

In a few moments Captain Hawk was fast asleep.

The young girl in the magnificent chamber at the Lady Deliva's—Lady Deliva herself, and the horrors of the chamber of death in her mansion, were all forgotten now by Hawk, and he was only aroused by a sudden crash in the room that made him start with surprise and apprehension to his feet.

Joe was there, and a large tureen which had contained some rich-looking soup lay in fragments on the floor.

"Now, you have done it," said Joe. "There you go again!"

"You scoundrel!" cried Hawk; "what do you mean by this?"

"Oh, go it—go it; lay it to me!"

"You?"

"Yes; I can bear it,—say it was me—say I broke it. Oh, dear, I quite expected you would when I saw it go."

"Explain yourself, scoundrel. What do you mean? Did you not drop the tureen, which I don't know how you had here at all? Did you not drop it while I slept for a few minutes, you unmitigated rascal?"

"A few minutes! Oh, lor! Why, it's two o'clock."

Captain Hawk staggered back a step or two, as he repeated Joe's words—

"Two o'clock!"

"Yes, to be sure; you have been asleep in that easy chair just seven hours and a half."

"Seven hours and a half?"

"Just so."

"She is lost—she is lost! Oh, fool —fool that I am!"

"Well," said Joe, "that's yourself, mind. Don't say I called you a fool. It's all your own doing, you know."

"Wretch! idiot! Why did you not awaken me?"

"Well, now, that is a good one. Here have I been abused and called all sorts of things a little while ago, because I did wake you, and now I'm a wretch, and an idiot, because I didn't. Well, this is too bad."

Captain Hawk felt strongly inclined at the moment to rush upon Joe, and throttle him, but he controlled the impulse, which was a thing he very seldom did regarding any of his impulses, and making a great effort to appear calm, he said—

"Tell me at once the truth. Is this some nonsense of your own? is it, indeed, two o'clock in the day, Joe?"

"It is as true as gospel."

"And I came in about seven, or earlier. Oh, what may not have happened in all these hours? Oh, why did I give way to this fatal inducement to sleep? I that had upon my hands such a momentous affair—I that knew so well what I had to do—I that brought the relics of death with me as evidence of what horrors I had seen! Oh, fatal —fatal sleep!"

As he spoke he took from his pocket the officer's gorget, and the ring, that he had brought away from the room of murder at the Lady Deliva's, and cast them upon the table in the centre of the room.

Joe looked at him and then at the articles with amazement. He picked up the gorget, and turned it over and over without being able to make anything of it, and then he looked at the ring and shook his head, and then he looked at Captain Hawk, who he began to entertain strong suspicions had gone out of his mind.

Hawk strengthened this idea in a few moments, by exclaiming—

"Joe—Joe, I shall go mad!"

"You won't have far to go," said Joe.

"What do you say, you villain?"

"Oh, nothing. Take it easy, that's all I have to say. But I'll just tell you how the soup came to go down. You see, the landlord came, and says he— 'It's lunch time, it is,' says he, 'and there's some of the finest soup in the world ready for the prince, if he will have it,' so I says to him, 'Dish it up at once,' says I, 'for he may wake up by the time it's all ready;' so the fellow brought it, and then, as you didn't wake, I thought I should like to have a taste, but I wasn't going to be such a beast as to use the spoon that you would have to use, so I just took up the tureen itself to take a drop out of, and at that very moment, who would believe it, you gave a sort of a kick and a groan, and says you—'No —no,' says you, 'I will save her!' Well, this took me a bit by surprise, so the blessed soup-tureen being rather greasy, came through my fingers like a piece of soap, and down it went, as you see it, and if that wasn't all through you, I don't know what was."

"Two o'clock!" groaned Hawk, as he paced the room to and fro, without paying the least attention to what Joe was saying. "Two o'clock. Alas! alas!"

"A lass, is she?" said Joe.

"Silence, wretch! Stop. Something must be done at once. It is just possible that it may not be too late."

"Oh, yes, it is too late," said Joe. "The soup has all soaked into the carpet, and all the mops in the world would not get it up now."

"Joe?"

"Yes. Here you is."

"If you don't be quiet, I'll blow the few brains you have out. You know me, and that I am very likely to fulfil such a promise when once I make it, so if you value your existence, you will only answer me when I speak to you."

Joe knew the captain too well to think for a moment that any such threat from him could be considered in the light of a joke; so in reply to it, he just nodded his head, and was silent.

"Now be quiet for half-an-hour, if I

don't speak to you," added Hawk, "and if I do, be attentive."

Joe nodded, again.

Captain Hawk then took a chair, and placed it next to one of the walls of the room, and sitting down in it with his face to the back of it, and resting his arms there, he hid his face completely, and amid darkness and abstraction from everything in the room, he deeply thought over what was the best course to pursue with regard to the Lady Deliva and the young girl, who could not be now, at all events, considered in any other light than as her captive.

In ten minutes Hawk sprang to his feet.

"Joe?"

"Here you is."

"Writing materials."

Joe placed before Hawk a little table, upon which were pens, paper, and ink; and then Hawk wrote as follows:—

"To the Secretary of State for the Home Department.

"My lord,—On condition that your lordship will give me your word of honour that an incognito, which it is my humour to observe in this business, shall be respected by the police, and by all acting with them, I can and will disclose what has become of the two gentlemen, one of whom owns the gorget I enclose, and the other the ring.

"A few words to the effect I have stated, given to the messenger of this note, will satisfy me, and I will be with you as soon as possible with my information.

"Hoping your lordship will excuse the character of this note, as the appearance of want of respect in it is only apparent, and not real, I remain, my lord,—

"Your lordship's obedient servant,
"MASK."

This note Captain Hawk rapidly wrote and wrapped up along with the gorget and the ring that he had taken from two of the dead bodies in the Lady Deliva's chamber, and he addressed the packet to the Secretary of State for Home Affairs.

"Now, Joe," he said, "attend to me."

"Rather," said Joe.

"You must take this to Downing Street, and wait for an answer. If the secretary is not there, you will say that the matter is of such importance that one of the messengers or clerks must go with you to his house. They will be afraid to refuse your request. When you get there, you are to refuse to to answer any questions; but if you get a note addressed to 'Mask,' you will bring it to me at once."

"All's right."

"You are sure, now, that you understand all that?"

"Quite."

"Then be off with you."

Joe ran out at the door of the room down the stairs, and at a swinging trot on he went to the office of the secretary of state in a minute.

"That is done," said Hawk, "and I hope well done. I could have done it in another way; but then I should have missed the chance of looking upon that young girl again, and that I would not have missed for worlds. Oh, she is truly beautiful! If, now, it should be too late?—If it should really happen that the Lady Deliva and her odious waiting-maid have sacrificed her to their interest?—I must not think of that, or I shall go distracted. No, I will not think of that."

CHAPTER CXII.

THE LADY DELIVA STANDS UPON A MINE, BUT KNOWS IT NOT.

CAPTAIN HAWK could not take upon himself exactly to say how his letter would be received by the secretary of state, so he prepared himself accordingly.

Of one thing, however, he felt quite assured, and that was, that they would get nothing out of Joe; and, therefore, that, let the reception of the letter be what it might, they would not be a whit the nearer the discovery of who it was that had sent it.

With this feeling, or rather conviction, Captain Hawk knew that he had nothing in the world particularly to fear.

"And now," he said, "for the proceedings that will be necessary. If the proposal I have made to give the information should be entertained just in the way that I point out, I must be ready to lose no time."

In the small vallise that Captain Hawk had brought with him to London, there were many little articles which he would not exactly have been desirous should have been seen by all the world.

Among these things were materials for so disguising his really handsome and youthful face, that those who knew him best would have failed to recognise him. Of course, with the police, admitting that he should have been in their power, such disguises would be useless, because they would easily discover which was false in feature and which was true; but he did not now set to work to metamorphose himself with any idea of imposing upon the police, except as they might merely look upon him without thinking of laying hands upon him. He was just making himself up in case the answer of the secretary of state should be in accordance with his wish.

He thought it would be.

From the vallise Hawk took a pair of false moustachoes, with which he graced his upper lip. Whiskers, of which he had various, were likewise added to his face; and then he covered all the upper part of his face down to the end of his nose with a close-fitting mask of black velvet.

With such a disguise he felt quite certain no one could possibly recognise him, let them know him ever so well.

A glance in the large chimney-glass quite satisfied him as to that fact; and he felt quite at ease as to his incognito.

All his anxiety now was for the speedy return of Joe.

To be sure, Joe had not been gone long enough to get back, even if all had gone quite well with him, and if none of the delays and difficulties of transacting business with great official personages interposed to delay him. But Hawk walked to and fro with hasty and impatient steps in the gorgeous apartment at the hotel, notwithstanding.

"Confound him!" he muttered; "why don't he come? Is it a failure or not, I wonder? What on earth can detain him? Shall I or shall I not have an opportunity of looking again into the eyes of that fair being, who, with all her innocence and all her beauty, I saved from the merciless Lady Deliva?"

Each moment now that passed without the arrival of Joe was an hour of agonising anxiety to Captain Hawk; and at last, when he heard his footstep upon the stairs, or what he supposed was it, he made a rush at the door of the room; and opening it rapidly, sprang on to the stair-landing, and cried out—

"Well, the answer?"

"Oh, lor!" cried a waiter, who was just coming up with a rather heavy tray of glasses, and whose cautious and rather heavy footsteps with such a load had been mistaken by Hawk for the clumsy tread of Joe—"oh, lor!". and then backwards he went with all the glasses; and the crash in the hall below when he reached it was something truly tremendous.

"The devil!" said Hawk, as he returned to his room again. "Confound the fool!—what is he alarmed at, I wonder?"

Hawk caught a glance of himself in one of the mirrors, and then he recollected the mask that he had on, and which, no doubt, had struck the waiter as being such an extraordinary object, that he fell, as we have described, in sheer fright.

Hawk took off the mask, and flung himself into a chair.

"Everything crosses me," he said. "Now it will go all over the house that I wear a mask at times. Curses on—Ah!—another footstep! No—I will not go out to that. It may be some other blundering fool, and not Joe."

It was Joe, though, this time, for in another moment Joe entered the room.

Captain Hawk sprang at him as though he intended to knock him down, as he cried—

"The answer—the answer!"

"Murder!" said Joe. "Don't hold a feller by the throat in that 'ere sort of way, I beg—oh don't!"

"The answer, then!"

"Very good. I'll tell you."

"Quick—quick!"

"Now, do let a fellow draw his breath just a little, now. You know, that it's always best to let a man tell his story his own way. I've had, rather, I should say, a race for it."

"A race?"

"Yes, to be sure."

"Why—why—they did not attempt to arrest you? They are not such absolute idiots as to carp at information of consequence, just because they did not happen to know who it came from? You have not had to run for your life, or your liberty?"

"Well, I don't know about life and liberty. You see, captain—I mean my lord count—but there has been a fellow with such long legs as never was seen after me all the way here; and if I had not doubled upon him, he would have found out where I was coming to, and that was what I didn't intend."

"Certainly not. Well?"

"Well, in the first place, I'm as thirsty as possible."

Captain Hawk at once flung a jug of cold water in the face of Joe, as he said—

"Now go on."

"Oh, lor!" said Joe, as he wiped his streaming face. "Now, isn't that like him? If anybody had told me he would have done that, I should have said, 'In course he will—in course he will.'"

"Go on! Have you seen the secretary?"

"I have. You see, when I got to the office of the secretary, the first person I saw was a fellow with a golden collar to his coat, and he cried out, 'Hilloa! where are you going, now? Stop!—hoi!' But I only put out my foot, and down he fell on his nose; and then another came up, and says he, 'Who are you?'"

"You barbarous wretch!" cried Hawk, "never mind what you said to a parcel of flunkies, or what they said to you. Come to the point."

"I'm a-coming. Well, there was a row, and in the middle of the row up came a carriage, and a little gentleman he gets out of it with a pair of silk stockings on, and a sword by his side; so up I went to him, and I said, 'My little one, I have got a letter for the secretary of state. Where can I find him?'

"'Give it to me,' he said, 'and I'll take care he has it.'

"'You had better,' said I; 'for if I find you play any tricks with it, I'll break every bone in your skin.'

"Well, the little man only bowed and smiled, and in he went, and I sat down in the hall to wait; and the flunkies, they kept chattering and laughing to themselves, and grinning at me, till I was half a mind to have a right go-in among them, and just teach them some manners, when out flew the little man who had had the letter, and he came out as if he was mad.

"'Who brought this ring? Who brought this ring? Where is the man? Oh, where is he?'

"'There, my lord!' cried all the flunkies at once; and then I found out that the little man was the secretary of state himself."

"Common sense might have told you as much," said Hawk.

"Oh, might it? Well, it didn't, then, and more shame for it, as you seem to think it ought."

"Go on—go on."

"Well, says he to me, all in a fluster-like, while his little wig seemed to be standing up on end on his little head, 'Did you bring this letter?'

"'I did,' says I.

"'Seize him!' said he.

"Well, thereupon three or four of the flunkies made a rush forward, and laid hold of me; but I pretty soon made clear work of them, for I took them up one after the other, and flung them into the street; and then the little secretary called out—

"'Stop! stop! I will soon give you the assurance you require.'

"'I don't know what you mean,' says I, 'by giving me the assurance. All I can say is, that I have had so much of the assurance of your men, that I don't want any more of it.'

"'Excuse them,' says he, 'and step this way.'

"Well, I followed him into a sort of a room that had a lot of maps hanging on the wall, and on the table in the middle of the floor such heaps of papers and letters, that if you wanted any particular one among all the lot, you might go on wanting it for I don't know how long before there would be any chance of finding it. The little man here then sat down, and giving a sort of groan, he said—

"'My good sir, I do not defend Charles; but the fact is, he was my brother, and so I felt rather severely his disappearance.'

"'Oh, did you?' said I.

"'Yes,' says he, 'I did. This ring is a dreadful confirmation of his death. Alas! alas!'

"'Very likely,' said I.

"'There,' he said, 'there,' as he wrote a few words, 'that is the protection you require. And now I wait your direction what to do.'

"'My lord,' said I, "this is some slight mistake. I am not the man.' Upon that he made quite a start; but I told him that I came from my master, who was a gentleman, and that I would take him back the answer, and that I myself knew nothing about what he was talking of.

"'True,' he said, 'the note said that you were but a messenger; but I thought that you were in all probability the principal himself; but as it is not so, here is the note required, and you can say to your master that I will wait here till he comes.' So after that, off I came with the answer."

"Where is it?"

"Here, to be sure. In my hat—no—yes, here it is. But I must tell you that just as I came out of his room, I saw him touch a funny little piece of wire that was on the chimney-piece, and then a small bell rang. I didn't take any notice of it at first; but I soon found what it meant."

"What did it mean?"

"Why, that I was to be followed, for I saw a fellow coming after me; but I soon got the better of him, I promise you."

"You have conducted the affair very well, Joe. Now, just be quiet while I read the note."

Captain Hawk hastily opened the secretary's note, and found it to contain the following words:—

"To Mask.

"The secretary of state promises to hold 'Mask' harmless in all that may occur with relation to his communication, and to respect his incognito himself, and cause all under his control to respect it."

"That will do," said Hawk. "Joe?"

"Yes, captain—I mean, my lord."

"Order a hackney-coach; but don't bring it to the door of the hotel. Be with it at the corner of the street."

Joe was off in a moment; and then Hawk, who had taken off the little half mask of velvet with which he had unwittingly frightened one of the waiters, put it on again, and wrapping a cloak about him, and slouching his hat down upon his brows, he left the house.

At the corner of the street Joe had a hackney-coach in readiness, and Captain Hawk at once sprang into it.

"Get up with the coachman, Joe," he said, "and tell him to drive to the secretary of state's."

CHAPTER CXIII.

THE NIGHT EXPEDITION TO THE HOUSE OF THE LADY DELIVA.

A BOLDER manœuvre of Captain Hawk's than this to visit the secretary of state in disguise could not very well, considering the very ticklish situation in connexion with the police that he, Hawk, was in, be conceived.

Nothing but the intense desire to see the beautiful young girl again who was in charge of the Lady Deliva could possibly have induced him to make such a movement in the affair.

Of course, there was as well the desire to bring the Lady Deliva to justice for the murders that she and her waiting-maid had committed of such a dastardly and truly wicked character, that even he, Captain Hawk, who, as the reader well knows, was not very particular, felt shocked and horrified at her base conduct.

The coach went rather more rapidly than hackney coaches usually did, for the directions to drive to the office of the secretary of state had got up an idea in the mind of the coachman that his fare was some passenger of great importance.

Acting upon this notion, the coachman put his horses to their mettle, and eventually drew up to the door of the secretary of state's office with quite a rush.

The hall was quite crowded by foot-

HAWK ADMIRING THE BEAUTY OF THE MARCHIONESS OF POODLETON'S DAUGHTER

men now, and as Hawk alighted he felt the full danger of his position.

A gentlemanly-looking man, in plain clothes, stepped up, and in a low voice said to him--

"Are you Mask?"

"Behold!" said Hawk, as he slightly raised his hat and lowered his cloak, so that the velvet mask might be seen.

"That will do, sir. Please to follow me."

"I will."

The private secretary of the minister, for such this man was, led the way to the same room in which Joe had had his audience with the great men; and then turning to him, he said—

"Pray be seated. His lordship will be here in a few moments. He has been rather indisposed."

"Since my messenger was here?" asked Hawk.

"Yes, sir."

"Tell him I will wait his leisure, but that yet it will be as well to move in this affair as quickly as possible. I am sorry that by accident I have lost too much time."

"I will, sir."

The private secretary left the room, and Captain Hawk had time to look about him a little. There was the room, just as Joe had described it, with the maps upon the walls, and the table in the centre, so covered with papers, that to find any particular one seemed as if indeed it would be a work of serious labour.

In other respects, the room was but meanly furnished, and it was evidently one devoted entirely to business.

While Hawk was slowly turning in his seat in order to look about him the more easily, another door opened than that at which the private secretary had left him, and two gentlemen entered the room.

One of them was the secretary of state, and Captain Hawk, if he had not often seen him before, would have known him by Joe's description of him. The other was a tall, soldier-like looking man.

They both advanced to Hawk, who rose and bowed to them.

"Sir," said the secretary, "did you bring this letter—or, I should rather say, did you send this letter about an hour ago?"

Captain Hawk took a glance at the open letter in the hands of the secretary, as he said—

"I did."

"Then I implore you——"

"Stop, George," said the tall gentleman; and then advancing to Captain Hawk, he said—"Hark you, sir; you bring or you send information, accompanied by such a token as stamps your communication with an air of truth, that the brother of his lordship here is murdered. Now, I need not, I daresay, tell you that you stand in rather an awkward position in this affair."

"I don't see it," said Hawk. "But pray go on, sir. Let me have the benefit of all you have to say."

"You shall, sir. I think that you ought to be immediately taken into custody; but his lordship is induced to be lenient, and to give you the opportunity of making the disclosures you promise; so mind that we have nothing but the truth from you, or you will repent it."

"You are insolent, sir," said Hawk.

"Insolent? Dare you speak so to me?"

"Dare I? Indeed, I dare. I am the one to say, how dare you speak as you have done to me? Again I say, sir, you are insolent; and were it not that I wish the guilty to be brought to justice, and to satisfy the feelings of his lordship as far as I can respecting the fate of his brother, I would from this moment decline giving any further information upon the subject."

"Give him into custody!—give him into custody at once!"

"Why, you blundering ass!" said Captain Hawk, "what on earth induced his lordship here to call you into counsel?"

"What, sir!" cried the military-looking man, stamping with rage. "Do you call me an ass?"

"A blundering ass!" said Hawk.

"Do you know who I am, sir."

"I have just told you."

"I am the Duke of Montrose, sir!"

"If you were ten Dukes of Montrose, you would still, in this matter, be a blundering ass. You are the commander-in-chief of the army, I believe; but it is quite clear you are very much out of place in such an affair as this."

"Come—come," said the secretary. "Don't let us have any quarrelling."

"My lord," said Hawk, sharply.

"Yes—yes."

"Is this, or is this not your handwriting?"

As he spoke, Hawk produced the letter that Joe had brought to him.

"It is," said the minister.

"Then do you mean, or do you not mean, to abide by its conditions?"

"I—a—that is——"

"Pshaw!" said the duke, as he took up the letter that Hawk had laid upon the table before the secretary. "Of course this is of no consequence now. It was quite necessary to write it to get you here."

"I beg to inform your grace," said Hawk, "that that note is mine."

"Stuff!"

"Please to hand it to me."

"No such thing."

With a bound like a lion springing upon his prey, Captain Hawk flew at the Duke of Montrose, who measured his length upon the floor, while Hawk then calmly put the note into his pocket.

"Help!—help!" cried the secretary.

"Oh, my lord, there is no danger," said Captain Hawk—"none in the least, I assure you."

The private secretary rushed into the room, and the Duke of Montrose slowly rose to his feet.

"What has happened, my lord?" said the private secretary.

"Nothing, I think," said the minister. "Montrose, are you hurt?"

"So much that somebody's blood must pay for it, and so little that I shall be able to avenge an insult."

"Your grace is quite a conjurer," said Captain Hawk. "I congratulate you upon your keeping your temper. I will give you all the satisfaction you can possibly desire at any time."

"If I could but think or know that you were a gentleman," muttered the duke, "I would soon send to you."

"Your grace may be easy upon that score. I believe that there has been a duel at the back of Moutague House recently that has deprived fashionable society of one of its ornaments, if a professed duellist could be called such. I was there."

"Ah, did you kill the colonel?"

"They say he is dead."

"And Lord Noddie was your second?"

"His lordship did me that honour."

The duke and the secretary looked at each other, and then the private secretary, who had left the room, came into it again, and handed the minister a slip of paper, at which he smiled as he handed it to the Duke of Montrose, who smiled likewise.

"You are very polite, gentlemen," said Hawk, rather sarcastically.

"Excuse us," said the minister, as he took the slip of paper from the duke, and handed it to Hawk; "read it for yourself."

Hawk saw with some surprise and amusement these words upon the paper—

"He wears the same stockings and knee-buckles that the supposed Prince of Austria wore at the entertainment in Spring Gardens."

"Oh, indeed!" said Hawk.

The minister now bowed, as he said, "Pardon me for penetrating your incognito; but I rather think I speak to the prince of the house of Austria, who is in London upon some mission for which he has not yet received his credentials."

"I have not yet received my credentials," said Hawk.

The Duke of Montrose looked a little confused at the turn that the affair had taken, and he said—

"Well, how should I have known who it was?"

"Your grace might, at least, have been liberal enough to be assured that I might be a gentleman before you could possibly have any evidence to the contrary," said Captain Hawk; "but if you are satisfied, I am."

The duke bit his lips, as he said—

"I will consider."

"Do so, your grace; but don't fatigue your intellects too much in the effort."

"Sir?"

"Well, sir?"

"Really—really," said the secretary of state, "allow me to hope that this truly ridiculous quarrel may not go any further."

"I don't know that," said the duke. "But in the meantime, I think that I can be of no further service here."

"And I am sure of it," said Captain Hawk.

"I take my leave," added the duke, as he cast a furious look at Captain Hawk—"I take my leave, and perhaps the prince of the house of Austria will hear from me."

"Well, I hope not," said Hawk; "for if I do, I am quite certain it will be something very foolish."

The duke was boiling with rage, and rushed out of the room, and left the house in such a state of aggravation, that the flunkies in the hall looked at each other aghast as he passed them.

Captain Hawk then, in a mild, sweet tone of voice, such as he knew well how to assume, now addressed the secretary, saying—

"I am sorry, my lord, that you took one into your counsel who is so singularly unfitted for any rational exercise of thought; but now I am quite ready to enter fully into this affair, and can only deeply regret that so much valuable time has been wasted."

"So do I," said the secretary; "but the fact was, that the gorget you sent belonged to a cousin of the duke's, and that was what made me send to consult with him on the matter."

CHAPTER CXIV.

CAPTAIN HAWK SUCCEEDS IN RESCUING THE YOUNG LADY FROM DELIVA HOUSE.

The manner of the secretary of state towards Captain Hawk was now so very different to what it had been in the first instance, that Hawk could not fail being highly amused by the effect that his assumption of the princedom of Austria produced.

The secretary would make him come into his own private apartment, which was fitted up with great splendour, and then pressed him to be seated, and urged him to take some refreshment.

Now, the fact was, that Hawk was beginning to feel quite faint for want of something to eat, for the agitation and the worry of mind that he had been in for so many hours had prevented him from taking proper care of his stomach; so he said at once—

"I shall be grateful, my lord, for a glass of wine and something to eat; and I can manage to tell you what it is necessary for you to know while I take a slight repast, for I am indeed in want of one."

His lordship seemed delighted that the Prince of Austria should make himself so much at home as he now did. A silver tray was soon produced with wine and a cold collation upon it, to which Hawk took good care to do justice, for he could not exactly say how long it might be before he had another opportunity of satisfying his appetite, since he had quite made up his mind to go with the party that, no doubt, would be soon got together for the attack of the house of the Lady Deliva.

"Now, my lord," he said, "let me tell you all."

"I shall listen with profound interest."

Captain Hawk felt the necessity of mentioning some other motive than his real one for visiting the Lady Deliva, so he said—

"The fact is, my lord, that by accident I became aware of the fact that in a certain house in this great city a young girl of surpassing loveliness was kept in a state of bondage, and cruelly treated at times. I have always been something of a knight-errant, and I made up my mind to see her, and if I found the circumstances such as I had heard, to rescue her."

"And very proper too."

"I am glad your lordship thinks so. Well, after trying many devices and finding them all fail, I hit upon one that succeeded."

"What a good thing."

"That one was to ingratiate myself into the good graces of the old female sinner who held the young girl in bondage, and, under the pretence of visiting her as her admirer, so get admission to the house, which otherwise I found was, with my limited knowledge of the locality and of the topography of it, quite impregnable."

"Capital—capital! And you succeeded, prince?"

"I did, as you shall hear."

After this point in the story, Captain Hawk was not at all embarrassed in what he had to say, for he had nothing to conceal except that he had induced the Lady Deliva to give him the cheque for the two thousand pounds. The colouring he gave to that part of the transaction was, that the Lady Deliva had forced the money upon him as a present, in testimony of her regard for him.

With this exception, then, he told the whole story, and the secretary of state listened to it with the most profound attention. At its conclusion, he said—

"Good Heavens, who would have thought there could be such wickedness in the soul of woman?"

"The Lady Deliva, my lord," said Captain Hawk, "is an exception to what woman usually is, and only proves the rule that she is an angel."

"You are very gallant to the sex, prince; but, really, the waiting-maid is another exception, I presume?"

"Quite so."

"Well, in return for the kind confidence you have had in me, I will tell you that the ring you sent in the packet that so luckily reached my hands, for I was going out of town in an hour, was the property of my brother, Lord Marsh. I scarcely need tell you that the life he led was anything but creditable to his family, and that he was a perpetual source of anxiety and vexation to me. About four months ago he suddenly disappeared, and from that time to the present nothing whatever has been heard of him. There can be no doubt now, though, of his fate."

"I fear not, my lord."

"He lies in that dreadful chamber, at the house of the Lady Deliva, from which you alone have escaped to tell the tale of horror."

"Even so, my lord."

The secretary seemed to be for a few moments deeply affected, for even secretaries of state have at times actual hearts to feel like ordinary men, notwithstanding the absence of such a commodity is a great element in the success of a public man in this as well as in other countries.

"Well, well," he said at length, "if he had not fallen in the way he has, there is no doubt but that some duel would have been the end of him, for he was perpetually engaged in some such transaction with enraged fathers, husbands, brothers, or lovers."

"Was he, indeed?"

"It is too true that he was."

"But what, my lord, could have been his inducement to seek the Lady Deliva? Surely he did not fall in love with her? Did he, too, like me, hear of the paragon of beauty she had hidden in her house?"

"It is possible. But I am afraid a baser motive took him there, and that he went just to get money out of the old woman, under the pretence of admiring her; and that, then, she finding out the hollowness of his professions, treated him as she tried to treat you."

"To a cup of poisoned coffee?"

"Just so. That, I fear, is the fact. But it is my duty now to lose no time in the arrest of this woman. What do you advise as the best mode to set about it, prince?"

"I have thought over that," said Captain Hawk. "The days are but short, now, and it is nearly five o'clock. In an hour and a half longer it will be absolute twilight; so I would, although it goes much against me to do so, advise that we wait till then, and at that hour get together a party of four or five men, who can be thoroughly depended upon, to enter the house by the garden—in fact, by precisely the same way that I left it."

"That will do; and you may depend that I will inform you quickly of the result of the expedition."

"No, my lord, I will inform you. I cannot stay away. I will go with the party."

"Oh, but, prince, suppose some accident should occur to you? It would be a lasting source of regret to us all if anything took place in our capital to take the life of so illustrious a personage as yourself."

"Do not think of that, my lord. I will take care of myself. I think I am pretty well qualified to do that; and, besides, I shall be the most efficient guide the party can possibly have."

"Then, if it must be so, let me hope that you will be my guest till the hour of action comes."

"Nay, I am by so doing keeping you in London."

"Oh, I gave up at once going out of town when your letter with its sad enclosures came. I was going to Windsor, but I sent a messenger with an excuse at once."

"In that case, then, my lord, I accept your kind offer."

"Do so; and I will send to the police at once."

"My lord, allow me to offer a suggestion?"

"With pleasure."

"I think if your lordship will let me have under my command an officer of the army, and a file of soldiers, I will manage this affair better than by the aid of the police. It is a fixed determination with me that I will not appear in the matter before any tribunal. My family would be very much enraged if I were, so that that is out of the question; and for such a reason I would rather not come into contact with the police at all."

"But will you not, prince, give me your evidence to help to commit these two wretches—the Lady Deliva and her maid?"

"I cannot. Surely, the four dead bodies are sufficient evidence of her acts without me compromising my position by appearing in the matter?"

"Prince, I can easily understand your scruples, and I will take care that they are respected. The plan of operation you propose shall be adopted."

"My lord, I am greatly obliged to you; and all I wish in addition is, that the officer and soldiers just be told that I am to be obeyed, but not told who I am, further than that I am a person of distinction; and in that case I no longer need wear a mask."

As he spoke, Captain Hawk took off the velvet mask that he had worn for fear of coming into contact with any of the police, who might have known him as Hawk, the Highwayman.

"Well, prince," said the secretary of state, "it is quite a comfort to see you in your own proper form, without disguise."

It was wonderful the deference which was paid to Captain Hawk. An officer of the guards was sent for in the course of the next half hour, and the secretary explained to him that he would have to accompany, with a file of men that he was desired to pick from his company, an exalted personage, and act under his orders entirely.

The officer at first thought it was some political plot that had been discovered, but he was soon undeceived in that; and perhaps he would not much have liked the job if it had not been that it was so exalted a personage who was to accompany him in the affair.

As it was, he looked very much gratified; and when the secretary of state hinted that if the affair went off well, he would find himself in the next gazetted list of promotions, he was as brisk as a bee in the matter.

The hour and a half that it wanted to the twilight soon passed away, and, as it happened, the evening set in very gloomily. The sky was covered by dark clouds.

A cool wind from the south-west swept through the trees of St. James's Park; but few people were abroad. Indeed, take it for all in all, a more favourable night for the enterprise that Captain Hawk, with the officer and his file of men, were going upon could not very well have been found.

The secretary of state forced upon Hawk all kinds of hospitalities and civilities; so that it was quite a relief when the officer arrived with his men, and reported himself quite ready.

Little did the secretary of state imagine that all this time he had been entertaining the notorious Captain Hawk, the highwayman, who had only escaped conviction for the murder of one of the judges of the land by the most remarkable *alibi* upon the records of the courts—an *alibi* of which the lord chief justice expressed himself to the effect that no man could help acquitting the prisoner legally upon it, while no man in his senses could believe a word of it.

And yet this very highwayman, upon whose head a price was set, had had the singular effrontery to obtrude himself upon the minister of the country, and to be the man who professed an abhorrence of the crimes of the Lady Deliva.

It is rather a singular phase of human nature that it feels a horror of those crimes in others which it by no means scruples to commit itself.

Thus, although Captain Hawk was a murderer, we find him most anxious to bring the Lady Deliva to justice, who, after all, had but committed a similar crime!

CHAPTER CXV.

THE LADY DELIVA HAS MADE UP HER MIND TO GET RID OF HER FAIR PRISONER.

The officer of the guards who was to accompany Captain Hawk upon his mission to the house of the Lady

Deliva had received a hint from the secretary of state that he, Hawk, was a rather great personage, who did not want to be known.

This communication had all the desired effect upon the captain, who forthwith treated Hawk with quite a distinguished deference in the course of the proceedings.

The sergeant and his men, too, took their cue from the officer, and considered that the service they were on could not be otherwise than very important, while so distinguished a personage led them to it.

"Now, my dear sir," said the secretary of state, as he pressed Captain Hawk's hand quite affectionately, "I hope you will allow me the pleasure of seeing you again soon."

"When my credentials come to hand," said Hawk, "I hope to appear before the society of the English metropolis in my proper character."

"Certainly—oh, certainly. But we have a little entertainment to-morrow night, and I am quite certain that it will be to the general delight if you will honour it with your company."

"I am afraid that my incognito might not be respected."

"Oh, but it will. I assure you it will; and who knows, after all, but that your credentials from Vienna may arrive before the hour when I hope to have the pleasure of presenting you to my guests?"

"That is possible."

"Then, prince, you will allow me the pleasure of being able to assure myself that you will come?"

Captain Hawk hesitated a moment or two; and then he said rather abruptly—

"I will come."

"I am exceedingly gratified," said the secretary, "and will no longer detain you from the prosecution of the enterprise upon which you are so anxious. Farewell until we meet again."

In another minute Captain Hawk was in the park.

At that hour, and entering the park as Captain Hawk and the soldiers who were with him did by a private mode of getting into it near the Birdcage Walk, but very few persons noticed the little party. A chance straggler or two might turn and look after them with some degree of wonder as to where an officer's guard could be going at such a time; but that was all.

The few sentries they passed drew themselves up, and with a rattle of their musketry saluted the officer.

In this way they proceeded for some time in silence until they were close to the Green Park, and then Captain Hawk thought that it was rather ungenerous upon his part to say nothing to the officer of the nature of the expedition upon which he was coming with him.

Respect for his supposed rank had evidently kept the officer silent; but that silence had lasted long enough to be rather awkward to both parties.

Hawk considered that it was his business to break it.

Turning to the officer with a slight bow, he said—

"Sir, I will commit to you as much as I know of this matter upon which we are engaged, so that you will be better able to act in the business than as if you were in ignorance about it."

"You are very good," said the officer, and Captain Hawk thought that there was a slight tone of sarcasm in the reply.

"I expect," said Hawk, "that we shall make two prisoners."

"Indeed, sir?"

"Yes, and both women."

"Women?"

"Exactly so. One, very likely, and perhaps both, might take some exception to the term, in so far as they might call themselves ladies; but that does not alter the case at all."

"Not at all, so far as that goes," said the officer; "but I did hope that the duty upon which an officer in the guards and some of his company were called out upon would be a little more dignified than the arrest of a couple of females."

"I am very sorry that you should have been troubled in the matter," said Captain Hawk, "but I beg to assure you, sir, that there are reasons of an all-sufficing nature which has induced me to wish the affair conducted in this precise manner."

"Very good, sir. I am under your

orders, and will obey them, I assure you, in all particulars."

"Then, sir, allow me to state to you that I will take you and your men to a garden wall, over which we must all get. The men must proceed through a garden to a tree that grows by the side of a wall in which there is a window—up that tree and in at that window to the house will be our course.

The officer looked at Captain Hawk as well as the darkness would permit him, as he said—

"But is there no door to the house?"

"Oh, yes, but were we to arrive at it by that means, those whom I wish to have captured would most undoubtedly escape."

"Well, sir, your orders must be obeyed. I don't know exactly how far my powers of ascending a tree may serve me, but, at all events, as it is in the way of my duty, I will attempt it."

"To attempt it is to succeed, captain. This way, if you please."

Captain Hawk now, without any further hesitation, led the way to the garden-wall of the Lady Deliva's house, and there he paused in the darkness that reigned close to it. The wall was not a very high one, but yet as the top of it was beyond reach, it was not the easiest thing in the world to get over it.

"If a few moments' delay," said the officer, "be not of much moment just now, they can be amply made up by the increased facilities that a light ladder would afford us for the purpose of scaling the wall and ascending the tree you have mentioned. One of my men can fetch one from the barracks by St. James's, in a few minutes."

"Let him do so, then," said Hawk.

The officer despatched one of his men accordingly, who in a very short space of time, indeed, for he had been urged to speed in the matter, returned with a light scaling-ladder, which he placed against the garden-wall.

"Now, sir," said the officer, "we shall all be over much more quietly and quickly than if we scrambled over the brick-work. It was quite ludicrous to see the soldiers mount to the top of the wall, and then descend on the other side, dropping as though they had fallen into the profound darkness of some deep cavity from which it would not be possible for them ever to emerge again in this world.

The soft garden ground that they came upon on the other side of the wall returned no souud, so that the descent was quite perfect. When they had all gone over, the officer said to Captain Hawk, as he proceeded to the ladder—

"You or I next, sir?"

"As you please."

"I will follow you, then."

Captain Hawk was over in a moment, and then the officer followed him, and one of the soldiers who had remained on the top of the wall for that purpose, drew over the ladder, so that there trey were all in Lady Deliva's garden without having created any alarm.

"Now, sir," said Captain Hawk, "it will be necessary to accost every person that we may meet in the place, and to secure them, so that they give no possible alarm."

"That shall be done, but you will excuse me for asking if this is not the garden belonging to a large house with Corinthian columns in the front of it, and which looks into Pall Mall?"

"It is."

"Then it is the house of the Lady Deliva?"

"You are right, Captain."

"May I further ask, sir, if her ladyship is to be one of the prisoners we are expected to take this evening?"

"She is."

"Well, I am not at all sorry for that. I have reason to believe that a comrade of ours narrowly escaped death in her house. She is a violent and most dangerous woman, I assure you, sir."

"I know it. Come on."

Captain Hawk was certainly not displeased to hear that the officer had no sort of distaste to the job of arresting Lady Deliva, so they proceeded with some alacrity through the garden. Captain Hawk led the way now, and as his object was to get into the house as quietly as he could, he had no sort of objection to tread on the flower-beds, as the soft mould effectually prevented the footsteps of the party from making any noise.

HAWK, PERSISTS IN TAKING THE SNUFF BOX TO GET IT REPAIRED.

"Who goes there!" suddenly cried a voice. "Thieves! thieves!"

"Halt!" said Hawk

The soldiers drew up in a moment.

There was now the flash of a lantern through the bushes, and Captain Hawk saw the dusky figure of a man advancing.

"Who is there?" cried the voice again. "If you don't answer at once I will fire my carbine at you."

"There's no occasion for that," said Hawk. "I give up."

"Oh, do you, my fine fellow. We shall soon then see who and what you are. I suppose a person must not have a garden near one of the parks without vagabonds getting over the wall to steal the fruit and flowers."

As the man who then spoke, and who was the Lady Deliva's gardener approached, and got close to the bushes,

Captain Hawk suddenly sprang upon him, and caught him by the throat, holding him with a force that effectually prevented him from not only giving no alarm, but very nearly made an end of him at once by strangulation.

"Take care of this man," said Hawk, to the soldiers. "Gag him, and tie him to one of the trees. We can call for him if we should happen to want him, as we come back."

The soldiers were not at all slow or inactive in the carrying out of this order, to the discomfiture of the gardener, who found himself severely gagged, and his arms tied behind him, by the aid of a belt, in the short space of about half a minute.

He tried to implore them to be merciful by making gestures to that effect, and by attempting to kneel upon the damp ground; but as it was tolerably dark, they did not see the agonised supplication he put on.

The attempt to kneel, they looked upon as a villanously cunning attempt to escape, by reeling among their legs.

The only thing, therefore, that the gardener got by his movement, was a kick, so that when he was tied by the ancles likewise, and then thrown into a bed of tulips, he felt that his last hour had all but come.

"All right, sir," said the sergeant of the party to Captain Hawk. "The prisoner is disposed of, sir."

"You have not killed him?"

"Oh, no, sir; but he is in what we call limbo, sir, and wont get out of it in a hurry, I take it."

CHAPTER CXVI.

HE LADY DELIVA TAKES THE ALARM AND TRIES TO DISPOSE OF HER WAITING-MAID.

As Captain Hawk neared the house, his thoughts ran upon the beauty and the innocence of the young girl named Angela, who was there a prisoner, and who he dreaded to think might, by that time, have suffered from the revengeful feelings of the Lady Deliva, and her accomplice, the waiting-maid.

He had but one hope that Angela might have escaped from any very serious ill usage, and that arose from the feeling that as the Lady Deliva had every reason to think him, Captain Hawk, dead, surely even her angry nature would be somewhat satisfied by having made one victim.

This was rather a hope, though, than a persuasion of his mind.

The officer, after they had got close to the tree that now partially shielded the windows of the house, thought it was time to rouse the distinguished personage from the state of abstraction in which he appeared to be in, and so touching Hawk lightly upon the shoulder, he said—

"Sir, we are at the house."

Hawk started.

"What say you?"

"Simply, sir, that the corporal, who is in advance, says he cannot get any further, for he has reached a brick wall."

"Pardon me for my inattention. The fact is, my thoughts were rather busy, and I was not, indeed, sufficiently alive to present events.

"Don't mention it, sir. We are under your orders, and will obey you with pleasure."

"Wait here, then, for a few moments. As I am well acquainted with the spot, or, at all events, sufficiently well acquainted with it to know it much better than you or your men can, I will go forward and reconnoitre myself. Where is the ladder?"

"It is here, sir," said the sergeant.

"Very good. We shall want it when I return."

Captain Hawk upon this went forward in search of the particular tree which had been of such essential assistance to him in his descent from the window of the chamber of death.

It was no easy thing upon such a night as that to find, in a garden rather overrun with vegetation, a particular tree; and yet, Captain Hawk considered that the aspect of that side of the house, even amid the uncertain night light that was around him, would aid him in his discovery of the spot he sought.

The house stood up, tall and black, against the sky; and now and then as one of the more dense of the clouds that were coming fast, under the influence of a north-west wind swept by, he could see very distinctly the whole outline of the tall edifice.

"Oh! if I can but rescue Angela," he said to himself, "this will be, after all, a happy night's work!"

The fear that the Lady Deliva had by that time executed her promised vengeance against Angela, came, however, each moment more strongly upon the mind of Hawk, and he trembled to think of the possible, and we might go so far as to say, probable fate of that young and beautiful being.

The dread, however, was but an additional reason to activity; and, after a search for about five minutes, Captain Hawk felt quite sure that he saw the dim outline of the window of the death chamber, from which he had made his escape.

It was quite necessary, however, to guard against the possibility of a mistake, so he examined the tree carefully all round, and, by standing between it and the window and looking up, he was convinced that it was the very one whose branches actually touched the glass.

"This will do," he said, as he turned back to where he had left the officer and his men.

"Who goes there?" cried the officer, as the sound of Captain Hawk's footsteps returning came upon his attentive ear.

"A friend. It is I. Do you not know me?"

"Yes, sir; by your voice. But—but ——"

"But what?"

"There has been a little alarm in your absence."

"An alarm? Of what character?"

"That we hardly can take upon ourselves to say, but about two or three minutes ago something white and tall seemed to come from behind one of the hedges, and to look at me. It then gave utterance to a smothered sort of cry, and on the instant disappeared."

"Who could it be?"

"Oh! what could it be?" said a voice.

"Listen, sergeant," said the officer. "You will have it that it was an apparition, but that is too absurd."

"Confound it!" said Hawk, for the idea came ac[illegible] on the moment that it might have been the waiting-maid.

"So say I, sir," said the officer. "The fact is, that under ordinary circumstances while on duty, a shot or two would, no doubt, have at once solved the mystery; but the discharge of a musket would, as you know, sir, have had an effect the direct contrary to your injunctions to keep quiet."

"True—true."

"So we were compelled to satisfy ourselves with hunting the ladies, and upon finding nothing, to let the affair wait till you came."

"You did all you said, sir?"

"In truth, I did."

"I know it. It can't be helped, now. But I much fear the alarm is given by this time to those whom we wish to seize; and yet, we may manage to steal a march upon them. Follow me at once with the ladder. I have found the window by which we must enter the house."

They lost no time in carrying out this order of Captain Hawk. The sergeant took possession of the scaling ladder, and kept quite close upon Hawk's heels; and the rest of the party followed. As soon as Hawk got past the tree, he took the ladder, and placed it against the wall, and found that it would be just long enough to reach to the sill of the window.

"This is fortunate," he said.

"It is, sir," said the sergeant. "That is the window?"

"Yes."

"Then, if you will give me leave I will go up to it."

"Nay," said the officer, advancing, "I will lead, and you can follow, sergeant. It is my duty to go first."

"No," said Captain Hawk. "There is no danger here, and, therefore, you are not called upon, sir, to do what I feel assured you would always do in danger, namely, take the lead. I know the place, and understand what there is to do when I get to the window, so I will go first."

The officer merely bowed to the compliment that Captain Hawk had paid to him, and then he stepped aside to allow him to take his own views in the matter.

Hawk sprang up the ladder with rapidity, and in a few moments was at the window of that awful room, which was so full of horrors, and of which he had so very vivid an appreciation, that he certainly did not at all wish to trouble it again with his presence unnecessarily.

The present, however, was a case of emergency, so he did not scruple to quietly raise the sash.

All was as still as the grave in the room, and although Captain Hawk put his head into it, and listened attentively, he could not hear the slightest sound coming from any part of the house.

It takes us longer to tell the stirring incidents than it actually took them to transact, and Captain Hawk feeling that now there was no time to lose, descended a few steps from the ladder, and said in a low tone to those below—

"Hist! hist! are you there?"

"Yes—yes."

"Follow me, then."

"We will, sir."

The officer sprung up, and the sergeant, and the men followed him closely. Captain Hawk made his way into the room, and then helped the others, at the same time cautioning them to tread lightly upon the floor, for he did not feel quite sure what apartment was under that dreadful one which had been, by the Lady Deliva, converted into a charnel-house.

In a few moments there was a sufficient force in that chamber to put at nought all ideas of any danger to those who had thus taken the house of the murderess by storm.

"What an odd smell," said the officer.

"There is a good reason for that," said Captain Hawk.

Hawk was provided with a few phosphorus matches, and he now ignited one, and held it up to burn freely.

As the blue flame changed its colour upon the little slip of wood of which the match was made from igniting, they could all take a rather hurried glance around them, and the officer with a start, said—

"There is somebody in that corner."

"And somebody down by the sofa," said the sergeat, as he drew his sword. "Soldiers, attention!"

"Silence!" said Hawk.

The match went out.

"But I see some one," said the officer. "How is this?"

"It is the dead," said Hawk. "This chamber contains some of the victims of the poisons that the Lady Deliva has given to those who were imprudent enough to come to the place, and then to offend her. There is no less than four corpses in this one room."

"What!" said the officer, "is the house full of dead men?"

"No. I have reason to believe that here only are to be found the victims of the Lady Deliva, but they are quite sufficiently numerous for all that."

"They are, indeed. But how, sir, did you manage to find out this fearful secret?"

"That is a long story which I will tell you at another time. It is now a great duty to arrest the women, and I want to get that work accomplished before she can execute revenge upon one who is in this house, and who I would give my own life to save."

"Another victim, sir?"

"Yes, but not one like these. The person I speak of is a young lady."

"Oh!"

"And so beautiful—so innocent—so——"

Captain Hawk felt that he was rather imprudently falling into a state of rapture with regard to the charms of Angela, to those who could not feel with him upon the subject, inasmuch as they had not seen her, and who, if they had, could only rival him in loving her, so he stopped short, and a rather ludicrous silence ensued.

The officer felt the awkwardness of saying nothing, so he very quietly remarked.

"Sir, we are at your orders."

"Yes. Thank you. There is a secret door leading from this chamber if I could but find it in the dark. Ah!"

"Hush!" said the officer.

They were all as still as death, while a bright spot of light came into the room from a little opening in the secret panel, that looked as if it had been caused by the displacement of a knot in the wood itself. One thing was quite clear, and that was that somebody was on the other side with a strong light.

"Sir," whispered the officer to Hawk, "sir——"

"Oh, silence!" said Hawk.

The spot of light moved up and down in the darkness of the room, and it struck Captain Hawk that whoever had the light on the outside was looking for the spring that fastened the secret door. If that were so, another minute might bring him face to face with, perhaps, the Lady Deliva or her waiting-maid.

With that hope he kept close to the panel, intending the moment it was opened to spring upon whoever it was, and take them prisoner.

The soldiers were evidently impressed with superstitious terror, for the hard breathing of some of them could be powerfully heard in the stillness of that horrible chamber.

A voice now broke that stillness, and in a moment Captain Hawk recognised the voice of the Lady Deliva.

"Dare I—oh, dare I enter this room?" she said. "Oh, dare I do it? What sights may meet my eye. Oh, conscience! conscience! did I even think that you could make a coward of me?"

Captain Hawk touched the officer's arm.

"That is the Lady Deliva," he said in a whisper. "Pray, attend to what she says, and recollect it."

"I will."

"Oh, it was but a dream," said the Lady Deliva, with a strange, screaming voice. "What could it have been but a dream, after all? But do such dreams come only to those who have dipped their hands in human blood? Am I to dream for ever in such a fashion? Oh, horror! horror!"

It seemed from the strange tone in which the Lady Deliva gave utterance to these words, that she must have risen from her bed under the effect of some fearful vision of the imagination, and was thus in anything but her ordinary state of self-possession.

Surely, there was in this world a retribution which overtook that deeply guilty woman.

The officer whispered in Captain Hawk's ear—

"Would it not be better, sir, to take her at once?"

"Perhaps it would, but there is some difficulty. The opening of the panel might not be accomplished in a moment; and the attempt to do it, if it alarmed her, would lead her to fly from the spot, and then we should have what I do not want, namely, a race after her through the house. When we take her we ought to be able to lay hands upon her at once."

"True. That would be better."

"Listen!—She speaks again."

The Lady Deliva did speak again, and from the tone and manner in which she so spoke, it was quite clear that she was not recovering from her agitation.

CHAPTER CXVII.

ANGELA FEELS GRATEFUL TO HER DELIVERER FROM DEATH.

"Where are you now?" cried the half-maddened Lady Deliva—"where are you all now? But a little while since you all stood by my bed-side, and pointed at me with your shrunken, bony fingers. I saw you all. Why do you not come forth from the chamber where you all lie in death and in corruption? I am not mad—I am not mad, I tell you all, nor shall you drive me so, even if you confined me as you are with death—horrible death in all your looks!"

She struck the panel fiercely.

"She is mad," said the officer.

"She looks like it," said Captain Hawk.

"Ha!—ha!" screamed the Lady Deliva, "I did the deed!—I was the death of all of you! I own it. I poisoned you all; and amid your pangs—pangs too horrible to bear, made you know that I had had my revenge!—yes, my revenge! And you come in the night, when my eye-lids are weighed down by sleep, to fright me—to set fire to my brain—to drive me mad, so that I may rush into the very streets and shriek out the fact that I am a murderess!"

She banged at the door again, and then after the silence of a few moments, she uttered a piercing scream; and the lights disappeared, and they heard her fall to the floor heavily.

"What is she about now?" said the

officer. "Why, that woman is as mad as it is possible for any human being to be."

"I don't think it," said Captain Hawk. "There are times and seasons when the fancy getting the better of the reason in a brain which has long hoarded up the memory of guilt, will play such havoc with the mind, that all will be unconnected, and wild, and vague, and full of terror, until the paroxysm has passed away; but that is not what can be called madness."

"Sir, you are right."

"She speaks again."

There came a voice to their ears; but it was not the voice of the Lady Deliva now. To the surprise of Captain Hawk, it was the voice of the waiting-maid.

"My lady—my lady, I say! Good Heavens! what do you here? Is this a place to be in? By this door, too! There is danger, I tell you. I am cold as death with fright. I tell you there is danger. I was forced to come to seek you as I could. I lost my shoes in the garden, and that was what made you, I suppose, not hear my tread. It is I. I touched you on the shoulder. You need not have screamed so."

The cause of the sudden scream, and the dropping to the floor of the Lady Deliva was now clear enough. The waiting-maid had come suddenly behind and touched her on the shoulder, making her think at the moment that it was one of her victims who was endowed with the terrible power of answering her call, and appearing to her.

"My lady — my lady! Speak to me."

A low murmur was all that the Lady Deliva gave utterance to.

"And the light is out, too," added the waiting-maid. "No—no, I think I can revive it. I have blown a light in at times for mere sport, and now I will see if I can do it that I really want it."

There was, no doubt, a red wick to the candle; for as the maid blew at it, a faint illumination lit up the crevices in the panel, and then all at once it came to a flame.

"Ah, that will do," she said. "I have a light now. My lady, I have something to tell you which will rouse you. Do you hear me?"

"Yes," said Lady Deliva, faintly.

"Well, that's a good job. I never knew you to faint, so I could not think you had done so now."

"Where am I?"

"Where are you? Why, you are by the door of the panelled room.

"Oh, no—no!"

"Oh, yes, my lady. If you will only look up, you will see that you are there."

"Why—oh, why did you bring me here?"

"I bring you? Indeed, I did not. I have as little a liking for the place as you can possibly have, my lady. Indeed, I wish with all my heart I was well out of it. I found you here, and I hope you will come away."

"You found me here?"

"Yes, my lady, and you appear to be terribly frightened, but you can't be more so than I am. There are men in the garden."

"Men in the garden?"

From the manner and tone of the Lady Deliva, it was quite evident that her wits were not sufficiently clear just then to be fully aware of the importance of the communication of the waiting-maid.

"Oh, what shall I do?" said the latter. "I do think she is out of her mind. There is but one thing open to me, and that is flight."

"Oh, no—Stop!" cried Lady Deliva. "What did you say?"

"Nothing, my lady."

"You did—you did; you spoke of flight. You would leave me, but I tell you, you must not. We must live together—die together—we must go down—down—down——"

"Oh, where?"

"To perdition together!"

"You terrify me. I thought you thought that after death there was no such a thing as—as——"

"Hush! I have said so. But there is something even now at my heart and brain that gives the lie to the idle words. Oh, there is—there is a hereafter; I know it—I know it. Oh, what a terrible knowledge that is to such as we are."

"What can we do?"

"Hush! What's that. I thought I heard a noise. Did I dream that there were men in the garden?"

"No, I told you so."

"Ah!"

The Lady Deliva sprang to her feet.

"Help! murder!" cried the waiting maid. "Oh, my lady, don't look like that! What is the matter with you?"

"Nothing—nothing! Stop a little. I am calm now and collected. There is danger. Are you sure you too were not dreaming?"

"Oh, quite. I could not sleep, and so I rose and went to walk in the garden, for the sake of getting thoroughly cool, for I have found that then, upon returning to bed, I have slept well enough, and I came suddenly close to some men, I feel certain of it. I came here at once to seek you."

"How many?"

"What?"

"How many men, idiot?"

"Oh, I don't know."

"Five!"

"Why should there be five? What puts that into your head, my lady? How very odd you do look, to be sure. Oh, my lady, speak to me."

"If there were five of them we should know who they were. They would be the five who came in this room. We know that—oh, yes, we know that."

"What, the five dead men?"

"Oh, yes—yes."

"Madam, this is indeed monstrous, and I shall be compelled to look to my own safety and leave you to your fate. Have you so soon again forgotten what I told you about there being in the garden? Living men and not the mere shadows of your imagination. There is no time to lose if you are to escape; they may be enemies."

"Hush, Margaret—hush!"

"Ah, now you speak in something like your natural tone of voice. What is to be done?"

"Did you see the men?"

"Yes, sufficiently distinctly to know that there were some eight or ten of them, as I guess. They made an effort to pursue me, but with my knowledge of the garden it was not at all difficult for me to elude them, and I did so effectually, and came to you at once. I would advise you to leave the house at once by the front of it."

"Stop. Perhaps so; but——"

"But what, my lady?"

"Would it not be better to get rid of one who may be a witness to all that has happened here with regard to that Austrian Prince? Angela can guess well enough his fate, and she lives."

"Why, yes, madam, she does—live—at present."

"Ay, at present."

"Yes, madam, but——"

"Well?"

"Oh, I have nothing to say except that I quite agree with your ladyship, I can see, and from what I know of Angela, and from what you know, we may be well aware that the moment she has an opportunity there is nothing that she knows that she won't tell."

"Most certainly."

"Of course, my lady, it is for you to make up your mind what to do and it is not for me to presume to advise you; but if I were to take that liberty I would pack up my jewels and leave, and before I left I would not leave any one in life to say wicked things of me. Dead men tell no tales, and the saying holds good, you may depend, with girls, my lady."

"It does—it does. She dies!"

"Hem!"

"I will not live in constant dread of the revelation of that young girl; she knows too much already—oh, a great deal too much, and so I will take your advice—she shall die."

"Oh, don't say I advised it."

"You did—you know you did. But what does that matter so that it is done? It shall be done, and then all will be well as far as she is concerned—all will be very well, indeed. You will do it?"

"Oh, I—could not."

"You could not—you say you could not, and yet you hesitate. You mean you will, for I know that you hate her; you always did hate her for her beauty, and you always hated her, too, for her virtue and her innocence—you hated her for the possession of those qualities in which you were yourself deficient."

"Yes, my lady, we both hate her upon that account."

"Silence! No insolence. It is for

me to say what I think and for you to listen. Go, now, to the cabinet in my chamber and bring me from it a silken cord, and a knife that you will find in one of its drawers—the knife has a silken sheath."

"What drawer, my lady?"

"It is numbered twelve."

"I will find it. Be tranquil till I return."

The waiting-maid left the room, and the moment the sound of her footsteps died away the Lady Deliva muttered in a deep tone between her teeth—

"She shall die, too. I will leave the house, but I will leave nothing but death within it. She shall die as well as Angela. Of late I have noticed that there is an insolent familiarity—a growing assumption of power upon the part of this woman arising from the fact that she knows so much. It is time that she should die. Tools that are used for unholy purposes sooner or later will wound their master if they be not in time thrown aside."

CHAPTER CXVIII.

THE LADY DELIVA LOOKS AFTER HERSELF IN THE MIDST OF HER REMORSE.

The great malignity with which the Lady Deliva uttered the words with which our last chapter concluded, was such that there could be not the shadow of a doubt upon the minds of any of those who listened to her of the fell purpose of her soul.

She really meant to murder her waiting-maid and accomplice in crime, and, likewise, the fair Angela.

One was to be murdered for her guilty knowledge, and the other for her childish innocence and candour of disposition.

Little did the Lady Deliva fancy that there were so many listeners to her diabolical intentions.

"Yes," she added, as she paced the apartment to and fro, "guilt like mine is never secure if the secret of it is lodged in more than one bosom. I have always felt that, and yet the necessity of an accomplice has kept me for so long in the society of that woman. Well—well, her time had not come, but it has now—oh, yes, it has now."

"Of all the wretches that ever wore the garb of humanity," whispered the officer of the guard to Captain Hawk, "I do think this woman is the very worst."

"She is bad enough, indeed, sir."

"Indeed and in fact she is. What are we to do; recollect that we are under your orders."

"Yes, I am not unmindful of that fact, and will take care that all is well shortly. There is time enough; I am desirous of seeing further what may be the plan of this odious woman."

"What can detain her?" said Lady Deliva, suddenly; "what on earth can detain her? Is it true that there are men in the garden, or is it but some false alarm upon the part of Margaret? Ah, it may be so, and yet I do not give her credit for so much tact. There is a window in the adjoining room that will enable me to see."

"She will come here," said the officer.

"No," said Hawk, "she means another room: she could not speak so calmly about this one."

Lady Deliva passed through a doorway opposite to that at which the waiting maid had taken her departure, and she had hardly been gone a moment when the waiting-maid returned, saying, as she entered the apartment hurriedly—

"Here is the knife, madam, it is a regular dagger, and here is the cord. Will you strangle her with it? Why—why, where is she? Gone! Ah, no, in the next room looking out into the garden. Hem! she is suspicious. I wish that she was right in suspecting that I had deceived her, but if I have my own eyes deceived me first. Oh, if I can but get her to pack up all her jewels, I will soon take her life and possesss myself of them."

"A sweet pair," said the officer; "like mistress like maid."

"The one is quite as bad as the other," replied Hawk.

"Madam," called the waiting-maid, "do you see them now?"

"No, but I hear a strange voice like some one moaning in pain."

"Indeed."

"Yes; do you not hear it now? There, did you hear that?"

"Yes, I heard a groan."

"That was it. I cannot understand that, but I am convinced that there is danger. It will not do to remain longer in this house. I had yesterday half resolved to go, and my dream of to-night has quite determined me."

"I am so glad to hear you say so, madam. Will you pack up all your jewels first, though?"

HAWK WATCHING THE ARRIVAL OF HAMILTON AND HIS SECONDS.

"Yes; follow me at once and assist me."

"Oh, with pleasure."

"We can come back and finish the affair connected with Angela. Let the knife and the cord lie upon this chair; upon our route we must pass through this chamber necessarily."

"Yes, my lady."

They both hastily left the room now,

and in the course of half a minute there was not the faintest sound of their retreating footsteps to be heard.

Then it was that Captain Hawk said boldly and clearly to the officer who was waiting his orders—

"Now, sir, I do not see any further hindrance to our proceeding. We will open this panel in the wall at once, and I can rescue the young lady I spoke of, who, I rejoice to hear, is yet alive and uninjured by the Lady Deliva."

Captain Hawk twisted up tightly a piece of paper, and then lit one of the phosphorus matches he had with him. He set the folded paper into a flame, and it made a pretty good temporary torch; and one of the soldiers held it while he, Hawk, looked for the secret spring which opened the panel in the wall.

The great thing in such a secret consisted in knowing just where to look for it; and Captain Hawk very soon touched the little nob, which caused the panel to fly open.

"Come on," he said. "Let us get out of this place at once, which, I suppose, you are none of you very sorry to leave."

"I am anything but sorry," said the officer. "The very atmosphere seems to be loaded with murder in that room."

It was rather ludicrous to see the alacrity with which the sergeant and the soldiers got out of the chamber of death, as it might be fairly enough called.

"Now, sir," said the officer, "we follow your orders."

"Come on, then, if you please, gentlemen, and we shall soon find her whom I chiefly seek."

"The paper is all consumed, sir," said the soldier who carried it, as he dropped the last burning fragment to the floor.

"Never mind," said Hawk. "I can lead you some distance by the light of another match; and you will then be in a narrow passage, from which you cannot deviate; and you have nothing to do but to come direct on."

The passage leading from that room towards the boudoir of Angela was soon found, for Captain Hawk, when he had been in that house before, had taken good care that no little circumstance should escape his observation which would enable him successfully to find his way at another time; and now he felt the full advantage of his knowledge of the premises.

The officer, with his drawn sword in his hand, followed Hawk closely; and the sergeant, with his men, brought up the rear.

It was with a feeling of great delight that Hawk, at each footstep that he made in advance, told himself that he was nearing the abode of Angela, whose beauty had made so deep an impression upon his imagination. He quickened his pace, so that the officer and the soldiers had almost to run to keep up with him; and then he suddenly touched the curtain that he knew hid the apartment of Angela from him.

"Halt!" he said, in a low tone.

They all stopped on the moment, and then he said to the officer—

"Keep your men quiet here, sir, if you please, for a few minutes. I shall be within call if I am wanted; and I will not detain you for any length of time."

"As you please, sir," said the officer.

Captain Hawk now carefully felt over the folds of the massive curtain till he came to the edge of it, which he only pulled aside sufficiently wide to enable him to pass it, and then he was in the boudoir chamber of the beautiful and artless Angela.

There was but a very dim light, indeed, in that chamber, which came from a little silver hand lamp that stood upon the superb toilette table. Captain Hawk cast an anxious and hurried glance around the room, but no Angela was to be seen.

His heart sank within him.

"Gone! gone!" he gasped. "They have taken her from me!"

He staggered to a chair, and held by the back of it, while he again looked around him. In an alcove, at the farther end of the room, he saw that there was some sort of bedstead, concealed, for a mass of white satin drapery hung partially over the foot of it, which was richly gilt. The idea struck him that there in repose he might find Angela.

The hope that, after all she was there and he might be in time to save her, was so delicious to him, that he feared to banish it from his mind by the risk of finding it a delusion; and it was some few minutes before he could muster courage enough to advance and satisfy himself one way or the other in the matter.

With a cautious step he at length crept towards the bedstead, and laid his hand upon the hangings of it. He moved them gently on one side, and then he saw Angela lying asleep, and looking as calm and as still as some sculptured saint.

"She is here!" he gasped.

Yes, there she was in all her beauty. Her long hair hung in disordered masses over her pillow, and one arm was outside the clothes, looking almost as white as the satin coverlet it rested upon.

Captain Hawk could have stood there gazing upon the fair girl for hours; but he was not forgetful of what was to be done to rescue her yet from the Lady Deliva.

"I must awaken her," he said—"yes, I must disturb that sweet and happy slumber. Ah! she smiles!"

Some gentle, happy thought must have crossed the mind of the young girl, for a light smile played for a moment like a sunbeam upon her lips, and then all was still again.

"Angela!" said Captain Hawk—"Angela! Dear, beautiful Angela!"

She smiled again. It was still in her sleep that she heard his words, and the soft eyes did not open.

"Angela, oh! Angela, I love you!" he said.

He spoke very softly and gently.

After a few moments, then, when he found she did not awake, but only smiled again and again with the joy of her young heart, he leant over the bed and kissed the fair cheek of the sleeper.

That kiss awakened her, and with a cry of surprise and alarm she started up in the bed.

"Angela, be not alarmed, I come to save you"

"To save me?"

"Yes, dear one. Do you not know me—do you not recollect me?"

"Oh, thank God you are not dead! My aunt was not wicked enough to kill you."

"Wicked enough she was, Angela, but I was fortunate enough to escape her evil intentions; she would now kill you, but I am with you, and you need have no fear. All the world in arms against you should not harm you now, or if they did, it is only through my heart that they should find a road to yours."

"Oh, how good, how kind of you!"

The heart of Captain Hawk smote him a little at these words of Angela's, for, after all, he could not conceal from himself the fact that his goodness and his kindness to Angela mostly, if not entirely, arose from his admiration of her marvellous beauty.

"Dress quick," he said, "this is no longer a home for you; rise and follow me. Where is your out-door apparel? I see that you are dressed."

"Oh, yes; I had such a fear of my aunt, that after sitting up until fatigue overpowered me, I sunk into a deep sleep just as you see me. Oh, what joy it will be to go from this dreadful house."

CHAPTER CXIX.

ANGELA FANCIES THAT THE WORLD IS VERY DIFFERENT FROM WHAT IT IS.

In the sweet simplicity of her innocent heart, Angela never for a moment thought of asking herself the question of whether or not it would be a prudent or a proper thing for her to go with Captain Hawk from under her aunt's roof. She only felt that he spoke kindly to her, and that she was unhappy and in danger where she was.

Alas, poor Angela!

"Rise, dear one," repeated Hawk. "Here is a cloak; place it about you, and we will soon leave this place far behind."

"Oh, what is that?" said Angela. "I hear a noise."

Captain Hawk, too, heard a noise, and he stepped towards the massive curtain that hung before the entrance to the room and drew it wide. As he did so he heard footsteps in the passage, and in a moment the officer in command of the little party of soldiers made his appearance.

"Sir," he said, "one of my men is dead."

"Dead, sir?" said Hawk, with some asperity, for he did not want the officer there, although he hardly liked to tell him so.

"Yes. He saw a decanter upon a table in one of the rooms, and incautiously drinking of it, immediately expired."

Before Captain Hawk could make any remark upon this statement of the officer's one of the men came forward, and in rather a hurried manner said—

"Sir, there are two women coming this way, and one of them carrying a light."

That these two women were the Lady Deliva and her infamous waiting-maid Captain Hawk could not doubt, and he formed his plan of operations in a moment.

"Come in here, all of you," he said, "and hide in the best manner you can. It will be well to see what the women mean."

The officer and the soldiers easily hid themselves in Angela's pretty boudoir, and in a few moments the Lady Deliva, with a dagger in her hand, entered the room, followed by her waiting-maid, who said to her—

"All is ready, madam, and you have nothing now to do, since you have determined upon the deed, but to put an end to Angela, and then to leave the house."

"I will do it now," said the Lady Deliva.

At the moment that she approached the bed to put her villanous design into execution, Captain Hawk sprang forward and seized her.

"You are my prisoner!"

The Lady Deliva gave a shriek and fell to the floor.

The waiting-woman fled, but being pursued by a couple of the soldiers she was soon brought back again, and then Captain Hawk said to the officer—

"Sir, your duty is over now; all you have to do is to take these two women and deliver them to the civil power. I will communicate the whole of the night's proceedings to the secretary of state."

The officer merely bowed in answer to this, and then ordered his men to leave the house with their prisoners, so that Captain Hawk had accomplished the apparent object of his visit to the Lady Deliva's mansion, and was alone with Angela, in a very short space of time after making good his entry to the house of murder.

That Angela would have been sacrificed to the rage of the Lady Deliva upon that most eventful night if Captain Hawk had not come to her rescue, does not admit of the shadow of a doubt; and the young creature, as she looked now at her deliver, felt all the gratitude that such a heart as hers was sure to feel upon such an occasion.

"Oh, my friend," she said, "it would indeed have been hard to die, and I so young. They tell me that the world is very beautiful, although I have seen but little of it."

"It is beautiful, Angela."

"If you say it is, why then it must be."

"Why so?"

"Because you are all truth and goodness, and it is quite impossible that you can say a word that is not right. You see, I know you."

Captain Hawk turned pale and red by turns, and looked confused.

"How little does she really know me," he thought.

"Yes," added Angela, "I know you well, my good friend; and much as you dislike to hear your own praises, which I can perceive by your confusion when I speak of your good and noble qualities, I cannot deny myself the pleasure of so doing. Who but you would have come here to save the poor girl who had no one but you in all the world to befriend her?"

"You—you wrong human nature at large," said Captain Hawk. "I think that there are many thousands who would have felt the greatest pleasure in flying to you rescue."

"But then they might not have been, like you, solely actuated by pure and holy motives in so doing. I have been told that there are bad men, who will seem to do great and noble things for such as I am, merely from the idea that I am beautiful. But you are not one of them, my dear friend."

"What the deuce is the girl talking about?" thought Captain Hawk. "Is this art, or is it the very perfection of innocence?"

One glance in the soft, mild, ingenuous,

child-like face at his side, convinced him that it was innocence. He trembled as he replied to her—

"Angela, there are such men as you allude to. But now let us leave the place at once. The very atmosphere of the house seems full of murder. I pray you let us go, I wish to see it no more."

"And it will be a joyful thing to me to bid it adieu for ever," said Angela. "for it has been the scene of much suffering to me. I am quite ready now."

She wrapped the cloak about her which Captain Hawk had handed to her some short time before, and taking a hat from a side table on which it lay, she placed it upon her head, and looked so charming, as the long drooping feather that was in it hung half over her cheeks, that Captain Hawk gazed at her with so great a feeling of admiration, that for the moment he forgot even where they were.

"Will you not come?" said Angela.

Captain Hawk started.

"Oh, Angela! Angela!" he said. "Why are you so beautiful, and being so beautiful, why are you so innocent?"

"Alas!" said Angela, "would you not have me innocent?"

"Yes—yes, I know not what I say to you—I would, indeed."

"And it is only the partiality of one who loves me, that will call me beautiful."

"No—no. Do not say that. There never was such beauty—there never was such innocence. Angela! Angela! were you born to be my curse or my salvation?"

The young girl looked alarmed.

"My dear friend," she said, falteringly, "you are unwell. All that you have gone through in this house, and all the anxiety you have suffered for my sake, have had the effect of making you speak thus."

"Angela, answer me one question."

"Oh, yes, a thousand if you wish."

Captain Hawk tried to speak several times, before he could shape the words that at length came faintly from his lips, and then he said—

"Angela, do you think that you could love me?"

"Love you?"

"Yes—oh, yes. Tell me, now, at once, in that pure spirit of candour which is all your own—tell me, do you think that you can ever love me?"

"Why, I love you now," said Angela, without the least appearance of embarrassment. "I love you now."

"You love me now?"

"Yes—oh, yes. Are you not entitled to all the love that gratitude can bestow? Have you not saved me from the cruelties of my aunt Deliva? Cruelties that would and that could only have terminated with my life. It would be strange, indeed, of me if I did not love you."

From the tone and manner in which Angela uttered these words, Captain Hawk felt convinced that, however he had awakened all the noble feelings of the young girl's mind in his favour, that her heart was as yet quite untouched. If she had loved him as he wanted her to love him, she could not possibly have looked him in the face as she now did, and spoken with such composure.

"Be it so," he said to himself. "I am bad enough, but yet I shudder at the mere thought of losing the respect of this girl—this all but child. I will wait until time has, perchance, lit up in her fair bosom a different feeling for me."

We do not, after all, give Captain Hawk much credit for coming to this determination, for it arose in his mind rather from pride and vanity than from any other cause. The fact was, that he could not bear to fall from the pinnacle of greatness to which Angela had raised him in her imagination.

Then again, it is a fact, that those who have made the human heart much their study will readily admit that there is a something about truth and innocence that is so lovely—so truly great, that even the most hardened guilt shrinks abashed in their presence, and never hardly shows itself.

Thus, then, was it that Angela owed her safety—the safety of her honour and of her peace of mind, not to any strength or to any planning and flattery for her defence, but really to her innocence, and if we may so express it, to her absolute weakness.

There she was alone in that house, with a man who never yet had shown pity to a human being—a man whose own dark and evil passions had hitherto lighted him to a course of iniquity, but he had never yet met with such confiding innocence as Angela's, and now that he did meet with it, it completely confused him.

"Come, Angela," he said, with a tone that was almost one of sadness. "Come, dear one, all shall be well. Will you come with me?"

"Oh, yes."

"And will you trust me?"

"With all my heart."

"What! Without really knowing who or what I am—without the slightest inquiry as to where I am about to take you?"

"Why should I not trust you? Oh, may the time, indeed, be far distant when I shall feel that I ought not to trust you. I do not think, my dear friend, that any one but yourself could awaken me from my dream of trustfulness as regards you."

"It quite unnerves me," muttered Hawk to himself. "Her innocent prattle gets the better of all the subtilty in the world."

"Come, then, Angela, may I perish before I ever give you cause to mistrust me. Lean upon my arm, dearest, and we will leave this wretched house together with the hope of never looking upon it again."

Angela took the arm of Captain Hawk with all the ease in the world. It was as clear as possible that in her innocent heart she thought herself perfectly safe with him.

"Is there anything," he said, as he glanced round the room, "that you would like to take with you from the place?"

"Oh, no, no; there is nothing now. I had a bird that used to sing to me and love me; but my aunt found that the little creature was a companion and a joy to me, so she killed it."

"The wretch!"

"It was, I think, very wicked of her, in good truth; and now that the poor bird is dead, there is nothing that I wish to have that would recall to me the memory of this place that I would gladly forget."

"Be it so. then, Angela; we will go at once. There is now no occasion for any concealment in our flight, so we will go out of the house by its ordinary mode of exit. Do you know the way through the intricacies of all these rooms to the outer door?"

"Alas! no!"

"Then we will find it by exploring our way as best we can. Cheer up, dear one! You are safe now."

"Oh, yes, I am so safe! You will be like a brother to me."

"A brother?"

"Yes; will you not let me call you so? Oh! do take me for a sister! I will be so good a one to you."

"Be it so," said Hawk, speaking thickly; "for the present you shall be my sister, dear Angela, and I will be your brother. Where I am about to take you I will introduce you as such; and be you careful not to contradict the statement."

CHAPTER CXX.

CAPTAIN HAWK IS HIGHLY COMPLIMENTED BY THE SECRETARY OF STATE.

After some trouble—for the mansion of the Lady Deliva was, in truth, rather complicated in its design—Hawk and Angela found their way to the street-door, and safely emerged from the house.

"Free at last!" said Hawk, as he drew a long breath. "It seems quite a relief to breathe the fresh air."

"Oh, yes, brother!"

That word, brother, jarred a little upon the feelings of Hawk; but, since he had consented that it should represent the species of connection between them, he felt that he had no right to complain of it; so he replied as well as he could, saying—

"Dear sister Angela, I am still in doubt where to take you."

"Indeed?"

"Yes. Large as this city is, and ample as my resources are, I still hardly know where now to bend my steps with you. Perhaps you know some one?"

"I, brother? Alas! no! not a soul!"

"Good!" thought Hawk.

The fact was, that he had asked the question for the purpose of discovering if Angela did know any one in London, and he was very well satisfied with the answer in the negative.

"Do you mean to say that the Lady Deliva never took you anywhere?"

"Never of late."

"Nor brought any one to see you?"

"Oh, no, no, not for a long time, indeed. So, you see, brother, I have no one to love but you."

Captain Hawk strove to look in her sweet face as she spoke; but the darkness in the streets was too great to let him do so; and he only pressed the slender arm in his, as he said—

"It is a great joy to me, dear one, to hear you say that you will love me; and now I have determined upon taking you to a house where you will be surrounded with every respect and every comfort."

"Anywhere with you, brother. But what shall I name you, for I must speak of you, you know, when I say my prayers?"

Hawk was rather puzzled for a moment or two what reply to make to this; but at last he said—

"Call me Gerald. It is my real name, and, therefore, I cannot forget it; but to others it will be as well to name me just The Count. It will only be to each other that we will be Gerald and Angela."

"That will be delightful!" said Angela. "Well, now, I like the name of Gerald. There is something frank and noble sounding about it."

"Ah, dear Angela, you associate it with me now that you have heard that it is my name, and that is why you like it, is it not?"

"Perhaps a little."

While this conversation was proceeding, Captain Hawk, for want of any other place to take Angela to where she would be in safety and immediately under his own special care, took his way towards the hotel, where he knew that she would meet with every possible attention upon the statement that she was his sister. Of course, he knew that it would look rather odd to the landlord and the servants of the establishment that the sister of one of the Princes of the House of Austria should arrive in so very undignified a manner at a hotel; but when he came to consider how firmly convinced they were of his rank and wealth, he considered that, after all, the objections that occurred to him were but trivial.

Still, before arriving, it was necessary that Angela should know something of the position in life she was supposed to fill; and he said to her—

"As my sister, dear one—for it will be supposed by others that you are my real sister, and not merely one by adoption—you will be considered to be a lady of rank, and, therefore, it will be well to leave people in this delusion as regards that circumstance. Do you understand me?"

"Then you are of rank?"

Captain Hawk could not, for the life of him, bring himself to utter to that young girl a deliberate falsehood, so he just replied—

"They say so, and I don't contradict them, and that is the course I wish you to pursue. There is another thing, too, that I wish you to bear in mind, and that is, that my means are quite ample, so that you need not restrict yourself in nothing that your fancy may dictate. I hope in a few days to be able to think of some plan of living that will be pleasanter than a sojourn for any length of time at a hotel."

Angela was as easy as possible in his hands to make say or do anything that he wished, for she had such an opinion of him, that what he thought right she was quite ready to give up her own judgment concerning, and to believe it right, just upon that account.

When they reached the door of the hotel, the first person they encountered was Joe, who, seeing upon Captain Hawk's arm a young and beautiful girl, started back in amazement.

The lights in the hall of the hotel were quite sufficient to reveal to Joe and to the attendants who were there the astonishing beauty of Angela, and there was a great gaze of admiration and amazement.

Captain Hawk turned to Joe, and spoke.

"Send the landlord to me," he said sharply.

"Oh, lor, yes," said Joe. "Oh my eye!"

Hawk darted at him an angry glance, and Joe, seeing that his master was not pleased at his manner, made a low bow, and said—

"Your lordship's orders shall be obeyed—I mean your grace—that is to say—dear me, what a fool I am—I mean, your royal highness's orders."

Hawk, with Angela still upon his arm, ascended the grand staircase, to the suite of rooms he occupied, and placing her upon a couch, he said—

"This shall for a time be your home. I will likewise order a suite of private rooms for you, and even I will not visit you without your leave."

"How good you are to me."

"No—no. It is you who are good, I only wish, Angela, that I were but half so good as you are."

"And I, brother, wish—"

"Hush, dear, some one comes."

Joe flung the door of the saloon open, and the landlord, who had been sitting up waiting the return of his princely guest, entered the room, almost bent double with the respectful feelings that actuated him.

The landlord of the hotel passed Joe at the same time that he gave him an impulse with his foot that very nearly sent him into Angela's lap.

"Murder! Oh dear! A thousand pardons, gracious sir," said the landlord. "I rather think your man pushed me."

Joe had made good his retreat at this moment, or it is probable enough he would have had something thrown at his head by Captain Hawk, who had seen his conduct to the landlord. Making up his mind, however, at some future opportunity to let Joe know that he was not to play tricks with impunity, Captain Hawk smothered his anger at the moment, and said to the landlord—

"This young lady is my sister."

The landlord bowed, till his nose very nearly touched the carpet.

"Have you a wife?" added Hawk.

"I have that honour and satisfaction, noble sir, if you wish it."

"Very well, that is so far fortunate, for my sister will live for some time here, and I should, of course, like her to be in the care of your wife. I wish her to have a suite of rooms to herself, and every possible care and attention I wish lavished upon her that money can pay for. She is dearer to me than my life."

"Oh, how deeply affecting," said the landlord. "This is, indeed, one of the most rare examples of brotherly af—"

"Silence!"

Nothing was so annoying to Captain Hawk as to have himself praised for feelings and motives which he knew he had no sort of pretence to. The landlord suddenly stopped short in his speech, and concluded by a profusion of bows.

"I think you quite understand me," added Hawk, "that this young lady is to be the most honoured guest in this house?"

"Oh, yes, your highness—oh, yes. I will fetch my spouse, who will only be too happy to attend to the illustrious young lady."

"Do so."

The landlord left the room, and Angela could not help laughing, in the gaiety natural to her innocent young heart, at the manner in which he had conducted himself to her new brother.

"Do they all act thus, Gerald?" she said.

"Yes, Angela, you have only to let them know in this country, past a doubt, that you are willing to pay everything they please, and you may command the utmost possible servility in the attentions that will be paid to you."

"But that is not right."

"It is not, indeed, dear; but it is ever the case. Here comes the landlady of the hotel, though, and you will, no doubt, soon see that you will be loaded with compliments by her, as well as by the landlord."

Captain Hawk found himself just a little mistaken in his estimate of the landlady of the hotel, for she was a quiet, sensible woman, certainly respectful enough, but by no means fulsome in her flatteries. She curtsied to Angela, and to Captain Hawk, and said gently—

"I shall have pleasure in making the stay of the young lady here as comfortable as possible. Do I understand that she is the sister of your highness?"

"Just so," said Hawk.

"Then she requires separate apartments?"

HAWK ACCOSTED IN THE STREET BY LADY DELIVA'S COMPANION.

"By all means. Sometimes we shall take a meal together, but not always."

The landlady, now that she saw the affair was to all appearance all right, looked well pleased, and said to Angela—

"If your ladyship will have the goodness to follow me, I will conduct you to your rooms, which I hope will meet with your approbation."

"Good-night, Angela," said Hawk.

"Good-night, dear brother," said Angela, as she flung her arms around him, and kissed him on the cheek. "Good-night, and God's blessing attend upon you."

Captain Hawk was too much taken by surprise by that artless caress and kiss to return another.

The door closed upon Angela, and

he then sunk into a chair, and resting his head upon his hands, he drew a long breath as he said—

"Where is all this to end?"

That was a question which, in good truth, it was much easier to ask than to answer. That he loved Angela to positive desperation he could easily have told himself; and that he was awed from a full and free expression of that love by the innocence and simplicity of the young creature, was likewise true.

What was he to do? How, indeed, as he asked himself, was it all to end? Could it be possible that he would continue to exercise so much self-control?

Agitated by such feelings, Captain Hawk paced his room for an hour or two, instead of retiring to rest, in the vain hope of seeing some way out of the difficulties of his present position.

Once or twice he thought of getting together all the money he possibly could, and leaving England altogether with Angela. Then, again, the idea struck him that he ought to allow her to remain the innocent and gentle creature she was, and get some other person than himself to afford her an asylum.

And yet who would think so well of her as she really deserved to be thought of, now, after she had been, as it were, in his society, and residing with him? If they did, though, and if some one were to love and marry her?

This thought that she might be another's was to Captain Hawk positive madness, and clenching his hands, he cried out—

"No—no! Never shall she be another's! It shall be death to any one to look at her with eyes of too great affection. She is mine, and mine only. I saved her from death, and she is mine!"

Captain Hawk sank upon a couch in a state of great exhaustion.

CHAPTER CXXI.

CAPTAIN HAWK GETS SOME NEWS OF WHO ANGELA REALLY IS.

The sunshine was beaming upon his face when Captain Hawk awoke on the morning following the night of excitement that he had passed through. For a few moments Captain Hawk was so confused that he could hardly be said to have a very clear notion of where he was; but this was in consequence of the sunlight having been strongly in his eyes.

Springing to his feet, he went to a decanter of cold water, and quite heedless of the elegant carpetting of the room, he deliberately poured it over his head and face.

The shock and the coolness had the effect of instantly reviving him.

"Ah, home," he said. "Yes, I am at home."

Then there came with a full rush back to his mind all the remembrances of the former night; but when he came to recollect how he had rescued Angela from the Lady Deliva, and how he had brought her to the hotel, and how she had kissed and embraced him before retiring to rest, he thought that surely all must be nothing but a very vivid dream.

The memory of the caress, though, that the young creature had so innocently bestowed upon him was too delightful to be unreal; and after gazing about him for a few moments, he sunk back upon the couch again, saying—

"Oh, if indeed and in truth this be all a dream, it is one that I would most willingly never awaken from."

The sound of a footstep startled him, and he looked at Joe, who was standing by the door within a few paces of it.

"Joe?"

"Yes, capt—no, I mean, your highness."

"Did I or did I not last night bring a young lady to this place?"

"Rather."

"Then it is no dream!"

"Who said it was?"

"Silence, idiot!"

"Oh, very good; but I ain't sich a

idiot as to bring a gal home, and then have to ask somebody else whether it was a dream or whether it wasn't."

Hawk turned upon him a fierce look.

"Hark you, my fine fellow," he said. "Of late, you seem to fancy that you can say what you like to me, and you have given a licence to your insolence that I do not feel at all inclined to put up with. I warn you."

"Very good."

"Beware, I say, for if you do not, it may happen at some moment when you least of all expect it that you will find you have gone too far."

"A nod's as good as a wink any day to a blind oss," said Joe. "Here is a letter for the Count Astral."

"That is for me. Who brought it?"

"A fellow with a gold shoulder knob bobbing about, and a pair of red plush breeches, and a powdered vig—a white coat, and a waistcoat as long as to-day and to-morrow."

"Ah," thought Hawk, "the livery of the secretary of state, I think. But how could he by any possibility have discovered that I was staying here? You may leave the room, Joe."

"Much obliged," said Joe. "What a tail our cat has got, to be sure."

Now, Joe would not have wished even in the lightest whisper to have said one half that he did, only that he had indulged himself with a morning glass, and it had had its usual effect upon him. It was well that Hawk was too busily engaged in breaking the seal of the letter that had been placed in his hands to attend to what Joe was muttering.

The letter was, indeed, as he had suspected, from the secretary of state, and ran as follows :—

"Downing Street.

"MY DEAR COUNT,—First let me ask your pardon for taking the liberty of addressing you at all at a place of residence which you did not think proper to communicate to me ; but the fact that having by the merest of accidents in the world heard from a gentleman that you were residing a the hotel to which I send this note, I venture upon writing it.

"In an interview which I have had the honour of having with his majesty, I took occasion, as, in fact, I was bound in duty to do, to mention that the fate of my poor brother was no longer involved in obscurity, and to state what I knew of the details of the proceedings of the infamous Lady Deliva.

"His majesty, thereupon, was pleased to say that, as he was about to-night to give a grand masked ball at the palace, he would be happy in the course of the evening to receive you, and to hear from your own lips the curious story you have to tell.

"I hope that you will feel inclined to attend St. James's, any time between the hours of ten and four—that is, ten at night and four in the morning.

"If in any way I have said too much of the affair, I beg you, my dear count, to consider to whom I was talking, and how difficult it was to evade the questions of the king, and to believe me, with all sincerity—Yours truly,

"ADDINGTON."

"P. S. The accompanying slip of paper will procure you admission, together with whoever you choose to bring with you."

Upon the slip of paper that was in the letter were the words—

"Pass for me.

"GEORGE R."

"The king's signature," said Captain Hawk, as he looked at the pass. "Well, to go, or not to go, that is the question. As for the accident that made Lord Addington acquainted with my place of residence, I presume it arose from likewise the accident of his sending a spy to dog me. Well, well, after all, that don't a great deal matter, so long as they think me to be what I have made them for the time believe."

Still Hawk could not quite make up his mind what to do, for the fact was, he felt so jealous of the possession of Angela, that he was fearful of saying that she was with him at all, and he was not without some fear that her residence with the Lady Deliva might be sufficiently notorious to induce inquiry.

What if, after all, the invitation to the palace were but a trap, as it were, in which to catch him, and force from him an account of what had become of the young girl?

The latter idea all but induced him at once to forego the notion of accepting the invitation, but still he did not quite decide upon so doing. The whole day was before him, in which to think it over.

Captain Hawk rang his bell, and Joe appeared.

"Joe," he said, "inquire how the princess is, and whether she is up."

"Oh, lor!" said Joe.

"Do you hear me, wretch?"

"Yes, I does—oh, I'll do it."

"You had better; and tell her if she is disposed so to honour and oblige me, I shall be very happy of her company at breakfast."

"That's the way to do it," said Joe. "All's right."

"I must check that fellow's growing familiarity," thought Captain Hawk, "and yet, I know not how to do it, without spoiling his efficacy as a follower. He is as faithful as the dog, and as brave as a lion. I cannot forget, either, that I owe him my life. Well, well, I must put up with as much as I can from him."

Joe returned.

"Well? Well?"

"Why, her ladyship says, with her love to her brother, meaning you, that she will be here directly."

"That is well. Order the breakfast, and tell them to let it be of the best they can lay before me."

"I will. But I say, captain?"

"What, now?" roared Hawk.

"You don't mean to go for to say that that is your little sister, now, and no sort of gammon, do you?"

"Joe?"

"Here you is."

"If you have the slightest personal regard for yourself, I advise you, as a friend, to be careful of your conduct. It seems to me that of late something or another has disgusted you with the world."

"Lor! what makes you think that?"

"Just from this simple reason, that I think you have resolved upon suicide, only have not the courage to carry out the determination; and, therefore, you are trying all you can to get me to blow your brains out."

"Oh, that's it?"

"Yes, Joe; and I can only inform you, if it be any sort of satisfaction for you to know the fact, that you are gradually but surely succeeding."

Joe was, as he himself not unfrequently said, not such a fool as he looked, and so he quite understood what Captain Hawk meant. With a very low bow, that had something so very ludicrous about it that Hawk had to turn to the window to hide the smile that would come to his lips, despite his wish to avoid it, Joe quitted the room.

"By Heaven!" said Captain Hawk, as he paced the room, waiting for the appearance of the lovely Angela, "I do not know what to make of that fellow at times. I almost suspect that he knows me too well, and that the day will come when he will thwart me."

CHAPTER CXXII.

CAPTAIN HAWK TAKES ANGELA WITH HIM TO THE KING'S ENTERTAINMENT.

If Captain Hawk had seen Joe when the latter got outside the magnificent breakfast room, he, perhaps, would have had a still further reason for the idea that was just dawning upon his mind, to the effect that some day or another he and his follower would come into collision with each other.

The half comic, half respectful manner of Joe vanished as soon as the door was shut upon Hawk; and then, rising to his full height, Joe shook his head rather scornfully, and muttered to himself—

"I don't mean to deny, captain, but that I like you—you are the sort of reckless devil-may-care chap that just suits me; but I know you are a bad one, for all that; and if this pretty little innocent looking creature you have brought here, from Heaven only knows where, should want a friend, she will find one in me, despite all your big looks and your threatenings, Captain Hawk. You are but a man, after all, and I am another; and of the two I am rather the biggest; so look out."

It will be seen by this mode of discourse of Joe's that he was far, very far from meditating anything in the shape of treachery towards Captain Hawk, but that he was resolved along with his fidelity to the captain to thwart him in any extraordinary villany that he might think himself at liberty to carry out.

It was well, as the sequel of this little episode in the life of Captain Hawk will show, that Providence or accident raised up such a defender for the innocent Angela as the susceptible and courageous Joe.

Perhaps there was hardly another person in the world who could have coped with Captain Hawk with one half the chances of success that would be Joe's.

After thus slightly giving utterance to his feelings upon the subject, which was as uppermost in the thoughts of Hawk as it was in his, Joe took the message with which he had been charged to the landlady of the hotel.

A very short time sufficed, with the large resources of that establishment, to lay a magnificent breakfast in the room where Hawk was sitting; and the landlady took the message of the pretended brother to Angela.

That message, couched as it was in language rather of distance and respect, was in the mind of the landlady yet a further proof of the exalted rank of the parties.

"Dear me," she said to her husband, "you see now how princes and princesses behave to each other, though they are brothers and sisters."

"Well, but ain't it foolish, now?" said the landlord.

"Foolish? Certainly not."

"Oh, but it is, after all. Why, if my sister was staying here, I should first go and knock at her room door and cry out, 'Hilloa!'"

"You are a fool."

"No, I should not."

"I didn't say you would, but I say you are a fool; and if you bring your sister Sarah here any more, I will be the death of you."

"But, my dear, I ——"

"Hold your tongue, and attend to your business. I don't want to have anything to say to such a wretch as you are."

These little disturbances between the landlord and the landlady were too common even to create much attention in the household of the hotel. All the waiters and the chambermaids did was to laugh with each other at the discomfiture of the master, and there was an end of it.

The doors leading from the adjoining apartments to the one in which Captain Hawk's magnificent breakfast was laid were now thrown open, and the landlord himself with a low bow ushered in Angela.

"Dear Angela!" cried Hawk.

"Dear brother Gerald!" said she; "are you well and happy this morning?"

"I am well, dear one; and how can I be otherwise than happy when I see you with that enchanting smile?"

"Ah! you flatter, now!"

"Oh!—oh!" cried the landlord, "this is too—too much. Oh!"

"What is the matter?" cried Hawk.

"Oh, excuse me, your royal highness, but my feelings just for the moment overcame me, that was all, to see such exquisite, and beautiful, and nice affection between you and your lovely sister. That was all, noble and illustrious sir."

"Be off," said Hawk.

"I will do myself that honour."

The landlord closed the door upon Captain Hawk and Angela.

"These people are so very intrusive," said Hawk, rather petulantly, "although I believe that they mean all for the best."

"Bear with them patiently, Gerald," said Angela, with a sweet smile.

"For your dear sake, Angela, I could bear with anything. But tell me—have you received here all the attention that you required? Have they been kind and considerate to you?"

"I have been treated like a princess. In fact, they will have it that I am one. Ah, dear Gerald, I think you have kept secret from me your real rank, and that, after fancying that I know you so well, I am really deceived in you."

Hawk's colour went and came quickly.

"Deceived in me, you think, do you?"

"Yes, Gerald. Come, now, tell me who and what you really are."

"It is better not."

"Shall I try to guess?"

"If you please to do so, dear one, although it will be but an unprofitable waste of your time."

"Well, then, I will. You are a prince?"

"No."

"You are not a prince? Then you are a king?"

"Oh, no."

"Then I can guess no more, and there's an end of it."

"Do not trouble yourself to guess, dear one, what I am. Only do you be content with the knowledge that I am your own Gerald, and that I love you. Is not that sufficient for you?"

"It is. Oh, yes, it is indeed."

Captain Hawk was more enraptured with the beauty and the charming simplicity of this girl the more he saw of her, and making her sit next to him at the breakfast-table, he took a delight in attending upon her as if she had been some charming little child, the care of which devolved entirely upon his kindness.

Angela was far from being insensible to this attention upon the part of Captain Hawk, and she smiled and talked to him in such a pleasant way, and with so much of the purity and innocence of her guileless heart, that more than once he asked himself—

"What can I say to this young creature that shall be other than as pure and as holy as she is herself in all her thoughts and all her actions?"

It was with a feeling nearly approaching to the aggravation of despair that Captain Hawk found Angela so perfect a being. If she had but had some of the faults and the foibles incidental to others of her sex whom she had encountered, and still possessed all her beauty, he would have much preferred it.

"Angela," he said, "you are really too like an angel, and that is the sober truth."

"I an angel?"

"Yes, dear one, you are indeed; and there are times, as I look at you, in which I can scarcely bring myself to believe that you are mortal."

"That is the conceit of one who loves me," said Angela.

"It is, indeed. But what is that you wear round your neck, Angela, by that plain thin piece of white ribbon?"

"Oh, that is—I know not what; but one of my earliest recollections consisted in having it placed upon my neck, and being told never to part with it."

"Indeed?"

"Yes, and I have a vivid recollection that it was in the midst of some great conflagration that this happened, and that then I was let down from some window a great height, and caught in the arms of some one, who, instead of being kind to me, beat me dreadfully, until I became insensible, and when I recovered, I found the Lady Deliva sitting by me in a handsome room."

"This is a strange story."

"It is. Oh, Gerald—my adopted brother—you would give me great joy if you could tell me what it means."

"Alas! I cannot. What did the Lady Deliva say to you when you recovered in the way you state?"

"She told me that, as my aunt, she had now the care of me, and that I must obey her in all things for my own peace and comfort, for that if I did not, she would be compelled to adopt such means of forcing me as would let me see that I was completely in her power. She spoke much more at the time, which I paid but little heed to, for I began to cry bitterly."

"Then she is your aunt?"

"Oh, yes, she said so."

"But have you no other evidence of the fact than her own assertion?"

"No—no!"

"Then, Angela, the probability is, that she is not your aunt at all. Who knows but that you may have some parents even living?"

Captain Hawk saw reason, so far as his own selfish views with regard to Angela were concerned, to regret the having started this idea the moment he gave utterance to it, for clasping her hands with a sudden joy, Angela cried out—

"Oh, is this, indeed, possible? Have I a mother, do you think, Gerald? What a world of new ideas you give me!"

She commenced sobbing as though her heart would break.

"Cheer up," said Captain Hawk. "It was but the vague suggestion of a moment, and I had no special reason for thinking what I said."

"But is it possible?"

"Certainly possible; but it is better to banish such a thought from your mind now, as it will distract you much."

"Oh, no—no! I cannot banish such a thought from my mind, Gerald, now that it has once found a home there; and far from at all distracting me, it will be to me a constant solace under all affliction. It is a dear and pleasant thought."

"Well, well. Leave all this to me to inquire for you concerning. I think you may safely trust me with all you know of your history."

"You know it all. Lady Deliva, from the time that she announced herself to be my aunt, kept me as you found me, only that at times, without my being accused of any fault, she would come, attended by her waiting-maid, and cruelly beat me, so that, you see, I have suffered much."

"How strange a heart must she have had to raise her hand against you, Angela. It seems to me as if it were quite impossible there could be any human being so wicked in all the world. But you have not yet told me what it is that is attached to the end of the ribbon round your neck."

"No more I have, Gerald. Here it is."

"A ring?"

"Yes, it is a mourning ring, as you see, and it has the initials of some one upon it, but whose they are I cannot tell."

Captain Hawk took the ring in his hand, and looked at it attentively. It was of solid gold, and on the inner surface was engraved the words—

"*In memorium.*"

After those words, there was the initials, L. L. P. and a ducal coronet, but beyond all this there was nothing about the ring to lead to a discovery of whom it had belonged to.

Captain Hawk, though, felt very much disturbed at all this, for the conclusion that he came to concering it was, that Lady Deliva was not the aunt of Angela, but had, from some selfish purpose, or from some revenge, stolen her from her parents.

CHAPTER CXIII.

CAPTAIN HAWK TAKES RATHER AN ILL-ADVISED STEP.

After regarding the ring for a few moments in silence, Hawk returned it to Angela, saying as he did so—

"My dear Angela, I can make nothing of it."

She placed it in her bosom again with a sigh, as she replied—

"Alas, I feel melancholy when I look at it, and something seems to tell me, that in some way it is intimately connected with my destiny."

"Do not let it disturb you, Angela. Wait patiently, until some circumstance may occur to afford you a clue to the mystery, and in the meantime, as you do not know whether it be a story of joy or of sorrow that you might have to hear in connection with that ring, you should not let it cast a cloud upon your young heart."

"I will strive not, Gerald."

The breakfast was taken at intervals, while this interesting conversation was going on between Captain Hawk and Angela. But while Hawk was thus talking to her, he was considering what he should do about the invitation of the secertary of state to attend the king's entertainment at St. James's that evening.

That he should contrive to make some profit by the affair, he hardly doubted it he went at all; and now that he had Angela to look to, he was more than ever anxious that his resources should be as large as possible, for he could not bear the idea of keeping her at all in a different style to that which he had shown her he lived in.

There was a vague idea in the mind of Hawk of establishing Angela in some splendid house where he could visit her when he chose so to do, and from which, without her ever knowing what his real pursuits were, he could sally forth to make money on the road, for the support of her state and dignity.

The idea was not encouraged though, and now his whole thoughts were about the entertainment at St. James's.

The fact was, that Captain Hawk felt with regard to Angela, now that she was with him, something like a miser feels with his money. He could not bear to have her out of his sight for any length of time, and it was from this feeling that he was prompted to conceive the idea of taking her to the king's entertainment at night.

The idea of taking her there, would never have found a home in the mind of Captain Hawk for many moments had it not been that the entertainment was a masked ball, so that the fair face of the young girl would be concealed from the general gaze.

A masked ball, too, encouraged the discretion of going in any costume one pleased, and though Captain Hawk could not only put on some dress that would conceal him from any curious eye who might otherwise rather disagreeably recognise him, but he could get a costume for Angela that would conceal her beauty and her youth.

"Angela," he said, "I don't want you to feel dull while you reside with me, and, therefore, I think of taking you to a ball to-night."

"A ball? Oh, how delightful!"

"But will you go on the conditions I shall make with you?"

"Oh, yes."

"Hear them first, Angela. Perhaps you will not like them."

"Well, brother," said Angela, quite in raptures at the idea of a ball, "what are the conditions? Are they very hard ones?"

"Not difficult at all, Angela, are they. First, I want you to dance with no one but with me."

"That I consent to."

"Then I want you to take care not to lose sight of me, for if I should lose you in the throng, I should be very unhappy."

"And so should I, so I consent to that, too."

"The third condition is, that you go in disguise. It is a masked ball, and you may do so with perfect propriety. I want you to go in male costume."

"As a page?"

"Oh, no—no. I want you to go in a costume not nearly so fascinating. In fact, I want to disguise both your youth and your beauty. Will you permit me to do so?"

Angela laughed, and there was just the least perceptible glance at herself in a mirror close at hand, and she seemed as if she would have said, "My youth and my beauty are beyond all powers of disguise."

"Well, brother," she said cheerfully, "I consent to whatever course you please to adopt for me. You shall have the full direction of the whole affair, and whatever dress you require me to put on, or whatever part you require me to act, I will do it to the utmost of my ability."

"That is like my own Angela! So you will see the ball and the rich and princely rooms in which it will be held. During the day I will make all the necessary arrangements for our going."

This being so far settled, Captain Hawk left Angela to amuse herself while he went about several affairs that required instant seeing to.

The cheque that the Lady Deliva had given to him while she had had a confidence in his protestations, or chose to delude herself into a belief that she could purchase his constancy, he changed into gold and notes, so that he was excellently provided with ready money against any emergency.

During some portion of the day, too, Captain Hawk looked about for a house in which he might place Angela, for the plan of keeping her to himself for his own purposes began to grow more and more pleasant to him the more he reflected upon it.

He saw a mansion standing in some very beautiful grounds at Kensington, which he thought would suit him, but he wished not to be precipitate about it, but to await the events of a few days.

It will be seen that it was just as well he, Captain Hawk, did wait for a few days, as things did not go exactly as he would have wished during even that short period of time.

As the evening approached, though, he turned his whole attention to the making his arrangements for taking Angela to the ball at the palace, and for that object he visited one of the first costumers of the metropolis, and after considerable trouble selected for her the dress of a Tartar officer, which was so constructed as quite to conceal the figure, and which assisted the covering up of the face to such an extent that it would be almost impossible

for any one to have recognised the fair young girl in such a disguise.

For himself he chose a Venetian dress of great beauty.

In fact, Captain Hawk was pleased to think that no one could suspect Angela when in the dress of the Tartar officer to be other than some well-looking youth, for he costume involved the necessity ot wearing a false moustache, which he considered would alter the whole aspect of her face.

While Hawk was away from the hotel, though, Angela was not without some company, for Joe made his appearance in the saloon where she sat, and carefully closing the door, he marched up to her and said—

"Miss, I don't know who you are, but I know what you are, and that is, one of the sweetest little creatures that ever the sun shone upon, and now if you tell His Royal Highness Gerald, as I heard you call him, that I have spoken to you he will try to kill me, and, of course, I will try to take care of myself, which will make a row that may be the end of both of us; so say you won't tell him."

"Certainly not," said the beautiful Angela. "Oh, no, not for worlds."

"That will do," said Joe. "He won't be back for some little time, and if he should, you can say you rang for some books, and that I came in answer to the bell."

"Yes—yes. But go away if there is danger."

"Oh, no, there's no danger, unless you go from your word, miss, and make it, and that I don't think you will do."

"My word? What do you mean?"

"Why, you have promised that you won't tell him that I spoke to you, and that if he should come in while I am here you will say you rang for me."

"Did I—oh, did I?"

"To be sure you did."

Poor Angela was really so frightened at the serious manner of Joe, that she hardly knew what she had said or promised at the moment.

"To be sure you did," added Joe; "and now, miss, I am a pretty good judge of such articles as you are. I think—indeed I will say that I know that you are an innocent young girl."

"I am—indeed I am."

"I knowed it. Well, where's your mother?"

"My mother?"

"Yes, don't you understand? Where's your mother, and your father, and your brothers, and your sisters, and your cousins, and your aunts, and your uncles, and all those sort of people?"

"Alas, I have no one in the whole world to cling to but to Gerald, and he is so good and so kind."

"Oh, is he?"

"Yes, you who are a follower of his, for he said you were, must know that in all the wide world there is no one to compare with him."

"You don't say so?"

"I say so because it is true."

"Very good, miss; it's true as long as you think it, but no longer. What I have to say to you is just this: if it should happen—mind, I don't say that it will, but it may for all that—if it should happen that in any sort of way you want a friend to stand between you and any harm, and you don't at the time think that Gerald, as you call him, is just the proper person to appeal to, you may depend upon me, for I shall not be far off."

"Oh, what do you mean?"

"Never you mind that, miss. It isn't at all necessary that I should tell you now what I mean; you will find that out, if so be the occasion should arise, and if it shouldn't—and I hope it won't—if it shouldn't, there's no occasion for you to know any more about it."

"You alarm me."

"Never mind that neither."

"But—but you ought to have said nothing or you ought to say much more."

"No, all I wanted to say I have said, and that just is, that you may depend upon a friend in any emergency, and that friend is Joe."

"I cannot but feel grateful to any one who proffers to me friendship, but yet I feel so secure in the love and the goodness of my adopted brother, your master, that I am certain I shall never require any other friend than he."

"Very good," said Joe, "that's right enough as long as it lasts. Joe is my name—it ain't a very long one, is it?"

"Certainly not, Joseph."

"Oh, don't call me Joseph. Lor love you, I have never been called Joseph since I was christened, and then it was the parson who would be so mighty particular about nothing at all. When you want me, you sing out 'Joe! Joe!' and you will soon see me."

"Sing?"

"I mean, call out. Oh, dear, you don't seem to know a very great deal, you don't, with all your pretty face. Oh, what a thing it is now to be so beautiful; I could look at you, miss, all day, that I could—but I mustn't. Now you remember what I have said to you, and don't tell nobody."

"I will be secret."

"That's right, then, and all's safe. Now my mind feels a little easier nor it did, for all day I have been so put out to see you here like a babby a going into a slaughter-house, that I have been regularly off my feed."

"Off what?"

"Couldn't take my *wittles*, miss, that's what I means. But it's all right now, and I'll go and take a slight snack of a couple of pounds of chops, and a bottle of stout, just to pamper up my stomach a bit, for you see I means to be precious careful and moderate now, in case you should call out, 'Joe, I want's you.'"

"I thank you," said Angela. "I fully believe you have some good motive in coming thus to me to warn me of possible danger, but I will yet hope that it only exists in your own imagination."

"My what?"

"Your imagination."

"Lor love you, miss, and your pretty face, and bright eyes, I never had none."

CHAPTER CXXIV.

ANGELA GOES TO THE BALL AT THE PALACE WITH CAPTAIN HAWK.

Joe ought to have taken himself off as soon as he had said all he had to say to Angela, but the real fact was, that the more he looked at the sweet, innocent, child-like face of the young girl, the more fascinated he became, and the more difficult he felt it to tear himself away.

It is so rare a thing that one meets with that exquisite beauty of expression which reveals the purity of the soul, such as bloomed in the features of Angela, that it is not in human nature not to glory in the sight, and to gaze upon it with eyes of the intensest admiration.

Thus, then, was it that Joe, with all his rough nature, felt an affection for the young and helpless girl, and continued gazing at her when he ought to have gone from the room, and not run the risk of Hawk coming back.

"You have nothing more to say to me then, Joseph?" said Angela.

"Nothing, miss, only that it's Joe, and not Joseph."

"Joe, then, be it."

"Ah, that's right. Bless you, good bye. Take care of yourself, for I'm blessed if there's many such as you is. You may go a duece of a way on a long summer's day, and not see—Oh!"

The door of the saloon opened rather sharply, and Captain Hawk made his appearance in the gorgeous apartment.

Poor Angela, who was as guileless as it was possible for any human being to be, and who was about the worst person in the world to be engaged in any plot that required a good face to be put upon matters, and ample presence of mind, uttered a faint shriek, and Captain Hawk paused with a look of astonishment that gradually grew to one of rage.

It was well, though, that Joe did not lose his presence of mind, and it was equally well, too, that before coming to the room at all to speak to Angela he had provided himself with an excuse for so doing.

Without betraying the smallest embarrassment at the sudden appearance of Captain Hawk, or heeding in any way the scowl that was upon his brow, Joe coolly took from a very capacious pocket of his coat an elegantly bound book, and holding it towards Angela, he said—

"The landlady says that this is the only book she has that may amuse you, and so I have brought it."

Angela looked rather pale, but she recollected what Joe had told her, namely, that the want of a book upon her part was to be the excuse for his presence there if it should chance that Gerald, as she called him, should come to the hotel unexpectedly, so she managed to say—

"I thank you. I am sorry I troubled you."

"What is all this?" said Captain Hawk, advancing.

"All what, your lordship?" said Joe.

"This intrusion, sirrah."

"Oh, that's it? I did not comprehend at the moment. The young lady rung the bell, and I answered it. She wanted a book, and I got one. I am exceedingly sorry to have committed such a very terrible offence."

Captain Hawk pointed to the door, as he said—

"Do you see that?"

"Certainly I do. It's a very nice door, with gilt mouldings."

"Go."

"With great pleasure, my lord. Have you any commands for your most humble and devoted servant, who, of course, loves you all the same, let your conduct to him be just what it may, you are such a quiet man."

Captain Hawk's face turned white with rage, as he said—

'I will talk with you another time."

"When you please," said Joe. "Only don't hurry yourself, because I feel quite certain it makes you ill, and spoils your digestion."

With these words, Joe left the room, and after the conduct of Hawk to him, it cannot be wondered at that his respect and admiration for him was hourly upon the decrease, and if the captain should go on in this way, treating Joe like a dog, it is to be expected that he will end by converting him into an enemy instead of a friend.

The fact was, that Captain Hawk was a most disagreeable, overhearing-tempered man, and he had not sense enough to know when to be civil.

Angela had not before during her brief acquaintance with Captain Hawk had any opportunity of observing that he could look so desperately savage as he did while speaking to Joe, and she was rather alarmed to find that one of whom she had had so very high an opinion could give way to such an amount of passion, and as it appeared to her, too, all about just nothing at all.

Poor Angela, tremblingly, held the book in her hand, and when the door was fairly closed upon Joe, she looked at Captain Hawk with the tears starting to her eyes; but she said nothing.

Hawk made quite an effort to speak with composure, as he said—

"My dear Angela, I don't like that man to speak to you. How long has he been here, my darling?"

"He brought this book."

"Yes, but——"

"Oh, Gerald, you terrify me."

"Do not say that. Nothing can possibly be further from my intention, I assure you, than to do so; but I am compelled to put on harsh looks, which are not my nature, and to speak in a manner that is very contrary to the dictates of my heart, to such people as the one who has just been here."

"Oh, I am so glad to hear you say that it is contrary to your nature to look as you looked just now, and to speak as you spoke. I hardly knew you."

"Indeed?"

"No; and you did not look nice and handsome at all."

Captain Hawk tried to smile as he took the book from the hand of Angela, and opened it. It was a little volume of sentimental poems, and about as rubbishy as such efforts usually are.

Casting it from him with an expression of contempt, Hawk said—

"I shall be very seldom out, Angela; but when I am, for the time that we shall stay here, I would rather you remained in your own rooms, and then when you ring some of the female servants of the hotel will wait upon you."

"As you please, Gerald. But you are not angry now?"

"No—no. Not at all, and never at all with you, dear Angela. Ah, if I were angry with all the world, I do think that one of your sweet looks would alter my feelings entirely, and make me forgive them."

"That is like yourself."

A very slight noise outside the door of the room came upon the ears of Captain Hawk, and a sudden idea seemed to strike him that Joe was there listening to what he was saying to Angela.

The young girl saw the change of countenance that came over him, and clinging to his arm, she said—

"Oh, Gerald—Gerald, now you look angry again."

"Not with you, Angela—not with you. I pray you to let me go."

Withdrawing his hand from her grasp, Captain Hawk stepped to the far end of the saloon, and from a corner took a sword that he had purchased the day before. Drawing it from its sheath, he approached the door of the room with it, and laying his hand upon the lock, he suddenly flung the door wide open, and made such a thrust with the sword on the other side of it, that if any one had been there they must have been run through the body.

To the mortification, though, of Captain Hawk, the landing-place outside the door was quite vacant, and he was muttering some curses to himself, when from the stairs some distance below the landing Joe called out—

"Did your royal highness condescend to want anything?"

Hawk made a step forward as if he would have gone after Joe; but he saw the latter place his hand in the breast of his apparel, and he felt from that moment convinced that he had bullied and threatened Joe until he was on his guard against him.

The idea of a fight with Joe upon the staircase of the hotel was one that Captain Hawk even in his anger had sense enough left to feel would be one of the most imprudent things he could possibly engage in; so he withdrew into the saloon, swearing in a low tone to himself to be the death of Joe at some fitting opportunity.

It generally happens that your very angry and irascible people, when they run a chance of getting the worst of any encounter, can always call up sufficient discretion to their aid to put it off to another opportunity, and so it was with Captain Hawk in the present instance.

He saw, though, that Angela was very much alarmed, and he began to fear, not without good reason, that a few more such exhibitions of his temper and his violence would go far towards toppling him down from the pinnacle on which he had stood in her affections.

Fearful of such a result, he put on, as well as his anger would permit him to play the part, quite an amiable look, and said—

"Come, Angela, don't let this little matter vex you, but think of the entertainment you will derive from the ball at the palace to-night."

"But who did you mean to kill?"

"Kill?"

"Yes, with that sword, Gerald, which you still hold in your grasp."

"Pshaw! don't think of it," said Hawk, as he threw the sword from him. "I only thought it possible that some one was hiding and listening to you and me, that was all. The fact is, the fellow I brought here is a very bad one."

"Is he, indeed?"

"Yes, I keep him out of charity, you see, and I once saved his life, and that made me foolishly have a sort of attachment to him."

"And is he ungrateful to you?"

"Yes, very ungrateful to me. But he is an ungrateful subject of discourse. Let us think no more of him, dear Angela."

Angela said no more of Joe; but she could not help wondering which was right, Joe or Gerald, since the former by implication gave the latter a bad character, and the latter more boldly declared Joe to be everything but what he should be. The faith that she had in her adopted brother, Gerald, was not quite so great as it had been. The fact is, that about Joe there was a rough honesty of tone and manner that, with all his education and all his art, Captain Hawk could not counterfeit; and so was it that Joe had a decided advantage over him.

Hawk was rather in doubt about how he should dispose of Joe; for when he come to think that subject carefully over, he had in his own mind a kind of suspicion that now Joe was on his guard, the killing him would not be such an easy matter as he, Hawk, in his transactions with Joe had always affected to think it.

The necessity, however, for getting everything in readiness for the ball at the palace soon withdrew Hawk's attention from Joe and his affairs. He considered that whatever he intended to do with his old friend and follower would keep; for he had no thought for one moment that Joe would set about doing him any injury by betraying him or otherwise.

In this Captain Hawk was quite right. Joe only, as it were, stood upon the defensive in the matter.

Hawk had engaged one of the female assistants at the costumer's to come to the hotel with Angela's dress, and to assist her in attiring herself in it; for it was otherwise too complicated to be made use of by any person who did not quite understand it.

This young person arrived at about nine o'clock in the evening; and Angela, with childish glee, was prepared to be quite delighted.

"I will wait for you in the saloon," said Hawk. "There is ample time;

and I promise both you and myself much entertainment from where we are going."

"Oh, I am sure of that, brother."

Angela tripped off along with the attendant quite in a state of pleased excitement, for all this was so very different to the quiet, dreamy kind of life she had led at the Lady Deliva's, that to her it had all the charms of novelty added to its legitimate pleasures.

Hawk had no difficulty in soon attiring himself in his sumptuous dress, in which, to do him but common justice, he certainly did look noble. It set off his fine figure to admirable advantage.

CHAPTER CXXV.

CAPTAIN HAWK MAKES A DISCOVERY OF PECULIAR INTEREST TO THE FAIR ANGELA.

At the hour of nine o'clock upon that night Captain Hawk's gilded carriage, which he had hired, stood at the door of the hotel, ready to convey him and Angela to the ball at the palace.

It was no secret where they were going, as, indeed, he had told Angela to make none of it; for, if he had attempted to keep it secret, he would have failed in so doing, since the coachman, when he returned, would have proclaimed the fact.

Besides, it made the people of the hotel more and more convinced of his rank to see that he was among the invited guests upon that splendid occasion to St. James's, where it was known that all the *elite* of the nobility would be congregated.

The hall of the hotel was lined with the servants of the establishment, waiting to see the prince, as they called Hawk, from thence to his carriage, with the princess, his sister, who they firmly believed Angela to be.

Hawk paced the saloon anxiously, expecting the appearance of Angela in her male disguise, which took longer to arrange than his impatience would have had it take. At length the door opened, and Angela, with a smile of childish delight at her strange metamorphosis, made her appearance.

"Well, Gerald," she said, "how do I look?"

Captain Hawk was amazed at the change that the dress had made in her appearance. It was, certainly, a most gorgeous dress; but, as he had wished it to do, it had the effect of quite hiding the figure; and the little moustache upon her upper lip was put so cleverly on that no one could suspect it to be other than such.

"You look excellent," he said.

"Do I, dear Gerald? Do you know I anticipate great amusement in going with you to the palace."

"I hope you will not be disappointed, Angela. But have you a full remembrance of what you promised me?"

"Oh, yes, perfectly."

"That is well. If you do but follow my directions and take care to recollect what I have said to you, all will be well. Come, now, the carriage is at the door, and we shall soon be under the king's roof."

Angela placed her arm within that of Captain Hawk, and they descended the staircase of the hotel together. The spectators in the hall were numerous enough, but they all affected to be seized with so much reverence for the supposed Austrian prince and his sister, that it would have been very difficult to have quarrelled with them, even had Hawk felt inclined to do so, on account of their curiosity.

"To St. James's Palace," said Hawk, as the door of the carriage was closed.

The footmen ran by the side of the vehicles to which they belonged in those days, and at night carried torches, for London was indifferently lit by the miserable oil lamps, one half of which generally went out one hour or so after being lighted; so Captain Hawk's servants, that he had hired for the occasion, ran on by the side of the vehicle, and St. James's Palace was quickly gained.

The bustle and the excitement in Pall Mall and St. James's-street upon the occasion of the entertainment being given by the king exceeded all description. The thoroughfares were nearly blocked up by carriages of all sorts and descriptions, and the confusion at times reached a height that was absolutely deafening.

Angela, notwithstanding she was sitting with Hawk, in whose power to protect her she had great confidence, looked several times alarmed at the riot, and Hawk had once to look from the window and call to the constables of the high bailiff of Westminster, who were upon the spot, to interfere to get his carriage on.

After about half an hour's squabbling of this character the carriage fairly reached the entrance to the palace, and was allowed to roll into the court-yard, then as now called the Colour Court.

A strong body of the Yeomen of the Guard were there drawn up, and the bands of music of the foot regiments of guards were playing enchanting airs. The throng was very great in the Colour Court, but, as may be supposed, it was of a more select character than that without, inasmuch as it only consisted of the official personages connected with royalty, and the invited guests.

There was a long strip of elegant carpet laid right out into the court-yard for the distinguished guests to tread upon as they alighted from their carriages; and in a few moments Captain Hawk and the fair Angela were making their way to the entrance.

After passing through the door-way, they came to a small apartment, in which sat some gentlemen in plain clothes, and in which a guard of some twenty men, of the gentlemen of the royal body guard, were likewise. It was in this room that a kind of scrutiny took place of all who proffered their cards or orders of admission to the royal entertainment; for it was feared that the Jacobites might try to make some disturbance, as they had done recently upon several occasions.

"Your order, sir?" said one of the gentlemen to Hawk.

"It is here."

Hawk took from his pocket the pocket-book in which he had placed the order sent to him by the secretary of state, and opened the only pocket that was in it, where he had placed the rather important document.

It was gone!

"Your order of admission, sir?" said one of the gentlemen who were seated at the green table in that small apartment, rather sharply.

"I had it."

"It is a pity, sir," said another of the persons who sat at the table—"it is a pity that you are compelled to speak of it in the past tense."

"It is, sir."

"Well, sir," added the gentleman, rather sarcastically, "perhaps you will have the kindness to say what you would yourself do if you were in our places?"

"My duty, sir."

"Just so. Then it is with regret that I have to inform you you cannot be admitted. Please to go back, sir."

Captain Hawk was excessively provoked at the nonchalant mode of ignoring his right to an entrance; but what could he do or say under the circumstances? There he was quite unknown to the person whose duty was quite imperative upon the occasion, without the order, which would, no doubt, have admitted him at once.

It was truly provoking.

"Angela," he whispered, "I am afraid you will be disappointed."

"Heed it not," she said. "What does it matter?"

"Stand aside, sir!" cried a voice in authority, as a couple of gentlemen ascended the stairs. They were both masked; but one of them happened to say to one of the persons at the table—"How are you, Ansterthens?" and Captain Hawk thought he knew the voice to be that of the secretary of state.

Stepping up to him at once, Hawk said—

"My lord, this is a fortunate meeting. Do you know me?"

"What, the prince ——"

"Hush, my lord! I am the Count Astral here; but I regret to say that I shall not be able to visit the king to-night."

"Not able? Why, my dear count, you are here. How do you mean by saying you are not able, when I have the pleasure of seeing you now before my very eyes?"

"Just so, my lord; but I have lost or mislaid the order you were good enough to send me."

"Oh, if that be all," said the minister, with a smile, as he took the arm of Captain Hawk, "I think we can manage to arrange that. This is a friend of mine."

"If I had known that, my lord," aid the gentleman who sat at the table, and who had been so sarcastic in his treatment of Hawk, "I should, of course, not have hesitated a moment; but the gentleman will understand that my duy here is rather onerous."

Hawk merely inclined his head in reply, and took Angela by the arm, saying to the minister as he did so—

"A young *protege* of mine from Austria, my lord. I hope I may be permitted to give him a glimpse of the English court."

"By all means, count."

The difficulty was over as regarded the entrance of Captain Hawk and Angela to the saloons of the palace; but the minister had not got very far from the ante-room when he was overtaken by the person whom he had named Ansterthens, and who said, in rather an anxious whisper, as he presented him a scrap of paper—

"Was this the order, my lord?"

"Yes, surely. Where did you find it?"

"Nowhere, my lord. It has been presented."

"Presented?" said Hawk; "and by whom?"

"A gentleman richly dressed and masked. A few moments only before you, sir, made your appearance this order was presented, and the bearer of it was, as a matter of course, allowed to pass."

Captain Hawk looked rather confounded at this information, and so did the minister. Angela, seeing that something was amiss, although she hardly knew what it was, trembled as she hung upon the arm of Captain Hawk.

"This is very odd," said the minister. "It is exceedingly vexatious, too, for it goes a long way to prove that we have, at all events, an uninvited guest here to-night. I hardly know what to do."

"Should you knew the person again?" said Hawk.

"Yes, if he wore the same cloak, but not otherwise."

"Provoking."

"It is provoking," said the minister; "but it can't be helped, my dear prince. I will give some instructions, so that the secret police that we have here on the look-out to-night may be put in possession of the fact that there is some suspicious person in the saloons. Pardon me for a moment."

"Certainly, my lord."

The minister went to the table in the ante-room, and was engaged in conversation for a few moments with one of the parties there seated; and then he returned to Hawk, who, during the period of his absence, had been puzzling himself to think how and where he had lost the ticket of admission, and whose hands it could possibly have fallen into.

All the conjectures of Captain Hawk upon this occasion were, as he afterwards discovered, wide of the truth.

"Come, prince," said the minister, when he returned to Hawk, and saw that he had an anxious look upon his face. "Dismiss, I pray you, this little incident from your mind. It is not, after all, of much importance, I daresay. I hope you will enjoy your evening. Is your young friend Austrian?"

"Yes, my lord."

"A member of your own family, doubtless?"

"Even so."

"Ah, I thought as much. This way, if you please, prince. His majesty will only be too happy to receive you, I am sure. In about an hour, if a gentleman usher should accost you with such a request, you will have the goodness to follow him, and in the meantime to excuse me."

"Certainly."

The minister bowed and left Captain Hawk, who was a good deal relieved at his absence, for he began not to like the way in which he inquired who and what Angela was. The attention of Hawk was, however, now completely taken up by the scene which opened to his view in the old royal saloons of St. James's Palace. It was a scene which was in every way calculated to elicit admiration, and to distract the mind from other objects of contemplation.

HAWK CONSOLING ANGELA.

CHAPTER CXXVI.

CAPTAIN HAWK IS HAUNTED IN THE KING'S SALOONS.—AN ADVENTURE.

After passing through a guard room, a couple of pages drew aside a massive curtain of purple velvet, and in another moment Captain Hawk found himself in one of the principal saloons of the palace.

The saloon was about seventy feet in length, and about forty in width, and the only fault which a critical eye could possibly find with it, was one that is common to all the larger apartments of the old palace, namely, the low pitch of the roof. An apartment of such extent as that, lost much of its grandeur of appearance, owing to being so low, and the effect was bad in the extreme when you stood at one end of the saloon, and looked its entire length.

The walls were hung with tapestry of the most brilliant and gorgeous description, and a row of chandeliers, each carrying some thirty or forty wax candles, illuminated the scene.

But it was the moving throng upon the floor that attracted soon all the attention of Captain Hawk, for there he felt was congregated all that was illustrious and great in England. The show of court dresses, of military and diplomatic warfare, and of fancy costumes, was immense, and many of the ladies and gentlemen had taken off their masks for the sake of coolness, as the temperature of the saloons was anything but a low one.

To Angela there can be no doubt but that the scene was one partaking of all the beauty of enchantment; for considering the sort of life she had led while in the custody, as we may call it, of the infamous Lady Deliva, such an assemblage as that she was now mixed with must have been to her a novelty of the most gorgeous description.

Even Captain Hawk, satiated as his mind was by all that he had seen in that great world, which to him was so familiar, could not help looking about him with interest at the passing scene.

In addition to the fact that the guests in the saloons of the palace were attired in the most gorgeous costumes and blazing with rich jewels, there was the truth that could not be forgotten, that there were assembled in that building those historical personages who by their fiat controlled the fates of nations.

It was no empty pageant that which presented itself to the eyes of Captain Hawk, but there was the real thing and these were the real people. In fact, he looked about him with a conviction that no country in the world could produce a spectacle at all equal to that which those saloons presented.

And then the thought occurred to him of how strange the system of government in this country was that could induce so many men, illustrious for their intellect and attainments, to crowd with reverence around a man whom they called a king, and for whose mind and general conduct they could not but entertain the most profound contempt.

Captain Hawk thought that it must be that human nature in all its varieties and conditions was fond of plunder, and that the reason why royalty, with all its ridiculous state, was kept up, was because that was the established mode by which money and honours were dispersed to others.

The joyous noise in the saloons soon put an end to Hawk's political and philosophical reflections, and Angela, as she hung upon his arm, whispered to him—

"Oh, brother Gerald, how good and kind it was of you."

"Good and kind! What mean you?"

"To bring me here."

"Then you are pleased?"

"Indeed and in truth I am. Did you ever see such a brilliant assmblage as this, brother Gerald?"

"It is brilliant, my dear Angela, but, no doubt, it has to you more of the charms of novelty than to me."

"Oh, yes, Gerald, that I can easily conceive, for you are a great prince."

"What makes you think that?"

"Can I think otherwise?"

"Well, well, we will talk about who and what I am some other time. Perhaps it is as you say; but if I am a great prince, I desire only the love of one person, and that is yourself."

"I do, indeed, love you."

"With all your heart?"

"Yes, Gerald. Did you doubt it?"

Angela took her mask from her face, and Captain Hawk saw that tears had started to her eyes as she spoke.

"By Heavens! an angel!" cried a voice close at hand; and Captain Hawk, with a feeling of great vexation, perceived that some one had then obtained a glance at Angela's face, and had so discovered that the seeming young Tartar officer was, in reality, a beautiful girl.

He turned hastily, and tried to find out in the crowd who it was that had spoke; but, although several masked figures were sufficiently close at hand to have made the remark, he could not pitch upon any one in particular as the actual utterer of it.

Angela had replaced her mask.

"Do not remove your mask again,"

said Hawk. "Do you hear me, Angela?"

"Ah, yes, you are angry with me, now?"

"No, no."

"Yes. You speak so differently when you are angry. I wish I were dead, brother Gerald."

"How can you be so foolish, Angela? I am not angry with you, I tell you; but, really, one would think that you wished to make me so. You ought not to hastily conclude that I am angry with you because my voice is a little harsh, on account of my anger at others."

At this moment a figure, attired in a long cloak of crimson velvet, approached Hawk, and said—

"His majesty will see you, sir."

"His majesty?"

"Yes. Follow me."

Captain Hawk hesitated for a moment, and then he followed the figure. It was not exactly the mode by which Hawk expected to be introduced to the king; but, at all events, he felt pretty sure that the figure in the robe must be some messenger from the minister, or how could he know that it was he who was to be introduced?

Angela whispered to Hawk, as they proceeded—

"Shall we see the king, then?"

"Yes. Angela, I presume so. Don't laugh when you do see him."

"Laugh?"

"Yes, for you will see a fool with such a look of ridiculous importance upon his face, that your happy spirit will be sorely tempted to indulge in mirth."

"You surprise me, Gerald."

"And so, you supposed that kings were really something great? Why, don't you know, that in this country any idiot may be king, since it is a hereditary dignity. My poor Angela, you have suffered yourself to be misled sadly, if you think that a king is in any way different to his fellow mortals."

Angela did not reply, but clung close to the arm of Captain Hawk, and they together followed along the saloon the figure in the cloak that had summoned them.

The figure suddenly stopped at a small door, which it opened, and then beckoned Hawk to follow.

Captain Hawk did so, but the figure turned, and laying its hand upon the arm of Angela, said—

"But you will come alone, prince. My orders extend to no other but yourself."

"Then I must be excused," said Hawk.

"Excused? Why, it is to have an audience of his majesty that I now take you. Excused, did you say?"

"Indeed, I did, sir, for fearfully afflicting and heart-breaking, as the fact of being so near having an audience of the king, and yet avoiding it, may be, I decline to leave this young gentleman, who is in my care."

"But the young gentleman is quite safe, sir, in the saloons of St. James's, I should think."

"Possibly."

"Then you will follow me, sir?"

"With him?"

"No—no, I really cannot. It is contrary to all form and etiquette, I assure you, sir. Of course, as far as I am concerned, it matters nothing, but I should subject myself to discredit, I assure you."

"Farewell, sir."

Captain Hawk turned aside, but at that moment, from the side of the little door, there came the secretary of state, who at the sight of Captain Hawk broke into smiles, saying—

"His majesty is impatient, prince. What is the cause of this delay—eh? Speak loud."

The messenger, who was, in fact, one of the royal pages, had begun to explain to the minister in a whisper why it was he had not brought Hawk with him, but being told to speak loud, he said—

"My instructions were to convey the gentleman pointed out to me to the king; but he will not come alone."

"Is this so?"

"It is," said Hawk.

The minister looked vexed for a moment or two, and then he said—

"Perhaps, prince, you have an objection to leave this young gentleman in the saloon? Would that difficulty be removed if he were to remain in this room while you saw his majesty?"

The room to which the minister alluded was that immediately through the small door in the wall of the saloon, and into which they had all four strayed, as it were, unconsciously, while talking. It was a small apartment, but exquisitely furnished and decorated, and was lighted by an opal lamp, that hung from the ceiling.

The door had closed; and it did not appear that there could be the least danger to Angela.

Hawk hesitated; and then he said to Angela in a whisper—

"You shall decide this. Shall I go, and leave you here for a few minutes, or shall I still refuse?"

"Go, Gerald; go at once. I can wait here easily."

"Be it so, then." Turning to the minister, Hawk bowed, as he said, "My young friend will wait here for me, where, I trust, he will not be intruded upon; and I will follow you, my lord."

"A thousand thanks!" said the minister, bowing to Angela. "Now, prince, if you please. No doubt you are aware of the fact that his most gracious majesty is of rather an impatient temper, and don't like to be kept waiting even for a moment."

Hawk smiled as he followed the minister and the page from the room. They took him through two other apartments, and then across a narrow corridor to a door, at which stood another of the royal pages, who made way for the minister and Hawk.

The door was opened, and then there appeared a heavy curtain, quilted very thickly. The minister moved it aside, and made a low bow.

"Forward!" he said to Hawk, in a whisper.

In another moment Captain Hawk was in the royal presence. Those who have chanced to see some of the early portraits of George the Third, no doubt have had a good look at that serio-comic face of idiotic wonder that that monarch possessed. The characteristics consisted of a low forehead, a pair of protruding eyes, and a large development of all the lower part of the face; and, added to these peculiarities, the head and face were generally turned on one side, and projected upwards in a comical fashion; while the expression was one of constant surprise, mingled with obstinacy and petulant enmity.

Such was the king to whom Captain Hawk was introduced with so much state and dignity.

"Well—well, what—what?" cried the king. "Eh?—eh? Has he come? What—what?"

"He is here, your majesty."

"Oh, very well. Eh? What—what? How do you do? So, you are very well? So am I. Eh? what did you say? A prince of the Austrian house are you? Yes—very well. Eh? what's your name?—Very well—eh?"

"I have the honour," said Captain Hawk, "to compliment your majesty upon your good looks. The Emperor of Austria has sent me to England upon a delicate mission."

"Delicate mission? Nothing improper, I hope—as you say—oh, very well. How are you? Very well? So am I."

"The Emperor of Austria is desirous," added Captain Hawk "of availing himself of your majesty's advice, by which he will be guided, in an affair of the greatest moment; for, as he said, 'I will take the advice of the wisest monarch and the most wonderful man in all Europe, who is, no doubt, George the Third of England, and what he says I will abide by.'"

"Eh?—oh, clever fellow the Emperor of Austria—eh? Quite a charming fellow he is. Very well is he? Yes. Glad to hear it. What's it all about?—Out with it. I rather think I am the most remarkable monarch in Europe, as he says—eh?"

"I must only commit to your majesty's private ear what I have to say."

CHAPTER CXXVII.

CAPTAIN HAWK ASTONISHES GEORGE THE THIRD OF BLESSED MEMORY.

At these words of Captain Hawk that he could only tell the king in private what he had to say, the minister looked a little vexed, and the king jerked up his comical, bullet-looking face, and tried to think; but soon gave it up as by far too laborious a process.

"Eh—eh? Private, did you say?"

"I did, your majesty."

"It is," said the minister, "for your majesty to decide upon the propriety, or otherwise, of such a step. Of course the prince does not come with any political object?"

"It is quite clear," said Captain Hawk, "that by the manner of my presence in this country I have taken every care to deprive the visit of any official or political significance. I come purely on a domestic affair."

"In that case, then, there can be no objection."

"Stop," said the king. "I have an idea."

It was so unprecedented a thing for the king to have an idea, that the minister quite leant forward to listen to it, and his majesty said, rather in a solemn tone of voice—

"In that case there can be no objection."

At any other time and place the minister and Captain Hawk must both have laughed to hear this echo of what had just been said given forth by the king as an idea; but as it was, they both kept their countenances very admirably, and the minister said—

"That, indeed, throws a new light upon the subject."

"Stop," said the king. "I may add further, that that indeed throws quite a new light upon the subject."

The minister bowed.

Captain Hawk really had to bite his lips to keep himself from laughing outright at these efforts of the royal wisdom; and they were accompanied by looks of such profound stupidity—such solemn stolidity of brain, that no one who had not seen that gracious monarch act in such a manner could believe it possible.

"Shall I leave your majesty?" said the minister.

"Yes—oh, yes. What—what?—How are you, prince, quite well? Yes—Glad to hear it. Eh?"

The minister bowed out of the royal presence, and Captain Hawk was alone with the king.

When Captain Hawk found that he was really alone with the king, he approached close to him, and said in a low tone—

"Can any one overhear us?"

"No—God bless me, no."

"Then, your majesty must know that at the court of Austria there is a young lady named Jacoretta."

"What?"

"Jacoretta."

"Oh!"

"And one day as the king was thinking, as your majesty might be, of nothing at all, this young lady asked an audience of him and got it; and when they were quite alone——"

"Yes—yes?"

"And nobody could possibly hear what she said, or have the least idea of what she was doing, she—but I ought to tell you that she was the most beautiful young creature you ever saw, and only fifteen years of age. Her cheeks were like roses, and her figure and face were so perfect, so exquisite——"

"But what did she do?"

"I will tell your majesty. She was only attired upon the occasion in a robe of gray silk, fastened round the waist by a silver girdle, and to the surprise of the king she took off the——"

"God bless me, you don't say so?"

"Yes, she actually took off the silver girdle——"

"Oh, the silver girdle, and the a—the a—eh?—the gray robe—the a—a—Eh? She—she took off the a—a—the gray robe, and had nothing—dear me!"

"No. Oh, dear, no."

"No?"

"Certainly not. What could have put such an idea into your majesty's head, I wonder, about a perfectly virtuous and decent young lady?"

"God bless me, I don't know."

"It was the girdle she took off, and she approached the emperor, and said, 'Your majesty will, I am sure, accept this in exchange for your rings, your watch, and what money you may have about you;' and with that she took his watch with a jerk out of his pocket, this way."

As Captain Hawk spoke, he laid hold of the magnificent seals attached to the king's watch, and with an ingenious jerk, had it out of the watch-pocket.

"Oh, dear," said the king, "did she?"

"Yes, and then she laid hold of his hands, and off she took a couple of diamond rings that he had on his fingers, just in this sort of way."

Captain Hawk dexterously enough took a couple of rings from the king's hands of immense value.

"Then she said to him, 'If you don't hand over what money you have about you, I will blow your brains out.'"

With this, Captain Hawk took a small pocket pistol from the breast of his apparel, and held it close to the nose of the king, who shrunk back as far as he could in his chair, and looked quite of a livid colour in the face.

"Oh, dear, no—don't! I say—murder!"

"Silence! Another word and you are a dead man. Your money quickly. Be alive."

The king drew a pocket-book from one pocket and a purse from the other, and handed them to Hawk in speechless terror.

"That," said Hawk, "was just what she did, and then holding up her finger in this sort of way, she said, 'If you by word or look, or implication, in any way give notice until two hours have expired of what has taken place in this interview, I will find a mode of again getting a private interview with you, and as sure as you live I will then lodge an ounce of lead in your stupid cranium.' Good night."

The king sat with his mouth wide open, and his eyes an inch or so further out of his head, and his tongue projecting from the side of his mouth, looking the very picture of distress.

Captain Hawk had pocketed the various articles he had taken from the Majesty of England, and then he coolly walked to the satin curtain that hung over the doorway, and lifting it aside, he passed out of the room.

The two pages that were there bowed to him as he passed out, and then Hawk said to one of them, in a most courteous tone—

"It is his majesty's order that you show me the way back to the grand saloons by the way I came."

"With pleasure, sir," said the page.

"Where is the secretary of state?"

"His lordship will be here shortly, sir."

"Very well. When you see him, you can say he will find me in the grand saloons with my friend."

The page bowed, and led the way by the same route that Captain Hawk had been conducted to the royal closet. But it now becomes necessary that we should detail to the reader what happened to Angela while Captain Hawk was away from her.

His absence lasted about half an hour altogether, and during that time she had by no means been left alone in the little apartment leading from the saloon.

The young girl, although she had given Hawk leave to go without her, still felt some degree of disappointment at not seeing the king. She did not, however, consider for a moment that there was anything to be afraid of in being there left alone.

Angela looked around her, and thought that she could not sufficiently admire the beautiful decorations of the little apartment in which she was. The ceiling was painted in some allegorical subject, that was cast into strong light by the chandelier, and the walls were covered with tapestry of the most costly description.

"This is, indeed, a palace," she said to herself. "Ah, how tedious, though, appears the time when Gerald is away from me!"

These reflections were suddenly interrupted by a slight movement of one of the pieces of tapestry on the wall opposite to which she sat, and then a voice said, in accents of the most friendly character—

"Be not afraid, I pray you. No harm is intended you."

The arras was moved aside almost at the same moment, and a gentleman, magnificently attired in a Spanish costume, entered the little room.

It was not alarm so much as wonder and curiosity that took possession of Angela, for the intruder was both young and handsome, and his manner was as respectful as possible, as he advanced towards her and said—

"In the grand saloons, by mere accident, as you chanced to remove your mask, my eyes were ravished by the sight of your beauty. From that moment I felt that my heart was yours and yours only. I make to you this frank avowal, with the hope that if you cannot love me now at once, that you will yet permit me to hope that time will do something for me, and you will perhaps let me know who you are, and I will be equally frank with you."

There was an engaging candour about this young man, that was exceedingly fascinating to Angela, and she did not feel at all alarmed as he thus spoke to her so freely.

As the sound of the voice of this young and handsome cavalier rang in her ear, poor Angelia forgot all the caution that Captain Hawk had given to her to speak to no one, and to let no one see her face; and she replied with all the simplicity and artlessness of her disposition—

"Sir, I do not know you. If you would cultivate my acquaintance, it can only be through the medium of my brother."

"Your brother? Then that is the gentleman I saw with you. Oh, how happy you make me by telling me that he is your brother."

"Indeed? It is very strange that that should have any influence upon your happiness. I cannot understand that."

"Cannot you, dear one? Then I will tell you that I was maddened by apprehensions that he might be your lover."

"Ah, no—no; and yet——"

"Why do you pause?"

Angela felt very sad, and after a few moments' thought, she said—

"I pray you to leave me, sir; it is much better that you should do so, I assure you. I do not wish to converse with you. My brother will soon return, and he will be angry with me. I dread his anger. Oh, sir, I pray you to leave me now, and at once."

"Sweet innocence, you said, that if I would know you better, I should seek to do so through an acquaintance with your brother. Tell me, I pray you, who and what he is, that I may still cherish that dear hope."

CHAPTER CXXVIII.

ANGELA BEGINS TO MAKE SOME FAMILY DISCOVERIES CONCERNING HERSELF.

Angela was now thoroughly apprehensive that she was transgressing the orders that Captain Hawk had given to her, and she trembled very much. Upon this the young cavalier placed his arm tenderly around her, and said, in cheering accents—

"I will protect you against the whole world. Oh, sweet engaging girl, do not tremble, I beg of you."

"Oh, leave me—leave me! My brother is a prince."

"A prince?"

"Yes, but I am I know not what. Oh, would that I did know who and what I was! Alas! alas! have I a father? Have I a mother?"

Angela burst into tears.

The young man was evidently quite bewildered by this seemingly frantic behaviour of Angela, and for a few moments he did not know what to do or to say. She did not repulse him when he placed his arm around her waist, and now he drew her gently towards him, and lifted the mask from off her face, and looked upon that rare beauty that had by the momentary glance he had had of it so fascinated him in the saloon.

"Dear girl," he said, "from this moment I devote my life to your service. I am one who can and who will protect you; but I implore you to cease these terrors, for they will break my heart if you do not."

"Do you, too, love me, then?" sobbed Angela.

"Love you? Oh, can you ask such a question of me? Sweet girl, I adore you!"

"How good people are to me now, after all that I have suffered," said Angela, as she looked up in the face of her young admirer. "Will you tell me who you are?"

"Yes, I am the Marquis of Brereton. My father is a duke, and so I have the title of Marquis from courtesy. Now tell me who you are, my darling girl?"

"Alas, I cannot. That is just what I should like to know. If I could find out who I am, I think I should be very happy indeed; but in truth I cannot."

"Have you no friends?"

"Oh, yes, I have a friend; you saw me with him."

"Your brother?"

"In affection."

"Ah, is he not, then, your real brother?"

"Oh, no."

The young Marquis of Brereton dropped the hand of the young girl, and a vague suspicion flashed across his mind for the moment that he was being made the victim of some one who unblushingly led a life of iniquity; and yet another glance at the face of Angela was sufficient to convince him that nothing but truth and innocence could by any possibility reside in such a form.

"You are a lovely riddle," he said. "Have you no knowledge of your parents at all?"

"None but this."

As she spoke, she took from her bosom the ring which she had shown to Captain Hawk, and held it up to the eyes of the young marquis for his inspection. At sight of it he changed colour and had to hold to a chair for support.

"Good Heavens!" he exclaimed.

"Ah, you are ill," said Angela; "let me call for aid."

"No—no. I implore you not to do so. Tell me, how came you to be possessed of this ring? Oh, is this a dream? Can it be true—can it be possible? I know not what to think or what to say."

Angela was both surprised and alarmed at this passion of emotion upon the part of the young nobleman, and she looked at him with tears in her eyes, as she said—

"Have I committed any fault that appears heinous in your eyes, my friend, or what is it that now ails you? Oh, tell me!"

"Will you lend me that ring for ten minutes? I promise you, on my soul's salvation, that I will return to you with it at the end of that period of time."

"No, no; I dare not—indeed, I dare not! I feel if I were to part with this I part with the only chance that remains to me of ever discovering my parents. Do not ask me to let you have it."

"Nay, hear me. It is to further that very object that I ask it of you. I have a supposition concerning it, and concerning you, which there is a person now in the saloon who can answer at once in the affirmative, or otherwise; and, before I say more to you of your origin or name, I wish to show him this ring. I implore you to trust me with it."

"Ought I?"

"Indeed, and in truth, you ought. You say that by its means you yet hope to discover who were your parents? Only consider if by withholding it from me for the short space of time I mention to you, you make the greatest obstacle to such a discovery."

"Take it—take it."

"Depend upon my honour. And now, my dear girl, promise me one thing, upon your soul's best hopes."

"What is it?"

"That you will keep this affair secret."

"No, I cannot, I dare not promise that. The dear friend you saw me with saved me from death, and I cannot consent to keep anything that may concern me a secret from him. You must not ask me that, for I cannot—indeed I cannot consent to it."

"Let the issue of this affair be with Heaven," said the marquis, as with the ring in his hand he hastily left the apartment.

Now that he was gone, and that she was no longer fascinated by his appearance and words—now that she was able to reflect without any interruption upon what had taken place, Angela began to feel the keenest regret at having so easily parted with the ring.

The moments appeared lengthened into hours as they passed, and she paced the room with a feeling of despair. She would have made her way into the saloon, and rushed to and fro in frantic search for the young marquis, but that she was restrained by several reasons, which she could not stultify herself sufficiently to disregard even in that period of wild anxiety.

In the first place, she had promised to wait there for Gerald, that self-constituted brother of her affections, and she dreaded what would be his feelings if he should return to that room and

CAPTAIN HAWK DECIDING UPON THE DEATH OF THE MARQUIS.

find her gone. Then, again, while she might be looking in vain for the marquis, he might return with the ring by some route she was unacquainted with, and not finding her there, might return again and leave the palace, and so destroy her only chance of getting it back again from him.

The manner of his entrance to the room showed that he knew of a route to it and from it different from that at which she and Gerald had got to it.

All these considerations kept her where she was, although her anxiety increased every moment.

In the midst of all this Captain Hawk made his appearance, looking just a little flushed and hasty. The page opened the door that led to the room, and then said—

"Have you any further commands, sir?"

"No—no," said Hawk, "I thank you. That's all."

Angela rose at the sight of Captain Hawk, and she sprang forward to him, exclaiming as she did so—

"Oh, brother—brother, how glad I am to see you once again! But what has happened?"

"Happened? I may ask that question. Why do you cast your eyes round the room so earnestly?"

"Did I?"

"In faith you did."

The fact was, that Angela expected each moment to see the young marquis, who had effected a precipitate retreat only just in time to escape being seen by Captain Hawk; but she was not aware of the amount of excitement and anxiety that was exhibited in her countenance.

"What has happened?" said Hawk again. "Yet why do I ask her? It is time for us to go, Angela. Follow me quickly."

"Oh, no—no!"

"No?"

Captain Hawk looked at her in astonishment. He could not comprehend what had come over her that so suddenly had seemed to alter her whole style of thoughts and behaviour to him. With difficulty he suppressed a hasty expression of his dissatisfaction, and said with assumed calmness—

"You have seen some one?"

"I have—I have."

"Ah, I thought so. Who was that?"

"That I know not, brother Gerald, except that he said he was a marquis; but you will too be glad when I tell you all."

"Shall I?"

"Oh, yes. Nay, now, you look vexed. But do you think that I would keep a secret from you? No—no; when he asked me to do so I refused, and I will tell you all that passed."

"Not here, my dear Angela. Not in the atmosphere of this place. Something has occurred which induces me to leave the palace as quickly as I can. Do not ask me what it is just at present, but follow me through the saloons. You can tell me what you have to tell, as we go home. Come, Angela. Come quickly."

"I cannot—oh, I cannot!"

"You cannot? What do you mean? Have you lost the power to walk that you say you cannot?"

"No, but—but——"

"But what? Oh, Angela, I implore you to answer me. Do you forget that I am the saviour of your life?"

"No—no, think anything but that I am ungrateful to you; but I dare not leave this place till the return of the gentleman whom I have spoken to in this room."

"Curses on him!"

"No, do not curse him; he is good and noble, I feel assured, and when I tell you all you—you——"

Captain Hawk gulped down his rising rage as best he could, and, although he looked deadly pale and held the wrist of Angela with a force that was positively painful, he said with an affectation of calmness—

"Well—well, tell me all."

"Yes. He came here, and I can hardly tell you, for I hardly know myself, how it came about, but he saw the ring that I wore round my neck, when, as he looked at it, he was struck as with some sudden and strange emotion, and implored me to let him take it with him to show to some one, and gave me his word of honour that he would come back with it, so I promised him that I would wait here till he did come back, and that is all—all."

"Confusion!"

"Oh, no. You are—you surely are happy at the idea that I may discover my parents? Only think how delighted they will be to welcome you as the preserver of their child from the cruelties of the Lady Deliva. You are not angry with me, dear brother Gerald?"

CHAPTER CXXIX.

A SCENE OF CONFUSION TAKES PLACE IN ST. JAMES'S PALACE.

As Angela spoke, she flung her arms round the neck of Captain Hawk and kissed his cheek.

There was no such thing as resisting the caresses of that fair and innocent girl. It was not in human nature to do so. Moreover, even in his rage, Captain Hawk had sense and reflection enough left to feel that nothing that had happened was really any fault of Angela's, although it might very materially interfere with his views. He adopted a line of policy at once which was heartless, but very likely to succeed. That line of policy was by no means to quarrel with Angela, but by violence even to death to clear the way of all obstacles towards the accomplishment of his own purposes and designs.

He recollected that he had dared the king for two whole hours to give any alarm of the robbery that had been practised upon him, and an eighth of that period of time had certainly not yet elapsed, so there was yet a hope that danger was sufficiently far distant for Captain Hawk to escape even after he had so far yielded to Angela as to let her wait the return of the marquis she had mentioned.

In pursuance of this rapidly concocted plan of operations, Captain Hawk said to her—

"Well, my dear Angela, since it is your wish to wait the return of this gentleman, be it so. I will wait here with you; but I tell one thing, and that is, if the time be much prolonged, it may be at the risk of my life."

"Your life?"

"Even so, Angela."

"Oh, Heaven! what am I to do? Oh, why did I part with the ring even for a moment? Now, indeed, am I justly punished. What will become of me? I struggle between the impulses of a divided duty. Did you say your life?"

"I did."

"But—but do you, indeed, mean your life? It is no mere metaphor, is it?"

"No, it is my existence. I speak literally."

"Then come away at once, Gerald. Let the ring be lost, and so finish all my hopes of a father's blessing and a mother's caress. What is all the world to me compared with you? I am ready, Gerald."

Even Captain Hawk was struck with the matchless goodness of heart and the generosity of this young girl whom he had resolved to destroy if he could, and he shrunk from her gaze with a feeling of the terrible guilt he had in contemplation towards her. For a moment or two he could not speak, and when he did, it was in rather a strange and altered tone—

"Angela, you are too good—too innocent."

Captain Hawk paused, and paced the room for a few moments in silence; and then suddenly striding up to her, he said—

"Angela, we will fly from the world together. We will be to each other everything. You shall not regret kindred, friends, or every joy that you may fancy the world possesses, while you are with me. Come, dear Angela, come at once, and all will yet be well."

They moved towards the door leading towards the saloon; but at the moment that Captain Hawk placed his hand upon the brass bolt that held it shut, the tapestry at one of the walls was moved aside, and the young marquis made his appearance.

"Dear girl," he cried, "I have news for you. Ah! May I ask, sir, who are you?"

Captain Hawk confronted the young man with a calm and steady glance, as he replied—

"That question, sir, might as well come from me to you."

"The Marquis of Brereton, sir!"

"Indeed? And your business with this young lady?"

"Oh, brother Gerald, let him speak. Let him tell me what he has to say. It is of the ring he speaks. See, it is in his hands. Oh, sir, have you, indeed, made for me the discovery you say you have? Have you found that I am not a nameless, desolate being? If you have, I pray you speak at once."

"Yes; oh, yes, I will speak."

"Silence, sir!" said Hawk. "This young lady is under my protection, and any communication concerning her is more properly to be made to me. I will speak with you at another time. Now that I know your name and rank I shall have no difficulty in finding you."

"This is absurd!" said the marquis. "I have information to give to that young lady, and not to you, sir. How dare you interfere?"

"Oh, peace! peace!" said Angela. "You know him not. He is my friend, my very dear friend."

"I like not the title as applied to

him," said the marquis; "and my heart sickens within me as I hear it. Woe! woe! to the man who under such a mask has dared, possibly, to trifle with the innocence of such a being as you are!"

"Do you threaten, sir?" said Captain Hawk.

"Ay, do I with all my heart and soul. Nay, sir, you need not place your hand upon your sword. The palace of my sovereign is not the place in which I can engage in a brawl. I will not hastily jump at any conclusion; but if it be true that you are only the friend of this young lady, in the real and pure significant of that term, I can, I believe, advance a yet higher claim to her confidence."

"What claim?"

"That of a relative."

"Oh, Heaven! is this so?" cried Angela.

"Pho! pho!" said Captain Hawk; "a weak invention, that, to enthral your young heart. I—do not believe it. You are my sister, my own sister, you know. Death and fury! sir, stand aside, and let me pass, or it will be the worse for you!"

The marquis had stepped between Captain Hawk and the door leading to the saloon.

"This passion, sir, is misplaced. A just cause requires no such fury to assert it. I doubt much your rank in life; and, probably, it gives you little pretence to earn the acquaintance of this lady."

"You wrong him there," said Angela. "He is a prince."

"A prince?"

"Yes; and were any of the attendants of the palace here, or the minister of state, you would soon perceive that the Prince of the House of Austria, although living incognito in London, was entitled to your respect. These words I am bound to say for one to whom I owe much."

It will be seen that the generosity of Angela was such that she would not allow Captain Hawk to be spoken lightly of in her presence, although his present conduct was to her as mysterious as it appeared to be selfish and reprehensible, since she could not conceive why he should place himself in the way of her receiving information of her origin, and of her family.

These few words of Angela's, though, made a great impression upon the young marquis, and put the affair in a very different light in his mind. He, in common with all the nobility of the court, had heard of the fact of the presence in London, upon some secret mission of an undiplomatic character, of a prince of the House of Austria; and now that he heard this was the man, he was not so much inclined to doubt his honour.

"Sir," he said, "you stand in too high a position to do a very dastardly or very wicked action. What is your wish?"

"That you communicate to me what you have to say concerning this young lady, while she waits in the saloon. Her disguise will protect her for the space of five minutes."

"It will. If she be willing, I am."

"Angela," said Captain Hawk, "will you so far gratify me, as to wait in the saloon for a few moments, while I settle matters with this gentleman?"

"Yes, Gerald."

Captain Hawk opened the door, and Angela passed through it into the saloon. Hawk bolted the door again, and then turning to the marquis, he said—

"Now, sir—your information."

"That young lady is my cousin. She is the only daughter of my father's brother, the Earl of Cliffdale. Her name is Emmeline, and she is a peeress in her own right. All this I know to be true."

"It's a lie," said Hawk.

A flush of colour came to the face of the young marquis, and he half drew his sword from its sheath.

"Out with it," said Hawk, "coward that you are—coward and liar!"

Captain Hawk drew at the same moment. There was a flash of the weapons, and the young marquis fell, run through the body.

"That will do," said Hawk as he pushed the body under a sofa in the room. He then opened the door, and Angela glided in. Captain Hawk looked keenly at her, and she trembled as she gazed around her. It seemed as if the very atmosphere of the room suggested terrors to her soul.

After all this, it was not very likely that St. James's Palace would be the safest place in the world for Captain Hawk to stay in; and his great object was to get out of it as quickly as he possibly could.

Seizing Angela by the arm, he whispered to her—

"Follow me, or you are lost."

"Lost?"

"Yes, Angela. You know not your own danger. Follow me, I say, at once, or all is over with you."

"Tell me, Gerald. Is the danger to me, or is it to you?"

"Does that make a material difference, Angela? If it does so, stay where you are, ungrateful girl, and let these be the last words that I may say to you—farewell for ever."

"Oh, Gerald—Gerald, how can you be so cruel to me as to speak in such a fashion? It was of my parents that the young cavalier wished to speak. Oh, let me return to him, I beg of you, for as yet he has not told me all that I wish to know."

"He is gone."

"Gone?"

"Yes, I tell you he is gone. Circumstances prevented him from staying any longer here, and, I assure you, he is gone."

"But he will return."

"It is not at all likely. Come this way. Don't parley with me further, but come this way."

Captain Hawk placed his hand upon the handle of the door that led into the saloon, now, but as he opened it an inch or two he heard a loud clear voice say—

"By order of the king, no one is to leave the saloons. The doors will be kept by the yeomen of the guard."

"Ah, is it so?" said Hawk, as he drew back and closed the door again, but he had hardly done so when it was attempted to be opened from the other side. By the dim light of the nearly expiring lamp Captain Hawk saw there was a brass bolt at the bottom portion of the door, and he at once shot it into its socket.

"Not caught yet," he said. "We will see if wit and courage may not be sufficient even to contend against all the force collected in the palace of England's king."

CHAPTER CXXX.

CAPTAIN HAWK IS ASSISTED BY A MYSTERIOUS PERSONAGE TO ESCAPE FROM THE PALACE.

Sounds of great confusion in the saloons came plainly upon the ears of Captain Hawk and Angela.

"Oh, Heaven," said Angela, "what has happened?"

"Nothing."

"But those cries—those orders in rough tones of command—the confusion in the saloons, when so short a time ago all was gaiety and pleasurable excitement. Can all that take place and nothing be the matter?"

"Yes."

"Oh, no—no, brother Gerald, you know that I rely upon you. Oh, tell me if I or if you are in any way concerned in this tumult."

"No."

"Then perhaps the marquis has met with some obstruction and cannot return to me. Is that it?"

"He has met with an obstruction to his return to you," said Captain Hawk, and as he spoke his brows were settled into an awful look of gloom. "He has met with such an obstruction; but that is not the cause of the confusion in the saloons."

"What then—oh, what then? My mind is full of terrible imaginings. Are you in danger, brother Gerald?"

"I am."

"Ah! that is it. Those two brief words at once afford to me a key to my distressful feelings. You are in danger. You suffer under some misapprehension as to your thoughts and your feelings. Is it not so?"

"It is; and in this emergency I have but one question to ask of you."

"Of me?"

"Yes. Listen: I love you, Angelina."

"Ah! I know that."

"But it is not with the love of a brother."

Angela changed colour, and trembled.

"Not with the love of a brother?"

"Not with such a love do I love you, Angela," added Captain Hawk, speaking with vehemence. "I love you as man loves woman. You understand me now, surely; but I tell you that my life is in danger. It is my life only that is in danger. I am sought for to be sacrificed; and if you feel that you can never love me, I pray you to leave me so to be sacrificed, for life will have no charm for me."

"Oh, this is terrible!"

"Speak! your decision. Will you leave me or not?"

"Leave you?"

"Yes. Oh, remember that it was I who stepped between you and the murderous intents of the Lady Deliva."

"No — no, I will not leave you, Gerald."

"It is well. Ah!"

A violent shaking at the door leading to the saloons now took place, and then a loud, clear voice cried out in a tone of command—

"Send a couple of the guard here with the axes to break this door down. It must be opened forthwith."

"Lost! Oh, God, he is lost!" said Angela.

"Hush! it is not so. Come this way."

Captain Hawk took Angela almost off her feet in the eagerness with which he conducted her across the room to the door through which the marquis had entered. He dashed aside the tapestry. The door was open. All was dark beyond it; but Hawk plunged on with Angela in his arms.

If Captain Hawk, now, had had the free use of his intellect, so to speak, and had not been so far warped from such a condition by the passion he felt for the beautiful Angela, there can be no doubt but that he might have done much better for his own safety by deserting her than by keeping with her, or, rather, keeping her with him.

He might, too, have left her in the palace, without being at all open to the charge of deserting her interests, or endangering her safety; for there could be no question at all in his own mind, if he had chosen to think about it at all, but that Angela would be much safer left to what casual protection she would meet with in the palace of the king, than in the hands of Captain Hawk, the notorious highwayman.

But pride as well as passion interposed to induce Hawk, as long as he possibly could, to keep the young girl with him.

That there was some contesting influence to rescue her from him, either of a natural—that is to say, a human or a divine nature, he felt, and that fact only increased the obstinacy of his disposition, and made him mutter to himself—

"Death—death in any shape rather than have this girl wrested from my hold. She is mine, and mine only."

With this feeling, then, and a total disregard of what crimes he might commit—what blood he might shed, Captain Hawk still held Angela by the hand, and seemed prepared to defy both earth and Heaven to tear her from his grasp.

The first act of Captain Hawk, when he found that he had got fairly out of that chamber in which there was the dreadful evidence of the deed of blood he had committed, was to feel for some mode of fastening the room door, so that their pursuers should not come so speedily, if at all, upon their track.

He pushed the door shut, and it closed with a snap, giving evidence by so doing that there was some spring attached to it.

A crash came upon their ears, and Hawk felt that the door from the saloons had been broken open, without any further ceremony than the brief and energetic order that had been given by the person whom they had heard speak of it.

"On—on!" said Hawk; "this is no place for us."

Angela was in too great a state of agitation to say to Captain Hawk what no doubt she would fain have said, and she allowed him to carry her along a narrow passage till a glare of light came upon their senses, and they emerged on to a landing-place at the head of a small flight of winding stairs.

The light came from below, and sent a faint radiance far up to a roof of dome-like shape.

Captain Hawk paused and listened; and then the young girl, as she clung to him, spoke—

"Oh, tell me, I implore you," said Angela—"tell me what all this means? Why—oh, why should they seek your life?"

"Silence!"

"No—no! There is no one here. Why should you implore silence upon me, Gerald? Have you been trustful? Have you been candid with me?"

"What on earth do you mean?"

"I mean, have you told me who and what you are?"

"No!"

"God! I thought not. Tell me now, I implore you, or I shall go quite mad—oh, do tell me all. These scenes of tumult and of strife are all unfitted to me. I implore you, ere we advance another step, to tell me who and what you are instantly."

"At a more fitting time and place I will. Not here—not now."

"Yes, yes, now and here."

Captain Hawk let go the arm of the girl. Angered as he was at her pertinacity, he felt that now there was but the one chance of retaining his influence over her, and that was to act as he had done before, by appealing to her generosity and her gratitude.

"Angela, listen!"

"I do—I will."

"You think wrong of me. That is a fact, that, with such agony as I feel, will soon terminate my existence. Go, you are quite free. Go now at once, and leave me."

"Oh, cruel—cruel!"

"No, it would be cruel to detain you, since your heart stays not. Go at once and forget me, and leave me to my fate."

"Never! No—no—never!"

"My Angela—my own—my beautiful!"

Captain Hawk folded her in his arms, and kissed her vehemently. She was cold and passive in his embraces. Hawk felt the conviction come like a chill to his heart at the moment, that he had not the affection of that young girl.

Wounded pride for the moment urged him to quit her, but passion dictated another course, and he thought to himself—"It will be time enough to leave her when I am no longer enamoured of her; but I will not leave her now."

A rapid step approached them, and they again fled along a narrow passage. A door in it suddenly opened, and a voice said, in strange, unearthly accents—

"Take the staircase to the right. It will lead you to temporary safety. I will soon be with you."

Captain Hawk started back.

"Who and what are you?" he cried. "Who speaks to me?"

There was no answer to the question, but hearing footsteps still approaching, Hawk went in the way directed, and after ascending a staircase reached an apartment at its top.

The room of old St. James's Palace in which Captain Hawk now found himself, with the fair Angela, was one that had evidently not been used, or even entered, for a considerable space of time. Yet it was one that at a distant period had no doubt been of importance.

By the dim morning light that stole through the coloured glass of its window, on the outer side of which appeared the branches of trees, Hawk could just manage to see about him, and to prevent himself from running foul of any of the furniture of the room.

The apartment was about eighteen feet square, and upon the floor had been what no doubt at the time was considered a very rich carpet. The dust lay upon it now as thick as soot, that might have been purposely sprinkled over it, with the intention of making a thick coating of such a material over its beauty.

The walls of the room were hung with tapestry, and as Captain Hawk ran his eye along the wall furthest from him, he saw that the current of air upon the narrow staircase waved a particular portion of the tapestry to and fro in a manner to lead him to the conclusion that there was an opening in the wall that was only hidden by the hangings.

Angela clung to Captain Hawk in a paroxysm of fear.

"Oh, my friend—my brother," she said, "what will become of us? When will all this evil end? Can it be possible that any one would raise a hand against your life? Oh, no—no! There must be some mistake."

"Perhaps so," said Hawk; "but in the meantime they would kill me. I am puzzled to think who that could have been who directed us up here. Did you see the figure?"

"I did, Gerald."

"Well, tell me, on your soul's hopes, did you know the man? Speak freely, and I will not be angry."

"I did not know him. Oh, Gerald, how could you think it at all likely that I should know him?"

"It is me, then, with whom he is acquainted. Who on earth can it be that has recognised me? That is a question that gives me even now more uneasiness than all else."

"Hush, Gerald—oh, hush! There is some one coming."

Captain Hawk placed his hand upon the hilt of his sword, and stood in an attitude of defence, fully expecting an attack now.

CHAPTER CXXXI.

CAPTAIN HAWK MAKES A PROPOSITION TO ANGELA, WHICH SHE REJECTS.

The sound of footsteps coming up the little winding staircase which Captain Hawk and Angela had, by the advice of the tall man in the cloak and mask, ascended, now was too perceptible to admit of a moment's doubt.

"I will sell my life dearly," said Hawk, as he drew his sword. "One thing I have determined upon, and that is, never again to be taken with life."

"Again?" said Angela; "of what do you speak?"

Captain Hawk looked a little confused. He had rather incautiously spoken before Angela of a matter which he never intended she should know.

"It is nothing," he replied, "nothing."

A flash of light came up the staircase, and in another moment, to the relief of Captain Hawk, there appeared the same tall figure in the cloak that had met him on the landing-place below. In its left hand the figure carried a lamp, and in its right a sword.

Placing the lamp upon a bracket that was fastened to the wall just above the entrance to the room, the figure placed itself by the side of Captain Hawk, and in the same strange sepulchral tone of voice that it had before spoke in, it said—

"Courage—the enemy is coming—courage!"

"Who and what are you?" said Hawk.

"Ha! ha! You would tremble at my name. Let it suffice that in you I recognise a friend whom I am willing to aid. Ha! ha!"

The laugh was a hideous one, and Hawk felt as if all the blood in his veins paused for a moment as he listened to the voice of this singular being. There was no time, however, for speculation as to who or what he was, for the confused sound of armed men ascending the stairs proclaimed sufficiently that the warning of the mysterious personage in the cloak was not to be disregarded.

Captain Hawk, although he felt an intense fear tugging at his heart with regard to the man in the cloak and the mask, yet was not a likely person to hold back when there was positive danger; so with his sword firmly in his grasp, he placed himself by the side of the stranger, saying—

"I will fight to the last; and be you man or fiend, I am obliged to you for your help."

"Ha! ha!" laughed the mysterious personage. "Good. Ha! ha!"

The approaching persons on the stairs now showed themselves, and Captain Hawk saw that they consisted of three yeomen of the guard in their quaint costumes. Two of them came first, and the third followed with a light, which he held above the heads of his comrades.

The yeomen of the guard did not expect to find any one in that portion of the palace; but in pursuance of the general orders they had received to leave no portion of the building unsearched, they had sought that tower and its apartments.

It was not till they had reached the head of the stairs that they saw Captain Hawk and his mysterious friend.

"Hold!" cried one of the yeomen, "Here he is, I do think."

HAWK CONCEALING HIMSELF FROM THE GARDENER.

"Surrender!"

"Not with life," said Captain Hawk. "You may have my dead body and welcome, if you can get it."

The two yeomen of the guard made a sudden rush forward, and one of them, with his tall battle-axe, made a blow at the head of Captain Hawk, which, very likely, if it had chanced to hit him, would have at once put him out of this world; but the mysterious man in the cloak and mask made a dart forward, and caught the handle of the axe, and at the same moment ran the yeoman of the guard through the body.

"Ha! ha!" he said, "so much for one. The other is your game."

Captain Hawk rushed at the other guard, who turned to try to escape, as the man with the light, too, was doing; but Hawk caught him, and made a thrust at him in the back with his sword.

The man uttered a shriek, and fell headlong down the narrow staircase, upsetting his comrade with the light as he did so. The battle was thus cleverly won by Captain Hawk and the mysterious stranger, who quite calmly wiped the blood off his sword in the folds of his cloak.

Poor Angela was so horrified at the struggle that had taken place, that she dropped upon her knees, and was engaged in prayer, when Captain Hawk took hold of her by the arm, saying—

"Rise, Angela—rise; the danger is over."

"But how is it over?" she said. "Oh, Gerald, Gerald, can you justify to yourself the death of those men?"

"Yes."

"No—no! Oh, do not dream that you can do so. Has not the Almighty said, 'Thou shalt do no murder?'"

"Ha! ha!" laughed the man with the cloak in his hideous fashion.

Captain Hawk felt sick at heart as those words came from the sweet and innocent lips of Angela. He felt that there was a gulf between him and her, which he might in vain attempt to cross. Madly in love with her as he was, still his intellect told him that by fair means, after what she knew of him, and what probably she suspected, she never would be his.

"Ha! ha!" laughed the stranger again.

"Peace, fiend!" said Hawk. "Peace, I say! You have forced your services upon me. I have not yet sold my soul to you."

"I don't ask you. It is mine already."

Hawk shuddered, and the idea occurred to him of trying the temper of his sword upon this man or devil; but he abstained from so doing, and almost dragging Angela to her feet, he said—

"This is no safe place for us. We cannot stay here. Come, Angela. Let us still make an effort to leave the palace. If we can only get into the garden, we may make our way into the park, and so get free."

"Go, then," said the mysterious stranger, as he proceeded down the stairs where the yeomen of the guard had disappeared. "Go to your destruction if you will go."

"No," said Hawk, "there is a door this way. I saw it when first we reached this apartment. Come, Angela, courage, and all may yet be well."

The mysterious stranger made no opposition to this proceeding of Captain Hawk's, but quietly let him take the light, and lead Angela towards that part of the room where, by the swinging to and fro of the hangings, he had suspected the existence of some opening.

Captain Hawk was not wrong in the supposition. After drawing aside the tapestry, he saw a tall, narrow slit in the wall of the room, and by the light he carried he perceived that there was another staircase similar to the one by which he had entered that apartment.

A noise in the room caused him to look round, and he saw the mysterious stranger bolting the other door on the inside. This, as an ordinary means of precaution against peril by that way, was all very well; but to the apprehension of Captain Hawk it had another meaning, and that was, that the stranger meant to accompany him, which he, Hawk, began to have the strongest objection to, notwithstanding the great service he had rendered to him in the recent conflict with the yeomen of the guard.

Turning to the stranger, Hawk spoke with as much calmness and decision as he could command at the moment—

"Sir, I thank you for the service you have already rendered, but now would consider that service much enhanced by your absence. Good night."

"Indeed!"

"Yes, sir, I trust that I am speaking to a gentleman who would scorn to intrude himself where he was not welcome."

"I saved your life."

"I admit it; but surely that is not a sufficient plea for persecution?"

"No. Therefore, you will no longer urge it to the fair Angela as a reason why she should cling to you and follow your evil fortunes, for you have no other plea whatever to urge. She is free to leave you; she ought not to be persecuted."

Captain Hawk was thunderstricken at this speech, for it proclaimed at once that the mysterious stranger knew his situation, and the only bond of union there was between him and Angela. The notion that he had been for the last ten minutes struggling against that this mysterious being was supernatural, arose again in full force, and a sickness of the heart came over Captain Hawk at the idea that he was so far steeped in crime as to be obnoxious to such a fearful visitation.

"Leave me—oh, leave me now," he said. "I implore you to leave me! I would rather encounter any fate than be indebted to you for further aid. I do not know you—I will not know you!"

"Ha—ha! You cannot help it. I know you, and that is sufficient. I cannot afford to lose you yet, you are too useful. I pray you go on—I will follow you."

Angela, during this brief but strange discourse, clung to Hawk with looks of wonder; and now when goaded to desperation he placed his hand upon his sword, she cried out—

"No—no! Oh, no more bloodshed!"

"Calm yourself," said the stranger. "As easily could I disarm him as hold up my hand; but I look upon him as a friend, and although he may, from a certain peculiarity of temper, vex me at times, yet I can and do forgive him. It is for you to think."

"To think?"

"Yes. You are yet innocent; remember that."

Angela trembled.

"Fiend!" cried Captain Hawk, stamping with his foot hurriedly upon the floor, "what would you have?—what do you want with me? Speak out at once your hellish command! What is it? I am in life yet, and you have no power over me: you must wait."

"We shall see. Go on. This rage is but folly. Already I can hear, although you cannot, the tramp of feet. There comes this way a force that will laugh to scorn your puny opposition, and, perhaps, I may not choose to aid you. They come!—ah, yes, they come!"

The mysterious man put himself into an attitude of listening; and imagination, if not reality, made Captain Hawk think that he, too, heard the tramp of armed men approaching the staircase, on the other side of the door, which was made fast.

The necessity for immediate action, in the way of escape, came strongly to his mind. Placing his arm round the waist of Angela, he fairly lifted her off her feet, and darted through the narrow opening in the wall.

"Ha! ha!" laughed the mysterious personage, as he followed him with quick but noiseless steps.

If the devil in *propria personæ* had followed Captain Hawk, the circumstance would not have given him the disquietude that this mysterious personage gave him. There seemed to be about him a terrible knowledge of who and what he, Hawk, was; and while in the presence of that strange being, Captain Hawk felt that more than half his strength and courage was gone.

The questions of "who is he?" and "what does he want with me?" were upon the surface of Captain Hawk's thoughts; but they were questions much easier to ask than to answer; and, at all events, he did not think it likely, even if he paused to ask them, that he would get anything like a satisfactory reply.

The circumstances of danger and of difficulty in which he was now placed, though, were, in good truth, so eminent, that Captain Hawk could not afford to be at all particular with regard to where the aid came from that promised to extricate him from them; so the footsteps of his mysterious friend behind him was certainly more welcome than the tread of the yeomen of the guard in that direction.

Immediately upon passing through the narrow door in the wall of the apartment, Captain Hawk found himself in a narrow passage, for the wall all but touched his clothing upon each side as he traversed it. The darkness was most intense.

CHAPTER CXXXII.

CAPTAIN HAWK FINDS OUT WHO THE MYSTERIOUS UNKNOWN REALLY IS.

The first feeling of Captain Hawk upon passing out of the room which, no doubt, would be so soon filled with his foes in pursuit of him, was, of course, one of great congratulation that there was such a mode of escape from it and from them at all open to him.

This feeling, however, soon gave way before the gloom and the intensity that surrounded his progress in that dreary and most uncomfortable passage.

After proceeding about twenty paces, Captain Hawk came to a pause; and in a low tone he certainly uttered some maledictions that it would have been quite as well if he had kept from the ears of Angela, who certainly was not used to such energetic modes of capricious opinions upon any subject as Captain Hawk was.

"Oh, Gerald, Gerald, do not speak so! You shock and terrify me!"

"Pardon me," he said. "It was but the forgetfulness of a moment."

"But have you to remember not to use words of that kind, Gerald?"

"No, no, do not ask me now, dear Angela. Recollect that at present all we have to think of is our escape from this truly detestable palace, in which I deeply regret I ever set foot."

"And so do I, Gerald, since it has brought disquietude upon you; although it has awakened a hope in my breast that I may yet live to have the satisfaction of presenting you as my dearest and best friend, and adopted brother, to those who are bound to me by the ties of relationship. Will not that be a joy, brother Gerald, if ever it can be brought about?"

"Oh, amazingly," said Hawk.

Angela did not exactly like the tone of voice in which he replied to her; but she was not disposed to quarrel about trifles, or to be very particular concerning what, after all, might only be a mere idea of her own; so she made no remark upon the tone in which she thought he spoke.

Captain Hawk came to a stand-still, for he thought that he heard some sound in advance of them, although at a considerable distance.

"Angela," he said, "what do you hear? Listen, and tell me if any noise comes upon the night air. I fancy I hear voices and footsteps in abundance."

"So do I, Gerald. I am certain of that"

"Then we must not pursue this track."

"Ha! ha!" laughed their now invisible friend with the mask in the dark, for the darkness of the passage completely hid him from the sight of Captain Hawk and Angela. "Ha! ha! are you troubled which way to proceed?"

"I am," said Hawk.

"Do you ask advice of me?"

"I do."

"Oh, no—no!" cried Angela. "I tremble at the idea of asking help of you."

"You must not," said the voice. "I will now advise. You, Gerald, as you call yourself, leave the girl with me. I will undertake that she is placed in honour and safety, and I can then direct you to a mode of escape; but upon no other terms can I act."

"Angela, what say you?" said Hawk.

"Oh, Gerald, do you think that I would leave you?"

"No, Angela, I did not think you would. You know that I love you."

"Ha!" laughed the stranger; "you think so? Well, I can tell you different from that. He does not love you with a brother's love. It is with the love of a man for one so fair and young and full of beauty as you are that he loves you."

"Villain!" cried Hawk, as he made a sudden lunge in the direction of the voice with his sword—"villain! take the reward of your insolent meddling."

The point of the sword struck against the wood panelling which formed the side of the narrow passage; and then with the greatest composure the voice said—

"It is useless, captain, for you to try to injure me. You might as easily attempt to cut the air into pieces as to hurt me with your sword; so put it up like a wise man; and if you wish me to tell you why I consider that your love is not likely to be very brotherly, why, I will."

"Silence, fiend!"

"Ha! ha! Well, people are ever ready to cry out 'Silence, fiend!' to any one who is about, as they think, to utter unwholesome truths."

"Oh, Gerald," sobbed Angela, "what is the meaning of all this? and where is it all to end? You do not know how terrified I am."

"Fear nothing, dear one—fear nothing. Come with me. We will yet find our way out of this place without the aid of this mocking devil. Come on. I do not now hear the voices and the footsteps so plainly as I did, and, perhaps, we may yet, by pursuing this passage, reach a place of safety."

"I trust to you, Gerald."

"Do so, dear Angela, and all will yet be well. Come, dear one, do not tremble. Lean upon me. I can and I will protect you from all harm."

There is very little doubt, now, but that Captain Hawk would rather have encountered any ordinary amount of danger, so that he could, by so doing, have got rid of the mysterious personage who had dogged his footsteps, and who seemed to be much more enlightened regarding him and his affairs, both past and present, than was at all agreeable.

Captain Hawk made up his mind that he would not speak to this personage if he could avoid it; and yet, as he proceeded, it was with a shuddering kind of awe that he felt certain the mysterious man stalked behind him.

The roof and the walls of the narrow passage were so covered with dust that the progress of Captain Hawk and Angela through it disturbed much of that subtle substance, so that the air they were compelled to breathe was quite impregnated with it, and at times they felt half choked by it.

"Courage, courage!" whispered Captain Hawk to Angela. "We cannot remain long in this place; it must come to an end shortly."

"I will not sink while I am with you, Gerald."

"This noble confidence," whispered Hawk again, "shall not go unrewarded, Angela. You will be even dearer to me than life itself, and we shall be very happy, indeed."

"Yes, dear Gerald, as brother and sister."

The pertinacity with which the young girl clung to this idea that their affection for each other was to be of the brother and sister order was excessively provoking to Captain Hawk; but that was not exactly the time at which to bring such an affair to an issue, so he said no more, but hurried on.

By feeling his way with his extended sword in his right hand, Hawk prevented the great likelihood of their either encountering any obstacle to their progress, or their falling down some staircase that might be thereabouts; and it was as well that he was so cautious, for suddenly he fancied that the even course of the floor ceased.

"Hold! hold!" he said, as he held Angela back. "We are, for all I know, at the brink of some precipice."

"A precipice in a house, Gerald?" said Angela. "Oh, no—no. It must be a staircase merely if the passage ceases."

"My brains are bewildered," said Captain Hawk. "It is probably what you say, I will soon discover if it be so. Ah, yes, it is a staircase. Come on, dear one, and be careful how you descend. How thickly the dust lies upon each stair, and how ominously they creak as we press them."

The stairs did, indeed, creak ominously, and the dust felt like snow, or wool beneath their feet, rather, as it did not make the sound that trodden snow must make to some degree, however slight.

It seemed pretty clear that this was the mode by which the lower portion of the palace was again reached from the turret room, in which Captain Hawk, by the advice of the mysterious stranger had taken refuge. After descending twenty steps, though, a new source of alarm presented itself. It was quite evident that they were each moment approaching some portion of the palace which was in possession of either some of the domestics—some of the guards, or some of the guests, for the sound of many voices came in a confused manner upon their ears, and they likewise heard the trampling of feet passing to and fro.

"When—oh, when," said Captain

Hawk, "shall we breathe the fresh air and feel that we are out of the perils of this palace?"

"Not yet," said the mysterious man.

"You then still persist?"

"Oh, yes, I have my mission to fulfil, and I must do it."

"As soon as there is sufficient light for me to get a good look at you," responded Captain Hawk, "it strikes me you will find your mission a more dangerous one than you contemplated."

"Ha—ha!"

"You laugh now in the dark, but it will be my turn to laugh probably when you will not feel the inclination so to do."

"Attend to your own position, captain," said the voice, "and do not waste time in idle threats against me. I know you."

Hawk trembled as, in a confused voice, he replied—

"You do not know me, for you call me captain when you should call me prince."

"That is so," said Angela.

"No," said the voice. "The Hawk naturally is a bird of prey, and tries to disguise itself."

At these words a cold perspiration broke out upon the brow of Captain Hawk, for he felt that, indeed, he was well known to that most mysterious personage, be he whom he might.

The effect of the shock of feeling upon the part of Captain Hawk was to induce him to urge Angela forward, despite of any dangers that might be in their progress; for he seemed as if he would gladly have encountered any risk or pursuit from those who knew him not rather than chance the disclosures that the mysterious stranger might make to the trembling girl who hung upon his arm, and who, at all events, whatever she might think of his intentions could have, as yet, no sort of idea of who he really was.

Suddenly Angela paused, and pressing the arm of Hawk, she said—

"I am certain that we are approaching the voices and the footsteps that we have heard at intervals. If there be from them danger to you, Gerald, let us rather try to retrace our steps than further advance."

"No—no, I cannot go back. Ah, we are at the foot of the stairs."

As Captain Hawk spoke a voice, that appeared to be in startling proximity to his, spoke in rather a loud tone. It took a minute or two for Captain Hawk to convince himself that that voice was on the other side of a wooden partition in which there did not appear to be the slightest vestige of a door, a fact which Captain Hawk concluded from the natural enough idea that whoever was upon the other side of it conversing so freely and so loudly could not be in the dark, and so if there had been any door in the wall some ray of light must have found its way sufficiently through to penetrate that part.

As it was, the same impenetrable darkness surrounded Captain Hawk and Angela that had accompanied them since they entered that long, dreary, and dusty passage, from the turret chamber.

The voice jarred upon the ears of Captain Hawk, as it said—

"Murder has been committed, my lords, within the precincts of the palace, and it is a duty we owe to ourselves as well as to his majesty to discover the offender, at all hazards. So atrocious an offence must have had some fearful motive to occasion it."

"That is true," said another. "Rest in peace, my lords, as the palace is now surrounded it is quite impossible that any one can leave it without the watchword, with which the sentinels are all provided.

"I will endeavour to be calm," said the first speaker; "but there are things that so much interest us that it is difficult to preserve any equanimity while speaking of them. But I will endeavour to be calm, for as you say no one can pass out without the watchword."

"And what is the watchword?" said another. "Really I have not heard it."

"Oh, it is merely the number twenty-four."

"That is easily remembered."

"Yes, but by no means easily to be hit upon by any one who has not heard it. The sentinels have been all doubled, and strict orders are given to arrest every one who cannot give the pass, and in the event of their making any resistance to use force, even to death, if necessary.

"Let us go," whispered Captain Hawk.

"Oh, Gerald, they spoke of murder!"

"Yes, dear, but that is no reason why we should let them murder us."

CHAPTER CXXXIII.

CAPTAIN HAWK ESCAPES FROM THE PALACE, AND WOUNDS THE MYSTERIOUS PERSONAGE.

ANGELA trembled, she scarcely knew why, as Captain Hawk caught her up in his arms and fairly ran down a continuation of the flight of steps which had seemed to end on the landing they had come to; but had not so ended in reality.

The word, murder! rang in the ears of the young girl, and yet she did not dare to confess to herself that she associated it, in some way, with the person of whom she had thought so highly, and who was, indeed, the protector of her life from the Lady Deliva, but whose conduct since had been rather equivocal.

But what shall we say of the exultation of Captain Hawk at finding that accident had so far favoured him as to put him in possession of the watchword, by the means of which, provided he could find any outlet at all from the palace, he might at once escape? He felt as if animated by fresh strength, and reached the foot of a tolerably long flight of stairs with the speed of an antelope.

"We shall be saved yet, Angela," he said. "Be joyful, dear girl, for we shall yet be saved."

"But, Gerald—Gerald?"

"Yes—yes."

"I do not yet know from what we fly. Those whom we heard, even now, conversing, spoke of murder. We have done no murder, Gerald!"

"Oh, no—no! That had nothing to do with us. Ah, Angela, I thought you trusted me?"

"Why should she?" said the voice of the mysterious stranger, whom Captain Hawk for a few moments had really began to think he had got quite rid of.

"You here again?"

"No."

"I say you are. Why do you deny it?"

"You said again, while I have never left you. I like to be correct. If you go right on, now, you will get into the palace yard. You have but then to cross it, and you will come to a gate leading into the park. There you will find a couple of sentinels. You know the word of the night. You can give it, and then you will be free."

"I knew all this, without the devil telling it to me," said Captain Hawk.

"Yes; but after that, I have something to say to you."

"After what?"

"After you have escaped from the palace."

"Then I decline the communication. I have done with you; and if you consult your own safety you will have done with me. You are some foolish masquerader, who by accident happens to know something, as you think, of us; but you mistake me for some other person."

"Oh, dear, no. Ha! ha!"

"We shall see."

"Yes, if we live long enough," said the stranger. "When that young lady, Angela by name, wants aid, she knows who to call upon."

Angela uttered an exclamation of surprise, and Captain Hawk cried out to her immediately—

"What is this?—What does this mean?—Do you understand him?—What is all this, Angela?"

"Nothing."

"Do not tell me that. It is something. You are too truthful and too ingenuous to conceal from me anything to which the speech of this man, or fiend, be he which he may, refers. Tell me all."

"Beware!" said the stranger.

"Peace, fiend! I will not have you interfere between me and this pure young spirit."

"Ha! How long will the pure spirit be entitled to that mode of description, if in your society, Captain Hawk?"

"Captain Hawk?" said Angela.

"Nothing—nothing," said Hawk. "Come on—oh, come on. Let me but gain the park, where I can feel that I am in the open air, and I will speak to this wretch in another fashion. He is your foe, Angela—your worst foe—I give you my word that he is. He can't say anything against me. There is no one can say anything against me."

"Oh, no, Gerald, I should not think there was, indeed."

"Generosity," said the mysterious stranger, "might even induce the once bright-eyed and moon-faced May Boyes to be silent."

Captain Hawk staggered as though some invisible but powerful hand had struck him a blow upon his breast.

"Now do I know," he gasped, "that you are, indeed, a fiend incarnate; but I will grapple with you. Life for life—my soul against your powers of hellish mischief. Come on, devil! I will no longer be tortured by you. Come on, and fight!"

"Not yet," said the mysterious man. "Look to the lady."

"No—no, Gerald!" cried Angela, in a voice which, considering the position of danger in which they stood, was a degree or two too high for prudence. "No—no! For my sake, command your feelings, and do not resent what this man may say."

"It is not a man!"

"Go—oh, go, I implore you!" added Angela, turning to the mysterious unknown. "Go at once. If you come here as a friend to me, I ask you by that friendship to go; and if thus invoked you will not, I repudiate at once your good offices. I reject them! Let that suffice to induce you to leave me."

"No," said the stranger.

"Oh, what can I do?" sobbed Angela.

"Leave him to me," said Captain Hawk, making a slight effort to free himself from the grasp that Angela had of his arm.

"No—no!"

"Yes, leave him to me, and this most unwarrantable interference with me and my affairs will soon end. Let me go, Angela."

"No, I will have no violence. I tell you, Gerald, I will voluntarily leave you if you attempt any violence. Recollect, that this person has done us some service, although he has angered you likewise."

"You waste precious time," said the unknown. "You seem to think that the danger in which you are in here is not at all thickening round you; but I can tell you that it is. If you wish to quarrel with me, do so when we reach a place of comparative safety to you. A bout here would fatally enthral you. Be prudent in your anger."

There was really by far too much truth in this for it not to have some effect even upon Captain Hawk, and he cooled down.

"Well," said Captain Hawk, smothering his rage as best he could, "be it so. I will wait till we get into the park."

"Ah, do."

"Yes, I will wait till then; and when only a little time since my principal desire was that you should leave me, I now wish that you should have the courage to follow me, which I doubt."

"We shall see."

"Yes, we shall see. Come, now, Angela, do not tremble. Foolish girl! what can you possibly have to fear while I am with you? Come—come, assure yourself that all is well."

"I would that I could think so," said Angela.

"You will think so. You are mine, and mine only.

"Yes, brother—yes, Gerald, as brother and as sister, we——"

"Bah!"

Angela stopped abruptly. Never before had Captain Hawk uttered to her an angry or a rude expression, and to find that now he would not even hear what she had to say, both surprised and shocked her.

"Pardon me," added Hawk. "Do not fancy that that interjection was applied to you."

"To whom, then, brother Gerald?"

"Do not ask me just now, dear Angela, but let me get clear of the palace, and then you shall hear all the explanation you can, by any possibility, desire of me."

Angela said no more, but kept up as

LADY DELIVA LISTENING AT THE PANEL OF THE DEATH-CHAMBER.

well as she could with the rapid rate at which Captain Hawk now proceeded along the passage of the palace in which they were.

In the course of half a minute they came to a door, through the upper portion of which, which was of glass, they could see trees moving to and fro, which could only be in the palace garden Animated now by the hope of escape, Captain Hawk laid his hand upon the door, and flung it open.

At that instant a couple of yeomen of the guard sprang forward and laid hands upon him.

"Hold! you are our prisoner!"

"Prisoner?"

"Twenty-four!" cried a voice in sharp, clear accents, and the mysterious stranger stood by their side.

"Ah, yes," added Hawk; "how could I forget it? Twenty-four is the password that the duke gave me."

Hawk knew well what a magic power in England even the mention of a title has upon all connected with the court, so he put in this about the duke on the spur of the moment.

The two yeomen of the guard let go their hold of him; and an officer stepping up, said—

"I hope it is all right, gentlemen?"

"If you have any doubt, sir," said Hawk, "pray act at once; but, remember, it is upon your own responsibility that you do so. I give you the password."

"My duty is clear enough," said the officer. "Pass on!"

Without another word, Captain Hawk and his party passed on into the garden. They did not speak to each other as they traversed it, for they knew that there was yet another guard to pass ere they could get into the park.

"Who goes there?" cried a rough voice.

"Twenty-four," said Captain Hawk.

"Twenty-four? Pass on!"

Right glad to do, so they did pass on. Some one whom they could not see opened a gate for them; and in another moment or two they were in St. James's Park.

The night now was tolerably clear, and the moon had risen and was shining down between some light fleecy clouds, that, even if they had been before its disc, would not have had sufficient power to hide its beams. Lower down, though, in the southern sky, from whence the wind came, there was rather a threatening black cloud or two.

Captain Hawk went right across the grand Mall of the park; and then, when the palace was left sufficiently far off to make any interference from that quarter quite futile, he turned and cried out—

"Now, Sir Mask, where are you?"

"Here!"

"Oh, 'tis well. What, now, have you to say for your impertinence in following me this night?"

"Nothing to you," said the mysterious stranger, "but much to that young lady. I warn her that you are not the man, either by station, or by mind and intention, that you represent yourself! I warn her that if she does not fly from you, it will be to her own destruction that she stays with you! I warn her, as she values honour, virtue, and peace, to no longer consort with you!"

If anything could be calculated more than another to raise the utmost ire of Captain Hawk, these words from the mysterious personage who had followed him from the palace, were just what would do so.

With an exclamation of rage he drew his sword; and, stepping a pace or two before Angela, he cried out—

"Villain! how dare you thus address me while I have my right arm at liberty, and a weapon in my hand?"

"It's the truth!" said the mask.

"Defend yourself!"

"There will be no occasion."

"No occasion? What are you?"

"Why, if you bawl out in the way you are doing you will have the guard upon you."

CHAPTER CXXXIV.

JOE CALLS UPON MAY BOYES, AND TELLS HIS STRANGE STORY.

This caution from the man in the cloak and the mask was, by no manner of means, thrown away upon Captain Hawk. Nothing could be very well more disagreeable to him than the idea of being taken by the park guard, after he had, at such great personal risk, managed to get out of the palace.

Turning completely round, in order to make sure that no one was at hand, he said in a more subdued tone—

"It is well. Let me hope that you, too, have a wholesome dread of the guard, and that you will step aside, and fight like a man in this dark alley."

"No."

"Do you say no? Coward!"

"Your calling me such does not, by any means, prove the fact. It is you who are the coward, for you are seeking to destroy when you ought to protect. Look at that pale young girl clinging to your arm. She is now tortured by a thousand doubts."

"Doubts of what?"

"Of whether she ought to believe you to be her preserver or a villain."

"I can bear this no longer."

"Oh, hold—hold!" said Angela; "for my sake hold!"

"Unhand me! I must and I will punish this most extraordinary insolence This fellow shall die!"

"No—no, Gerald, he does not know you, or he would not say what he does."

"Humph!" said the man in the mask.

"I tell you, Gerald, that we ought to give him credit for good feelings and intentions. If he knew you better than he does, do you think that he could for one moment conceive that you would betray me? Ah, no, I feel, dear Gerald, that my innocence and my honour are safe in your hands."

Captain Hawk trembled. The mysterious man in the mask laughed bitterly, as he said—

"You will tell another tale, girl, before twenty-four hours have passed over your head, I fear, unless I save you."

"Enough," said Hawk; "take the reward of your meddling and audacious interference."

As he spoke, Captain Hawk by a sudden movement shook off the hold that Angela had of his arm, and darting forward he made a pass with his sword at the figure in the cloak before it could defend itself.

"Ah!" cried the man in the mask.

"I hit you now. Ah, you are mortal, after all."

The mysterious man staggered back and held for a moment by the trunk of a tree, and then he trembled violently.

"This—is — murder!" he gasped, "foul murder! I was not quite prepared for this. Angela—Angela, fly - or you are lost—lost - as—as I am! Oh, death death!"

He fell to the ground, and Captain Hawk, seizing the moment when with surprise and horror Angela could make no resistance, placed his arm round her waist and hurried her from the park. Angela felt like one in a dream, and it was not until they reached the steps of the hotel, which they did on foot, that she recovered herself sufficiently to cry out—

"Gerald—Gerald, it was murder!"

"Hush—oh, hush!"

"No—no, I cannot be hushed to silence after that deed of blood. Let him have been who or what he may, I yet cannot conceal from myself that it was for my sake he came by his death. It was to save me from some real or fancied evil that he followed us."

"Silence, I say. Will you be my destruction?"

"No, no, I do not wish that; but it is a murder, Gerald, after all."

"Then, Angela, I tell you what will be your course, if you are so prepossessed in favour of that man, and against me. Here we are upon the steps of the hotel. The morning is coming fast, and there are sufficient persons about to make my escape all but impossible. You have but to call out lustily for aid, and you will have the satisfaction of possibly seeing me, after two or three more human beings have fallen beneath my sword, overpowered and covered with wounds, and taken into custody."

"Oh, horror! horror!"

"That is your course. Try it."

"No—oh, God! no!"

"There is another course, then, dear Angela Come with me quietly, and let me explain to you how all this has come about. Let me prove to you, as, believe me, I can, that this man, for whom you feel so much sympathy, deserves none of it Let me prove to you that he was your arch foe as well as mine."

"Can you, Gerald?"

"I can."

"Oh, but it was terrible to take his life in such a way, was it not? Oh, Gerald, I think I see him now!"

"Where?—where?"

Captain Hawk gave such a start, and looked around him with so much alarm, that Angela might, even from that alone, have gathered the fact that his conscience did not by any means acquit him so easily and glibly of the act he had committed in the park as his words would fain lead her to suppose it did.

"I did not mean that I saw him here, Gerald. I meant that my imagination conjured up his appearance as he leant, faint and ill from the death-wound you gave him, against a tree."

Angela began to weep now; and Captain Hawk seized the opportunity of half carrying her into the hall of the hotel.

The night-porter and watchman of the hotel, who had not yet gone off duty, was as fully impressed as the rest of the establishment with the idea of Captain Hawk's great importance; and he passed the word to the landlord, who was only lounging on a sofa in one of the rooms on the ground-floor, that the prince had come home.

With officious zeal, Hawk found himself now surrounded by the landlord and several waiters; and, to his chagrin, the landlady, too, appeared upon the scene of action; and the moment Angela saw her, she left the care of Captain Hawk, saying as she did so—

"I will bid you good-night, now, brother; and in the morning we will talk further of those things that to-night there is not time to discuss."

Captain Hawk uttered an execration, for he had hoped at such an hour as that to get Angela into his own room, and even as it was he did not like to give up the idea, but approaching her, he whispered in her ear, in the most engaging accents he could command—

"Dear Angela, I have much to say to you—much to explain, if you will but now give me half an hour of your company."

Angela looked in his face, and there was a peculiar flash of his eye that made her shudder.

"To-morrow — to-morrow," she cried.

"It may be too late."

"Oh, no—no, impossible. Good night, brother."

Angela took the arm of the landlady, and left him. Hawk bit his lip with vexation, and then with rapid strides went to his own room, and closed the door with a violence that shook the whole house, and awakened everybody in it.

"Dear me," said the landlord, "his royal highness, the prince, seems to be rather out of sorts. I'm glad that my nose was no nearer to the door, or it certainly would have had a severer blow than it got."

It would be impossible to repeat the awful maledictions that now for some few minutes or so flowed from the lips of Captain Hawk, as he flung himself on a couch in his gorgeous room; but he found it a relief to utter such fearful words, and after a time becoming more calm, he raised his clenched fist in the air, and muttered—

"I swear it, she shall be mine, though all the angels in heaven, and all the devils in the other place, were to come and try to take her from me. The greater the difficulty I have in this affair, the more enamoured I am of her. Oh, she is beautiful! Mine and mine only shall she be, in spite of all the world. To-morrow? Well, let it be to-morrow; but I did hope that to-night would have made her mine. It cannot be, though, now. To-morrow I will take a house, and at once in the morning remove her to it. There shall be but few attendants, and those shall be wholly devoted to me. Angela shall be the beautiful toy and plaything of my leisure hours. I do love her. Ah, yes, she is beautiful!"

Captain Hawk closed his eyes, and falling upon the sofa, he gave way to a sense of fatigue, and was soon fast asleep,

While all this was going on, the unfortunate stranger in the park who had been wounded by Hawk, in rather a dastardly manner, lay upon the gravel-walk close to the Grand Mall.

And now we may communicate to the reader a fact, which he may or may not have guessed before, namely, that the mysterious man is no other than our old friend, Joe.

Captain Hawk thought he knew Joe well, but it appears that he did not, for beneath the rough exterior and apparent utter ignorance of all polite language and acts that Joe exhibited, there lay quite a different character. The fact was, that Joe possessed an amount of education that Hawk never gave him credit for, and the manner in which he had acted the part that he had undertaken sufficiently testified to that fact.

It was Joe who had possessed himself of the ticket of admission to the king's assembly which had been lost by Captain Hawk, and which had well nigh been the means of preventing him from getting admission to the palace at all.

Joe had made his way to a costumier and procured a dress that completely disguised him; and before Captain Hawk arrived, he had passed into the saloons of St. James's with the king's order. By keeping close to the entrance, Joe had been able to see when Hawk and Angela entered the rooms; and he had kept by them like their shadows the whole evening.

What was Joe's motive for all this? Was he pitiful to such a degree that he could not bear to see a young creature like Angela so betrayed? Yes, that was part of the feeling; but the greater part remains behind. For the first time in his life, Joe really loved. The young girl had touched his heart with the magic of her wondrous innocence and beauty; and Joe had resolved that Captain Hawk should not sacrifice her to his passions.

After making this determination, Joe was quite prepared to chance his life upon the result. Alas! poor fellow, it seems as if he had done so, and lost the game!

CHAPTER CXXXV.

MAY BOYES FEELS THAT SHE HAS A DUTY TO PERFORM.

It was some half hour after Captain Hawk had left the park that, with a deep sigh, and holding his hands tightly to his side, Joe partially rose.

"He has killed me!" he gasped. "The sword went too far for any recovery. Oh! if I had but life enough left me to do something for Angela—to save her yet—for she is friendless now—quite!—oh, quite friendless! Help me, Heaven!"

Joe, by a great effort, although the pain he endured in doing so was truly excruciating, managed to struggle to his feet; and then, after leaning for a time against the trunk of the tree that was nearest to him, he managed to struggle on for a few paces, and then he fell.

"No—no," he gasped, "I must die here! It will not do! Oh, God! she is lost while I die here—here! with none to hear the story of her danger, and of my murder! Ha! what is that? A light among the trees! More lights! I hear the tread of feet! Some one comes! I will speak—I will speak!"

Along the Grand Mall there came now in the direction towards the old gate at Spring Gardens a troop of footmen, bearing a sedan chair, in which, no doubt, there was some lady coming from the palace entertainment.

Those of the servants who were in advance carried lanterns, so that the route of the cavalcade was quite well lighted; and as they came rapidly on, Joe saw that the sedan chair was a very rich one, and he could even see a portion of the head-dress of the lady who was within it.

"Help—oh, help!" cried Joe.

The foremost of the footmen stopped.

"Something the matter," he said. "Hilloa, here's a dead man on the Mall calling out for help."

"Who is it?" said another.

"How should I know, eh? Don't ask me. Let us get on. The duke told us to get Miss Boyes home all safe, and that is our business, now, you, know; come on."

"Help! Mercy!" said Joe.

"My good fellow, we will tell the first sentinel we meet of your condition, and a guard will be sent to take you up, no doubt. Be quiet, do."

One word of explanation.

The Boyes family had been invited to the entertainment, and the Duchess of Kingston had sent to Lady Boyes specially to say that she would introduce May to the queen; and although poor May, with the remembrance of the past, and all its afflictions still green and fresh in her mind, would gladly have abstained from availing herself of any such honour, yet her father would not have it so.

"To be introduced to the queen," said Sir John, laying his fingers by the side of his nose, "is all but acquainted—indeed one may say, in a manner of speaking, that it is much the same thing as being made slightly acquainted with a royal personage."

So poor May was compelled to go to London with Sir John and the rest of the family, and to take up her abode with the Duchess of Kingston.

Little did Captain Hawk think that May Boyes and her father and brother and Lady Boyes had all arrived at the entertainment at the palace five minutes after he had gone with Angela into that little room where the young marquis had come to so tragical an end.

But so it was; they all reached the saloons just too late to encounter the man who had been the destroyer of the peace of their family.

May was soon tired of the gaudy glitter of the scene about her, and after the presentation to the queen was over, she begged of the duchess to allow her to go home—that is to say, to the duchess's house; and as the duchess was compelled to stay in attendance upon the queen, she gave orders to her servants to take May home in her sedan-chair, and then to return for her to the palace.

Thus was it, then, that with such apparent state and dignity, May Boyes, escorted by the servants of the duchess in their state liveries, came through the park at such an hour as that.

Hearing something was the matter, May looked from the sedan-chair, and inquired what it was.

"A man killed in the Grand Mall, if you please, miss," said one of the footmen.

"Killed, did you say?"

"Why no, miss—he is not dead quite."

"Alas, poor fellow!"

Now, as May looked from the sedan-chair, the light of some of the flambeaux that the footmen carried fell full upon her sweet face, and Joe knew her at once, and called out—

"It is May Boyes—yes, it is she! Oh, this is the work of Heaven! If anybody in all the world will help Angela, it will be May Boyes. Oh, speak to me—speak to me!"

Surprised to hear her own name uttered by a man of whom she knew nothing, May alighted from the sedan, and walked up to Joe.

"Who and what are you," she said, "that you seem to know me, and to think that I can and will save any one?"

"I am dying! Hawk—Captain Hawk—Gerald Clifton, as he often called himself."

May turned deathly pale, and in a choking voice she said—

"What would you say of him? Oh, why recall that terrible recollection? Is it needful to do so?"

"Dead, miss," said one of the footmen, as he lifted the arm of Joe, and then let it fall quite helplessly—"quite dead."

May shuddered, and then returned to the sedan chair.

"Do me the favour, some of you," she said, "to take charge of the body, and to convey it to some place more fitting for it than the Mall of the park. God help the poor creature! I know him not."

May's request was complied with, for two of the footmen staid behind, while the rest took her home to the duchess's house in the Strand, close to Northumberland House.

Much did May ponder over all this; but she found it impossible to come to any conclusion or opinion as to who and what the man could be who had died in the park. There were times when, with a shudder, she asked herself if it could be Captain Hawk himself so disguised, partly by remorse and partly by art, that she even did not fully recognise him; but when she came to think how well she had known him, and how impossible it would be for him to disguise himself from her, she gave up that supposition as merely the coinage of a heated imagination, and she was still lost in doubt and perplexity.

This state of mind was anything but favourable to repose, and poor May passed a sleepless night, and rose in the morning looking pale and ill.

About the first thing she met with, upon descending to the breakfast room of the duchess's house, was a note addressed to her, and which ran as follows:—

"To Miss May Boyes.

"He who in the park last night fainted from pain and loss of blood is this morning able to say what he fain wishes to say to May Boyes. He would send her upon an angel's errand—one of mercy and of salvation; then let him hope that she will hear him."

May read the note with surprise, and upon questioning one of the servants, the man said—

"Yes, miss, the note was brought an hour ago, by a man who is now in a sedan-chair at the door of the house. He looks very pale and ill, and is rather richly dressed in some foreign costume."

"The duchess! Oh, where is the duchess?"

"Not up yet, miss."

"And there is no onea bout? Stay—no. I will see the man here. Yet no—I will go down stairs to one of the refreshment rooms. Admit him. Tell him that I will see him."

"Yes, miss."

May hurried down to the ground floor, and in one of the refreshment rooms she saw sitting upon a chair the ghastly figure of the man she had seen in the park. He made an effort to rise, but May prevented him, saying—

"Be seated, and God grant you strength to say to me what you wish."

"Amen!" said Joe. "There is a young, and fair, and innocent girl, almost a child—she is in the hands of Captain Hawk, at the Royal Hotel near Charing-cross. He means mischief—she will be lost. Nothing will convince her but that he is a prince—the son of a king. He calls himself the Prince of Austria. She will fall—fall, unless you see her, and convince her of what he really is. Oh, save her! She is so young, and her name is Angela. She is so beautiful—so innocent—so full of nature's sweet simplicity. Oh, save her—save her from the destroyer, who, body and soul, will hunt her to destruction! Save her—save her! Oh—God!"

Joe's head dropped upon his breast, and May uttered a scream, as her brother Ratchley entered the room.

"What is this, May?"

"Oh, is he dead—is he dead?"

"Dead? A dead man? Good God, yes, he is dead. May, I have seen this man's face before He was a kind of servant to—to——"

"Gerald Clifton."

"To Captain Hawk, the highwayman, sister."

May burst into tears.

"Ratchley—Ratchley! do you love me?"

"Do you doubt it, May?"

"No—no, brother, I do not. I never doubted it; but now I want your help. Listen to me, and do not interrupt me."

"I will listen."

May hastily told him what Joe had communicated to her; and when she had concluded, Ratchley said with a sigh—

"When will the wicked career of that man end? Oh, May—May, you have something to answer for!"

"I, brother?"

"Yes. You saved him from the punishment of his crime—you saved him from death for the murder of Judge Holme."

May trembled.

"But that is past, sister. I do not wish to raise up in your mind distressful images. I know what you feel, and I can guess what you wish. It is to save this girl, Angela."

"Oh, it is—it is!"

"I will help you to the best of my ability so to do. You shall see her, if it be possible that you can see her without coming into contact with Hawk. The fact that Captain Hawk and this Prince of Austria that all the fashionable world is mad about are one and the same astounds me: but after what I have heard I cannot doubt it. I will think over the best mode of arranging your visit to the hotel. Come, sister, be of good cheer."

"And you will be secret, Ratchley?"

"As the grave."

"Oh, brother, I cannot thank you; but it will be a great thing to save this human soul."

CHAPTER CXXXVI.

RATCHLEY BOYES COMMUNICATES WITH THE SECRETARY OF STATE.

When Ratchley had conducted his sister to her room, and was returning to the apartment below to see to the disposal of the dead body of Joe, a gentleman accosted him on the stairs.

"Mr. Boyes," he said, "do you know me?"

Ratchley looked at him for a moment in surprise, and then said—

"Ah, it is Hastings, my old Oxford friend. They told me that you were private secretary to the home minister. Is it so?"

It is; and I am glad I have met with you. A footman of this house has just made a communication to me, in which your name and that of your sister is mixed up."

"Indeed?"

"Yes; he says that—that, in plain language, he was listening at the door of one of the reception-rooms, and he heard the words—'This Captain Hawk, then, and the supposed Prince of Austria, concerning whom the fashionable world are so curious, are one and the same person.' These may not be the exact words; but such is the substance of them."

Ratchley was silent.

"Come, my old friend, be candid with me. What did such words mean? or have they no meaning?"

"Hastings, will you answer me a question first?"

"Certainly."

"What course do you consider you ought to adopt in this matter?"

"I will tell you freely. If by any accident I had myself overheard the words, they would have remained buried in my bosom, unless you gave your free consent to my reporting them; but, as they were brought to me as public information by another, you see, I——"

"I understand. You feel that you must demand from me their explanation?"

"I must. It is my duty to do so."

"Well, Hastings, to tell the honest truth, I don't know whether to be glad or sorry about it."

"You speak in riddles."

"I do. But since you know what you know, I think I will see the secretary of state, and make a communication to him. It is, after all, better as it is. Of course you have made up your mind to some step in the business?"

The private secretary took out his watch, and after glancing at it for a moment he said—

"Within the next quarter of an hour the royal hotel in which the Prince of Austria resides will be surrounded by the police, so that all possibility of his escape will be cut off."

"You are prompt."

"It is fit that I should be so, my dear Ratchley, in these troublesome times. But come, you shall see his lordship at once; I will take you to him."

"I follow you. Alas! poor May! I cannot keep your secret longer; and it is better for your peace, I feel convinced, that I should not do so."

While Ratchley is adopting a line of conduct that he has no objection to follow now that he is forced, as it were, into it, but which he certainly would not have followed if he had not been so forced, for he would have respected the promise he gave to his sister, May, she was waiting with some anxiety for him to arrange the mode by which she was to see Angela.

The few words that poor Joe had uttered previous to his decease had been quite sufficient to the purpose, at all events, to enable May to understand sufficient of the case to act in it.

After waiting for Ratchley about half an hour, she received the following note from him—

"Dear May,—Take a sedan-chair, and tell the men to wait with you and it at the corner of Pall Mall, by Marlborough House. I hope to be there as soon as you will; but, if not, I will come to you within a few minutes of that time.—I am yours,

"Ratchley Boyes."

May at once ordered the chair, for she had made up her mind so thoroughly to rescue the young girl that Joe had mentioned, that it was quite a relief to her to commence the undertaking.

A few minutes sufficed to take her to the spot mentioned in Ratchley's note, and there she found him waiting for her. In rather hurried accents Ratchley said—

"I have ascertained that Hawk has not left the hotel, but that he is about to do so. The girl is indisposed, and no one has yet seen her this morning. As soon as Hawk goes out I will give you notice, and you can go to the hotel. I will keep guard in the sedan, so that if Hawk should come home before you leave it I can act as circumstances will require."

"Yes, Ratchley; but, remember, no violence."

"Oh, no—no. Ah, keep your head back, there he is."

Captain Hawk, wrapped in a large brown cloak elegantly trimmed with silk braid, passed close to the sedan chair. He was going to look for a house to remove Angela to. Her plea of indisposition had prevented their meeting that morning, but cool and calm as he then was he did not mind that

CAPTAIN HAWK'S ENCOUNTER WITH THE GARDENER.

much, as he considered that she could not possibly escape him.

At the sight of Captain Hawk poor May thought for a moment that she should have fainted; but greatly recovering herself she ordered the men to wait with her brother and the sedan-chair, and she ascended the steps of the hotel and demanded to see the landlady.

There was an appearance about May which always commanded respect, and the landlady bowed to her very humbly.

"I want to see the young lady who is here," said May, "I mean the sister of the Austrian Prince. Go and tell her that a lady has called to see her or, stay, it will be as well if you point out her room to me."

The landlady was a little puzzled, as Captain Hawk had threatened awful consequences if they admitted any one to see Angela; but then as this was a lady, and as the landlady's ideas of danger all were upon men, she thought there could be no harm, so she showed May into the magnificent saloon which Captain Hawk usually sat in, and went to inform Angela, or the princess as she called her, that there was a visitor for her.

Angela was surprised, but upon the assurance of the landlady that it was a lady, she hastily threw over her shoulders a cloak and entered the sitting-room from her own apartments, having to cross the landing at the head of the stairs to do so.

At the first sight of the charming young girl, who looked to be so near to absolute childhood, poor May was deeply affected, and she asked herself if it were possible that even Captain Hawk could be such a villain as to seek the destruction of such a being. There is a tact about human nature which enables it to distinguish true innocence from guilt, and one glance at the face of Angela was enough to convince May that as yet she had not fallen.

"You wished to see me," said Angela. "Pray be seated."

"I did wish to see you," said May. "I come, I hope, to save you."

"To save me! Oh, from what—from whom?"

"From him who would destroy you; from the man whom you think a prince, or, if not that, at least an honourable gentleman! Girl, you tremble. I know not how many moments I may have to spare to speak to you, but as one of your own sex, and a lady, I ask you while you are still innocent—still pure, to fly from this man as you would from some hideous monster. He will betray you, and destroy you, if you not."

"Oh, you do not know him. You cannot mean Gerald?"

"I do—I do. It is you who do not know him. This Gerald, as you call him, is a highwayman—his name is Hawk. He is worse than that—he is a murderer!"

"Oh, God!"

"Yes, a murderer. Judge Holme fell by his hands, and God forgive me for being the means of shielding him from the just consequences of that offence. On, come with me at once. My brother—my father—my mother, will aid you. My name is Boyes. Come, Angela—oh, come. You do not know the precipice upon which you stand."

"Nor do you, May Boyes," said Captain Hawk, as flinging open the door, and then terribly dashing it shut again, he stood before the astonished eyes of May and Angela.

"Returned!" said May.

"Yes," added Hawk, "returned to your confusion. So, May Boyes, you are—ha! ha!—jealous, are you?"

"Monster!"

"Oh, a fine word that—A monster, am I?"

"Stop, Gerald!" cried Angela. "Are you a thief and a murderer?"

The scowl that came over the face of Captain Hawk was truly horrible, as advancing to May, he said—

"So, May Boyes, I owe this fine character to your kindness? But know that I will have revenge. What do you here, wretch?"

"I come to save this girl, and I will save her."

"Ha! ha! Good! Why, Angela, you see, this poor girl fell in love with me, and I was forced to repulse her, and get rid of her fulsome attentions, and it turned her wits, that's all. A lunatic asylum is the only fitting place for you, May Boyes. Begone at once, and do not trifle with me."

"To do more murders, I suppose," said May. "Oh, Gerald Clifton, I do repent me now."

"Of what?"

"That I saved you. But your time has now come. You must perish, that the innocent may be saved."

"Pshaw! This jargon is all nonsense. Away with you, or, perhaps, May, you have come to throw yourself into these arms? Oh, for shame! I am really surprised at you. Respect the innocence of this young creature, I beg of you."

"Angela!" cried May. "Oh, Angela, come with me!"

"Not if I know it," said Captain Hawk, as he strode to the door of the room. "Hilloa, landlord! Waiter, here is a mad woman. Remove her instantly. Mad—quite mad!"

He flung open the door; but started back when he saw the landing-place covered with armed men. A couple of stalwart officers of the police flung themselves upon him, and a clear voice called out from the landing—

"Gerald Clifton, alias Captain Hawk, I arrest you in the king's name!"

"Ah!" screamed Hawk, "death—death! Not in life will I be taken—not in life! Cowards!"

"All's right," said one of the officers, after a brief struggle with Captain Hawk—"all's right, old fellow; now you may kick as much as you like."

They had placed handcuffs upon his hands, and manacles upon his ankles; so that he was perfectly helpless.

"Now, my men," said the person who had taken the command of the officers, "off with him."

Captain Hawk was carried down the stairs, and placed in a hackney coach.

"Where to?" said the driver.

"Newgate!"

Off went the coach at a brisk trot of the old pair of hacks that drew it.

CHAPTER CXXXVII.

THE ARREST OF CAPTAIN HAWK, AND HIS RE-ARRAIGNMENT FOR THE JUDGE'S MURDER.

The following paragraph appeared in the *St. James's Chronicle* on the evening of the arrest of Captain Hawk:

"The notorious Captain Hawk, who was acquitted some time since of the murder of Judge Holme, is again arrested, and will a second time be placed upon his trial for the offence, as it has been discovered that, beyond all doubt, the *alibi* by which he was acquitted was a tampered-up one. Although contrary to the usual course to try a man twice for the same offence, we understand that the law officers of the crown have raised a point which enables them to do so in this instance. If, however, they should fail, there are other offences of equal magnitude to lay to the charge of the prisoner."

This paragraph pretty accurately stated how the case stood. Captain Hawk was to be again put upon his trial for the murder of Judge Holme, and if again acquitted, there were other indictments pending against him.

The Old Bailey Sessions were on, and the grand jury brought in a true bill against Hawk; so that within three days of his arrest at the hotel he again stood, pale and wan, at the bar of the Old Bailey to take his chance of life or death.

The arrest of Hawk again had made quite a sensation among all the thieves in London, and the same witnesses who had proved the *alibi* at the former trial were sought out, and came forward in his behalf.

The point raised by the attorney-general to get a new trial was, that Hawk was not tried in his right name on the former occasion, and, therefore, that although as regarded him a conviction would have been good, an acquittal was not so. What his real name was, though, did not seem to be easily to be got at.

There was the difficulty in the case; so the indictment charged him, he being a person unknown, but a subject of his majesty's, with the murder, &c., &c., of Judge Holme!

The trial proceeded, and a declaration was put in for May Boyes, who was very ill, but who had made it upon oath to the effect that she had substituted herself for Captain Hawk upon the night of the murder, and so misled the witnesses.

The trial created an immense degree of interest, both among the legal profession and the public, and the issue seemed to be very doubtful indeed, till the judge summed up in favour of the prisoner, by saying—

"It is quite clear to my mind, and I think it is equally clear to the mind of every one in this court, that the prisoner at the bar did the deed for which he is this day arraigned before us; but it is contrary to the spirit of the English law that any one should be harassed by repeated trials for one and the same offence.

"We cannot rid our minds from the fact that the prisoner at the bar has been tried once for this identical murder, and I think that it would be straining a point against the subject were the law and the crown to decide that, under any circumstances whatever, he could be again tried and convicted.

"It is for you, gentlemen of the jury, to come to a decision upon this matter in the way your judgments may direct you. There seems to be no knowledge of what the prisoner's name really is; but if there were, I don't think that would help us out of the difficulty at all. I have to regret extremely the course which a young lady——"

"Hem!" said Sir John Boyes.

"Which a young lady of a highly respectable family took upon the night of the murder—a course which she has at last found it to be necessary to testify to, under her own hand, attested by her solemn affidavit."

"Hem!" said Sir John. "What's o'clock?"

"Silence!—silence!"

"That young lady may be very much entitled to our pity," added the judge; "but, sooner or later, it was quite certain that she would bitterly repent the course she pursued; and if there be any here who have allowed their imaginations to be carried away by the seeming heroism of the act, I do think that if they in the bosoms of their own family watch——"

"Family watch!" cried Sir John Boyes. "My lord—my lord, I did think I had heard the last of that family watch. Don't allude to it, I pray."

"What is the meaning of all this?" said the judge.

"The watch of the family, my lord, the—a—the—a family watch I allude to. We are all distracted and in the family way—God bless my soul, no! What am I saying?"

"That lunatic," said the judge, "will have to be removed if he again interrupts the court. Gentlemen of the jury, the case is with you."

"Now he is on about the case," groaned Sir John. "He won't leave that watch alone. Oh, dear—oh, dear!"

The jury did not retire from the box, but after a few minutes' consultation among themselves they intimated that they had agreed upon their verdict.

"Gentlemen of the jury," said the clerk of the arraigns, "what say you? Do you pronounce the prisoner at the bar guilty or not guilty?"

"Not guilty!"

There was a death-like silence in the court. Every one there present felt that those words, "Not guilty," had in reality been pronounced in favour of a murderer.

Captain Hawk cast a glance around him, and he did not see one face that looked sympathisingly upon him. There he stood the observed of all observers, and the shunned by all. In a remote corner of the court, now that the trial was over, there arose a veiled figure, and the veil was for a moment placed aside.

Captain Hawk saw that it was May Boyes.

"Not guilty," he cried, as he held up his hand. "Again not guilty, despite of all! Ha—ha!"

"Hold!" said the judge. "Prisoner at the bar, do not prejudice your future fate. Wretched man!"

"Take back the taunt," cried Hawk. "I am not wretched. I demand my freedom. I am not guilty!"

"My lord," said the attorney-general, "the prisoner at the bar appears quite to forget, or chooses to seem to do so, that there are other indictments against him. We have evidence of two other murders committed by him."

"'Tis false!" cried Hawk.

"One," continued the attorney-general, "was committed in the Palace of St. James's—the other in the park adjoining that palace. It is quite out of the question that such a man can possibly be let loose again upon the society he has so grievously outraged by his crimes."

"Are these indictments ready?" said Hawk's counsel.

"Yes."

"Where are the true bills as found by the grand jury?"

"The true bills? Oh, they will be found in the course of the day."

"Then until they are my client is free. I don't see why he is to be kept here while you perfect your evidence. Take him before a magistrate in the regular course, if you have any charge to make against him."

"Oh, this is too absurd," said the attorney-general.

"Yet a moment," said the judge; "let me speak to the prisoner at the bar. Will you attend to me, prisoner?"

"At your service, my lord."

"It is quite clear that your doom is near. It is quite clear that your career of crime, unexampled as it has been, is at an end. There are other offences to be proved against you, the lightest of which will condemn you to a felon's death. It is for you to consider whether you will give yourself the protracted agony of a second appearance in this court, or now, by admitting your guilt in either of the instances mentioned, change the proceedings against you to a matter of form."

"Wherefore should I? What do I gain?"

"Peace."

"No, my lord—no. I do not submit. I may be crushed by force and by numbers, but I do not submit."

"As you please. But will you now declare, as it can make no difference to you, who and what you are?"

"Never!"

"We shall solve that mystery, I daresay," said the attorney-general, "by the time we have the prisoner here again, my lord. Of course his alias has been adopted to try to screen him."

"I don't know that," said Hawk's counsel; "that is a very unfair suggestion, indeed."

"Why so?"

"I will give you an instance. Judge Holme we know, from family circumstances, changed his name. That is a fact sufficiently well known to the profession, and no one ever thought of attributing any unworthy motives to him for doing so."

CHAPTER CXXXVIII.

CAPTAIN HAWK FINDS THAT THERE IS IN THIS WORLD A RETRIBUTION.

"It is true," said the judge, "that my lamented friend, Judge Holme, did, from family disagreements with his son, I believe, change his name, but that is a very different case indeed. The act in one case was quite innocent—in the other it was with guilty objects. Judge Holme's name was Hesketh!"

Captain Hawk uttered a shriek.

"Speak—speak!" he gasped; 'speak again! Did—did you say Hesketh? for, if you did—*he was my father, and I am his murderer!*"

Even as he spoke, all power of self-support seemed to fail him; he reeled back a pace or two, and then fell headlong in the dock, while blood gushed from his mouth, giving him the appearance of having broken some blood vessel, which would soon terminate his earthly career.

All was then in an instant commotion; the sort of mental paralysis that seemed to have seized upon every one in court when first he uttered that frightful cry, had passed away. Some shrieked, some endeavoured to escape, battling their way through the dense crowd; others fell, and were trodden upon by their excited companions; and, amid all, May Boyes stood up with her hands clasped, and a look of despair upon her countenance, as she cried aloud—

"Lost—lost—lost! all is lost! Heaven have mercy on me now!"

The judge rose from his seat, and in vain implored for order. The counsel rushed forward among the crowd, and some of them were the first to raise the highwayman from where he had fallen.

He seemed perfectly insensible, and from the rigidity of his muscles, and the fixed and awful expression of his face, they thought that he was dead. A surgeon, who was present, bled him, and then he opened his eyes, and breathed a faint sigh, as the life-blood trickled from his arm.

"Father—father," he said, "this is a frightful dream. I left you in anger, but I come to you again to stir within you, with the affection of a son, whatever reminiscences of early affection that may yet linger in your bosom."

"He is not dead!" said May Boyes. "God of Heaven, why is he not dead? What now is life to him? what now prolonged existence to the wretch who feels himself a parricide?"

She let her head drop upon her hands, and shook as with a strong convulsion of grief. It was in vain that her sister, her mother, and her brother, strove to cheer her, and bid her look up; she only muttered—"Lost—lost! all lost!" and they could do nothing with her, but let the tide of grief have its way, even if, upon its stormy billows, it should wreck the noblest, gentlest heart Heaven ever placed in a human breast.

A dozen hands held up the highwayman, and there, ghastly and grim, he stood again at that dock confronting the judge.

But, oh, what a change was there! Where, now, was the gallant bearing?—where, now, the haughty brow—the eagle eye?—where was the slightly curled lip, speaking of scorn, and the ineffable smile, as if of conscious superiority, that was wont to sit upon his face?—all lost! all lost! And there stood, at the bar of justice, instead of one possessing these attributes and qualities, a trembling, shrinking, ghastly, looking wretch, bearing more the appearance of one risen from the grave, into whose veins, for a brief space, life-blood had been ejected, than a living, breathing man, and one of a great crowd of humanity around him.

The old judge moved his lips, but he could not speak for many minutes. His head shook and his hands trembled ere he could say, in broken accents—

"Prisoner at the bar, is this frightful fact uncontradicted? Is your name Hesketh?"

Captain Hawk's fingers played tremulously upon the front of the dock. Twice, thrice, he tried to speak, but could not.

"The mind is gone," said the attorney-general "Heaven keep me from witnessing such a scene again."

"Hesketh, Hesketh!" said Hawk. "Wallis Hesketh—father! Is this blood upon my hands?—your blood—my blood! God! God! God!"

The counsel for the defence rose, and, in a low voice towards the judge, he said—

"I have my duty still to do—the prisoner is free."

"He is," said the old judge.

"No—no!" cried Hawk, stretching forward his hands—"no, no! kill, slay, destroy me! I did the deed. Guilty—guilty—guilty! A hundred lives could not appease Heaven's vengeance. I am guilty. He was my father; I slew him upon the heath; but, oh! I knew him not. I swore to stop Judge Holme: I kept my oath. There was resistance; he fired at me; but I knew him not. On the impulse of the moment, I fired again. I saw his white hair dappled in gore; but then I knew him not. I hovered round the spot; a frightful influence kept me moving in that hideous circle round the dead; the odour of the fresh-spilt blood came upon my senses, as the sweet morning air blew across the heath; and then they took me. All that has happened here to-day is but a hideous delusion. I am guilty. I knew him not; but I am guilty; and now I think that I am mad!'

"My lord," said the counsel, "I understand that the prisoner at the bar is free?"

"No—no—no!" cried Hawk; "give me death!"

"Free to leave this court as any person within it?" added the counsel.

"Quite free," said the judge.

"I am guilty!" shrieked Hawk. "If you have a dungeon deeper than another, place me in it. Life for life—blood for blood! and—oh, God! that that should be the blood of my father!"

"My lord," said the counsel, "I submit that the time of the court is being wasted. Being retained in the next case, I hope your lordship will order any person to be removed who makes a disturbance."

"Set the prisoner free," said the judge.

The attorney-general rose.

"With your lordship's permission," he said, "I shall press the other indictments; and, owing to the extraordinary and conflicting nature of the evidence, as well as the most unlooked-for statement made by the prisoner himself, I have to beg that those indictments be traversed to next sessions."

The judge was silent for a moment, and then he said, with a deep sigh—

"Be it so—be it so. Officers, remove the prisoner. The court is adjourned."

CHAPTER CXXXIX.

THE CELL.

The judge was so overcome—for he was an aged man—with the frightful proceedings which had taken place within the court, that he had to be assisted from the bench, and it was said that, when he reached his private room, he fainted.

Captain Hawk, too, was half carried from the dock. All he seemed now to comprehend was, that he was not to be set free; and so that, of course, he should suffer for the dreadful deed that he had done.

The crowd that was then in court were as anxious to leave it, to carry far and wide the news of the most awful and singular termination of the trial, as they had been early in the morning to get a place within its precincts. The struggle to get out was immense, and the wondering witnesses, who on the former trial had so successfully proved an *alibi* for the highwayman, were most of them carried out with the throng.

As for the turnpike-man and the landlord of the Goat and Boots, they both seemed perfectly bewildered; the sudden admission by the prisoner that he had really done the deed, appeared to them perfectly inexplicable, and they retired at once to a neighbouring public-house, where they both got profoundly drunk, without being able to come to a more satisfactory conclusion.

The attorney-general, and most of the counsel, probably including the one who had been retained for the defence, eagerly adopted the hypothesis which had been started for the prosecution, namely, that the party who had commenced proceedings by robbing Sir John Boyes of his watch, and then proceeded to London, was a confederate of Captain Hawk, and that so far the affair was planned of eventually proving an *alibi*.

And now that we have incidentally mentioned Sir John Boyes, let us for a moment imagine the state of intense wonder into which he was thrown by the new and extraordinary light which had fallen upon the proceedings.

He had listened to the judge's exhortation to the prisoner at the bar with much the same stolid, stupid-looking gravity with which he was accustomed to attend to the drowsy sermons at the parish church; but when the sudden interruption ensued, and that horrible cry sounded in his ears, poor Sir John for the whole space of five minutes knew not whether he was upon his head or his heels.

He first of all started up, and then down he sat upon the floor, instead of his seat, so that his head only came upon a level with the wainscot which enclosed the box to which he and his family had obtained admission.

Then he laid hold of the ankle of Mrs. Boyes, fancying that it was some part of the wood-work of the court, which it was highly necessary for him to hold tight of, for fear he shou'd get any lower; and there he listened to all, turning his great gray sleepy-looking eyes first upon one, and then upon another of the speakers.

"Gracious Providence!" said Lady Boyes, "something dreadful's got hold of my ankle;" but Sir John paid no attention, and it was not until the crowd had nearly left the court, and an officer came to show the Boyes' family out, that he released her.

"My friend," said Sir John, to the officer, "I don't wish to give you any unnecessary trouble, but if you can tell me, in a manner of speaking, what it's all about, which will be equivalent, you understand, to letting me know, I shall be much obliged."

"Didn't you hear?" said the man, who had been employed upon the principle of set a thief to catch a thief; "the rummy cove has peached on himself, and says as he's scuttled the governor."

"Indeed," said Sir John; "the governor of where?"

"Why, just the governor, to be sure."

"Oh, the governor of Newgate, I suppose?"

"Well, I'm blowed! here's artifice—pretends that he doesn't understand the English language—oh, you ass!"

Away walked the officer.

"Well," said Sir John, "it is one of the most extraordinary things in the world"—and he tapped his head several times as he said it—"that, within these last few weeks, I have been more repeatedly called a donkey and an ass, than I think the whole Boyes' family ever were before. There's something wrong in the state of society, which is just as bad as if there were something erroneous; and my private opinion of all this is—ah, and that's my private opinion. God bless my soul, stop thief! The family watch—the family watch is gone at last!"

Sir John patted himself all over as he spoke, as if he were nothing but one mass of pockets, into any one of which the family watch might surreptitiously have crept.

"My lady, my lady," he added, "do you hear the family watch? It seems to me that nobody has the slightest sympathy for the dignity of the Boyeses."

"I'm quite sure, Sir John," said Lady Boyes, "that you brought it into the court, because, you know, you showed it to me, and I remarked that it was an hour and twenty minutes wrong, as it always is."

"My lady, my lady, it is as impossible for the family watch of all the Boyses to be wrong, as it is, in a manner of speaking, for me to be wrong. It's gone, however, and that's the very thing why somebody's stolen it, because it's always right. Bless my heart and life, what dishonesty there is in the world. Ratchley, my dear, as the representative of the great Boyes, you ought to have watched."

"Father, my attention," said Ratchley, "was too painfully otherwise engrossed. What do you intend to do?"

"Do? Why, offer a reward, to be sure."

"Nay, I do not mean about the watch, but as respects this unhappy man, who unexpectedly finds he has committed so awful a crime?"

"Do! what shall I do? Why, let me see—ah! to be sure, I'll do nothing; that'll be most dignified; and I rather think I'll go home."

"But not until to-morrow. It would be far better to go home in daylight than so late as it is now. Consider the danger of the road."

"Danger!"

"Not to you, but to others, who seeing you proceeding home, would fancy there was a sort of protection thrown over them by travelling the same route."

Sir John drew himself up, and touched his head with his forefinger.

"There's something in that, Ratchley," he said.

"You really think so?" said Ratchley, with a quiet sarcasm.

"Yes, there is; I won't go home to-night; you've convinced me. When a Boyes convinces a Boyes it's all right, and the world jogs on as usual. I won't go home to-night."

"May," whispered Ratchley to his sister, "I have won this point for you as you desired me; though what use you intend to make of it, Heaven only knows. Why, oh, why, dear May, will you not confide all to me? Is it my affection or my prudence that you doubt?"

"Neither, Ratchley, neither," said May. "But do not ask me yet; you shall know all, perchance, to-morrow—trust me, Ratchley, you shall. And now I've another request to make of you."

"Name it, dear May, name it. God knows there is no request of yours from which I would shrink."

She placed both her small hands in one of his, and looked imploringly in his face, as she said—

"Ratchley, you will, by some means or another, and at once, too, procure me a written orders to see—him."

"The prisoner in Newgate?"

"Yes, yes, yes."

"I doubt my power, May, to obtain this; and most frightful appears to me the imprudence of the step."

"Do not reason with me—do not reason with me."

"Nay, but, sister——"

"Ratchley! Ratchley! look in my face—my heart is nearly broken; will you complete such a catastrophe by denying that which I ask of you?"

Ratchley Boyes pressed the small hands he held in his, and, in a voice of deep emotion, he replied—

"No, dear May, I will not refuse you—I cannot, I dare not—although I know not how it is to be obtained—the order you speak of."

May passed her hand across her

LADY DELIVA CONSCIOUS-SMITTEN AT HER INIQUITIES.

brow, and then she said, in a lower tone—

"Listen! Misfortune, and such mental agony as I have gone through, have taught me artifice. You must go to the judge who presided at the trial, you must tell him that, in the prisoner at the bar, you fancy you recognise one who robbed and tried to murder you on Hounslow Heath, then, with only an amount of interest which shall seem sufficient for the occasion, and no more, you will ask him for an order to admit the bearer, mind."

"I will try, May, to do so; but I must confess that, even now I have made you a promise I shall not attempt to retract, I do view with sentiments of great dislike your visit to this desperate man."

"Enough—enough, brother! I know all—I feel all that you would say; there is nothing that you can urge that I have not thought over too painfully. Say no more; but let me feel that I have yet to live for something, by making what endeavour you can to provide me with the means of ingress to that dreadful building, which has ever filled so horrible a place in my imagination."

"To Newgate—but you will not go to-night?"

"Yes, to Newgate—and to-night. Ratchley, Ratchley, again I implore you not to reason with me; it seems like paltering with my soul's welfare to hesitate upon this enterprise."

"It shall be done, May, if it can be done."

"What are you talking about?" said Sir John. "I suppose it's about the family watch. Perhaps you think it's singular that I should be robbed of it? but never mind, great minds are not to be understood every day. Who are you?"

This was addressed to a man who came up before Sir John, and saluted him with a broad grin.

"Who am I?" said the fellow; "why, don't you know me? Why, I called upon you, and represented myself to be Long the officer, and told you what an ass you were. Ha! ha! Sir John, I got the better of you there; and secured just the reception for the real Long that I wished. But I take no credit for it—oh, dear, no; because, you see, out of all hand, you are the most desperate donkey that ever I came near. D—e! it's a disgrace to do you. Good day."

"There's a villain!" said Sir John. "He mistakes me for somebody else. I've a great mind to go home, after all. There'll be a revolution in this country soon, and all the ancient institutions will be completely rooted up."

After this gratuitous insult, Sir John and his family proceeded to their lodgings in quiet.

The reader who has followed us thus far in tracing what may be called the fortunes of Captain Hawk the highwayman, will be at no loss now to unravel the mystery of our tale.

By referring to some chapters back, we shall find that there was an interview recorded as happening between a stern father and a reproachful son: They met, but to exchange a few words of an unsatisfactory nature, and then they parted, as each probably thought, for ever.

That father was he who afterwards became Judge Holme—the son was Wallis Hesketh, better known as Captain Hawk, the notorious highwayman, who had, in the disguise which introduced him to the family of Sir John Boyes, won the gentle heart of May.

The change of name on the part of both father and son had hindered each from knowing the other even by repute—a stern pride, and a kind of family obstinacy peculiar to them both, stopped all inquiry on either side.

They had not met for years, until on that fearful night when they met on Hounslow-heath, in the character of the assailer and the assailed, the highwayman and the traveller, the murderer and his victim.

Alas! looking at these affairs with a philosophic eye, which of them are we most to pity?—the father who fell by the hand of his son, or the unconscious parricide, who now, with all the horrors of his crime upon his conscience, lay in Newgate, a melancholy wreck of what he once had been?

Most truly, the terrific crime of which Captain Hawk was really guilty admitted of no extenuation. It was "murder most foul, as in the best it is. But this most foul, strange, and unnatural;" and all we can say of him, and for him, is, that he knew not who his victim was.

It may be that, in the eyes of a beneficent and a just Providence, the crime of such a murder could not be made greater by the fact of the unknown relationship of the individuals; but still the parricide himself was not in a condition to reason logically upon his vast offence. No; he could only feel all the stings of a remorse, which soon must hurry him to that grave which his thoughts had never until that day turned upon.

We will fancy now Sir John Boyes established at his lodging, and May having retired to her chamber on the sufficiently valid plea of fatigue. Ratchley Boyes has been absent more than an hour—he returns pale and agitated, and his eye glances round the small family circle.

"Where is May?" he said.

"Why," said Sir John, "as I understood, she has gone to repose for an hour or so after her fatigues."

"Oh! indeed," said Ratchley; "no wonder."

He took an opportunity, some few moments after, of leaving the room, and then he inquired of one of the servants of the house which was May Boyes's bed-chamber. It was indicated to him, and with rapid steps he reached the door, at which he tapped gently. It was opened by May herself instantly.

"It is you, Ratchley," she said! "come in—and, and—tell me at once have you succeeded?"

"I have, and without difficulty."

"The order, the order—give me the order."

"It is here, May; but, oh! reflect again! You have thrown me into such a state of feverish anxiety by this projected visit of yours to Newgate, that I know not what to do or say."

"Hush! hush!" said May; "enough."

She hastily threw over her shoulders a cloak and hood, and was in a few moments ready for the streets. Ratchley gazed upon her until she reached the door of the apartment.

"You are determined?" he said.

"Quite, quite."

"And will you not allow me to go with you?"

"Do not ask it. Heaven must be the only witness of our interview. Ratchley, God bless you! Farewell, brother—farewell!"

"Why do you say farewell?"

"Nay, I know not, for we shall soon meet again. It is very foolish to say farewell. Adieu, adieu; it is a gentler and a better word."

She passed out of the room, and he heard her light footstep tripping down the stairs. He clasped his hands, and, in a tone of great anguish, he said,—

"My poor May, my poor May, I will follow thee. If you will adventure upon this mad interview, I cannot find it in my heart to thwart you; but at the door of Newgate I will wait your coming forth again."

May Boyes had very nearly described all she felt by those despairing words she uttered in court, when she said,—

"All is lost—all is lost."

And, indeed, now there was no hope; if we may except that faint one with which she sought the dreary prison-house of him that she had loved so well.

She wished now but to see him once again, to implore him to think that the mercy of Heaven was infinite, to beg of him not yet to despair of that serenity in a life to come, which in this he had robbed himself of. She wished to tell him all that she had done, and all that she had striven to do, to save him; and she thought then, that if she could awaken one tear of genuine repentance, and see it but for an instant glittering in those once haughty, flashing eyes she would have performed her mission, and have liked to die.

It was with such thoughts and feelings as these, little heeding the lateness of the hour, or any remark of chance passengers upon her hurried mien, that she sought the gate of Newgate.

Her object lifted her far above all such considerations. In her mind's eye she looked through those dreadful walls into the very cell where he, who first had won her eyes, and then her heart, she knew was lying. She paused not a moment, but, as ten o'clock was pealing forth from the bell of St. Sepulchre's church, she, with the judge's order firmly clutched in her grasp, tapped at the wicket gate of Newgate. It was instantly opened, and a rough visage appeared at the small aperture.

"Well, what now?" said a man; "you know now, as well as I do, that it's no use knocking here?"

May held up the paper.

"Ha! bother," said the man; "what's it all about?"

"Read it," said May, "and see."

There was something in the voice that awed him; he picked up a lantern from the stone floor, and held it to the paper.

"Admit the bearer to an interview alone with Captain Hawk. Hum! Charles Anderton, the judge, by all that's good! What a start! There's no saying no to it, though. Well, mum, come in."

The door was opened, and May Boyes stood within the precincts of Newgate.

"I begs your pardon, mum, for being 'tickler. We has rum 'uns here to deal with, and rum 'uns comes to see 'um; and in course we don't expect a lady at such a time of night, nor more does Captain Hawk seem to expect any company. He's as comfortable as ever mortal man was, mum, and I calls his a perfectly blessed state, and I wishes I could say as much for myself."

"Comfortable!" ejaculated May.

"Yes, mum; he says he ain't hungry, and he ain't dry, and he doesn't want nothing of nobody; and if that ain't something like a remarkable genteel independence, mum, blow my whiskers. I only wishes I could say so much—to be sure, I can't say as I'm hungry, and I don't tickler want nothing of nobody; but atween you, me, and the post, mum, I'm thundering dry—that's the only difference atween us. Eh! mum? did you speak, mum?"

"No."

"Oh! I begs your pardon; I thought you said, here's a crown to drink. What a blessed illusion, to be sure—an illusion of the senses, mum."

"Alas! he does not expect me," sighed May.

"Eh—eh! d——d if she ain't thinking of something else. It's no use—come along, mum—this way, mum—mind you don't fall into the well. I sees I shan't get nothing out of her. Pious, I should think. Comes to talk to him about his soul, no doubt, or else she wouldn't have had the order."

With a surly mien, and carrying with him an enormous bunch of keys, the man strode on, followed closely by May, who was not at all alarmed at his mock warning concerning the fictitious well, for she really did not hear it—her thoughts were with the prisoner in his lonely cell. What to her was the whole world and all its hopes, its fears, its anticipations, and its regrets?

The tide in her existence which might have led her on to happiness had but wrecked all her dearest and best hopes upon the rocks of despair. She was one of those who love but once, and that once with a fervour and devotion akin to that spiritual affection which it may be supposed ministering angels feel for each other in that realm beyond the sky, where there are no jealousies and no doubts. She was as some adventurous merchant, who embarked all his fortune in one frail vessel, and, being overtaken by the storms of fate, had as a consequence of that too free venture lost all. She had played her only stake in the great game of existence, and she stood defeated and despoiled of the means of again making such a venture.

It was not likely that such a being as May Boyes should pass entirely through existence, with no one to whom she could render up that rich store of affection which she had garnered in her heart; but, oh! far, far better had those holy and delightful feelings slumbered for ever, lending only the faint halo of their full glory to her thoughts and actions, than that she should have loved so well one who was so unworthy of that love.

We doubted if the murderer or his victim was to be pitied; but what is pity for them, compared to that anguish of regret which all must feel for the heart-desolation of poor May Boyes?

She was one of those beings whose very faults make them, perhaps, the more admirable; her errors were but exaggerated virtues—noble pieces of generosity, uncurbed by prudence.

How she had clung, even it the face of a conviction of his worthlessness, to him whom she had loved; and yet it was not with the feeling of an earthly passion that she clung to him—it was not that she loved the man, and was disposed to gloze over his vices, that she did so; no, from the first moment that she became aware of who and what he was, she felt as if Heaven itself had sunk a chasm between them, which she would not, and which she dared not cross.

But out of that affection and that abundance of love, which would, had all prospered and gone happily, have made her such a gentle helpmate to Gerald Clifton as the world never saw, arose another and perhaps as noble, if not a nobler, feeling. She resolved to do all that in her lay to save him, not for the purpose merely of saving him from the mortal consequences of his crimes, but to save him from himself, and to save him for Heaven. She thought it possible that she might wean him from the evil of his way, and lead him, by the gentle influence of some affection which surely he must feel for her, to those pleasant paths of virtue which are strewn with Heaven's sweetest flowers.

And when she started on her enterprise—when, attired in that costume which made her look the daring highwayman so well that she deceived even practised eyes, it will be borne in mind that she knew not, and that she never for a moment surmised, the extent to which Captain Hawk's criminality that night would go.

There was no frightful murder present to her imagination; she saw not, and suspected not, that those exertions she was making were for any one about to commit so terrific an offence against both God and man.

All she had heard and all she had read of highwaymen consisted of daring robberies, characterised by boldness on the one side, and pusillanimity on the other. The deed of blood took her by surprise, and then it was that, perhaps, with the sophistry taught her by her affection, she said to herself—

"The greater the crime, the greater the need of a long period of repentance. What will his death avail?—nothing, nothing; while his future life may suffice, in some measure, to make his peace with an offended Providence."

And thus it was that she had persevered in her attempt to rescue him from the consequences of his criminality—a perseverance which we have seen would have fully attained its object, but for the unexpected denouement of the trial.

Thought, in its rapidity of mental expression, pays little heed to time. During the brief space in which May Boyes was following the turnkey, her imagination ran riot, and she was lost almost in a maze of anticipation as to the result of the coming interview.

A number of intricate winding passages were threaded, here and there dimly lit by a lamp suspended from the ceiling; cold and chilly moisture exuded from the walls, and the silence of the place seemed ominous and dismal.

Suddenly the turnkey paused, and, addressing her, he said—

"We had heard of Captain Hawk before he came here, and we're bound to take good care of him. He's in the coffin cell."

"The coffin cell!" said May.

"Yes, it's a name we give to one of the strong boxes, partly in consequence of the roof being shaped like a coffin lid, and partly in consequence of nothing. Here you are, and there he is."

"No light?" said May.

"Not a bit of it. We should soon be singed out of old Newgate, if we gave lights in the cells."

He opened a door. May crossed the threshold, and she heard the ponderous lock shot into its place.

CHAPTER CXL.

THE SHADOW OF DEATH.

THE coffin cell was dark; there was a narrow grating through the roof, which looked upon the sky, for it was placed aslant, and carried the eye of any weary prisoner far above the surrounding buildings. But now that sky was dark as a funeral shroud; and, before her eyes became accustomed to it, the cell, to May Boyes, was a dense mass of gloom, the extent of which was left wholly to the imagination.

But does the prisoner move not?—are his senses so dull and deadened that he knows nothing of the fact of this disturbance of his solitude, or has he already bidden, with deep sincerity, the world and its affairs adieu? He moves not—he stirs not—and, indeed, scarcely seems to breathe.

Is there nothing at his heart which tells him of the presence of her he loved?—does she bring with her no atmosphere of beauty, and intelligence, and devotion, into the recesses of that gloomy place? It would seem not; and, if he had really heard his cell-door move upon its hinges, he, probably, thought it but an official visit from some of the prison authorities.

May stood for several minutes unable

to utter one word of salutation, and, perhaps, more unnerved by the fact that she was unchallenged by the inhabitant of that dreadful place, than as if he had at once spoken, and demanded who it was that intruded upon his loneliness.

But she had much to say, and time was waning fast. She heard the departing tread of the gaoler, as it grew fainter and fainter in the intricate passages that led from the cell. How soon he might return again she knew not, but the thought that his presence might rob her of the opportunity of saying something of that which was sitting brooding at her breast, warned her to be quick, and, advancing yet another step into the cell, she said, in something of her old accents, when love and joy and many anticipations of delight were the fair dreams of her imagination—

"Gerald Clifton!"

Those words seeemed a spell of wondrous power. With a cry of surprise, the prisoner sprang to his feet from where, in the darkness, he had been reclining. She could just see dimly his figure within a couple of arms' lengths of her, and the cell echoed to his words, as he cried—

"Fiends! fiends! mock me not with such a sound as that; but that I am here alone a prisoner, and nearly mad, I should tell myself that I had heard the voice of May Boyes."

"Gerald Clifton," said May, "you have heard the voice of May Boyes. You may be deserted by all the world beside; but I have come to you even here, not from woman's weakness, which induces her still to cherish the idol of her heart, though proved unworthy, but from higher and nobler motives have I sought you."

"It is—it is," he gasped—"it is the living likeness of the best, the truest—"

He could say no more; but in that dim light, to which her eyes were now beginning to get accustomed, she saw him sink at her feet. He clasped one of her hands in his; she felt that they were icy cold. He covered it with kisses, and she felt that there were tears—perchance, for the first time for many a year—gushing from those eyes, the sparkle of whose happy intelligence had ever made them look so beautiful.

"My own—my beautiful!" he ejaculated. "Oh, May—May! I do not deserve this, and as little expected it. And you can love me still; even now, the felon, the murderer, you can love. Oh, could I have but guessed at such a world of devotion!"

"I expected, as well as feared, this," said May. "I do not love you, Gerald Clifton, for by that familiar name I still wish to call you. I do not love you—disabuse yourself from that delusion."

"Delusion, May—not love me, and yet here, at such an hour, too, and in the condemned cell of the self-accused murderer? No—no, May, you have not come here to tell me that you do not love me."

"Gerald Clifton, this is not a time for ceremonies or reserves. I—I did love you, but I loved you for what you seemed, as now I love you not for what you are. Still do I think that the consummate actor, who can play a part so well that it shall look like nature's self, must possess something of the nature of that part in his own person; and so, because to me you played the part of nobleness, of greatness, and of virtue, I will cling to the thought that the elements of those feelings may be yet within you; that yours in a perverted nature, Gerald Clifton, not a bad one."

He trembled, and dropped the hand that till now he had held in his grasp, as he said faintly—

"Go on—go on."

"Joining this faith to a feeling which has grown out of a reminiscence of my fond affection, I have come here, Gerald Clifton, with the hope of being the mediator between your conscience and your God. Do you understand me now?"

"Yes," he said—"yes;" and he rose with a staggering movement to his feet. "I understand now; and the partial vanity of the moment, in believing that it was woman's love that brought you here, is properly rebuked. You forget who and what I am. Dare you trust yourself here with the parricide—the man whose hands are dyed in the blood of him who gave him life?"

"You see, Gerald Clifton, that I dare do so."

"Your errand, May, is a vain one.

I am sunk too low to be raised by thee. I want no preaching. I have enough here in my own breast already, to tell me that there is a hell on earth, if there be not one hereafter. I will not believe in, nor will I think of, a future state."

"You do both, Gerald Clifton," said May; "even now your guilty soul trembles at the dim perspective of the world to come."

"No; well aware am I that the minor crimes laid to my charge will bring me to death—to a felon's death, amid a gaping crowd, who will make high holiday to see the show. The memory of the doom which I have escaped will enable those who are my judges, with easy consciences, to condemn me; but they will fail—their victim, as they think me now within their grasp, will yet escape them."

"Yes," said May, "their victim may escape them."

"And he will."

"But how? There is a road, Gerald Clifton, the road which leads to the footstool of the Omnipotent, and that is the road which you must take; there is an ear which will not turn away from your supplication, and that alone is the ear which you must address."

"May Boyes—May Boyes, you cannot add one pang to those which I already suffer, nor can you diminish one by thus talking to me upon a subject which, from other lips, I would not have heard so long. I am one who has lived, fearing nothing, and believing nothing. You might have moved me by speaking to me of your love; and I should have wept to think that so much beauty and so much gentleness should have been cast away upon such a wretch as I; but now you have commenced a theme which awakens no sympathies in my heart."

"Oh, Gerald Clifton—Gerald Clifton! can you utter such words as these to me? Can you forget the past, and yet have no hope for the future? Is there no lingering expectation in your heart that we may meet again?"

"Meet again!"

"Yes; but not here—not beneath earthly skies."

"No, no, May—that is madness; we can never meet again. If all that men say of religion and of that life which is to come be true, you and I can never meet. The abodes of the blessed, in which joy eternal would be yours, can be no home for me; while you are listening to strains from heavenly lutes, the shrieks of doomed wretches like myself will be my melody; and if all be false—if all that is said upon these subjects be but the vain dreams of enthusiasts, then there is oblivion, and we can never meet again."

"I can well see," said May, "from whence your unbelief arises; it is because you despair of mercy—it is because you have no hope; but my visit here is to give you that hope, Gerald Clifton—to pour into your ears, and fill you with a better faith than that you have declared."

"You forget my crime, May."

"No — no, I do not; but—but, Gerald, you did not know it was your father."

"No—I call God to witness——"

"What! do you call upon that God to witness your denial, whom you have yourself denied? Oh, shake off this bravado of opinion, and, standing upon the smallest space of hope that imagination can give you, look up to Heaven, and tell yourself how infinite is its mercy."

"May Boyes, I will not say that any one could move me to think as you would wish me but yourself. Sometimes I doubt that I have done the deed, which, at others, my own conscience attributes to me with an accusing voice that appals my intellect. There are circumstances and mysteries connected with the whole transaction which I cannot unravel, and which make me feel like a man in a dream."

"These circumstances, Gerald Clifton, I can explain to you. There is nothing in your dreadful position but cold reality; but you tremble, and your voice sinks—you are ill."

"Hush—hush! do not say so. It is better that I should be ill. Death—death may be near at hand. I should like to die with the sound of your voice, May, in my ears. It is said that the dying sometimes hear pleasant music. What strains of melody would equal those to me?"

He staggered to a wooden seat that was in the cell, upon which he sank with a deep sigh, and then he added, faintly—

"Is it fancy, or does the cell grow lighter?"

"It does grow lighter," said May; "the moon is nearly at its full, and, as it rises in the sky, its reflected beams will penetrate even to such a place as this. I can see your face now, Gerald. How pale and sad you look; you will listen to me; you will think again; better thoughts will usurp the place of those that you have uttered. Gerald, Gerald, I think—I know you love me."

"I did, as Heaven is my judge!"

"There again, as Heaven is your judge. Why, Gerald, when you are in earnest, you at once appeal to that Heaven which your pride denies."

"Will you sit beside me, May, and go on speaking to me? This is—quick—quick! I did not think it would be so soon."

"What, Gerald, what?"

"Ay—ay, what!"

"You spoke of something?"

"No—no, it was nothing; go on. Let me hear you speak."

"Your own voice grows fainter; shall I get you help?"

"Not for worlds," he cried, as he sprang to his feet and grasped her wrist; "not for worlds! You shall not, you dare not, you—you will not."

At that moment, the moon must have emerged from behind some dense and shadowy clouds, for, as if by magic, there streamed in at the grating of the dungeon's roof a beam of silvery light, which fell upon the wall on the opposite side to that on which they sat.

A half shriek burst from May Boyes' lips as, by the reflected light of this beautiful moonbeam, she looked upon Gerald Clifton's face. It was of a death-paleness; the very lips were white, and cold drops of perspiration stood upon the ample brow.

"God! what is this?" she exclaimed; "can mental agony, in a few hours, have worked this wondrous change?"

His lips parted, but it was a moment or two before he could speak, and then he said—

"What change? Hush, hush! I am quite well; I shall be better. Oh, do not stir—make no alarm; 'tis better, ay, a million times better, as it is. Did they think that I would live to make a show at Tyburn?"

"What is the meaning of these dreadful words?" cried May. "Speak to me—confide in me, Gerald Clifton."

"Hush, hush!" he cried; and he clutched her convulsively by the wrist. "What is that—what is that?"

"Where—where?"

"On the wall—on the wall, in the moonlight. Do not you see it creeping round the cell?"

"It is but a shadow."

"Yes, yes, it is but a shadow; but it is the shadow of the dead—it is the spirit of the murdered, come to look upon me as I breathe my latest sigh. Do not mock me—do not look upon me thus. Wait but another hour—ay, or less, and I shall be even as thou art. There, there! look at it, May Boyes! Do you not see it? It is creeping to the door. It is the shadow of my father! It will not leave here alone; one shadow has entered the coffin cell, but two will depart."

May Boyes trembled as she looked in the direction indicated by Gerald Clifton. The moonbeams threw the shadow of some object upon the wall; it might be a chimney-stack, part of a church spire, or the exaggerated outline of some architectural ornament; but most certainly, with a little aid from the imagination, it assumed a human form, looking like some figure enveloped in massive drapery, and gliding slowly along the wall, as the moon took its path along the starry heavens. They were both silent several minutes, gazing upon the seeming apparition.

"Yes—yes," said Gerald, in a low tone, "I come. We shall pass out together. I did not know you. Do not look so stern upon me. Horror! horror! Is this blood that is floating in the air? The poison! the poison! It will do its duty. Shadow of the dead, I will come with thee; in the wide realms of space I will listen to your accusing voice. I knew you not, but you shall drag me to perdition!"

"Poison—poison!" cried May. "Oh, Gerald—Gerald, you have not——"

"Hush! I was prepared. I would not—I could not be the rabble's spectacle."

Her head sank upon her hands, and

HAWK AT THE BED-SIDE OF ANGELA.

she sobbed bitterly; then, springing to her feet, she flew to the cell door, and beat at it frantically with her clenched hands, calling loudly for help.

It was in vain, no one heard her. The utmost stretch of time allowed for an interview with a prisoner had not expired, and so there she remained locked up with the dying in the coffin cell.

But what could not a love, such as May Boyes had felt, accomplish, when she indeed found that it was hopeless to attract attention, and so procure aid for him whom she now felt convinced had taken some deadly drug? She returned again to his side, and, taking his hand in hers, she strove to wean him from his dreadful thoughts. He heard her, though his eyes were fixed upon the shadow on the wall.

"Gerald Clifton, you will pray—you

will utter the name of God, not as an exclamation, but as a man deeply repentant of that which he has done, and hopeful of mercy of the Great Judge of all."

"Look at the shadow—look at the shadow!"

"Gerald—Gerald, turn your thoughts on other subjects. You said you loved me; by that love, I adjure you to repentance! You had a mother once—can you remember her? if so, in her name, and by her memory, too, I call upon you for repentance! Let me hear, Gerald—oh! let me hear one heartfelt appeal to Heaven, and I shall dream you may be happy."

"The shadow seems to beckon me!"

"I will tell you all. 'Twas I, Gerald, who followed you upon the heath, when, perchance, you thought some form of evil beckoned you onwards and haunted your footsteps: 'twas I, Gerald Clifton—'twas I! I saw you leave the house of my father, on your dreadful errand; and I saw you change from what you had seemed to be, to what I had been told, but believed not, that you were."

"See! see! it nears the door. It looks sterner now I am dying!"

"No, no; not yet—not yet, Gerald."

"Shadow of death, you will have ample vengeance!"

"Look not on it!—look not on it! It is a delusion! Listen! listen! 'Twas I, disguised in clothing that you had left at the hall, who rode to London, deceiving, by a mockery of your presence, those who, while they have not forsworn themselves, yet have not sworn the truth."

"Look! look! look! can you doubt it now? The face, May Boyes—the face! God! I ought to know that face!"

"Will no one come?—will no one come?" said May, and she wrung her hands frantically.

"No one—no one," said Gerald; "no one but the dead! Look at it now! See with what a glassy stare it now regards me! My time is nearly come! Stay, shade, stay! Let me linger for a brief space by her whom I have loved!"

"Yes," said May, for she caught at the gentler accents in which he spoke, and felt at last that there, indeed, was the only point on which she could move him—"yes, yes; you have loved me, and you do love me, Gerald Clifton. Do you remember our walk upon the terrace of the old hall, where the sweet garden lay stretched far beneath us? Do you remember how the soft evening air then fanned our cheeks, and you talked to me of love?"

"Yes," he said, "before my hands were of this crimson colour."

"By the remembrance of that love, then, Gerald, it is that I adjure you to say something, to do a something yet which will give the ministering angels around the throne of God a cause to plead for you! They shall say that even at the last it was from the memory of the best and gentlest feelings of your life that you sued for mercy. Gerald! Gerald! will not the hope that we may meet again where there is no sorrow induce you to say, 'God, have mercy upon me!'"

"If—if," he gasped, "it were not for the shadow on the wall ——"

"Heed it not, heed it not. I will walk up to it, and place my hand upon the seeming face!"

"Yes; you are innocent! Your hand is spotless, and gentle as a babe's. Look at mine! dyed with the life-blood of a father! Since that fatal night, as I have held them up 'twixt me and the light, they have ever worn a crimson hue; while, 'twixt me and the glorious sunshine, a blood-red mist has seemed to float! Look at the shadow!—look at the shadow!"

The moon had sped on her gentle course, and the seeming likeness of the murdered man was within a pace or two of the cell door. May Boyes flung herself at Gerald Clifton's feet—she clasped his knees.

"Gerald! Gerald!" she cried, "you will utter these words that I have put into your mouth?"

"And so—and so," he said, faintly, "it was you, my beautiful May, who saved me from my doom? Was ever such devotion! Leave me—leave me! The shadow creeps towards the door, and we must part for ever!"

"I cannot leave you, nor would I if I could. Gerald, you have not prayed yet, nor yet acknowledged, as I hoped you would acknowledge, your deep sinfulness. Gerald! Gerald Clifton! he sinks! he's dying! Help! help! help! Oh!

horror! horror! Madness will come now! Gerald Clifton, speak again!"

In hissing whispers, he said—

"The shadow! the shadow! the shadow of death!"

The strange shade reached the cell door, and at the moment a heavy tread sounded from without. There was the rattle of a key in the lock—the gaoler had come. Gerald Clifton's head had sunk upon his breast, a spasm seemed to seize him; all her former love returned, and May sprang to her feet, and flung her arms round him.

"Gerald! Gerald! dear Gerald!" she cried, "I do love you still!"

"My May, my May," he said, faintly; "God have mercy upon me!"

He slipped from her hold, and fell heavily upon the floor of the cell.

"Time's up," said the man.

"Yes," said May; "time's over."

She walked from the cell without another word, and it seemed as if she and the shadow of death had left it together. She followed the man through the intricate passages like some automaton. He spoke to her, but she heard him not; he opened the wicket-gate, and she passed out into the open air. Some one sprang forward to meet her—it was her brother, Ratchley. She held him for a moment convulsively by the breast, and she tried to speak. The effort was a vain one; she swung round, and would have fallen but for his supporting arm.

CHAPTER CXLI.

THE SEQUEL.

We say now that virtually our tale is over; he, whose fortunes we have followed through the stormiest period of his life, has ceased to breathe—the brief drama of his existence is at an end, and the dread curtain of eternity has dropped between him and the world. But we still have a lit le more to say of those in whom we are interested, although we, for our own parts, consider that with the death of the prisoner in the coffin cell we have little more to do, except to utter a few words concerning the beautiful May Boyes, who had passed through so dreadful an ordeal, and who might never expect again such another episode in her existence.

We left her in the arms of Ratchley Boyes, and it was a thousand mercies indeed that he had thought of coming to meet her as she passed out of the prison.

Had he not done so she must have fallen, for succour and assistance, into the hands of perfect strangers, who, however much they might sympathise with her on account of her beauty, and her evident distress of mind, could not be expected to feel for her as did Ratchley, or to be able to take such immediate care of her.

When she fainted in his arms, it was a result that he expected, although a sad one, for he could well imagine that a scene of much distress must have taken place between her and the prisoner, although his wildest dreams of imagination could not have pictured it to be what it really was.

Little did he suspect that May Boyes had left in the condemned cell at Newgate a dead instead of a living man. Perhaps when she uttered those few inarticulate sounds which she did to him at the moment when she fainted in his arms she meant to tell him what had occurred, but lacked the power to do so.

The consequence of this was, that hours must elapse before any but herself could become aware of the dreadful catastrophe. Not that it mattered now, for no regrets, official or domestic, could again recall to life that man who, with all his errors on his head, had at last consummated his career of crime by self-murder, thus carrying out to its full extent the same description of pride which had been his strongest feeling throughout the whole of his career.

Too haughty to bend his energies to any of the arts of life, he preferred criminality and a sort of predatory warfare upon society to any other mode of existence; and at length, carrying out that same principle of dogged, obstinate resistance to what he was, he had chosen rather to take his own life, than justify the laws of his offended country in the eyes of its people.

Ratchley Boyes immediately procured a vehicle, for the purpose of conveying his sister home. He did not attempt to seek medical aid for her, because he knew that those who would proffer it could not minister to a mind diseased, or pluck out a rooted sorrow from the soul.

Home, rest, and gentle words, were the remedies which he proposed to himself to bring her, if not back to happiness, at least to serenity. He procured a hackney-coach, and having, notwithstanding his recent wound, had, as Sir John would have remarked, a great deal of the strength of the Boyes about him, he lifted May into the vehicle, and at once directed the driver to proceed to the lodgings of Sir John.

Perhaps Ratchley scarcely regretted that this period of insensibility had so closely followed upon her interview with the criminal in Newgate. It seemed as if nature by such a means was attempting to restore the tone of her mind, which must have been so cruelly shaken by recent events. The distance was not great, for Sir John, when he came to town upon the business that required him at the Old Bailey, naturally enough sought for some temporary abode in its immediate vicinity.

His object was to get her to her own apartment without apprising Sir John, or even Lady Boyes, of what had occurred, and in this, to his satisfaction, he succeeded, for Lady Boyes had retired to rest, fancying that May had done so likewise, and Philippa was waiting the arrival of her sister, having a sort of perception of the errand she was gone upon.

Sir John had solaced himself with a goblet of spiced wine, and after a great many sage remarks, he had fallen asleep in his chair, and was snoring just like the representative of all the Boyes.

"Philippa," said Ratchley, as he surrendered May to her care, "it is mental affliction that has produced this state in her, not bodily affliction. Do not be alarmed, for she will soon recover, and then your best plan will be for you to lead her to tell you all that has happened; such a confidence will tend more to relieve her mind than anything else, and should she weep abundantly, do not strive to check her tears, she will be the better for their flowing."

Philippa promised to obey his directions, and he left the sisters together.

It was not until the following morning that the news began to spread over the city of the death in his cell of Captain Hawk, the renowned highwayman. In those days people were not so sharp in detecting death by poison as they are at present, and as he had succeeded in taking some subtle drug, which presented no outward appearances of its malign influence, a hasty inquest upon his remains returned a verdict of *felo-de-se*, and he was buried at a junction of several roads, somewhere about the spot upon which those magnificent mansions now stand, which lend a grace to the neighbourhood of Hyde-park.

Although it was midnight when the ceremony of his interment took place, the officials connected with the prison had whispered it to so many persons, and they again to others, that there was a considerable concourse.

The man at Tyburn turnpike, who had professed so violent an admiration for Captain Hawk, left that ancient and now extinct gate in charge of a boy, while he went to see the last of what he considered one of the greatest geniuses of the age. Of course the boy left likewise, the moment his master's back was turned, so that for one evening everybody went through Tyburn gate free.

Ratchley, when he heard of the death of Hawk, or rather, as we ought to call him now, Hesketh, mentioned it to May, but she only slightly inclined her head in reply to him, which was quite a convincing proof to him that on the evening before she had known of the fatal act.

He scarcely thought it possible; but yet there was a disagreeable suspicion in his mind that she might possibly have supplied Hawk with the poison. To have such a suspicion of one whom he loved, was sufficient to make him unhappy until it was dispelled; so with all the honest frankness of his nature, a frankness which he knew she liked much better than any other mode of conduct, he put the question to her. Her simple answer in the negative was sufficient; he was abundantly satisfied that he was wrong.

We cannot say that May Boyes was ever restored to what might be called serenity. It was likely that such a being as her would speedily recover from the shock she had experienced; and although she made no violent exhibition of her mental agony, yet that became a further argument to those who knew her best, in favour of the supposition that her melancholy would be of a lasting character.

She retired with her father and family again to Boyes Hall. There needed no injunction to Ratchley to keep secret what he knew of the affair: his affection for May was quite sufficient to induce him to do so; so that Sir John knew as little as possible of the real circumstances connected with the matter, which had really produced so much confusion in his family.

He offered a reward for the family watch, and got it back again; but with great cleverness, fancying it was the thief who brought it, he dodged him to London to take him into custody; but somehow or another, he lost sight of him for a moment in the streets, and then pounced upon somebody else by mistake, who brought an action for false imprisonment against him, which he was forced to compromise, for fear the old story of the watch should be again brought before a public court of justice.

After that he kept the family chronometer safely locked up in a drawer, looking only now and then at it. There is very little doubt, though, but that Sir John looked upon the family watch as a sort of necromancer, who was in some way mixed up for good or for evil with his destiny.

To be sure, Sir John could not take upon himself to say that he found anything practically in the old authors, which he was wont to consult in his library, upon the subject of family watches, and that fact rather distressed him than otherwise. Indeed, so much so that he said to his son Ratchley, some time after the events we have recorded—

"Ratchley, have you consulted any of the old authors of late?"

"No, sir."

"Then I wish you would, for the express purpose of ascertaining what they have, in the profundity of their wisdom, to say about family watches."

"Family watches, sir?"

"Yes, my son, so now go at once."

"But, sir——"

"Speak! What would our son say?"

"I would merely remark, sir, that there occurs to my mind a reason why the old authors have said nothing of family watches."

"A reason?"

"Yes, sir, a good and sufficient reason."

"What is it?"

"Simply, sir, that I don't think the ancient authors had any watches."

Sir John placed his fingers by the side of his nose, and said slowly—

"You don't think that the ancient authors had any watches?"

"Just so."

"Why, that is equivalent to—a—a—their being without, and to—a—a—their not knowing the time of day."

"I really think it is, sir."

"Good," said Sir John, rising with dignity, and shaking some crumbs from his cravat. "Good. I will give that subject my best consideration."

CHAPTER CXLII.

GIVES THE READER SOME NEWS OF ANGELA.

Amid the hurry and the whirl of the many striking events that have occurred to Captain Hawk, and to some of those who were closely and personally connected with him, we have been compelled, although reluctantly, to leave in the shade the fair and gentle Angela.

That her pure and compassionate nature would be very much shocked by the arrest, and the death of Captain Hawk, may well be supposed by all who have paid any attention to the peculiar bias of her mind.

There are generous natures, who cannot bear to find that the confidence they have been in the habit of bestowing upon human nature is ever liable to be abused. Of such was Angela.

There was, to be sure, no such thing as

disputing the facts that appeared now quite clearly before her as highly criminatory of Captain Hawk, alias Gerald Clifton; but yet in her own mind she strove to find something like an extenuation for some of his offences, even if she could not get so far as positive excuse.

It was not likely that any one whom she would encounter would go out of their way for the purpose of shocking to a greater extent than it had been shocked her feeling for the man who, at all events, had, in a brave and gallant spirit, saved her from the cruel and most indecent persecutions of the infamous Lady Deliva.

Hence was it, then, that this young creature, in common with May Boyes, took a kindlier view of the character of Gerald Clifton than probably was at all warranted by the utmost stretch of Christian charity.

Immediately after the arrest of Captain Hawk, the police laid their hands upon Angela; for it looked so like as if she were an accomplice in the guilt that seemed to hang over all his actions, that they considered themselves justified in arresting her.

The youth, the beauty, and the artless simplicity of Angela's manner, soon won for her hosts of friends; and when she had told her tale, it did not take a long time to restore her to those relatives from whom, for purposes of her own, which could in their fullest extent scarcely be guessed at, the Lady Deliva had torn her.

It was a great relief to Angela to find it thoroughly established that not the slightest relationship existed between her and that woman.

But for the immense interest which the case of Captain Hawk had created in the public mind, there can be no doubt but that the iniquities of the Lady Deliva would have taken the people by storm; but it was well for the lovers of the curious and the terrible that the trial of Lady Deliva upon five distinct charges of murder did not take place until the popular excitement regarding the life and the death of Captain Hawk was to a great extent over.

The whole of the bodies in that dreadful chamber of death, to which she thought she had so successfully consigned Captain Hawk, were identified, and so was cleared up the fate of various missing members of what is called the fashionable world of London.

It would appear that all who had met with death at the hands of the Lady Deliva must have been attracted to her house by the exaggerated accounts that were current of her great wealth and unbounded liberality, and that, as the stepping-stone to the enjoyement of some portion of her resources, they had feigned to be in love with her, and had promised her marriage.

The hollowness of these pretensions the Lady Deliva, by the aid and assistance of her fiend-like waiting-maid, had discovered, and then she had herself not scrupled to execute the sentence of death that she passed upon them.

It was believed by some that one of the reasons why she kept Angela in the house in such a state of imprisonment was just because she could at any time make use of her as a test of the sincerity of her pretended lovers.

If they resisted falling at the feet of Angela, and bowing down to her youthful charms, the Lady Deliva might well have something like a good opinion of their constancy. If otherwise, death was their portion.

There were others, again, who inclined to the opinion that Angela was kept as a something upon which she, the Lady Deliva, could at any time she pleased exercise her cruelties upon; for it is well known that there are people in the world who would be quite unhappy if they had not some one upon whom they could exercise the petty tyranny of their disposition.

The truth, perhaps, was not to be found in either of these suppositions, and it did not seem that the Lady Deliva herself would take the trouble to enlighten any one concerning it.

When put upon her trial for one of the murders that it was so very clear she had committed, she listened to the indictment with great calmness, and at its conclusion she said, in a very easy and unrestrained voice—

"I plead guilty to the killing of that dog!"

"Dog?" said the judge. "Unhappy

woman, how can you speak of one of your victims in such a fashion?"

"That is my business," she replied, still with perfect calmness. "I wish to ask if the police have thoroughly searched my house?"

"That has been done."

"Have they found a small octagonal casket made of mother-of-pearl and inlaid with silver?"

One of the sheriffs who was upon the bench whispered to the judge that such a casket as the prisoner mentioned had certainly been found in her house.

"I ask again," said the Lady Deliva, "has such an article come to light, or has it been stolen?"

"Stolen by whom?"

"The police."

"In order then," added the judge, "to free the police from even the suspicion of such an act, I will, although this proceeding is very irregular, say that such a casket is found."

"It is well; you can now go on."

"Prisoner at the bar," said the clerk of the arraigns, "do you plead guilty or not guilty to the charge as set forth against you?"

"I cannot plead until I have that pearl casket," she replied. "I wish to do one act of justice and of mercy to a human being yet, and in that casket there is a letter which I took from the pocket of the man you accuse me of murdering, which I should be glad to restore to his friends."

"There is no such letter," said the sheriff. "The casket has been, of course, carefully examined."

"There is a secret receptacle in it," said Lady Deliva, "which may very well escape the vigilance of a sheriff. Give me the casket, and I will produce the letter."

The judge now consulted with a colleague who was upon the bench with him, and then he said, in rather a doubting voice—

"If the ends of justice can be best answered by allowing the prisoner to produce the document she speaks of, the court can [illegible] no objection, since it may be, f[illegible] we know, necessary to her defenc[illegible]

"It is [illegible]

"T[illegible]w, then, of the case, and a[illegible]pirit of that English law which gives all possible facilities to any one accused for his or her defence, I order the police to place the casket mentioned in the hands of the prisoner."

There was some little trouble and delay in procuring the casket that the Lady Deliva wanted, inasmuch as it was at the Mansion House of the city; but, finally, an officer, who had been hastily dispatched for the purpose of getting it, arrived in court with it.

"Prisoner," said the judge, "is that the casket you want?"

"It is."

"Hand it to her."

All eyes were now upon the Lady Deliva, as the casket, which was a very beautiful and costly-looking article, was duly handed to her in accordance with the order of the judge.

She took it with all the calmness in the world, slowly turning it round and round as if anxious thoroughly to identify it.

"It is the same," she said. "The readiness with which this request of mine has been granted shall not be without its reward, for in what I am about to do I shall save you, my lord, great trouble."

"Think of yourself," said the judge. "Not of me."

"I will—I will. I am thinking of myself."

The Lady Deliva pressed her thumb-nail upon one of the narrow little pieces of silver with which the pearl box was inlaid, and what appeared to be the solid lid of it suddenly sprang open into two portions, disclosing a small cavity about two-eights of an inch in depth between them.

"Here is the secret."

All eyes were turned upon the Lady Deliva, as now, taking a folded paper from the secret cavity of the casket, she handed the box to one of the officers, and proceeded slowly to unfold the paper.

"My lord, and you all, gentlemen," she said, "who have come here to consign a woman to death, after fatiguing her by all your power both in mind and body, I have said that I would save you trouble, and I will do so just for one reason only. That reason is because I cannot save myself trouble without saying it to you likewise, and so I am compelled to this course. My curse—my dying malediction light on you all!"

As she uttered these words, she flung the paper to her feet, and placed something in her mouth that she had taken from the paper.

"Seize her!" cried the judge, who saw too late the error of judgment he had fallen into. "Seize that woman!"

The officers dashed forward; but it was too late. The prisoner only smiled calmly, and looked at them with disdain.

"Wretched woman!" said the judge, "you have poisoned yourself."

"I have. What then?"

"The resources of art are great. We may yet counteract your intention. Are there any medical men in court?"

"Yes, my lord," cried three or four of that fraternity, and they struggled through the crowd to get to the prisoner.

Even as they did so the Lady Deliva uttered one shriek, and fell a corpse to the floor.

Every possible means for upwards of an hour were tried to restore the form of that wicked woman to animation again; but it was all in vain. The poison had done its work, and never more would the breath of life animate the cold, lifeless form of Lady Deliva.

Thus ended the career of that woman whose crimes, if she had not had the art to devise the means of ridding herself of life, would have speedily brought her to an ignominious end.

The confusion and excitement at the Old Bailey that day was, if possible, more apparent than they had been even upon the occasion of the declaration from the lips of Captain Hawk that in the murdered judge he recognised his father; and for many days afterwards the painful subject of conversation in all classes of society was the strange career and the terrible end of the Lady Deliva.

The news of the death of that woman whom she knew so well, gave to Angela a kind of shock which, although it differed very much from any feeling of regret, yet affected her; but in the society of those who soon loved her to excess, she soon forgot the direful events that were connected with her residence beneath the roof of the false and the wicked Lady Deliva.

"I tremble," Angela would say, "if I awaken in the night and think of Lady Deliva; but when I have said a prayer, and looked around upon every object that convinces me how truly I am surrounded by kind and dear friends, I then sleep again, and feel happy."

The circumstances that had occurred in the young life of Angela had tended very much to get up a community of feeling between her and the Boyes family; so much so, indeed, that when she heard the whole story, so far as any one could tell, of May Boyes, she felt that she would like to be to her a sister in affection, and she wrote to her.

The letter was one that touched the heart of May from its simplicity and tender trustfulness, and for the first time since the tragical events that had occurred to her she wept freely.

Those tears were the first signals of the fact that May Boyes was weaning from the blight that the conduct of Gerald Clifton, or Gerald Hesketh, as we may rightly call him, had cast upon her soul. From that time she got better.

With the full consent of Sir John and the whole of the family, May wrote a reply to Angela, in which she asked her as a favour to come to Boyes Hall for a time, and to stay with her, excusing herself for not coming to London to see her upon the ground that she was yet "very weak" and "a sad invalid."

Alas, that such a young and joyous creature as May Boyes should live to pen such words as those!

CHAPTER CXLIII.

RATCHLEY BOYES SETTLES IN LIFE, AND MAY IS MUCH HAPPIER.

Perhaps this invitation was what Angela expected; but whether it was so or not, certain it is that she wrote a long and kind letter back to May again, accepting it.

The arrival of Lady Angela slow-

bray, for such was the real rank and title of Angela, at Boyes Hall was quite an event of importance there, considering the very retired life that the family led.

Sir John Boyes partook of the general feeling of excitement, and Ratchley suspected that he had positively wound up the family watch in honour of the auspicious event.

As for Ratchley himself, he had once in London seen Angela; and when he began, as he did at times, to talk of her beauty to the listening circle at Boyes Hall he got quite vehement upon the subject.

"It strikes me," said Sir John, "that you don't know what you are saying, Ratchley, which is equivalent to not having a clear idea of your ever marrying."

"Perhaps I don't, sir."

"Perhaps you don't, sir? I say you don't, sir."

"As you please, sir."

"No, sir, it is not as I please, for as an old author judiciously remarks—hand me the toast—there can be no greater bondage than being made to do just as you please."

"You don't say so, sir."

"Sir, I do say so. Hem! when I say anything it ought to be considered in this family as beyond all dispute—hem! which means that it is indisputable. I hope I make myself understood?"

"Perfectly so, sir. Hilloa! Hurrah! There she is!"

A travelling carriage had appeared coming up the long avenue in front of Boyes House, and Ratchley had at once jumped to the conclusion that it could be no other than Angela, who had arrived a little sooner than she had been expected.

It was so unexpected, though, that in his hurry Ratchley ran against Sir John, and upset half a cup of rather hot tea in his lap.

"Bless my soul!" cried Sir John, "what is that? The representative of the Boyes is scalded to death! Murder!"

"I beg your pardon, sir; but, really——"

"Silence, sir!"

"Yes, sir, I——"

"Don't speak to me, sir. Look at my what's-their-names."

"Your what, sir?"

"D—n it, my satin small-clothes!"

"Really, sir, I am so extremely sorry. Yes, there she is! Bravo! I'll go and meet her. There she is—there she is!"

Ratchley made another rush, and caught his foot in one of the hind legs of Sir John's chair with such force and violence, that he dragged it from under him, and down went Sir John on to the carpet.

"Fire!" cried Sir John. "Fire! The world is at an end! What is going to happen next? I rather believe that I am sitting on the floor, which is equal to my occupying a low position. Fire! Murder!"

"Lady Angela!" cried Ratchley, throwing the folding-doors at the end of the breakfast-room wide open.

"Bless my soul!" cried Sir John, as in an effort to rise, he just reached a position of all-fours as Angela stepped into the room, and then Sir John got so jammed between the table and a chair, that Lady Boyes heartily wished, that he would not get up at all.

Angela acknowledged the introduction of Ratchley with all that grace that was peculiar to her; and then she folded poor May in her arms, as she said—

"Shall we be sisters?"

"If you—" said May, and then she could get no further for her tears.

And now Ratchley met with the reward of his precipitancy, for in stepping back two steps to allow himself room to make a very graceful bow to Angela in, as she left the room with Lady Boyes and May to go to the chamber allotted to her to change her travelling dress, over he went backwards on Sir John's back, and so upon the floor at one time was to be seen both Sir John and his heir.

"What the devil is this?" said Ratchley.

"Murder! He wants the title too soon!" said Sir John. "The son and heir of the Boyes title is murdering the possessor of it!"

"My dear Sir John," said Ratchley, as he sprang to his feet and lifted his father up, "what on earth made you get down there?"

"What made me, sir?"

"Pray excuse me, if I have seemed to want in respect to you, sir; but the presence of—of——"

"Of whom, sir?"

"The young lady who has honoured us with her presence, has just a little unsettled my nervous system. I have a very great favour to ask of you though, sir."

"Hem! what is it?"

"It is, that you would have the kindness, sir, to consult the ancient authors, and see if you can find any passage applicable to the situation of our fair young guest."

"Consult the ancient authors?" said Sir John. "Why that is equivalent to reading their remains."

"Just so, sir."

"Reading their remains—Hem! The works left by the ancient authors may be said to be their remains, for their real remains perish."

"While their works, sir, are immortal as the emanations of that genius which can know neither decay nor death."

"My very words," said Sir John. "Upon my life, Ratchley, I do not approve of your taking the words out of my mouth in that way. But I will go, nevertheless, and consult some of the most ancient of the authors, and let you know the result."

With this promise, Sir John stalked majestically to his library, to the great relief of Ratchley, who quite dreaded that his father would expose some of his little peculiarities before their fair visitor, to the detriment of the family.

Angela, as she quite wished that they should all call her, did indeed look lovely in a dress of white satin, and a pretty gossamer looking scarf of fawn-coloured gauze, when she sat down to luncheon in the old oaken parlour of Boyes Hall.

How Ratchley did look at her, to be sure! and what dreadful blunders he did make! He need not have been afraid of what Sir John might do or say, for the worthy baronet, in comparison with the confused Ratchley, was quite the pink of politeness and propriety. At one time Ratchley did nothing but glare at Angela and eat the salt, till Lady Boyes upon seeing how he was employed, uttered quite a scream and snatched it from him.

"What are you doing, Ratchley?"

"Nothing, nothing. Oh, how sweet!"

"What! Do you call salt sweet?"

"Salt did you say, mother? I was alluding to the—the ——"

"The what?" cried everybody.

"The roses, and the lilies, and the carnations, and the little pearls that peep out of the rose-buds, and the—the——"

"Mad!" said Sir John—"our son is mad, which is equivalent to his being out of his senses."

"No," said Ratchley, "pardon me, sir, for contradicting you, but I am in complete possession of my senses, I assure you. Will you allow me the happiness of pouring you out a glass of this old hock, Angela?"

"If you please," returned Angela.

Upon this permission being given to him with such a smile as never was seen, the bewildered Ratchley actually poured out for Angela to drink a glass of the best Durham mustard, and gravely presented it to her.

"I can recommend my father's hock," he said.

"But," cried Sir John, raising his arm, "can you recommend your father's mustard?"

"Mustard, sir?"

"Yes," said Angela, with the most provoking *naivete* in the world, as she held the glass up to Ratchley's eyes and nose; "only look! Oh, Mr. Ratchley Boyes, your sister, May, told me that you were disposed to make quite a pet of me; and when I asked her what that meant, she said that you would spoil me, and I suppose this is the beginning of the process?"

"I am mad!" said Ratchley; and, darting from the table, he made a precipitate rush from the room.

"Our son," said Sir John, "is in a state of lunacy, and he must be taken care of."

"The family must watch him," said Angela, laughing

"Eh? Did you say family—watch?"

"Yes, Sir John.

"Hem! it won't go. Don't ask for it, I beg of you. Smith—no, I mean Jones—or Thomas, or some such highly remarkable person, has got it to mend. Drop it—drop it."

"Dear me, Sir John, I thought you had dropped it," said Lady Boyes, "if you mean the family watch; but I don't think that Angela at all referred to it."

"Lady Boyes?" said Sir John.

"Yes, Sir John?"

"I beg your pardon, madam. Angela did refer to it, I beg to state—hem!—most distinctly. And now, if it be agreeable, come for a walk; we will woo the flowers and walk in the garden of the hall.'

CHAPTER CXLIV.

RATCHLEY BOYES SHOWS THAT THERE IS A METHOD IN HIS MADNESS.

The visit of Angela to May Boyes seemed as though it were calculated to have the happiest results upon all the Boyes family.

In the first place, it certainly roused May from the state of apathy into which she had fallen, and which must have had the most dreadful results had it continued.

Partly the duties of hospitality, and partly the fact that she, Angela, knew the man who had been the blight upon the sunshine of her own existence, May felt irresistibly attracted towards Angela, and in the course of a few hours loved her as if she had known her for years.

Such a gentle and affectionate disposition as Angela's was sure to reciprocate the feeling that was awakened in the breast of the desolate May.

The story of May was tolerably well known to Angela, but not in all its details; and the young girl thought that if May could only once be brought to speak freely to her of the past, that it would lose most of its power to harm her mind and to inflict suffering upon her.

The reasoning of Angela upon this subject was singularly felicitous.

"The recollection of a grief," she said, "such as May suffers from is like the dread of a spectre, which we dress up in all sorts of terrors, but which if we had but the courage to meet face to face, and to question, would, in all probability, lose by far the greatest amount of its terrors; so I want to induce May to speak to me quite freely and candidly about her affairs, and then they will lose half their power to harm her."

With this view it was, then, that Angela tempted May to wander with her into the recesses of a plantation in the domain of Boyes Hall, which was purposely made rugged and wild to imitate some forest of nature's own planting.

It was for this object that she separated her during that day from her family and friends, and strove to engage her in earnest talk that might lead to [illegible] recollection of the past.

This sort of tactics rather astonished [illegible] for she had seen, as it was quite [illegible] not to see, that the whole [illegible]r family and friends had been [illegible] apparent recollection of [illegible]hich had cost her, May, [illegible] crush a [illegible]

Hence it had followed, as a thing of course, that, deep in the recesses of her own bosom, May had cherished those recollections, and allowed them to feed, as it were, upon her thoughts hour by hour.

There was an old spring in the plantation to which May and Angela went hand in hand; and the Boyes' family had from time to time done all that art could enable them to do to surround the spot, from which the clear and sparkling water dashed into a little marble basin, with every sylvan charm that could be imparted to it.

The graceful birch-tree scattered its transparent foliage about the spot—the tall poplar lent its feathery beauty to the scene; and the back-ground was shut in by a screen of Spanish chestnuts, of extraordinary beauty.

The green turf, quite up to the little fountain, was of quite an emerald tint, and looked at a short distance off like a rich piece of velvet laid upon the spot.

"Ah!" said Angela, as she came in sight of the rustic beauties of this place. "Whither are you leading me, May? Is this a fairy region?"

"No, Angela; but it is, to my thinking, one of the prettiest spots in all the place."

"It is truly charming!"

"I am glad, since you admire it so, that I have brought you to it. There is a pretty rustic seat close to the spring, where you may sit upon a summer's day with coolness and shade about you, and listen to the melody of the tumbling water, as it flows down yonder mimic cascade."

"Oh, beautiful!—most beautiful!"

May was pleased with the enthusiasm of her young companion; and, as she looked into her sweet girlish face, she breathed a mental prayer that when she did love she might never know the heart's agony which her feelings in that way had brought upon her.

The reader will bear in mind that Angela had never been in love with Captain Hawk, and that with instinctive terror she had shrunk from him so soon as she became fully aware of the fact that the feelings with which he chose to regard her were different from what she had at first supposed.

It had been the delight of Angela at

the commencement of her intercourse with Hawk to call him brother; and it had suited his purpose very well, in order to get a hold of the imagination and the confidence of the young girl, to agree with that title and to make his conduct accord with it; but he had soon cast aside the mask, and although for a time it had seemed as though Angela would be his victim, yet that only lasted until she was fully aware of what it meant.

The little rustic seat that May had mentioned was soon reached, and the two young girls sat upon it, and listened, as May said they might, to the fall of the cascade that, at the instigation of herself and of Ratchley, Sir John had gone to the expense of having constructed.

It was then that Angela felt that her mission began, and that if she was to save May from the agony of concealed grief, a fairer opportunity of commencing the process could not arrive than the present.

But although Angela felt this, and although no idea of abandoning the task she had set herself occurred to her, yet never until that moment had she felt its extreme difficulty and delicacy. As she looked into the sweet, suffering face of May, she felt how rude and rough would seem to be the hand that would tear aside the curtain that hid her inmost griefs; and yet she felt that it was necessary so to do.

"If some one," thought Angela, "will not awake her to the present by making the past appear painful to her, she will die, or go distracted; so I must do it."

There had subsisted a silence of some few minutes' duration between the two young girls, and then May said—

"I fear, Angela, that you will find me but a poor and dull companion, and that you will make yourself cheerless."

"No—no! But is there any likelihood of any one coming here?"

"To the hall?"

"No, I mean to this spot."

"Oh, no—no! Not the least."

"We are quite secure from interruption?"

"Quite, Angela. But why do you ask?"

A slight flush of colour came to the cheek of Angela, and it was no small effort for her to say—

"Then, May, I wish to speak to you of Gerald Clifton!"

If a thunderbolt had suddenly fallen at the feet of May Boyes she could not have been more truly astonished than she was at this abrupt mention of a name she never thought to hear again from mortal lips. After gazing in astonishment at Angela for a few minutes, she clasped her hands, and said—

"Cruel—cruel!" and then she burst into tears.

"I repeat," said Angela, "I want to speak to you about Gerald Clifton—alias Gerald Hesketh—alias Captain Hawk, the highwayman, and I don't think it is cruel at all."

May sobbed, as if her heart were bursting.

"As for these tears," added Angela, "they will do you good, I know. Oh, May, May!"

The young girl twined her arms around May's neck, and in her turn sobbed, as she clasped her to her bosom and whispered—

"Do you think I have said what I have for the purpose of giving you a moment's pang? No, May, I have spoken so for the purpose of saving you from many hours, days, months, and years of misery. You cherish in your breast a remembrance of the occurrences connected with that bold, bad man, which you ought not to cherish. I tell you, May, that your seclusion and your grief will become a disease, if your better nature and your innocence does not fight out against it. Speak freely of him, and of the past. You lovedhim?"

"Loved him? Oh, God!"

"Well, you loved him, because you thought him worthy."

"I did."

"But you found him unworthy, and then you were weak enough to love him still."

"Weak, said you?"

"To be sure I did."

"Nay, you wrong me; I am not weak."

"But I say that you are weak, May Boyes. Nay, do not look at me so unkindly. Let me tell you how and why you are weak. You saw this man who is now no more—this Gerald Clifton as you thought him, and you thought you saw that he possessed high and noble qualities, and for those high and noble qualities you loved him. Well, in time you found out that you had made a grievous mistake, and that he did not possess one of those qualities you thought he had in such perfection. In lieu of his being a gentleman, you found that he was a heartless libertine—you found that he was actually dishonest, and that he gained his living by rapine and robbery—you found that he had all but taken the life of your brother, and that then, with a hypocrisy that only such a man could or would stoop to have affected, to be wonderfully sympathetic upon the occasion. Then, finding he was all that you had not thought him, what did you do?"

"What did I do?"

"Yes, what did you do?"

"Spare me!"

"No, you are so selfish that you must not be spared."

"Selfish? I selfish?"

"Yes, to be sure you are, for do you not, for the gratification of indulging in tears, and woe, and regrets for a man who must be detested by everybody, make your whole family and friends uncomfortable?"

May was silent.

"Of course you do," added Angela, "and you know it. You know that the man whom you sigh for, and for whom you shed such tears, and for whom you walk about like a ghost, is utterly and completely unworthy of a thought. You know that he has committed the most terrible of crimes. He is a parricide."

"I didn't know that till lately."

"But you know it now."

"Yes, yes—I—do."

"Then shake of this monkish servility. Let shame step in to cure you of regrets for a man whose very name should not be mentioned to the ears of honour and of virtue. Have you consented to become the widow of such a man as Gerald Hesketh?"

"Oh, Angela, you are right. Oh, God, what a mist seems to be cleared from before my eyes!"

"Dear! dear May! I have been cruel to you, but it was to be kind; that was my only object. You will be restored to yourself, to your friends, and to the world as once you were, and you will no longer be the weeping victim that you formerly were. Is it not so?"

"It is—it is! You have made me think, and I begin to see all the subject you have spoken of in a new light. I do think that I shall be happier and calmer now."

CHAPTER CXLV.

THE MARRIAGE OF RATCHLEY, AND THE SNOW-STORM AT THE TALBOT.

May clasped Angela in her arms, and wept for a long time; but when those tears were over she looked up in the face of her young friend with a faint smile, as she said—

"I am better, dear Angela."

Angela was so delighted at the effect that her plan of operations with May had had, that she could not reply to her, the tears gushed so to her eyes. No longer was she the inspired intellectual girl arguing in the cause that she felt to be right, but once again she looked like the tender child that could be led whither any one chose to say to her it was good to go.

"Who," said May, as she kissed her fervently, "who would have thought for a moment that you were what you are, Angela!"

"Ah, May, what am I?"

"Shall I tell you?"

"Yes."

"Then you are a bold, fearless, fair-spoken, noble-minded girl, with more sense and moral character and genuineness than——"

"Hush, May; I must hear no more. I did not—oh, believe me I did not mean to ask you for compliments. I thought that you were going to tell me of my friends."

"You have me."

"You are too good and too patient to me. But now will you come to the house again? and will you ever remember our conversation by the little spring?"

"I shall never forget it. This place will be sacred to me as one in which I found the truth freely uttered for my own good by one whom I roughly repelled."

"No more of that. Come, dear May—come."

They walked together to the house, and upon the broad lawn in front of the drawing-room window they met the whole of the Boyes family assembled. May walked up to them, and with quite a smile upon her face—such a smile as they had not seen for many a long day—she said—

"I intend to be happy for the time that is to come. The past is no longer to hang upon my soul like a cloud. A kind and gentle spirit has lit again the pure spirit of serenity in my heart. Father—mother—sister—brother, your May will be all to you that once she was, and strive if she can find a means of making a fitting return for all your love."

Amazement sat upon the countenances of the whole party, and then Lady Boyes folded her daughter to her heart, and wept with joy, and Philippa turned aside to hide her tears.

Sir John was deeply affected, and rubbed his nose so fearfully, that he made the end of it red for the rest of the day.

"My dear," he said to May, "we rejoice once more to see you happy; because by being so, we come to the conclusion that you are no longer wretched. God bless you, my dear—God bless you. I feel that I shall be better after half an hour's converse with the old authors; for, as some one of them says somewhere, 'When you don't feel as if your feelings inclined you to company, you had better sit alone for some time until you feel disposed to get up again.'"

Ratchley only remained with the family group until he heard May make the speech that we have recorded; and then, to the surprise of everybody, off he ran as if he were mad.

Poor Ratchley! His feelings got the better of him, and he wept alone. It was a couple of hours before he could venture to emerge from the shrubbery into which he had plunged, and then, just as he turned the angle of a hedge, he met Angela.

The young girl was sobbing and smiling like an April day.

"Angela!" he exclaimed.

"Oh, Mr. Ratchley, pardon me. I fear I have intruded upon you."

"Oh, no. But you weep?"

"Do I?"

"Yes, surely, there are tears upon your cheeks."

"They are tears of joy. Why, I declare, Mr. Ratchley, you, too, look as if you had been crying."

Ratchley turned aside his head, and said nothing.

"Adieu!" said Angela, as she turned to trip away, but Ratchley called after her.

"Angela—Angela, in mercy stay!"

"What would you?"

"Angela, you have saved May—you have restored her to us as if it were from the grave. God's blessing be upon you for ever and ever—you—you have been so good—so kind——"

"Nay, Mr. Ratchly, I won't hear any more in that strain."

"But—but—oh, do not go."

"Wherefore should I stay?"

"Unhappy Angela!"

"Unhappy? What mean you?"

"Alas—alas! you think that you have done good by coming here—you fancy that your visit here has been one that will be remembered with the most gratified feelings by this family; but, oh, mistaken Angela, you know not what you have done!"

"What have I done?"

"Mischief."

"Mischief? Oh, no—no!"

"I am very sorry to be obliged to say, oh, yes—yes. You have, it is true, saved the sister from a mournful state of melancholy: but, alas—alas! you have destroyed the brother!"

"Destroyed the brother—you?"

"Yes, me. Dear—dear Angela! your mission is but half accomplished. In me you will behold one who will soon be in a much worse state than May ever was, and you—you alone can save me from it."

"I really do not comprehend you."

"Angela, I love you!"

"Oh, get up."

Ratchley was kneeling at her feet.

"Dearest and best, I love you. Beautiful, but not so beautiful as you are good and great, I love you, Angela!"

"Mr. Ratchley, is this fair?"

"You are fairer."

"Oh, rise. Some one is coming. To see you thus, what will they think?"

"Let them come. I care for nothing but the hope that you may some day say as kind things to me as you said to May."

"Oh, what shall I do? Come, now, Mr. Ratchley, just for fear they should laugh at you now, I will say what you like. What is it to be?"

"Oh, joy—joy! You will say, 'Ratchley——'"

"Ratchley——"

"'I will try to love you.'"

"I will try—to—to—hate you!"

"Hate me?"

"Yes; but as I know I shall fail in that, I won't try it any more; but I won't try to love you."

"Oh, do—do!"

"No—no!"

"Why—oh, why will you not even try to love me?"

"Because — because I am rather afraid that, to tell the truth, I do love you a little already."

With a cry of joy, Ratchley sprang to his feet, and clasped Angela in his arms, and before she could prevent it, he had kissed her some dozens of times.

"May the blessing of the head of the Boyes' family light upon you, my child!" said a voice.

They both started, and upon looking round, they saw that Sir John Boyes was on the other side of the hedge, and was projecting his long arms over the top of it in the form of a benediction upon them, while tears were coursing each other down his cheeks.

"We are all here," cried May.

"Yes," said Philippa, "I wish you joy, Angela; but you must not let Ratchley have too much of his own way."

"My dear children," cried Lady Boyes, "how happy you have made us!"

"Yes," cried Sir John. "Tol de rol—de rol!"

"Bless me, father," said Ratchley, "that must be some modern author you are quoting now."

"Never mind, my son—never mind what author it is. In me you see the author of your being, and I have only to hope that you will be an author in due time in the same way, and that——"

"Silence, Sir John!" cried Lady Boyes. "How very improper you are talking, to be sure!"

"Never mind, Lady Boyes—never mind. All I stipulate for is that the eldest boy shall be named Cicero. And now I propose, as he is not ready yet, so it is of no use bothering about him, that we all go to the Talbot to-night, and give a grand treat to the whole neighbourhood and a ball; for owing to certain events, the one annually held there has been put off."

This was a proposition that was fully in accordance with the wishes of all parties; and as they had none of them ever seen Sir John in such a state of hilarity before, they were quite delighted to find that he had such a fund of humour in his disposition.

It was a funny thing to see him seize Angela round the waist, and commence the execution of some curious dance, which must have been of his own invention, for nobody had ever seen the like of it before.

Well, the Boyes' family was very happy now; and if any one had looked in upon them that day after dinner, they could hardly have supposed that such a cloud had passed over them.

The servants soon saw that things were very different with the household; and when it got hinted about among them, as it soon did by some mysterious means, that Ratchley was going to be married to the sweet young lady they all called Angela, there was such kissing, and bustling, and laughing in the mansion as never was known.

The promised ball was given at the Talbot, and a rare night's entertainment it was. Sir John danced the minuet, in which he thought he excelled so much, and a lot of country lasses persuaded him to make one in the cushion dance, and so pushed him about, and worried him, that at last he sat hopelessly upon the cushion in the middle of the place, calling to Ratchley to come and rescue him.

A happier party than was assembled in that old inn upon the occasion could not have been found; and Ratchley,

as they went home by the light of the moon, said to himself—

"Is this all a dream, or has the past been one? I shall be some time before I can fully believe in this great happiness."

CHAPTER CXLVI.

THE CONCLUSION.

THE episode of human existence, called "Captain Hawk; or, the Shadow of Death," is over.

Ratchley and Angela were duly married, and were as happy as it was possible for any two human beings to be. They continued to reside at Boyes Hall, although Angela had princely estates in different parts of the country, having brought to her husband one of the most extensive properties in all England.

Sir John Boyes lived to a good old age, and the contemplation of the happiness of his child did much to rid him of many of the stately prejudices with which, at the period of the reader's first acquaintance with him, his mind was crowded.

Philippa was married to a country gentleman, and went to live in Buckinghamshire.

May remained with her brother and Angela, and she continued to enjoy the serenity of soul that Angela had restored to her. She had many offers of marriage, but she rejected them all, kindly but firmly; and as the children of Ratchley increased, and the sounds of youthful laughter soon became tolerably rife in the house, May found her time pleasantly and fully occupied in attending to them; and no one had a greater share of their best affections than Aunt May.

At Sir John's death, the ministry of the day made Ratchley an earl, with the title of Lingstenteir, which was the name of an estate that belonged to Angela. If anything could have aroused poor Sir John Boyes from his eternal rest, it would have been this accession of honour to his family; but—

"After life's fitful fever he slept well,"

and was remembered with much love by those he left behind him. He desired that the sculptured form of an angel should be placed on his tomb, and his last words were—

"Let it be as like our Angela as possible, for she has been the guardian angel to us all."

The death of Captain Hawk in the condemned cell at Newgate was, in its actual integrity, sufficiently mysterious to excite a considerable amount of attention both upon the part of the authorities and of the public.

[illegible], of course, soon ascertained beyond the shadow of a doubt that the victim of the law had escaped, and, therefore, there was nothing further to be done but to give the notorious criminal christian burial—for, after all, it would have been hard to deny him that.

With such sombre solemnity, then, as befitted the occasion, the remains of Captain Hawk were committed by the prison authorities to the grave; but as he lead a restless life, so was it his fate, even after death, not to rest even in his grave.

The question arose publicly, and was largely and fully discussed in the public papers, regarding the mode and the manner of his death.

Some would have it that he had not died at all in the coffin-cell at Newgate, but had been taken away, and enabled to leave the country by the aid of the friends and the family of the late Judge Holme.

Others, again, insisted upon it that he had been assassinated in the cell, in order that while he was put out of the world as he ought to be the family to which he so incontestably belonged might not be disgraced by the fact in their recorded annals that one of their members was hanged.

These rumours and disputes got to such a height, and were pronounced by most newspapers with such acrimony, that at last the secretary of state sent to the county coroner for his account of the inquest on the body of one Gerald Clifton, alias Gerald Holme, alias Gerald Hesketh, alias Captain Hawk.

This was just what the coroner for the county wanted, and afterwards people went the length of saying that it was the coroner who, in an anonymous letter, had suggested the course to the home secretary; but be that as it may, it enabled the coroner to send a reply to the effect that there was no inquest at all held upon the mortal remains of Captain Hawk, and that the prison authorities at Newgate were in the habit of burying persons who expired in that prison without any inquest, and that once when he interfered upon the subject he only got laughed at for his pains.

This brought up the whole subject again, and finally [illegible] led to disinter the body of Captain Hawk, alias all that we have stated, and hold an inquiry, *secundum artem,* over his remains.

In the old church-yard at Stamford Hill, the city authorities had a portion of ground that belonged to the corporation, and in it had been placed Hawk.

Armed, then, with the coroner's warrant, and a letter from the secretary of state, and the leave and licence of the bishop of the diocese, a party went to Stamford Hill, accompanied by an immense crowd, to disinter the body of the malefactor.

The news of what was about to take place spread like wildfire about the city and the eastern suburbs of it; and by the time the party reached the burial ground, it was computed that there could not be less than three or four thousand persons present.

The operation was quickly commenced, and the rector of the parish, in his robes, attended on the spot. The coffin, with its rough plate, bearing the inscription of the name of the occupant, was brought to light, and a complete sea of heads surrounded it, as the grave-digger inserted the corner of his shovel between the lid and the edge of the last narrow home of human nature, and said—

"Now, gentlemen, say the word, and open it goes."

"Open it," cried the rector, as he took off his hat.

This was a signal to every one to do so likewise, though they did not know very well what it was for, since not one among them had the smallest respect for Captain Hawk, either in life or in death.

With one wrench of his spade the grave-digger loosened the lid of the coffin at that corner, for the screws had but a slight hold, and they had already begun to rust in this place. With his hands, then, the man was able to raise the lid and throw it aside.

The people fought and struggled for foremost places. Cries of "Shame! shame!" resounded through the crowd, and the greatest excitement prevailed for a few moments.

Then it was ascertained that all the coffin contained were six or eight bricks, wrapped up in an old torn quilt.

The people, upon this, did not know whether to be pleased at the mystery attached to the affair, or enraged at the idea of having come so far to see a dead body, and being, after all, disappointed; so, after finding that there was no one in particular upon whom, with any show of reason, they could wreak their vengeance, they began throwing the bricks at each other, and a regular row of some hours' duration ensued, which only wore itself out when night came.

Now all this was duly reported to the secretary of state, and a great inquiry was made concerning it; but nothing came of the inquiry, and at last it died away.

Popular superstition, however, would not let the matter rest, and it was asserted that sometimes in the depth of winter, when the snow covered all the ground, and the north-east wind was moaning and howling amid the branches of the leaf-deserted trees a shadowy form would gallop along the road by Boyes Hall upon a sprite charger, shrieking as it went, and calling out—

"Parricide—parricide—parricide!"

Who could this be but the ghost of Captain Hawk?

Then, again, it was said that near the corner of a little wood, not far from Boyes Hall likewise, a shadowy form would be seen in the soft moonlight sitting upon a horse as still and motionless as a statue, and that the trees and the sky could be seen right through both horse and man, and that one who knew Hawk well by sight fainted when he saw the vision, and after being restored, by sundry glasses of something hot and strong, declared it was Captain Hawk.

The Boyes' family carefully kept these rumours and strange reports from poor May. They would only have distressed her, so it was just as well that she knew them not; and, as she did not care for the newspapers, they, happily, never disturbed her serenity.

But, still, there are old people on the Western-road, who, to hush their refractory children to repose, threaten them with Captain Hawk, or the ghost of that individual; and it is said that if you go to Hanger Hill, near Acton, on the twenty-third of June, and wait from half-past twelve to one you will see the spirits of both Captain Hawk and May Boyes slowly pass down a verdant lawn, that is close to the orchard of an old farm-house there.

"Thus superstition doth awake wayward fancies
in the brain,
And mocks at stern reality."

If any of our readers should feel at all inclined to make the experiment of trying to obtain a sight of the ghost of Captain Hawk at the corner of the old lane by Hanger Hill, we can only say that we wish them all the success in the world. But if they should chance to light upon the dreary sight of the shadow of the parricide, let it awaken sympathy for the poor heart that he so cruelly destroyed. We allude to the kindly spirit of May Boyes, which, although for a time wrecked amid the quicksands of doubt and despair, at length rose superior to all such inducements, and regained that serenity of soul which is the only true happiness that this world can afford.

THE END.

PRINTED BY E. LLOYD, SALISBURY SQUARE, FLEET STREET, LONDON.

www.ingramcontent.com/pod-product-compliance
Lightning Source LLC
Chambersburg PA
CBHW080943020726
47505CB00009B/2127

* 9 7 8 1 5 3 5 8 0 2 4 0 6 *